Paul Sussman read Histo............................lso won a Boxing Blue. From......................on has been archaeology. He................................lo- gist, in particular in Egypt where he was part of the first team to excavate new ground in the Valley of the Kings since Tutankhamun's tomb was found in 1922. His first two novels, *The Lost Army of Cambyses* and *The Last Secret of the Temple*, are international bestsellers, while his journalism has appeared across the media, notably in the *Independent*, *Big Issue*, *Evening Standard* and on CNN.com. He lives in London with his wife and two sons.

Acclaim for ***The Last Secret of the Temple*** and ***The Lost Army of Cambyses:***

'The **intelligent reader's answer to *The Da Vinci Code***: a big, fat satisfying archaeological puzzle'

Independent

'Not just a tightly-plotted, richly-observed, thought-provoking thriller, but one with a soul . . . The **compelling mix of tough, page-turning suspense, archaeology, history and characters caught up in the brutal politics of the Middle East**, make this a timely and authentic novel . . . comfortably blends historical mystery with unflinching contemporary suspense'

RAYMOND KHOURY, author of *The Last Templar*

'**A brilliant detective novel**, hidden within a medieval saga, tucked inside an archaeological mystery, surrounded by a modern-day Middle East terrorist thriller . . . **a multi-layered quest** where all the characters are real and alive, and we should expect the completely unexpected'

KATHERINE NEVILLE, author of *The Eight*

www.rbooks.co.uk

'Spine-chilling, fast-paced . . . it **has all the ingredients of a James Bond adventure** . . . and it keeps you guessing right up until the final chapter'

Sunday Business Post

'Adrenaline-packed . . . combines **all the elements of a truly great adventure story** – a 2,000 year-old historical mystery, buried treasure, a race against time . . . superbly evocative, with a huge epic sweep'

Crime Time

'An enjoyable adventure story, **replete with archaeological lore**'

Spectator

'A **tough, sometimes brutal, but always engrossing** thriller. Sussman knows his Egypt, past and present, and he has the gift for creating engaging heroes of both sexes and really, really vile villains'

DR BARBARA MERTZ, archaeologist

'A textured, **well-researched and expertly paced** debut . . . truly inventive'

Publishers Weekly

'The twists in this detective story span 3,000 years and the credible surprises show the writer is a loss to the Secret Intelligence Service. **Frederick Forsyth has a worthy contemporary**'

The Week

'A **cinematic, rip-roaring adventure** mystery, brimming with details of Egyptian archaeology and history'

Booklist

'Satisfyingly **full of ruthless characters, difficult situations and impossible odds**'

WBQ

'**Excellent twists** . . . this is Harrison Ford country . . . Sussman's knowledge of Egypt – past and present – is **really impressive**'

Shots

Also by Paul Sussman

THE LOST ARMY OF CAMBYSES
THE LAST SECRET OF THE TEMPLE

and published by Bantam Books

THE
HIDDEN
OASIS

𓄿 𓏏 𓅓 𓊖 𓈖 𓏏 𓊹 𓏏 𓅓 𓏏

PAUL SUSSMAN

BANTAM BOOKS

LONDON • TORONTO • SYDNEY • AUCKLAND • JOHANNESBURG

..., London W5 5SA
A Random House Group Company
www.rbooks.co.uk

THE HIDDEN OASIS
A BANTAM BOOK: 9780553818734

First publication in Great Britain
Bantam edition published 2009

A CIP catalogue record for this book
is available from the British Library.

Addresses for Random House Group Ltd companies outside the UK
can be found at: www.randomhouse.co.uk
The Random House Group Ltd Reg. No. 954009

The Random House Group Limited supports The Forest Stewardship Council
(FSC), the leading international forest certification organisation. All our titles
that are printed on Greenpeace approved FSC certified paper carry the FSC
logo. Our paper procurement policy can be found at
www.rbooks.co.uk/environment

Typeset in 11/14pt Caslon 540 by
Falcon Oast Graphic Art Ltd.
Printed in the UK by CPI Cox & Wyman, Reading, RG1 8EX.

4 6 8 10 9 7 5 3

I am blessed to have found the most perfect oasis on earth, a place of shelter and warmth and joy unbounded. It is called my family: Alicky, Layla, Ezra and Jude.

This book is for them, with love, always.

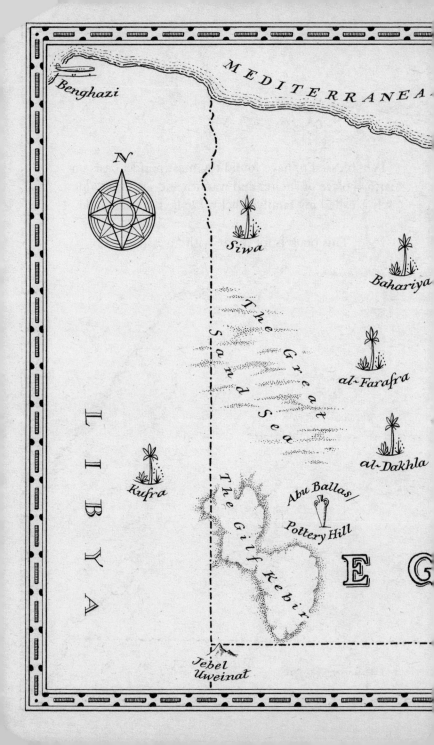

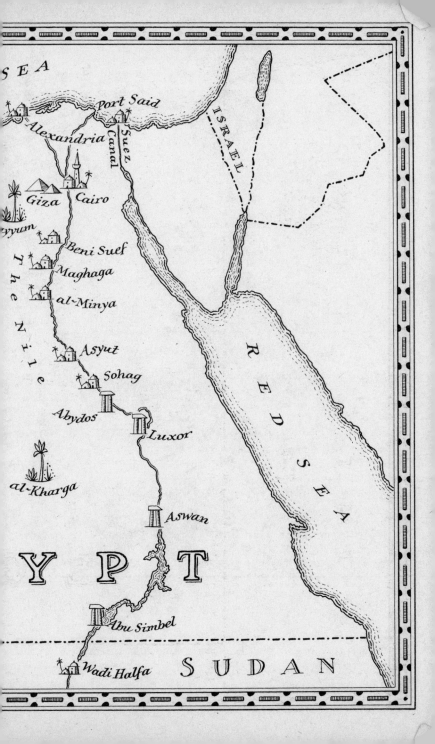

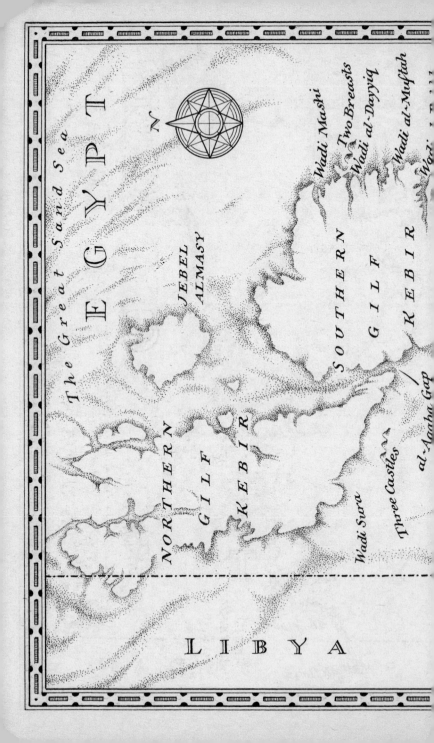

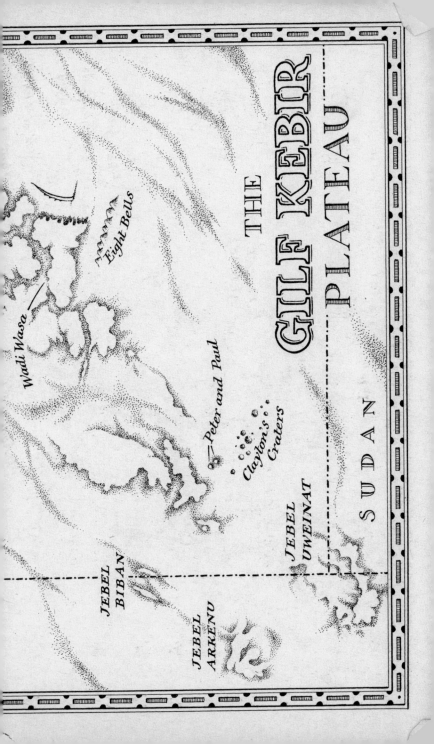

THE
HIDDEN
OASIS

2153 BC – EGYPT, THE WESTERN DESERT

They had brought a butcher with them out into the far wastes of *deshret*, and it was a cattle-slaughtering knife rather than a ceremonial one that he used to cut their throats.

A savage implement of knapped yellow flint, razor-sharp and as long as a forearm, the butcher went from priest to priest expertly pressing its blade into the soft angle between neck and collarbone. Eyes glazed from the brew of *shepen* and *shedeh* they had drunk to dull the pain, their shaved heads glistening with droplets of sacred water, each man offered prayers to Ra-Atum, imploring Him to bring them safely through the Hall of Two Truths into the Blessed Fields of Iaru. Whereupon the butcher tilted their heads backwards towards the dawn sky and, with a single, firm sweep, slashed their necks from ear to ear.

'May he walk in the beautiful ways, may he cross the heavenly firmament!' the remaining priests chanted. 'May he eat beside Osiris every day!'

Blood spattering across his arms and torso, the butcher

lowered each man to the ground and laid him flat before moving to the next priest in line and repeating the process, the row of bodies growing ever longer as he went about his business, blank-faced and brutally efficient.

From a nearby dune top Imti-Khentika, High Priest of Iunu, First Prophet of Ra-Atum, Greatest of Seers, gazed down at this choreographed slaughter. He felt sorrow, of course, at the deaths of so many men he had come to know as brothers. Satisfaction as well, though, for their mission was accomplished and every one of them had known from the outset that this was how it must end, so that no whisper should ever be spoken abroad of what they had done.

Behind him, in the east, he sensed the first warmth of the sun, Ra-Atum in His aspect as Khepri, bringing light and life to the world. He turned, throwing back his leopardskin hood and opening out his arms, reciting:

'Oh Atum, who came into being on the hill of creation,
With a blaze like the Benu Bird in the Benben shrine at Iunu!'

He raised a hand, fingers spread as if to clasp the narrow rim of magenta peeping above the sands on the horizon. Then, turning again, he looked in the opposite direction, westwards, to the rearing wall of cliffs that ran north to south a hundred *khet* distant, like a vast curtain strung across the very edge of the world.

Somewhere at the base of those cliffs, in the thick mesh of shadows that the dawn light had yet to penetrate, was the Divine Gateway: *re-en wesir*, the Mouth of Osiris. It was invisible from where he was standing. And it would have been to an observer positioned right in front of it, for he,

Imti, had uttered the spells of closing and concealment and none but those who knew how to look would have been aware of the gateway's presence. So it was that the place of their ancestors, *wehat er-djeru ta*, the oasis at the end of the world, had guarded its secrets across the endless expanse of years, its existence known only to a select few. Not for nothing was it also named *wehat seshtat* – the Hidden Oasis. Their cargo would be secure there. None would find it. It could rest in peace until more settled days should come.

Imti scanned the cliffs, his head nodding as if in approval, then he pulled his gaze back, to the warped spire of rock that burst from the dunes some eight *khet* from the cliff face. It was a striking feature even at this distance, dominating the surrounding landscape: a curving tower of black stone bowing outwards and upwards to a height of almost twenty *meh-nswt*, like some vast sickle blade ripping through the desert surface or, more appropriately, the foreleg of some gigantic scarab beetle clawing its way up through the sands.

How many travellers, Imti wondered, had passed that lone sentinel without realizing its significance? Few if any, he thought, answering his own question, for these were the empty lands, the dead lands, the domain of Set, where none who valued their lives would ever dream of venturing. Only those who knew of the forgotten places would come this far out into the burning nothingness. Only here would their charge be truly safe, far from the reach of those who would misuse its terrible powers. Yes, thought Imti, despite the horrors of their journey the decision to bring it west had been the right one. Definitely the right one.

Four moons ago now that decision had been taken, by a secret council of the most powerful in the land: Queen

Neith; Prince Merenre; the *tjaty* Userkef; General Rehu; and he, Imti-Khentika, Greatest of Seers.

Only the *nisu* himself, Lord of the Two Lands Nefer-ka-re Pepi, had not been present, nor informed of the council's decision. Once Pepi had been a mighty ruler, the equal of Khasekhemwy and Djoser and Khufu. Now in the ninety-third year of his reign, three times the span of a normal man's life, his power and authority had waned. Across the land the nomarchs raised private armies and made war on each other. To the north and the south the Nine Bows harried the borders. For three of the last four years the inundation had not come and the crops had failed.

Kemet was disintegrating, and the expectation was that things would only get worse. Son of Ra Pepi might have been, but now, at this time of crisis, others must assume control and make the great choices of state for him. And so their council had spoken: for its own protection, and for the safety of all men, the *iner-en sedjet* must be taken from Iunu where it was housed and transported back across the fields of sand to the safety of the Hidden Oasis, whence it had originally come.

And to he, Imti-Khentika, High Priest of Iunu, had fallen the responsibility of leading that expedition.

'Carry him across the winding waterway, ferry him to the eastern side of heaven!'

A renewed swell of chanting rose from below as another throat was cut, another body lowered to the ground. Fifteen lay there now, half their number.

'Oh Ra, let him come to you!' called Imti, joining in the chorus. 'Lead him upon the sacred roads, make him live for ever!'

He watched as the butcher moved to the next man in line, the air echoing with the moist whistle of severed windpipes. Then, as the knife sliced again, Imti turned his eyes away across the desert, recalling the nightmare of the journey they had just undertaken.

Eighty of them had set out, at the start of the *peret* season when the heat was at its least fierce. With their cargo swathed in layers of protective linen and lashed to a wooden sled, they had travelled south, first by boat to Zawty, then overland to the oasis of Kenem. Here they had rested a week before embarking on the last and most daunting stage of their mission – forty *iteru* across the burning, trackless wastes of *deshret* to the great cliffs and the Hidden Oasis.

Seven long weeks that final leg had taken them, the worst Imti had ever known, beyond even his most terrible imaginings. Before they had even reached halfway their pack oxen were all dead and they had had to take up the load themselves, twenty of them at a time yoked together like cattle, their shoulders streaked with blood from the bite of the sled's tow-ropes, their feet scorched by the fiery sands. Each day their progress had grown slower, hampered by mountainous dunes and blinding sandstorms, and above all by the heat, which even in that supposedly cool season had seared them from dawn until dusk as though the air itself was on fire.

Thirst, sickness and exhaustion had inexorably reduced their numbers and when their water had run out with still no sign of their destination he had feared their mission was doomed. Still they had trudged on, silent, indomitable, each lost in his private world of torment until on the fortieth day out of Kenem, the gods had rewarded their perseverance with the sight for which they had so long been praying: a hazy band of red across the western horizon marking the line of the great cliffs and the end of their journey.

Even then it was a further three days before they reached the Mouth of Osiris and passed through it into the tree-filled gorge of the oasis, by which point there were only thirty of them still standing. Their burden had been consigned to the temple at the heart of the oasis; they had bathed in the sacred springs; and then, early this morning, the spells of closing and concealment recited, the Two Curses laid, they had trooped back out into the desert and the throat-cutting had begun.

A loud clatter snapped Imti from his reverie. The butcher, a mute, was banging the handle of his knife against a rock to attract his attention.

Twenty-eight bodies lay on the sand beside him, leaving just the two of them still alive. It was the end.

'*Dua-i-nak netjer seni-i,*' said Imti, descending the dune and laying a hand on the butcher's blood-drenched shoulder. 'Thank you, my brother.'

A pause, then:

'You will drink *shepen*?'

The butcher shook his head and handed over his knife, tapping two fingers against his neck to indicate where Imti should cut before turning and kneeling in front of him. The blade was heavier than Imti had imagined, less easy to control, and it took all his strength to lift it to the butcher's throat and drag it across the flesh. He sliced as deep as he could, an explosion of frothy blood arching outwards across the sand.

'Oh Ra, open the doors of the firmament to him,' he

gasped, manhandling the body to the ground. 'Let him come to you and live for ever.'

He arranged the butcher's arms at his sides and, kissing his forehead, trudged back to the top of the dune, feet sinking into the sand almost up to his knees, the knife still clutched in his hand.

The sun was now just a fraction off being fully risen, only the very bottom of its circumference still flattened against the line of the horizon; even at that early hour its heat caused the air to buckle and throb. Imti gazed at it, eyes narrowed as if calculating the length of time it would take to elevate itself completely, then he turned west, towards the distant spire of rock and the dark mass of cliffs beyond. A minute passed, two, three. Suddenly, he lifted his arms to the sky and cried out:

> *'Oh Khepri, Oh Khepri,*
> *Ra-Atum at the dawn,*
> *Your eye sees all!*
> *Guard the* iner-en sedjet,
> *Hold it in your bosom!*
> *May evildoers be crushed in the jaws of Sobek*
> *And swallowed into the belly of the serpent Apep,*
> *So let it rest in peace and silence,*
> *Behind* re-en wesir, *in the* wehat sehstat!'

He turned once more towards the sun, threw the leopard-skin back over his head and, again struggling with its weight, drew the knife across each of his wrists.

He was an old man – sixty years and more – and his strength swiftly drained away, his eyes dimming, his mind clouding with a confused procession of images. He saw the girl with the green eyes from the village of his youth (oh how he had loved her!), his old wicker chair atop the Tower of Seshat at Iunu, where he had used to sit at night observing the movement of the stars, the tomb he had had made for himself in the Necropolis of the Seers which would never now hold his body, although his story at least had been left so that his name would live in eternity.

Round and round the images swirled, weaving in and out of each other, merging and splicing and becoming more fragmented until eventually they faded altogether and all that was left was the desert, the sky, the sun and, from somewhere nearby, a soft fluttering of wings.

Initially he thought it must be a vulture come to devour his corpse, but the sound was too delicate for such a large creature. Looking groggily around, he was surprised to see that on the dune top beside him was a tiny yellow-breasted bird, a wagtail, its head cocked to one side. What it was doing out there in the emptiness of the desert he had no idea, but, weak as he was, he smiled, for was it not as a wagtail that the great Benu had first manifested itself, calling in the dawn of creation from its perch atop the mighty Benben stone? Here, surely, at the very end of things, was confirmation that their mission was blessed.

'May he walk the beautiful ways,' he murmured. 'May he cross . . .'

He failed to finish the sentence, his legs buckling under him and pitching him face forward onto the sand, dead. The wagtail hopped about a moment, then fluttered up onto his shoulder. Raising its head to the sun, it started to sing.

November 1986 – Kukesi Airstrip, north-eastern Albania

The Russians were late for the rendezvous which meant that the weather window was gone. Thick racks of cloud streamed eastwards across the Šar mountains, blackening the late afternoon sky. By the time the limousine eventually pulled up at the airfield gates the first snowflakes were drifting down and in the two minutes it took the vehicle to speed out to the waiting Antonov AN–24 and come to a halt beside the boarding steps at the rear of the plane, the flakes had worked themselves up into swirling flurries, powdering the ground with white.

'*Verfluchte Scheiße!*' muttered Reiter, dragging on his cigarette and peering out of the cockpit window at the thickening storm. '*Schwanzlutschende Russen*. Cock-sucking Russians.'

The cockpit door opened behind him, revealing a tall, dark-skinned man in an expensive-looking suit. He had slicked-back hair and smelt strongly of aftershave.

'They're here,' he said, speaking in English. 'Start the engines.'

The door closed again. Reiter took another drag and started flicking switches, his fat, nicotine-stained fingers moving with surprising dexterity across the instrument panels in front of him and above his head.

'*Schwanzlutschende Ägypter*,' he spat. 'Cock-sucking Egyptians.'

To his right, his co-pilot chuckled. He was younger than Reiter, blond, handsome save for the heavy scar that ran across the top of his chin parallel to his bottom lip.

'Spreading sunshine and goodwill wherever you go, Kurt,' he said, twisting in his seat and gazing out of the cockpit's side window. 'How is it possible for one man to contain so much love, I ask myself?'

Reiter grunted but said nothing. Behind them their navigator was leafing through his flight charts.

'You think we'll get off in this?' he asked. 'It's looking pretty bad.'

Reiter shrugged, fingers still dancing over the instrument panels.

'Depends how long Omar Sharif spends fannying around out there. Another fifteen minutes and the runway's going to be buried.'

'Then?'

'Then we get to spend the night in this godforsaken shit-hole. So let's just hope Omar gets his skates on.'

He hit the starter buttons. With a sputter and a whine, the twin Ivchenko turboprops blasted into life, the propellers slicing at the snow-filled air, the fuselage trembling around them.

'Time, Rudi?'

The co-pilot glanced at his watch, a steel Rolex Explorer that had seen better days.

'Coming up to five.'

'They've got till ten-past and then I'm shutting down again,' said Reiter, leaning sideways and drilling his cigarette out into an ashtray on the floor. 'Ten-past and that's it.'

The co-pilot twisted round further and craned his neck, watching as the man in the suit descended the boarding steps, a chunky leather holdall clutched in his hand.

Another man followed him down, this one wrapped in a heavy coat and scarf. The limousine's rear door swung open to meet them and the man in the suit disappeared inside, his companion taking up position at the bottom of the steps.

'So what's the deal here, Kurt?' asked the co-pilot, still gazing out. 'Drugs? Guns?'

Reiter lit another cigarette and rolled his head, vertebrae clicking.

'Don't know, don't care. We pick up Omar in Munich, fly him here, he does whatever he's got to do and then we take him on down to Khartoum. No questions asked.'

'The last no-questions-asked job I did some bastard tried to cut me a new mouth,' muttered the co-pilot, reaching up and touching the scar underneath his bottom lip. 'I just hope they're paying us well.'

He threw a glance over his shoulder then returned his gaze to the window, watching as the limousine's bonnet slowly disappeared beneath a thin carapace of snow. Five minutes passed, the car door swung open again and the suited man re-emerged. His holdall was gone. In its place he was now clutching a large metal case, heavy to judge by the way he was struggling with it. He handed it to his companion, another case was passed out to him and the two of them trudged up the boarding steps into the plane. A moment later they came back out and collected two more cases before once again clambering back up into the Antonov. The co-pilot caught a momentary glimpse of someone inside the limousine, swathed in what looked like an ankle-length black leather coat, before a hand reached out, slammed the door and the vehicle sped off.

'OK, they're done,' he said, turning away. 'Get us closed up, Jerry.'

While the navigator headed back into the cabin to retract the steps and secure the door, the two pilots donned headsets and ran through their final checks. Behind them the suited Egyptian loomed in the cockpit doorway, his head and shoulders dusted with snow.

'The weather will not prevent us taking off.'

It was phrased more as a statement than a question.

'You let me be the judge of that,' growled Reiter, cigarette clamped between his teeth. 'If it's blowing too hard on the runway we're shutting down and sitting it out.'

'Mr Girgis is expecting us in Khartoum tonight,' said the Egyptian. 'We will take off as planned.'

'If your Russian friends hadn't been late it wouldn't be a fucking issue,' snapped Reiter. 'Now get back to your seat. Jerry, get them strapped in!'

Reaching down he released the brakes, eased the mixture control forward, then the throttle levers. The engine's pitch rose to a roar as the revs shot up. The plane started to move.

'The weather must not prevent us taking off!' came the Egyptian's voice from behind them in the cabin. 'Mr Girgis expects us in Khartoum tonight!'

'Kiss my arse, rag-head,' muttered Reiter, taxiing the plane out to the end of the cinder runway and turning. The navigator came back in, closed the cockpit door and sat down, buckling his seatbelt.

'What do you think?' he asked, nodding out of the window at the worsening blizzard. Reiter just pulled back on the throttle, gazed a moment at the spiralling snow, then, with a muttered 'Fuck it!' pushed the throttle forward again, grasping the control column with his other hand.

'Grab your balls, boys,' he said. 'This is going to be bumpy.'

The plane rapidly picked up speed, bumping and swerving on the uneven cinder surface. Reiter's feet wrestled with the rudder pedals as he struggled to counter the crosswinds now whipping across the airfield. At 80 knots the Antonov's nose came up, only to drop again and with the end of the runway looming ever nearer the navigator yelled at Reiter to abort. The pilot ignored him, holding the plane steady, pushing the speed up to 90 knots, then 100, then 110. At the last minute, as the speed indicator hit 115 and the end of the runway disappeared beneath them, he yanked the control column back towards his chest. The plane's nose lurched upwards, its wheels bumping across grass before rising sluggishly into the air.

'Jesus Christ,' coughed the navigator. 'You mad fucking . . .'

Reiter chuckled and lit another cigarette, taking them up through the clouds and into the clear sky above.

'Easy,' he said.

They refuelled in Benghazi on the North African coast before setting a course south-east across the Sahara, cruising at 5,000 metres, the plane on auto-pilot, the desert below glowing a dull silver in the moonlight as though it had been cast out of pewter. Ninety minutes into the flight they shared a thermos of tepid coffee and some sandwiches. An hour after that they cracked open a bottle of vodka, the navigator easing the cockpit door ajar and throwing a glance into the cabin behind.

'Asleep,' he said, clicking the door closed again. 'Both of them. Spark out.'

'Maybe we should take a look in one of the cases,' said the co-pilot, swigging from the vodka bottle and handing it across to Reiter. 'While they're both out of it.'

'Not a good idea,' said the navigator. 'They're packing. Or at least Omar is. Saw it under his jacket when I was strapping him in. A Glock, I think, or a Browning. Didn't get a proper look.'

The co-pilot shook his head.

'I've got a bad feeling about this. Have had from the start. A very bad feeling.'

He stood, stretched his legs and, stepping to the back of the cockpit, removed a canvas shoulder bag from the wall locker. He sat down again and started rummaging inside it.

'You want to get one of my cock?' asked Reiter as the co-pilot pulled out a camera.

'Sorry, Kurt, haven't got a big enough lens.'

The navigator was leaning forward.

'Leica?' he asked.

The co-pilot nodded.

'M6. Bought it a couple of weeks ago. Thought I'd get some shots of Khartoum. Never been there before.'

Reiter gave a disparaging snort and, taking a long gulp, passed the vodka bottle over his shoulder to the navigator. The co-pilot fiddled with the camera, turning it over in his hands.

'Hey, you know that bird I've been knocking off?'

'What, the one with the big arse?' said the navigator.

The co-pilot smirked and waggled the camera.

'Got some pics of her before we left.'

Reiter turned, interested suddenly.

'What sort of pics?'

'Kind of artistic,' said the co-pilot.

'What does that mean?'

'You know, Kurt, artistic.'

'I don't fucking know.'

'Artistic. Tasteful. Stockings, suspenders, legs round her neck, banana up her . . .'

Reiter's eyes widened, his mouth shaping itself into a lustful pucker. Behind them the navigator grinned and started humming the tune to Queen's 'Fat-Bottomed Girls'. The co-pilot joined in, then Reiter as well, the three of them breaking into song as one, belting out the chorus, slapping time on the armrests of their seats. They sang it once, twice, and were just starting on a third round when Reiter suddenly fell silent, leaning forward and peering out of the cockpit window. The co-pilot and navigator sang on for another couple of lines until their voices too trailed off as they realized Reiter was no longer with them.

'What?' asked the navigator.

Reiter just nodded ahead, to where what looked like a vast mountain had suddenly loomed in the distance, directly across their flight path – a dense, bulging mass of shadow rearing from the desert floor high into the sky and stretching from horizon to horizon. Although it was hard to be sure, it seemed to be moving, drifting towards them.

'What is that?' asked the navigator. 'Mist?'

Reiter said nothing, just watched through narrowed eyes as the darkness came steadily closer.

'Sandstorm,' he said eventually.

'God Almighty,' whistled the co-pilot. 'Look at it.'

Reiter grasped the handles of the control column and started to ease it back.

'We need to get higher.'

They climbed to 5,500 metres, then 6,000 as the storm advanced inexorably in their direction, devouring the ground, blotting it out.

'Fuck, it's moving fast,' said Reiter.

They climbed higher, right up to their service ceiling, almost 7,000 metres. The wall of shadow was now close enough for them to make out its contours, great folds and billows of dust creasing around and into each other, tumbling silently across the landscape. The plane started to bump and tremble.

'I don't think we're going to get above it,' said the co-pilot.

The bumping became more pronounced, a faint hissing sound percolating into the cockpit as grains of sand and other debris started to impact on the windows and fuselage.

'If any of that gets in the engines . . .'

'. . . we're screwed,' muttered Reiter, finishing the co-pilot's sentence. 'We'll have to backtrack and try to go round it.'

The storm seemed to be gathering speed. As if aware of their intentions and anxious to catch them before they could turn, its face surged forward like a tidal wave, eating up the intervening distance. Reiter started to bank the plane to port, beads of sweat glistening on his forehead.

'If we can just get her round we should be—'

He was cut short by a loud bang, outside, to starboard. The plane yawed sharply in the same direction and started to roll, its nose dropping, the master caution indicators bursting into life like the lights on a Christmas tree.

'Oh Christ!' cried the navigator. 'Oh Jesus Christ!'

Reiter was fighting to stabilize the aircraft as their dive steepened, the cockpit turning almost 40 degrees on its side. Equipment tumbled out of the locker behind them, the discarded vodka bottle span across the floor and smashed against the starboard bulkhead.

'Fire starboard engine,' yelled the co-pilot, throwing a backward glance out of the window. 'A lot of fucking fire, Kurt!'

'Fuck, fuck, fuck,' hissed Reiter.

'Fuel pressure dropping. Oil pressure dropping. Altitude six thousand five hundred and dropping. Turn-and-slip – Christ, it's all over the place!'

'Shut it down and hit the fire bottle!' shouted Reiter. 'Jerry, I need to know where we are. Fast.'

While the navigator scrambled to locate their position and the co-pilot furiously flicked switches, Reiter continued to battle the controls, the plane losing height all the time, spiralling downward in a series of broad circles, the storm coming ever closer, looming in and out of the cockpit window like a towering cliff face.

'Six thousand metres,' cried the co-pilot. 'Five thousand seven hundred . . . six hundred . . . five hundred. You've got to get the nose up and turn us, Kurt!'

'Tell me something I don't already fucking know!' There was an edge of panic in his voice. 'Jerry?'

'Twenty-three degrees 30 minutes north,' called the navigator. 'Twenty-five degrees 18 minutes east.'

'Where's the nearest airfield?'

'What the hell are you talking about? We're in the middle

of the fucking Sahara! There aren't any airfields! Dakhla's three hundred and fifty kilometres, Kufra's—'

The cabin door flew open and the suited Egyptian staggered into the cockpit, grasping at the navigator's seat to steady himself as the plane bucked and rolled.

'What is happening?' he cried. 'Tell me what is happening!'

'Christ Al-fucking-mighty!' roared Reiter. 'Get back to your seat, you mad—'

He got no further because at that moment the storm lunged forward and enveloped them, flinging the Antonov up and then down as though it were made of balsa. The Egyptian was pitched face forward against the armrest of Reiter's seat, slicing his head open; the port engine sputtered, coughed and died.

'Get out a Mayday,' cried Reiter.

'No!' coughed the Egyptian, pawing at his shredded scalp. 'Radio silence. We agreed there would be—'

'Call it, Rudi!'

The co-pilot had already flicked on the radio.

'Mayday, Mayday. Victor Papa Charlie Mike Tango four seven three. Mayday, Mayday. Both engines out. Repeat, both engines out. Position . . .'

The navigator repeated their GPS co-ordinates and the co-pilot relayed them into his microphone, sending the message over and over as Reiter wrestled with the controls. With no power and the storm buffeting them from all sides it was a hopeless battle and they continued to plummet, the altimeter's needle spinning relentlessly anticlockwise, its gauge clicking downwards past 5,000 metres, then 4,000, 3,000, 2,000. Outside the howling of the wind grew louder, the turbulence ever more violent as they plunged into the heart of the maelstrom.

'We're going down!' cried Reiter as they dipped below 1,500 metres. 'Get Omar secure.'

The navigator dropped the folding chair on the back of the co-pilot's seat and heaved their blood-soaked passenger onto it, strapping him in before lurching back to his own seat.

'*Estana!*' the Egyptian called weakly to his companion in the cabin. '*Ehna hanoaa! Echahd!*'

They were now under 1,000 metres. Reiter dropped the landing flaps and activated the wing spoilers in a desperate bid to reduce their speed.

'Undercarriage?' shouted the co-pilot, his voice all but drowned out by the raging of the wind and the clatter of debris against the plane's fuselage.

'Can't risk it!' yelled Reiter. 'If it's rocky down there it'll flip us over.'

'Chances?'

'Somewhere south of nil.'

He continued to pull on the control column, a chant of '*Allah-u-Akhbar!*' echoing from the cabin behind, the co-pilot and navigator watching in horrified fascination as the altimeter whirred its way downwards through the last few hundred metres.

'If we get out of this you make sure you share those photos, Rudi!' cried Reiter at the very last moment. 'You hear! I want to see that woman's tits and arse!'

The altimeter hit zero. Reiter gave the control yoke a final yank, the nose by some miracle responding and coming up so that although they hit the ground at almost 400 km/hour, they at least did so level. There was a ferocious, bone-shattering thud: the impact ripped the Egyptian out of his seat and smashed him first into the ceiling of the cockpit and then against its rear wall, his neck snapping like a twig. They bounced, came down again, the cockpit lights cut out and the port window exploded inwards, shearing off half of Reiter's face like a scalpel. His hysterical screams were all but obliterated by the raging of the storm, a suffocating cloud of sand and debris pouring in through the opening where the window had been.

For 1,000 metres they careered across flat terrain, bucking and jolting but just about keeping a straight line. Then the plane's nose glanced against some unseen obstruction and they went into a spin, the 14-tonne Antonov whirling around like a leaf in a breeze. A fire extinguisher tore itself from its holder and cannoned into the navigator's ribs, shattering them as though they were made of china; the door of the wall locker flew from its hinges and crunched into the back of Reiter's head, pulping it. Round and round they went, all sense of speed and direction lost in the choking murk of the cockpit, everything kaleidoscoping into a single chaotic blur. After what seemed like an age but must have been only seconds, they started to slow, the plane's revolutions slackening as the desert's surface grasped at the underside and finally brought the plane to a halt, leaning backwards at a precarious angle as though on the edge of a sharp slope, the nose pointing upwards.

For a moment everything was still, the sandstorm continuing to hammer against the fuselage and windows, the acrid stench of super-heated metal suffusing the cockpit; then, groggily, the co-pilot shifted in his seat.

'Kurt?' he called. 'Jerry?'

No response. He reached out, fingers touching something warm and wet, then started to unbuckle himself. As he did so he felt the plane tilt. He stopped, waited, then continued to fumble, throwing off his harness and levering himself out of his seat. Another tilt, the plane's nose see-sawing up and then down. The co-pilot froze, trying to sense what was happening, peering into the blackness. Again the plane pivoted before, with a groan and a creak, its nose started to rise and this time kept on going, rearing almost vertical as the Antonov started to slide backwards. It snagged on something, stopped, started sliding again and then it was plummeting tail-first through open space. The sandstorm disappeared and the windows suddenly cleared to reveal tangled glimpses of shadowy rock walls to either side, as though they were falling into a gorge of some sort. The plane bounced and cartwheeled downwards until with a deafening crunch it slammed belly-first into a dense mass of trees. For several moments the only sounds were the crack and hiss of tortured metal. Then, gradually, other noises started to fade in: a rustle of leaves, a distant tinkle of water and, soft at first but growing steadily louder until it filled the night, the startled twittering of birds.

'Kurt?' groaned a voice from inside the wreckage. 'Jerry?'

WASHINGTON. THE PENTAGON BUILDING. THE SAME EVENING

'Thank you all for coming. I apologize for bringing you here at such short notice, but something has . . . cropped up.'

The speaker drew heavily on his cigarette, wafting a hand to dispel the smoke and gazing intently at the seven men and one woman gathered round the table in front of him. The suite was windowless, sparsely furnished, non-descript, the same as hundreds of other offices within the cramped catacomb of the Pentagon, its sole distinguishing feature a large map of Africa and the Middle East covering most of one wall. That and the fact that the only lighting came from a battered Anglepoise lamp sitting on the floor at the foot of the map, so that while the map itself was illuminated everything else in the room, including those in it, was sunk in deep shadow.

'Forty minutes ago,' the speaker continued, his voice low, throaty, 'one of our stations picked up a radio message from over the Sahara.'

He reached into his pocket and produced a hand-held laser pointer, directing its eye towards the map. A jerky red dot appeared in the middle of the Mediterranean.

'It was sent from about here.'

The dot slid down the map, coming to rest in the south-west corner of Egypt, close to the intersection of the borders with Libya and Sudan, over the words *Hadabat al Jilf al Kabir* (The Gilf Kebir Plateau).

'The message came from a plane. A Cayman-registered Antonov, call sign VP–CMT 473.'

A pause, then:

'It was a Mayday.'

There was an uneasy shifting in chairs, a muttered 'Jesus Christ.'

'What do we know?' asked one of the listeners, a burly man with a balding head.

The speaker sucked out the last of his cigarette and drilled the stub into an ashtray on the table.

'At this stage not much,' he replied. 'I'll give you what we've got.'

He talked for five minutes, tracing lines across the map with his pointer – Albania, Benghazi, back to the Gilf Kebir – occasionally referring to a sheaf of papers scattered in front of him. He lit another cigarette, and then another, chain-smoking, the atmosphere in the room growing steadily thicker and more acrid. When he finished everyone started speaking at once, their voices merging into a confused cacophony from which certain words and half-sentences leapt out – 'Knew it was crazy!' 'Saddam!' 'World War Three!' 'Iran-Contra', 'Fucking catastrophe', 'Gift to Khomeini' – but from which no overall sense could be made.

Only the woman remained silent, tapping her pen thoughtfully on the tabletop before rising to her feet, walking over to the map and gazing up at it. Her body cast a slim silhouette, her bobbed blond hair glowing in the lamplight.

'We'll just have to find it,' she said.

Although her voice was soft, barely audible amidst the hubbub of male argument and counter-argument, there was an underlying strength to it, an air of authority that commanded attention. The other speakers quietened down until the room was silent.

'We'll just have to find it,' she repeated. 'Before anyone else does. I'm assuming the Mayday went out on an open frequency?'

The speaker acknowledged that it had.

'Then we should get to work.'

'And how exactly do you propose we do that?' asked the

burly, balding man. 'Phone Mubarak? Put an ad in the paper?'

His tone was sarcastic, confrontational. The woman didn't rise to it.

'We adapt, we improvise,' she said, still gazing up at the map, her back to the room. 'Satellite imaging, military exercises, local contacts. NASA has a research unit in that part of the world. We use whatever we can, however we can. If that's OK with you, Bill?'

The balding man muttered something, but was otherwise silent. No one else spoke.

'That's it then,' said the original speaker, pocketing his laser pointer and shuffling his papers into a neat pile. 'We adapt, we improvise.'

He lit another cigarette.

'And we'd better do it quickly. Before this whole thing turns into even more of a disaster than it already is.'

He picked up his papers and swept from the room, followed by the rest of the group. The woman alone remained, one hand held at her neck, the other reaching up to the map.

'Gilf Kebir,' she murmured, touching a finger to the paper, holding it there a moment before placing her foot over the lamp's On–Off button. Pressing down with the toe of her shoe, she plunged the room into darkness.

FOUR MONTHS LATER, PARIS

They were waiting for Kanunin in his hotel suite when he got back from the nightclub. The moment he stepped through the door they took out his bodyguard with a single, silenced shot to the temple and punched him to the floor, his ankle-length coat tangling around him in a swirl of black leather. One of the hookers started screaming and they shot her as well, a 9mm dumdum into her right ear, the entire left side of her head exploding away like a shattered eggshell. Waving a pistol at her companion to indicate that if she said a word the same would happen to her, they forced Kanunin onto his belly and yanked his head back so that he was staring up at the ceiling. He didn't bother to struggle, knew who they were, knew it was pointless.

'Just get on with it,' he coughed.

He closed his eyes and waited for the bullet. Instead, there was a rustle of paper followed by the feel of something – lots of things – pattering down onto his face. His eyes flicked open again. Above him hovered the mouth of a paper bag from which was dribbling a steady stream of pea-sized steel ball-bearings.

'What the—'

His head was forced back further as a knee pressed into the base of his spine, huge hands clasping vice-like around his forehead and temples.

'Mr Girgis invites you to dine with him.'

Other hands clawed at his mouth, prising apart his jaws, yanking them open, the bag coming closer to his face so that the ball-bearings dribbled directly down into his mouth, choking him. He bucked and writhed, his screams no more than a muted gurgle, but the hands held him tight and the pouring continued, on and on until the bag was empty and his jerking had grown weaker and eventually stopped altogether. They dropped his body on the floor, steel trickling from between his bloodied lips, put a bullet through his head just to be certain and, without even glancing at the girl hunched against the wall, left. They were already speeding away into the dawn traffic when the hotel suddenly echoed to the crazed soprano of her screaming.

THE WESTERN DESERT, BETWEEN THE GILF KEBIR AND DAKHLA OASIS – THE PRESENT

They were the last Bedouin still making the great journey between Kufra and Dakhla, a 1,400-kilometre round trip through the empty desert. Using only camels for transport, they carried palm oil, embroideries, and silver and leather-work on the way out, and returned with dates, dried mulberries, cigarettes and Coca-Cola.

It made no economic sense, such a journey, but then it was not about economics. Rather, it was about tradition, keeping alive the old ways, following the ancient caravan routes that their fathers had followed, and their fathers before them, and their fathers before them, suviving where no one else could survive, navigating where no one else could navigate. They were tough people, proud, Kufra Bedouin, Sanusi, descendants of the Banu Sulaim. The desert was their home, travelling through it their life. Even if it did make no economic sense.

This particular trip had been hard even by the harsh standards of the Sahara, where no journey is ever easy. From Kufra, the trek south-east to the Gilf Kebir and through the al-Aqaba gap – the direct route east would have taken them into the Great Sand Sea which even the Bedouin dared not cross – had passed off uneventfully.

Then, at the eastern end of the gap, they had discovered that the artesian well at which they would normally have filled their water-skins had dried up, leaving supplies dangerously tight for the remaining three hundred kilometres. It was a concern, but not a disaster, and they had continued north-east to Dakhla without any great sense of alarm. Two days on, however, and still three from their destination, they had been hit by a ferocious sandstorm, the feared *khamsin*. Forced to hunker down for 48 hours until it blew over, their water supplies had in the process dwindled to next to nothing.

Now the storm was gone and they were on the move again, pushing hard to cover the remaining distance before their water ran out completely, their camels lolloping across the desert just short of a full trot, driven on by cries of '*hut, hut!*' and '*yalla, yalla!*'

So intent were the Bedouin on reaching their journey's end as swiftly as possible that they would almost certainly have missed the corpse had it not appeared directly in their path. Rigid as a statue, it protruded waist up from the side of a dune, mouth open, one arm extended as though imploring them for help. The lead rider shouted, they slowed to a halt and, bringing their camels down onto the sand and dismounting, gathered around to look, seven of them, *shaals* wrapped around their heads and faces against the sun so that only their eyes were visible.

It was the body of a man, no doubt about that, perfectly preserved in the desert's desiccating embrace, the skin dried and tightened to the consistency of parchment, the eyes shrivelled in their sockets to hard, raisin-like nuggets.

'The storm must have uncovered it,' said one of the riders, speaking *badawi*, Bedouin Arabic, his voice coarse and gravelly, like the desert itself.

At a signal from their leader three of the Bedouin dropped to their knees and started to scoop sand away from the corpse, freeing it from the dune. Its clothes – boots, trousers, long-sleeved shirt – were worn ragged, as if they had undergone an arduous journey. A plastic thermos flask was still clutched in one of its hands, empty, the screw-top gone, the rim scarred with what looked like teeth marks, as though in his desperation the man had chewed at the plastic, hopelessly biting for whatever tiny drop of moisture remained within.

'Soldier?' asked one of the Bedouin doubtfully. 'From the war?'

The leader shook his head, squatting down and tapping the scratched Rolex Explorer watch around the body's left wrist.

'More recent,' he said. '*Amrekanee*. American.'

He used the word not specifically, but to denote anyone of western, non-Arab appearance.

'What's he doing out here?' asked another of the men.

The leader shrugged and, rolling the body onto its front, tugged a canvas bag off its shoulder and opened it, removing a map, a wallet, a camera, two distress flares, some emergency rations and, finally, a balled-up handkerchief. He unfolded this, revealing a miniature clay obelisk, crudely made and no longer than his finger. He squinted at it, turning it this way and that, examining the curious

symbol with which each of its four faces was incised: a sort of cross, its top arm tapering to a point from which a thin looping line curled upwards and over like a tail. It meant nothing to him and, balling it in the handkerchief again, he laid it aside and turned his attention to the wallet. There was an ID card inside, bearing a photo of a young, blond-haired man with a heavy scar running parallel to his bottom lip. None of the Bedouin could read the writing on the card and, after gazing at it a moment, the leader returned it and the other objects to the knapsack. He began patting the man's pockets, and pulled out a compass and a plastic canister with a roll of used camera film inside. These too he dropped into the knapsack, before tugging the watch off the man's wrist, slipping it into the pocket of his *djellaba* and coming to his feet.

'Let's get going,' he said, swinging the knapsack onto his shoulder and heading back towards the camels.

'Shouldn't we bury him?' one of the men called after him.

'The desert'll do it,' came the reply. 'We need to get on.'

They followed him down the dune and mounted their camels, kicking at them to bring them upright. As they moved off, the last rider – a small, wizened man with pock-marked skin – turned in his saddle and looked back, gazing at the body as it slowly receded behind them. Once it had faded to no more than a blurred lump on the otherwise featureless desert he fumbled within the folds of his *djellaba* and pulled out a mobile phone. Keeping one eye on the riders in front to ensure no one was looking round at him, he pressed at the keypad with a gnarled thumb. He couldn't get a signal, and after trying for a couple of minutes gave up and returned the phone to his pocket.

'*Hut-hut!*' he cried, slapping his heels into his camel's quivering flanks. '*Yalla, yalla!*'

CALIFORNIA, YOSEMITE NATIONAL PARK

It was a five-hundred-metre wall of vertical rock rearing above the Merced Valley like a billow of grey satin, and Freya Hannen was just fifty metres from its summit when she disturbed the wasps' nest.

She had toed into a small rock pocket near the top of her tenth pitch and, reaching up onto an overhanging ledge, was feeling for purchase around the roots of an old manzanita bush when she accidentally swiped the nest, a cloud of insects erupting from beneath the bush and swarming angrily around her.

Wasps were her primal fear, had been since she had been stung in the mouth by one as a child. A ridiculous fear to have, given that she made her living climbing some of the world's most dangerous rock faces, but then terror is rarely rational. For her sister Alex it was needles and injections; for Freya, wasps.

She froze, stomach tightening, her breath coming in short panicked gasps, the air around her a mesh of skimming yellow-jackets. Then one stung her on the arm. Unable to stop herself, she snatched her hand away from the ledge and barn-doored outwards from the rock, her lead-line flapping wildly, the ponderosa forest 450 metres below seeming to telescope up towards her. For a moment she swung, hinging on her right hand and foot, her left limbs flapping in space, carabiners and cams jangling on her harness. Then, gritting her teeth and trying to ignore the burning sensation on her arm, she heaved herself back to the wall and locked her hand around a protruding rock knuckle, pressing into the warm granite as though into a lover's protective embrace. She remained like that for what felt like an age, eyes closed, fighting the urge to scream, waiting for the swarm to calm and dissipate, then traversed swiftly to her right beneath the ledge and climbed up further along, beside a stunted pine that lurched outwards from the rock like a withered arm. She anchored herself there and sat back against the trunk, panting.

'Shit,' she gasped. And then, for no obvious reason: 'Alex.'

It was eleven hours since she had received the call. She had been back at her apartment in San Francisco when it had come, just after midnight, totally out of the blue, after all these years. Once, early in her climbing career, she had lost her footing and fallen from a two-hundred-metre rock face, plunging vertiginously through open space before her line caught and held her. That's how the call had felt: an initial giddy sense of bewilderment and disbelief, like plummeting from a great height, followed by a sudden, sickening jerk of realization.

Afterwards she had sat in darkness, the late-night sounds of North Beach's bars and cafés drifting in through the open windows. Then, going online, she had booked herself a flight before throwing some gear into a bag, locking up the apartment and roaring off on her battered Triumph Bonneville. Three hours later she was in Yosemite; two hours after that, with the first pink of dawn staining the heads of the Sierra Nevada, at the base of Liberty Cap, ready to start her ascent.

It was what she always did in times of turmoil, when she needed to clear her head – climbed. Deserts were Alex's thing: vast, dry, empty spaces, devoid of life and sound; mountains and rock were Freya's – rearing, vertical land-scapes through which she could clamber up towards the sky, pushing mind and body to the limit. It was impossible to explain to those who had never experienced it; impossible to explain even to herself. The closest she had come was in an interview with, of all things, *Playboy* magazine: 'When I'm up there I just feel more alive,' she had said. 'Like the rest of the time I'm half asleep.'

Now, more than ever, she needed the peace and clarity

that climbing brought her. Thundering east along Highway 120 towards Yosemite her first instinct had been to free-climb a route, something really tough, punishing: Freerider on El-Capitan, perhaps, or Astroman on Washington Column.

Then she had started thinking about Liberty Cap, and the more she had thought about it, the more attractive it had seemed.

It was not an obvious choice. Parts of it were aided, which necessitated extra equipment and denied her the absolute purity of a free-climb; technically it wasn't actually that difficult, not by her standards, which meant that she would not be pushing herself as hard as she wanted: not right to the very edge and beyond.

Against that, it was one of the few Yosemite big walls she had never attempted before. More important, it was probably the only one that at this time of year was not going to be covered with a scrabble of other climbers, thereby ensuring absolute peace and solitude – no one talking to her, no one trying to take her photo, no amateurs blocking her way and slowing her down. Just her and the rock and the silence.

Sitting on the ledge now, the midday sun warming her face, her arm still smarting from the wasp sting, she took a gulp from the water bottle in her day-pack and gazed down at the route she'd just ascended. Apart from a couple of aided sections it hadn't thrown up too many problems. A less experienced climber might have taken a couple of days to summit, overnighting on a ledge halfway up. She would do it in less than half that time. Eight hours tops.

She still couldn't escape a vague twinge of disappointment that it hadn't stretched her more, taken her to that heady, intoxicating plateau reached only through extreme physical and mental exertion. Then again the views from up there were so spectacular, the sense of removedness so complete she could forgive the lack of challenge. Yes, she thought, in the circumstances Liberty Cap had been just what she needed. Holding on to the anchor rope she extended her legs – long, tanned, toned – rubbing at the muscles, pointing the tips of her Anasazi climb shoes to stretch out her feet and shins. Then, standing and turning, she scanned the rock above ready to start her eleventh and final pitch, fifty metres up to the summit.

'Allez,' she murmured, rubbing chalk onto her hands from the pouch at her waist. 'Allez', and then, as if prompted by the similarity in sound, 'Alex' again, her voice all but lost in the roar of Nevada Falls below.

Later, back down at her motorbike, the climb done, she bumped into a couple of guys she knew, fellow wall rats, one of them pretty good looking although at this moment that was the last thing on her mind. They chatted for a while, Freya describing her ascent – 'You soloed Liberty Gap? Jesus, that's impressive!' – before she cut the conversation short, explaining that she had a flight to catch.

'Anywhere nice?' asked the good-looking one.

She rolled the bike off its stand and swung her leg over the saddle.

'Egypt,' she replied, starting the engine, revving it.

'To climb?'

She clicked the bike into gear.

'For my sister's funeral.'

And with that she roared off, her blond hair whipping behind her like a flame.

CAIRO – THE MARRIOTT HOTEL

Flin Brodie adjusted his reading glasses and glanced up at the audience: fourteen elderly American tourists scattered amongst the fifty or so chairs in front of him, none of them looking especially interested. He ventured a quip about how he was glad they'd all managed to find a seat, which brought a guffaw of laughter from his tourist-guide friend Margot, but was otherwise greeted with blank stares.

Oh Christ, he thought, fiddling nervously with the pocket of his corduroy jacket. *It's going to be one of those.*

He tried again, explaining that years of working as an archaeologist in the western desert had got him well used to large empty spaces. Again, the joke fell horribly flat, even Margot's supportive laughter starting to sound strained. He gave up and, hitting a button on *his* laptop to bring up the opening Powerpoint slide – a shot of the receding dune ridges of the Great Sand Sea – was about to start the lecture when the door at the side of the room clicked open. An overweight man – extremely overweight – in a cream-coloured jacket and bow-tie, leaned in.

'May I?' His voice was curiously high-pitched, almost feminine, the accent American, Deep South. Flin glanced at Margot, who shrugged as if to say 'why not?' and waved the man forward. The newcomer closed the door and sat down in the seat nearest to it, removing a handkerchief and dabbing at his forehead. Flin allowed him to settle, then, clearing his throat, began talking, *his* accent English, the diction clipped and clear.

'Ten thousand years ago the Sahara was a considerably more hospitable place than it is today,' he told them.

'Radar imaging of the Selima Sand Sheet by the Space Shuttle *Columbia* has revealed extensive fluvial topography – basically the outlines of long-lost lakes and river systems. This was a landscape much like the savannah of modern-day sub-Saharan Africa.'

Next slide: the Serengeti National Park in Tanzania.

'There were lakes, rivers, forests, grasslands – home to an abundance of wildlife: gazelles, giraffes, zebras, elephants, hippos. And to humans as well – itinerant hunter-gatherers for the most part, although there is also evidence for more permanent Middle and Upper Palaeolithic settlements.'

'Speak up!'

This from a woman right at the back of the room, a hearing aid clamped to her ear like a plastic barnacle.

Why in God's name do you sit at the back if you can't bloody hear properly? Flin thought.

'I'm sorry,' he said aloud, lifting his voice. 'Is that better?'

The woman waved a walking stick to indicate that it was.

'More permanent Palaeolithic settlements,' he repeated, trying to pick up the thread of what he was saying. 'The Gilf Kebir Plateau in the south-western corner of Egypt – an upland region covering an area roughly the size of Switzerland – is particularly rich in remains from this period, both material . . .'

Slides of, respectively, rearing orange cliffs, a grinding stone and a collection of flint tools.

'. . . but also votive and artistic. Some of you may know the film *The English Patient*, which featured the prehistoric rock paintings in the so-called Cave of the Swimmers, discovered in 1933 by Hungarian explorer Ladislaus Almasy in the Wadi Sura, on the western side of the Gilf.'

A picture of the cave came up: stylized red figures with bulbous heads and stick-like limbs appearing to swim and dive across the uneven limestone walls.

'Anyone seen the film?'

General murmurs of 'No', which persuaded him not to bother with the brief critique of the movie he usually slipped in at this point. Instead he pushed straight on with the talk.

'Towards the end of the last ice age,' he said, 'around the Middle Holocene, about 7000 BC, this savannah-like landscape underwent a dramatic change. As the northern ice sheets retreated so aridification set in, the verdant plains and river systems giving way to the sort of landscape we see today. The desert peoples were forced to migrate eastwards into the Nile Valley . . .'

Scenic slide of the Nile.

'. . . where they developed the various pre-dynastic cultures – Tasian, Badarian, Naqada – that would eventually coalesce to form a single unified state. The Egypt of the pharaohs.'

One of the listeners, Flin noticed, a jug-eared man in a New York Mets baseball cap, was already starting to nod. And he hadn't even finished the introduction. Christ, he needed a drink.

'I have travelled and excavated in the Sahara for well over a decade,' he continued, running a hand through his unkempt black hair. 'Primarily at sites in and around the Gilf Kebir. In this lecture I wish to put forward three propositions based on my work. Three rather controversial propositions.'

He emphasized 'controversial', scanning the audience for

any sign of interest. Nothing. Not a flicker. He might as well have been talking about vegetable-growing. Would probably have done better if he had been. *Christ*, he needed a drink.

'Firstly,' he went on, struggling to sound enthusiastic, 'I believe that even after they had migrated eastwards into the Nile Valley, the ancient Sahara dwellers never entirely forgot their original desert home. The Gilf in particular, with its dramatic cliffs and deep wadis, continued to exert a strong religious and superstitious influence on the early Egyptian imagination, its memory kept alive, albeit in allegorical form, in a number of myths and literary traditions, notably those relating to the desert gods Ash and Set.'

Slide of the god Set – human body surmounted by the head of some indeterminate animal with a long snout and pointed ears.

'Secondly I intend to demonstrate that not only did the ancient Egyptians preserve memories of their former home in the Gilf Kebir, but also, despite the formidable distances involved, actual physical contact with it, sporadically return-ing across the desert to worship at sites of special religious and sentimental significance.

'One wadi in particular, the so-called *wehat seshtat*, the Hidden Oasis, seems to have been held in particular reverence. Although the evidence is scanty, this latter site appears to have continued as an important cult centre right the way up to the end of the Old Kingdom, almost a thousand years after the emergence of Egypt as a unified state.'

The listener who had been nodding, Flin noticed,

had now fallen asleep. He raised his voice another couple of notches in a vain effort to jolt him out of his slumber.

'Finally,' he went on at something just short of a shout, 'I will argue that it it this mysterious and to date undiscovered wadi that served as the inspiration and model for a whole series of subsequent legends of lost Saharan oases, notably that of Zerzura, the Atlantis of the Sands, for which the aforementioned Ladislaus Almasy spent much of his career vainly searching.'

Last slide of the introduction – a blurred black-and-white shot of Almasy in shorts and military cap, the desert stretching away behind him.

'So, ladies and gentlemen,' he said, 'I invite you to join me on a journey of discovery – out across the desert, back through time, and in search of the long-lost temple-city of the Gilf Kebir.'

He fell silent, waiting for a reaction, any reaction.

'There's no need to shout,' came a voice from the back of the room. 'We're not deaf, you know!'

Bollocks, thought Flin.

He ploughed on to the end of the lecture, jumping and cutting wherever he could so that the normal running time of ninety minutes was reduced to less than fifty. Compared to most of his fellow Egyptologists he was considered an exciting speaker, capable of bringing a dry and complex subject to life, holding people's attention, enthusing them. In this instance, no amount of editing and simplification seemed to have any effect. Halfway through, one couple stood and left the room; by the end those who remained were openly fidgeting and glancing at watches. The man with the jug ears slept peacefully right the way through, head cradled on his wife's shoulder. Only the overweight latecomer in the bow-tie seemed genuinely interested. Occasionally dabbing at his forehead with his handkerchief, he focused unswervingly on the Englishman, eyes bright with concentration.

'In conclusion,' Flin said, bringing up the final slide of the talk, another shot of the towering orange flank of the Gilf Kebir, 'no sign of the *wehat seshtat*, non Zerzura, nor any of the other legendary lost oases of the Sahara has ever been found.'

He turned slightly, looking up at the slide, smiling wistfully as if in acknowledgement of a long-time sparring partner. For a moment he seemed to disappear into his own thoughts before shaking his head and turning back to the audience.

'Many people have argued that the whole idea of a lost oasis is precisely that. An idea, a dream, a figment of the imagination, no more tangible than a desert mirage.

'I hope the evidence I have presented tonight will persuade you that the basis for all these stories, the *wehat seshtat*, certainly *did* exist, and was regarded by the early Egyptians as a cult centre of paramount significance.

'Whether its location will ever be revealed is another matter. Almasy, Bagnold, Clayton, Newbold – all scoured the Gilf Kebir and returned empty-handed. In more recent times satellite imaging and aerial survey have likewise drawn a complete blank.'

Again he threw a glance up at the projected slide, again smiled that wistful smile.

'And maybe it is better that way,' he said looking forward again. 'So much of our planet has now been studied and mapped and explored and laid bare, stripped of its magic, that it somehow makes the world a more interesting place to know that one small corner of it at least is still beyond our reach. For the moment the *wehat seshtat* remains exactly that – a hidden oasis. Thank you.'

He sat down to scattered, arthritic applause. The overweight man was the only one to show any real appreciation, clapping loudly before rising to his feet and, with a grateful wave, slipping out of the door. Flin's friend Margot stood and came to the front of the room.

'What an absolutely fascinating talk,' she said, addressing the audience in a loud, schoolmistressy sort of voice. 'I for one wish we could get straight into our coach and drive out to the Gilf Kebir for a good look around.'

Silence.

'Now Professor Brodie has kindly agreed to answer any questions you might care to put. As I said before, he is one of the world's leading authorities on the archaeology of the Sahara, author of the seminal *Deshret: Ancient Egypt and the Western Desert* and a legend in his field – or perhaps that should be a legend in his Sand Sea! – so do make use of this opportunity.'

More silence, then the man with the jug ears, now awake, piped up:

'Professor Brodie, do you think Tutankhamun was murdered?'

Afterwards, once the tourists had trooped off to dinner, Flin packed up his notes and laptop while Margot hovered around him.

'I don't think they were especially inspired,' he said.

'Nonsense,' insisted Margot. 'They were absolutely . . . riveted.'

He'd only done the lecture as a favour to her, old university friends and all that, filling in at the last minute for some other event that had fallen through. He could tell she was embarrassed by her party's reaction, was trying to make up for it and, reaching out, he squeezed her arm.

'Don't worry yourself, Margs. Believe me, I've had an awful lot worse.'

'At least you only had to put up with them for an hour,' she sighed. 'I've got them for the next ten days. Was Tutankhamun murdered! Christ, if the ground could have swallowed me . . .'

He laughed. Zipping his laptop into its carry case, the two of them walked across the room, Margot threading an arm through his. As they reached the door there was a sudden, discordant cacophony of clarinets and drums from the foyer outside. They stopped and watched as a wedding party processed past in front of them – bride and groom followed by a crowd of clapping relatives, a video-camerman walking backwards at the head of the group, shouting instructions.

'My God, look at her dress,' murmured Margot. 'She looks like an exploding snowman.'

Flin didn't respond; his eyes were drawn not to the newlyweds but to the back of the group. A young girl, aged no more than ten or eleven, was jumping up and down trying to see what was happening ahead. She was excited, pretty, her long black hair whirling around her. Just like . . .

'You OK, Flin?'

He had swayed against the doorframe, grasping at

Margot's arm for support, sweat glistening across his neck and forehead.

'Flin?'

'Fine,' he mumbled, straightening and releasing her arm, embarrassed. 'Fine.'

'You're white as a sheet.'

'I'm fine, honestly. Just tired. Should have eaten before I came out.'

He smiled, not entirely convincingly.

'Let me buy you dinner,' said Margot. 'Get your blood sugar up. It's the least I can do after tonight.'

'Thanks, Margs, but if you don't mind I'm going to head home. Got a lot of papers to mark.'

It was a lie, and he could tell she knew it.

'Just feeling a bit out of sorts,' he added, trying to explain himself. 'Always have been a moody bugger.'

Margot smiled. Leaning forward, she enveloped him in a hug.

'It's your moodiness I love, my darling Flin. That and your looks, of course. God, if only you'd let me . . .'

The hug tightened momentarily and then she broke away.

'We're in Cairo till Thursday, then down to Luxor. Call you when we get back?'

'I'll look forward to it,' said Flin. 'And don't forget to tell them about how the Pyramids are aligned with Orion because that's where the alien builders came from.'

She laughed and bustled off. Flin stared after her, then returned his gaze to the wedding party. It was now passing into a room at the far end of the foyer, the young girl still hopping up and down at the rear. Even after all these years small things like that still pole-axed him, brought it all flooding back. If only he'd bloody got there on time.

He watched a moment longer as the wedding guests disappeared into the room and the doors slammed shut behind them, then, intending neither to go home nor to mark essays, but to get as drunk as he possibly could in what remained of the evening, hurried out of the hotel, followed a few moments later by a rotund, waddling figure in a cream-coloured jacket.

Freya only just made her flight: midnight from San Francisco International to London, and then a connection on to Cairo. She should have had plenty of time, but somehow, as was always the case when she had plenty of time, the clock mysteriously seemed to speed itself up and everything turned into a frantic rush. She was the last person to check in, and one of the last to board the plane, jamming her knapsack into the already crammed overhead locker and squeezing herself into her seat between an overweight Hispanic man and a lank-haired teenager in a Marilyn Manson T-shirt.

Once airborne she flicked through the in-flight entertainment: repeats of *Friends*, an inane-looking comedy with Matthew McConaughey, a *National Geographic* documentary about the Sahara, which, given the reason for her journey, was the very last thing she felt like watching. She went through the menu a couple of times, then switched off the screen, reclined the seat and drilled the headphones of her iPod into her ears: Johnny Cash, 'Hurt'. Appropriate.

Famous female travellers – that's who their parents had named them after. In her case Freya Stark, the great Middle Eastern traveller, in her sister's the Himalayan explorer Alexandra David-Neel. Ironically, each had ended up emulating not their namesakes, but that of their sibling, Alex, like Stark, drawn to heat and deserts, Freya, like David-Neel, to cliffs and mountains.

'Nothing with you two ever goes to plan,' their father had joked. 'Should have swapped you round at birth.'

He had been a big man, their dad, bear-like, jovial, a geography teacher in their home town of Markham, Virginia. Aside from jazz and the poetry of Walt Whitman the outdoors had been his great love, and from an early age he had taken them on expeditions: hiking through the Blue Ridge Mountains, canoeing on the Rappahannock River, sailing off the coast of North Carolina, pointing out birds and animals and trees and plants, teaching them about the landscape and everything in it. It was from him that they had inherited their spirit of adventure, their fascination with wild places. Their looks, on the other hand – slim, blonde; translucent green eyes – they inherited from their mother, a successful artist and sculptor. Looks, and also a certain reservedness and introspection, a dislike of inane chatter and big crowds. Their father had been a gregarious man, delighting in conversation and social gatherings. The Hannen women, by contrast, were always more comfortable inside their own heads.

Alex was the older of the two by five years, not as obviously attractive as Freya, but cleverer – academically at least – and also less moody. They were never inseparable in the way some siblings are, the difference in age meaning that both were inclined to go their own way and do their own thing rather than spending every hour in each other's company.

The family's old clapboard house out on the edge of town had contained a treasure trove of maps, atlases, guides and travel books and on rainy days each would load themselves up with their favourite volumes and disappear into their own secret corner to plot future adventures: Alex into the loft, Freya the tumbledown summerhouse at the end of the garden. When they were outdoors – which they were most of the time – they would likewise head off in separate directions, Freya tramping for miles through the local woods and orchards, scrambling up trees, building rope-swings, timing herself to see how quickly she could complete a hiking trail or climb a mountain, always pushing herself.

Alex, too, loved to walk and explore, although in her case there was more of an intellectual edge to her rambles. She would take a notebook and colouring pens with her, maps, a camera, an old army compass that had, apparently, once belonged to a marine in the battle of Iwo Jima. When she returned home – invariably late in the evening – it would be with extended notes on her day's travels, drawings, a precise record of the route she had taken, all manner of specimens she had picked up on the way – leaves and flowers, pine cones, curiously shaped rocks and, on one memorable occasion, a dead rattlesnake that she had draped triumphantly around her neck like a scarf.

'And there's me thinking I was bring up two young ladies,' their father had sighed. 'What in God's name have I unleashed on the world?'

Independent they may have been, forever engaged in their own private adventures, Alex trying to map the world, Frey to conquer it, but that in no way diminished their love for each other. Freya worshipped her older sister, trusted and looked up to her, told her things she told no one else, not even their parents. Alex, for her part, felt a fierce protectiveness towards her younger sibling, sneaking into her room at night to comfort her when she had had a nightmare, reading to her from the books of travel and adventure they both so loved, braiding her hair, helping her with her schoolwork. When, aged five, Freya had been stung in the mouth by a wasp it was to her sister rather than her parents that she had run for comfort. A few years later she had been hospitalized with meningitis and Alex had insisted on moving in with her, sleeping on a cot-bed on the floor and clutching her hand when she had had to undergo a lumbar puncture (it was this, and Freya's accompanying hysteria as the needle was driven into the base of her spine, that had sparked Alex's lifelong horror of anything to do with injections). When, just shy of her seventeenth birthday, Freya had stunned the climbing world by soloing the Nose on Yosemite's El Capitan, the youngest person ever to do so, who had been waiting for her at the top, a bunch of flowers in one hand and a Dr Pepper in the other? Alex.

'I'm so proud of you,' she had said, wrapping Freya in a tight embrace. 'My fearless little sis.'

And of course when, just a few months later, their mother and father had been killed in the car accident, it was Alex who had stepped in as surrogate parent. By that point her own career as a desert explorer was starting to blossom:

Little Tin Hinan, her account of the eight months she had spent living and travelling with the Tuareg Berbers of northen Niger, had briefly topped the bestseller lists. But she had put it all on hold and moved back into the family home to look after her sister, taking a job in, of all places, the CIA's cartographic department over at Langley so she could put Freya through school and college, fund her climbing career, support and protect her.

And after all that Freya had repaid her love with betrayal. As her ears echoed to the gravelly croak of Johnny Cash, singing of pain and loss, of failing those for whom you most care, she closed her eyes and saw again the shock on Alex's face as she walked into the room. Shock and, worse, the terrible, reproving sadness.

Seven years and Freya had never once said sorry. She had wanted to. God, she had wanted to. Not a day went by when she didn't think about it. But she never had. And now Alex was dead and the opportunity was gone. Her beloved Alex, her big sister. *Hurt*. It didn't even get close to describing it.

Reaching into her pocket she pulled out a crumpled envelope, postmarked Egypt, gazed at it for a moment then snatched the headphones out of her ears and switched on the Matthew McConaughey film. Anything to help her forget.

CAIRO

Flin didn't drink much any more, certainly nothing like he used to. On the rare occasions he did drink, it was invariably in the bar of the Windsor Hotel on Sharia Alfi Bey, and that was where he headed tonight.

A quiet, sedate room on the first floor of the building, all polished wood floors, deep armchairs and soft lighting, it was a throwback to an earlier age of colonial gentility. The staff sported crisp white shirts and black bow-ties, a writing desk sat in one corner, the walls were hung with the sort of whimsical oddments you might find in an up-market bric-à-brac shop – a giant turtle shell, an old guitar, mounted antlers, black-and-white photographs of scenes from Egyptian life. Even the bottles behind the bar – Martini, Cointreau, Grand Marnier, crème de menthe – spoke of a different age, an era of cocktail parties, aperitifs and post-prandial liqueurs. Only the piped Whitney Houston music spoiled the illusion. That and the jean-clad backpackers huddled in corners reading their Lonely Planet guides.

Flin got there just after eight and, taking up position on a stool at the end of the bar, ordered a Stella. When the beer arrived he stared at it, as a diver might before plunging off the high-board into the water far below, then brought the glass to his lips and emptied it in four long gulps, immediately ordering another. This too he knocked back swiftly and was just starting on his third when he happened to glance in one of the mirrored panels behind the bar. Sitting on a sofa behind and to his left, a newspaper clasped in his hands, was the overweight man from the lecture. Flin didn't remember him being there when he had come in. Not wanting company, he started to shift stools so as to bring a pillar between the two of them. As he did so, the man looked up, clocked him and waved, laying aside the paper and walking over.

'That was a fine talk, Professor Brodie,' he said in that curious high-pitched drawl of his, coming up to Flin and extending a hand. 'Very fine.'

'Thank you,' said Flin, taking the hand and shaking it, groaning inwardly. 'I'm glad someone enjoyed it.'

The man proffered a business card.

'Cy Angleton. Work over at the Embassy. Public Affairs. Love ancient Egypt.'

'Really.' Flin tried to sound enthused. 'Any particular period?'

'Oh, all of it, I guess,' replied Angleton with a wave of the hand. 'The whole package. Although I do find the Gilf Kebir thing fascinating.'

He pronounced it 'gilf kay-beer'.

'Real fascinating,' he continued. 'You should let me take you to lunch some time. Pick your brains.'

'Love to,' replied Flin, forcing a smile onto his face. There was a silence, then, feeling he had no other option, he asked the American if he wanted to join him. To his relief the offer was declined.

'Got an early start tomorrow. Just wanted to say how much I enjoyed the lecture.'

The briefest of pauses, then:

'We really must have that chat about the Gilf.'

Although it was said innocuously enough, something about this last remark made Flin feel uncomfortable, as if there was more to the comment than Angleton was letting on. Before he could pursue the matter, the American gave him a pat on the shoulder, complimented him again on the lecture and wandered out of the room.

It's the girl in the hotel, Flin told himself, draining the rest of his beer and waving at the barman to indicate he wanted another. *Got me on edge. That and every other bloody thing.*

'And a Johnnie Walker as well,' he called. 'A double.'

He drank on for the rest of the evening, turning things over in his mind – the girl, the Gilf, Dakhla, Sandfire – losing track of how much booze he got through, drowning himself, just like the old days. A group of English girls materialized at a nearby table, one of them – elfin, dark haired, pretty – shooting glances in his direction, trying to make eye contact. He had always been attractive to the opposite sex, or so people told him, his slim, muscular frame and large brown eyes marking him out from most of his fellow Egyptologists, who tended towards the physically bland. Despite that he had never been especially confident around women, incapable of making the ice-breaking small talk at which some men excelled. And even if he had been, he certainly wasn't in the mood for it tonight. He acknowledged the girl's attention with a half-smile, then lifted his eyes to the pair of antlers mounted above the bar and kept them there. Twenty minutes later she and her companions left and a group of Egyptian businessmen took their table.

Around eleven, by now heavily drunk, Flin decided to call it a night and started fumbling for his wallet. As he did so he felt a hand on his shoulder. For an unpleasant moment he thought it was the fat American again. It was only Alan Peach, a colleague of his from the American University. 'Interesting Alan' as they called him on account of his being the most boring man in Cairo, a pottery expert whose conversation rarely ventured beyond the realms of early dynastic red-ware ceramics. He greeted Flin and, indicating a group of other university colleagues who had sat down at a table on the far side of the room, invited him to join them. Flin shook his head and explained that he was just leaving; he pulled out his wallet while Peach launched into a rambling story about an argument he'd had with one of the curators at the Egyptian Museum over a pot that in his opinion was almost certainly Badarian rather than Naqada II as it had been officially labelled. Flin zoned out, nodding every now and then but not really paying attention. It was only when he had counted out the correct money, placed it on the bar and gathered up his laptop that he realized Peach had moved on and was talking about something completely different.

'. . . at Sadat Metro. Couldn't believe it. Literally bumped right into him.'

'What? Who?'

'Hassan Fadawi. Literally bumped right into him. Was on my way up to Heliopolis to help with some ceramics they'd found, Third Dynasty they think, although stylistically—'

'Fadawi?' Flin looked shocked. 'I thought he was . . .'

'So did I,' said Peach. 'Got early release, apparently. Looked a broken man. Absolutely broken.'

'Hassan Fadawi? You're sure?'

'Positive. I mean he's got family money by all accounts, so financially he's not going to—'

'When? When did he get out?'

'About a week ago, I think he said. Thin as a rake he was. Remember having an extremely interesting chat with him once about some Second Dynasty hieratic wine jar dockets he'd found down at Abydos. Say what you like about him, he certainly knew his pottery. Most people would have dated them Third or even Fourth, but he'd figured you wouldn't get that sort of rim structure . . .'

He was talking to himself, Flin having already turned and left the room.

He should have gone straight home. Instead, unable to stop himself, he diverted via the duty-free alcohol shop on Sharia Talaat Harb, picking up a bottle of gut-rot Scotch before flagging down a taxi and giving directions back to his apartment block on the corner of Mohamed Mahmoud and Mansour.

Taib the caretaker was still up when he got back, sitting in his armchair just inside the building's entrance, a *shaal* draped over his head, grimy feet thrust into old plastic sandals. They had never got on, and, drunk as he was, Flin didn't bother to acknowledge him, walking straight past and into the ancient cage lift which rumbled its way up to the top floor.

Inside his flat he grabbed a tumbler from the kitchen, filled it with whisky and weaved his way into the living room. Flicking on the light he slumped onto the sofa. He emptied the glass, poured himself another and emptied that too, really gulping at it, aware that he was accelerating down a slippery slope, but unable to stop himself.

For five years he'd kept it under control, had barely touched the stuff. There had been cravings, of course, especially in the early days, but she'd helped him through and thanks to her he'd somehow stayed on track, slowly piecing his life back together again, like one of Alan Peach's reconstructed pots.

Five years, and now he was chucking it all away. And he didn't care. He just didn't care. The girl, the Gilf, Dakhla,

Sandfire and now Hassan Fadawi – it was all too much. He couldn't hold it together any more.

He refilled the glass, emptied it again, swigged straight from the bottle, eyes veering drunkenly around the room. Random objects blurred in and out of focus – his El-Ahly football scarf, a copy of Stephen Quirke's *The Cult of Ra*, a fist-sized lump of Libyan desert glass – round and round before eventually his gaze latched on to a photograph sitting on the coffee table beside the sofa. It was of a young woman. Blonde, tanned, laughing, she was wearing mirror shades and a battered suede jacket; an expanse of flat desert gravel stretched away behind her towards a distant whale-back dune. Flin stared at it, swigged, looked away and immediately back again, an expression of pained humiliation arranging itself on his face as though he had been caught doing something he had promised faithfully not to. Five seconds passed. Ten, twenty. Then, with a growl of effort, his entire body trembling as though pushing against some unseen force, he swayed upright and stumbled over to the window. Opening the shutters, he launched the whisky bottle out into the night.

'Alex,' he slurred, the crunch of shattering glass echoing up from the alley below. 'Oh, Alex, what have I done?'

Cy Angleton swept a handkerchief across his forehead – Jesus, the heat in this city! – and called for another Coca-Cola. Everyone else in the café was drinking glasses of ruby-coloured tea or viscous black coffee but Angleton wouldn't touch the stuff. Twenty years he'd been working this type of gig – Middle East, Far East, Africa – and always the same rule: if it ain't in a can, don't drink it. His colleagues laughed at him, called him paranoid, but it was he who did the laughing when they were doubled up with food poisoning, intestines flying out of their arseholes. If it ain't in a can, don't drink it. And, also: if it ain't cooked by Americans, don't eat it.

The Coke arrived. Angleton opened the can and took a long sip, eyeing the teenage serving boy as he wandered away among the tables, admiring the narrow hips and muscular arms. He sipped again and looked away, focusing on the matter in hand.

It had been a useful evening. Extremely useful. Part of him wondered if he hadn't gone too far in the Windsor Hotel, shouldn't have been quite so pointed with Brodie about the Gilf Kebir, but on balance it had been a risk worth taking. In this business you sometimes had to trust your instincts. And his instincts had told him that Brodie's reaction would be informative. As indeed it had been. He knew something, definitely knew something. Piece by piece by piece. That's how he liked to work. Building up a picture, teasing out the facts. That's what he got paid for, why they always used him for this sort of thing.

Aftewards he had followed Brodie back to his apartment where he'd got chatting with the old caretaker. The man clearly disliked the Englishman, and he'd played on that, winning his confidence, slipping him some cash, which would make things easier when the time came to have a look round Brodie's flat, as it soon would. Yes, all in all, an extremely useful evening. Piece by piece by piece.

He sipped at his Coke and gazed around at the other

customers in the café. Some puffed on shisha pipes, others played dominoes; all were male. The boy walked past again and Angleton's eyes tracked him, scenarios playing lazily through his mind, imagined embraces, wetness and sweat. He smiled and shook his head, throwing some money onto the table before standing and setting off down the street. Although he had needs, he had no intention of indulging them in a place like this. Maybe when he got back to the States, but for the moment he'd make do with his own hand. Such were the rules he lived by: don't drink the water, don't eat the food, and above all, don't ever touch the meat, however fierce the temptation.

Freya landed at Cairo International at 8 a.m. local time. Waiting for her at the arrivals gate was a woman named Molly Kiernan, a friend of Alex's and the one who had called two nights back to break the news of her death.

Late fifties, with greying blond hair, sensible shoes and a small gold crucifix hanging round her neck, Kiernan came forward and hugged Freya, telling her how very sorry she was for her loss. Then, taking her arm, she shepherded her out of the international terminal and across to the domestic one for her flight down to Dakhla Oasis. This was where Alex had lived and where her funeral was to take place the following day.

'You're sure you won't stay in Cairo and fly down with me tomorrow?' Kiernan asked as they walked. 'I've got a spare bed.'

Freya thanked her, but said she would prefer to head

south immediately. She wanted to see her sister one last time before the funeral, to say her goodbyes.

'Of course, my dear,' said the older woman, squeezing Freya's hand. 'Zahir al-Sabri will meet you at the other end – he worked with Alex. He's a good man, a bit surly. He'll take you to the hospital and then over to her house. If you need anything, anything at all . . .'

She handed Freya a card: Molly Kiernan, Regional Co-ordinator, USAID. A mobile number was scribbled on the back.

At the domestic terminal Freya checked in, one of only four people to do so. Flashing some sort of pass and speaking to the security men in fluent Arabic, Kiernan was allowed to accompany her through to the departures lounge, where she waited with her until her flight was called, neither of them saying very much. Only when they had started to board and Freya had joined the queue for the bus that would take her out to the plane, did she vocalize what had been tearing at her ever since she had received the news of her sister's death:

'I just can't believe Alex would kill herself. I just can't believe it. Not Alex.'

If she was looking for an explanation she didn't get it. Kiernan simply hugged her again, stroked a hand down her hair and, with a final 'I'm so very sorry', turned and walked away.

Once airborne Freya stared distractedly down at the desert below, an endless expanse of dirty yellow dissolving into the haze of the far horizon. Here and there its surface was scored by the branching, scar-like courses of long-dried-up wadis, but for the most part it was wholly featureless. Blank, empty, desolate – just like she felt.

Morphine overdose – that's how Alex had done it. Freya didn't know the precise details, didn't really want to, it was just too painful to contemplate. She'd had multiple sclerosis, apparently, a particularly aggressive form of the disease, had already lost the use of both legs and one arm, part of her sight too – Christ, it was just so heartbreakingly cruel.

'She couldn't bear it any more,' Molly Kiernan had told her when she'd called to break the news. 'Couldn't go on. Decided to act while she still could.'

It didn't sound like the Alex Freya knew, giving up hope like that, quitting without a fight. But then all she really had was a memory: the Alex of their childhood, with her notebooks and rock collection and old army compass from the battle of Iwo Jima. The Alex who had held her close at their parents' funeral, and given up her career to look after her, loving and supporting her. A past Alex. A lost Alex. It was seven years since they had last spoken, and who could say how much her sister had changed in that time.

True, she'd written to Freya, once a month, regular as clockwork, dozens of letters over the years, all in that curious handwriting of hers that somehow managed to be both wild and neat at the same time. The letters had steered clear of any personal stuff, however. As though the events of that last day in Markham had somehow slammed shut the door on any deeper level of involvement between the two of them. Dakhla, the desert, the work she was doing on dune movements and the geomorphology of the Gilf

72

Kebir Plateau, whatever the hell that was – these were the things Alex wrote about. Surface stuff, external, never delving too deep. Only the last letter, the one Freya had received just a few days before news of her sister's death, had been different, opening up again, allowing Freya back in. But by then it was too late.

And of course Freya, convulsed with shame, had never replied to any of the letters. Not once, in seven years, had she made an attempt to reach out, to say how sorry she was, to try to repair the damage she had done.

That's what tormented her now, even more than Alex's actual death. The fact that she had been suffering, terribly by all accounts, and that she, Freya, had not been there for her, as Alex had always been there for her. The wasp sting, the lumbar puncture, the day she had soloed the Nose on El Capitan – her sister had never let her down, always supported her. But she had not done the same for her sister – she had failed her. For a second time.

Reaching into her pocket she pulled out the crumpled envelope with the Egypt postmark, gazing at it before again putting it away unread and staring back down at the desert below. Blank, empty, desolate. Just like she felt. Had felt for the last seven years. Would probably now always feel.

As arranged, she was met at Dakhla airport – a remote huddle of orange buildings surrounded by desert – by Alex's colleague Zahir al-Sabri. Thin, wiry, hook-nosed, with a pencil moustache and a red-checked Bedouin *imma* wrapped around his head, he muttered a curt greeting and, taking her holdall – she kept her knapsack – led her across the arrivals hall and out through a set of glass doors. The mid-morning heat thumped into her as though a scalding towel had been pressed hard against her face. It had been hot in Cairo, but this was something else: the burning air seemed to drive deep down into her lungs, sucking the breath out of her.

'How do people live in this?' she gasped, slipping on her sunglasses against the glare.

Zahir shrugged.

'Come in summer. Then is hot.'

There was a car park in front of the terminal building, fringed by weeping fig trees and pink-flowered oleander bushes. Zahir padded across to a battered white Toyota Land Cruiser with a luggage rack clamped to its roof, its left headlamp smashed out. Hefting her bag into the back, he threw open the passenger door and, without saying a word, climbed in the driver side and started the engine. They moved off, passing through a security point and out onto a tarmacked road – the only road – that wound away through the desert like a slash of dirty grey paint. Ahead loomed the green blur of the oasis. Behind, hemming it in and curving the length of the horizon like the rim of a giant saucer, reared a steep, cream-coloured escarpment.

'Gebel el-Qasr,' said Zahir. He didn't expand on the comment, and Freya didn't ask.

They drove fast and in silence, gravelly dunes giving way first to scatters of scrub grass, then to irrigated fields interspersed with palm, olive and citrus groves. After ten minutes a sign in Arabic and English announced they were entering Mut which, from Alex's letters, Freya knew was Dakhla's main settlement. A sleepy affair of two- and three-storey whitewashed buildings, it was all but deserted, its dusty streets lined with casuarina and acacia trees, its pavement edges painted with minty bands of white and green, the town's predominant colours.

They passed a mosque, a donkey-drawn cart with a group of black-robed women sitting in the back and a line of camels wandering aimlessly along the side of the road; occasional wafts of dung and woodsmoke pushed in through the open windows. Under other circumstances Freya would have been fascinated: it was all so different, so completely alien to her own experience. As it was she just sat there gazing distractedly out of the window as they followed a wide boulevard through the town, crossing a succession of mini-roundabouts from which other boulevards radiated off in different directions so that she had the curious sensation of pinging around a giant pinball machine.

In a matter of minutes they were out the other side and speeding through a patchwork landscape of maize fields and rice paddies. Dovecotes and palm groves drifted by, irrigation canals, strange twisted outcrops of rock until at last they came into a village of densely packed mud-brick houses. Zahir slowed and swung left through an open gateway, coming to a halt in a yard hemmed in by high mud walls topped with palm fronds. He tooted the horn and cut the engine.

'Alex's house?' asked Freya, trying to match the yard and attached, ramshackle dwelling with the descriptions in her sister's letters.

'My house,' said Zahir, opening the door and getting out. 'We drink tea.'

Freya had no desire whatsoever to drink tea, but she

sensed it would be impolite to refuse – Alex's letters had made much of the importance Egyptians attached to hospitality. Tired as she was, she grabbed her knapsack and alighted as well.

Zahir led her into the building and along a corridor – dark and cool, smells of smoke and cooking oil – and into a gloomy, high-ceilinged room with pale blue walls and a mat-covered floor. Other than a cushioned bench along one of the walls and a television sitting on a table in the far corner, the space was empty. He waved her onto the bench, shouted something towards the back of the house and squatted down on the floor in front of her, his *djellaba* riding up to reveal white Nike trainers. Silence.

'I hear you worked with Alex?' she said eventually, Zahir showing no sign of starting a conversation. He grumbled an affirmative.

'In the desert?'

He shrugged as if to say 'where else?'

'Doing what?'

Another shrug.

'We drive. Far. Out to Gilf Kebir. Long way.'

He flicked his eyes up at her and then away, cricking his neck and brushing at something on his *djellaba*. She wanted to ask him more: about Alex's life here, her illness, her last days, anything he knew about her, everything, desperate to gather in whatever tiny fragments of her sister she could. She held back, however, sensing that he wasn't going to be particularly forthcoming. Molly Kiernan had warned her he was surly, but it felt like more than that. Almost antagonistic. She wondered if Alex had told him what had happened between them, why they hadn't spoken for so long.

'You're a Bedouin?' she asked, pushing the thought from her mind and making a renewed attempt to break the ice.

A nod, no more.

'Sanusi?' It was something she vaguely remembered from Alex's letters, a name somehow associated with the desert peoples. If she was hoping to impress him with her knowledge she was disappointed. Zahir let out an exclamation of disgust and shook his head vigorously.

'Not Sanusi,' he spat. 'Sanusi are dogs, scum. We al-Rashaayda. True Bedouin.'

'I'm sorry,' she mumbled. 'I didn't mean—'

A clinking from the corridor outside interrupted her. A boy of no more than two or three came toddling into the room, followed by a young woman – slim, dark-skinned, attractive. She carried a shisha pipe in one hand and a tray with two glasses of reddish-brown tea in the other. Freya stood to help, but Zahir waved her back to the bench, motioning to his wife – or so Freya assumed – to lay the tray and pipe down beside him. For the briefest of moments her gaze met Freya's, and then she was gone.

'Sugar?'

Zahir emptied a spoonful into Freya's glass without waiting for a reply and handed it to her before sweeping the boy into his arms.

'My son,' he said, smiling for the first time since they had met, the tension of a moment earlier apparently forgotten. 'Very clever. Aren't you clever, Mohsen?'

The boy laughed, feet kicking beneath the hem of his miniature *djellaba*.

'He's beautiful,' said Freya.

'No beautiful,' said Zahir, wagging a finger disapprovingly. 'Women is beautiful. Mohsen handsome. Like father.'

He chuckled and kissed the boy's forehead.

'You have children?'

She admitted that she didn't.

'Start soon,' he advised. 'Before you too old.'

He spooned three sugars into his own tea, sipped and, lifting the mouthpiece of the shisha, puffed it into life. A cloud of dense blue smoke drifted ponderously up towards the ceiling. There was another uncomfortable pause – or at least Freya found it uncomfortable; Zahir seemed oblivious. Then, raising the mouthpiece, he pointed above her head to a curved knife hanging on the wall, its bronze scabbard inlaid with intricate silvery tracery, its ivory handle tipped with what looked like a large ruby.

'This belong my family in-sis-teer,' he said. Freya was momentarily confused before realizing what he meant.

'Ancestor,' she corrected.

'This what I say. In-sis-teer. He name Mohammed Wald Yusuf Ibrahim Sabri al-Rashaayda. Live before six hundred year, very famous man. Most famous Bedouin in desert. Sahara like his garden, he go everywhere, even Sand Sea, know every dune, every water-hole. Very great man.'

He nodded proudly, hugging an arm around his son. Freya waited for him to continue, but that seemed to be all he wanted to say and they lapsed into silence again. The distant cough of an irrigation pump drifted through the open window and, from closer, the squawk of geese. She gave it another couple of minutes, sipping at her tea, the young boy staring up at her. Then she put her glass down, stood and asked if she could use the bathroom. Not because she needed to, just to get away from him for a while. Zahir waved a hand, indicating that she should follow the corridor they had come in along, towards the back of the house.

She stepped out of the room, relieved to be alone. Passing a couple of bedrooms – bare walls and floors, curiously ornate wooden beds – she swished through a bead curtain and out into a small internal courtyard. A pile of bamboo cages was stacked against one wall, crammed with rabbits and pigeons. From an opening directly ahead came the clank of pots and the sound of female voices. To her right were two closed doors, one of which, she assumed, must be the bathroom. She crossed the yard and opened the nearest one. It was either an office or a storeroom, she couldn't tell which, a desk, chair and ancient computer suggesting the former, sacks of grain, a rusted bicycle and various farming implements the latter. She started to close the door only to stop, her attention drawn to the far side of the room where the desk was pushed into a corner. Sellotaped to the wall above it was a photograph. She stepped into the room, staring.

The picture was in colour, blown up to several times its normal size by the look of it so that even from the doorway she could make the image out clearly: a towering curve of glassy black rock erupting from an otherwise featureless desert like some enormous scimitar ripping its way through the sands. It was a dramatic formation, gravity-defying, its uppermost end tapering to a point, its sides notched and serrated from millennia of weathering giving it a curiously barbed appearance. Part of Freya couldn't help thinking what an amazing climb it would make, although it was less the rock itself that drew her attention than the person standing in the shade at its base. She crossed to the desk and leant over it, gazing up. Although the figure was tiny, dwarfed by the curving monolith overhead, the smile, the battered suede jacket, the blond hair were all unmistakable. Alex. She reached out a hand and touched her.

'This private.'

She spun. Zahir was standing in the doorway, his son beside him.

'I'm sorry,' she mumbled, embarrassed. 'I got the wrong door.'

He said nothing, just stared at her.

'I saw Alex.' She indicated the picture, feeling inexplicably guilty, as though she had been caught doing something she shouldn't, like that day back in . . .

'Bathroom next door,' he said.

'Of course. I didn't mean to . . .'

She paused, flustered, unable to find the right word. Intrude? Trespass? Snoop? She could feel tears starting to well up.

'Was she happy?' she blurted, unable to stop herself. 'Alex. She sent me a letter, you see, just before she died, said things . . . she seemed happy. Was she? Do you know? At the end. Was she happy?'

He continued to stare at her, face blank.

'This private,' he repeated. 'Bathroom next door.'

She felt a surge of anger.

She's dead! she wanted to scream. *My sister's dead, and you bring me here to drink tea and won't even let me look at her picture!*

She said nothing, aware that her fury was directed as much at herself as at Zahir – for what she'd done to Alex, for not being there for her, for everything. She took a last glance at the photo, then walked back across the room and stepped out into the yard.

'I don't need the bathroom any more,' she said quietly. 'I just want to see her. Will you take me, please?'

He gazed at her, expressionless, giving nothing away, then, with a nod, pulled the door closed. He propelled his son across the yard to the kitchen before leading Freya back through the house to the Land Cruiser. They didn't speak on the journey back into Mut.

CAIRO

It was nearly midday when Flin woke. He was on his sofa, fully clothed, his head pounding, his mouth dry and crusty as though it had been rammed full of chalk. For a terrible moment he thought he'd missed his morning lectures, before remembering it was Tuesday, and on Tuesday he didn't start teaching until early afternoon. With a muttered 'Thank God' he sank back into the cushions.

For a while he just lay there, gazing up at the slats of sunlight that sliced across the ceiling, mulling over the events of the previous night while an incessant orchestra of car horns blared up from the street below. Then, heaving himself to his feet, he trudged through to the bathroom and took a cold shower, the apartment's ancient plumbing groaning and rumbling as it delivered a heavy cascade of water onto his face and torso. He gave it fifteen minutes. His mind slowly clearing, he towelled himself off and brewed up some coffee – thick, black Egyptian coffee, as sharp and sour as lemon juice. Wandering back into the living room, he threw open the shutters. A chaotic mass of buildings spread away in front of him, sweeping eastwards like a surge of muddy froth before crashing into the distant, hazy wall of the Muqqatam Hills. To his right the dome of the Mohammed Ali mosque glowed dirty silver in the midday sun. Everywhere minarets speared upwards from the confusion beneath, like needles through coarse fabric, their loudspeakers filling the air with the ululating wail of the city's muezzin, calling the faithful to noon prayer.

He had lived here for the best part of a decade, renting from an old Egyptian family who had owned the entire block since it was first built, back at the end of the nineteenth century.

From the outside it wasn't much to look at, the once proud colonial façade – ornate balconies, intricately carved window surrounds, florid glass and ironwork doorway – cracked and weathered and stained a dung-coloured brown by the smoggy air. Inside the common parts of the building were also well past their prime, gloomy and depressive, the walls scratched and chipped and scored with graffiti, the paintwork flaking.

It was conveniently located, though – only a few streets away from the American University where he taught. And the rent was low, even by Cairene standards, an important consideration given that he only lectured part time. And if the block itself had seen better days, his apartment, on the top floor, was an oasis of calm and light, its rooms high-ceilinged, its windows affording spectacular views east and south across the city. He would always be most at home out in the desert, where he spent four months of the year, well away from everyone and everything, but so far as he could be happy in a city he was here. Even with that surly bastard Taib lurking downstairs.

He knocked back his coffee, poured another and returned to the window, staring out across the jumbled flux of rooftops. Most of them, like the streets below, were covered with mounds of litter, as though the metropolis was sandwiched between twin layers of rubbish. He tried, and failed, to make out St Simon the Tanner and the other Coptic churches cut into the cliffs above the Zabbaleen quarter of Manshiet Nasser, then dropped his eyes to the alleyway directly below, where the remains of last night's whisky bottle lay scattered in the dust. A cat sniffed inquisitively around them. He wasn't sure whether to feel disgust at himself for so spectacularly falling off the wagon, or relief that he'd somehow managed to clamber back onto it again. A bit of both, he guessed.

'Thanks, Alex,' he murmured, knowing that if it hadn't been for the photo, he'd still be drinking now. 'What would I do without you?'

He gazed out for a while longer, the coffee continuing the work of the cold shower, clearing and ordering his mind. He then returned the cup to the kitchen, dressed and padded along the corridor to his study at the far end of the apartment.

Wherever he had set up home in his life – Cambridge, London, Baghdad, here in Cairo – he always laid out his work space in exactly the same way. His desk sat just inside the door, facing across the room towards the window. There was a row of filing cabinets lined up beside the desk, floor-to-ceiling bookshelves along the side walls and an armchair, lamp and portable CD player in the corner, with a clock on the wall above them. It was exactly the same arrangement his father – also an eminent Egyptologist – used to have in his study, right down to the pot plants on top of the filing cabinets and the kilim rug on the floor. More than once Flin had wondered what a psychoanalyst would make of the similarity. Probably the same as they'd make of him following his old man into Egyptology: a sublimated need to please, to emulate, to be loved. All the usual crap psychoanalysts came out with. He tried not to dwell on it. His father was long dead, and when all was said and done he was by now so used to that particular furniture configuration it was easier to just let things be. Whatever the emotional subtext.

Coming into the room now he paused, as he always did, to look up at the framed print hanging on the wall above the desk. A simple ink line drawing, it depicted a monumental gateway – two trapezium-shaped towers with between

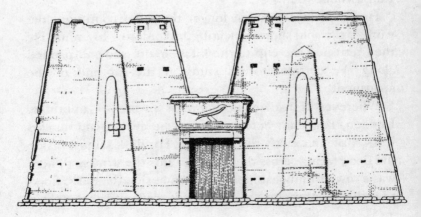

them, about half their height, a pair of rectangular doors surmounted by a lintel. Each tower bore on its face the image of an obelisk with inside it a cross and looping line symbol – *sedjet*, the hieroglyphic ideogram for fire. The lintel also bore an image, this time of a bird with a small beak and long sweeping tail. At the bottom of the print, in flowing script, ran the legend:

The city of Zerzura is white like a pigeon, and on the door of it is carved a bird. Enter, and there you will discover great riches.

He stared at it, repeating the legend to himself – as he always did – and then, with a shake of the head, crossed to the armchair and threw himself down, flicking on the CD player. The melancholy, tinkling strains of a Chopin nocturne rose around him.

It was a ritual he followed every morning, and had done since he was an undergraduate (apparently the spy Kim Philby had sworn by it): a still, meditative thirty minutes at the start of the day – or in this case the middle of it – when he would sit back, block out the world and focus on what-ever intellectual problem happened to be preoccupying him at that moment, while his brain was still fresh. Sometimes it might be an abstract problem – how to interpret the mythical struggle between the gods Horus and Set, for example; at other times something more specific: an argument he was developing for an academic paper, per-haps, or the translation of a particularly obscure inscription.

More often than not he would end up pondering some aspect of the Hidden Oasis mystery. This, more than any other subject, was what had occupied his mind these last ten years. And it was the one to which, in the light of recent events, his mind turned this morning.

It was a complex problem, impossibly complex he sometimes thought: an intricate jigsaw from which most of the pieces seemed to be missing and those pieces that did exist refused to fit into any sort of recognizable pattern. A handful of textual fragments, most of them ambivalent or incomplete; a couple of pieces of rock art, again open to interpretation; the Zerzura stuff; and, of course, the Imti-Khentika papyrus. Not a lot to go on, all things considered; the Egyptological equivalent of trying to crack the Nazis' Enigma code.

Closing his eyes, the Chopin swirling gently around him, Flin let his mind drift, going back into it all for the ten-thousandth time, meandering through the scattered evidence as though through a field of ancient ruins. He mulled over the various names by which the oasis had been known – the Hidden Oasis, the Oasis of the Birds, the Sacred Valley, the Valley of the Benben, the Oasis at the End of the World, the Oasis of Dreams – hoping that by scrolling through them again he might stumble upon some hitherto overlooked clue. Likewise the *Iret net Khepri* reference, the Eye of Khepri, which he was convinced was more than just one of those figurative phrases so beloved of the ancient Egyptians, but indicated something specific, something literal. If it did he hadn't yet worked out what it was – and didn't come any closer to doing so today.

Thirty minutes went by, and then another thirty – the Mouth of Osiris, the Curses of Sobek and Apep: what the hell were they? – until his mind started to cloud and his eyes popped open again. For a moment his gaze wandered around the room, then came to rest on the drawing above the desk: *The city of Zerzura is white like a pigeon, and on the door of it is carved a bird. Enter, and there you will discover great riches.* Standing, he walked across to it, took it off the wall and carried it back to the armchair, sitting again and balancing it on his knees.

It was the frontispiece – or rather a copy of the frontispiece, the original Arabic script rendered into English – of a chapter from the *Kitab al-Kanuz*, the Book of Hidden Pearls, a medieval treasure-hunter's guide to the great sites of Egypt, both real and fanciful. This particular chapter was concerned with the legendary lost oasis of Zerzura – aside from a brief and rather cryptic mention in a thirteenth-century manuscript, the earliest known reference to the place.

Although of no intrinsic value, the print was one of Flin's most treasured possessions, a gift from the great desert explorer Ralph Alger Bagnold, whom he had met shortly before the latter's death in 1990. Flin had been studying for his doctorate at the time (on Palaeolithic settlement patterns around the Gilf Kebir) and their mutual fascination with the Sahara had meant the two men clicked instantly. A series of happy afternoons had been spent together discussing the desert, the Gilf, and, most fascinating of all, the whole Zerzura problem – magical conversations that had first sparked Flin's interest in the subject.

He gazed down at the print, smiling, even now – almost two decades later – still feeling the thrill of excitement he had experienced at being in the great man's presence.

Bagnold had been in no doubt: Zerzura was just a legend, the descriptions of it in the *Kitab al-Kanuz* – heaps of gold and jewels scattered everywhere, a king and queen asleep in a castle – pure fairy tale, no more to be taken literally than Hansel and Gretel or Jack and the Beanstalk.

There was no question that the *Kitab* was in large part fantasy, crammed full of sensational accounts of hidden riches. Despite that, the more Flin had researched the subject the more convinced he had become that when you stripped away the obvious embellishments, the Zerzura of the *Kitab al-Kanuz* was in fact a real place. Not only that, but – as he had outlined in his lecture the previous evening – it was one and the same as the Hidden Oasis of the ancient Egyptians.

The name itself provided a clue. Zerzura came from the Arabic *zarzar*, or little bird, a clear echo of one of the ancient variations on *wehat seshtat*: *wehat apedu*, Oasis of the Birds.

The image of the gateway was also intriguing: an almost perfect facsimile of a monumental Old Kingdom temple pylon. The obelisk and *sedjet* symbols likewise signalled an ancient Egyptian connection, as did the bird on the lintel, a clear rendering of the sacred Benu bird.

It was, admittedly, all fairly tenuous, and when Flin had talked it through with Bagnold, the older man had been unconvinced. The similarity in names was almost certainly a coincidence, he had argued – all oases had birds in them – while the ancient architecture and symbols could easily be explained by the *Kitab*'s author having simply copied things he had seen in the temples of the Nile Valley, with which he would most likely have been familiar.

And of course there remained the obvious problem of how – even if Zerzura did exist and was one and the same as the Hidden Oasis – the *Kitab*'s author had come about his information. The oasis was, after all, supposed to be hidden.

Curiously it had been Bagnold himself who had provided an answer of sorts. There had long been rumours, he told Flin, that certain desert tribes knew of Zerzura's whereabouts, Bedouin who had stumbled on it by accident and had guarded the secret of its location ever since. For himself he didn't believe a word of it, but if Flin was looking for explanations that, in Bagnold's opinion, was the most likely one: the *Kitab*'s author had heard about the oasis second, third or fourth hand from a Bedouin who had actually been there.

'It's a fascinating tale,' he had said. 'But be careful. More than one person has been driven mad by the search for Zerzura. Keep it as an interest. Don't let it become an obsession.'

And Flin hadn't. Not in the beginning. He had continued to explore the subject, to turn up whatever information he could, but it had never been more than a hobby, a diverting sideline to his main area of study. And then he had finished his doctorate and moved out of Egyptology and Zerzura and the Hidden Oasis had been all but forgotten.

Only when his life had gone tits-up and he had returned to Egypt, got involved in Sandfire, had he started looking into it all again, going back over the evidence. Only then had it really sunk its claws into him, his interest ballooning into obsession, and obsession into something bordering on full-blown mania.

It was out there, he knew it, he could feel it. Despite what Bagnold and a hundred others had said. Zerzura, the *wehat seshtat*, whatever you wanted to call it – it was out there in the Gilf Kebir. And he couldn't find it. He couldn't bloody find it. However hard he looked.

He stared down at the print, his brow furrowed, his teeth clenched, then glanced up at the clock on the wall.

'Fuck it!' he yelled, leaping to his feet. Only fifteen minutes before he was due to start his Advanced Hieroglyphs class. He replaced the print, snatched up his laptop and rushed from the building, in such a hurry that he failed to notice the rotund figure sitting in the window of the juice bar next door, dabbing at his face with a hand-kerchief and sipping from a can of Coca-Cola.

DAKHLA

'Al Dakla Central Hospital', as the sign on its roof pro-claimed, sat on the main thoroughfare through Mut: a modern, two-storey building surrounded by dum palms, and painted green and white like most of the rest of the town. Leaving the Land Cruiser on the forecourt Zahir and Freya went inside where Zahir spoke to a nurse at the reception desk. She motioned the two of them to a row of plastic seats and picked up a phone.

Ten minutes passed, people drifting in and out of the foyer around them, a faint sound of music echoing from somewhere deep within the building. Then a balding, middle-aged man in a white doctor's coat approached.

'Miss Hannen?'

Freya and Zahir stood.

'Dr Mohammed Rashid,' said the man, shaking her hand. 'I am sorry to have kept you waiting,'

His English was fluent, a faint American twang to his accent. He spoke briefly in Arabic to Zahir, who nodded and sat down again. With a 'Please follow me,' he ushered Freya down a corridor towards the rear of the building, explaining as they went that he had cared for her sister during her final few months.

'She had what we call Marburg's Variant,' he told her, adopting that sympathetic yet detached tone doctors always use when describing terminal sickness. 'A rare form of multiple sclerosis in which the disease progresses extremely rapidly. She was diagnosed just six months ago and by the end had lost the use of almost everything except her right arm.'

Freya trailed along beside him, only half registering what he was saying. The closer they came to her sister the harder she was finding it to believe any of this was happening.

'. . . easier for her in Cairo or back in the States,' Rashid was saying. 'But this is where she felt at home and so we did what we could to make her comfortable. Zahir was very good to her.'

They turned right through a set of swing doors and descended a staircase into the hospital basement then followed another corridor, their footsteps echoing on the tiled floor. About halfway down Rashid stopped, removed a set of keys and unlocked a door – thick, heavy, like the door to a cell. Pushing it open, he stood aside to allow Freya through. She hesitated, the temperature around her seeming to drop suddenly. Then, with an effort of will, stepped past him into the room.

It was a large, green-tiled space, unnaturally cold, with strip lights in the ceiling and a vague smell of antiseptic in the air. In front of her, on a trolley, lay a body-shaped form covered in a white sheet. Freya raised a hand to her mouth, her throat tightening.

'Would you like me to stay?' the doctor asked.

She shook her head, afraid that if she spoke she would start sobbing. He nodded and started to close the door before leaning back in again.

'People here in Dakhla don't always warm to strangers,' he said, his voice gentler than it had been, less officious. 'They did to Miss Alex. *Ya doctora*, they called her, the doctor. An expression of great respect. *Ya doctora*, and also *el-mostakshefa el-gameela* – it's hard to translate precisely but basically means "the beautiful explorer". She will be greatly missed. I shall wait for you outside. Please, take as much time as you want.'

The door clicked as he pulled it to. Freya stared at it a moment before turning and crossing to the gurney. She stretched out a hand and laid it on the sheet, pressing down, shocked by how skeletal the body beneath felt, as though there was barely any flesh on it.

For a while she just stood like that, overwhelmed, biting her lip, her breath coming in short gasps. Then, tentatively, she grasped the top corner of the sheet and pulled, revealing first her sister's face and neck, and then the rest of her body down to the waist. She was naked, her eyes closed, her skin translucently pale save for around the left shoulder where the flesh was stained by a heavy epaulette of bruising.

'Oh God,' she murmured. 'Oh Alex.'

Curiously it was the small things, the obscure details that

caught her attention rather than the body as a whole, as though to have taken it all in would have been too much and only by dealing with it jigsaw-like, piece by tiny piece, could she come to terms with the enormity of what she was looking at. Of *who* she was looking at. The mole on the side of her sister's neck, the sickle-shaped curve of scar tissue on her left hand, where she had slashed it against barbed wire as a child, and another bruise, this one much smaller, just beneath the bend of her right elbow, no bigger than a thumbprint.

Detail by detail she took the body in, piecing her sister together, reclaiming her, until eventually her eyes came to rest on Alex's face.

Despite all the pain and distress of her final few months her expression was curiously peaceful and contented, the eyes closed as though in restful sleep, the corners of the mouth turned slightly upward in what looked like the beginnings of a smile. Not the face of someone who had died in pain and despair.

Or so Freya tried to tell herself. She thought of her parents, in their caskets at the funeral home following the car accident that had killed them both, remembered that they too had had that same look about them. Maybe it was just how corpses were, the physical default setting of death. Maybe she was reading too much into it.

She couldn't help herself, however. Needed some re-assurance that her sister's suicide was not quite as hopelessly, unutterably bleak as it seemed. That at the end Alex had found something good to cling to. That she had, in her own way, died happy. That's what Freya wanted to believe; needed to believe. The alternative – that she had died alone, in agony and despair – was just too terrible to contemplate. There had to be something more. Some flicker of hope.

She reached out and touched her sister's cheek: the skin was cold and smooth to the touch, like alabaster. She remembered the time when, aged thirteen and out on one of her extended rambles around Markham, she had stumbled across Alex and Greg – the boyfriend who would later become Alex's fiancé – lying asleep in each other's arms in the corner of a hayfield. They had been on their side, bodies curved into each other like spoons in a drawer, Greg's arm clutched around Alex's waist, a faint smile tweaking the corners of her mouth. That same expression as she now wore in death. Greg and Alex – Freya started to sob.

'I'm sorry,' she choked. 'Oh God, I'm so, so sorry. Please, Alex . . . please . . .'

She wanted to say 'Forgive me' but the words wouldn't come. Instead, leaning forward, she kissed her sister's brow and laid her cheek momentarily against her forehead. Then she drew the sheet back up and hurried from the room.

CAIRO

The US Embassy compound is a walled, heavily guarded affair just off Midan Tahrir. More akin to a high-security prison than a diplomatic residence, it is dominated by two buildings.

Cairo 1, as staff call it, is an ugly dun-coloured tower rearing fifteen storeys from the centre of the compound and home to most of the Embassy's core services: the Ambassador's office, governmental liaison, military affairs, intelligence gathering.

Cairo 2, just a short hop across the compound, is altogether less obtrusive than its sister building, with a façade of pale cream stone, slit-like windows and a pair of satellite dishes sitting on its roof like giant jug-ears. Here are housed the back-up departments that keep the Embassy functioning – Accounts, Administration, Press, Information. And here, on the third floor, was where Cy Angleton had his office.

Sitting behind his desk now, the door locked and the blinds drawn, he slotted a needle into the insulin-dispensing pen. Lifting his shirt he grasped a handful of rubbery flesh, the compression causing the skin to turn even whiter than it already was.

Things had moved on since he was a kid growing up in the sixties in Brantley, Alabama. Back then injections had involved a vial, a syringe and a needle the length of his finger. Now it was a neat little cartridge and a dispenser no larger than a fountain pen. If the technology had improved, however, some things never changed. As a lifelong Type 1 diabetic he still had to inject himself four times a day, regular as clockwork ('Pincushion pig boy!' the kids at school had used to chant at him). And even now, after almost forty years, he still hated doing it.

He gritted his teeth and started humming Hank Williams's 'Your Cheating Heart', giving it a few bars before banging the pen down firmly onto his stomach. The needle pierced the skin with a sharp, transient sting. He held it there a moment as the insulin pumped out into the fatty tissue, keeping him alive; then, with a sigh of relief, he returned the pen to its holder. Buttoning his shirt he waddled across to the window, raising the blind. Sunlight flooded the office.

It was a small, cramped space, the furniture – desk, chair, sofa and bookcase – bland and ugly: GI furniture, they called it. He would have been more comfortable over in Cairo 1, where the offices were bigger and better appointed, but his secondment was to Public Affairs, and Public Affairs was in Cairo 2, so that's where he was. Fewer questions that way. It wouldn't be for too long, hopefully. Once the whole Sandfire thing was resolved he'd pack up and be on the first plane out.

Below him two figures charged back and forth across the Embassy tennis court, the rhythmic thud of the ball echoing dully around the compound. He watched them, wondering, in a detached sort of way, what it felt like to move so freely, before returning to his desk. He sat down and reached for the file he'd been working on before his insulin shot. On the front, stamped diagonally in red, was the word 'Classified'. Below that was a name: Alexandra Hannen. He flipped it open and started reading.

DAKHLA

There was paperwork to be gone through, forms to be signed releasing the body for burial, a landslide of bureaucracy. It was getting on for late afternoon before it was all done and Freya was able to leave the hospital. The sharp, piercing sunlight of earlier in the day had softened to a rich, honey-coloured haze, although the heat was just as intense.

'I take you Doctor Alex house,' said Zahir as they climbed into the Land Cruiser.

'Thank you,' she replied.

After which they were silent.

They followed what appeared to be the main axis road north-west through the oasis. Fields of maize and sugar cane stretched out to either side, irrigation canals, groves of olive, palm and what Freya thought might be mulberry trees. She wasn't really paying much attention, her mind still struggling to cope with what she had seen back in the morgue.

After twenty minutes they turned left onto a smaller road which took them into a village; Qalamoun, according to a dual Arabic–English sign planted on its outskirts. There was a mosque, a cemetery, a couple of dusty fruit and vegetable stalls and, rather incongruously, a glass-fronted shop with a neon Kodak sign outside and a board proclaiming 'Fast Foto devilp here'.

Just beyond the village they turned again, this time onto a rutted, rubbish-strewn dirt track. Freya clutched the door handle as the Land Cruiser lurched back and forth, watching distractedly as the farmlands gave way to desert, verdant green dissolving into scorching hues of orange and red. Up and down they bumped as the track wound through a messy, disordered landscape of sand hummocks and gravel flats before climbing up onto a low ridge beyond which the desert opened out dramatically. Freya leant forward, the trauma of the hospital receding fractionally as she took in the panorama ahead – a vast undulating ocean of sand stretching away as far as the eye could see, the dunes seeming to rise and sharpen the further out they went so that what began as gentle swells had, by the time they reached the horizon, surged into towering knife-edged waves. Beneath, in the broad plain between the ridge and the first of the dunes, lay a small subsidiary oasis of fields and palm groves shimmering lushly amidst the surrounding emptiness.

'This Doctor Alex house,' said Zahir, slowing and pointing to a white dot near the far side of the greenery.

Despite herself Freya smiled, thinking how perfectly suited it was to her sister, how happy she would have been there.

'It's beautiful,' she said.

Zahir just grunted and, gunning the engine, took them down and across the plain.

They crossed some outlying fields, newly ploughed, what looked like white egrets pecking at the chocolatey soil, and entered the oasis. Now that they were nearing her sister's home Freya took more notice of her surroundings, her head turning this way and that as they jolted and slewed along the sandy track. Trees pressed in all around, tangled spiderwebs of light and shade dappled the ground. They passed a brushwood animal enclosure, a stack of cut sugar cane and a rectangular threshing floor before a donkey cart piled high with olive branches appeared round a corner ahead and Zahir was forced to pull over to allow it to pass. An elderly, sunburnt man in a straw sunhat leered at them as he went by, a cigarette dangling from his toothless mouth.

'This Mahmoud Garoub,' said Zahir once the cart was gone. 'He no good man. You no talk to him.'

He flicked his eyes at Freya to make sure she had got the message, then shifted the Land Cruiser back into gear and carried on, the undergrowth gradually thinning until eventually the track petered out in a glade of lilac-flowered jacaranda trees. Ahead, near the far edge of the glade, stood Alex's house – single-storey, whitewashed, with a satellite dish on the roof and a bougainvillaea-framed front door. Zahir pulled up, got out and, grabbing Freya's bag from the back seat, crossed to the front door.

'You sure you no want stay in hotel?' he asked, pulling a set of keys from his *djellaba* and unlocking the door. 'My brother have good hotel in Mut.'

She thanked him, but said she was quite happy here.

He shrugged, threw open the door and dropped the bag inside.

'Housekeeper leave food,' he said. 'You heat on cooker, very easy.'

He handed her the keys and gave her his mobile number which she keyed into her own phone.

'No walk in trees without shoes,' he warned. 'Many snakes. And no speak Mahmoud Garoub. Very bad man. I come tomorrow morning seven and half take you Doctor Alex—'

He broke off, as if reluctant to say the word.

'Funeral,' she said. 'Thank you.'

They stood for a moment, Zahir shuffling his feet as if building up to saying something. Freya just wanted him to go. Seeming to read her thoughts, he gave a curt nod, climbed back into the Land Cruiser and, swinging it around, drove away.

*

Once the car was out of sight Freya went into the house and closed the door behind her. The roar of the Land Cruiser's engine slowly faded, leaving just the distant putter of an irrigation pump and, intermittently, the soft, rattling hiss of palm fronds as they swayed in the breeze.

The building's interior was cool and dim and for a moment she just stood there, relieved to be on her own at last. Then, crossing a large living area, she opened a set of shuttered doors and stepped out onto a veranda at the back of the house. It was a beautiful spot, shaded by a giant jacaranda tree and with fabulous views out over the desert. The air was redolent with the scent of blossom and citrus. She imagined Alex standing there, and started to smile, only for the smile to fade as she caught sight of the wheel-chair parked up at the far end of the veranda. She winced, staring at it in horror as though at some item of torture equipment, then turned and went back inside.

A series of rooms – kitchen, bathroom, bedroom, study, storeroom – opened off the main living area and she wandered from one to the other, taking the place in. There was little by way of furniture or ornament – Alex had always been like that, living simply, hating clutter – but it was unquestionably her sister's home, her character stamped everywhere and on everything. It was there in the CD collection (Bowie, Nirvana, Richard Thompson, her beloved Chopin Nocturnes); the maps Blu-Tacked all over the walls; the labelled rock samples lined up along every windowsill. There was even a smell of Alex, invisible to a stranger, perhaps, but unmistakable to Freya who had grown up with it: Wright's Coal Tar Soap mingled with

Sure deodorant and just the faintest hint of Samsara perfume.

She came to the bedroom last. Draped from a hook behind the door was Alex's old suede travelling jacket – Christ, how many years had she had that? Freya wrapped her arms around it and pressed her face into the worn material, then went over to the bed and sat down. On the bedside table were three books: *The Physics of Blown Sand and Desert Dunes*, by R.A. Bagnold; *The Heliopolitan Tomb of Imti-Khentika*, by Hassan Fadawi – since when had Alex been interested in Egyptology? – and, most poignantly, Walt Whitman's *Leaves of Grass*, the battered, dog-eared copy that had once belonged to their father. Three books and, also, three photographs: one of their parents; one of a handsome, dark-haired man, something vaguely academic-looking in his round spectacles and corduroy jacket; one . . .

She leant forward and lifted this third photo. It was of her, Freya, smiling uncomfortably and clutching the climbing world's highest accolade, a Golden Piton award. She'd only won it last year so God knows how Alex had got hold of the photo. There it was, though, with a second, smaller photo tucked over it in the corner of the frame – a passport-booth shot of the two sisters, taken when they were in their teens, pulling faces at the camera and laughing. She clutched the photo to her chest, eyes blurring with tears.

'I miss you,' she whispered.

Later, much later, when she had composed herself, Freya left the house and walked out onto the desert. Climbing to the top of the nearest dune, she sat down cross-legged on the sand. For a while she gazed at the sun as it inched its way down towards the western horizon, then she pulled out the crumpled envelope with the Egypt postmark and opened out the letter inside. The last letter Alex had written her. 'To my beloved sister Freya,' she read.

CAIRO – THE AMERICAN UNIVERSITY

At the end of the afternoon, having completed his day's lectures – Advanced Hieroglyphs, Theory and Practice in Field Archaeology, Ancient Egyptian Literature and, filling in for someone on annual leave, English for Beginners – Flin slipped into 'Interesting' Alan Peach's office to try to find out more about the latter's recent encounter with Hassan Fadawi.

'Apparently Mubarak himself called for early release,' Peach said distractedly, eyes focused on the desk in front of him where he was piecing together the fragmented sherds of a large earthenware pot. 'Past services to Egyptology and all that. Still, even three years is bad enough. Would you . . . ?'

He nodded towards a tube of Duco Cement sitting on the corner of the desk. Flin removed the cap and passed it over. Peach ran a thin line of the adhesive along the edge of a sherd and pressed it firmly against another, holding the two pieces together while they bonded.

'He'll never work again, of course,' he went on. 'Not after what he did. Still can't think what on earth possessed him. Absolute tragedy. Brilliant man. Really knew his pottery.'

He turned the fragments back and forth underneath his desk lamp, making sure they were smoothly aligned.

'Bedja mould?' Flin hazarded, knowing that the best, and indeed only way to keep his colleague in the conversation was to humour him with chat about his beloved ceramics. Peach nodded, laying the glued fragments carefully on the table and holding up another piece of the pot.

'From the workers' village at Giza,' he said. 'Take a look at this.'

The sherd was stamped with a badly faded cartouche, the hieroglyphic signs – sun disc, djed pillar, horned viper – barely visible.

'Djedefre,' read Flin.

'Apart from the boat pit cartouches, the only direct mention of Khufu's son ever found at Giza,' beamed Peach. 'Sexy or what!'

'Very sexy,' agreed Flin.

He gave it a moment while Peach laid aside the inscribed fragment and started to work through the other pieces searching for matches, then:

'So what else did he say?'

'Hmm?'

'Fadawi. When you bumped into him. What else did he say?'

'Oh, right.'

Peach seemed slightly nonplussed by the question, as though he had thought that particular line of conversation over and done with.

'Well to be honest he was rambling a bit. Looked absolutely dreadful, poor man, thin as a rake. You know how fastidious he always was about his appearance, bit of a ladies' man by all accounts – I think playboy's the technical term although I wouldn't know myself. Anyway, to look at him now – aha!'

He held up two more sherds, the jagged edge of one marrying perfectly with that of the other.

'Fadawi,' coaxed Flin, trying to keep him to the point in hand.

'What? Oh yes, yes. Kept going on about how he was innocent. How it was all a misunderstanding, that he'd been framed. Sad, really. I mean from what I heard the evidence was pretty damning. Even had some Tutankhamun stuff by all accounts. I just can't imagine what possessed him.'

He shook his head and, leaning forward, trailed a snail-like streak of glue along the side of one of the sherds, clamping it against the other and, as before, holding them under the lamp to ensure the connection was neat.

'Did he mention me?'

Flin tried to keep the question casual, matter-of-fact.

'Hmm?' Peach was squinting at the join, turning it back and forth.

'Did he mention me?' Flin repeated, louder.

'Yes he did, as it happens.'

Peach's eyes flicked up and then down again.

'Said some rather unpleasant things, actually. Very unpleasant. I mean I know it was you who blew the whistle and all that, but . . .'

He trailed off as he realized the join was uneven. With an annoyed click of the tongue he leant right into the lamp and delicately tried to ease the pieces into alignment.

'What did he say?' asked Flin.

No response.

'What did Fadawi say, Alan?'

'I really don't think I want to repeat that sort of language here,' muttered his colleague, driving the sherds hard against each other. 'He'd got himself rather worked up and – oh sod it!'

The sherds had come apart in his hand. He threw an annoyed look across the desk as if to say 'If you weren't distracting me with damn fool questions that wouldn't have happened' and reached for the tube of Duco. Before he could grasp it Flin leant forward, picked it up and moved it out of the way, forcing Peach to look up at him.

'What did he say, Alan?'

Their eyes held, then, with an exasperated sigh, Peach laid the two fragments on the table and sat back in his chair.

'If the rumours I heard were true, pretty much what he said to you in court when they sentenced him. I'm sure you remember what that was.'

Flin certainly did remember. How could he forget?

'I'll kill you, Brodie!' Fadawi had screamed. 'I'll cut off your balls and kill you, you filthy treacherous bastard!'

'I wouldn't take it too personally,' said Peach.

'How the hell else am I supposed to take it?'

'Well I'm sure he didn't mean it. He's an archaeologist, after all, not a gangster. Well, an ex-archaeologist. Never work again after what he did. Really can't think what on earth possessed him. Can I . . . ?'

He indicated the Duco. Flin passed it over and Peach bent down over the table again.

'Are you going to Donald's book launch tonight?' he asked,

changing the subject. 'Should be quite a jolly affair, provided that bloody boyfriend of his doesn't turn up.'

Flin shook his head, and rose to his feet.

'Got a 5 a.m. flight down to Dakhla. Enjoy.'

He raised a hand in farewell and made for the door.

'Mentioned something about an oasis.'

Flin stopped and turned. Peach was still hunched over his pot, apparently oblivious to the effect this throwaway comment had had.

'Couldn't make much sense of it, to be honest,' he continued, absorbed in his work. 'Gabbling he was, very emotional. Claimed he'd found something. Or was it knew something? Can't remember exactly. One of the two. About an oasis, anyway. And wasn't going to tell anyone and that would be his revenge. Very worked up, he was, very emotional. And thin as a rake. Tragic when you think about it. Did I ever tell you about the Second Dynasty hieratic wine jar dockets from Abydos? Thief or not, he certainly knew his pottery, you've got to give him that.'

Peach looked up, but Flin was no longer there.

DAKHLA

Sitting on top of the dune, a sudden, sharp breeze causing the sand around her to whisper and hiss, Freya went through Alex's last letter, her sister's voice ringing clear inside her head.

Dakhla Oasis, Egypt
3 May

To my beloved sister Freya,

I begin with those words because although it has been many years since we last spoke or saw each other, and there has been much pain and anger, they have never for one moment ceased to be true; nor have you for one moment ceased to be in my thoughts. You are my little sister, and whatever has passed between us, whatever has been said and done, my love has always been there, and always will be.

I want you to know this, Freya, because lately I have come to realize the future is an uncertain place, full of doubt and shadow, and if we do not speak our hearts now, in the present, the chance to do so might be lost for ever. So I say it again – I love you, little sis. More than I can possibly express; more than you could ever possibly know.

It's late evening now, and there's a full moon up in the sky; the biggest, brightest moon you ever saw: so clear you can make out the craters and seas on its surface, so big you feel you only have to reach out a hand and you could touch it. Do you remember that story Dad used to tell? About how the moon was actually a door, and if you climbed up there and opened it you could pass right through the sky into another world? Do you remember how we used to dream of what it was like, that secret world – a beautiful, magic place full of flowers and waterfalls and birds that could talk? I can't explain it, Freya, not clearly, but just recently I've looked through that door and glimpsed the other side, and it's just as magical as we ever imagined it. More magical. When you've seen that secret world you can't help but feel hope. Somewhere, little sis, there's always a door, and beyond it a light, however dark things might appear.

There's so much I want to say, so much I want to tell you, to share and describe, but it's late and I'm tired and I don't have the energy I used to. Before I stop, however, there is one thing I want to ask of you – have wanted to ask for many years now – and that is your forgiveness. What happened, happened, and however great my pain at the time I should have seen it coming and done more to prevent it, to protect you. Should, also, have had the courage to reach out sooner and say what I am now saying. The fault is mine, Freya, and now the years have passed and the pain is locked in and I have not been the sister I ought to have been. I hope, in some small way, this letter can make amends.

I shall finish here. Please, don't be sad. Life is good, and there is so much beauty in the world. Be strong, climb high, and know that whatever happens, wherever you are, I will always, in one way or another, be there with you. I love you so much.

Alex xxx

P.S. The enclosed flower is a Sahara Orchid. It is, I am told, very rare. Treasure it, and think of me.

Wiping the tears from her eyes Freya laid the letter on the dune top and removed the flower from the envelope; its dried petals were thin as rice paper and coloured a deep, golden orange, like the sands around her. She gazed at it, then, folding it carefully inside the letter, wrapped her arms around her knees and watched as the sun inched its way slowly down towards the horizon, a soft breeze hissing across the sand, the desert rippling and swirling away into the distance like an expanse of crumpled taffeta.

They buried her early the next morning, not far from her house, in a grove of blossoming acacia trees, right on the very edge of the little oasis. There were flowers on the ground – zinnias and periwinkles – and a smell of honeysuckle in the air, and, from somewhere beyond the grove, the soft plash of water trickling into a cistern. It was, thought Freya, one of the most beautiful, peaceful places she had ever been.

There was only a small group present, which is how Alex would have wanted it: herself, Zahir, Dr Rashid from the hospital, Molly Kiernan and a handsome, slightly dishevelled man in a crumpled corduroy jacket, whom she recognized from the photo on Alex's bedside table – Flin Brodie, as he introduced himself. There was a scatter of local people too. Farmers mostly, come to pay their respects, hanging back from the main group, and three Bedouin women, one of them Zahir's wife, dressed in traditional costume – black robes, headscarves, intricate silver jewellery. As Alex's coffin was lowered into the ground they came forward and started to sing – 'Aloosh', Zahir explained, a Bedouin love song 'about very beautiful woman'. Their clear, nasal voices wove in and out of each other, rising and falling, one moment low and barely audible, the next swooping upwards so that the whole grove echoed to the music. There were no words to the song, or at least none that Freya could make out, just a winding thread of sound that nonetheless, in the way the tune shifted and contrasted, sometimes dark, sometimes light, seemed to tell a story she could understand: of love and loss, joy and pain, hope and despair. She felt Molly Kiernan's hand reach out and clasp hers, squeezing it tight, the song wafting over and around them until it dropped away and faded into silence, leaving just the tinkle of water and, from above, the low twitter of a pair of hoopoes.

For a moment everyone just stood, lost in their own thoughts. Then, releasing Freya's hand, Kiernan cleared her throat and stepped forward to the head of the grave.

'Freya has asked me to say a few words,' she said, throwing a glance first at Freya, and then Flin, who was gazing down at the coffin. 'I promise that it *will* be just a few words, because as everyone who was privileged enough to know Alex will be aware, she hated fuss and chatter.'

Although soft, her voice seemed to fill the entire glade.

'Thirty years ago now, I myself lost someone I loved very much. My husband, as it happens. In that dark time two things helped me through. The first was the love and support of my friends. I hope, Freya, you can feel our love here today in this special place, both for Alex, and for you too. We are here if you need us, however, whenever, wherever.'

She cleared her throat again, fingering the gold cross at her neck.

'The other thing that eased my pain in that time of sorrow was the Holy Bible and the words of our Lord Jesus Christ. I would quote from it now, but I know Alex wasn't a believer, and although the love of Jesus is universal, I won't insult her memory by dwelling on sentiments with which she herself did not feel comfortable.'

It was fleeting and barely noticeable, but as she said this

there was the faintest tightening around her mouth, as if of disapproval.

'Instead,' she went on, 'I would like to read you something that was close to Alex's heart, and that is a poem by Walt Whitman.'

She fumbled in the pocket of her jacket, pulled out a printed sheet and slipped on a pair of spectacles.

'O Me, O Life,' she read, holding the sheet out in front of her.

O Me! O Life! of the questions of these recurring,
Of the endless trains of the faithless, of cities fill'd with the
*   foolish,*
Of myself forever reproaching myself (for who more foolish than
*   I, and who more faithless?)*
Of eyes that vainly crave the light, of the objects mean, of the
*   struggle ever renew'd,*
Of the poor results of all, of the plodding and sordid crowds I
*   see around me,*
Of the empty and useless years of the rest, with the rest me
*   intertwined,*
The question, O me! So sad, recurring – what good amid these,
*   O me, O Life?*

Answer

That you are here – that life exists and identity
That the powerful play goes on, and you may contribute a verse.

She folded the sheet and removed her glasses, wiping an index finger across her eye.

'There is so much I could say about Alex. Her beauty, her intelligence, her courage, her sense of adventure. I think Walt Whitman puts it best, though, when he talks about contributing a verse. Alex contributed a verse to all our lives, a very special verse, one that enriched and uplifted us all. Sister, friend, colleague – the world is a poorer place without her. Thank you, Alex. We miss you.'

She returned to Freya's side and took her hand again as two of the local men stepped forward with shovels and started filling the grave. The thud of dirt on coffin echoed dully around the grove, a harsh, discordant sound at odds with the otherwise idyllic atmosphere. For a brief moment Freya's eyes met Flin's, the latter giving the faintest of nods as if to convey that he both understood and shared in the grief she was feeling, before the two of them looked away again. The grave was rapidly filled until all that was left was a raised rectangle of sandy earth surrounded by flowers.

'Goodbye,' Freya whispered.

Afterwards Dr Rashid made his excuses and hurried off, explaining that he was on call and needed to get back to the hospital. Most of the local people drifted away too, leaving just Freya, Molly, Flin, Zahir and a young, bearded man whom Zahir introduced as his brother Said. As the five of them walked back along the path to Alex's house, Flin came up beside Freya.

'Not ideal circumstances, I know,' he said. 'But I'm glad to meet you at last.'

She nodded, but said nothing.

'Alex told me a lot about you,' he went on. 'About your

climbing and everything. Scared the shit out of me, to be honest. I get vertigo just standing on a step-ladder.'

She gave the faintest of smiles.

'Did you know her well?'

'Pretty well,' he replied, thrusting his hands into the pockets of his jeans. 'We shared an interest in the desert. Became friends. Good friends.'

She glanced at him, raising her eyebrows.

'You and Alex were . . . ?'

'Christ no!' Flin gave an amused snort. 'Neurotic English bookworms weren't her thing at all. As far as I could make out she was more into the hippie-surfer type.'

An image of Greg, Alex's former fiancé, flashed into Freya's mind – blond, tanned, toned. She shook her head to dislodge it.

'She was very good to me,' Flin was saying. 'Helped me through some . . . difficult times. She was more like a sister than a friend.'

He kicked at a stone in the path, then turned to her, frowning.

'I'm sorry, I didn't mean . . . inappropriate analogy.'

She waved a hand to indicate that the apology was unnecessary. Their eyes met and held a moment before they both looked away again. The path led them through a shadowy olive grove, the ground carpeted with manure pats and dusty black olives, before at last bringing them to Alex's house.

Someone – the housekeeper, Freya assumed – had laid out a simple breakfast on the table in the main room: cheese, tomatoes, onions, beans, bread and flasks of coffee. They gathered round and picked at it, only Zahir and his

brother showing any real appetite, faltering bursts of conversation petering out into extended silences. Thirty
minutes passed, then both Flin and Kiernan announced
that they had to be leaving to catch their flight back up to
Cairo.

'You're sure you'll be all right?' Kiernan asked as they
walked out to Zahir's Land Cruiser, her arm threaded
through Freya's. 'I could hang around if you like.'

'I'll be fine,' Freya replied. 'I'm going to stay here for a
couple of days, get Alex's stuff together, then head home.
My flight's not till Friday.'

'Why don't I meet you at the airport when you come back
into Cairo?' said Kiernan. 'We can have lunch, say goodbye
properly.'

Freya agreed and they embraced, the older woman kissing her on the cheek before pulling away and climbing into
the Toyota's rear passenger seat. Flin stepped forward and
handed her a card: Professor F. Brodie, American University
in Cairo, Tel: 202 2794 2959.

'I doubt it'll happen, but if you ever find yourself at a
loose end do look me up. You can scare me with climbing
stories and I can return the compliment by boring you rigid
with tales of Neolithic rock inscriptions.'

He leant forward and for a moment it looked as if he was
going to embrace her. As it was, he just gave her a quick
peck on the cheek and, walking round the other side of the
4x4, heaved himself up beside Kiernan. Zahir and his
brother climbed in the front, the engine roared into life and
they were just moving away when Freya suddenly reached
through the open window and grasped Kiernan's wrist.

'She didn't suffer, did she?' Her voice had become choked,

urgent. 'When she ... Alex ... you know, the morphine ... When she took it. It was quick, wasn't it? No pain.'

Kiernan squeezed her hand.

'I don't think there was any pain at all, Freya. From what I heard it would have been very swift, and very peaceful.'

Beside her Flin seemed about to add something, his mouth half opening before closing again. Freya withdrew her hand.

'I just needed to know,' she mumbled. 'I couldn't bear it if . . .'

'I understand, dear,' said Kiernan. 'Believe me, Alex didn't suffer in any way. Just a small prick when the needle went in and that was it. No pain, I promise.'

She leant forward and touched Freya's arm, then nodded to Zahir and they drove off. Only when they had disappeared among the trees and Freya was walking back towards the house did it strike her exactly what the older woman had said. She spun round, the colour draining from her face.

'Alex would never have . . .'

But the roar of the engine had faded away, leaving just the hum of flies and, in the distance, the soft coughing of the irrigation pump.

CAIRO

Using his elbow Angleton nudged shut the door of Flin Brodie's apartment. The rhythmic slap of the caretaker's plastic slippers slowly faded on the stairwell outside as he descended to the ground floor again. He'd wanted to stick around, see what Angleton was up to, but the American had added an extra wad of notes to the money he'd already paid him for opening the door and told him to scoot. He was old and dirty and clumsy and Angleton didn't want him moving stuff around, alerting Brodie to the fact he'd had visitors. This was business, not just a bit of casual snooping. Keep it professional, keep it focused. That's what they paid him for. That's why he was the best.

The door closed with a muted click. Reaching into his pocket, he pulled out a pair of latex gloves and tugged them on, the rubber hissing and snapping as he stretched it up over his wrists. Along with the shoe covers he'd donned on the landing outside, they would ensure there were no traces, no indication of any sort, that he'd been there. He was almost certainly being over-cautious. Brodie had no reason to expect an intrusion of this sort, or to be on the lookout for one on his return. You could never be too careful, though. On the thousand-to-one chance the Englishman *was* more paranoid than Angleton was giving him credit for – and with his background the possibility was always there – he wasn't going to risk blowing the whole operation by leaving unnecessary clues.

He glanced at his watch – plenty of time; the Dakhla flight hadn't even taken off yet – and started wandering around. He wasn't looking for anything in particular, just trying to get a feel for Brodie, a sense of what he knew, how he tied in with the whole Sandfire thing. Living room, kitchen, bathroom, two bedrooms, study: he examined them all, snapping shot after shot with his digital camera, recording his thoughts on a handheld Olympus Dictaphone.

To the untrained eye the apartment wouldn't have revealed a great deal about its owner: a self-contained, bachelor Egyptologist with an interest in classical music, desert exploration, current affairs – particularly Middle Eastern current affairs – and, judging by the scarf and signed team photograph in the living room, El-Ahly Football Club. Those and a few other details – Brodie kept himself fit, read at least five languages, steered clear of alcohol and had a social conscience (thank-you letters from a children's orphanage in Luxor and a Zabbaleen outreach programme over in Manshiet Nasser) – would probably have been about the sum total of things. A join-the-dots sort of portrait, giving a basic character outline but without any great depth or meat to it.

But Angleton's eye *was* trained. As he moved around the rooms he was able to read between the lines of their contents, teasing out the underlying information. In the bathroom, for instance, tucked into one of Brodie's heavily worn Kayano trainers, he found a state-of-the-art speed and distance monitor, its computerized memory recording details of all the Englishman's runs over the last fortnight. Ten kilometres in 36:02 minutes, 20 kilometres in 1:15:31, 15 kilometres in 53:12 – Brodie, it seemed, wasn't just fit, but seriously so. In the bedroom the battered lamp on the bedside table, the marks on the wall directly behind it, the three-quarters-empty pack of Xanax tablets, all likewise spoke to Angleton. Brodie, they told him, was someone who had nightmares, flailing in the dark for the light switch before popping anti-anxiety pills to calm himself down again. All confirmation of what the American's research had already told him about the man.

The photo of Alex Hannen in the living room was interesting. Whether the two of them had been lovers or not Angleton couldn't be sure. On balance he'd say no – lovers, in his experience, usually possessed multiple images of each other, especially if they lived separately, whereas here there was only the one photo. Brodie clearly cared for her – deeply, to judge by the expensive silver frame in which the picture was enclosed – but if pushed Angleton would have gone for close friendship over romance.

Either way, what intrigued him more were the telling little clues tucked away in the corners of the photo. It had clearly been taken out in the remote desert – the western desert, he assumed, given their mutual interest in the place – and by Brodie himself, whose reflection could just be made out in the mirrored lenses of Hannen's sunglasses.

In the background, off to the left and slightly blurred, were a couple of orange equipment cases (there was a similar case in the apartment hallway, containing some sort of radar or sensing device). Even more intriguing, behind Brodie in the reflection in Hannen's shades, almost invisible – Angleton had to peer very hard with the mini-magnifying glass he always carried – was what appeared to be the tip of some sort of wing or sail, way too small for a plane. A kite? A hang glider? A microlight? He couldn't tell, and there wasn't time to take the photo away for digital enhancement. It was informative nonetheless, suggesting, when you factored in the equipment cases and remote desert setting, that as well as being personally close, Brodie and Hannen had also been working together in some way. A one-off trip? Part of some bigger project? Again, he couldn't be sure, but it was another fragment of the picture. Piece by piece by piece.

He spent almost twenty minutes poring over the photo before glancing again at his watch – still plenty of time – and heading back into the study. He'd already given it the once-over, but it was clearly the nerve centre of Brodie's world so he wanted to have another nose round before he left, see if anything more could be gleaned from it.

He stared again at the framed print on the wall behind the desk, repeating its legend – *The city of Zerzura is white like a pigeon, and on the door of it is carved a bird* – into his Dictaphone even though he'd already done so on his earlier sweep of the room.

The wooden filing cabinets lined up beside the desk also received a second inspection. Each was divided into five drawers, each drawer crammed with sheaves of notes, articles, photographs, charts, print-outs and maps, separated out into alphabetically headed sections, starting with Almasy in the top drawer of the first cabinet, and finishing with Zerzura in the bottom drawer of the last one.

There was way too much stuff to go through it all in detail. Instead he contented himself with opening each drawer in turn and walking his latex-gloved fingers over the protruding section headings, pulling out a folder here, a folder there – Bedouin; Khepri; Long Range Desert Group; Pepi II; Wingate – before moving on again, never lingering too long on any one subject, skimming.

Only two files caused him to pause for a more in-depth perusal. One, labelled Gilf Kebir/Satellite Imaging, contained a sheaf of colour pictures. Starting with wide-scale shots of the entire south-west corner of Egypt, the images homed in, in ever greater detail, on specific areas of the Gilf, the desert landscape becoming progressively clearer and more defined. The last twenty or so shots were so sharp Angleton could make out the actual cliff faces along the Gilf's eastern edge. Occasionally there would be a prick of green – probably just a couple of trees or a clump of desert bushes – but otherwise the area was utterly lifeless and empty. No sign, certainly, of Brodie's mysterious oasis.

The other file that caught his attention was labelled Magnetometry Data (was that what the sensing device in the hallway was? A magnetometer?). The file's contents – sheet after sheet of meaningless monochrome speckles and smudges – meant nothing to him. The data itself wasn't important. What gave him pause for thought was the fact that Brodie was using a magnetometer at all. Magnetometers, so far as Angleton was aware, were used for sub-surface imaging and metal detection. And yet in his talk the other evening Brodie had specifically stated that the Stone Age inhabitants of the Gilf had not yet developed metal-working technology. There was doubtless some perfectly innocent explanation, but all the same it was curious.

'Why the magnetometer?' he drawled into his Dictaphone, pausing the machine before almost immediately pressing Record again.

'And where does he get all the satellite stuff from? NASA? Oil companies? Check who would have this material.'

He finished going through the cabinets and ran his eyes over the bookshelves again. It was all Egyptology, so far as he could see, save for one section devoted to current affairs – lots of stuff on Iraq – and, slotted in behind a row of leather-bound volumes on ancient Egyptian architecture, which is why he'd missed it before, a book on, of all things, Russian aeroplanes.

'*Osprey Encyclopedia of Russian Aircraft,*' he intoned into his recorder. 'What the hell's that doing here?'

He returned to Brodie's desk last. It was a large affair, old-fashioned, polished oak, with a phone, lamp, blotter, paper tray, pen holder – all the usual stuff, neatly arranged. No desktop computer, which suggested the Englishman worked off his laptop. And he must have taken his laptop with him to Dakhla since there was no sign of it in the flat. Annoying. Angleton scouted around for a memory stick in case Brodie had backed his work up but there was no sign of one. With time ticking away he abandoned the search, turning his attention first to the contents of the paper tray, none of which were especially revealing, and then, finally, to the book sitting on the blotter at the centre of the table: *Cuneiform Texts of The Hermitage Museum.*

There was a sheet of A4 paper sticking up about halfway through. Opening the book at that page Angleton found himself looking down at a photograph of a toffee-coloured clay tablet, badly eroded and covered in rows of small wedge-shaped marks. Underneath was a caption: 'The Egypt Tablet. Royal archive of Lugal-Zagesi (*c.* 2375–50 BCE). Uruk. From collection of N. Likhachev'.

He stared at the photograph, then turned his attention to the A4 sheet. On it Brodie had painstakingly transcribed the wedge-marks on the tablet, or at least those that were legible. Beneath he had then written out what Angleton assumed was a transliteration of the original cuneiform, rendering the text phonetically into Latin characters. And beneath that – again Angleton was guessing, although it seemed a fairly safe bet – a straight English translation, with rows of dots where the cuneiform was marred or damaged, and bracketed guesses and question marks alongside the words of whose meaning Brodie seemed to be uncertain:

... west beyond *kalam* (Sumer) beyond the horizon ... great river *artiru* (Iteru/Nile) and the land of *kammututa* (Kemet/Egypt) ... 50 *danna* from *buranun* (Euphrates?) ... rich in ... cows, fish, wheat, *geshnimbar* (date palms?) ... city called *manarfur* (Mennefer/Memphis?) ... king who rules all ... in great fear by his enemies for ... *tukul* (weapon?) called ... from an (heaven/sky?) in the form of a *lagab* (stone?) and carried into battle before the king's armies ... *bil* (burn?) with a blinding light and *u-hub* (deafen?) ... pain and dizziness ... With this thing the enemies of *kammututa* in the north are destroyed and in the south are destroyed ... east and west are beaten into dust so that their king rules all the lands around *artiru* and none shall stand against him nor come against him nor ever defeat him for in his hand is the *mitum* (mace?) of the gods ... most terrible ... ever known to ... beware and go not ever against the king of *kammututa* for in his wrath he will ... utterly destroyed.

Angleton read through this a couple of times, unable to make head or tail of it.

'Weird shit about stones,' he said into his recorder, shaking his head in bemusement at the things people found interesting. He paused a moment, then added: 'Probably not relevant.'

Replacing the A4 sheet he closed the book and shifted it

fractionally across the blotter so that it was exactly as he had found it. He gave the room one last sweep, planted the GSM listening devices – one in the phone, one behind the bookcase, one underneath the living room sofa – and left the flat. He'd been in there for just under ninety minutes, and by his reckoning Brodie's flight wouldn't even be halfway back to Cairo yet. Good, precise work, he thought to himself. That's what they paid him for. That's why he was the best.

DAKHLA

'Alex would never have injected herself. Not in a million years. There's something wrong here. You have to believe me. There's something wrong.'

Dr Mohammed Rashid furrowed his brow, tweaking at his left earlobe.

'You have to believe me,' Freya repeated. 'Alex had a phobia about needles. I would have said something before but I assumed she'd swallowed pills or drunk something. She could never have injected herself. Never.'

She was wound up, agitated, had been ever since Molly Kiernan's parting comment about the needle prick. The moment she'd registered what Kiernan had said she'd tried to call Zahir on his mobile, ask him to come back, explain things to her. His phone had been switched off. The same with Kiernan's and Brodie's. She hadn't bothered leaving messages. Frantic, she had just grabbed her knapsack and started running, through the palm and olive groves and

along the desert track back towards the main oasis. She
didn't know what she was going to do, just knew that something was terribly wrong and she had to do something. After
about a kilometre she heard a rattle and a clatter behind her
and a donkey-drawn cart had come up alongside, driven by
the elderly, toothless man she and Zahir had passed on their
way to Alex's house the previous afternoon – Mohammed,
Mahmoud, something like that. Zahir had warned her not to
have anything to do with him, but too worked up to care she
accepted his offer of a ride, desperate to get to Mut
as swiftly as possible. He had jabbered at her and
squeezed himself up unnecessarily close, allowing his
hand to brush against her thigh, but she had barely noticed.

'Mut,' she kept saying to him. 'Please, Mut, hospital,
quickly.'

In the mud-brick village at the head of the track he had
pulled up in front of the Kodak shop with its 'Fast Foto
devilp' sign and flagged down a pick-up truck which had
driven her the rest of the way. Dr Rashid was on his ward
round, they had told her when she reached the hospital,
wouldn't be available until past midday. She had insisted on
seeing him, had made a scene, and eventually calls had
been made, pagers bleeped and he'd come down and led
her up to his office.

'You have to believe me,' she said a third time, struggling
to control her voice. 'Alex couldn't have killed herself. Not
like that. It's impossible.'

In front of her, the doctor shifted in his chair, eyes flicking from his desk to Freya and back again.

'Miss Hannen,' he began slowly, still tweaking at his earlobe, 'I know how difficult—'

'You don't know!' she snapped. 'Alex could not have injected herself. She couldn't! She couldn't!'

Her voice was becoming shrill. He gave her a moment to calm, then tried again.

'Miss Hannen, when a loved one dies . . .'

She started to interrupt but he raised a hand, requesting that she give him a chance to speak.

'When a loved one dies,' he repeated, 'especially in this manner, it can be very hard to accept. We do not want to believe it, to acknowledge that someone we care for – care for deeply – could be in so much pain that taking their own life becomes preferable to continuing with that life.'

He clasped his hands on the desk, shuffled his feet.

'Alex had an incurable, degenerative condition. One that had already, in a very short space of time, robbed her of most of her movement, and one that was inevitably going to kill her, most likely in a matter of months. She was a courageous, strong-willed woman, and took the decision that if she was going to die, she at least wanted to control where, when and how it should happen. I am not happy about it, I wish she hadn't done it, but I understand her reasons, and I respect her decision. Painful as it is, you must try to do so as well.'

Freya shook her head, clasping the armrests of her seat.

'Alex would not have injected herself,' she insisted, spelling out the words, emphasizing the 'not'. 'If she'd taken an overdose, or hanged herself, or . . .'

She broke off, overwhelmed by the scenarios she was describing.

'Ever since we were kids Alex was terrified of needles,' she continued after a moment, fighting back the tears,

125

struggling to keep her voice steady. 'I know we hadn't seen each other for a long time, but I also know that sort of fear doesn't just go away. She couldn't even look at a needle, let alone fill one with morphine and stick it in herself. It's impossible.'

Dr Rashid looked up at the ceiling, then down again, exhaling slowly.

'Sometimes, when you are very ill, you make the impossible happen,' he said gently. 'This I have seen many times as a doctor. I am not suggesting you are wrong about your sister, or that her fear was not what you say it was. Simply that when you suffer as she was suffering, fear becomes relative. What terrified her when she was in good health probably did so less when measured against the greater terror of a slow, lingering, painful death, one that day by day was stripping her of what little dignity she had left. By the end Alex had become desperate, and desperate people do desperate things. I am sorry to be so blunt about it, but I do not like to see you adding to your grief in this way. Alex took her own life. We have to accept—'

A loud bleeping from his pager interrupted him. Apologizing, he lifted the phone and hit a button, turning away from her and speaking in hushed tones. Freya rose and crossed to the window. She gazed down into a large paved courtyard with a towering India laurel at its centre. A family were breakfasting in the shade beneath the tree; a man in blue pyjamas was shuffling around wheeling a drip-trolley, a cigarette dangling from the corner of his mouth. She watched him, fingers drumming on the windowsill, waiting for the doctor to finish his call.

'Did Alex tell you she was going to do something like

this?' she asked the moment he'd replaced the receiver, jumping straight back into the conversation. 'Did she say anything to you about it?'

Rashid adjusted the position of his chair, clasped his hands on the desk again.

'Not in so many words, no,' he replied. 'It had come up a couple of times in a . . . how do you say? . . . abstract sort of way. She certainly didn't ask for my help, if that is what you mean. And I certainly wouldn't have given it if she had. I am a doctor. My job is to save lives, not take them. She knew my views on this.'

Freya took a step forward.

'Who found her body?'

'Miss Hannen, please, these questions . . .'

'Who?'

Her tone was blunt, insistent.

'The housekeeper,' he said with a sigh. 'When she arrived in the morning.'

'Where? Where did she find Alex?'

'On the back porch, I believe. In her wheelchair. She liked to sit there, look out at the desert, particularly towards the end when she found movement difficult. The morphine bottle and syringe were on the table beside her. Exactly as would be expected.'

'Was there a suicide note?'

'Not so far as I know.'

'That didn't strike you as strange? Someone kills themselves and doesn't leave a note, a letter of explanation.'

'Miss Hannen, it was obvious what she had done and why she had done it. She had already made it known that if anything should happen to her you were to be contacted, that she wanted to be buried in the oasis near to her house. There was no reason for her to leave a note.'

'The morphine bottle?' Freya pushed. 'The syringe? What happened to them?'

He shook his head, a faintly exasperated expression creasing his face.

'I have no idea. I think the housekeeper threw them away. Given the circumstances it would have been morbid to—'

'There was a bruise on her shoulder,' said Freya, cutting him off, changing tack. 'A big bruise. How did she get that?'

'I really can't tell you,' he replied helplessly. 'She fell over, she bumped into something. Her condition made her very unsteady. People with multiple sclerosis often have bruises. Please believe me, Miss Hannen, if there was anything—'

'Where did she do it?' snapped Freya, again cutting him off.

'I'm sorry?'

'Inject herself. Where did she inject herself?'

'Miss Hannen . . .'

'Where?'

The exasperated expression became more pronounced.

'In her arm.'

'Her right arm?' Freya thought back to the morgue, her sister's naked body on the trolley. 'Just below the elbow. Where there's a small bruise.'

He nodded.

'How did she do that?'

His eyes narrowed, not understanding what she was asking.

'How did she do that?' she repeated, harder this time. 'You told me she could only use her right arm; that her left arm was paralysed. But she couldn't inject herself in her right arm with her right hand. It's physically impossible. She would have had to do it with her left hand. But you said that hand was paralysed. So how? How? Tell me.'

He opened his mouth to reply, then closed it again, frowning. The question clearly hadn't occurred to him before.

'How can someone inject themselves in their right arm with their right hand?' she pushed. 'It can't be done. Look!'

She demonstrated, flexing her right arm at the elbow, bending the wrist, her fingers only just able to brush the top of her biceps. Dr Rashid was still looking perplexed, eyes blinking as he struggled to come up with an answer.

'Multiple sclerosis can be a very uncertain condition,' he said after a moment, speaking slowly, hesitantly, as though still trying to think through what he was saying. 'Symptoms come and go, sometimes very rapidly. It's hard to predict what is going to happen.'

'You're saying her left arm suddenly got better?'

'I'm saying that with a condition such as this strange things happen, unexpected things, sudden relapses and remissions . . .'

He didn't sound convinced.

'It's hard to predict,' he repeated. 'It can be a very . . . confusing illness.'

'You've seen cases like that?' Freya pressed. 'People with . . . what did you call it, Malburg Syndrome?'

'Marburg's Variant,' he corrected.

'You've seen this happen? People suddenly recovering the use of a limb? You've seen it, you've heard of it?'

A long pause, and then he shook his head.

'No,' he admitted. 'No, I haven't. With other forms of the disease, less severe forms, yes, perhaps. But with Marburg's . . . no, I've never heard of it.'

'So how?' she repeated. 'How could my sister have injected morphine into her right arm? Even leaving aside the fact that she was right-handed and terrified of needles . . . how could she have done this?'

Dr Rashid opened his mouth, closed it again, rubbed his temples, sat back in his chair. There was a long silence.

'Miss Hannen,' he said eventually, 'can I ask . . . what exactly are you saying here?'

She stared straight at him, holding his eyes.

'I think someone killed my sister. That she didn't commit suicide.'

'Killed as in murdered?' he asked. 'This is what you are saying?'

She nodded.

He held her gaze, fiddling with the cuff of his white jacket. From outside came the twitter of birds and, very faintly, the hum of cars. Five seconds passed. Ten. Then, leaning forward, he lifted the phone, dialled and spoke rapidly in Arabic.

'Come,' he said, replacing the receiver and standing.

'Where?'

He held out an arm, indicating the door.

'Dakhla police.'

Between Dakhla and Cairo

'More coffee, sir?'

'Please.'

Flin placed his cup on the proffered tray; the flight attendant filled it from a plastic flask and handed it back to him.

'Madam?'

'I'm fine,' said Molly Kiernan, holding a hand over her cup. 'Thank you.'

The attendant nodded and moved away. Kiernan continued with the *Washington Post* article she was reading on Iran's nuclear programme; Flin sipped his drink and dabbed half-heartedly at the keyboard of his laptop. The cabin around them reverberated with the low, monotonous growl of the plane's engines. A couple of minutes drifted by, then, shifting in his seat, Flin looked across at his companion.

'I never knew.'

She glanced at him over the top of her reading glasses, raising her eyebrows questioningly.

'That you were married. All these years and I never knew.'

He indicated the ring on her left hand.

'I always assumed it was to ward off unwanted admirers. That you were, you know . . .'

It took her a moment to get his meaning. When she did she let out an exclamation of mock outrage.

'Flin Brodie! Do I look like a lesbian?'

He gave an apologetic shrug.

'Can I ask his name?'

She lowered her paper and removed her glasses.

'Charlie,' she said. 'Charlie Kiernan. The love of my life.'

A brief pause, then:

'Died in the line of duty. Serving his country.'

'He was . . . ?'

'No, no. Marine corps. A pastor. Killed in Lebanon, '83. In the Beirut barracks bombing. We'd only been married a year.'

'I'm sorry,' said Flin. 'I'm so sorry.'

She shrugged and, folding the newspaper, slid it into the pocket of the seat in front then leant her head back and stared up.

'Would have been his sixtieth birthday tomorrow,' she said quietly. 'We used to talk about it all the time, what we'd do when we got old. A little spread up in New Hampshire, porch, rocking chairs. Kids, grandkids. Slushy stuff. Charlie sure was slushy.'

She sighed and, sitting upright again, made a show of putting away her glasses, the movement indicating that she'd said as much as she wanted to on the subject.

'Oasis stuff?' she asked.

'Hmm?'

She nodded towards his laptop, the file he was working on.

'Oh, no. A lecture I'm giving at ARCE next week. Pepi II and the decline of the Old Kingdom. Even I'm bored by it, so I pity the poor buggers who've got to sit there listening.'

She smiled and, resting her head against the window, gazed down at the desert below, the distant miniature hump of Djoser's Step Pyramid drifting past like some dirty brown iceberg.

'Fadawi's out,' she said after a moment, not looking round.

'So I heard.'

'You think—'

'Not a chance,' he cut in, sensing what was on her mind and dismissing it before she'd even had a chance to vocalize the thought. 'Even if he knew anything he wouldn't tell me, would rather cut out his own tongue. Blames me for what happened. Rightly, to be fair.'

'It wasn't your fault, Flin,' she said, turning. 'You weren't to know.'

'Whatever.'

He shut down his laptop and zipped it into its carry-case. Above them there was a muted ping as the fasten seatbelt sign came on.

'It's never going to be found, you know,' he said. 'Twenty-three years . . . it's never going to be found, Molly.'

'You'll get there, Flin. Trust me. You'll get there.'

A voice sounded over the plane's tannoy system, speaking first in Arabic, then English:

'Ladies and gentlemen, we are now beginning our final approach into Cairo. Please ensure your seatbelts are fastened and all loose items stored in the overhead lockers.'

'You'll get there,' she repeated. 'With God's help you'll get there.'

I don't think God has any more bloody idea where it is than any of the rest us, thought Flin.

He kept it to himself, knowing that Kiernan would disapprove of the blasphemy. Leaning his head back, he closed his eyes and started wading through it all over again – Eye of Khepri, Mouth of Osiris, the Curses of

Sobek and Apep – his ears popping as the plane dropped down low over Cairo.

DAKHLA

By the time the Bedouin came to the top of the dune ridge and spied the distant shimmer of Dakhla Oasis, they had not drunk for two days. Exhausted, they brought their camels into a line abreast, and as one raised their hands to the sky:

'*Hamdulillah!*' they cried, their voices hoarse, their mounts panting and honking beneath them. 'Thanks be to God.'

If they had had water they would have dismounted there and then and brewed tea to celebrate the completion of their journey, enjoying the moment perched thus above the desert with the wilderness stretching out on one side of them and civilization looming on the other. As it was their water was long gone, and anyway, they were too weary and battered to think of anything other than reaching their destination as swiftly as possible. Without further ado they urged their camels down the far side of the ridge and continued on their way, silent save for the occasional encouraging cry of '*hut hut*' and '*yalla yalla*'.

For the last three days, ever since the discovery of the mysterious corpse, the desert had tormented them, blocking their line of travel with an endless succession of mountainous dune walls, lashing them with a heat fiercer than any of them had ever known at this time of year. Now, finally, it seemed to have relented. It was cooler today and, as if bored with toying with them, the landscape began to flatten and fragment, the dune labyrinth breaking up into scattered swirls and hummocks of sand interspersed with stretches of flat gravel, easy on the camels and swift to traverse. Within an hour the indeterminate shimmer of the oasis had solidified into a heavy green blur backed by the pale sweep of the Gebel el-Qasr escarpment. Within two hours they were able to make out individual groves of trees and the white dots of houses and pigeon lofts. They broke into a lolloping trot, the lead rider out ahead, his companions strung out behind him in a staggered chain, robes billowing, driving their camels ever faster the closer they came to water and to safety.

Only the last rider failed to keep up the pace, slowly dropping back from the group until there was over a hundred metres between his camel and the one ahead. Satisfied that he was out of earshot he removed his mobile phone and, as he had done every few hours for the last two days, checked the display. He grinned to himself. He now had a signal. He dialled, bent down low over the saddle so no one could see what he was doing and, when the connection was made, started talking excitedly.

CAIRO – MANSHIET NASSER

'Our honoured guest today needs no introduction, ladies and gentlemen. As you know, he was born into our community and remains an esteemed and respected member of it, even if his life has taken him elsewhere. Over the years his generosity has made possible numerous health and education projects here in Manshiet Nasser, of which this drop-in clinic is merely the latest, and although he has achieved both wealth and success, he has never forgotten his roots, nor abandoned his fellow Zabbaleen. He is both friend, benefactor and – I am sure he will not mind me saying – father to us all. Please give a warm welcome to Mr Romani Girgis.'

There was applause and a sour-faced, sallow-skinned man in dark glasses and an immaculately tailored suit rose to his feet. With his lank, greying hair oiled back across his scalp, there was something distinctly lizard-like in his appearance: the hollow cheeks, the pencil-thin lips, the way his tongue kept nudging out of the corner of his mouth. He acknowledged the assembled dignitaries with a nod, and, stooping to kiss the cheek of the Coptic bishop who occupied the seat next to his, came forward and shook the hand of the woman who had introduced him.

'Thank you,' he said, turning to the audience, his voice deep and slow, like the rumble of a heavy lorry – not at all the sort of voice one would expect from someone of his slight physique. 'I am honoured to be here to open this new medical centre. To Miss Mikhail . . .'

He motioned towards the woman.

'. . . His Grace Bishop Marcos, to the board and trustees of the Zabbaleen Metropolitan Development Fund, I say again thank you.'

There was a muffled clicking as a photographer manoeuvred around, getting shots of Girgis and the rest of the guests.

'As Miss Mikhail has told you,' he intoned, 'I am a Zabbal, and proud to be so. I was born here in Manshiet Nasser, just a few streets from this spot. As a child I worked the rubbish carts with my family, and although my circumstances have, through God's grace, changed and improved . . .'

He glanced at the bishop, who smiled and nodded, stroking a hand through his beard.

'. . . Manshiet Nasser nonetheless remains my home, its inhabitants my brothers and sisters.'

Polite applause. More camera clicks.

'The Zabbaleen are integral to the life of this city,' he went on, pulling at the cuffs of his shirt, adjusting them so that exactly the same amount of white protruded from each jacket sleeve. 'For the last fifty years they have collected, sorted and recycled its garbage in a model of sustainable waste management. Because they sort by hand they achieve an efficiency rate that no mechanized operation can match. For the same reason, they are also uniquely susceptible to hepatitis infection from cuts and scratches incurred while carrying out the sorting. Both my father and my grandfather died from this terrible disease, and I am thus delighted to be associated with a project that will help lower infection rates by providing free hepatitis vaccinations to all who need them.'

Murmurs of approval from the audience.

'I have already spoken for long enough, and so I shall merely thank you again for your presence here today and without further ado declare the Romani Girgis Manshiet Nasser Inoculation Centre . . .'

He spread his hands, indicating the courtyard in which

they were gathered, the surrounding buildings, the glass
doors with red crosses painted on them.

'. . . open!'

Accepting a pair of scissors from Miss Mikhail, Girgis
turned and, as the guests applauded, cut into the heavy
ribbon that had been strung across the courtyard, the
photographer going down on one knee to capture the event.
For some reason the material resisted the blade and he was
forced to cut again. And then again, hacking at the fabric,
trying to slice it apart. Still it wouldn't sever, and as the
seconds ticked by and he continued to fumble the clapping
behind slowed and faltered, giving way to embarrassed
whispers and the odd giggle. His hands started to tremble,
face creasing into a rictus first of annoyance, and then anger.
Miss Mikhail came forward to help, tugging at the ribbon
while Girgis continued to struggle with the scissors.

'I give you money and you make a fool of me,' he hissed
underneath his breath.

'I'm so sorry, Mr Girgis,' she mumbled, hands trembling
even more than his.

'And tell that *koos* to stop taking pictures.'

Furious, he chopped again at the ribbon and it finally
came apart. Rearranging his expression into a magnanimous
smile he turned back to the assembled guests and held up
the scissors. The applause picked up, echoing around the
courtyard. He gave it a moment, then, reaching for Miss
Mikhail's hand, laid the scissors in her palm, placing them
in such a way that their point pushed hard into the cushion
of flesh beneath her thumb, indenting the skin, hurting her,
the action carried out in such a way that only the two of
them were aware of what was happening.

'Don't ever embarrass me again, you fat bitch,' he murmured, the smile never leaving his face. Giving the scissors an extra push to emphasize his point, he let them go and walked back to his chair. The woman clasped her hands together in front of her, lower lip quivering.

'Mr Romani Girgis!' she sputtered, struggling to regain her composure. 'Our beloved benefactor. Please show your appreciation!'

The applause redoubled as Girgis sat down, leaning forward to brush a smudge of dust off the tip of his shoe before sitting back again, head bowed modestly. Beside him the bishop leant over and laid a hand on his arm.

'You are an example to us all, Romani. How lucky these poor souls are to have you as their protector.'

Girgis shook his head.

'It is I who am lucky, Your Grace. To have the means to help these, my own people, to improve their lives . . . Truly, I am blessed.'

He lifted the bishop's hand and kissed his ring of office, then, as if embarrassed to be talking about himself in this way, faced forward again. A group of girls in matching dresses and headscarves came to the front and started singing.

It was bullshit, of course, all of it. Manshiet Nasser his home; the Zabbaleen his brothers and sisters – utter bullshit. Girgis had loathed the place when he was growing up here, and loathed it even more now that he had clawed his way out. Vile, filthy, shit-filled, stinking, peopled by uneducated simpletons who worked their fingers to the bone, obeyed the law, said their prayers, and all for what? A life of excruciating hardship spent scrabbling

PAUL SUSSMAN

over rubbish heaps and living in cockroach-infested tenements, society's outcasts, the lowest of the low. Proud to be a Zabbal? He might as well have said he was proud to have cancer.

Appearances: that and that alone was why he still came back here, funded the various aid projects he lent his name to, played the humble son of the Church. Because it made him look good, nothing more, nothing less. Distracted attention from the less salubrious activities in which he was involved. He smiled. Amazing, really, what a bit of philanthropy could do for your image. A clinic here, a school there – Christ, even Susan Mubarak was a fan ('A pillar of Egyptian society,' she'd called him). For the Zabbaleen themselves he felt no more than he felt for the herds of pigs snuffling around among the Manshiet Nasser garbage dumps. Business, that's what mattered. All that had ever mattered. That's why he was what he was – a multi-millionaire – and they were what they were: stinking paupers who spent their days sifting crap and dying of hepatitis.

The song came to an end and the girls started to troop away again, Girgis's gaze tracking them from behind his sunglasses. They were pretty, all big green eyes and small, pert breasts, and he made a mental note to source names and addresses. Copts always commanded a greater premium in his brothels than Muslim Arabs, particularly the younger ones. Although it was years since he had been directly involved in that side of his affairs, preferring to focus his energies on higher-end activities – arms dealing, antiquities smuggling, money laundering – he nonetheless liked to keep a hand in. Bribe the girls' parents – or failing

140

that snatch them – and put them to work, make him some money. They wouldn't last long, what with AIDS and the rough stuff many of his clients liked, but that wasn't his concern. Profit was his concern. And anyway, Zabbaleen life being what it was, they probably wouldn't do much better if they stuck around here. His smile broadened, a thin unpleasant expression as though someone had slashed his face with a scalpel.

The girls gone there were more speeches and an interminable violin recital by some overweight blind kid. Girgis did his best to look enthusiastic while taking increasingly frequent looks at his watch. When the recital was finally over everyone stood and started to file indoors for refreshments and a look around the clinic. Girgis alone declined the tour, citing work commitments, very sorry, would have loved to stay, etc. He accepted the thank-yous of the clinic's staff, made his farewells – pointedly ignoring Miss Mikhail – and, relieved to be getting away at last, crossed the courtyard and passed through a high wooden gate out onto the street, his nostrils recoiling at the dense, sweet-sour stench of rotting garbage.

As he emerged he clicked his fingers. Two figures peeled off the wall where they had been leaning and bustled up to him. Rotund yet at the same time brawny, squat spheres of muscle, they wore grey Armani suits and, incongruously, red and white El-Ahly FC football shirts. One had a flattened boxer's nose, the other a shredded left earlobe; other than that they were identical in every feature, each a mirror image of the other: same ring-covered fingers, same ginger hair slicked sideways across the scalp, same air of brooding menace. They hovered as Girgis removed a handkerchief

141

and dabbed at his nose, then fell into step beside him as he started walking.

They were on a steep hill, the road dropping away below them, its dirt surface pitted and strewn with litter. Higgledy-piggledy buildings pressed in on either side, the brickwork uneven and badly laid, the balconies hung with festoons of multi-coloured washing. Donkey-drawn carts rattled past, piled with giant polypropylene sacks of paper, cloth, plastic, glass and other waste; similar sacks lay heaped against every wall like mounds of engorged larvae, clogging the already narrow thoroughfare. There were wafts of woodsmoke, and the rumble of granulators, and women in black robes and bright headscarves, and everywhere – in every doorway, down every alley, through every window, up every stairwell – heap upon heap of mouldering, fly-blown, malodorous garbage, as if the whole quarter was some enormous vacuum-cleaner bag into which all of the city's trash had been inexorably sucked.

This was the world in which Romani Girgis had spent the first sixteen years of his life, and this was the world he had spent the subsequent fifty years trying, and failing, to scrub out of his system. Parisian aftershaves, Italian face creams, soaps and balms and scented emollients – no matter how much money he laid out, no matter how hard he washed and scoured it just wouldn't go away. Never, ever could he be truly disinfected, free of the hellish filth of his youth: the stench, the germs, the rats, the cockroaches. Everywhere cockroaches. A multimillionaire and he'd give every piastre of it just to feel clean.

He speeded his step, clutching his handkerchief to his nose, his twin bodyguards barging people out of his path.

The street continued steeply downwards before taking a sharp turn to the right. As it did so the buildings to either side suddenly dropped away and they emerged onto a broad, sun-drenched terrace cut into the hillside. Above, like bulging slabs of yellow cake, reared the Muqqatam cliffs, their faces carved with polychrome images of Christ and the saints. Below, the confusion of buildings and rubbish heaps swept on downwards before coming to an abrupt halt at the Al-Nasr Autoroute and the Northern Cemeteries.

A limousine – long, black, with smoked-glass windows – was parked at the side of the road, the closest it had been able to get to the clinic above. A black-suited chauffeur was standing beside it. The moment he saw them he hurried forward and opened the rear door. Girgis clambered in, letting out a gasp of relief as the door was closed behind him, sealing him within the cool, leather-scented cleanliness of the car's interior. He pulled a packet of wipes from his pocket, ripped a couple out and began frantically to rub them over his hands and face.

'Disgusting,' he muttered, his body twitching as though at the feel of tiny creatures scurrying over his skin. 'Disgusting.'

He continued wiping as the twins and chauffeur climbed into the front and the limousine pulled away, manoeuvring slowly down through the narrow streets. Outside the world drifted past – grime-blackened men hefting vast garbage sacks; women and children sorting heaps of plastic bottles; a sty full of slithery black pigs. Only when they had reached the bottom of the slope and bumped their way across a railway track onto the Autoroute, picking up speed as they headed back towards the centre of the city, did Girgis start to relax. He gave his hands a final swab and put away the wipes. Pulling out his mobile phone he checked the voice-mail. One message. He pressed the keypad and listened. Thirty seconds went by. Frowning, he pressed the key again, hearing the message through a second time. By the time it had finished the smile had returned to his face. He waited for a moment, then punched in a number and lifted the phone to his ear.

'Something's come up,' he said when the connection was made, speaking in English. 'Looks like it could be one of the crew. Call me, usual number.'

He rang off and, lifting a flap on the limousine's armrest, took out an intercom phone.

'Have the Agusta meet us at the house. And tell the twins they're going down to Dakhla.'

He replaced the phone and laid his head back against the leather neck-rest.

'Twenty-three years,' he murmured. 'Twenty-three years and finally . . . finally . . .'

DAKHLA OASIS

It was mid-afternoon when Freya eventually arrived back at Alex's house. By this point she had all but persuaded her-self she was imagining things and that her sister's death had been suicide after all.

She had spent the best part of four hours at Dakhla police station – a nondescript, lemon-coloured building surrounded by watchtowers, just down the road from the hospital. Initially she had been dealt with by a local policeman. He had seemed to understand only a fraction of what she was trying to tell him and in the end someone else had been found to conduct the interview: a detective over for the day from Luxor on other business and a fluent English-speaker.

Inspector Yusuf Khalifa had been kind, efficient, and had taken her suspicions seriously, displaying an attentiveness that had, paradoxically, served to make those suspicions appear increasingly ill founded. He had gone through everything she had told Dr Rashid about Alex's needle phobia, while scribbling notes and chain-smoking – he must have got through a pack or more of Cleopatra cigarettes over the course of the interview – before broadening the questioning.

'Did your sister have any enemies that you know of?' he had asked.

'Well I hadn't seen her for a long time,' Freya replied, 'but I don't think . . . She never mentioned anything in her letters. She wasn't really the sort of person who made enemies. Everyone . . .'

She had been going to say 'loved Alex' but the words caught in her throat, tears welling up in her eyes. Khalifa had pulled a tissue from a box on the desk and handed it to her.

'I'm sorry,' she had mumbled, embarrassed.

'Please, Miss Hannen, no apologies are necessary. I myself lost a brother some years ago. Take as much time as you need.'

He had waited patiently for Freya to compose herself, then continued with his questions, taking things slowly, gently. Did she know if her sister had been in trouble of any sort? Was there any sign that her sister's house had been broken into? Had Freya noticed anyone acting suspiciously near the house? Was there any reason she could think of why someone would have wanted to harm her sister?

On and on it had gone, the detective covering every possible angle, exploring every conceivable motive and scenario. By the end of the four hours it had become apparent, firstly, how little Freya knew about her own sibling, and secondly how feeble her suspicions were when viewed objectively and dispassionately. Everything, it seemed – the bruise on Alex's shoulder, her terror of injections, the absence of a suicide note, the fact that she hadn't seemed the sort of person to take her own life – could be explained away rationally, just as Dr Rashid had done when she had spoken to him in his office earlier.

Almost out of desperation Freya had brought up Mahmoud Garoub, the old farmer who had given her a lift on his donkey cart, the way he had leered at her and touched her leg, how she had been told to steer clear of him.

'Maybe he's involved in some way,' she had suggested, scrambling round for something to keep her doubts alive.

When Khalifa had asked around the station, however, that line of inquiry had been closed off too.

'This Garoub is well known to the police,' he had informed Freya. 'A notorious . . . how do you say? . . . peeping Joe?'

'Tom,' she corrected.

'Exactly. A dirty man, according to my colleagues, but harmless. Certainly not capable of murder.'

He lit another cigarette, adding: 'Apparently it's his wife who's the violent one. Mainly towards him.'

In the end it had all boiled down to the issue of where Alex had injected herself: how could someone with a paralysed left arm stick a needle into their right arm? It had been a major stumbling block, and the reason the interview had become so protracted. Then, towards the end of the afternoon, Dr Rashid, who had returned to the hospital, had telephoned and spoken to Khalifa. He had been in touch with colleagues, Rashid explained, neurological experts in the UK and the US, far more experienced in this sort of thing than he was and, contrary to what he had earlier told Freya, it transpired there *were* recorded instances of people with Marburg's experiencing a sudden and unexplained remission of symptoms. One case was eerily similar to Alex's. Three years earlier, a Swedish man who had lost motor function in all four limbs had woken up one morning to discover that he could use his right arm again, a window of opportunity he had exploited by removing a pistol from his bedside drawer and blowing his brains out.

Why, if she was right handed, Alex should have chosen to inject herself with her left hand – that the doctor couldn't explain. The point was that from a medical perspective it was perfectly feasible that Alex could have injected herself in the way she had. Unusual, certainly, but feasible nonetheless.

Khalifa had relayed all this to Freya once he had put the phone down.

'I feel stupid,' she said.

'No, no,' he admonished her. 'You were quite right to ask questions. Your doubts were perfectly justified.'

'I've wasted your time.'

'On the contrary, you have done me a considerable favour
– were it not for you I would have had to spend the afternoon in a conference on policing systems in the New Valley
Governate. I am for ever in your debt.'

She had smiled, relieved that her suspicions seemed to
be baseless.

'If you still have any concerns,' he said.

'I don't, really I don't . . .'

'Because there are other avenues we could explore. What
happened to the morphine bottle and syringe, where the
morphine was purchased . . .'

It now seemed to be he who was trying to persuade her
that Alex's death needed more investigation.

'Honestly,' she said, 'you've done more than enough. I'd
just like to get back to Alex's house. It's been a long day.'

'Of course. I will arrange for a driver.'

Opening the door of the office in which they had been
talking, the detective led her along a corridor and down a
staircase to the ground floor. There he spoke in Arabic to
the uniformed officer on the front desk; requesting a car,
Freya assumed. By way of reply the officer had nodded
towards the front entrance, through which Zahir could be
seen sitting in his Land Cruiser on the street outside,
fingers drumming on the steering wheel. How he had found
out she was at the police station Freya didn't know, but as
soon as he saw them he leant across and opened the
Toyota's passenger door, in the process throwing Khalifa a
not entirely friendly look.

'You know this man?' asked the detective.

'He worked with my sister,' said Freya. 'He's been . . .'

She was about to say 'looking after me' but hesitated, before continuing:

'Driving me around.'

'I will leave you in his hands, then,' said Khalifa.

He walked her out of the police station.

'Please, don't hesitate to contact us should you have any further worries,' he said as they came up to the car.

'Thank you,' replied Freya. 'You've been so helpful. I'm just sorry to have—'

The detective waved a hand, cutting her off. He nodded a greeting at Zahir, who just grunted and looked straight ahead, then took a step back as Freya climbed into the Toyota and pulled the door shut.

'It has been a pleasure meeting you,' Khalifa said. 'And please accept my condolences on the death . . .'

Before he could finish Zahir floored the accelerator and sped away, eyeballing the policeman in the rearview mirror.

'Police no good,' he muttered as they swung round a corner, narrowly missing a cart piled high with watermelons. 'Police no understand things.'

He had been unusually talkative on the drive back, bombarding her with all manner of questions about Alex's death, why she had been suspicious, what the police had said, his eyes all the while flicking across at her. It had made her feel uncomfortable, even more so than his reticence the previous day, and her answers had been terse and monosyllabic, evasive, although what exactly she was trying to evade she couldn't be sure. When he finally pulled up in front of her sister's house, she couldn't get out of the car fast enough. Mumbling a curt thank-you she disappeared inside, slamming the door and leaning her back against it, relieved to be rid of him.

Now he was gone and she was on her own, and exhaustion suddenly enveloped her, as though, with her sister buried and her suspicions allayed, her body was finally holding up its hands and saying 'Enough!' For the first time in three days, she realized, she didn't have something to worry and obsess about. She'd got herself to Egypt, she'd buried Alex, she'd resolved the questions surrounding her death. Everything that needed to be done had been done. Except for the grieving. And the guilt. Of those there was plenty to come.

A sharp cheesy odour hung in the air from the breakfast remains still sitting on the living room table. She went over to them and piled some bread, tomatoes and cucumber onto a plate. Then, dragging an armchair outside to the veranda, she sank down and curled her legs under her, gazing out across the desert, picking at the food with her fingers. She was hungry – she hadn't eaten properly for the last three days – and in a matter of minutes the plate was empty. She could have eaten more, but by then the exhaustion had become so intense the prospect of covering even the short distance back to the living room table seemed too much. She laid the plate on the ground, snuggled further down into the cushions of the chair and, resting her head on her arm, closed her eyes and was asleep almost instantly.

'*Salaam.*'

Freya jerked awake, startled, thinking that she was dreaming, had only just nodded off. Then she noticed how red the sun had become, and how low it had dropped in the sky, almost to the level of the horizon. She must have slept for an hour or more. Groggily she stretched out her arms and legs, yawned, and was just rising to her feet when she saw the figure standing three metres away at the end of the veranda. She froze.

'Salaam,' the voice repeated, a man's voice, gruff and guttural, his face wrapped in a linen scarf so that only the eyes were visible.

For a moment they just stood like that, looking at each other, neither saying anything. By now wide awake, Freya began to back away, hands coming up protectively in front of her, bunching into fists, her eyes dropping to the large curved knife slotted into the stranger's belt. He must have realized what she was thinking because he raised his own hands, palms outwards, gabbling something in Arabic.

'I don't understand,' Freya said, her voice more shrill than she would have liked. She backed away another step, glancing around for something to use as a weapon should he come at her. There was a rake leaning against the bole of a jacaranda tree away to her left. Stepping carefully off the veranda, she edged towards it. Again the man seemed to realize what was going through her mind because he shook his head and, reaching down, slipped the knife from his belt and placed it on the ground, taking a step backwards away from it.

'No danger,' he said, speaking in halting, heavily accented English. 'He no danger you.'

They stared at each other, the air echoing with the twitter of birds and the rasping chirrup of cicadas. Slowly he reached up and tugged away the linen scarf to reveal a long, bearded face, the skin deeply lined and dark as ebony, the cheekbones so high and prominent, the cheeks beneath so sunken it looked as if someone had scooped the flesh out with a spoon. His eyes were red with exhaustion; his beard, Freya noticed, speckled with flecks of sand and grit.

'He no danger you,' he repeated, patting his palm against his chest. 'He friend.'

Freya's hands came down slightly, although her fists remained bunched.

'Who are you?' she asked, her voice more assured now the initial shock at his appearance had passed. 'What do you want?'

'He come Doctor Alex,' he said. 'He . . .'

His eyes narrowed as he tried to find the word he wanted. With a frustrated click of the tongue, he gave up and instead mimed knocking on a door.

'No person,' he explained. 'He go back of house. You . . .'

Another mime, this time of hands pillowed underneath a head. That was how he had found Freya, asleep.

'He sorry. He no want scare you.'

It was clear by now that he meant her no harm and Freya's hands opened up and dropped to her sides. With a nod she indicated that he should pick up his knife. Leaning down he tucked the blade back into his belt before slipping a canvas bag off his shoulder and holding it out to her.

'This find,' he said, tilting his head towards the desert. 'For Doctor Alex.'

Freya bit her lip, her chest tightening.

'Alex is dead,' she said, the words sounding curiously dull and emotionless, as if she was trying to distance herself from what she was saying. 'She passed away four days ago.'

The man clearly didn't understand. Freya rephrased the sentence, with no more success, and in desperation she ran a finger across her neck, the only mime she could think of to indicate death. His eyebrows shot up and he muttered something in Arabic, raising his hands towards the sky in a gesture of shock and disbelief.

'No, no, not murdered,' she said quickly, shaking her head, realizing he had got the wrong end of the stick. 'She took her own life. Suicide.'

Again, her words meant nothing to him and it took another thirty seconds of explaining and gesturing before awareness finally seemed to dawn. He broke into a broad, brown-toothed smile.

'Doctor Alex go away,' he said triumphantly. 'Holiday.'

How she had managed to give him that impression she had no idea, but it would have been too much to correct him again and so she just nodded.

'Yes,' she said. 'Doctor Alex has gone away.'

'You *okht*?'

'Sorry?'

He clasped his hands together, indicating closeness, connection.

'*Okht*?' he repeated. 'Sister.'

'Yes,' she said, smiling despite herself, amused by the absurdity of the situation. 'Yes, I'm Doctor Alex's sister. Freya.'

She held up a hand in greeting and he mirrored the gesture before holding out the canvas shoulder bag again.

'You give Doctor Alex.'

Freya came forward and took the bag from him.

'This is Alex's?'

He frowned, confused. Then, realizing what she was saying, shook his head.

'No Doctor Alex. He find. In sand. Far.'

He chopped a hand out towards the desert.

'Far, far. Half to Gilf Kebir. Man.'

He slit a finger across his throat, as Freya had done. The man of whom he was speaking must be dead, although whether he meant that he had been murdered or was simply deceased she couldn't be sure.

'Doctor Alex give money,' he continued. 'Doctor Alex say he find man in desert, he find new thing in desert, he bring.'

He reached into the pocket of his *djellaba*, pulled out a steel Rolex watch and handed this across as well.

'I don't understand,' said Freya, clutching the bag in one hand and the watch in the other. 'Why would Alex want these things?'

'You give Doctor Alex,' he repeated. 'She know.'

Freya continued to press him, asking why Alex had paid him money, who the man in the desert was, what it was all about, but having handed the objects over, he clearly considered the purpose of his visit had been achieved. With a final 'You give Doctor Alex,' he bowed, turned and disappeared around the corner of the house, leaving Freya staring helplessly after him.

EGYPT – BETWEEN CAIRO AND DAKHLA

The Agusta helicopter flew fast and low, just a few hundred metres above the desert, its shadow sweeping along the dune tops. The thrub of its Pratt & Whitney-powered rotor blades echoed dully across the sands like the thudding of distant drums. All of its eight seats were occupied, one by the pilot, five by hard-faced men cradling Heckler & Koch submachine-guns in their laps, and two – the rearmost seats – by Girgis's twin henchmen in their grey Armani suits and red and white El-Ahly FC football shirts. The pair of them were gazing intently at the football fanzine one of them was holding in his lap, utterly engrossed. Throwing a half-glance over his shoulder to make sure they weren't listening, the pilot nudged the man beside him.

'No one's ever found out their names,' he whispered. 'Seven years they've been with Girgis and no one's ever found out their names. Even he doesn't know, apparently.'

The man said nothing, just gave a slight shake of the head, indicating that this was not the time or place to talk about such things.

'They killed one of his pimps,' continued the pilot, ignoring the warning, warming to his subject. 'Cut him up and dumped him in the Nile because he said El-Ahly were shit and el-Hafeez takes it up the arse. Girgis was so impressed he gave them a job.'

Another shake of the head, more vigorous this time, accompanied by a cutting motion of the hand to signal that the conversation should go no further. Again the pilot didn't take the hint.

'Mother's a smack-head, apparently. They absolutely worship her. Forty people they've killed and—'

'Shut the fuck up and fly,' came a voice from behind.

'Or it'll be forty-one,' came another almost identical voice.

The pilot's hand tightened around the steering column, face turning the colour of milk, thighs squeezing together as if to protect his crotch. He didn't speak for the rest of the journey.

DAKHLA

Back inside Alex's house Freya opened the mysterious
canvas bag and removed its contents one by one, laying
them out on the living room table alongside the Rolex
watch. Map, wallet, camera, film canister, distress flares,
emergency rations, handkerchief with miniature clay
obelisk wrapped inside and, lastly, a green metal compass
with a folding lid. She held on to the latter, opening it up,
smiling sadly to herself. It was exactly the same model her
sister had owned when they were children: a lensatic military compass, with a dial, bezel, magnifying lens and, in its
lid, a slot with a hair-thin brass wire running through it.
('You line the wire up with the point you're aiming for, then
read the bearing through the lens,' Alex had explained to
her. 'It's the most accurate compass you can get.')

Whether this particular version was so reliable Freya
doubted, for its sighting wire had snapped in two, making it
almost impossible to take a precise reading. Despite that
she cradled it in her palm as though it were some priceless
antique, its feel and weight pitching her back to her youth,
to those magical, carefree Markham summers, before it had
all gone wrong, before she had broken her sister's heart. She
held the compass up, aligning the lens, dial and sighting-
slot, just as Alex had taught her, watching as the needle
swung lazily around, hearing Alex's voice again, the stories
she used to tell about how her compass had once belonged
to a marine in the battle of Iwo Jima. Almost a minute
passed, then, with a sigh, she closed the case, put it down
on the table and turned her attention to the other objects.

The wallet contained some German banknotes, a couple

of credit cards, a wad of receipts – all dating from 1986. And there was an identity card. It showed the wallet's owner: a handsome, blond-haired man with a heavy scar cutting across his chin beneath his mouth.

'Rudi Schmidt,' she read aloud.

The name meant nothing to her. A friend of Alex's? A colleague? After repeating it a couple of times she returned the card to the wallet and moved on. She examined the clay obelisk with the curious motifs inscribed on each of its sides, the film canister, the camera, which had another roll of film still inside its chamber, all but two of its pictures used up according to the exposure counter. Finally, she opened out the map, pushing the other objects aside and spreading it flat on the table.

It was Egypt, the western half of the country from the Libyan border to the Nile Valley, 1:500,000 scale. The paper was crumpled, the creases where it had been folded starting to split from overuse.

She gazed down, her eyes drawn to the bottom left-hand corner where a circle had been pencilled around the words Gilf Kebir Plateau. She frowned. Wasn't that where Alex had been working? She cocked her head to one side, trying to remember what her sister had said about it in her letters, then looked back at the map, bending over it, examining the diagonal line that extended north-east from the Gilf towards the nearest patch of green, Dakhla Oasis, which had also been circled. Five small crosses bisected the line, starting near the Gilf and extending about a third of the way to Dakhla, each cross accompanied by a pair of numerals: a compass bearing in degrees, and a distance in kilometres. While the bearing was always the same, 44 degrees, the distances appeared to diminish the further the crosses moved away from the Gilf – 27 km, 25 km, 20 km, 14 km, 9 km.

The record of a journey, that was Freya's immediate impression. A five-day journey, on foot to judge by the relatively short distances covered, starting at the Gilf and continuing for ninety-five kilometres before ending abruptly amid the blank yellow emptiness of the open desert. Who Rudi Schmidt was, what he was doing out there, whether the map was in fact telling an entirely different story – these were questions she couldn't answer. What she did know was that it didn't feel right. None of it. Why should her sister be interested in these things? Why should she pay money for them? The more she thought about it the more odd it all seemed. She found herself going over Alex's suicide again – her paralysed left arm, her horror of injections – and the doubts of earlier that day started to creep back in. All the explanations she'd been given suddenly seemed unconvincing. She wondered if she should return to the police station – that nice detective had told her to get in touch if she had any further concerns – but then what could she say? Someone turned up at my sister's house with a dead man's belongings? It sounded so para- noid, so . . . flimsy. And anyway, the detective had told her he was only in Dakhla for half a day and would probably be on his way back to Luxor by now. Which meant that she would have to start from scratch not only with someone else, but in a language none of the other detectives seemed to speak properly. Maybe she should call Molly Kiernan? Or Flin Brodie? But again, what was she supposed to tell them? That she thought something suspicious was going on?

Christ, it made her sound like a character in some schlock B-movie.

Freya stared at the map for a while longer, then folded it up and started returning the objects to the canvas shoulder bag, trying to decide what to do, wondering whether her doubts were valid or not. She paused for a moment to gaze again at the miniature obelisk – some sort of souvenir or good luck charm, she assumed – before dropping that in as well, followed by the camera, compass, and, finally, the plastic film canister. Once everything was in she started to do up the bag's buckles. Almost immediately she undid them again, brow furrowing as if she had been struck by a sudden thought. Delving in she retrieved the canister and camera, weighing them in her hands, pondering. Several seconds passed, then, with a nod, she reached for her knapsack and placed both objects inside it, tucking them down into the fleece she kept there. She retrieved the compass as well, wanting to keep it with her, a connection, however tenuous, with her sister and better days. Leaving the canvas bag on the table, she closed up the house and set off back towards the main oasis, hoping the Kodak shop in the village would still be open. That whatever was on the films in the canister and camera might offer some clue as to who Rudi Schmidt was, why he had been wandering around in the middle of the Sahara and why on earth her sister should have been interested in him.

The Bedouin remained in Dakhla long enough to refill their water-skins, collect firewood, and purchase a goat and other provisions. Then, preferring to keep their own company, they withdrew into the desert and set up camp about a mile outside the oasis, beside a tangled clump of acacia and *abal* bushes that had somehow found purchase amid the surrounding emptiness.

By the time their leader returned from Alex's house the camels were tethered and munching on heaps of fresh *bersiim*; the goat had been slaughtered and was roasting over a fire and the men were sitting in a circle around it, singing an old Bedouin song about an evil desert *djinn* and the boy who cleverly outwits him. Tying his mount with the others the leader joined the circle, his companions shuffling around to give him room. His rich sonorous voice took up the song's verse while the others came in with the chorus, the first evening stars twinkling in the sky above, the air heavy with smoke and the rich, fatty scent of roasting meat. When the song was finished they passed round cigarettes and fell into a discussion about the route they should take on the journey home. Some argued that they should go back the way they had come, others urged a more northerly line around Jebal Almasy and the top end of the Gilf. Their voices became increasingly loud and animated, rising and clashing until someone shouted that the meat was ready, and the tension evaporated. Hefting the goat away from the fire, they drove one end of the spit down into the sand so that it was standing upright and started to hack at it with their knives, slicing off long, slippery chunks. They ate with their hands, their voices dying away until all that was left was the crackle of the fire, the rhythmic sound of their chewing and, from somewhere away to the north, barely audible, a puttering, droning sound, like the flight of some enormous insect.

'What is that?' asked one of the men. 'A water pump?'

No one answered as the sound grew steadily louder.

'Helicopter,' said their leader eventually.

'Army?' asked another of his companions, frowning, relations between the Bedouin and the military never having been particularly good.

The leader shrugged and, laying aside his food, rose to his feet. He gazed north, hand clasped around the grip of his knife. Thirty seconds passed, then he raised an arm and pointed.

'There.'

One by one the others stood, peering into the distance. They watched as a vague, juddering smudge slowly extricated itself from the twilight gloom, its outline gradually hardening until it could be made out clearly – a black helicopter, long and sleek, arrowing through the evening sky just a few hundred metres above the desert surface. It came straight at them, nearer and nearer before sweeping directly overhead, the downdraught of its blades causing their robes to billow wildly and sending sprays of sand into their faces.

The helicopter swung around, pivoting in an impossibly tight arc and flying back over them. Lower this time, forcing the Bedouin onto the ground, their cries of protest lost within the clattering hammer of the rotors.

The moment it had passed, the leader sprang to his feet and raced to the camels, untying an old bolt-action rifle that was lashed to one of the saddles. The chopper circled back again, surging forward before abruptly rearing up and dropping to the ground. Shadowy figures leapt out and ran towards them.

The other Bedouin were now up as well. Tugging away the last of its ties, the leader threw the rifle to the nearest of them. The man caught it two-handed and, in a single fluid motion, cocked the bolt and swung towards the approaching figures, raising the muzzle and aiming. Before he could pull the trigger there was a crack of gunfire and he spun, the rifle flying out of his hands, his arms flailing as he wheeled around and smacked face down onto the desert. A black stain spread across his robes like ink through blotting paper. There was more gunfire, the sand jumping and spitting around the Bedouin, forcing them to freeze where they were. As they stood motionless the men from the helicopter came up and arranged themselves in a line beside the fire, submachine-guns held in front of them. For a moment the two groups faced each other, silent, an acrid metallic stench mingling with the sweet aroma of roasted meat. Then the newcomers shifted slightly and parted to make room for two figures who had come up behind. Squat and brawny, they were identical in almost every feature, their neatly slicked ginger hair, grey suits and El-Ahly football shirts wholly out of place in the wild desert setting.

'You found some things,' said one of them, his tone matter-of-fact, unfazed by the violence of a moment earlier.

'Out in the desert,' said the other.

'Where are they?'

No reply. The twins glanced at each other, then, as one, raised their guns and opened fire on the nearest camel. The Bedouin cried out in horror as the bullets tore into its neck and flank, shredding the flesh. The shooting continued for five seconds, then ceased, the crackle of gunfire fading away into intense, shocking silence. Calmly the twins broke out their empty clips and slotted in new ones.

'You found some things,' repeated the first brother, his tone exactly the same as it had been before.

'Out in the desert.'

'Where are they?'

'*Taala elhass teezi, ya kalbeen*,' spat the leader of the Bedouin, eyes glinting in the firelight. 'Kiss my arse, you dogs.'

Again the twins glanced at each other. Again they opened fire, dropping two more camels before turning their guns on the man standing closest to the leader. The force of the fusillade lifted him off his feet and threw him backwards onto the sand where he twitched a moment before going still.

'He took them away!'

The voice was shrill, terrified. One of the Bedouin had stepped forward, arms raised above his head – a small, wizened man with a scrawny beard and heavily pockmarked face.

'He took the things away,' he repeated, motioning towards his leader, hands trembling. 'I saw it.'

The twins eyeballed him.

'It was me who called you,' the man whined, waving his mobile phone to prove the point. 'I am your friend. I help you!'

The Bedouin leader gave a snort of disgust and his hand moved towards his knife, then quickly pulled away as more bullets chewed up the sand at his feet.

'Your mother always was a whore, Abdul-Rahman,' he spat. 'And your sister a dog-fucker.'

The man ignored him and moved forward another step.

'I was promised money,' he said. 'If I called. Mr Girgis promised me money.'

'In return for the objects,' said one of the twins.

'Where are they?' asked the other.

'I told you, he took them away. They were in a bag and he took them away.'

'Where?'

'Into the oasis. He gave them to someone. I don't know who, he wouldn't say. I've done what I promised. I want my money.'

'Fuck you.'

A thunder of bullets punched into his face and chest, killing the man instantly. His body was still crumpling to the ground as the twins turned on the other Bedouin, slaughtering all of them save for their leader, who alone was left unharmed. He stood where he was, weighing his options, the heavy desert silence once more enveloping them, the fire's embers glowing an angry red as twilight slipped into darkness. Then he snatched the knife from his belt and launched himself forward, letting out a high, ululating yell of fury and defiance, thinking to take out at least one of the attackers before he himself was killed. As he did so men swarmed around him, seizing his arms, tearing the knife from his hand, punching and kicking him, dragging him across to the fire where they forced him to his knees and yanked his head back, mouth and nose streaming blood. The twins leant over him, one to either side.

'You found some things.'

'Out in the desert.'

'Where are they?'

*

He was tougher than they had anticipated. And braver. They had to burn off both of his feet and one hand before he broke and told them everything they wanted to know. They put him out of his misery and shot the remaining camels – it was a remote spot and it would be days if not weeks before the massacre was discovered. Their business complete, the gunmen returned to the chopper and took off, speeding south over the desert and away into the night.

Chuckling to himself, his dirty brown *djellaba* already bulging at the crotch in anticipation, Mahmoud Gharoub carried the wooden ladder through the olive grove towards Doctor Alex's house. It was dark, the moon not yet risen, the grove shrouded in an inky fog of gloom and shadow. More than once he stumbled, his feet crunching on the carpet of dried leaves with which the ground was covered, the end of the ladder clattering loudly against the tree trunks all around. He wasn't concerned by the noise. He had watched the American woman jogging up the track towards Dakhla, knew he had plenty of time to get himself positioned before she came back, and continued on his way untroubled by the racket he was making. He chattered to himself, occasionally breaking into tuneless bursts of song:

> *'Oh pretty little woman with firm young breasts*
> *Come, open your legs and let me taste your peach!'*

When he reached Alex's house he worked his way round to the far end, pushing between a pair of flowering oleander bushes and leaning the ladder against the wall. He began to climb, up and up until he reached the flat roof. The distant scattered lights of Dakhla glittered on one side, the empty grey billow of the desert rolled away on the other. Pulling a bottle from the pocket of his *djellaba* he took a swig, then crossed to the small skylight above the bathroom and squatted down beside it. The tingling in his crotch grew more intense.

He'd watched the woman's sister many times, even after she'd become ill and lost her looks. His own wife was fat and ugly, more water buffalo than woman. Anything was better than that, even a cripple who had to sit in a special chair to shower. When she'd died he'd been sad, assuming all the fun was over. But now her sister had arrived, young and blonde and fit. Wanton, like all western women. Mahmoud Gharoub could barely control himself. He would have come sooner but his wife had been suspicious, and it was only because she was with her family tonight that he had been able to get away. He took another swig from the bottle, gazing down through the skylight into the room beneath. It was pitch black now, a well of impenetratable darkness, but once the light was on he'd be able to see everything: shower, toilet, every movement, every contour, his own private show. He broke into song again, rubbing at his groin:

> '*Lie down, my sweet, and close your eyes,*
> *Let me enter you now, so deep, so . . .*'

He broke off, head coming up and tipping to one side, listening. What was that? The noise grew louder, a spitting, droning sound. Helicopter. Heading straight towards him by the sound of it. He stood, suddenly nervous, fearful it might be the police. He'd have some explaining to do if he was found up here on someone else's roof, both to the authorities and, more worryingly, to his horror of a wife. His erection sagging, the bathroom forgotten, he hurried back across the roof to the ladder, swinging himself onto it and starting down, anxious to get away. He only managed a couple of rungs before a pummelling rush of wind enveloped him, his *djellaba* flapping wildly, dust and sand blowing into his eyes. There was a blinding flash as the helicopter's searchlight came on, rotating this way and that before picking him out and locking onto him. Gharoub clutched the ladder, moaning in terror, shouting out that he had just been sweeping the roof, that it was all a misunderstanding. Then the force of the downdraught caused him to lose his grip and he pitched backwards away from the wall, plummeting with a high-pitched scream and a crash of snapping branches three metres into the bushes below. The helicopter hovered overhead like some monstrous dragonfly, eyeing the old man as he squirmed and floundered beneath, still calling out that it was all a misunderstanding, he'd just been sweeping the roof, there had been leaves up there, lots of messy leaves, whole drifts of them . . .

The Kodak shop had turned out to be a complete waste of time, although the forty-minute walk back along the track to Dakhla at least allowed Freya to stretch her legs and clear her head a bit.

It had still been open when she got there, its brightly lit glass windows visible from half a mile away. The air-conditioned interior – all marble floors, chrome furniture and framed, soft-focus photographs of grinning newlyweds and overweight babies – had looked promising, as had the fact that the young woman behind the counter actually spoke English. From there it had all been downhill. The developing machines at the rear of the shop didn't work; had never worked, apparently. As for the 'Fast Foto devilp' promised by the advertising board outside, that meant 'fast' in the Dakhla sense of the word: about a week. Fighting to suppress her frustration, Freya had chatted with the woman for a while, allowing her to touch her blond hair, trying to explain why at twenty-six she still didn't have a husband, and then left. She had briefly toyed with the idea of trying to hitch a ride into Mut to see if she could get the films developed there, before deciding it was too late, too much hassle, and setting off back towards Alex's house.

Now she was walking along the track again, the sky over-head ablaze with stars, the only sounds the soft crunch of her footsteps and the distant braying of a donkey. A gentle breeze had come up, pushing away the last heat of day; the moon was slowly rising behind her, its buttery glow turning the desert sepia so that she felt as though she was trudging through some old-fashioned photograph. The solitude calmed and relaxed her, and the further she walked the more her spirits lifted. She'd get back, have something to eat, maybe listen to some music, get a good night's sleep and then review things in the morning. Things were always clearer in the morning.

She came to the top of the ridge from which Zahir had

pointed out Alex's house the previous afternoon. The miniature oasis loomed below, a dark, elongated oval stamped on the otherwise featureless landscape, the ghostly outline of the house clearly visible. She descended the slope and crossed the flat, passing through the oasis's outlying fields before plunging into the trees. Dense walls of vegetation crowded in on either side of her, shutting out what little light there was and leaving her in almost complete darkness. Pausing a moment to allow her eyes to adjust to the gloom, she became aware of a distant whining, chopping sound. It grew steadily louder – a helicopter. Closer and closer it came, louder and louder. The air vibrated to the thud of its rotors, the branches around her started to sway and hiss as it flew in low over the treetops away to her right, its silhouette just visible through the tangled canopy above.

Freya stood where she was, expecting the sound to recede. Instead it held steady, its volume neither increasing nor decreasing, as though the helicopter was now hovering. A couple of seconds passed, then, from ahead, roughly the direction of Alex's house, there came a sudden sharp burst of illumination. Misty shreds of light filtered back through the undergrowth towards her, throwing parts of the surrounding foliage into clearer focus, plunging others into even deeper shadow. At the same moment, all but lost behind the heavy throb of the engines, she heard what sounded like a scream. More from instinct than any conscious decision, Freya stepped off the track and onto one of the small paths that ran away from it. She moved further into the trees, trying not to dwell on Zahir's warning about snakes, listening as the rotors gradually slowed and quietened. The light disappeared. The helicopter must have landed. There were muffled voices, another scream and then the dull clank of breaking glass.

It was dark again now, black. Freya stood motionless, her heart pounding, trying to work out what was going on. Thirty seconds passed. As the leaves and branches came back into murky focus around her, she started to move. Slowly, trying not to make too much noise, she pushed deeper into the trees, following the path as it twisted and turned before plunging through a bank of reeds and emerging into an open field beyond.

There was more light here, the moon higher in the sky than it had been when she'd begun her walk back from the village, its glow bathing everything in a wash of muted silver. She paused to get her bearings, then crossed the field and picked up another path at its far corner, circling her way around through the oasis until she came into a shadowy olive grove beyond which she could see the pale outline of Alex's house. The lights were on. More voices.

She hesitated, wondering if it wouldn't be better just to lie low, wait for whoever was there to leave. Then there was another scream – a man's scream, feeble, terrified. Her curiosity getting the better of her, she continued forward, treading carefully so as not to disturb the dried leaves littering the ground, moving from tree to tree, her breath coming in short, nervous pants. She reached a low brushwood fence at the edge of the grove and squatted down behind it. The voices were louder now, clearer, and again she wondered if she shouldn't just keep watch from a safe distance. Again curiosity got the better of her. She crept through a gap in the fence and on towards the house, freezing every couple of metres as though she was playing grandma's footsteps, ready to turn and run should anyone come out. No one did, and she was able to skirt round the building, pressing herself behind one of the jacaranda trees that shaded the veranda at the back. Now she had a clear view through the living room window.

There were men in there, muscular, hard-looking men. Three that she could see, although a clatter of opening drawers and cupboards from Alex's study to her left suggested there were more of them. Two of the three were physically identical: same brawny build and slicked ginger hair, their ring-covered fingers glinting in the lamplight. They seemed to be addressing someone on the other side of the room, out of her line of sight. The words 'camra' and 'film' were repeated over and over again. A terrified voice jabbered back at them. On and on it went, always the same words, always the same wailing response until, with an annoyed shake of the head, one of the two clicked his fingers. There was movement, and three more figures came into view: two of them broad and tough-looking, like the others. Between them, cowering and wringing his hands, a scrawny dog tormented by a pack of larger animals, was Mahmoud Gharoub, the wizened farmer who had given her a lift on his cart earlier in the day. Freya pressed herself harder against the tree, staring in horrified fascination, her hand coming round and touching the knapsack on her back, where the camera and film were sitting.

At a signal Gharoub's *djellaba* was hoicked up around his waist, revealing scrawny legs and grimy white underpants. In the same motion, arms were hooked around his back and under his thighs and, struggling feebly, he was hoisted off the floor and his legs levered open as though he was about to give birth.

'*La!*' he moaned, eyes so wide with terror it looked as if they were going to spring right out of the sockets. '*La! Minfadlak, la!*'

His interrogators came up to him, faces blank, as though they were engaging in some mundane household chore. To Freya's disgust one of them hooked a finger beneath the gusset of the old man's pants, yanking it aside; the other clicked open a flick-knife. Leaning right in between the man's legs, he touched its tip to the exposed flesh. Their victim howled in shock, hips bucking up and down. More questions were asked. When the required answers weren't forthcoming, pressure was applied to the blade. Freya's throat filled with a sharp acidic taste as the knife was forced into the old man's perineum, the skin depressing and then splitting.

'No!'

Her voice filled the night. There was a fractional pause, a second, no more, the scene in the room freeze-framed, then shouting and a stampede of feet. The veranda doors crashed open, figures spilled out, there were flashes of red as guns opened fire and bullets thudded into the jacaranda tree where Freya had been standing. But she was no longer there. Sprinting round the side of the building and back towards the olive grove, she hurdled the low brushwood fence and slalomed on through the trees, stumbling on the uneven ground, her heart hammering, sounds of gunfire and shouting behind her.

She reached the far end of the grove and hurdled again, plunging headlong into a dense bank of reeds. She fought her way through and into a field beyond. The gunfire had stopped, although the shouting continued. Half a dozen voices, all coming from slightly different directions as her pursuers spread out, hunting her. Also, a menacing whine and thud as the helicopter powered up.

She crossed the field and scrambled down and through a deep irrigation ditch, feet sinking ankle deep in mud, her hands slithering and clawing at the opposite bank as she pulled herself up and out. She stumbled onwards. First through a grove of lemon trees, then a field of towering maize plants, then a seemingly endless expanse of tangled undergrowth, her arms sweeping and flailing at the vegetation as though she was swimming until suddenly the greenery came to an abrupt halt. She was right at the very edge of the oasis, the desert lapping against her feet. Away to her left, swathed in shadow, stood some sort of barn. Breeze-block walls with a palm-thatch roof. Running up to it, she tried the door, but it was padlocked. She looked around, frantic, then squatted down beside an old wooden cart parked up against one of the barn's walls, her entire body trembling, her breath coming in short, painful rasps.

The helicopter was in the air now and circling low over the tree-tops, its searchlight slashing through the shadows beneath. The pounding of rotors drowned out all other sounds although every now and then Freya thought she caught a shout and, once, unmistakably, the crackle of gunfire.

'They killed Alex,' she mumbled to herself, the scene she had just witnessed leaving her in no doubt about what had happened to her sister. 'They killed Alex, and now they're going to kill me. And I don't even know why.'

She wiped the sweat from her forehead, cursing herself for leaving her mobile in Alex's house, trying to figure out what to do. It was possible all the commotion had attracted attention back in Dakhla and would bring people out here to investigate, but she couldn't count on it. Nor could she just play cat and mouse for the rest of the night. The oasis was small, there were only so many places she could hide. Even in the dark and with all the dense vegetation, they'd track her down in the end, especially with the helicopter hovering above.

'I have to get to Dakhla,' she thought, gulping air. 'I have to get away from the oasis and back across the desert to Dakhla.'

How, though? With the helicopter overhead and the moon brightening all the time they'd spot her the moment she stepped out of the trees.

She stood, looking around, orientating herself, then squatted again. She seemed to be at the very southern tip of the oasis. To her left, eastwards, some five kilometres away as though across a broad channel of water, lay the main body of Dakhla, its scattered lights twinkling, the ghostly wall of the Gebel el-Qasr escarpment looming behind.

It was the obvious direction to take and offered the shortest route to safety. But the terrain was completely open, all gravel flats and low sand hummocks. There was no protection whatsoever, nowhere to hunker down against the probing eye of the helicopter's searchlight. She'd be spotted immediately, skewered, like a rabbit in the headlamps of a car.

Things didn't look much better to the south, although the landscape was more broken and varied, the desert swirling into high dunes and twisted rock formations, its surface scattered with boulders and clusters of vegetation. It was still exposed, but a lot less so and offered the possibility, if not of complete concealment, at least some vague shelter. She could trek a few miles to the south, she thought, well away from the oasis, and only then turn east to Dakhla, by which point she hoped she would be outside the radius of her pursuers' search.

Freya decided it was her best option. Her only option. The problem was that between the derelict barn where she was cowering and the first cover – a tall clump of desert grass – lay two hundred metres of flat, compacted sand. Crossing it would leave her horribly visible, like standing alone in the middle of an ice rink.

Every rock climb has its crux, the hardest part of the ascent beyond which the rest of the route suddenly opens out and becomes easier. This was the crux of Freya's escape. If she could negotiate those two hundred metres she'd have a chance. If she was spotted, either from above or by one of the men on the ground, she was finished.

The thud of the chopper grew louder as it came in almost directly overhead, its searchlight scanning back and forth, the downdraught from its rotors causing the trees to sway madly. Freya rolled underneath the cart, wafts of sand and dust spitting into her face, thin wafers of light cutting down onto her through the cracked wooden planking above. The machine hovered a moment, then swung away, swooping north towards the other end of the cultivation. The sound of its engines faded only to grow louder again as it turned and came back towards her. That seemed to be the pattern of its flight: up and down the oasis, end to end, as though doing lengths in a pool, seeking her out, thirty seconds one way, thirty seconds the other. If she was to have any hope of making it across the sand flat she'd have to synchronize her run with that pattern, starting the instant the helicopter began its run in the opposite direction, towards the far end of the oasis and finishing before it turned and flew back again, when she would come directly into its field of vision.

She pressed her palm against her forehead, calculating. Thirty seconds to cover two hundred metres. On a track it would have been easy – as a schoolgirl she had run for Markham County and done the distance in just under twenty-five. But this was across sand, and at night. It was going to be close, painfully close. And that was without factoring in the men on the ground. What if one of them spotted her? What if they'd already fanned out into the desert to watch for just this eventuality? She bit her lip, suddenly doubtful, scared, wondering if it wasn't too big a risk. There hadn't been that many of them, after all. And it was dark, the undergrowth was heavy in places – surely she'd be able to evade them, stay one step ahead.

Then she heard a shout. Tensing, she peered into the gloom, ears straining, trying to work out where it had come from. Somewhere behind her, beyond the tangled mass of vegetation she'd fought her way through a few moments earlier. Still a way off, but not that far. It was answered by another shout, and then another. Three of them, and all coming her way, converging. One she might be able to dodge, two even, but three . . . no chance. Decision made. She'd have to run. If it wasn't already too late.

A clattering roar and the helicopter swung in overhead again, its search beam carving blinding avenues of light around and across the barn. On its previous run the chopper had moved on almost immediately. This time, agonizingly, it just hovered where it was. Freya clasped her ears against the noise, the cart above her rattling madly as if it was being shaken by invisible hands, the blast of the rotors lifting part of the barn's thatch roof and whirling it off into the night. On and on it went, every second bringing the men on the ground closer, narrowing her window of opportunity. She had all but given up hope, accepted that she would be cornered here like a rat in a trap, when finally the roar started to lessen and the air around her to still as the machine rolled away and began its run back up to the top end of the oasis.

She was out and on her feet immediately. Barely aware of what she was doing, driven by an elemental, adrenalin-fuelled instinct for self-preservation, she sprinted past the barn and onto the desert. She had no idea where her pursuers were, just prayed they were still struggling through the undergrowth behind the barn and wouldn't be able to see her through the heavy curtain of leaves.

The sand was flat, compacted, almost as firm as a cinder track, and she covered the first hundred and fifty metres easily, elbows pumping, legs powering her forward towards the clump of desert grass ahead.

She was just starting to believe she might make it when her feet began to drag. The desert surface was loosening beneath her, the sand sucking at her shoes, slowing her down. The going became harder with every stride, her lungs heaving, her thighs burning as the muscles flooded with a surge of lactic acid.

When they were young she and Alex had played a game of dare, knocking on people's doors and then running away, every step an agony of anticipation as they waited for the home-owner's angry shouts behind them. She had that same feeling now, but amplified a thousand-fold – a breathless, desperate hope that she would not be caught twinned with the sickening expectation that she almost certainly would be.

Slower and slower, feet slipping and sliding and fighting for traction, she kept going. The malevolent throb of the helicopter rotors held steady as it hovered at the far end of the oasis before gradually swelling again as the chopper turned and came back towards her. Freya knew she was out of time, was going to be spotted, couldn't fail to be now that she was directly in the helicopter's line of sight. She powered on regardless, her body continuing to run even as her mind seemed to slow and give up hope. Scrabbling over the last ten metres of flat, she pitched headlong through the clump of grass and down a steep incline, tumbling to a halt in a shower of sand.

For a while she just lay there, chest heaving, legs screaming in pain, waiting for the helicopter to swamp her with light. It remained dark. Rolling onto her front, she crawled back up the bank and carefully parted the wiry stems of grass to make a small gap. Two hundred metres away the chopper was now hanging directly above the barn, swaying this way and that. Below, caught in its searchlight, three suited figures were holding their arms up as if to say 'She's not here.' There was some gesticulating and waving, and then the helicopter sped off back across the oasis and the three men disappeared into the undergrowth.

She'd made it.

*

Dakhla Oasis

Having said his evening prayers – bowing and kneeling in the inner courtyard of his house – Zahir ate dinner with his wife and son, the three of them sitting cross-legged on the floor of their living room, silently picking with their fingers at bowls of rice, beans and *molocchia*. When they had finished the woman fetched a shisha pipe and placed it at her husband's side before leading the boy away, leaving Zahir alone. For fifteen minutes he sat thus, motionless, lost in thought, the only sound the soft popping of his lips as he pulled at the shisha's mouthpiece. Then, laying the mouthpiece aside, he stood and walked back through the house and out into the internal courtyard. Crossing to the first door on his right, he opened it and switched on the light. In front of him, on the wall above the desk, was the photograph Miss Freya had seen: the curving arm of rock, with Doctor Alex standing in the shade beneath it. He stared, fingers drumming nervously on the doorframe.

'What is troubling you?'

His wife had come up beside him and laid a hand on his arm. He said nothing, just continued gazing at the picture.

'You are not yourself,' she said. 'What is wrong?'

Still he didn't reply, but put his hand on his wife's, squeezing gently.

'Is it the American girl?' she asked.

'She went to the police,' he murmured. 'Thinks someone killed her sister.'

'And?'

He shrugged.

179

'You should talk to her,' said his wife. 'Find out what she knows.'

He nodded.

'Tomorrow,' he said. 'I'll go tomorrow.'

He kissed her forehead, running a finger down her cheek, then indicated that she should leave him. When she was gone he stepped into the room and, closing the door, went over to the desk and sat down, eyes never leaving the picture.

'Sandfire,' he murmured.

Freya gave it a few minutes, crouching behind the clump of grass, the sound of the helicopter waxing and waning as it patrolled up and down the oasis. She checked that the camera, film canister and compass were all still safe inside her knapsack, and dabbed away the worst of the blood on her arms and neck, which had been badly scratched during her headlong charge through the undergrowth. She then began working her way south.

It was a clear night, cool bordering on cold, the moon now fully risen, the desert an expanse of icy silver. Terrified of being seen, she moved only when the helicopter was going in the opposite direction, sprinting from one piece of cover to the next – boulder to dune to rock formation to bush – before cowering down again. A couple of times she heard gunfire, and once the helicopter came out beyond the oasis, flying almost directly overhead as she curled herself into a ball beneath a thin rock shelf. It seemed the pilot was only chancing his arm, taking pot luck that he might spot her, and after flying round for a while the chopper turned and

180

headed back. After that there were no more signs of pursuit.

She continued south for almost two hours, cautiously at first, then with more confidence as the oasis dropped out of view behind her, lost among the dunes and gravel hills. The air turned bitterly cold and she removed her fleece from the knapsack and pulled it on, breaking into a jog every now and then to keep herself warm. She tried to go over events in her head, searching for answers, but she was in shock and everything was confused and jumbled and meaningless. Beyond the fact that someone had killed her sister, and had tried to kill her, and that it was all tied up with the objects the Bedouin man had brought to the house that afternoon, she could make no sense of it whatsoever.

She covered about five kilometres, then judged it was safe enough to turn east back towards the distant glinting lights of Dakhla proper. It took her a further hour to reach the first outlying fields, and another forty minutes beyond that to navigate her way through a maze of reed banks, fish ponds and irrigation canals. Eventually, more by luck than design, she emerged from a field of densely packed sugar cane and found herself on a tarmacked road, the main thoroughfare through the oasis.

Lights were approaching from her right. She hesitated, then stepped back among the cane stems, peering nervously out, fearful it might be her pursuers. Only when she saw that the lights belonged to a large oil tanker did she emerge again and frantically wave her arms, flagging the vehicle down. A horn sounded, and there was a wheeze of hydraulic brakes as the tanker slowed and came to a halt beside her. The driver wound down his window and leant out.

'Please help me,' she pleaded. 'I need to get to Mut. To

the police station. Someone's trying to kill me. Please, I need to get to the police station. You understand? Mut. Police station. Mut. Mut.'

The words spilled out of her in a garbled rush. The driver – a plump man with a whiskery, oil-smeared face – shrugged and shook his head, clearly not understanding.

'*El-Qahira*,' he said. 'Go *el-Qahira*. Cairo.'

He seemed to think she was a hitch-hiker and was thumbing a ride. Clenching her fists in frustration, she started to repeat herself, only to fall silent. El-Qahira. Cairo. Yes, she thought, maybe that would be better. Get out of the oasis altogether, as far away as possible, back up to Cairo where she could go to the Embassy, or call Molly Kiernan – fellow Americans, people who could speak English. People who could help her.

'Yes,' she said, throwing an anxious look over her shoulder. 'Cairo. Yes, thank you. Cairo.'

She hurried round to the passenger side, climbed in and slammed the door.

'They were trying to kill me,' she said as they started moving, her voice shaky, disbelieving. 'You understand? There were these men and they were trying to kill me.'

As before, the driver just shrugged.

'*Ingleezaya?*' he asked.

'What?'

'*Ingleezaya? Een-gleesh?*'

She shook her head.

'American. I'm American.'

He grinned.

'*Amreeka* good. Boos Weelis. Amal Shwassnegar. Very good.'

She so desperately wanted to explain, to make him understand – that they'd tried to kill her, and had killed her sister, and that she'd only just managed to escape and had been walking across the desert for hours and was cold and thirsty and frightened and exhausted. But it was pointless. She nodded at him, then brought her legs up, wrapped her arms around them and leant her head against the window, gazing out.

'Yes, yes, very good,' chuckled the driver, patting his palms appreciatively against the steering wheel. 'Boos Weelis. Amal Shwassnegar. Very, very good.'

As they picked up speed, the white dot of the helicopter's searchlight was briefly visible out across the desert before it dropped away behind them and they were rumbling off into the night, heading north.

CAIRO

The girl was young. Fifteen or sixteen, no more, drugged up and dressed in a school uniform. She sat on the bed, eyes glazed, bewildered, not quite sure what was happening. To murmurs of approval, the Ethiopians came in, strutting about a bit, doing some comic stuff with their penises, emphasizing their size and girth, before getting down to the serious business. They stripped the girl, slapping her about, forcing themselves into her mouth. The businessmen grinned and puffed on their cigars while the girl gagged and wept, pleading to be left alone.

In the next-door room Girgis watched through the one-way mirror, nodding in satisfaction. Not at the rape itself – he didn't care for such things; didn't particularly care for sex full stop – but rather at the deal that had preceded it. Everyone knew that if you did business with Romani Girgis he'd look after you, put on a good show, and that in turn meant business always went smoothly. As it had this evening. Almost too smoothly, if anything. Knowing the sort of entertainment that was being laid on for them, the North Koreans hadn't been able sign the contracts quick enough: fifty FIM-92 Stinger surface-to-air missiles, at $205,000 each, with Girgis taking a twenty per cent commission on the sale as middleman. He smiled, thinking maybe he ought to give the girl a cut, reward her for her exertions. But then the girl would most likely be dead by the end of the night, her body dumped in the Nile or somewhere out over the desert, so he might as well keep all the money himself. The thought made him smile even more.

He watched on for a while as the rape became increasingly frenzied and bestial. Then, glancing at his watch, he turned away and left the room, walking across the marble-floored hallway and up the grand staircase towards his study on the top floor. There'd be more shows after this one – young boys with an older woman, three girls together, a girl and a dog – after which his guests would be shown to private bedrooms, supplied with hookers, drugs, porn, whatever they wanted, the entertainment continuing well into the early hours. His people would see to it all. He had other business to attend to. More important business. Even more important than twenty per cent commission on $10.25 million.

At the top of the staircase he stooped to flick a crumb off the carpet – bloody cleaners, no attention to detail – before walking down a corridor and unlocking a door at the far end. He stepped into a large, wood-panelled study. A bank of closed-circuit television screens was arranged along one wall, each tuned in to a different room within the house. Crossing to his desk he sat down and, glancing at his watch again, lifted the phone, jabbing the loudspeaker button and placing the receiver on the desktop.

'Everyone there?'

Murmurs of assent as those at the other end of the line confirmed they were indeed present and ready to begin the conference call: Boutros Salah, his right-hand man; Ahmed Usman, his antiquities expert; Mohammed Kasri, his lawyer and link-man with the police and security services. The inner circle, his closest confidants.

'OK, let's get started,' said Girgis. 'Boutros?'

There was a cough as Salah cleared his throat.

'It's definitely the co-pilot,' came his voice, hoarse and wheezy – the voice of a heavy smoker. 'We've checked the details from the wallet and they tally. Looks like he was trying to walk his way out of the desert.'

'And he was coming from the oasis?' asked Girgis. 'We're certain of that?'

'Oh, no question about it,' came another voice, this one hesitant, slightly bumbling: Ahmed Usman. 'Really no question at all. We knew that's where the plane came down from the final radio message, of course, but the artefact confirms it beyond any doubt. A votive obelisk with the *sedjet* sign, found that close to the Gilf – it could only be Zerzura. Absolutely no question.'

Girgis nodded, clasping his hands on the desk in front of him.

'What about the camera film?'

Another cough as Salah again cleared his throat.

'The map should be all we need,' he wheezed. 'The twins are out looking for the co-pilot's body now. They got a good description from the Bedouin leader and the camel tracks are still visible so it shouldn't be that hard to trace. Once they've found it they just reverse the compass bearings on the map and follow them back to the Gilf. In theory they should lead us straight to the plane.'

'Theory?'

'Well the guy must have been in a pretty bad state by the end, so it's possible he didn't get the bearings exact. Either way they'll get us close, and once we're in the vicinity it should be easy to find with the helicopter, even in the dark. If everything goes smoothly they should have it in a couple hours, maybe less. If they end up having to go back to Dakhla to refuel, four or five. By dawn. We'll definitely have it by dawn.'

There was a knock on the door and a white-jacketed servant entered, carrying a glass of tea. Girgis waved him forward without looking up. The man placed the glass on the desk and left, all the while keeping his eyes firmly on the floor.

'What about the military?' Girgis asked. 'The Gilf's a security zone. I don't want any trouble.'

'All covered,' replied a third voice. Smooth, oily – Mohammed Kasri. 'I've spoken to the people who need to be spoken to; they'll give us a clear run. General Zawi was extremely helpful.'

'He bloody should be, given the amount we pay him,' said Girgis with a snort, raising his tea and taking a sip.

There was a pause, then Usman's voice came in again.

'May I ask about safety? I mean, we don't know what state it's going to be in after all these years, how the crash might have affected it. We really are going to need specialist equipment, people who know what they're doing.'

'It's in hand,' replied Girgis.

'Because this isn't just a consignment of guns we're talking about here. We can't simply box it up and fly it out. We're dealing with things . . .'

'It's in hand,' repeated Girgis, firmer this time. 'All necessary technical back-up will be provided.'

'Of course, Mr Girgis,' mumbled Usman, sensing that he had overstepped the mark. 'I didn't mean . . . I just wanted to be sure.'

'Well now you are,' said Girgis.

He sipped again, his lips barely touching the liquid, then set the glass down and dabbed at his mouth with a handkerchief.

'Which just leaves the girl,' he said. 'I take it we haven't found her yet.'

Salah acknowledged that this was the case.

'We've left five of the guys in Dakhla. And we've got local friends. If she's there we'll track her down.'

'The police?' asked Girgis. '*Jihaz amn al-daoula?*'

'I've alerted our contacts,' said Kasri. 'If she shows up they'll let us know. I'm assuming our American . . .'

'Alerted,' said Girgis.

He continued dabbing at his mouth before neatly folding his handkerchief and returning it to his pocket.

'I want her found,' he said. 'Even if the map gives us everything we need, I want her found. I haven't waited twenty-three years to see this whole thing screwed up by some little slut blabbing her mouth off. I want her found, and I want her removed. Clear?'

'Clear,' answered all three voices in unison.

'Call me as soon as you have news.'

The line clicked as one by one the other three rang off. For a moment Girgis was still, gazing across the room at the bank of closed-circuit television screens – a grainy mosaic of sex and violence – then he leant forward.

'Did you get all that?'

A barely audible murmur of acknowledgement emanated from the telephone. The tone was fractionally higher than those of the speakers who had just rung off; it was impossible to tell whether it belonged to a man or a woman.

'I'm going to need your help on this,' said Girgis. 'If the girl contacts the Embassy . . .'

Another murmur and the line went dead. Girgis stared at the phone, eyes narrowed, tongue flicking in and out of the corner of his mouth. With a nod, he replaced the receiver, stood and, taking his tea with him, wandered through onto the balcony where he gazed out over the ornamental gardens that ran down to the Nile at the back of the house.

Twenty years he'd lived here, a sumptuous colonial mansion right on the Zamalek waterfront. Even now it still amazed him: that he, the son of rubbish collectors, grandson of *Saidi fellaheen*, should live at one of the most exclusive addresses in Cairo, find himself hobnobbing with the elite. From Manshiet Nasser to this, from street-corner dope deals to a multimillion-dollar business empire – he'd certainly come a long way. Further than even he could have hoped or expected. Only the Gilf Kebir fiasco had marred an otherwise glittering career – a deal that should have been his crowning glory, audacious even by his standards, and all fucked up because of a freak weather event.

He frowned, his mouth tightening into an angry grimace. The expression only lasted a moment before rearranging itself into a smile.

Because the deal wasn't fucked up. Delayed, yes. But not fucked up. Far from it. The crash had, in the end, done him and his clients a favour, transforming an already ambitious venture into something even bigger. It had taken its time coming to fruition, but now, finally, he was poised to reap the rewards. Every cloud has a silver lining. Or in this case every sandstorm.

He sipped his tea and gazed across the Nile to the Carlton Hotel and the light-covered towers of the Egyptian National Bank building opposite as the sound of screams echoed up from below, pained and helpless. His smile broadened and he let out a chuckle. Say what you like, Romani Girgis always put on a good show.

CAIRO – THE AMERICAN EMBASSY

Having made himself a cup of warm milk Cy Angleton went through into the living area and settled himself down in the armchair, his paunch slumping out over the waistband of his pyjama bottoms, his hips pushing hard against the armrests

PAUL SUSSMAN

of the chair (who the hell designed this furniture? Midgets?). Most Embassy staff lived off site, in Garden City or across the river in Gezira and Zamalek, but he'd managed to bag one of the apartments on the top floor of Cairo 2. It was a tiny space, just a bedroom, living area, bathroom and kitchenette, with barely enough room to walk more than a few paces in any direction without slapping into a wall. But it was more secure than being outside the compound, less chance of people nosing around. And besides, it meant he could have all his meals sent up from the Marine Corps kitchen down in the basement, proper food, American food, including a steady supply of chef Barney's Mississippi mud pie. Damn, that pie was good. Almost made all the other shit worth it. Almost.

He took a long, slow gulp of the milk and, reaching for the remote control, activated the CD player. Adjusting the volume, he flicked through the tracks until he came to the one he wanted: Patsy Cline, 'Too Many Secrets'. A momentary silence, and then the familiar jaunty honk of clarinets as the song got started. He sighed with pleasure, leaning his head back and closing his eyes, drumming his fingers on the armrests.

He loved Country music; had always loved it, ever since he was a kid listening to crackly 78s on his ma's old Crosley radio-record player. Hank Williams, Jimmie Rodgers, Lefty Frizzell, Merle Travis: without these he would never have survived those early years – the bullying, the endless hospital visits, his pa's drunken rages. ('Look at you, for Christ's sake! I ask God for a son and what does he give me? A big fat pansy fucking hog!') Country had provided an escape, a refuge, a place where he didn't feel quite so alone.

Still did. If anything he needed it more today than he had back then, what with all the lies and suspicion and stinking corrupt filth he was forever having to wade through. 'Country ain't just music,' his ma used to tell him. 'It's what gets you through.' And she'd been right. The framed citation on the wall opposite proved it: 'The United States Department of State Award for Heroism is presented to Cyrus Jeremiah Angleton. For heroic service under circumstances of extreme danger.' It was Country that had got him that. He sure wished his ma was still around, so she could see how right she'd been.

He allowed the track to play through the first verse and chorus, then dropped the volume a few notches, finished his milk and leant forward, staring down at the floor. A large map of Egypt was spread out in front of him, the paper covered with a confusion of pencil scribbles: names, dates, phone numbers, sums of money, sequences of digits that might or might not have been bank accounts. There were photographs as well, lots of them, scattered across the country, all passport sized save for three larger images arranged side by side in the bottom left-hand corner of the map, above the words 'Gilf Kebir Plateau': Flin Brodie, Alex Hannen, Molly Kiernan. Reaching down, struggling to bend his body, he picked them up and sat back again, shuffling them in his hand like a pack of cards. He stared at each in turn: Brodie, Hannen, Kiernan, then back to Brodie again. Things were starting to open up, connections to appear, he could feel it, he could definitely feel it. There was still a way to go, but hopefully it wouldn't be too long before he could get the hell out of here. No more Sandfire, no more heat, no more creeping around – job done, money earned, employers satisfied. No more of chef Barney's Mississippi mud pie either, but he could live without that. Could live without anything except his beloved Country music. Throwing the pictures down he reached for the remote control and pressed replay, the room falling silent before once again filling with the song's jaunty instrumental opening, 'Too Many Secrets'. He chuckled. Story of his goddam life.

DAKHLA

The eastern sky was turning a cool shade of pink and the dawn birds were screeching in the trees as Fatima Gharoub stomped through the oasis, her capacious black robes flapping around her, her bulky frame moving with surprising speed. Every now and then she would stop and spit in the dust, muttering angrily, before moving on again, following the track as it switched back and forth through the palm and olive groves until eventually it brought her out in front of the American woman's house.

'Slut!' she bellowed, striding up to the front door. 'Where is he? What have you done with my Mahmoud?'

She raised a fist ready to hammer before noticing the door was already ajar. Kicking it open she barged through into the living area.

'Come on, I know you're in here! The donkey and his whore! Forty years of marriage and this is how he repays me!'

She stood listening, her face a rictus of indignant fury. Snatching up a plastic dustpan from the windowsill, she started towards the main bedroom, the pan held above her head like a weapon.

'Don't make me come and find you, Mahmoud Gharoub!' she yelled. 'Do you hear? Because believe me, if I have to come and find you, you'll regret it for the rest of your life!'

She was halfway across the living area when she sensed movement. A figure appeared in the bedroom doorway. She came to a halt, mouth dropping open in surprise.

'Zahir al-Sabri? My God, how many of you has she got in here?'

'I don't know what you're talking about,' snapped Zahir, scowling, clearly not pleased to have been found thus.

'Oh yes you do!' Fatima Gharoub cried. 'I know what goes on out here! Always snuffling around, he is. Bewitched! They've bewitched him, the dirty little whores! Mahmoud! Mahmoud! Oh my beautiful Mahmoud!'

She started wailing, tugging at her robe, banging the dustpan against her head. As suddenly as they had come, her hysterics ceased and her eyes narrowed.

'What are you doing here?'

Zahir shifted uneasily.

'I came to see Miss Freya.'

'At six in the morning?'

'I brought her breakfast.' He nodded towards a basket sitting on the living room table. 'The door was open. I came in to make sure she was OK.'

'You were snooping,' said the old woman, wagging an accusing finger. 'Poking around.'

'I came in to make sure Miss Freya was OK,' he repeated. 'She wasn't here. Her bed hasn't been slept in.'

'Snooping and poking,' she pushed, sensing a juicy bit of gossip. 'Looking at things you're not supposed to look at. Just you wait till I tell . . . What do you mean her bed hasn't been slept in?'

Zahir opened his mouth to answer, but before he could say anything the aggrieved wife had starting yelling again, tearing at her dress, slapping her palms against her forehead.

'Oh God, I knew it! They've gone away together. She's stolen my Mahmoud! Mahmoud, Mahmoud! My little Mahmoud!'

Throwing the dustpan across the room she swung round and, presumably intending to give chase to the eloping couple, rushed from the house, leaving Zahir standing where he was, shaking his head and looking distinctly uncomfortable.

CAIRO

Those who worked for Romani Girgis could sense when violence was imminent. They knew at such times either to keep out of his way or, if they couldn't keep out of his way, to keep their heads well down, get on with what they were doing and not attract attention to themselves.

It had been brewing all morning. A little after dawn Girgis had taken a phone call out on the terrace at the back of the house and according to the old gardener who was at the time watering geranium pots nearby, he hadn't been happy. Not happy at all, shouting at the person at the other end of the line, hammering his fist so hard on the wooden table that his cup of coffee had tumbled off and smashed on the ground, leaving an unsightly stain on the gleaming white marble. The gardener hadn't heard exactly what was being said, he later explained to one of the household cooks, hadn't dared look up or get too close, but he definitely heard Girgis use the words 'oasis' and 'helicopter'. And something about a black tower and an arch too, although by that point he had started to move away out of Girgis's line of sight, and might have misheard.

That had been the start. From there Girgis's mood had steadily worsened as the morning progressed. Around 8 a.m. his three lieutenants – Boutros Salah, Ahmed Usman and Mohammed Kasri – had arrived and disappeared into his study. A maid reported that she heard the sound of smashing glass and a yell of 'You said the map would be enough!' An hour later, at 9 a.m., a handyman mending a socket at the foot of the grand staircase had almost been knocked over as Girgis swept past him, mobile in hand as he bellowed, 'I don't care about the fucking fuel! Keep looking! You hear me! Just keep looking!'

Angrier and angrier he had become, the atmosphere ever more tense until just after noon there had been a thunder of rotor blades and Girgis's helicopter had landed on the garden helipad, the twins emerging and crossing to where Girgis was waiting for them on the lawn. Most of the staff were by now aware that something was amiss and were gazing surreptitiously out of the mansion's windows, although only the old gardener was near enough to hear what their employer said to the twins.

'Find her,' he cried. 'Find the girl, find the camera film,

cut her eyes out and dump her in the desert. You hear me? Find the bitch!'

'He's going to hurt someone,' the old gardener whispered to his assistant, keeping his face down over the flowerbed they were weeding. 'Mark my words, he's going to hurt someone.'

It was the thought on everyone's mind as Girgis stormed back into the house. His staff, like fish scattering before a predator, all withdrew to a safe distance as he marched across the hallway and up the staircase to his study on the top floor.

All except for Adara al-Hawwari. She had only worked in the mansion for three days, and knew nothing of its owner or his temper, was just grateful to have found a job. For a sixty-year-old widow employment was hard to come by and the chance to work in such beautiful surroundings, even if it was for only fifty piastres an hour, had seemed like a boon from Allah himself. For three days she had been waiting for an opportunity to thank her new employer, to tell him how very grateful she was for his kindness. And now here he was coming up the stairs towards her as she polished the teak balustrade around the first-floor landing. She was a shy woman, and it did not come naturally to her to address such a great and important man. She thought it her duty, how-ever, and as he reached the top of the stairs she stepped forward, touched a hand to her chest and, in a faltering voice, humbly thanked him for his kindness to an old widow. Girgis ignored her, walking straight past and down the corridor towards his study. He was halfway there when, suddenly, he turned. Striding back, he came up to her and slapped her hard across the face.

'Don't speak to me,' he spat. 'Do you understand? Don't ever speak to me.'

Adara al-Hawwari stood staring at him, a heavy red mark staining her cheek. Her silence seemed to infuriate him even more and he slapped her again: harder. The force of the blow caused her nose to crack and threw her back against the balustrade, blood dripping from her nostril onto the carpet.

'How dare you speak to me!' Girgis cried, his voice rising, his anger and frustration now homing in exclusively on the cowering figure in front of him. 'How dare you! How dare you!'

He hit her once more, across the side of the head. Snatching a pack of wet wipes from his jacket pocket, he ripped one out and rubbed it vigorously over his hands.

'And make sure you clean up your mess,' he panted, indicating the bloodstains on the floor. 'You understand? I want your filth cleaned up! I want it pristine! Pristine!'

He threw the wipe at her, wheeled round and disappeared down the corridor, leaving Adara al-Hawwari trembling in mortified silence and wondering whether working for Mr Romani Girgis was really such a boon after all.

Cairo – the Coptic Quarter

Humming 'What a Friend We Have in Jesus' to herself, her favourite of all hymns, Molly Kiernan made her way through the winding streets of the *Masr al-Qadima* – Old Cairo – and down a set of worn steps into the Church of St Sergius and St Bacchius.

PAUL SUSSMAN

Normally she worshipped at a small community chapel in the Maadi district of the city, where the USAID offices at which she worked were based and where she lived in a small two-bedroom bungalow shaded by flame and jasmine trees. Today, however – 7 May – was Charlie's birthday, and on this particular day she liked to go somewhere different, somewhere special. And so she came here, to the oldest church in Cairo, an ancient, crumbling basilica built, according to legend, on the site where the Holy Family themselves once stopped to rest on their journey into Egypt.

She always followed exactly the same routine on Charlie's birthday, had done for the last quarter of a century. She would make him a special birthday breakfast – bacon, eggs, grits, waffles and blueberry jam, Charlie's favourite – open the presents she had bought and wrapped for him, and spend a while with her photo albums, leafing through the story of their life together, smiling as she recalled all the good times they had enjoyed, what a handsome, special man her Charlie had been.

'Oh my darling,' she would sigh, 'Oh my darling, precious husband.'

Later she would make up a picnic and go to the zoo – that's where he'd taken her on their first date, to the zoo at Washington – and then to church. There she would spend the rest of the afternoon giving thanks for Charlie's life, trying to reassure herself that there was a reason why God had taken him in that terrible way, that it was all part of some wider scheme, although even after all these years she still struggled to fathom what that scheme was exactly. Such a kind, gentle man blown apart by

198

those murdering savages. Oh my darling. Oh my darling, precious husband.

Walking into the basilica now, Kiernan paused for a moment to gaze at the large icon of the Virgin Mary just inside the doorway, before moving forward and sitting down in one of the wooden pews. A pair of sparrows fluttered around the vaulted wooden ceiling above her.

She loved it here, just as she knew Charlie would have loved it. There was something about the tatty simplicity of the place: the faded frescoes, the threadbare rugs on the floor, the cool, musty smell of damp and dust and stone. It seemed to transport her right the way back to the very earliest days of Christianity: days when the faith was still young and pure, innocent, free of the terrible moral quandaries with which it had subsequently become burdened. Once, it seemed to her, to be a Christian had simply been a matter of love and belief, an acceptance that the goodness of Christ was all that was needed to cure the world's ills. That's how her Charlie had seen things – a simple, almost childlike conviction that if you had sufficient faith, trod as closely as you could in Christ's footsteps, then everything would turn out all right in the end, that good would triumph over evil.

But Kiernan knew that things were more complicated than that, more confused, as Charlie's death had proved. As everything these days seemed to prove. The Lamb of God was beset on all sides by jackals, and love alone was no longer enough to see you through. Long ago she had accepted that to be a Christian you had to walk a tightrope, find ways of living in Christ while at the same time standing firm against the evildoers. Meekness and strength, faith and conflict; it was all so very difficult, so very painful and troubling. Which is why Kiernan liked to come here. To lose herself, if only for an afternoon, in the cool, uncluttered simplicity of this beautiful ancient building. Just her and God and Charlie, united in silence, removed from the dilemmas with which her everyday life was choked.

She sat back and clasped her hands in her lap, gazing around the church, taking in the marble columns to either side of the central aisle, the exquisitely inlaid iconostasis at the head of the nave, the huge brass chandelier suspended overhead, all the while thinking of Charlie and their life together. All that they had shared in that too-brief time. All that she had lost.

They'd married late, both of them in their thirties. She was working for the government, he was a pastor with the 1st Battalion 8th Marine Regiment. She'd all but given up hope of finding anyone by that point, accepted that her work was going to be her life, spinsterhood her destiny. But the moment she'd clapped eyes on him standing beside her in the National Gallery of Art in Washington – in front of, appropriately, Carpaccio's *The Flight into Egypt* – she'd known instinctively that he was the one. The man she'd been waiting for all these years. They'd got talking, he'd asked her out, six months later they were engaged and five months after that they had married. There had been talk of children, of trips they would take, of growing old together – she had been so very, very happy.

Less than a year after their wedding, however, Charlie's battalion had been posted to Lebanon, as part of the international peacekeeping force. They'd had a final, magical fortnight together, and then one morning she'd made him his breakfast – bacon, eggs, grits, waffles, blueberry jam – he'd kissed her on the cheek and given her the cross she still wore around her neck and hefting his kitbag onto his shoulder, had walked out into the dawn. That was the last time she ever saw him. A month later, on 23 October 1983, news came through of an explosion in Beirut, a suicide bombing, marine barracks, massive casualties, and she'd known instantly that her Charlie was gone. Two years, that's all they'd had. Just two short years. The very best of her life.

A babble of voices interrupted her thoughts as a crowd of Italian tourists came trooping into the church, their guide ushering them into the seats around her, forcing her to move along to make space for them. They were young and seemed to have no interest in the place, no concept of its sacredness. Talking loudly amongst themselves, eating crisps, one of them was even playing with his Game Boy. She tried to ignore them, but then another group came in, Japanese this time and the church filled with an incessant strobe of camera flashes. Their guide's voice seemed to fill the entire space as she jabbered at them through some sort of portable amplifier. Unable to bear it – why couldn't they just be quiet, leave her to mourn in peace? – Kiernan stood and pushed her way out of the pew. As she came into the aisle a Japanese couple blocked her path, holding up a camera, grinning, bowing, asking if she would take a picture of them. She snapped.

'What's wrong with you people!' she cried. 'This is a church! Don't you understand that! Show some respect! Please, just show some respect.'

She rushed past the couple and out of the door,

stumbling up the steps and onto the narrow street above, eyes blurring with tears.

'I need you, Charlie,' she choked. 'I can't do this on my own any more. Oh God, I need you. My husband, my darling precious husband.'

It was past 1 p.m. when Freya eventually reached the outskirts of Cairo, and a further forty minutes before they had crawled their way through a crush of near-stationary traffic into the centre of the city. The tanker driver pulled over at one end of an enormous open square beside a swathe of litter-covered grass dotted with palm trees.

'Midan Tahrir,' he informed her, ignoring the toots of protest from the cars behind.

It had taken them the best part of sixteen hours to get here from Dakhla, an interminable journey made even more interminable by the driver's insistence on stopping off at what felt like every roadside café *en route* for tea. More than once Freya had contemplated ditching him and trying to hitch a lift with someone else. She had decided against it, paranoid that the men from the oasis might have colleagues out looking for her and that she would fall in with the wrong people. Slow he might have been, but at least the tanker driver seemed trustworthy.

She had dozed fitfully during the journey, an hour here, forty minutes there, but for most of the time she had been awake. Occasionally she had opened her knapsack and stared down at the camera, film roll and compass nestled inside. Mainly she had just gazed out of the window at the endless expanse of desert, watching as the mile markers counted them slowly through al-Farafra, Bahariya and on towards Cairo.

And now, at last, they were here.

'Midan Tahrir,' repeated the driver.

'Phone,' she said, miming holding a receiver to her ear. 'I need to make a call.'

He frowned, then smiled and pointed past her to a green and yellow public payphone.

'Menatel,' he said, rummaging in a locker under the dashboard and producing a disposable phonecard which he handed to her, waving away her offer of money. She thanked him, both for the card and the ride and, swinging her knapsack onto her back, dropped out of the cab onto the pavement. The driver gave a final cry of 'Boos Weelis. Amal Shwassnegar!' and moved off.

For a moment Freya stood there, exhausted, taking in her surroundings: the swirling traffic, the ant-like droves of pedestrians, the high dirty buildings capped with giant hoardings advertising Coca-Cola, Vodafone, Sanyo, Western Union. For all the infuriating slowness of the journey, there had been something secure and comforting about the inside of the tanker cab. Now, suddenly, she felt very alone and very exposed, like a snail whose shell has been torn away. At a nearby set of traffic lights a taxi driver was talking on his mobile. He seemed to be staring straight at her. So did an old woman selling lighters off an upturned crate just a few metres away. Dropping her head, Freya hurried over to the payphone, fumbling in her pocket and pulling out the card Molly Kiernan had given her when they had first met. She slipped the phonecard into the slot, selected the

English language option on the digital display and, cradling the receiver in the crook of her neck, tapped Kiernan's mobile number into the keypad. Silence, a ringing tone, then, to Freya's frustration, a voicemail message: 'Hi, this is Molly Kiernan. I can't take your call right now. Leave a message and I'll get back to you as soon as I can.'

'Molly, it's Freya,' she said the moment the record tone sounded, her voice tense, urgent, 'Freya Hannen. I'm calling from a payphone. Something's . . . I need help. Someone tried to . . . I think they killed Alex . . . They were . . . This man came to the house yesterday with a bag . . . there was a camera . . . he said he found them in the desert . . .'

She broke off, aware that she was gabbling and should have thought through what she was going to say before she called. Better to keep things short, explain it all face to face.

'Listen, I'm in Cairo,' she said. 'I need to see you. I'm in . . .'

Again she broke off, trying to remember what the driver had told her.

'. . . Midan something . . . it's a big open space . . .'

She looked around, searching for landmarks.

'There's a Hilton hotel, and some sort of fast food place called Hardees, and . . . and . . .'

Her eyes fell on a large, Ottoman-style building on the far side of the street. All arched windows, intricate wooden screens and ornate cornicing, it was surrounded by railings and a high dusty hedge. Emblazoned across the top of its façade in blue letters were the words THE AMERICAN UNIVERSITY IN CAIRO. Wasn't that where . . . ? She fumbled in her pocket again, um-ing and ah-ing into the phone, apologizing for the delay, removing the card that Flin Brodie had given her: Professor F. Brodie, American University in Cairo. She started to speak again, her voice more assured now.

'I'm outside the American University,' she said. 'I'm going to go in and try to find Flin Brodie. If he's not there I'll go to the Embassy. I think I'm in danger, I need to—'

The line went dead. The phone's digital display showed that she had no more credit left. She cursed, hung up and stepped back out onto the pavement. Pedestrians jostled past all around her. The taxi driver with the mobile had by now driven off, although the old woman selling lighters was still gazing fixedly in her direction. For a moment Freya wondered if it wouldn't be better just to go direct to the US Embassy, to seek some sort of official protection, but the prospect of having to deal with a load of bored bureaucrats and go through her whole story from the beginning dissuaded her. What she needed right now was a familiar face, someone she could trust, someone who would take what she was saying seriously. Admittedly she hardly knew Brodie, had only talked to him for a few minutes, but he had been a friend of her sister's and that was good enough for her. The Embassy could wait. Flin Brodie would help her, she was certain. He'd know what to do.

She patted her knapsack and threw a quick glance towards the lighter vendor, who continued to stare, her gold teeth glinting in the afternoon sun. Then, spotting a gap in the traffic, Freya jogged across the street and followed the fence round the side of the university building, anxiously looking for the main entrance.

They had some extremely advanced listening and surveillance facilities in the US Embassy, and some extremely skilled people manning them. Since his secondment was to Public Affairs, it wasn't feasible for Angleton to avail himself of those facilities. Not without all sorts of awkward questions being asked. He could have stuck his neck out, pulled strings, wangled the necessary permissions – might still have to do that – but for the moment it was easier for him to improvise. He didn't want to be giving the game away. Not yet at least.

And so he'd kitted out his own listening station, off campus, in a suite way up at the top of the drab orange tower of the Semiramis Intercontinental Hotel. The gadgetry wasn't as high tech as the kit they had back at the Embassy, and Mrs Malouff, who manned the station on a day-to-day basis, was competent rather than expert. But it did the job, allowing Angleton to listen in on phone calls and, with his insider knowledge of the various codes and passwords that were in use, hack into voicemails and e-mail accounts, building up a picture of who was saying what to whom and how they were all connected. He almost certainly wasn't getting the full story, there would be communication channels of which he was as yet unaware, but for the moment it was enough. Piece by piece by piece.

Angleton arrived this afternoon in a taxi; he went everywhere by taxi, never walked. Passing through the hotel's grand foyer, he stopped off at the ground floor pâtisserie and purchased two éclairs and some sort of outsize meringue with a slice of caramelized lemon on top, then headed towards the lifts.

He'd chosen the Intercontinental partly because it was a favourite with American tourists and his presence would attract little attention, mainly because it was a well-known hang-out for Cairo's high-class hookers. If anyone was following him – which he didn't think they were, but then you could never be too cautious – that's what they'd assume: he was here for the fun and games. It meant Mrs Malouff dressing up a bit, or down as she saw it, which she didn't like at all, but for the amount of money they were paying her she was prepared to grin and bear it.

The lift arrived, juddering slightly as he stepped in. He pressed the button for the 27th floor and moved back to make way for a group of elderly ladies in matching red T-shirts who between them pressed almost every other button on the panel.

'I'm afraid we're making it very slow for you,' one of them apologized as the doors closed and they started to rise, her accent pure Texas.

'The slower the better,' Angleton replied with a cheery grin. 'Gives me more time to enjoy you ladies' charming company.'

They clucked with pleasure, chattering away at Angleton, who really laid on the Southern charm, quipping and joking with them while at the back of his mind he mulled over his morning visit to the USAID building down in New Maadi, where Molly Kiernan worked and where he'd spent most of the day so far.

A large modernist structure of dark glass and polished steel, it sat in a gated, heavily guarded compound at the top end of Ahmed Kamel Street, looking out over an expanse of dusty, rock-strewn wasteland. Angleton had set up a meeting with the director, spinning him a line about how he was new in Public Affairs and believed they should be doing more to promote USAID's excellent work, greater synergy, added value, paradigm shift moving forward. A load of meaningless management guff which the director had absolutely lapped up, treating Angleton to an extended tour around the building, telling him everything he could possibly want to know about the organization, its employees, the various programmes it was involved in.

None of which remotely interested Angleton. He'd played along, though. He couldn't very well come right out and say: 'Tell me everything you know about Molly Kiernan.' Give the fish some line before starting to reel him in. And so he'd wandered around feigning interest, enthusing about the ground-water drainage projects and school exchange programmes, gaining the director's confidence before ever so slowly and ever so subtly nudging the conversation in the direction he wanted.

Kiernan was the hub, of that he was certain. Flin Brodie, Alex Hannen – they were both important, but it was Kiernan who was the key to Sandfire. He'd already been through her bungalow, one of his first ports of call when he'd got the brief, but it was clean, as he'd known it would be. She was too clever to leave anything lying around, too careful.

He hadn't got a whole lot more out of the director, which was in itself instructive. It confirmed what all his other lines of inquiry had indicated: that Molly Kiernan played her cards very close to her chest. She was one of USAID's longest serving employees, had been based in Cairo since late 1986, heading up various programmes out in the western desert: a family planning clinic in Kharga, an agricultural school in Dakhla, some sort of scientific research project over in the Gilf Kebir. The director wasn't entirely sure of the details.

'To be honest, Molly tends to get on with her own thing,' he had told Angleton. 'She files a six-monthly report and that's about it – no point in micro-managing someone that experienced. We just leave her to her own devices. Hey, how about I show you the new sewerage system we're funding down in Asyut? I've got a Powerpoint presentation back in my office.'

'Bring it on,' said Angleton.

As anticipated, the presentation had been mind-numbing. Fortunately he'd only had to sit through it for a few minutes before, as planned, the director had received a call from a journalist friend of Angleton's requesting a telephone interview. He'd waved away the director's apologies, said he'd just take a little wander around if that was OK, get a feel for the place. And headed straight down to Kiernan's office. It was at the end of a corridor on the third floor, locked of course, but he'd picked his way in, had a good rummage – nothing, absolutely nothing. He was out and back in the director's office before the latter had finished his interview.

Which had been the sum total of his visit. No new leads, no new information, a great big blank. Pretty much what he'd been expecting, although he'd had to make sure. He'd crack her in the end, of course, always did – that's why they employed him – but it wasn't going to be easy. Molly

Kiernan and Sandfire, it seemed, were shaping up to be one of his biggest challenges.

'This is us,' said the last two ladies in T-shirts as the lift doors opened on the 24th floor. 'It's been a real pleasure meeting you.'

'The pleasure's been all mine,' replied Angleton, pulling his mind back to the present. 'You ladies have yourselves a good holiday. And remember, go easy on the belly dancing.'

They giggled and stepped out into the hall. The doors closed and the lift rose silently to the 27th floor, where Angleton exited. He walked along a carpeted corridor, its walls hung with prints of nineteenth-century watercolours – camels and pyramids and men in turbans, typical tourist stuff – and stopped in front of a white wood door with a brass plate on it: room 2704. He gave five knocks – three swift, two slow – inserted a plastic card-key, opened the door and entered.

Inside everything was a chaos of technology: wires, cables, recorders, servers, computers, modems. The room's regular furniture had been shunted to one side to accommodate it all. Mrs Malouff sat at a desk against the far wall, one hand holding a pair of earphones to the side of her head while with the other she adjusted the dial of a large amplifier. A plump woman in her late forties, she sported an overly tight black cocktail dress and too much make-up, in keeping with her cover as a lady of the night, although in Angleton's opinion it would have to be a very dark night indeed before anyone found her remotely attractive. She gave him a sour-faced nod and, reaching across the desk, handed him a sheaf of transcripts of the day's recordings. He took them and went out onto the balcony. The Giza

Pyramids were just visible in the distance, hazy triangles hovering right on the very edge of the city. He didn't give them so much as a glance. Instead, sitting down on a chair beside a large satellite dish, he started working his way through the papers. Various calls to and from Brodie, most of them university business; a couple of anodyne messages on Kiernan's home answerphone, some stuff from the other taps he had in place, e-mails – none of it of any real use.

'This is it?' he called.

'Kiernan just had a call on her mobile,' replied Mrs Malouff. 'I haven't had time to transcribe it yet.'

She sounded harassed.

'Just play it to me.'

There was an annoyed hrumph followed by the click of buttons being pressed. A momentary burst of sound – high-pitched, gabbling, as the tape was rewound – then a female voice, tight, breathless, with a faint fanfare of car horns echoing in the background:

'Molly, it's Freya, Freya Hannen. I'm calling from a pay-phone. Something's . . . I need help. Someone tried to . . . I think they killed Alex . . .'

Angleton sat motionless, barely breathing, his eyes narrowing to slits as the message played itself through. When it was finished he instructed Mrs Malouff to rewind so he could hear it again.

'I'm outside the American University. I'm going to go in and try to find Flin Brodie. If he's not there I'll go to the Embassy. I think I'm in danger, I need to—'

A soft click as the recording ended. For a moment Angleton was still, exhaling slowly. Then, smiling, he fumbled in the box from the pâtisserie downstairs, removed an éclair and bit into it.

'Nice,' he murmured, small tongues of cream oozing from either side of his mouth. 'Very nice indeed.'

CAIRO – THE AMERICAN UNIVERSITY

The great temple complex of Iunu (the 'place of the pillars'), or to confer upon it its Greek name Heliopolis (the City of the Sun) was perhaps – nay, *sans doubte*! – the most important and top-hole religious scene in the whole of ancient Egypt. Today little retains of this glittering location, its once-paramount temples and shrines now obliterated into dust, interred profoundly beneath the Cairo suburbs of Ain Shams and Matariya (except for a single solitary obelisk of Senwosret I, so sad, so evocative). Hard it is to credit that for three whole thousand years, from the misty days of the Late Predynastic to the final advent of the Graeco-Roman, this unprepossessing joint was the pre-eminent cult-centre of the great sun-God Ra, home to the holy Ennead, worship-place of the Mnevis bull, the Benu bird, the mysterious and whacky Benben . . .

'For God's sake.' Flin Brodie let out a weary sigh and threw the essay onto his office desk. It was the first in a tall pile of papers he was due to mark by the following morning ('Explain and discuss the significance of Iunu/Heliopolis to the Ancient Egyptians'). As always with his students' work, they employed florid, antiquated prose to make up for the fact that English was not their first language. Thirty-three papers, each a minimum of four pages long. It looked like he was in for a long night.

He rubbed his eyes and stood. Crossing to the window, he gazed down at the university gardens where a group of students were lounging in wicker chairs, smoking and chatting. He could do with a drink – several drinks – but fought back the urge. The days when he used to keep a bottle of Scotch stashed away in the top drawer of his filing cabinet were long gone and, despite his lapse the other night, he intended to keep it that way.

Below, Alan Peach trotted into view, the students in the wicker chairs making yawning gestures as he passed, which annoyed Flin, even though he himself always joked about how boring Peach was. He watched his colleague disappear round a corner, then returned to his desk. He sat down, folded his hands behind his head and stared up at the ceiling.

He felt anxious, and it wasn't just at the prospect of having to mark thirty-three unreadable essays. Not full-on anxious – the sort of trembling, panic-ridden anxiety with which he was occasionally afflicted, when his guts would turn to lead and his entire world seemed to fold in on itself, crushing him beneath the unbearable weight of his past. No, this was a lesser order of worry, more a sort of carping background unease, a sense that something wasn't quite right. Although with the whole Sandfire thing nothing was ever going to be a hundred per cent normal.

The anxiety had been there since the other night, since that fat American had come up to him in the Windsor Hotel and made those pointed remarks about the Gilf Kebir. He felt in his jeans pocket and pulled out the card the man had given him: Cyrus J. Angleton, Public Affairs Officer, Embassy of the United States, Cairo.

If it had just been that one instance he would probably have dismissed it. The thing was, he had seen Angleton a couple of times since. Once, the day before yesterday, wandering through the grounds of the American University, and then again yesterday evening, in the stands of the Gezira Sporting Club where he went three or four times a week to train on the running track. The first of these could be explained away – there was nothing innately extraordinary about an American official visiting an American university. The Gezira sighting was more troubling. Admittedly he had only caught a brief glimpse of the man, way up at the back of the stands, and he'd disappeared as soon as Flin had started jogging towards him, but he was certain it had been Angleton. Same cream-coloured jacket. Same obese frame. There was no reason for him to have been there, none at all – as far as Flin was aware he was one of only a handful of westerners who ever used the club – and the fact that he had been was at the very least . . . unsettling.

Something else. It sounded crazy, but when he'd got back to his apartment yesterday afternoon, after returning from Alex's funeral, he'd had the curious feeling someone had been there. Nothing was missing or out of place. There were no obvious signs of intrusion, no disturbance of any sort to back up his suspicions. But a sixth sense had told him someone had been nosing around, and that someone had been Angleton. He'd gone downstairs, confronted Taib the caretaker about it. He'd denied all knowledge, although he'd had a furtive, guilty look about him. Then again Taib always had a furtive, guilty look about him so that wasn't in itself evidence of anything.

It was all wholly insubstantial, whispers and shadows. The anxiety was there nonetheless, and the fact was that nine times out of ten this sort of anxiety turned out to have some basis in reality. Maybe he was imagining things, maybe not. Either way he was keeping his eyes open, being even more cautious than usual. Maybe he should mention it to Molly, see what she thought.

He sat for a while longer. Then, giving his head a good shake as if to shunt his suspicions to the back of his mind, he leant forward, retrieved the essay and started to read again. He had managed only a couple of paragraphs before he was interrupted by a knock on the door.

'Could you come back later,' he called without looking up. 'I'm marking.'

The person obviously didn't hear him, because there was another knock.

'Could you please come back later,' he repeated, louder this time. 'I'm marking papers.'

'Flin?' The voice was hesitant, uncertain. 'It's Freya Hannen.'

'Good God!' He threw the essay onto the desk, strode across the room and flung open the door.

'Freya, what a wonderful surprise! I didn't think you were in Cairo for another . . .'

His voice tailed off as he clocked her mud-spattered jeans and trainers, the scratches on her arms and neck.

'Are you OK, Freya?'

215

She didn't speak, just stood there in the doorway.

'Freya?' He sounded concerned now. 'What's happened?'

Still she said nothing. He had just started to ask her a third time when the floodgates burst.

'Someone killed Alex,' she blurted out. 'And they tried to kill me too. Last night, in the oasis, a group of them, there were twins, they came in a helicopter and were torturing . . .'

She broke off, biting back tears, fighting to stay in control. Flin hovered a moment, not sure how to react, then stepped forward, wrapped an arm around her and drew her into the room. Nudging the door closed with his foot, he led her over to a chair and sat her down.

'It's OK,' he said gently. 'Calm down. You're safe.'

She wiped at her eyes, shrugging his arm away, a little too aggressively perhaps, but she was ashamed of her weakness, needed to assert herself. Flin stared down at her; Freya kept her eyes firmly on the floor as she struggled to regain her composure. Then, excusing himself, Flin left the room. He returned a couple of minutes later with a flannel and a steaming mug.

'Tea,' he said. 'The English solution to everything.'

She seemed to have calmed down a bit and gave a wan smile, accepting the cloth and dabbing at her bare arms.

'Thank you,' she said. 'I'm sorry, I didn't mean to . . .'

He held up a hand, indicating that no apology was necessary. Placing the mug on the corner of the desk he dragged his chair round so that he was sitting in front of her. He gave it a few moments before again asking what had happened.

'Someone tried to kill me,' she said, her voice firmer now.

'Last night, back in the oasis. They killed Alex too, it wasn't suicide.'

He half opened his mouth to speak, then thought better of it, letting her tell the story in her own way, in her own time. Freya laid aside the cloth, picked up the mug and sipped, gathering herself. Then she began to talk, going through everything that had happened the previous day, starting with Molly Kiernan's revelation about the morphine injection and moving on from there: Dr Rashid, the police station, the mysterious canvas bag, the twins, the chase through the oasis – everything. Flin sat listening, hunched forward, eyes narrowed in concentration, offering no comments, appearing outwardly calm although something in the intensity of his gaze, the way his hands were trembling slightly suggested her tale was affecting him more than he was admitting. When she had finished he asked to see the objects she had brought with her. She hefted her knapsack onto her knee and opened it, passing the items across one by one: camera, film canister, compass. Flin took each in turn, examining them.

'They killed Alex,' Freya repeated. 'And it's something to do with the man out in the desert and the things in his bag. Rudi Schmidt, that was the name in the wallet. Does that mean anything to you?'

Flin shook his head, still staring down at the camera, not meeting her eyes.

'Never heard of him.'

'Why would Alex be interested in his things? Why would someone kill her for them?'

'We don't know for sure that someone did kill her, Freya. We shouldn't jump—'

217

'I know,' she insisted. 'I saw them. I saw what they were doing to the old farmer. They murdered my sister, they injected her. And I want to know why.'

He looked up, holding her gaze. He seemed as if he was about to say something, but again thought better of it and just gave a reluctant nod.

'OK, I believe you. Someone killed Alex.'

Their eyes remained locked a moment, then he resumed his examination of the objects. He placed the camera and film on the desk and opened out the compass, sighting through the lens, tweaking its snapped brass sighting wire.

'Tell me about the other things in the bag again,' he said. 'The map, the clay obelisk.'

She described the mysterious symbols on the obelisk, the distances and compass bearings on the map. All the while Flin fiddled with the compass, appearing only to half listen to what she was saying although as before the barely perceptible trembling of his hand and the brightness of his eyes seemed to betray a greater degree of interest – of excitement, even – than his nonchalant manner was letting on.

'I think this Rudi Schmidt was trying to walk from the Gilf Kebir to Dakhla,' Freya said, staring across at the Englishman, trying to read him, work out whether or not he was taking her seriously. 'I know Alex was working in the Gilf Kebir, she told me about it in her letters. There's some connection between the two of them. I don't know what it is but there's definitely a connection and that's why she was killed.'

She picked up the camera and film canister, holding them up.

'And I think the answers are on here. That's why the men

218

in the oasis wanted the films. Because they'll tell us what's going on. We need to get them developed.'

Again there was silence. Flin continued to turn the compass over in his hand. Then, as if coming to a decision, he dropped it back into Freya's knapsack and stood.

'What we need is to get you somewhere safe,' he said. 'I'm taking you to the American Embassy.'

'After we get the films developed.'

'Now. I don't know what's going on, who these people are, but they're clearly dangerous, and the sooner you're off the streets the better. Come on, let's go.'

He held out a hand to help her up, but she remained where she was.

'I want to know what's on the films. They killed my sister and I want to know why.'

'Freya, those films have been lying out in the middle of the Sahara, probably for years. The chances of being able to develop them are a hundred to one. A thousand to one.'

'I still want to try,' she said. 'We do that first, then we go to the Embassy.'

'No.' His tone was sharp suddenly, abrupt. 'The films can wait, Freya. I want to get you somewhere safe. You don't know . . .'

He broke off.

'What?' she said. 'What don't I know?'

Although her eyes were red with exhaustion and her face pale and drawn, she was alert and energized, her gaze drilling into Flin.

'What don't I know?' she repeated.

He let out an exasperated sigh.

'Look, Alex was a very dear friend of mine . . .'

'She was my sister.'

'. . . and I owe it to her to make sure nothing happens to you.'

'And I owe it to her to find out why she was murdered.'

Their voices were starting to rise.

'I am not having you wandering around Cairo,' he snapped. 'Not after something like this has happened. I'm taking you to the Embassy.'

'After I get the films developed.'

'Now. You need protection.'

'Don't patronize me.'

'I am not bloody patronizing you! I'm trying to help you.' It was her turn to snap.

'I don't need helping and I don't need protecting. I need to know what's on those films, why someone tried to kill me. Why they killed Alex.'

'We don't know . . .'

'Yes we do know! I saw those men in her house, what they were capable of. They killed Alex and I'm going to find out why.'

She rose to her feet so violently she knocked the chair over. Shoving the camera and film into her knapsack, she threw open the door and crossed the corridor to the lifts. Flin came after her.

'Hang on, hang on.'

She ignored him, pressing her thumb against the lift's call button and holding it there.

'Freya, just trust me on this,' he pleaded. 'I live in Egypt, I know these sorts of people. Whatever else you owe Alex it's not to get yourself killed.'

The lift's wooden doors rattled open and she stepped

inside, pushing the button for the ground floor, still ignoring him.

'Freya, please, listen to me, I'm just trying . . .'

The doors started to close, but Flin blocked them with his foot.

'Christ, you're as pig-headed as your sister!'

'Believe me, Alex was the easygoing one,' she retorted angrily, poking at the buttons, trying to get the doors shut. There was a brief hiatus, Freya continuing to jab at the control panel, Flin to block the doors, before he suddenly let out a snort of amusement. She glared at him, then she too smiled. He took a step backwards, she followed him out of the lift and the doors clanked shut.

'Compromise,' he said. 'You humour me and go to the Embassy, I'll get the films developed. I've got a friend who works in the Cairo Antiquities Museum, in the photographic department, he'll be able to do them straight away. As soon as they're ready I'll bring them over. Deal?'

She pondered a moment, then nodded.

'Deal.'

'OK,' he said. 'Hold the lift, I just need to put some papers away and grab my wallet and mobile.

He disappeared into his office and the door closed behind him. The lift had by now been summoned by someone else and was clunking its way down to the ground floor again. Freya pressed the call button and wandered along the corridor, gazing first at a noticeboard – flyers for various concerts, a second-hand book sale, a Naguib Mahfouz symposium – and then out of a window. A faint sound of footsteps echoed up the stairs beside the elevator, barely audible behind the stairwell door.

Brodie's office was on the fourth and top floor of the building, in the English Department for some reason, and the window offered good views of the campus gardens – lawns, palm trees, herbaceous borders – and beyond, to the chaotic swirl of Midan Tahrir. She saw a group of students saunter past, followed by two burly men. Something about them – the rough faces, the lumbering, muscular gait – seemed out of place in the grounds of a university. She felt a sudden twinge of anxiety.

'Flin,' she called.

'Just coming,' came his voice.

The lift was rising again now, moving up through the building with a high-pitched whirr of machinery. She went over, pressed the call button again and came back to the window, wondering what was taking Flin so long. The two men were still down there in the gardens, standing around, one of them smoking, the other talking on a mobile phone. From the stairwell the sound of footsteps was growing louder. A rhythmic, echoing slap of shoes on linoleum, two or three people by the sound of it. Crossing the corridor again she opened the stairwell door and looked down. She could see handrails, a thin strip of stairs and, two floors below, a man's hand coming up the rails. A big, meaty hand half lost in a mass of chunky gold signet rings. Just like . . . She shrank back. Quietly closing the door, she ran to Flin's office and barged in.

'They're here!'

He was holding the telephone receiver in his hand: he seemed startled by her arrival.

'Freya! I was just—'

'They're here,' she repeated, cutting him off. 'The men

from the oasis. The ones who tried to kill me. They're coming up the stairs. And in the lift as well, I think.'

She was half expecting him to dither, ask if she was certain what she had seen, but he reacted instantly.

'Call you back,' he barked. Slamming the receiver down, he seized Freya's arm and pulled her back out into the corridor. As he did so there was a bump and a click and the lift doors started to slide apart. Again his reaction was immediate. Sweeping her protectively behind him he stepped forward. As the doors came fully open, a suited man emerged, gun in hand. Flin punched him, shockingly hard, his fist whipping out like a steel bolt and shattering the man's nose. He flew backwards, blood streaming across his mouth and chin, slamming into the lift's rear wall. Before he had even time to compute what was happening Flin had stepped forward and unleashed three more punches in rapid succession, one thumping into the man's stomach, doubling him up, one into his kidneys, knocking him sideways into the corner of the lift, and one into his jaw that sent him sprawling to the floor, where he lay dazed and groaning.

'Oh my God,' murmured Freya, stunned.

'I didn't get the impression he'd come for tea and a chat,' said Flin by way of explanation. Grabbing her arm again he steered her along the corridor and out of a fire door. As it closed behind them the stairwell door swung open.

They were at the top of a short flight of metal steps that led down to the roof of a slightly lower building below. They took them two at a time, leaping onto the roof's stone-tiled surface and running along a narrow walkway past a line of giant air-conditioning units.

'Where the hell did you learn to do that?' she gasped.

'Cambridge,' he replied, looking over his shoulder to make sure they weren't being followed. 'Double boxing Blue. The only thing that got me through three years of Middle Kingdom hieratic.'

They came to another set of steps. These took them up onto a much larger roof space with a small white dome at its centre and clusters of potted cacti grouped in its corners. As they started across it the fire door crashed open behind them. There were shouts and the thud of feet. They broke into a sprint, a group of students looking up in surprise as they careered past the bench on which they were sitting.

'You're late with your essay, Aisha Farsi,' called Flin, half turning and wagging a finger at a plump girl in a silk head-scarf. 'On my desk first thing in the morning.'

'Yes, Professor Brodie,' said the girl, trying to conceal the cigarette in her hand.

'And no smoking!'

They passed a prayer room, rows of men kneeling with their foreheads pressed to the carpeted floor, and ducked through another doorway and back into the building. Flin slammed the door and slid bolts across top and bottom to secure it.

'Quick!' he cried.

He led Freya along a dimly lit corridor, past a succession of classrooms and offices. The entire building seemed to vibrate as feet and fists started hammering at the door they had just secured. About halfway along the corridor a narrow staircase opened up to their right, flanked by a pair of water-coolers. They started down, only to backtrack as two figures appeared at the bottom – the men Freya had seen lingering in the grounds outside.

'Shit!' muttered Flin. Behind them the hammering grew louder and more furious. 'Shit, shit, shit!'

He looked wildly around. Seizing one of the water-coolers he shunted it across the floor and pitched it down the stairs at the men who were charging up from below. Their shouts were abruptly curtailed as the cooler slammed into them with a crash and a whoosh of water. The door still seemed to be holding.

'Come on!' Flin yelled, grabbing Freya's hand.

Sprinting on along the corridor, they barged through another fire exit and clattered down an external staircase to a courtyard beneath.

'Late for lectures again, Flin?' cried a familiar voice. 'Deary me, even the ancient Egyptians were better at time-keeping than you are!'

'Very funny, Alan,' Flin muttered, hurrying Freya past his colleague and into the campus canteen. They ran across the room, diners staring in astonishment as they slalomed between the rows of metal tables and chairs and through another doorway at the far end, back out into the university grounds. They slowed and stopped, heaving for breath. Almost immediately there were shouts to their left as three figures came charging round the side of the building, and more shouts behind as the twins burst into the canteen, bulldozing through the furniture, plates and cups cascading to the floor, diners yelling in protest.

'Christ, they're everywhere!' cried Flin, waving Freya down a trellis-covered walkway between tennis and volley-ball courts. They jinked right, then left along a broad alleyway lined with noticeboards and out through a tall iron gateway. They were on a street at the side of the university, cars and taxis rushing past in front of them.

Their pursuers had yet to turn into the alley, and for a brief moment Freya thought they would be able to lose themselves in the crowds thronging the pavement. Then, away to her right, she saw a gleaming black BMW parked up against the kerb. Two figures were leaning against it, both with the same menacing, rough-face appearance as those who were chasing them. An identical car sat directly opposite, outside a McDonald's; another two men were standing beside it, while a hundred metres to their left, loitering around a traffic light at the end of the street, were a further three heavies. A rush of feet, and their pursuers came in behind them, blocking the alley, slowing to a walk as they realized their quarry was trapped. Flin wrapped an arm protectively around Freya, drawing her into him.

'Bugger,' he said.

DAKHLA

At the beginning of Dakhla Oasis, to either side of the main desert highway, stand a pair of tall, rather crude metal sculptures in the shape of palm trees. Apart from a line of telegraph poles and a couple of road signs, they are the only man-made features in the otherwise empty landscape.

It was here that Zahir waited for his brother Said, his Land Cruiser parked up in a slim strip of shade at the foot of one of the sculptures, scrubby fields the only thing between him and the rolling dunes beyond. Ten minutes passed, then, in the distance, its shape warped and twisted by the heat, a motorbike appeared. The road along which it was travelling had dissolved into a glassy mirage so that it looked as if the rider was speeding across water. Closer and closer it came before suddenly tightening into clear focus, covering the last few hundred metres and skidding to a halt beside the Land Cruiser.

'Anything?' asked Zahir, leaning out of the window.

'*Mafeesh haga*,' replied Said, cutting the engine and brushing dust out of his hair. 'Nothing. I've been all the way down to Kharga and no one knows anything. Did you go to *el-shorty*? The cops?'

Zahir gave a dismissive snort.

'Idiots. They said she must have run off with Mahmoud Gharoub. Laughed in my face. They think because we're Bedouin we're fools.'

His brother grunted.

'You want me to keep looking? I could go up to al-Farafra, talk to people there?'

Zahir pondered a moment, then nodded.

'I'll keep asking around Dakhla. Someone must know something.'

His brother kick-started the bike, a battered Jawa 350, and, with a nod, roared away northwards.

Zahir watched him go, then started up the Land Cruiser. He didn't engage the gears immediately, just sat there with the clutch depressed and the engine running, gazing out across the desert. Fumbling in the pocket of his *djellaba*, he pulled out a green metal compass. Resting his wrists on the steering wheel he opened it and gazed at

PAUL SUSSMAN

the initials scrawled on the inside of the lid. AH. He fiddled
with the magnifying lens and rotating bezel, ran a finger
down the taut brass sighting wire, murmuring to himself.
Then, with a shake of his head, he pocketed the compass,
selected first and moved off, the Land Cruiser's wheels
skidding and churning on the gravel verge, dust billowing
behind it.

CAIRO

'What do we do?' asked Freya, looking desperately around.

'I'm really not sure,' said Flin, his fists clenched, his head
turning this way and that as he assessed the situation. Two
men leaning against a BMW along the street to their right;
two directly opposite, beside a second BMW; another three
at the traffic lights; and, coming up behind, five more, led
by the identical twins in their Armani suits and red-and-
white football shirts.

Their pursuers came to the university's gateway and
stepped through, stopping two metres away, separated from
Flin and Freya by a jostling eddy of pedestrians. They
pulled aside their jackets, revealing a glimpse of Glock
pistols. One of them pointed at Freya and grunted something in Arabic.

'What's he saying?' she asked.

'He told you to take off your knapsack and throw it over
to him,' replied Flin.

'Should I?'

'Seems we don't have much choice.'

The twin repeated his request, louder this time. Threatening.

'Take it slowly,' said Flin.

As Freya began to remove the knapsack, a taxi – a battered black-and-white Fiat 124 – pulled up at the kerb behind them. She got the bag off, clutching it in her hands, reluctant to let it go.

'*Yalla nimsheh!*' called the twin, waving at her to throw the knapsack over. '*Bisoraa, bisoraa!*'

The taxi driver had now got out of the car, leaving the driver door open and the engine running as he helped an elderly woman out of the back seat and onto the pavement. Flin's eyes jinked in that direction, as did Freya's.

'*Bisoraa!*' shouted the twin, losing patience: both he and his brother were opening their jackets right up, grasping their pistols.

'Better give it to them,' said Flin, turning to Freya and reaching for the knapsack, his eyes again flicking towards the taxi as the driver moved round to the boot, opened it and started heaving at an enormous suitcase.

'Come on, Freya, this isn't a game!' Flin's voice was unnecessarily loud, exaggeratedly so. 'Just give them the bag.'

He tried to pull the knapsack from her grasp. Freya sensed what he was doing and held on to it, buying them a few extra seconds as the driver manhandled the case onto the tarmac and slammed the boot shut. As he did so Flin gave the knapsack a yank, bringing his face right up against Freya's.

'Back seat,' he murmured. 'I'll drive.'

He pulled away again, shaking the bag and remonstrating

229

theatrically before suddenly letting the bag go and barging to his right, sending a man balancing a large tray of *aish baladi* on his head sprawling backwards into the twins. There were shouts, flailing arms and a loud clatter as the tray hit the pavement. In that brief instant of confusion, Freya dived headlong into the back of the taxi. Flin threw himself into the driver's seat. He didn't even bother closing the door, just flipped the knapsack over his shoulder to Freya, slammed the car into gear and thumped his foot down on the accelerator. The taxi's owner gazed on in mute bewilderment as his livelihood screeched away in front of him.

'Hold tight!' yelled Flin, his tall frame crushed into the limited space behind the steering wheel. He swerved round a bus, its right rear corner clipping the taxi's two open doors and slamming them shut. Yanking the gearstick into second and then third, he wove through the traffic, picking up speed, the taxi's meter ticking madly on the dashboard.

Freya scrambled into a sitting position, looking back. The twins were at the kerbside frantically waving at one of the BMWs while across the street the other was already moving off, smoke bursting from beneath its skidding tyres.

'They're coming!' she cried.

The taxi was now almost at the traffic lights at the end of the street, the vast chaotic expanse of Midan Tahrir opening up in front of them. The signals were on red, cars idling at the stop-line, a white-uniformed policeman standing in the middle of the road with one arm raised. Flin veered left into an empty lane and mounted the kerb, scattering the three heavies who were standing there and flying straight through the lights. There was a cacophony of hooting and a series of shrill blasts from the policeman's whistle as they slewed round the corner and into the traffic running up the side of the square. They skidded, straightened, skidded again, slamming into the flank of a pick-up truck which in turn cannoned into a minibus, forcing it off the road and into a fruit stall. Pedestrians leapt out of the way, shouting and gesticulating; oranges and watermelons cascaded across the ground like giant marbles.

'Anyone hurt?' called Flin.

'I don't think so,' replied Freya, staring back at the mayhem, her stomach lurching.

He nodded and sped on, feet dancing a mad jig across the brake, clutch and accelerator pedals, right hand ricocheting back and forth between the steering wheel and the gear-stick. Behind them one of the black BMWs came tearing around the corner. The second followed a moment later, the two cars slaloming through the traffic in fierce pursuit, other vehicles swerving out of their path, beeping furiously. More powerful than the old Fiat, the BMWs rapidly gained on Flin and Freya, closing to within twenty metres. Flin braked and wrenched the steering wheel to the right, skidding them out of the square and onto a broad street of what must once have been ornate colonial buildings. Signs flashed past – Memphis Bazaar, Turkish Airlines, Pharaonic American Life Assurance Company – as the taxi's speed-ometer strained to the limit of its gauge before Flin again stamped on the brakes, wheeling them around a large traffic island with a statue of a man in a fez at its centre and off along another street. The BMWs disappeared for a moment, then swept back into view.

'They're too fast,' cried Flin, shooting another look into the mirror. 'We're never going to outrun them.'

As if to emphasize the point the lead BMW put on a sudden burst of speed. Surging forward it slammed into their rear bumper, catapulting a screaming Freya into the back of Flin's seat.

'You OK?' he called.

'OK,' she said, tapping him on the shoulder, trying to sound less shaken than she was.

The BMW dropped back, sped forward and shunted them again, then swung out into the empty oncoming lane and moved in alongside them.

'He's got a gun!' she warned Flin as the man in the front passenger seat aimed a pistol through the open window: his face was close enough for her to make out his yellow teeth and a mole beneath his right eye.

'Hold on!'

Flin hit the brakes, the BMW flying ahead as he spun the Fiat into a side street. Swerving to avoid a group of school-girls, he smashed through a nut vendor's trolley – showers of nuts and seeds clattering down onto the windscreen like hail – before straightening and speeding on. There was a blare of sirens, although in the confusion it was impossible to tell from which direction it was coming.

'The other one's still with us!' cried Freya as the second BMW roared round the corner. It raced towards them, the twins leaning out of the windows and shooting. Pedestrians scattered along the pavements, screaming and diving for cover. One bullet punched out the taxi's back window, showering Freya with glass. Another whizzed past Flin's shoulder and shattered the dashboard meter.

'Guess I'll have to give you this ride for free,' he joked grimly, fighting to control the vehicle as it careered over a crossroads directly in front of an oncoming bus. Freya reeled across the back seat, glass crunching beneath her; cars dominoed into each other as the bus braked sharply to avoid a collision.

'At least we've lost the other one,' she shouted, righting herself again, her hair whipping madly in the wind.

'If only,' growled Flin, veering as the first BMW came flying back into view out of a side street, tyres screeching as it swept across the dusty tarmac and fell in behind the twins' car. The wail of sirens suddenly grew louder as first one, then two, then three police Daewoos joined the chase.

'For Christ's sake,' cursed Flin as a police motorcycle also locked onto their tail before almost immediately skidding, tumbling onto its side and crashing into a stack of wooden pigeon cages. Freya caught a brief glimpse of the rider clambering dazedly to his feet, feathers swirling around him like dirty snow, and then they rounded a corner and he was gone.

They were now speeding away from the centre of the city. Turn-of-the-century European architecture gave way to ugly concrete blocks interspersed with mosques and medieval-looking buildings with chunky masonry and intricately arched windows. The traffic started to grow heavier, choking itself into ever-tighter jams and tailbacks and forcing Flin into constant changes of direction as he struggled both to keep ahead of their pursuers and to avoid hitting pedestrians and other vehicles. Two of the police cars collided while trying to overtake the rear BMW, drinkers scrambling aside as one of them spun into the

233

furniture at the front of a café sending tables and chairs cartwheeling in all directions. The other hit the kerb and flipped over onto its roof, gliding down the street in a shower of sparks before thudding into a lamppost. The third Daewoo managed to keep up with them for a few turns longer before it too crashed out of the chase, misjudging a corner and ploughing into the back of a stationary cattle truck, terrified cows stampeding over the truck's tailgate and off down the road. Other police vehicles took up the pursuit, sirens blaring, lights flashing, but the pace was too intense and one by one they also dropped away and were lost. The BMWs alone stuck with Flin and Freya, remorselessly, mirroring their every twist and turn, refusing to be shaken off.

They hurtled into a square beneath a wall of towering ramparts and from there into a perilously narrow side street, crowds parting in panic as they bounced along the street's potholed surface. Shops and stalls rushed by to either side, a butcher's kiosk piled high with a mound of slippery pink offal, enormous sacks exploding with fluffy white cotton. The street got narrower and narrower, clogging them in, making it impossible to dodge the gunfire crackling from the BMWs behind.

'We've got to get out of here!' yelled Freya.

Flin didn't reply, just stared fixedly ahead, hammering the horn as they sped towards a massive stone gateway, its central arch flanked by a pair of rearing minarets. The gateway was undergoing some sort of restoration work, its façade covered with a matrix of rickety wooden scaffolding, the planking piled high with sacks of cement and huge blocks of stone.

'They're trying to take out the tyres!' Freya's voice was desperate, her gaze jerking back and forth between the BMWs and the gateway. 'Please, Flin, you've got to get off this street! You have to do it now!'

Still he said nothing, his eyes locked on the scaffolding, his jaw set. He glanced in the rearview mirror, eased off the accelerator a fraction to draw the BMWs in even closer and then forced it down again, tilting the steering wheel to the right. Freya screamed.

'What the fuck are you—'

'Duck and hold on!' he shouted, smashing the Fiat directly through the wooden props supporting the scaffolding. The structure teetered, slumped and began to collapse. The Fiat and the lead BMW just made it through before the entire structure came crashing down in billows of dust and debris, crushing the second BMW like an egg beneath a sledgehammer.

'And then there was one,' said Flin.

He braked and swung left, zigzagging through a labyrinth of ever-widening streets and up onto an elevated carriageway that led back towards the city centre. Although the road was busy, the traffic was still moving swiftly. With plenty of gaps between vehicles Flin was able to push the taxi up to 100 km/hour, swerving back and forth across the three lanes as he threaded his way through the maze of cars and trucks, the towers and advertising hoardings of central Cairo gradually crowding in around them. The BMW may have been faster, but the Fiat – small, box-like, easy to manoeuvre – was better suited to these tight conditions. Slowly and inexorably they started to pull away, the twins falling further and further behind. By the time they eventually left the carriageway, speeding down a slip road and back into the top end of Midan Tahrir, where the chase had started, they had put the best part of four hundred metres between them and their pursuers.

'I think we're going to make it,' said Flin, glancing over his shoulder.

'Watch out!'

He swung round, slamming on the brakes: the Fiat skidded to a halt a few centimetres away from the back of a pick-up truck piled with cauliflowers. Ahead, stretching what looked like the entire length of the square, was a solid jam of stationary traffic, blocking all three lanes. He crunched into reverse, thinking to get them into the outside lane from where they could U-turn away from the jam. But a tourist coach came in directly behind them and another one in the outside lane to their left, a cement lorry completing the blockade as it rumbled in alongside them to their right. Suddenly they weren't going anywhere.

'Bollocks,' spat Flin, pounding a fist on the steering wheel. And then: 'Out!'

He threw open his door and swung his feet onto the tarmac. Freya grabbed her knapsack and followed. Ignoring the shouts of the other drivers, they sprinted through the traffic and up onto the pavement.

They were at the northern end of Midan Tahrir, beside an enormous orangey-pink building surrounded by iron railings. Flin looked back, trying to get a fix on their pursuers, then grabbed Freya's hand and hurried her around the railings and through a gateway into the gardens at the front of the building. There were ornamental ponds, an array of ancient Egyptian sculpture and statuary, and crowds of tourists and schoolchildren. White-uniformed policemen stood around, cradling AK-47s. No one took any notice of them. Flin hesitated, eyes scanning back and forth, trying to decide what to do. A row of glass-fronted kiosks stood just inside the gateway, and one of them had just become free. He went over to it and purchased two tickets.

'Quick,' he said, steering Freya through the gardens and up the steps towards the building's arched entrance. As they came to the top she grasped his arm and pointed.

'Look!'

Back in the square they could just make out the twins' bobbing heads, the two of them jogging along between the lines of stationary vehicles, still some distance away from the abandoned taxi. They watched for a moment, then went quickly inside.

When Romani Girgis was angry he would shout and break things. When he was very angry he would hurt people, the suffering of others providing a welcome release from his own troubles. When he was truly incandescent, however, the sort of volcanic, white-hot fury that might cause other people to froth at the mouth or scream and rant, something curious happened to him. He would feel cockroaches. Hundreds upon hundreds of cockroaches crawling all over his face and limbs and torso, just as they had done when he was a kid back in Manshiet Nasser.

There were no cockroaches, of course, it was all in his head. Despite that, the sensation was horribly real – the loathsome tickle of their feelers, the scampering of their legs. He'd seen doctors, and analysts, and hypnotists and even, in his desperation, an exorcist. None of them had been able to help. Still the insects came, just as they had done when he was a child, and just as they did today when he got the call to say they'd lost the girl.

It started as a vague, barely noticeable prickling feeling across his cheeks and, as the call went on and the details came out, swiftly built and intensified until there was no part of him that was free of it, no nook or cranny of his body that hadn't been invaded: cockroaches on his skin, cockroaches in his mouth, cockroaches underneath his eyelids, cockroaches creeping their verminous way up into his anus – his entire being swamped with cockroaches.

Scratching and slapping at himself, trembling uncontrollably, he finished the conversation and made one further call, informing the person at the other end what had happened, instructing them to do everything they could to track the girl down. Then, throwing aside the phone, he rushed to the nearest shower room. Still fully clothed, he leapt beneath the nozzle and turned the jets on full, slapping at himself as though he was on fire.

'Get away!' he screamed. 'Get off me! Disgusting! Disgusting, disgusting, disgusting!'

Dabbing at his forehead with a handkerchief, Cy Angleton waddled up the steps to the main entrance of the American University, pausing a moment to take in the half-dozen police cars parked on the street outside before moving forward to the security desk blocking the threshold.

'The university is closed,' the guard on the desk informed him. 'No one allowed in or out.'

There had been an incident, he explained, the police were investigating, Angleton would have to come back later once the all-clear had been given.

Angleton was used to dealing with these sort of minor officials – all part of the job – and knew from experience there were two ways you could go: turn on the charm and try to sweet-talk them, or play the authority card and intimidate them into giving you what you needed. He eyed the man, sizing him up, calculating which option was going to work best in this case, then launched in.

'I know there's been a goddam incident,' he snapped, whipping out his ID and thrusting it forward. 'Cyrus J. Angleton, US Embassy. Just had a call from the principal. Apparently one of our nationals was involved.'

He was expecting at least a bit of resistance. As it was, the man crumpled immediately, apologizing and waving him straight through the rectangular arch of a metal detector which clearly didn't work because he had keys and pens and all sorts of other metal shit in his pockets and it didn't go off, not even a peep.

'You wanna get this thing fixed,' he said, banging a fist against the side of the machine. 'I'm not having American lives put in danger because your goddam security equipment doesn't work. Understand?'

The man whined an apology, said he'd get someone to look at it immediately.

'Do that,' said Angleton, glaring at him before turning and setting off across a long vestibule. Heavy brass lamps hung from the ceiling, their yellow glow giving the place a curiously soporific, dreamlike feel. At the end of the vestibule he climbed a couple of steps to the lift, which also seemed to be out of order. Forced to take the stairs, he puffed and wheezed his way up to the fourth floor.

There was a crowd of police up here, standing around not seeming to do very much. A line of yellow tape stretched across the lift's open door; there were bloodstains on the floor and back wall. He took all this in in a glance, then strode purposefully across to Brodie's office and threw open the door, as if he had every right to be there. Stepping inside, he pushed the door closed. Not one of the police said anything or tried to stop him.

He wasn't expecting to find anything in the office and he didn't. The one potentially useful piece of information came when he pressed the phone's redial button to discover that the last call Brodie had made had been to a mobile. He didn't bother taking the number down, didn't need to, recognized it instantly: Molly Kiernan.

He snooped around, opening drawers, poking in filing cabinets, having a quick look through the essays piled on Brodie's desk, then went back out into the corridor. Two newcomers had appeared while he was in the office, plain-clothes detectives – you could always tell. One of them asked what he was doing.

'Just leaving some essays for Professor Brodie. We teach a class together. Say, is everything OK? There's a lot of police around.'

No, everything wasn't OK, said the detective. He shouldn't be up here, this was a crime scene.

'A crime scene!' Angleton was all wide-eyed shock and amazement. 'Oh my goodness! Was somebody hurt?'

That's what they were looking into, the detective explained.

'Oh my goodness,' Angleton repeated. 'Please tell me nothing's happened to Flin. Professor Brodie.'

They weren't yet sure what had happened, the detective replied, although yes, Professor Brodie did seem to have been involved in some way.

'Oh my goodness!' said Angleton a third time, clasping a hand to his chest, for all the world the bumbling academic. 'Can I be of any assistance? I mean Flin's a good friend of mine, we work in the same department. If there's anything I can do, anything at all . . .'

And from there it was all plain sailing, like stealing candy from a baby. The detective started asking him questions about Brodie, he improvised the answers, playing the concerned friend. In the process he wheedled out of the detective everything they knew about the afternoon's events – Brodie's female companion, the chase, the twins, the taxi theft, all of it.

'And no one has any idea where they are now?' Angleton asked innocently. 'You're sure about that?'

Absolutely sure, the detective replied. If Professor Brodie happened to get in touch . . .

'You'll be the first to know,' the American assured him. 'Flin's a dear friend and I know he'll want to clear this up as soon as possible.'

Afterwards he went out onto the roof and walked the route of the chase, ending up at the side gate on the far side of the university campus, which also had a yellow police tape stretched across it. He got chatting to various people along the way, picking up a couple more titbits of information – the girl's knapsack was clearly important – but nothing that radically altered the picture the detective had given him or, more importantly, provided any clue as to where Brodie and the girl might be. He wandered around for a while longer, then decided to call it a day. Ducking under the police tape tied across the gate he set off down the street, prodding a number into his mobile and holding it to his ear.

THE CAIRO MUSEUM

'This is the museum, isn't it?' said Freya as they passed through the security point inside the entrance, the adrenalin of the car chase still pumping through her system. 'The Antiquities Museum.'

It was a statement of the obvious, given the array of statues and sarcophagi displayed all around them, and Flin simply nodded, leading her forward beneath a high domed rotunda. Long galleries ran away to right and left; ahead, down a set of steps, stretched a cavernous glass-ceilinged atrium. From its far end two colossal seated figures – one male, one female – gazed stonily back at them.

'We'll lose ourselves here for a while and then take a taxi to the Embassy,' said Flin. 'Preferably driven by someone other than me.'

He glanced at her, then started off along the left-hand gallery. Freya remained where she was.

'We can get the films developed,' she called after him.

He stopped and turned.

'You said you had a friend who works here, in the photographic department.' She held up the knapsack. 'We can get the films developed.'

She was expecting him to argue. Instead, after considering a moment, he nodded. Coming back, he took her arm and steered her in the opposite direction, into the right-hand gallery.

'Beats looking at Neolithic fish hooks, I suppose,' he said.

They walked past a succession of giant sarcophagi – granite and black basalt for the most part – their surfaces covered in neat ranks of hieroglyphs. Groups of uniformed schoolchildren were sitting on the floor beside them, drawing.

'All Late Period and Graeco-Roman,' he explained as they went, waving an arm around like a tour guide. 'Quality wise very inferior.'

'Fascinating,' muttered Freya.

At the end of the gallery was a security desk with a walk-through metal detector beside it. Flin spoke to the guard in Arabic, flashed some sort of card and led Freya past the detector and through a doorway. They were out of the public area of the museum and in what looked like an administrative section, rooms full of desks and filing cabinets opening up on either side. They followed a short corridor and climbed a spiral staircase, emerging into a cluttered, open-plan space with grimy windows and floor-to-ceiling shelves lined with rows of labelled box files.

'Papyri, Ostraca, Vases, Coffins,' read Freya, her gaze lingering a moment on the files before widening out to take in the rest of the space. There were half a dozen filing cabinets, a scatter of dilapidated furniture, a rusty paper guillotine and everywhere, stacked in corners and on shelves and underneath tables, a jumble of photographic and developing equipment, most of it old-fashioned and out of date, all of it shabby and covered in dust. Light-boxes, projectors, enlargers, teetering piles of Forte black-and-white photographic paper. It felt, Freya thought, more like a junk shop than a photographic studio.

A man sat at a desk on the far side of the room – plump, curly haired, with thick round glasses and a garish Hawaiian shirt – talking on the phone. They hovered, waiting for him to finish his conversation. When he showed no sign of doing so Flin gave an exaggerated cough. The man looked up, saw them and broke into a broad smile. Swiftly terminating the call, he slammed the phone down and bounced to his feet.

'Professor Flin!' he cried, bustling over. 'How are you, my friend?'

'*Kwais, sahebee*,' replied Flin, kissing him on each cheek. 'Freya, Majdi Rassoul – the finest archaeological photographer in Egypt.'

Freya and Majdi shook hands.

'Watch him,' the Egyptian warned, grinning. 'He's a terrible heart-breaker!'

Freya said she'd bear it in mind.

They made some polite small talk, Majdi launching into an extended description of how he'd recently unearthed a box of hitherto unpublished Antonio Beato glass negatives – 'A hundred and fifty years old and never seen before! Gold dust, absolute gold dust!' – before Flin steered the conversation round to the purpose of their visit.

'I need a favour,' he said. 'Some photos developed. Quickly, if possible. Can you do that?'

'I would hope so,' replied Majdi. 'We're a photographic studio after all.'

Flin nodded at Freya, who opened her knapsack and handed Majdi the camera and plastic canister.

'They've been out in the desert,' said Flin. 'Probably for years, so I'm not holding out much hope.'

'Depends what you mean by "in the desert",' said the Egyptian, turning the objects over in his hand. He examined the Leica first, then the canister, popping its cap and shuffling the used roll of film into his palm. 'If they've been sitting on top of a dune in direct sunlight then yes, the film'll be fried, impossible to develop. If they were covered up, on the other hand . . .'

'They were in a canvas bag,' put in Freya.

'In that case we might get something from them. I'll do the roll first – the film in the camera might be more complicated. Will you be wanting the develop-while-you-wait service?'

Flin smiled.

'That would be perfect.'

'Deluxe develop-while-you-wait with complimentary tea?'

'Even more perfect.'

Majdi shouted down the spiral staircase and, leaving the camera on the desk where he'd been sitting, crossed to a door on the far side of the gallery and opened it. Inside was a darkroom: sink, developing tank, drying cabinet, light-box, shelves lined with bottles of chemicals.

245

'Give me twenty minutes,' he said, throwing the roll of film in the air and catching it. He winked, stepped into the room and closed the door behind him. 'And no smooching on the sofa!' came his muffled voice.

For a moment they stood there, embarrassed by this last comment. Then Flin reached out and touched Freya's shoulder.

'You OK?'

She nodded. She felt calmer now, her pulse settling after the frenzy of the car chase.

'Sure?'

Another nod

'You?' she asked.

He opened up his hands.

'I'm in a museum. Couldn't be better.'

Freya smiled, more in acknowledgement of his attempt at humour than because she was amused by it. Their eyes held, neither of them quite sure what to say, how to vocalize the shock of what they'd just been through.

'Do you know who those men were?' she asked at last.

'Not the Marx Brothers, that's for sure.'

This time she didn't smile. Flin gave her shoulder a reassuring squeeze.

'It'll be OK,' he said. 'Trust me. We'll get out of this.'

They stood a moment longer, staring at each other. Then, as if uneasy with the intimacy, they broke away. Freya threw herself into a leather armchair and began flicking through a book of aerial images of Egyptian monuments; Flin wandered over to the box files lining the wall and ran his finger along their peeling sepia labels, pulling one out at random – Bas-Reliefs – and rummaging distractedly through its contents. An elderly man appeared with two glasses of tea, spooning sugar into each one before shuffling away again. A sparrow fluttered in through a window, perched a moment on top of a fan and swooped back out the way it had come. Twenty minutes passed. Twenty-five. Thirty. In the end it was almost three-quarters of an hour before the darkroom door opened again and Majdi put his head out.

'Success?' asked Flin, moving towards him.

His friend was frowning. He seemed rather less jovial than he had been before.

'Well I got the pictures developed, if that's what you mean, although I have to say . . . You know, I don't want to seem like a prude here, but . . .'

He shook his head and beckoned them over.

'You'd better come and see for yourselves.'

Flin and Freya glanced at each other and followed him into the darkroom. The light was on now, a single bare bulb hanging from the ceiling. Majdi opened the drying cabinet and removed a long strip of film negative. He laid it out over the light-box and switched off the overhead bulb while at the same time flicking a switch on the side of the box. A fluorescent glow welled up through its Perspex surface, illuminating the images.

'I mean, I'm as broad-minded as the next man,' he huffed, stepping aside to make room. 'But really . . . this is a museum, not a sex club.'

They leant over and stared at the negatives. It took them a moment to work out exactly what they were looking at. When they did both of them gawped in horror.

'Bloody hell,' murmured Flin.

PAUL SUSSMAN

The pictures – black-and-white – were of a large, not unattractive woman in stockings, suspenders, G-string and a half-cup bra, although after a couple of shots the bra and G-string disappeared, revealing breasts, luxuriantly-haired pudenda and, the focus of most of the shots, an extremely ample backside. She seemed to be in a hotel room, on a bed, sometimes lying on her back with her legs athletically akimbo, mostly kneeling with her posterior towards the camera, hand scooped between her thighs, probing at herself with an unnaturally fat banana.

'I'll never eat banoffee pie again,' said Majdi gloomily, fiddling with his glasses. 'What in God's name possessed you to take . . . ?'

'I didn't bloody take them!' Flin was outraged. 'Jesus, Majdi, you don't think I'd . . .'

'We don't know who took them,' said Freya, sounding rather less put out than the two men. 'The camera was found in the desert. We were hoping the pictures would tell us who the owner was, what he was doing out there.'

'Exploring, by the look of it,' said Majdi, twisting his head to one side as he assessed a particularly contorted posture. 'How on earth does she . . . ?'

'Don't,' snapped Flin. 'Just don't.'

There were thirty-six shots in total and they went through them one by one. Freya got about halfway before concluding it was a waste of time and going back out into the waiting area. Flin remained, hunched over the light-box. Majdi pottered around behind him as he worked his way methodically through the remaining images, peering intently at each in turn in the vain hope it might reveal

248

something useful. By the time he came to the last few shots even Flin had accepted it was a lost cause. He was starting to straighten when, suddenly, he tensed and bent down again, face hovering just a couple inches above the box's Perspex surface.

'What's she doing now?' asked Majdi, noting his interest and leaning over beside him.

Flin ignored the question.

'I need a print of this,' he said, tapping the very last image on the roll, his voice urgent suddenly, excited.

'Flin, you're an old friend, but this really isn't the place . . .'

'No bananas, Majdi, I promise.'

The Egyptian let out an exasperated sigh.

'OK, OK.'

He whipped a sheet of Ilford photographic paper from a pile on one of the shelves and, ushering Flin out of the darkroom, pulled the door closed.

'Did you find something?' asked Freya, looking up.

'Maybe, maybe not,' said Flin. 'Majdi's doing a print now.'

'What is it?'

'Let's wait for the print.'

She tried to push him further, but he batted away her questions and paced up and down before returning to the darkroom door and banging on it.

'Are you ready?'

'Give me a chance!' came the muted reply.

'How long?'

'Ten minutes.'

Flin resumed his pacing, up and down, up and down,

glancing constantly at the clock on the wall, tapping a hand against his thigh until finally the darkroom door opened and Majdi emerged, a glossy A4 sheet clasped in his hand. Flin walked swiftly over and practically snatched the print from his friend's hand. Freya looked over Flin's shoulder.

She didn't know what she had been expecting – dunes, perhaps. Or a picture of Rudi Schmidt, some indication of why her sister should have been interested in him, why that interest should have got her killed. The photograph provided none of the answers for which she was hoping. It didn't even seem to have been taken in the desert. Some sort of enormous stone gateway or entrance, that's what it showed, overgrown with lush eruptions of vegetation as if the building to which it gave access had long ago been abandoned and given over to nature. She leant in closer, trying to make sense of it, taking in the rectangular wooden doors, the outline of a bird carved into the lintel above them, the high trapezium-shaped towers to either side. For a moment she stared; then reached out and pointed to the image carved into the face of each tower: an obelisk enclosing a curious cross-and-looping-line motif.

'I've seen that before,' she said. 'On the clay obelisk in Rudi Schmidt's bag, the one I told you about.'

Flin just gazed down. The photo trembled slightly in his hand.

'*The city of Zerzura is white like a pigeon*,' he whispered.'*And on the door of it is carved a bird.*'

'What does that mean?'

He didn't respond. Instead, crossing the room, he snatched up the Leica, brandishing it at Majdi.

'We need to develop the film in here,' he said. 'We need to get it out of the camera and develop it.'

'Flin, I'm delighted to help but I do have other things I'm supposed to be—'

'We have to develop this film, Majdi. I need to know what's on it. Now. Please.'

The Egyptian blinked, rattled by his friend's brusqueness. Then, with a nod, he took the camera.

'If it's that important.'

'It is that important,' said Flin. 'Believe me.'

Majdi turned the camera in his hand.

'It's probably going to take longer than the other roll,' he said. 'The rewind's buggered, the casing's probably going to be full of sand and grit – Leicas are notoriously bad for that sort of thing – and even if I can get the film out there's no guarantee . . .'

He shrugged.

'I'll see what I can do. Give me forty minutes. I'll know by then whether its salvageable or not.'

He turned back towards the darkroom. Flin called after him.

'Thanks, *sahebee*.' He paused, then added: 'And sorry for being a wanker.'

Majdi waved a hand.

'You're an Egyptologist. Being a wanker goes with the territory.'

He turned, winked and disappeared into the darkroom, leaving the two of them alone again.

'Do you want to tell me what's going on?' asked Freya. 'What that place is in the picture?'

Flin was staring at the photograph again, his head

shaking slightly as if he could barely believe what he was looking at, the faintest of smiles playing around the corners of his mouth. There was a long silence.

'I can't be absolutely certain,' he said eventually. 'Not without seeing what's on the other film.'

'But you think you know.'

Another silence, then:

'Yes. Yes, I do.'

He looked up at her. Although his face was pale and drawn, his eyes were gleaming brightly, a combination that seemed to amplify his good looks.

'I think it might be somewhere called Zerzura,' he said.

'Which is where, exactly?'

To Freya's annoyance, he didn't answer. He looked back at the photo, then at his watch. Coming to a decision, he pulled his mobile out of his jeans pocket and dialled a number with his thumb, moving away to the far side of the room, out of earshot. She threw up her hands as if to say 'What the hell's going on?' but he just held a palm towards her and spoke rapidly into the phone. When he was finished he pocketed the mobile, crossed the room again and took her arm.

'What do you know about ancient Egypt?' he asked, leading her back to the spiral staircase.

'About as much as I do about quantum physics,' she replied.

'Time for a quick crash course.'

Yasmin Malouff had a secret, one that she kept from her parents, her siblings, her husband Hosni and also her American employer. She smoked.

As secrets go it wasn't especially earth-shattering. It was not, however, in her opinion, the sort of thing a lady should flaunt. While Hosni would probably not have been overly perturbed had he found her out, her family would most certainly not approve. And Mr Angleton had made it clear from the outset that he would not tolerate smoking on the job. She was welcome to do anything else she wanted in the hotel room, he had told her – 'Christ, you can even work in the buff if it'll help you concentrate' – but cigarettes were a strict no-no.

She wasn't a heavy smoker – just three or four Cleopatra Lights a day – and it was no great hardship to stay off them while she was manning the listening station. Only in the late afternoon did the craving become unbearable. Then she would lock up the room, take the lift down to the floor below and, positioning herself at the end of the corridor beside an open window, light up.

Today, for some reason, the craving was even stronger than usual. Having finished one cigarette she immediately lit another, her normal five-minute break as a result expanding into ten. Then she discovered she was out of mints and had to take the lift all the way down to the shop on the ground floor to restock. By the time she got back to the room, her breath suitably disguised, the traces of ash dusted off her dress, she had been gone for the best part of twenty minutes. Which wouldn't have been a problem had a call not come through to Molly Kiernan's mobile in her absence: the red warning light on the recorder that was monitoring that particular number was blinking furiously at her as she stepped through the door.

Any other call to any other number would not have been an issue. Following his visit earlier that afternoon, Mr Angleton had specifically told her that he was to be informed immediately of any traffic to Kiernan's Nokia. Slamming the door and throwing her handbag onto the bed, Yasmin Malouff hurried across to the recorder. Snatching up her notepad and pen, she pressed the Play button, sitting herself down ready to transcribe. A hiss of static, then a voice, hushed and urgent:

'Molly, it's Flin. I'm in the Egyptian Museum. With Freya Hannen. We're getting some photos developed – I'll explain later – and then I'm taking her to the American Embassy. Can you meet us there? This is urgent, Molly, really urgent. OK, thanks.'

End of call.

She played it through again, making sure she'd got the transcription right, that she hadn't missed or misheard anything. Then, picking up the special telephone Angleton had had installed in the room, she dialled. Her call was answered within two rings.

'Mr Angleton, it is Yasmin Malouff. There has been a call, on Kiernan's mobile. The transcript runs as follows . . .'

She held her pad up and began to read.

'Do you think it's safe?' asked Freya as Flin led her back into the museum. The image of their twin pursuers was still sharp in her mind, and the huge, crowd-filled gallery felt painfully exposed after the confined space of the photographic studio. 'What if they're still looking for us?'

'It's been over an hour,' Flin replied, stopping beside a giant stone sarcophagus and scanning the scene ahead. 'I'm guessing if they did think of coming in here they'll already have been and gone. I can't guarantee it, though, so keep your eyes open. If you see anything . . .'

'What?'

'Run.'

He looked around for a moment longer, then set off through the gallery, the photograph of the gateway still clutched in his hand. Freya trailed along beside him. He seemed, if not relaxed, certainly calmer and more assured than she did, as though the presence of so many ancient objects diluted the severity of the danger they were in. They covered about half the gallery's length, the vast interior echoing with the babble of voices and the slap of feet, then Flin started talking.

'Zerzura is a lost Saharan oasis,' he explained, moving aside as a horde of schoolchildren in matching blue uniforms poured towards them, led by a harassed-looking teacher. 'I've actually got quite a good Powerpoint presentation on it, but in current circumstances I'm afraid you'll have to make do with the edited version.'

'Fine by me,' said Freya, gazing around uneasily, half expecting one of the twins to leap out from behind a statue.

'The name comes from the Arabic word *zarzar*,' Flin continued, warming to his subject: 'which means starling, sparrow, a small bird. We don't really know much about the place, save that it was first mentioned in a medieval manuscript called the *Kitab al-Kanuz*, the Book of Hidden Pearls,

and supposedly lies somewhere in the vicinity of the Gilf
Kebir, although De Lancey Forth put it in the Great Sand
Sea, and Newbold . . .'

He saw that he was losing her and broke off, holding up
his hands.

'Sorry, too much information. One of the hazards of spending your life immersed in this stuff – you can never just tell it
simply. All you need to know for current purposes is that it's a
lost oasis and most of the early twentieth-century desert
explorers – Ball, Kemal el-Din, Bagnold, Almasy, Clayton –
tried, and failed, to find it. In fact it was the hunt for Zerzura
that drove much of that original exploration.'

They came to the high domed rotunda at the entrance to
the museum and continued directly ahead, into a gallery
marked 'Old Kingdom', its walls lined with statues and
carved reliefs.

'A lot of people have argued that Zerzura never actually
existed,' Flin went on, absorbed in what he was saying,
seemingly oblivious to the displays to either side and the
crowds all around. Unlike Freya, whose gaze continued to
flick nervously back and forth.

'That the whole thing's just a legend. Like El Dorado, or
Shangri-La, or Atlantis – one of those alluring but ultimately fictitious tales that wild places like deserts tend to
inspire. I've always believed it did exist, and that Zerzura is
simply another name, a much later name, for a place the
ancient Egyptians referred to as the *wehat seshtat*,
the Hidden Oasis.'

He glanced across to make sure he wasn't losing her.
Freya gave a nod to indicate she was keeping up with what
he was saying.

'Unfortunately, as with Zerzura, we don't really know a huge amount about the *wehat seshtat*,' said Flin, his brow furrowing slightly as if in frustration at this lack of information. 'With one notable exception, which I'll come to in a moment, the evidence is all extremely fragmentary and difficult to interpret: a few papyrus fragments, some badly damaged petroglyphs, a couple of inscriptions and a rather garbled mention in Manetho's *Aegyptiaca* – I won't bore you by going through it all. What we've basically managed to piece together – and I reiterate, much of this is open to interpretation – is that it was a deep gorge or wadi running off the eastern flank of the Gilf Kebir, and that from a very early date, before the Sahara even became a desert—'

'This is how long ago exactly?' asked Freya, interrupting. Despite her nervousness she was finding herself increasingly drawn into the story.

'Well, it's hard to give precise dates,' he said, apparently pleased by her interest. 'But we're talking at least ten, twenty thousand years BC, possibly even as early as the Middle Palaeolithic.'

The term meant nothing to Freya but she didn't pursue it, not wanting to hold things up.

'Way back in the mists of prehistory, anyway,' Flin continued, resuming the thread of his explanation. 'Even then this gorge, oasis, whatever you want to call it, seems to have been considered a place of supreme religious significance, its precise location a closely guarded secret. When and why it first came to be regarded as such we don't know, but it seems to have retained its status right the way through to the end of the Old Kingdom. About 2000 BC. After which knowledge of the oasis's whereabouts became lost and it disappears from history.'

They reached the end of the gallery and started up a staircase, the press of tourists thinning around them as they climbed to the museum's upper floor. It was quieter and less hectic here than on the building's lower level. Flin waved her back the way they had come, towards the rotunda, turning into a small, deserted side room with display cases full of simple stone and clay artefacts, all clearly of a much earlier date than everything they had passed so far. He stopped in front of one case and pointed. Inside, flanked by a pair of ivory combs and a large earthenware bowl were three objects Freya recognized: small clay obelisks, each about the height of a finger, each incised with the same symbol as the one in Rudi Schmidt's bag. She peered at the accompanying label: *Votive Benben miniatures, Predynastic (c. 3000 bc), Hierakonpolis.*

'What's a Benben?' she asked, thoughts of their pursuers moving ever further back in her mind.

'*The* Benben,' corrected Flin, leaning in beside her, his elbow just touching hers. 'I'm afraid this is where we have to sidetrack for a moment into the rather complex world of ancient Egyptian cosmology. I know it's not top of your interest list, but bear with me because it is relevant. I'll try to keep it simple.'

'Shoot,' she said.

A young couple wandered up to the case and glanced at its contents for a moment. Neither of them looked especially interested, and they moved on. Flin waited until they were out of earshot, then started talking again.

'The Benben was a central feature of ancient Egyptian

religion and mythology,' he explained. 'In many ways *the* central feature. Symbolically it represented the primordial mound of earth, the first small peak of dry land to emerge from Nun, the primal Ocean of Chaos. According to the Pyramid Texts – the oldest known collection of Egyptian religious writings – Ra-Atum, the creator God, flew across the blackness of Nun in the form of the Benu bird . . .'

He tapped the photo in his hand, indicating the long-tailed bird carved into the lintel above the doorway.

'. . . and landed on the Benben, from where his song ushered in the first sunrise. Hence the name, from the ancient Egyptian *weben*, "to rise in brilliance".'

The young couple wandered back past them, the girl now talking on her mobile. Again, Flin waited until they were gone before resuming his explanation.

'The Benben was more than just a symbol, however,' he said, his face pressed right up against the cabinet, his elbow still touching Freya's. 'We know from ancient texts and inscriptions that it was an actual physical object: a rock or stone shaped like an obelisk. There is some suggestion that it was originally a meteorite, or part of a meteorite, although the relevant texts are complex and open to interpretation. What we do know is that the Benben was housed in the inner sanctum of the great sun temple of Iunu and was, by all accounts, possessed of extraordinary supernatural powers.'

Freya let out an amused snort.

'I know, I know, it all sounds a bit *Raiders of the Lost Ark*, although we do have quite a number of corroborating sources – including one from royal Sumerian archives – that are remarkably consistent in their descriptions. They tell how the Benben would be dragged into battle at the head of the pharaoh's army and would emit a strange sound and a blinding light that utterly destroyed the opposing forces. Which possibly explains two of the alternative names that were used to describe it: *kheru-en Sekhmet*, the voice of Sekhmet – Sekhmet being the ancient Egyptian goddess of war – and *iner-en sedjet*, the Stone of Fire. That's what the symbol is, by the way' – he pointed at the motif on the side of the clay obelisk – 'Sedjet, the hieroglyph for fire. The cross-shaped terminal represents a brazier, with a flame rising . . .'

He broke off again, holding up his hands, as he had done before.

'But that's getting off the subject. The point is that the Benben and the *wehat seshtat* – the Hidden Oasis – were inextricably linked and you can't really discuss one without reference to the other. It would appear that the stone was originally lodged in a temple inside the oasis; as I said, we're talking tens of thousands of years BC here, long before the Nile Valley was even colonized. And although we can't be certain, there's some evidence to suggest that the reason the oasis was considered so sacred in the first place was because that's where the Benben was actually discovered. They're both part of the same package. Which is why, as well as *wehat seshtat*, the oasis was also referred to as *inet benben* – the Valley of the Benben.'

He glanced across, concerned he might have overwhelmed Freya with so much information. But she gave him the thumbs-up and after throwing a final look into the case he beckoned her away, leading her out of the room.

They passed beneath the museum's rotunda and along a balconied gallery overlooking the atrium.

'There's another reason the Benben's relevant to all this,' he said, holding up the photograph in his hand. 'And that is that by far the clearest and most detailed description we possess of the Hidden Oasis appears in a text specifically relating to the Benben. In here.'

They turned right into another room, also deserted, this one exhibiting a selection of hieroglyph-covered papyri. On the room's far side and stretching almost its entire width was a chest-high glass cabinet. Flin stopped in front of it and gazed down, a faint smile playing around the corners of his mouth. Inside was a papyrus covered from end to end in uneven columns of text in black ink. Unlike the other examples on display, most of which were exquisitely executed, with beautiful colours and intricate decoration, this document appeared bland and untidy, its hieroglyphs seeming to sway and knock into each other as if they had been written down in a hurry. Indeed they didn't even look like proper hieroglyphs, the symbols messy and scrawled, overlapping, more reminiscent of Arabic script than traditional Egyptian pictograms. Freya leant forward, reading the explanatory note on the wall behind the cabinet:

The Imti-Khentika Papyrus. From the tomb of Imti-Khentika, High Priest of Iunu/Heliopolis, 6th Dynasty, reign of Pepi II (c. 2246–2152 BC)

'Despite appearances, by some distance the most important papyrus in the room,' said Flin, nodding at the sheet. 'With the exception of the Turin King List and Oxyrhynchus texts, probably the most important Egyptian papyrus full stop.'

He laid a hand on the cabinet's glass top, something almost reverential about the way he stared down at its contents.

'It was discovered forty years ago,' he continued, smoothing his hand gently back and forth across the glass as though petting some rare animal. 'By a man named Hassan Fadawi, one of the greatest archaeologists Egypt's ever produced and an old . . .'

He was about to say 'friend of mine', or so it seemed to Freya, but after a fractional pause changed it to 'colleague'.

'It's an extraordinary story, right up there with Carter and Tutankhamun. Fadawi was only twenty at the time, just out of university. He was doing some routine clearance work in the Necropolis of the Seers – the burial ground of the high priests of Iunu – and stumbled on Imti-Khentika's tomb completely by accident. The door seals were unbroken which meant the burial was untouched, exactly as it had been left the day it was closed four thousand years ago. I simply cannot overstate how important a find this was, one of the few intact Old Kingdom burials ever discovered, pre-dating Tutankhamun by almost a millennium.'

Even though the papyrus was clearly familiar to him, its story one he knew well, he sounded awestruck, like an excited schoolboy. His enthusiasm was infectious, pulling Freya into the story, all her fears momentarily forgotten as if they were part of some different reality.

'And what was in it?' she asked, looking up at him expectantly. 'What did they find?'

Flin paused as if building up to some spectacular revelation. Then:

'Nothing,' he replied, his eyes glinting mischievously.

'Nothing?'

'When Fadawi broke through the doorway the tomb was empty. No decoration, no objects, no inscriptions, no body. Nothing – except for a small wooden chest, with inside it . . .'

He tapped a knuckle on the cabinet's wooden frame.

'It was a huge embarrassment. All the world's press were there for the opening, President Nasser – Fadawi was left with a lot of egg on his face. Until he actually read what was written on the papyrus, that is. At which point he realized the tomb was even more significant than if it had been crammed full of gold treasure,'

Something about the way Flin said this sent a tingle down Freya's spine. Curious, she thought, that with everything that was going on she should find herself so engrossed in a history lecture.

'Go on,' she urged.

'Well, it's an enormously complicated document, and one that was obviously written in a hurry. It's in hieratic – a sort of hieroglyphic shorthand. There's still a lot of argument about how exactly to interpret certain sections of it, but in essence it's both an account of Imti-Khentika's life and times – his autobiography if you like – and also an explanation of why his body was never interred in the tomb he'd had prepared for himself. I won't bother translating it from start to finish since the first part . . .'

He waved a hand to his left.

'. . . isn't particularly relevant, just a lot of stuff about

Imti's various titles, his duties as high priest, all standard formulations. It's from this point on . . .'

He touched the top of the cabinet where he was standing, about halfway down the length of the papyrus.

'. . . that it gets interesting. Apropos of nothing Imti suddenly launches into a long and rambling description of the contemporary political situation – the only remotely detailed account we have of the final years of the Old Kingdom and its collapse into the internecine chaos of the First Intermediate.'

Freya had no idea what he meant. As before she let it go, not wanting to interrupt him.

'It's all extremely garbled,' Flin went on, 'and I'm paraphrasing quite heavily, but basically Imti explains how Egypt is disintegrating. Pharaoh Pepi II is old and demented – he's been on the throne for ninety-three years by this point, the longest reign of any monarch in history – and central authority has collapsed. There is famine, civil war, foreign invasion, general lawlessness. In Imti's words: Maat, the goddess of order, has been usurped by Set, lord of deserts, chaos, conflict and evil.'

He had started to move along the cabinet, following the story as it unfolded on the papyrus.

'According to Imti, in the face of this general collapse the leading figures in the land come together in secret conclave and take a momentous decision: for its own safety, and to prevent it falling into the hands of what he refers to as "the evildoers", the Benben Stone is to be removed from the Temple of Iunu and, under Imti's guidance, transported back across the desert to . . .'

He stopped, bent low over the cabinet and began to read,

his voice becoming deeper and more resonant, as if echoing from far back in time: '. . . *set ityu-en wehat seshtat inet-djeseret mehet wadjet er-imenet er-djeru ta em-khet sekhet-sha' em ineb-aa en-Setekeh* – the Place of Our Forefathers, the Hidden Oasis, the Sacred Valley lush and green, in the far west, at the end of the world, beyond the fields of sand, in the great wall of Set.'

He looked up at her, his face slightly flushed.

'Extraordinary, don't you think? As I say, by far the clearest and most detailed description we have of the oasis.'

'That's clear?'

'Crystal by ancient Egyptian standards. The fields of sand refers to the Great Sand Sea, the wall of Set the eastern flank of the Gilf Kebir. Set, as I mentioned, being the ancient Egyptian god of the desert. Short of an actual postcode it doesn't get more precise than that. And that's not all.'

He started moving down the cabinet again.

'Imti goes on to describe the expedition itself – a rather interesting perspective, since he wrote the account before he actually set out and is thus recording events that have yet to happen. Again, I won't go through it word by word, but the last section is useful.'

He came to a halt near the very end of the papyrus, stooping once more and reading, his voice again assuming a deep, resonant timbre.

'And so we came to the farthest end of the world, to the Western Wall, and the Eye of Khepri was opened. We passed through the Mouth of Osiris, we entered the *Inet Benben*, we came to the *hut aat*, the great temple. Here is your home, oh Stone of Fire, whence you came at the beginning of all things, and whither you are now returned. This is the end. The gates are closed, the Spells of Concealment are uttered, the Two Curses are laid – may evildoers be crushed in the jaws of Sobek and swallowed into the belly of the serpent Apep! I, Imti-Khentika, Greatest of Seers, shall not return from this place, for it is the will of the gods that my tomb remain empty for all eternity. May I walk in the beautiful ways, may I cross the heavenly firmament, may I eat beside Osiris every day. Praises to Ra-Atum!'

He stopped and straightened. Freya waited for more, but it didn't come.

'That's it?'

She couldn't disguise her disappointment. After all the build-up, she had been expecting, if not a blinding revelation, at least some clarification, some hint as to what was going on and why it was going on. Instead everything seemed to be even more confused and opaque than it had been when Flin began his explanation. Eye of Khepri, mouth of whatever it was, curses and serpents . . . it meant nothing to her, none of it. She felt as if she had been led through an elaborate maze only to re-emerge precisely where she'd started, without ever getting close to the centre.

'That's it?' she repeated. 'That's everything.'

Flin gave an apologetic shrug. 'Like I said, there's not a lot of information out there. You now know about as much as I do.'

There was a sudden hubbub as a group of tourists trooped into the room, led by a woman holding up a folded umbrella. They walked straight through and out of the door at the other side without so much as a glance at the room's contents. Freya stared down at the papyrus, then reached out and took the photograph from Flin's hand.

'If this oasis is impossible to find . . .'

'How come Rudi Schmidt's been there?' Flin finished the sentence for her. 'That's the million-dollar question, isn't it? Not the least perplexing aspect of the whole Zerzura–*wehat seshtat* story is that despite the oasis being "hidden" . . .' – he lifted his hands and tweaked his finger-tips to indicate inverted commas – 'people do nonetheless seem to stumble on it occasionally. Rudi Schmidt for one. And whoever provided the information on which the description in the *Kitab al-Kanuz* was based for another – Bedouin probably: there have long been rumours that certain desert tribes know of its location, although personally I've never been able to corroborate that.'

'So how?' Freya asked. 'How do they find it?'

Flin threw up his hands.

'God knows. The Sahara's a mysterious place, mysterious things happen. Mugs like me spend our whole lives search-ing for the oasis, and someone else just happens to wander into it. There's no rhyme or reason to the thing. Believe it or not the most convincing explanation I ever heard was from a psychic, a very strange woman who lived in a tent down in Aswan, claimed she was a reincarnation of Pepi II's wife, Queen Neith. She told me that the oasis had had spells of concealment cast on it, that the harder a person looked, the harder it would be to find, that only those who *weren't* actually looking for it would ever discover its whereabouts. For which gem of wisdom I paid her fifty pounds.'

He gave a mirthless grunt and glanced at his watch.

'Come on, we should be getting back.'

They took a last look at the scrawled papyrus and started retracing their steps through the museum. A bell sounded somewhere, signalling that it was closing time.

'Did Alex know about all this?' Freya asked as they descended the stairs to the ground floor. 'The oasis, the Benben Stone?'

Flin nodded.

'We spent a lot of time together out at the Gilf Kebir and I used to bore her with it over the campfire. Although to be fair she gave as good as she got. If I never hear another thing about lacustrine sediments I won't be overly disappointed.'

They reached the bottom of the stairs and started back through the Old Kingdom galleries. Droves of visitors streamed towards the main entrance, herded along by uniformed guards.

'How important is the oasis?' Freya asked. 'I mean, is it . . . you know . . . ?'

'Full of jewels and treasure?' Flin smiled. 'I very much doubt it. The *Kitab al-Kanuz* claims anyone who finds it will discover great riches, but that's almost certainly hyperbole. Some trees and a lot of ancient ruins – that's all that's going to be there. Academically of huge significance, but to people who live in the real world . . .'

He shrugged.

'. . . not really important at all.'

'The Benben Stone?' she asked.

'Again, to egg-heads like me it would be a massive discovery. One of the totemic symbols of ancient Egypt –

absolutely massive. When all's said and done, however, it's just a piece of stone, albeit a unique one. It's not like it's made of solid gold or anything. There are a lot more commercially valuable artefacts out there.'

They had passed beneath the domed rotunda and were back in the gallery lined with giant sarcophagi. Freya stopped, held up the photograph of the mysterious gateway and asked the question that had been on her mind ever since she first clapped eyes on it.

'So why would someone kill my sister for this?'

Flin looked at her, then away again. It was a moment before he spoke.

'I don't know,' he said. 'I'm sorry, Freya, but I just don't know.'

Re-entering the museum's administrative section, they climbed the spiral staircase up to the photographic department. The darkroom door was still closed.

'How's it going, Majdi?' Flin called, knocking.

No response. He knocked again, harder.

'Majdi? You in there?'

Still nothing. He gave one final knock, then grasped the handle and opened the door. There was a fractional pause as his eyes adjusted to the gloom, then:

'Oh God! Oh no!'

Freya was behind Flin, her view blocked by his tall frame. Stepping forward, she looked around him. Her hand shot up to her mouth as she realized what he was looking at, and a horrified gagging sound issued from deep within her throat. Majdi was crumpled on the darkroom floor, his eyes wide open, his throat slit from ear to ear. There was blood everywhere, a viscous black wash of it – on the

Egyptian's face, his shirt, his hands, pooled all around his head like a halo.

'Oh Majdi,' Flin groaned, thumping a fist against the doorframe. 'Oh my friend, what have I done?'

'*Salaam.*'

Flin and Freya spun. The twins were sitting on a sofa on the far side of the room. One of them was holding a strip of developed film, the other a blood-smeared flick-knife. Both were blank-faced and unperturbed, as if the scene in the darkroom was no more shocking to them than the sight of someone sipping tea or playing ping-pong. A thud of feet and four more men appeared at the top of the spiral staircase, blocking off any escape. One had a black eye and a grotesquely swollen nose and lip – the heavy Flin had punched in the lift back at the American University. He shouted something to the twins and they nodded. Coming forward, he squared up to Flin, leering at him, then slammed his huge hands down on the Englishman's shoulders and drove a knee viciously into his groin.

'*Ta'ala mus zobry, ya-ibn el-wiskha*,' he growled as Flin slumped to the floor, gasping in agony. 'Suck my cock, you son-of-a-bitch.'

For a moment Freya was too shocked to react. Then, balling her fist, she swung for the man. Her punch didn't get close to connecting as her arm was seized from behind and yanked up her back. The photograph was ripped out of her hand. She struggled and kicked and swore, but they were too strong for her and when a pistol muzzle was pressed against her temple she knew it was pointless trying to resist and gave up. Still groaning in pain, Flin was hoisted to his feet and frisked, his mobile phone pulled from his pocket and crushed underfoot. He and Freya were pushed towards the staircase, the twins following on behind, the one with the flick-knife wiping the blade clean on a handkerchief as he went. As they started down the stairs Freya craned her neck, looking back first at Majdi's blood-drenched corpse, and then at Flin.

'I'm sorry,' she said, her voice hoarse with shock, her face grey. 'I should never have got you involved. Either of you.'

Flin shook his head.

'*I'm* sorry,' he croaked, barely able to get the words out he was in so much pain. 'Should never have got *you* involved.'

Before she could ask what he meant one of the thugs growled something and pushed the pistol harder into her neck, forcing her to look forward again. After that the only sound was the clatter of their feet on the metal stairs and the agonized rasp of Flin's breathing.

Outside the Museum of Egyptian Antiquities Cy Angleton sat on a plinth in a corner of the sculpture garden, watching as Flin and Freya were hustled out of a side door. Although Brodie was hobbling badly, and the men around them were pressing in slightly closer than was strictly necessary, there was nothing obviously untoward about the group of which they were a part, and no one – neither the tourists thronging the garden nor the white-uniformed police sentries stationed at intervals around its perimeter – gave them a second look.

PAUL SUSSMAN

Angleton alone stared at them, gazing intently as they passed through the gardens and out of the museum's main gate. He gave it a moment, then followed, tracking them as they turned right along the pedestrianized street in front of the museum, moving away from Midan Tahrir. Taxi touts and trinket sellers buzzed around him, offering postcards, carvings and the inevitable 'special trip no one else offer to Pyramid and papyrus factory'. Angleton waved them away, trailing the group past the Hilton Hotel and down to the Corniche el-Nil, where two cars – a black BMW and a silver Hyundai people carrier – were waiting, engines running. The twins climbed into the BMW while the two westerners were jostled into the Hyundai and the door was slammed behind them. As it did, Brodie happened to glance up, his eye momentarily catching Angleton's before the convoy moved off into the evening traffic.

'You want antiquity, mister?'

A young boy, no more than six or seven years old, had come up beside the American, proffering a crude and obviously modern carving of a cat.

'Twenty Egyptian pound,' said the boy. 'Very ancient. You want?'

Angleton said nothing, his eyes locked on the cars as they sped away down the Corniche.

'Ten Egyptian pound. Very good carving. You want, mister?'

'What I want,' murmured Angleton, 'are some goddam answers.'

He watched until the cars were out of sight. Then, reaching into his pocket, he pulled out a wad of notes and thrust

272

them at the boy before turning and lumbering back in the direction of the museum.

'You want go Pyramid, mister? You want go perfume shop? Real Egypt perfume. Very cheap, very good for wife.'

Angleton just waved a hand over his shoulder and continued walking.

In the grounds of the American Embassy Molly Kiernan paced anxiously up and down, her ID card flapping on its chain around her neck, her eyes flicking between her mobile phone and the Embassy's north gate. All staff and visitors had to pass through here and occasionally the door of the gate's security lobby would swing open and someone would emerge. Every time they did Kiernan stopped and stared, only to shake her head and resume her pacing, patting her phone against her thigh as if trying to force it to ring. Twice it did, Kiernan answering before the phone had even finished its first chime. The calls weren't what she was hoping for, and, politely but firmly, she cut them short.

'Come on,' she whispered. 'What's happening here? Where are you? Come on!'

CAIRO – ZAMALEK

'And how exactly will you get them out of the country, Mr Girgis?'

'I believe that is what you call a trade secret, Monsieur

Colombelle. All you need to know is that the sculptures will arrive in Beirut at the agreed time on the agreed date. And for the agreed sum of money.'

'And they're 18th Dynasty? You can confirm that absolutely?'

'I deliver what I promise to deliver. You have been told the pieces are 18th Dynasty and that is exactly what they are. I do not deal in fakes or reproductions.'

'With the Akhenaten cartouche?'

'With the Akhenaten cartouche, the Nefertiti cartouche and everything else that was described to you by my antiquities expert. Unfortunately Mr Usman is engaged on other business this evening and unable to join us, but rest assured the goods will more than live up to your expectations, if not exceed them.'

Monsieur Colombelle – a small, dapper Frenchman with unnaturally black hair – let out a satisfied chuckle.

'We're going to make a lot of money, here, Mr Girgis. A lot of money.'

Girgis opened his hands.

'That is the only reason I do business. If I might recommend, the lobster ravioli is particularly good.'

The Frenchman peered at his menu while Girgis sipped at a glass of water and glanced across the table at his two colleagues. Boutros Salah, a jowelly, thickset man with a bristling moustache and a cigarette dangling from the corner of his mouth, and Mohammed Kasri – tall, bearded, hook-nosed – met his gaze and all three gave a faint nod to acknowledge the deal was in the bag.

The dinner was an unwelcome distraction for Girgis, but Colombelle had flown into Cairo specially and with his clients waiting for delivery of the stolen sculptures it couldn't very well be put off. The sum involved – $2 million – was not enormous – negligible when compared with the whole Zerzura thing – but business was business and so the meeting had gone ahead. The four of them had worked through the details of the deal while underneath the table Girgis had tapped his foot impatiently, waiting for news of what was on the camera film, whether it would lead them to the oasis. He had hoped for a result sooner than this – his people had been looking at the negatives for over an hour now – but was trying to stay calm. At least they had the negatives, and Brodie and the girl as well, which was a step in the right direction. He took another sip of water, checked his mobile and started to peruse his own menu, trying to take his mind off things. As he did so a waiter approached and, leaning down, whispered into his ear. Girgis nodded. Pushing his chair back, he stood.

'You must forgive me, Monsieur Colombelle, but something unexpected has come up and I am required elsewhere. My colleagues will answer any further questions you might have and, should you wish it, arrange entertainment once the meal is over. It has been a pleasure doing business with you.'

He shook hands with the Frenchman, who looked slightly nonplussed by the abruptness of his host's departure, and, without further ado, turned and left the restaurant. Outside his limousine was waiting. The driver held open the rear door and a plump, dishevelled man with a pudding-bowl haircut and thick-lensed plastic spectacles shifted along the back seat to make room for Girgis: Ahmed Usman, his antiquities specialist.

'So?' asked Girgis once the door was closed.

Usman drummed the tips of his fingers together. There was something curiously mole-like in the action.

'Nothing, I'm afraid, Mr Girgis. Half the film was spoilt, and the other half . . .'

He handed over a sheaf of A4 photographic prints.

'Useless, completely useless. See, all the images are from inside the oasis – nothing to help identify the location. It's like trying to find a house in the middle of a city when all you've got to go on is a picture of the bathroom. Completely useless.'

Girgis flicked through the shots, his mouth curled into something midway between a grimace and a snarl.

'Could you have missed something?'

Usman shrugged, patted the tips of his fingers together again.

'I've gone through them extremely carefully, so I'd say not. Then again . . .' He gave a nervous laugh.

'. . . I'm not a world authority on the subject.'

'Brodie?'

'Professor Brodie is *the* world authority.'

'Then I think it's time to go and have a discussion with him,' said Girgis, handing the photographs back. Picking up the limousine's intercom phone, he issued instructions to the driver.

'I really can't see him helping,' said Usman as they started to move away. 'Even if he managed to spot something. From what I've heard he's a rather . . .'

Another nervous laugh.

'. . . stubborn character.'

Girgis adjusted the cuffs of his shirt, brushed something off his jacket.

'Believe me, once Manshiet Nasser's finished with Professor Brodie there's nothing he won't do for us. He'll be pleading to help. Begging.'

Cairo – Manshiet Nasser

'Gotcha,' murmured Freya, trapping the cockroach under the toe of her trainer. Its exoskeleton made a moist, crunching sound as she slowly ground it into the floor, smearing it across the dusty concrete, its yellowy-brown innards joining those of the other roaches she'd dispatched over the last hour.

'You OK?' asked Flin.

She shrugged.

'Not really. How's the . . . ?' She nodded towards his crotch.

'I'll live. Although I don't think I'll be doing any cycling for a while.'

She gave a weak smile.

'What do you think they're going to do to us?'

It was Flin's turn to shrug.

'On recent evidence, nothing particularly pleasant. They'd know better than me.'

He nodded towards the three men sitting silently opposite, sub machine-guns balanced in their laps.

'Hey guys, what have you got planned?' he called across at them.

No reply.

'I guess it must be a surprise,' he said, hunching forward and rubbing his temples.

They were on the top storey of what appeared to be a partially completed building – a large, shadowy space illuminated by a single fluorescent strip light lying flat on the ground close to the guards. Although the floor, ceiling, staircase and load-bearing pillars were all in place – bare concrete, with rusted iron reinforcing rods protruding here and there like fossilized branches – there were only three walls. The room's fourth side was open to the night, a gaping void staring out over the twinkling lights of Cairo like a cave mouth set high up in a cliff. Flin and Freya were at this end of the space, sitting on a pair of upturned crates. Behind them the floor came to an abrupt end and there was a long, sheer drop down to the street below. Their captors were in the centre of the room, beside the staircase. Even without the wall, the westerners were to all intents and purposes imprisoned.

'What the hell is this place?' Freya had asked when they were first brought here.

'Manshiet Nasser,' Flin had informed her. 'It's where the Zabbaleen live.'

'Zabbaleen?'

'Cairo's rubbish collectors.'

'We've been kidnapped by trash men?'

'I suspect we're just being held here,' said Flin. 'In my experience the Zabbaleen are decent people, if not the most hygienic.'

That had been almost an hour ago, and still they were waiting – for what exactly, neither of them could say. It had been light when they arrived, but the evening had closed in swiftly. Now everything was sunk in darkness, the strip lamp's sterile glow doing little to dispel the shadows bunched in the corners of the room. Moths and other bugs fluttered around the lamp's fluorescent tube; the air was heavy with heat and dust and hanging over everything – permeating everything, suffusing everything – was the dense, sweet-sour stench of rotting garbage.

Freya sighed and glanced at her watch: 6.11 p.m. Flin stood and turned, thrusting his hands into his pockets and gazing out into the night. They were at the back of the building, which sat on a steep slope. Below a jumbled mass of roofs cascaded away like a freeze-framed landslide, everything merging in a dim chaos of dirt and brick and concrete and trash-heaps. While the rest of Cairo was ablaze with light – a glittering carpet of white and orange spreading off into the far distance – this corner of it was swamped in gloom. There were a few dimly illuminated windows, meagre smudges of colour in the enveloping murk, and the street below glowed a sickly orange in the light of half a dozen sodium lamps. Otherwise all was dark, as if the buildings and alleyways and side streets and rubbish tips were submerged in black ink. There were occasional shouts, the clank of pans, a distant grinding of machinery, but no actual people, or none that Flin could see. The quarter possessed a curiously ghost-like feel – a village of phantoms tacked onto the edge of a city of the living.

Shuffling closer to the edge of the floor, Flin looked down at the street far below. A truck was creeping up the hill to his left, the low rumble of its engine counterpointed by a soft tinkle of glass from the mound of bottles it was transporting. It passed directly beneath where he was standing and lumbered on up the slope, disappearing round a corner as the street looped back on itself in front of the building. A minute went by, and then another truck appeared, this one piled with a spaghetti of old electrical wiring. Following behind it, distinctly out of place in the dilapidated surroundings, was a sleek black limousine. Flin watched as it manoeuvred its way around the corner and out of sight, then turned to Freya.

'Looks like we've got company,' he said. As he spoke a horn sounded outside and the guards rose to their feet. From down the stairs came an echo of footsteps, faint at first, but growing steadily louder as the newcomers – there seemed to be more than one – climbed up through the building towards them. Instinctively Freya's hand grasped Flin's. The footsteps came nearer and nearer until eventually two men emerged into the room. One was short and plump, dishevelled, with a pudding-bowl haircut and an A4 manila envelope clasped in his hand. The other was older and slighter, immaculately dressed, his grey hair slicked back across his scalp, his face sharp and sallow-skinned, the lips so narrow as to be almost non-existent. He seemed to be in overall charge: the other Egyptians moved respectfully aside to make room for him, the strip light on the floor enveloping the group in a cold bubble of light. There was a brief, tense silence, then:

'Romani Girgis,' murmured Flin underneath his breath.

'You know this man?' Freya released Flin's hand and turned to him.

'I know of him,' replied the Englishman, glaring across the room. 'Everyone in Cairo knows Romani Girgis.'

Another brief pause, then Flin raised his voice:

'A more grotesque piece of shit it would be hard to imagine.'

If he was angered by the insult, or even understood what it meant, Girgis didn't show it. Instead he motioned to his companion, who scuttled across the room and handed Flin the manila envelope.

'Not like you to do your own dirty work, Girgis,' said the Englishman, pulling a wad of photographs from the envelope and leafing through them. 'Where's Tweedledee and Tweedledum?'

It took Girgis a moment to get the reference. When he did he smiled, a thin, unpleasant expression, chilling, like a reptile about to bite at something.

'They are visiting their mother,' he said, his English fluent if heavily accented. 'Very dutiful sons, very soft-hearted. Much more so than me. As you will soon discover.'

His smile began to broaden only to morph into a grimace of disgust as a cockroach scuttled across the floor directly in front of him. He took a step back, muttering. One of his henchmen came forward and stamped on the insect, grinding it into the concrete. Only when he was sure it had been completely obliterated did Girgis seem to recover himself. Brushing at his sleeves, he again addressed Flin, his tone now cold and scalpel sharp. The other Egyptians stood silently beside him, their faces hard, their shadows bulging on the ceiling above.

'You will look at the photographs,' said Girgis, eyes gleaming malevolently. 'You will look at them, and then you will tell me where they were taken. Where *exactly* they were taken.'

Flin glanced down at the prints.

'Well this one's Timbuktu,' he said. 'This one's Shanghai, this looks like El Paso and this one . . .'

He held up a photo.

'. . . blow me if it's not my aunty Ethel in Torremolinos.'

Girgis stared at him, nodding as if he had been expecting such an answer. Removing a pack of wet wipes from his jacket pocket, he pulled one out and slowly rubbed it over his hands. For a moment he was silent, the only sounds the soft pop of moths hitting the strip light and, from outside, the clatter of a cart and the distant beeping of car horns. Then, throwing the wipe to the floor, the Egyptian spoke to his colleagues. One of the guards lifted the strip lamp and propped it against a chair, angling it towards the far corner of the room where a mound of giant polypropylene sacks were stacked from floor to ceiling. Beside them stood a machine resembling a large wood-chipper, with an opening at the top and various buttons and levers on the side. Girgis walked across to it, the plump man trotting along beside him like an obedient dog. Two of the guards hustled Flin and Freya over as well, jabbing at them with their guns. The third one, the man who had moved the light, disappeared downstairs, shouting at someone below.

'Do you know what this is?' asked Girgis as Flin and Freya came up beside him, patting the machine.

They didn't respond. Both of them stood stony-faced and defiant.

'It is called a granulator,' said the Egyptian, answering his own question. 'A common piece of equipment in this part of the city. Normally they are kept on the ground floor, but this one we have brought up here for . . . special occasions.'

He gave a grunt of amusement, his mouth again curling into a chilling reptilian smile.

'Let me show you how it works.'

He motioned to one of his men, who produced a flick-knife and snapped it open. Flin tensed and moved in front of Freya, ready to protect her. It seemed the knife was not intended for them. Instead the man went to the pile of sacks and slashed the blade across one of them. A rush of empty plastic bottles spilled out onto the floor.

'There's no great skill or science involved,' continued Girgis, removing another wipe from his pocket and again swabbing at his hands. 'It is child's play. Literally, since more often than not it is the Zabbaleen children who actually operate these machines. As my little helper will demonstrate.'

There was movement behind them and the man who had descended the staircase reappeared, accompanied by a young boy. Dirty-faced and malnourished, he could have been no more than seven or eight years old, his hands lost within the sleeves of an oversized *djellaba*. Girgis whispered to him and the boy stepped up to the machine. Reaching out with his left hand he pressed a mushroom-shaped red button. There was a rumble and a sputter, and the room filled with a deafening mechanical roar.

'We didn't have such things when I was young,' called Girgis, raising his voice to be heard above the clatter. 'But then it is only in the last few decades that they have really become necessary. So much plastic around these days. As always, the Zabbaleen have adapted to changing times.'

The boy had moved across to the pile of bottles and with his left hand collected a dozen of them in the hem of his *djellaba*. Returning to the granulator, he began feeding the bottles one by one into the mouth on top of it. There was a hissing, cracking sound and a spew of coin-sized plastic flakes rained down, spattering the floor like hail.

'As you can see, the bottles go in whole and are shredded by the blades inside,' explained Girgis, still shouting. 'They then re-emerge as a raw material that can be sold on to the city's plastic merchants. Very simple. And very efficient.'

The boy had now fed all the bottles into the machine and, at a signal from Girgis, hit the red button again, turning it off.

'Very simple and very efficient,' repeated the Egyptian, his voice sounding unnaturally loud in the silence that had now descended on the room. 'Although sadly not always very safe.'

He nudged the boy, who held up his right arm. The sleeve of his *djellaba* slipped back to reveal a bony stump where the hand should have been, scar tissue extending all the way up to the elbow as though the arm had been dipped in livid pink paint. Freya winced; Flin shook his head, both out of pity for the boy, and disgust that he should be paraded in this way.

'Their sleeves get caught in the blades, you see,' said Girgis, beaming. 'Their arms are dragged in, little hands all torn and chopped. Many can't get to hospital in time and bleed to death. A blessing in many ways. It's not as if they have especially bright futures ahead of them.'

He let this hang for a moment, still rubbing at his hands with the wipe. Then he turned to Freya.

'I understand you are a rock climber, Miss Hannen.'

Freya just stared at him, wondering where this was leading.

'I'm afraid I know little about such things,' continued Girgis. 'There is not much call for them in my line of business. I'd be interested to find out more. For instance, would I be right in thinking that it would be very hard to climb with only one arm?'

Flin took half a step forward.

'You leave her out of this. Whatever the hell it is you want you leave her out of this.'

Girgis tutted.

'But she is *in* this,' he said. 'She's very much in this. Which is why it is her hand that will go into the granulator if you don't tell me where those photographs were taken.'

'For fuck's sake,' spat Flin, holding up the photos, waving them at Girgis. 'It's just ruins. Trees and ruins. How the hell am I supposed to tell you where they were taken? It could be anywhere. Anywhere!'

'Well let's just hope, for Miss Hannen's sake, that you can tell me the precise location of anywhere. You have twenty minutes to look at the photographs and to come up with some information. After that . . .'

He banged his hand against the granulator's red starter button, allowing the machine to run for a moment before again turning it off.

'Twenty minutes,' he repeated as the echo of grinding blades slowly faded. 'I shall be waiting downstairs.'

He threw the wipe aside and, accompanied by his dishevelled companion, walked back across the room, veering around something on the floor – a cockroach, Freya guessed – before starting back down the stairs.

'You killed my sister,' she shouted after him.

He slowed and turned, eyes narrowed slightly as if he wasn't quite sure if he'd heard her right.

'You killed my sister,' she repeated. 'And I'm going to kill you.'

A pause, then Girgis smiled.

'Well let's just hope Professor Brodie can tell me where those pictures were taken or you'll be doing it one-handed.'

He nodded and disappeared down the stairs.

CAIRO – BUTNEYA

It was their mother who had taught the twins how to make lamb *torly*, a recipe that was, in the unanimous opinion of those who were lucky enough to have tasted it, the very best in Cairo, if not the whole of Egypt. The secret, she had told them, was to soak the lamb in *karkaday*, the longer the better, for an entire day if possible, the rich red juice not only helping to tenderize the meat, but also infusing it with a subtle, mouth-watering sweetness that both comple-mented and enhanced the casserole's other ingredients, the onions, potatoes, peas and beans.

'First we sit the lamb in its bath,' their mother used to sing when they were young, swirling the meat around in its hibiscus marinade, 'then we put it to sleep in the oven, and then it goes . . .'

'Into our mouths!' the twins would chorus, making a chomping sound and patting their bellies, their mother roar-ing with laughter, pulling her sons into her bosom, enveloping them in her arms.

'My little bears!' she would chuckle. 'My little monsters!'

Tonight, what with all the running around for Girgis –

flying out into the desert, chasing across Cairo – there hadn't been time to let the meat soak, not properly, and so they had just dunked it in the *karkaday* while they chopped and prepared the other vegetables before combining everything in a clay pot and putting the pot in the oven to heat.

They cooked for their mother at least twice a week, more often if they could manage it, back at her cramped, two-room hovel in Butneya, where they had grown up, amid the grim labyrinth of alleyways that snaked off the back of the al-Azhar mosque. They'd tried to persuade her to move out, to come and live with them, or at least allow them to rent her somewhere more comfortable, but she was happy here and so that's where she stayed. They gave her money, and had brought her new furniture – including a lovely big bed, and a wide-screen TV and DVD player – and the neighbours looked out for her, so she was well cared for. Despite that, they worried. Years of beatings from *el-Teyaban*, the Snake – they refused to call him their father – had left her frail and unsteady, and although the Snake had long since disappeared – after the two of them had given *him* a bloody good beating – the damage was done. Deep down they both knew she didn't have long left. It was something they neither talked about nor acknowledged. It was just too painful. Their *omm* was everything to them. Everything.

The *torly* done, they pulled it from the oven. The room filled with a fabulous, fatty aroma of cooked meat, tinged with just the vaguest hint of mint – another of their mother's secret ingredients. They carried it through to the living area and arranged it on the floor. The three of them sat cross-legged around the clay pot, ladling its contents into their bowls, their mother clucking and fussing, slurping at her spoon, her toothless old mouth puckering up like a dried slug.

'My little bears!' she cackled. 'How you spoil your *omm*! Next time you must let me do the cooking.'

'Next time,' they replied, glancing at each other and winking, knowing she was just saying it, that she loved to be waited on and pampered. And why not? She'd made enough sacrifices for them over the years. Best mum in the world, she was. Everything to them. Everything.

They chatted as they ate, or at least their mum did, filling them in on all the local news and gossip: how Mrs Guzmi had had another grandson, and poor old Mr Farid had had to have a second testicle removed, and the Attalas had just purchased a brand new cooker ('Six electric rings, would you believe! Six! And they got a free baking tray with it'). She didn't ask about their work and they didn't tell her. Something to do with community relations, that's all she knew. No point in getting her worried. And anyway, they wouldn't be working for Girgis for much longer. Over the years they'd saved up more than enough to realize their own dream: a food concession inside Cairo International Stadium, selling *taamiya* and *fatir* and, of course, their mum's legendary *torly*. Not long now and they'd be making the break. Girgis, they both agreed, was a complete and utter wanker.

Once the *torly* was finished they took the dishes to the sink and – each in a matching Red Devils apron – washed them while their mum settled herself in the reclining armchair they'd filched for her from an office furniture store over in Zamalek, rubbing her feet and humming to herself.

'And did you bring your *omm* a little treasure?' she asked coquettishly when they came back in to join her. 'A little something for dessert?'

'Mum,' they both sighed. 'It's not good for you.'

She whined and croaked and pleaded, squirming around on the chair, mewling like a hungry cat, and although they disapproved they didn't like to deny her, knew it was one of her few real pleasures. And so while one of them set the DVD player the other laid all the necessary equipment out on a tray – belt, spoon, water, lighter, alcohol swab, lemon juice, cotton wool balls – and, removing the syringe, needle and heroin wrap from his pocket, cooked up her fix.

'My little bears,' she murmured as the drug emptied into her arm, leaning her head back and closing her eyes. 'My little monsters.'

They held her hands, and stroked her hair, and told her they loved her and would always be here for her. Then, once she had drifted off into a world of her own, they settled down on the floor and started the DVD, clapping their hands in excitement even though they'd watched it fifty times before: El-Ahly's 4–3 victory over Zamalek in the 2007 Egyptian Cup Final, the greatest game of football ever played.

> '*El-Ahly, El-Ahly,*
> *The greatest team there'll ever be,*
> *We play it short, we play it long,*
> *The Red Devils go marching on!*'

They chanted softly to themselves while behind them their *omm* sighed and chuckled.

'My little bears,' she murmured. 'My little monsters.'

CAIRO – MANSHIET NASSER

'Every day for the last decade I've dreamt of seeing pictures like this,' said Flin, staring down at the photographs in his hand. 'And now I am seeing them I can think of nothing on earth I'd rather look at less.'

He shuffled the images, going through them one by one – again.

'It could be anywhere,' he groaned, shaking his head helplessly. 'Any-bloody-where.'

Freya cricked her neck and gazed out across the city through the wall-less void at the rear end of the room. She felt curiously calm given that their twenty minutes had almost elapsed. Behind her the three guards were playing cards at the head of the staircase, seemingly oblivious to their presence. At her side Flin pored over the photos, as he had been doing ever since Girgis had left, his eyes boring into them, his hands trembling.

Some of the images were general shots of a tree-filled gorge, its sheer walls rearing up towards a slit of pale sky high above, as though someone had sliced a scalpel deep through the rock. Others were more specific: a towering obelisk with the *sedjet* sign inscribed on each of its four faces. An avenue of sphinxes. A monumental statue of a seated figure with a human body and the head of a hawk.

There were pillars and parts of walls and three more shots of the gateway they had already seen, everything swaddled in a heavy jacket of vegetation – flowers and trees and branches and leaves, as though the mud-brick and carved stone of the man-made structures had over time begun to dissolve back into the natural landscape, reverting to their elemental state.

Mud-brick, carved stone, trees, rock walls – nothing, however, to give any hint of the wider context, of the oasis's actual location. And now their time was almost up.

They're going to cut my arm off, Freya thought, wholly unable to connect with the horror of what was about to happen to her. It was almost as if she was looking in on the scene from outside. As if it was someone else's limb that was about to be shredded. *They're going to cut off my arm and I'm never going to climb again.*

For some inexplicable reason she felt like laughing.

She glanced at her watch – a couple of minutes left, tops – and stepped up to the edge of the rough concrete floor, looking down at the street below. She thought about jumping, but it was way too long a drop. Thirty metres minimum, probably closer to thirty-five. It would either kill her or at the very least shatter her legs like matchwood. Nor was there any possibility of climbing to freedom – she'd already knelt and peered out over the edge of the floor, trying to assess a potential route down, but it just wasn't feasible. And anyway, the guards would clock what they were doing before they'd even started their descent. Shredded arm, shattered legs, shot: there were no appealing options.

'Do you think he was just threatening?' she asked,

looking round at Flin. 'You know . . . the granulator . . . do you think they'll actually . . . ?'

He looked up, then back at the photographs, unable to meet her eyes. It was all the answer she needed. Only about a minute now.

Away to her right there was a rumble of an engine and a slash of headlamps as a large flat-bed truck manoeuvred slowly around the corner at the top of the street. It jerked and juddered as the driver worked the brakes, trying to keep the vehicle under control. She wondered if she should shout out, cry for help, but what was the point? Even if the driver heard and understood her what was he going to do? Call the police? Charge up the stairs and rescue them single-handed? It was hopeless, utterly hopeless.

She wrapped her arms around herself, wondering how much it would hurt, whether it *would* hurt or if she'd just go into shock or pass out.

'Will you be able to get me to a hospital?' she asked out loud. 'Is there one near?'

'For Christ's sake,' said Flin, his voice taut to the point of breaking, his face sheened with sweat and drained of colour. Curiously, he seemed more worked up than she was.

Up the hill the truck had managed to negotiate the corner and was now descending slowly towards her, its brakes wheezing and squealing. Its bed was heaped with what from this distance looked like a mound of sand or rubble, although it was difficult to tell in the dim, unhealthy glow of the intermittent street lamps. Freya watched it for a moment, then suddenly jerked round as behind her one of the guards let out a triumphant cry, brandishing his playing cards at his two companions, making a rubbing motion with his fingers to indicate that they owed him money. Grumbling, they handed over the cash and were just about to deal again when from outside came three sharp blasts of a car horn. Time up. As if she had been slapped hard across the face, the reality of her situation burst on Freya. She started to shake, fighting back a strong urge to vomit. She turned to Flin.

'You'll need to get a tourniquet round my elbow.' Her voice was unsteady, her eyes dull with fear. 'When they've cut . . . when they've done it. You'll need to get something tight round my elbow or I'll bleed to death.'

'They're not going to do anything to you,' Flin said. 'You have my word. Just stay behind me. I'll . . .'

'What? What will you do?'

He didn't seem to have an answer.

'Just stay behind me,' he repeated impotently.

She stepped up to him, took his hand and squeezed it. For a moment they stood like that. Then, letting go, she reached out and undid the buckle of his belt, Flin remaining motionless as she slipped the belt out of the loops of his jeans and passed it to him.

'Tourniquet,' she said. 'As soon as it's done you have to get this round my arm. Promise.'

He said nothing.

'Please, Flin.'

A pause, then he nodded, taking the belt from her and touching her cheek.

'Just stay behind me.'

The men had packed away their cards and were peering down the stairway as from below came the echo of ascending feet. One of them looked over at Freya and grinned, chopping his right hand against his left wrist, making a growling sound as of grinding machinery. She shuddered and turned away, stepping back to the edge of the floor and gazing down at the truck again. It was now only forty-odd metres up the hill, still descending at a snail's pace. Maybe she *should* call out. Scream the place down. It wasn't like she had anything to lose. She took a deep breath and opened her mouth, but for some reason she couldn't make her voice work. Could only stand there staring as the truck rumbled ever closer, its flat-bed suddenly coming into clearer focus as it passed directly beneath one of the sodium lamps. It was not, as she had at first thought, heaped with sand or rubble, but with old material – loose shreds and scraps of cloth, offcuts of carpet, a fluffy mass of cotton, what looked like chunks of foam mattress: a deep, soft, cushioning . . .

'Flin,' she whispered, her shoulders tensing, electricity rippling down her spine. And then again, more urgent: 'Flin.'

'Hmm?'

He came up beside her. Freya nodded down at the truck, now less than twenty metres away.

'You ever see *Butch Cassidy and the Sundance Kid*?' she asked. 'That scene where they—'

'Jump off the cliff.' Flin finished the sentence for her. 'Oh Christ, Freya, I don't think I can. It's too far.'

'It'll be fine,' she said, trying to sound more confident than she felt.

'It's too far.'

'I'm not letting them cut my arm off, Flin.'

Behind them the echo of footsteps drew ever closer. Flin looked at her, then at the truck, then at Freya again.

'OK,' he said, wincing as if about to drink something he knew would taste disgusting.

He slipped the photographs inside his shirt and buttoned the shirt up to the collar, tucking it well down inside his trousers. One of the guards had wandered across to the granulator. The other two were still peering down the stairwell. None were looking directly at them.

'Count of three,' she murmured as the front of the truck came level with where they were standing. 'One ... two ...'

'In the film ... they survive the jump, don't they?'

She nodded. 'Although they both get shot later. Three!'

They clasped hands and stepped out into space.

For a moment the world around them blurred into a confused kaleidoscope of walls and roofs and balconies and washing lines before snapping into focus again as they thudded down onto the back of the truck. The mound of cloth and rags gave beneath them, breaking their fall. Freya was thrown sideways against the truck's tailgate, slamming into a sodden slab of mattress foam, jarring her neck, but otherwise unscathed. Flin was not so lucky. Bouncing off a roll of old carpet and over the side of the truck, he flailed through the air like a drunken gymnast, crashing sideways-on into a stack of plastic barrels and from there face-first into a heap of rubbish, some unseen object slicing a deep gash in his left arm.

They lay where they were for a few seconds, groggy, winded. Then shouts rang out above and they started scrambling. Freya heaved herself off the back of the still-moving truck and dropped to the ground. Flin slid and stumbled his way upright, his shirt sleeve soggy with blood.

Staggering over, he propelled her towards a narrow alleyway on the opposite side of the street from the building in which they had been held. The shouts from above were now answered by other shouts at street level, where men must have been stationed to watch the building's rear. They reached the alley and piled into its narrow black mouth, blundering forward through the darkness, gagging at the sour, suffocating stench of raw waste, feet crunching on a tide of rubbish.

'There are rats!' Freya shrieked, sensing something – lots of things – scurrying round her feet and ankles.

'Ignore them!' ordered Flin. 'Just keep going.'

They ploughed on through the murk, moving more by instinct than sight, the glow of the street lamps behind doing little to dispel the enveloping gloom. Flin tripped, fell, clambered upright again, sputtering in disgust; Freya's foot sank deep into something that felt horribly like a dead animal. She kept moving, the darkness growing ever more intense, the smell ever more unbearable until suddenly the alley took a sharp turn to the left and began to slope steeply downwards. There was light ahead, framed by the narrow slit of the alley's lower end. From behind, round the corner, came the sounds of pursuit: curses and yells and a bark of gunfire. They stumbled on, moving as fast as they could, the rubbish gradually petering out in a slide of old cans and paint pots. The opening drew nearer and nearer until the walls to either side fell away and they emerged on top of a vertical, three-metre embankment. Grim tenements pressed in all around; a floodlight mounted on a pole to their left cast a fierce, icy glare. From below they heard a muffled grunting, accompanied by a powerful waft of faeces.

'Jump,' cried Flin.

'It's a fucking pigsty!'

'Jump!'

He nudged Freya in the back and she dropped down, sprawling in a viscous soup of mud and straw. Her hands sank into the filth almost to the level of her elbows, the grunting gave way to alarmed squeals as slithery black shapes scattered around her. Struggling to her feet, she turned and looked up, slapping at a slime-covered snout as it butted into her thigh. Flin was still on the embankment, pressed against the wall just to the right of the alley mouth, his left arm soaked with blood, his fists clenched. The clatter of cans grew louder as their pursuers charged down after them, their descent accompanied by the sporadic crackle of gunfire.

'Over there!' hissed Flin, nodding towards a heap of straw bales on the far side of the sty. 'Go! Quick!'

'What about—'

'Just go!'

She waded through the mire, reached the bales and clambered over them, crouching down as the first of their pursuers burst from the alley, some way ahead of his companions. He started to turn, shouting back. As he did so Flin fell on him, unleashing a flurry of punches and pitching him head first into the sty where he landed with a squelch and a sharp crack as of something snapping.

Flin leapt down into the mud. Yanking the pistol from the man's limp grasp he swiftly frisked his pockets. He pulled out an extra ammunition clip, then stumbled across the sty and threw himself behind the straw bales, dragging Freya's head down out of sight just as the rest of Girgis's men came barrelling out of the passage. They skidded to a halt and looked around, seeking out their quarry in the glare of the floodlight. Unable to spot them, the Egyptians started shooting indiscriminately, raking the enclosure with deafening volleys of gunfire. Bullets whizzed and thudded around the two westerners, kicking up explosions of mud and straw; pigs stampeded in all directions, squealing in terror. On and on it went, Flin holding Freya close with one hand while with the other he fumbled with the gun, waiting for the barrage to ease off. The moment it did, without hesitation, he forced Freya's head down further, scrambled into a kneeling position and unleashed a volley of his own, his finger pumping rhythmically at the trigger, his arm tracking left and right as he sighted different targets. He emptied the ammunition clip, slotted in the new one and cracked off a few more rounds. Then, slowly, he lowered the gun. There was no return fire. He reached out and squeezed Freya's arm, breathing heavily.

'OK,' he said. 'It's over.'

For a moment she remained where she was, curled in the mud, the echo of gunfire gradually fading, leaving just the whimpering of injured pigs and the domino-like clack of shutters as around and above them people opened their windows to see what was going on. Then she unravelled herself and moved into a kneeling position, looking out over the straw bales. In front of her, splayed across the top of the floodlit embankment like corpses on a stage, were four crumpled bodies.

'Jesus,' she said, trembling. 'Jesus fucking Christ.'

There were voices now, and shouts, and the distant wail of a siren. Flin gave it a few more seconds, scanning the alley mouth in case any more pursuers should emerge. Then, jamming the gun into the back of his jeans and covering it with his shirt-tail, he pulled Freya to her feet.

'How did you do that?' she mumbled, her voice hoarse, disbelieving. 'All those men. How did you . . . ?'

'Later,' he said. 'We've got to get out of here. Come on.'

He helped her through the sty and over a low breeze-block wall, people shouting at them from above, gesticulating. The wail of the siren grew louder. They kept moving, skirting a rubbish tip and setting off down a dark narrow street, both too shocked to speak. After fifty metres a sound of running feet from around a corner ahead forced them to duck into a fetid doorway. A group of children scampered by, chattering excitedly, wanting to see what was happening. They waited for them to disappear, then hurried on, the road sloping downwards, twisting and turning, getting steadily wider. They passed a brightly lit shop, and then a fruit stall hung with fairy-lights, and then a café, more and more people materializing around them, more light and bustle, the street seeming to come alive the further down the hill they went. They knew from the way eyes bored into them that the gun battle had been heard, and that with their mud-caked clothes and Flin's bloody shirt they were being connected with the commotion. They quickened their pace, desperate to get away. Fingers pointed at them, voices jabbered, twice men came up and tried to stop them. Flin pushed them off, clutching Freya's arm and steering her through the crowds until at last the street dropped down a final steep slope and flattened out into a patch of waste ground. There were parked cars, a row of giant rubbish bins, a railway line and beyond that – like a roaring river dividing that particular corner of Cairo from the rest of the city – a busy three-lane highway with traffic careering past in both directions. They broke into a sprint, getting up onto the highway's verge and frantically flagging down a taxi.

Initially the driver was reluctant to take them. The car had just been cleaned, he explained, the seats only recently re-covered, he didn't want them getting everything dirty. Only when Flin produced his wallet and counted out a fat wad of notes did he relent and wave them in. Flin took the front passenger seat, Freya – pale, hollow-faced, exhausted – the back.

'Where you go?' asked the man.

'Anywhere,' replied Flin. 'Away from here. Just drive. Quickly.'

Throwing another glance at his passenger's bloodstained shirt, the driver shrugged, started the meter and pulled out into the traffic. Flin craned round and looked at Freya, their eyes meeting briefly before he turned away. Grabbing a handful of tissues from a box on the dashboard, he pressed them to his arm and sank back into the cheap plastic upholstery. As he did so he felt Freya lean in behind him, her face coming up close to his ear.

'I want to thank you for saving my life,' she said, her voice numb, subdued.

He gave a dismissive grunt, started to mumble that he was the one who ought to be thanking her.

'I also want you to stop bullshitting me,' continued Freya, cutting him off. Reaching down, she yanked the pistol from the back of Flin's jeans and pushed its muzzle into his kidneys. 'I want you to tell me who you are, what's going on and what the fuck you got my sister involved in. And so help me God if you don't the driver's going to be cleaning a lot more than pig shit off his new upholstery. Now talk.'

The twins weren't happy when they got the call from Girgis, not happy at all. The game had just gone into extra time after Mohamed Abu Treika's 88th minute wonder goal had brought El-Ahly level at 2–2 and there were still three more scores to come, including Osama Hosny's winning header. And now they were being ordered to drop every-thing and get themselves over to Manshiet Nasser without delay. If it had been anyone else they would have told them to fuck off. But Girgis was Girgis, and although they didn't like it – they hated being interrupted during football, hated it – he was still the boss. Grumbling, they packed away the DVD and covered their mother with a blanket. Checking there was food and drink left out for her when she woke in the morning and money on the kitchen sideboard, they got on their way.

'Wanker,' muttered one of them as they trudged down the tenement stairs to the street below.

'Wanker,' echoed his brother.

'We'll give it a few more months . . .'

'Then set up on our own.'

'No more bosses.'

'Just the two of us.'

'And Mama.'

'Of course Mama.'

'It'll be good.'

'Very good.'

They reached the bottom of the stairs and set off along the street, arms linked, discussing *torly* and food concessions and Mohamed Abu Treika and where on earth they could get plastic sheeting and a nail gun at this time of night so they could do what Girgis had instructed them to do once they'd tracked down the two westerners.

'Freya, I don't know what you think . . .'

'I'll tell you what I think,' she said, leaning right into Flin's ear and keeping her voice low so the driver couldn't hear what she was saying. 'I think it's a bloody strange Egyptologist who knows how to handle a gun like you just did. Get a Cambridge Blue in that as well, did you?'

'Freya, please . . .'

He started to turn towards her, but she pushed the pistol harder in under his ribs.

'I haven't met many Egyptologists but I'd lay good money there aren't a lot of them like you, Professor Brodie. I'm grateful for everything you've done for me, but I want to know who you are and what's going on. And I want to know now.'

He craned his neck round further, trying to meet her eyes. Then, with a nod, he shifted in his seat and faced forward again. He seemed suddenly weary.

'OK, OK. Just put the gun down.'

She sat back, laying the pistol on the seat beside her, her hand still on its grip.

'Talk.'

He didn't, not immediately, just sat staring out of the window as they motored along. The gloomy shadow of Manshiet Nasser slowly dropped away behind them, a wedge of darkness thrust up underneath the floodlit wall of the Muqqatam cliffs. The driver lit a cigarette and slotted a cassette into the taxi's dashboard stereo, filling the car with the sound of a wailing female voice accompanied by discordant bursts of violin. A motorbike drifted by on their inside, a sheep slung across the saddle behind its rider, a bored, resigned look on its face. Almost a minute passed and Freya was on the point of reminding Flin that she wanted some answers when he reached out towards the dashboard, picked up the driver's mobile and asked if he could use it. There were negotiations – his wife was ill, the driver explained, they were behind with their rent, calls were expensive. In the end Flin had to count out another large wad of banknotes before he was given the go-ahead. He keyed in a number and placed his thumb on the call button, only to lift it again.

'Who knew you were coming to see me?' he asked, staring down at the phone.

'What?'

'At the American University. This afternoon. Who knew you were coming to see me?'

'It's you who's answering the questions, remember?'

'Come on, Freya.'

She shrugged.

'Nobody. Well, Molly Kiernan. I left a message on her voicemail. You're not saying she's involved in all of this, are you?'

'Not in the way you're thinking,' he said. 'Molly and I go way back.'

'So what *are* you saying?'

Again he didn't answer her, just continued staring at the phone, then pressed Cancel, wiping the number he was about to call. Instead he keyed in a text message, thumb bouncing over the pad. Freya craned forward, trying to see what he was writing, but the phone's display was in Arabic and she couldn't read it. He finished tapping and pressed Send, murmuring '*Shukran awi*' to the driver and replacing the mobile on the dashboard.

'I'm waiting,' she said.

'Just bear with me, Freya. There's a lot of stuff . . . I can't . . . Not here. We have to go somewhere first. I will explain everything, I promise, but this isn't the right place. Please, trust me on this.'

He glanced round at her, then spoke to the driver in Arabic, issuing instructions before settling back in his seat again and staring up at the roof.

They drove for thirty minutes – half that time spent sitting stationary in a traffic jam – heading north, Freya thought although she couldn't be a hundred per cent certain. They passed cemeteries, and some sort of military base, and an enormous floodlit stadium before leaving the Autoroute and following a broad avenue lined with palm trees. From there they turned off into a grid of drab, dusty streets between uniform four-storey concrete apartment blocks. Roadside lamps suffused everything with a drab yellow glow as though the buildings and pavements were suffering from jaundice. The driver clearly had no idea where he was going, and it was left to Flin to direct him, instructing him to turn right here, left there, straight ahead at this crossroads until finally they pulled up outside one of the blocks, indistinguishable from its neighbours save for the slightly different patterns of washing hanging from its balconies. As Flin handed over a sizeable tip on top of what he'd already paid the driver, Freya slid the gun under the front seat, knowing she was never going to use it and there was no point taking it with her. They got out.

'Do you want to tell me where we are?' she asked as they walked towards the building's entrance, the blare of music receding as the taxi motored off behind them, leaving everything eerily silent.

'Ain Shams,' replied Flin. 'It's a suburb in northern Cairo. Appropriate, I suppose, given the circumstances?'

Freya raised her eyebrows, asked what he meant.

'Remember the papyrus we saw in the museum? Imti-Khentika wrote it in the great sun temple of Heliopolis, and the remains of the great sun temple of Heliopolis . . .'

He stamped a foot on the ground.

'The most important religious centre in ancient Egypt now propping up a housing estate.' He shook his head wearily. 'Such is progress.'

They passed into a dusty foyer area – a row of gas cylinders lined up along one wall, a stack of broken chairs against another – and started up a staircase.

'Is this where you live?'

Flin shook his head.

'Just somewhere they use.'

She waited for him to expand on this, explain who 'they' were, but he just led her up to the third floor and along a gloomy corridor, stopping in front of a door about halfway down. He paused, head cocked, listening – whether for sounds from within the apartment or from back along the corridor she couldn't tell – then, raising a hand, gave three sharp knocks. Almost immediately, as though someone was waiting on the other side, there was a soft scraping sound as the door's spyhole cover was drawn back, and then the door itself was thrown open. In front of them stood Molly Kiernan.

'Thank God,' she said, grasping Flin's hand and then Freya's, pulling them into the apartment and kicking the door closed behind them. 'I've been so very worried.'

Although it was less than 48 hours since Freya had last seen her, she seemed older somehow, more careworn, her eyes puffy from lack of sleep, her skin lined and grey. She gazed at them, taking in their filthy clothes, Flin's bloodied arm, then ushered them down a hallway and into a softly lit living area, Flin all the while filling her in on what had happened. No great detail, just a basic overview, starting with what Freya had told him about the body in the desert, the map, the photographic films, and then moving on to the events of that afternoon and evening. As he spoke Freya got the unsettling impression from the manner in which he described it all, the way he seemed to take it as read that Kiernan would know about such things as the Hidden Oasis and Rudi Schmidt and Romani Girgis and the Gilf Kebir, that while the specifics of what they had gone through might have been new to her, the characters and places involved most certainly weren't.

In the living room Kiernan sat them down on a sofa and disappeared. She returned a moment later with a bowl of warm water, a first aid kit and a steel surgical dish in which sat various syringes and glass ampoules.

'Flin texted me that you weren't in great shape,' she explained to Freya as she knelt in front of Flin and, clicking her fingers, motioned him to roll up his sleeve. 'There are towels and clean clothes in the bedrooms – I had to guess your size, I'm afraid – but first we need to get you both patched up. Ow!'

She winced as she saw the wound on Flin's arm, a gaping four-inch tear slicing down his forearm.

'Whole shirt off, please.'

He mumbled something.

'For goodness sake, it's nothing Freya and I haven't seen before. Come on, get it off.'

Reluctantly he stood. Undoing a few buttons, he pulled out the photographs of the oasis – unharmed save for some mud smears on the topmost one – and placed them on the floor before unbuttoning the rest of the shirt. He slipped it off his shoulders and sat down again. His torso was wiry and muscular, his chest matted with dark hair. Brisk and businesslike, Kiernan snapped on a pair of surgical gloves and set to work wiping down his arm with water and cotton wool before gently cleaning the wound with a disinfectant swab.

'My mother was a nurse,' she explained to Freya as she dabbed. 'I've been doing this sort of stuff my whole life. You up to date with your tetanus and hepatitis jabs?'

'I have no idea,' said Freya. 'Look, I want to know—'

'Let's get you cleaned up first, then we can talk.' Kiernan's tone was kindly but firm, matron-like, leaving no room for argument. 'I'm going to sort Flin out, then give you booster shots. You don't want to take any chances if you've been crawling round somewhere like Manshiet

Nasser. The place is home to every germ known to man. And probably a few that aren't as well.'

She finished cleaning Flin's arm and, pulling what looked like a large biro from the first aid bag, removed its lid and gently ran its tip along the lip of the wound. A transparent, glue-like liquid trailed out across the lacerated skin.

'Dermabond,' she explained, pinching the two edges of the gash together. 'Not ideal, but it will have to do till we can organize proper sutures.'

Flin had turned his head to one side and was gazing out of the window, trying not to look at his arm and what was being done to it. There was a brief silence, then:

'They can't find it.'

Initially Freya thought he was talking to himself, or to both of them, but when she looked across she saw that his eyes had swung towards Kiernan. That the comment was directed at her alone.

'They wouldn't have bothered showing me the photos otherwise. They can't find it.'

Kiernan was still pinching the lips of the wound, holding them together while the tissue adhesive bonded.

'What about Schmidt's map?' she asked. 'You said there were compass bearings, distances.'

'Obviously not accurate. It's hard enough navigating in the desert with proper equipment. By the looks of things Schmidt only had the single compass, and that had a broken sighting wire. He could have been fifty kilometres out. A hundred.'

It was surreal, as if Freya had ceased to exist.

'But Girgis has got helicopters,' Kiernan continued, checking that the wound was firmly closed before starting to bandage Flin's arm. 'Even if the bearings were a hundred kilometres out he should still be able to track it down. All he's got to do is to fly over the Gilf in the rough vicinity: a tree-filled gorge can't be that difficult to locate.'

'I can't explain it, Molly, any more than I can explain why every other bugger who's searched for the place over the years has come up empty-handed. All I know is that if Girgis had found the oasis he would have killed us straight away instead of playing name the picture. He's struggling, he's seriously struggling.'

Freya just sat there, bewildered. She felt as if she had slipped into some sort of dream state in which she was part of a scene and yet at the same time divorced from it, present but, for some inexplicable reason, barred from interacting with those around her. *I'm still here*, she felt like screaming. *I'm not invisible, you know*.

She said nothing, just allowed the conversation to unfold around her. When Kiernan had bandaged and inoculated Flin – who put his shirt back on despite it being caked in mud and blood – she instructed Freya to roll up her own sleeve and injected her as well. Two swift shots in the biceps, one for tetanus, one hepatitis B, in and out with barely a prick. Expert.

Only when all the medical stuff was out of the way and Kiernan had started talking about towels and clean clothes, explaining how to work the temperature control on the shower – 'It's a bit stubborn, I'm afraid. You have to play around with it' – did Freya finally snap.

'I don't care about the goddam shower!' she yelled, standing and backing away towards the door. 'Or towels or clothes or any of the rest of it. I want to know what's going on. You hear? I want you to tell me who you are and what the fuck's going on! Or so help me I'm walking out of this building and straight into the nearest police station.'

Flin and Kiernan exchanged a glance. Slowly and deliberately, Kiernan started gathering all the medical equipment together.

'Please sit down, Freya,' she said.

'I don't want to sit down! I want to know what's happening! How many times do I have to ask? Someone's just tried to cut off my arm and you're telling me to take a shower. What the hell's wrong with you people!'

Her voice had risen almost to a scream, her eyes wide with fury and frustration. Kiernan allowed her to finish, talk herself out, then again asked her to sit down.

'I appreciate how very difficult this is for you,' she said, calmly, but firmly. 'And please believe me, Freya, I am genuinely sorry for everything that has happened. If I had thought for one minute you were going to be in danger I would never have allowed you to stay alone in Dakhla.'

She crossed the room and dropped the used swabs, syringes and bandages into a wastepaper bin in the corner, staring down at them for a moment before turning back to Freya.

'Unfortunately one can't always foresee events,' she said, eyes fixed on the younger woman. 'One just has to deal with them as and when they occur. Which is what we are trying to do now. You have every right to demand answers, and you'll have them, I promise, but first I needed to get the full picture from Flin. Whatever you might think, you are with friends here. You're safe. Now please, Freya, sit down and we can talk.'

She extended a hand towards the sofa, the gesture at once both placatory and commanding. Freya hesitated, then sat, not on the sofa, but in an armchair opposite, perching right on the edge of the seat as though poised to leap up at any moment. Kiernan stared at her, the faintest hint of annoyance in her expression, like a teacher who has been deliberately disobeyed by a pupil. Then, with a sigh, she collected the water bowl, surgical dish and first aid kit and passed them through a serving hatch into the kitchen before taking the seat beside Flin, her hands clasped primly in her lap, her back ramrod straight. Something about the scenario, the way the two of them were positioned opposite her, made Freya feel as if she was in a job interview.

'So?' she asked.

'Well, as you've already guessed, there is more to recent events than either of us has let on to you,' said Kiernan, staring straight at Freya, her grey eyes unblinking, hard chips of flint. 'I apologize, both for myself and I'm sure for Flin as well, that you have been kept in the dark about certain things. Unfortunately there are issues of national security involved here – very considerable issues of national security – that have prevented us being wholly candid with you. I am only doing so now because after everything you've gone through continued evasion would seem both pointless and unfair. I'm going to explain what's going on, Freya, and I'm going to explain why it's going on. Before I do, however, I require your assurance that you will respect the highly sensitive nature of what you are about to hear. That no word of it will pass beyond these four walls. Will you give me that assurance?'

Freya said nothing.

311

'Will you give me that assurance, Freya?'

Still she didn't respond and Kiernan's tone hardened.

'Freya, if you can't guarantee . . .'

'She's not going to tell anyone, Molly,' said Flin. 'Not after what she's seen of Girgis. She has more reason to hate the man than either of us. She's safe.'

Kiernan continued to stare at Freya, her eyes narrowed. Then she nodded, her features softening slightly. When she spoke her voice was more gentle.

'I'm sorry, Freya, but you have to understand, this is an extremely delicate situation. I can't take any chances. There's just too much at stake here.'

Freya looked from her to Flin and back again. There was silence, then:

'You're some sort of spook, aren't you?' she said.

Kiernan unclasped her hands, smoothed down her skirt, laid her hands in her lap again.

'I work for the Central Intelligence Agency. Counter-terrorism. Flin is . . .'

'Ex-spook,' he said. 'I had a brief and distinctly inglorious career with MI6 after which it was decided the world would be a safer place if I stuck to pottery and hieroglyphs. Although they did teach me how to shoot, so I guess it wasn't a complete waste of time.'

For the briefest of moments his eyes met Freya's before veering away.

'And Alex?' she asked. 'Was she . . . ?'

Kiernan was shaking her head before Freya had even finished the question.

'Your sister was a desert explorer, not a spy. She was helping us, that's all. Just like Flin has been helping us.'

'Helping you with what, Molly? What the hell did you get my sister involved in?'

Kiernan held her stare, raising a hand to touch the small gold crucifix hanging round her neck.

'I think it's time I told you about something called Sandfire,' she said. 'The reason we're sitting here now, the reason I've been in Egypt for the last twenty-three years and the reason a singularly unpleasant man named Romani Girgis will stop at nothing to find the whereabouts of the lost oasis of Zerzura.'

DAKHLA

Although he lived in a house, with a kitchen and a bathroom and three fields behind – two growing vegetables, one *bersiim* – the desert was Zahir al-Sabri's true home. And it was to the desert that he always returned when his heart was heavy. As it was tonight.

He didn't go far, just a few kilometres out, his Land Cruiser rising and falling with the dunes like a coracle on the ocean, its one working headlight casting a pale glow across the sands. Although everything merged together in the darkness – a hazy collage of sand and rock and moonlight – he seemed to know exactly where he was going. Weaving his way through the uncertain landscape, he navigated the slopes and the troughs, the gravel pans and boulder fields as though they were streets in a city, eventually turning into a long valley between high dune walls and coming to a halt beside a solitary, stunted *abal* bush.

Removing wood and straw from the back of the Land Cruiser, he built a fire. The tinder burst alight the moment he touched a match to it, like a ragged orange flower opening and unfolding with the first warmth of the sun. He brewed tea in an old, fire-blackened pot and lit his shisha pipe. Wrapping a *shaal* around himself against the evening chill, he gazed into the flames, his lips pulling gently at the shisha's mouthpiece. The only sounds were the low crackle of burning wood and, from somewhere far off, the melancholy bark of a desert fox.

Often Zahir would come out here with his brother Said, or his son Mohsen, his beloved, his heir, the light of his life. Together they would camp under the stars, sing old Bedouin songs and tell and retell the story of their family, how they had come to Egypt all those centuries ago from the al-Rashaayda homelands in Saudi Arabia. So much had changed in the intervening years. So much had been lost. Tents had been replaced with concrete and mud-brick, camels with 4x4s, nomadic freedom with taxes and identity cards and paperwork and all manner of bureaucratic restrictions. For all that they remained Bedouin at heart, desert dwellers and desert travellers, and they had only to come out here for a few hours to remind themselves of the fact, to reconnect with their illustrious heritage.

Tonight, puffing on his pipe, Zahir dwelt upon that heritage. In particular upon the memory of his ancestor, Mohammed Wald Yusuf Ibrahim Sabri al-Rashaayda, the greatest of all Bedouin, the father of his tribe, who with his camels had crossed the Sahara from north to south, east to west, until there was no corner of the wilderness with which he wasn't familiar, no grain of sand that he hadn't at some point trodden underfoot.

There were so many wonderful stories about Old Mohammed, so many tales and legends that had been handed down through the generations. But for Zahir, one story stood out above all others, encapsulating everything that was noble about both his kinsman and his people as a whole. And the story was this: once, travelling deep within the Sahara, two hundred kilometres and more from the nearest oasis, Old Mohammed had come across a man staggering across the sands. He was without food or water or camel, and vultures were circling silently overhead in anticipation of his imminent death.

The stranger, it transpired, was a Kufra Bedouin, of the Banu Sulaim tribe, a sworn enemy of the al-Rashaayda. Mohammed's own brother had been killed by a Banu raiding party, and he would have been well within his rights to have cut the man's throat there and then with the knife that now hung on Zahir's living room wall. Instead he had given him water to drink even though his own supplies were dangerously short and lifted him onto his camel and carried him seven days to safety, by which point both of them were at death's door.

'Why have you done this?' the Kufra Bedouin had asked when at last they had sighted civilization. 'Saved me when there is such hatred between our tribes, so many wrongs that can never be righted?'

And Mohammed's answer: 'For the Rashaayda Bedouin there are many obligations, but none more precious than the duty of care to the stranger in need, whoever they might be.'

Usually this story was a source of joy and pride to Zahir. How many times had he recounted it to his son, enjoining him to live as Old Mohammed had lived, to show the same dignity and humility and compassion?

Tonight, after all that had happened lately, it made him neither joyful nor proud. Instead it caused him to feel the most unbearable sense of emptiness and self-reproach.

For the Rashaayda Bedouin there are many obligations, but none more precious than the duty of care to the stranger in need.

Fumbling in his pocket he pulled out the metal compass. He opened it up and gazed at the initials inscribed on the inside of the metal lid – AH – his dark eyes glowing in the firelight, the words of his ancestor echoing around his head, chiding and tormenting him. What use was knowing the desert as he knew it, keeping alive all the old stories and songs, if he could not live up to the most funda-mental precept of his people? He had a duty, and he had failed in that duty. The weight of his failure pressed down on him, so that tonight, instead of helping him to reconnect with his Rashaayda heritage, his presence out here in the wilderness only served to remind Zahir how unworthy he was of it.

For the Rashaayda Bedouin there are many obligations, but none more precious than the duty of care to the stranger in need.

He finished his tea and puffed a while longer on his pipe. Unable to find the peace he craved, he kicked sand over the fire, threw his equipment back into the Land Cruiser and set off home. The dunes rolled and turned around him as if the desert was shaking its head, letting him know how very disappointed it was.

CAIRO

'How much do you know about the Iran–Iraq War?'

Molly Kiernan's voice echoed from the kitchen where she was making coffee. It was not a question Freya had been expecting.

'Is this going to be a history lecture?' she asked. 'Because I've already had one of those today and, fascinating as it was, I'm not in the mood for another.'

Kiernan looked through the kitchen's serving hatch, uncertain what Freya was talking about.

'I gave her the Zerzura tour,' explained Flin. 'In the museum.'

'Ah.' Kiernan nodded, pouring steaming water out of a kettle. 'No, I'm not going to give you a lecture – I leave that sort of thing to the professionals.'

She tipped her head at Flin and continued pouring.

'Just a bit of background. No Benbens or papyri, I promise.'

There was a rattle of mugs as she lifted a tray and disappeared from view before reappearing in the living room doorway. She came over and placed the tray on the floor.

'It's only instant, I'm afraid,' she said, handing mugs up to Freya and Flin. 'And there's no milk or sugar, but I guess it's better than nothing.'

She took the third mug for herself and went over to the window, tweaking back the curtains and peering down at the street below before turning to face them.

'So?' she asked, blowing on her mug and sipping, her left hand perched on her left hip. 'You know anything about the war?'

PAUL SUSSMAN

Freya shrugged.

'Not really. Only what came out on the news when we invaded Iraq. Didn't we support Saddam, supply him with weapons?'

Flin grunted. 'Not the free world's finest hour. Propping up a genocidal, mass-murdering dictator in the interests of some warped notion of *realpolitik*.'

Kiernan tutted, gave an impatient shake of the head.

'Let's not get into a political debate here. Freya wants answers and I think we should focus on providing them.'

Flin stared into his coffee mug.

'The war lasted from '80 to '88,' continued Kiernan, 'and pitted Saddam's Iraq against Khomeini's Iran. Two utterly barbaric regimes, although Saddam's was marginally the lesser of evils, which is why, as you rightly said, we were prepared to offer him financial assistance, intelligence, weaponry—'

'Biological agents courtesy of special envoy Donald Rumsfeld,' interrupted Flin.

Again Kiernan tutted.

'We supported Saddam for exactly the same reasons that Britain, France, Germany, Italy, Russia and a dozen other countries supported him. Because the alternative, namely a victory for Khomeini and his revolutionary madmen, was just too terrible to contemplate. As Kissinger put it at the time, it was a shame they couldn't both lose, but if someone had to emerge victorious it was better for all of us that it should be Saddam.'

'And what a loyal ally he proved to be,' muttered Flin.

Kiernan threw him an annoyed look.

'Whatever,' she said. 'All that's relevant for current

purposes is that by the mid-1980s, after some initial successes, Iraq was militarily very much on the back foot. Although it had the more advanced weaponry and better trained troops, the war had by that point settled into a drawn-out conflict of attrition, and that favoured Iran, which had three times as many men on the ground and didn't give a hoot how many of them got slaughtered because there were always more to replace them.'

Her mouth puckered slightly, as if in distaste at the mind-set she was describing.

'The fact that a significant proportion of the Iraqi army was made up of Shia Muslims only added to Saddam's worries,' she added, 'given that he and his ruling regime were Sunni.'

In front of her Freya sipped at her coffee – weak, taste-less – wondering where the hell all this was leading. Flin had sat back and was gazing up at the ceiling, eyes tracing a thin crack that ran diagonally from one side of the room to the other.

'By 1986 Saddam was a seriously nervous man,' Kiernan went on, her left hand coming up and fiddling with the crucifix at her neck. 'It was clear that even with western support he was never going to win the war outright, and actually stood a good chance of losing it. He was like a boxer coming into the final rounds of a fight, knowing he's behind on points, his opponent's got more in the tank and the longer the contest goes on, the more vulnerable he is. What was needed, he decided, was a single knockout blow, a sucker punch that would end the conflict there and then and take out Iran in one fell swoop.'

She paused, her eyes fixed on Freya.

'And the obvious form for that sucker punch to take was a nuclear strike against Tehran.'

Freya looked up, surprised.

'But I thought . . .'

'Saddam didn't have the bomb?' Kiernan finished the sentence for her. 'He didn't. He wanted it, though, desperately. And despite what Blix and the other bleeding-hearts at the UN claimed, he came way closer to getting it than has ever been publicly acknowledged.'

From outside came the sudden, high-pitched shriek of cats fighting. Kiernan took another cautious look out of the window, then moved over and sat on the arm of the sofa beside Flin.

'Believe it or not, building an atomic device isn't tech-nically that difficult,' she said, sipping her coffee. 'Certainly not to someone with the sort of scientific resources Saddam had at his disposal. The problem is acquiring the necessary fissile material, specifically plutonium-239 or uranium-235. I won't go into the physics of it all – to be honest I don't even understand the physics – but producing either of these isotopes in sufficient quantity, and to a sufficient degree of purity for deployment in a weapon, is an enormously com-plex, costly, time-consuming process, and one that back in 1986, as today, was beyond all but a handful of countries. Saddam was never going to achieve it on his own, and what-ever other support the western governments were giving him they sure as hell weren't going to welcome him into the nuclear club. So he started looking elsewhere, putting out feelers to some of the world's more unscrupulous arms traders to see if they could procure the necessary goods for him. And in late 1986 one of those arms traders came up trumps.'

She drained off the remainder of her drink.

'That man was Romani Girgis.'

Freya had been on the point of butting in, demanding to know what all this had to do with her sister's murder, with everything that had happened to her these last 24 hours. At the mention of Girgis's name, she held off.

'Girgis is an arms dealer?' she asked.

'Among other things,' said Flin, sitting forward. 'Arms, drugs, prostitution, antiquities smuggling – there aren't many shit-pies he doesn't have a finger in. Arms trading's his main thing, though.'

'And he supplied Saddam Hussein with a bomb?'

'With fifty kilos of highly enriched, weapons-grade uranium, to be precise,' said Kiernan. 'Enough to construct two implosion-type atomic devices with the destructive power of the Hiroshima bomb. At a stroke Saddam could have flattened Tehran and Mashhad, ended the war, ended the Iranian Revolution, established himself as the dominant power in the entire region. In short, changed the course of history. And he almost did it as well.'

She allowed Freya to absorb this, then stood.

'More coffee, anyone?'

Flin handed up his mug, Freya kept hers. Kiernan disappeared back into the kitchen. For a brief moment Flin and Freya's eyes met, then they both looked away.

'Even quarter of a century after the event we're still not a hundred per cent clear about the precise details of the deal Girgis put together,' came Kiernan's voice. 'From what we can gather he acquired the uranium from a Soviet middleman named Leonid Kanunin – a distinctly unpleasant piece of work who got himself murdered in a Paris hotel suite back in '87 – who in turn seems to have sourced it from contacts in the Soviet military. Where exactly it came from originally we've never managed to pin down, nor is it relevant. What we do know is that in November 1986 Girgis chartered a Cayman-registered Antonov cargo plane piloted by a guy named Kurt Reiter, a veteran cold war drug and arms smuggler. That plane rendezvoused with Kanunin at an airfield in northern Albania where two of Girgis's representatives picked up the goods and handed over a down-payment of $50 million. To keep people off the scent the cargo was then to be flown round two sides of a triangle, first down to Khartoum and only then over to Baghdad, where its safe arrival would trigger a balance payment to Kanunin of another $50 million. Girgis would get his twenty per cent cut, Saddam his bomb, Iran would be obliterated. Smiles all round.'

She came back into the living room with two steaming mugs, handed one to Flin and again perched herself on the arm of the sofa. There was silence. Freya stared down at the floor, processing everything Kiernan had just told her. Then, looking up again, right into Kiernan's eyes, she put the question she had been on the point of asking five minutes earlier.

'I don't understand what any of this has to do with my sister. With this hidden oasis thing?'

'Well now we come to it,' said Kiernan. 'We'd got wind of the whole operation pretty early on, from informants in both Girgis's and Kanunin's organizations. But it was all broad-brush stuff. We knew what was being planned, who was involved – what we couldn't get hold of were precise dates, places, times. It was literally only a couple of hours before the Albanian rendezvous that we were finally able to nail down details of how the uranium was being moved, and where it was being moved to.

'By that point it was way too late in the day to intercept the Antonov before it took off. There was a slim possibility we could have caught it when it came down to refuel in Benghazi, but given our relations with Gaddafi at the time that would have presented a lot of complications. Better to keep a close track on the plane and catch it in Khartoum, before it started its final run up to Baghdad. We had a Special Forces unit stationed just across the Red Sea in Saudi, the Israelis were primed to help out. It should have been textbook. Would have been textbook if nature in her wisdom hadn't intervened.'

'Nature?' Freya shook her head, not understanding.

'The one thing we could never have planned for,' said Kiernan with a sigh. 'The Antonov got hit by a sandstorm as it was flying over the Sahara, lost both its engines. One of our listening stations picked up a Mayday from somewhere over the Gilf Kebir Plateau and then the plane dropped off the radar screens and disappeared.'

For the first time Freya caught a faint glimpse of light, of understanding.

'It crashed into the oasis, didn't it? That's what this is all about. Why Girgis wanted the photos. The plane crashed into the Hidden Oasis.'

Kiernan smiled although there was no humour in the expression.

'We didn't find that out immediately,' she said. 'All we knew was that the Antonov had come down somewhere in the vicinity of the Gilf, which is a pretty big area, 5,000 square kilometres of rock and desert. But about six hours after the first Mayday we picked up a second radio message, this one sent by the plane's co-pilot, a guy named Rudi Schmidt, who seems to have been the only survivor of the crash. The transmission was garbled and only lasted about thirty seconds, but in that time Schmidt was able to give a rough description of where the plane had crashed. In a tree-filled gorge, he said, with ruins everywhere. Ancient ruins, including some sort of enormous temple with a strange obelisk-shaped symbol carved all over it.'

'The Benben,' murmured Freya. Although the room was warm she felt goosebumps prickling her arms.

'Even without that little titbit it couldn't have been any-where *but* the *wehat seshtat*,' said Flin, taking up the story. 'There are no other known or reputed ancient sites within two hundred miles of the Gilf Kebir, and certainly none inside the sort of gorge he was describing. It's just about conceivable it was some unknown site, but the Benben motif put it beyond any doubt.'

He shook his head and bent forward, picking up the photographs he had dropped on the floor.

'A million-to-one chance,' he said, leafing through the images. 'A billion to one. With the whole Sahara to crash in, the Antonov comes down slap bang in the middle of the Hidden Oasis. Like dropping a piece of cotton over New York and it just happening to thread itself through the eye of a needle. You couldn't make it up, you just couldn't make it up.'

On the sofa-arm beside him Kiernan was also staring at the photos. It was the first time she had seen them, and her eyes were gleaming.

'We've been looking for that plane for nigh on twenty-three years,' she said, her head angled to one side to get a better view of the pictures. 'Sandfire – that was the operational name we used for the search. It was highly classified of course – even within the Agency there was only a small group of us who knew anything about it – and from the outset a decision was taken to not involve the Egyptian authorities for fear of someone tipping off Girgis we were on to him. Even so, given the available technology – satellite imaging, surveillance aircraft, UAVs – we should have been able to track the thing down in a matter of days.'

She sat up straight again, looking over at Freya.

'As it is we have scoured every inch of the Gilf Kebir and a hundred and fifty miles out into the desert 360 degrees around it, and we haven't found a bean. We've looked from the air, we've looked from space, we've looked on the ground, we've turned over what feels like every piece of rock from Abu Ballas and the Great Sand Sea down to Jebel Uweinat and Yerguehda Hill. And after all that . . .'

She gave a helpless snort.

'Nada. Nothing. An eighty-foot, twenty-ton aeroplane just upped and vanished. Believe me, I don't go in for occult superstition, but even I've started to think all that stuff in the Imti-Khentika papyrus about curses and spells of concealment might have some truth to it. I sure as goodness can't come up with any other explanation.'

Outside a car alarm started blaring, stopping almost immediately. Kiernan stood and took another peek through the curtains before turning back, folding her arms.

'For the first few years we threw everything we had at the problem. After that we started to scale back. If we couldn't find the oasis, we figured, it was highly unlikely Girgis or anyone else was going to. We obviously kept an eye on things, especially after 9/11 – it doesn't bear thinking about what would happen if a group like al-Qaeda got wind there was fifty kilos of highly enriched uranium sitting un-protected out in the middle of the desert. We still carry out regular satellite and U-2 surveillance sweeps, have a Special Ops unit on permanent standby down in Kharga in case something does turn up. But for the most part we've been relying on what we call ANOs, Amenable Non-Operatives: civilians who for whatever reason have a particular knowledge of, or involvement, with the geographical area we're interested in, and might conceivably stumble on something we've missed.'

She nodded towards the sofa.

'Flin I'd got to know back in the nineties, when he was with MI6. After he . . .'

A fractional hesitation, as if she was choosing the right words.

'. . . ended his association with British Intelligence and went back into Egyptology, moved out here, I got in touch, asked for his help. An obvious choice given the work he was doing.'

'And Alex?' asked Freya.

'Again, your sister was an obvious choice. Our paths had crossed back in Langley when she was temping in the CIA cartographic department. When I heard she'd settled in Dakhla I looked her up and outlined the situation. With the exception of Zahir al-Sabri I've never met anyone who knew the Gilf as well as Alex did. She agreed to get involved, in return for which we channelled some money into her research. Although to be honest, I think it was more the challenge that attracted her than the funding or a desire to protect the free world. Alex being Alex, I got the impression she looked on it all as a bit of a colourful adventure.'

Freya shook her head sadly. That was exactly why Alex would have got involved, she thought – because it was something different, something intriguing. She'd never been able to resist a mystery. And this one had got her killed. Poor Alex. Poor darling Alex.

'. . . kept everything as simple as we could,' Kiernan was saying. 'They reported to me and that was it, they had no involvement with the Agency *per se*. We'd just about convinced ourselves the plane was never going to be found. That it was just one of those inexplicable, Bermuda Triangle-type mysteries. And then suddenly after twenty-three years, Rudi Schmidt's body appears out of nowhere and the whole thing's blown wide open again.'

She sighed and rubbed her temples. She looked, thought Freya, even more careworn than when they'd first arrived in the flat.

'Unbelievable,' she said. 'And, obviously, extremely worrying. Saddam might be gone but there are plenty of others who'd be more than happy to pick up his end of the deal. And Romani Girgis is not the sort of man to quibble about who he does business with.'

She swivelled round and took yet another look out of the window, head craning back and forth before she turned back again. Silence.

'So what now?' asked Freya. 'What are you going to do?'

Kiernan shrugged.

'There's not really a whole lot we can do. We'll get those computer-analysed' – she indicated the photos in Flin's hand – 'ramp up our surveillance of the Gilf and Girgis. Aside from that . . .'

She threw up her hands.

'Watch, wait, twiddle our thumbs. That's about it.'

'But Girgis murdered my sister,' said Freya. 'He killed Alex.'

Kiernan's brow furrowed at this, her eyes flicking across to Flin, who gave a barely perceptible shake of the head as if to say 'Let it go.'

'Girgis killed my sister,' Freya repeated, her face flushing. 'I'm not just going to sit around doing nothing. Do you understand? I'm not just going to let it go.'

Her voice was starting to rise. Kiernan came over and squatted down in front of her. Reaching out, she squeezed her arm.

'Romani Girgis will get what's coming to him,' she said. 'If you trust me on nothing else, trust me on this.'

There was a pause, Kiernan holding Freya's eyes. Then, with a nod, she rose again.

'Right now, though, I think we've talked enough and you should go get that shower. Because from where I'm standing you don't smell so good.'

She smiled and despite herself Freya did too. Exhausted suddenly, she stood.

'You said there were clean clothes.'

'First bedroom on the right,' said Kiernan. 'On the bed. You'll find towels there as well. And do watch the temperature control on the shower – it's got a will of its own.'

Freya crossed to the door, stepping out into the corridor,

only to turn and put her head back into the room again.

'I'm sorry about the gun thing,' she said to Flin. 'In the taxi. I was never going to shoot you.'

He waved a hand.

'I know. You'd left the safety catch on. Try not to use all the hot water.'

After she'd left, Kiernan eased herself into the armchair Freya had just vacated. The hiss of the shower echoed from the far end of the flat.

'She's just like Alex, don't you think?'

Flin was working through the photographs again, still in his filthy shirt and jeans.

'Different as well,' he said, not looking up. 'Darker. She's definitely got baggage.'

He held one photo above his head, squinted at it.

'Alex never did tell me what happened between them,' he added, almost as an afterthought. 'It was the one thing she'd never talk about.'

He lowered the photo and held up another. Kiernan watched him, drumming her fingers on the arm of the chair.

'See anything?'

Flin shook his head.

'Although this one's interesting.'

He handed her the picture he'd been examining – a statue of a human figure with the head of a crocodile. It stood on a large, cube-shaped plinth on whose face – clearly visible – was a hieroglyphic text framed within the coils of a serpent.

'Sobek and Apep?' asked Kiernan.

Flin nodded.

'The same curse formula as in the Imti-Khentika papyrus. May evildoers be crushed in the jaws of Sobek, and swallowed into the belly of the serpent Apep. Except here there's something more. See.'

He leant forward and tapped a finger on the bottom of the picture.

'And inside the serpent's belly,' he translated, 'may their fears become real, their *resut binu* – that's evil dreams – a living torment. Not exactly revelatory, but intriguing from an academic point of view. Another tiny fragment of the mosaic.'

'Does it get us any closer to the actual oasis?'

He grunted.

'Not even a millimetre.'

He took the photo back, flipped through the rest of the pile one more time, then dropped them on the sofa and stood.

'By all means get them enhanced, but I can tell you now there's nothing here,' he said. 'You're wasting your time, Molly. They're useless.'

He rolled his neck and walked across to a wooden cabinet on the far side of the room. Opening it, he pulled out a three-quarters-empty bottle of Bell's whisky and a small tumbler.

'Medicinal,' he said, noting the disapproving look on Kiernan's face.

He filled the tumbler, knocked it back in one slug and refilled it, replacing the bottle in the cabinet and returning to the sofa. For a while he just sat there, swirling the whisky around, the liquid lapping the inside of the glass like a dirty gold tongue. The hiss of streaming water could still be heard from the bathroom. Then, downing half the drink, Flin fixed his eyes on Kiernan. 'There's something else, Molly.'

She raised her eyebrows, tilted her head slightly.

'I think someone might be hacking into your mobile.'

Kiernan said nothing, although the way her fingers suddenly stopped drumming suggested Flin's comment had taken her by surprise.

'When Freya arrived in Cairo she left a message on your voicemail,' he went on. 'Letting you know she was coming to see me at the university. Thirty minutes later a bunch of goons turn up and make straight for my office. It's conceivable someone on campus was looking out for her and tipped Girgis off, but then when we were at the museum I also left a message on your voicemail. Result: the same bunch of goons appear out of nowhere and a good friend of mine gets his throat slit. It's too much of a coincidence. Girgis has to be accessing your phone.'

Flin had known Kiernan for the best part of fifteen years, and in all of that time he had never once seen her look agitated. Until now.

'That's not possible,' she said, standing. 'That's simply not possible.'

'I can't see any other explanation. Unless Freya's lying or you're working for Girgis, both of which I somehow doubt.'

Kiernan strode over to the table where her shoulder bag was sitting and pulled out her Nokia. She brandished it.

'This is an Agency phone, Flin. It cannot be hacked. There are passwords, PINs, specialist IDs – it's ring-fenced. Even the goddam Russians couldn't get in.'

Another first. Never, ever had Flin heard Kiernan use an expletive. He took another sip of the whisky.

'Someone in-house?'

She opened her mouth, closed it and bit her lip.

'No,' she said eventually. And again: 'No. Not possible. The CIA does not go around gatecrashing its own operatives' private communications. Sure the technology's there, but to use it against an Agency employee – you're talking top-level authorization here. It's not . . . I can't believe it. I just can't believe it. There has to be some other explanation.'

Flin shrugged and downed the remainder of the whisky. Reaching into the pocket of his jeans, he pulled out the card Angleton had given him back in the Windsor Hotel and handed it across.

'Either way I think you should check this guy out.'

Kiernan took the card.

'He's been keeping an eye on me. Turning up in places he shouldn't be turning up. At the museum for example, just as Girgis's goons were hustling us away. I can't prove anything, but I'd lay strong odds however they found out we were there, that's how he found out. Whatever else he is, he sure as hell doesn't work in Public Affairs.'

Kiernan was examining the card, eyes boring into it, her face suddenly devoid of colour, as though this last revelation had agitated her more than anything that had come before. The hiss of the shower tailed off, leaving the flat silent. Then, stepping over to her bag, Kiernan dropped the card and mobile into it and swung back to face Flin.

'You're getting out of Cairo,' she said, her tone firm suddenly, authoritative. 'Out of Egypt. Both of you. Tonight. It's too dangerous. Things are getting out of hand. Have already got out of hand.'

'No offence, Molly, but I'm a civilian, you can't order me around. I do what I want.'

'You want to end up dead?'

'I want to find the oasis,' he said, his eyes hard and unblinking. 'And I'm not going anywhere till I do.'

For a moment it looked as if Kiernan was going to flare up at him. Instead she came over and put a hand on Flin's shoulder.

'Is this just about the oasis?'

He looked up at her and then down into his glass.

'Meaning?'

'Meaning is there more to this than just an interest in Egyptology and a desire to stop Girgis?'

'You're sounding dangerously like a psychoanalyst, Molly.'

'I was hoping I sounded like a friend who cares about you and doesn't want you to get hurt.'

He sighed and laid his hand on Kiernan's.

'I'm sorry, that was churlish. It's just, you know . . .'

He tailed off. Kiernan twisted her hand, clasped his.

'What happened with the girl happened, Flin. It's in the past, long in the past. And whatever debt of penance you might think you owe, you've more than paid it off by now. It's time to let go.'

He continued staring down, mute.

'I know how important this is to you,' she said, 'but right now I have enough on my plate without having to worry about you and Freya as well. Please, cut me some slack. Indulge an old woman and get out of town. At least until things have quietened down and I've dealt with all the fallout from the last twenty-four hours, which believe you me is going to be considerable.'

Flin lifted his glass to his mouth even though it was empty.

'There's more I can do,' he mumbled.

'Oh please, Flin!' Kiernan shook her head, exasperated. 'What more can you possibly do that you haven't already done in the ten years you've been working with Sandfire? What? Tell me?'

'I can go through my notes again. The satellite stuff. The magnetometry data – maybe I missed something.'

There was an edge of desperation to his voice, like a child trying to persuade a parent to let them stay up late, watch some forbidden television programme.

'There has to be something,' he insisted. 'There has to be.'

'Flin, you have gone through that stuff a thousand times. Ten thousand times and you've not yet found anything. It's a dead end.'

'I can go out to the Gilf . . . I can . . . I can . . .'

'The only place you're going is Cairo international airport where you're getting on the first flight—'

'I can go and see Fadawi.' He practically shouted it.

'I can go and see Hassan Fadawi,' he repeated, looking up at Kiernan. 'He's been saying he knows something. About the oasis. That's what I heard. It's probably bullshit but at least I can go and talk to him.'

Kiernan opened her mouth to argue, then closed it again. She stared at Flin through narrowed eyes, weighing things up.

'You said he wouldn't speak to you,' she said eventually. 'Said he'd rather cut out his own tongue.'

'So he tells me to bugger off. It has to be worth a try. With the stakes this high it has to be worth a try, you can see that.'

He could sense her starting to weaken and pushed home his advantage.

'I'll go and see him. If he sends me packing I'll do what you want – take a sabbatical, piss off back to England for a few weeks. Please, Molly, let me give it a go. I've come this far, for heaven's sake. Don't cut me out now. Not when there are still options open. Not now, not yet.'

She stood where she was, her hand coming up to the cross around her neck.

'What about Freya?'

'Well, in an ideal world she *would* get on the first flight out of here,' he replied. 'But from what I've seen of her so far she's not going to go quietly.'

Kiernan folded her arms. Another pause.

'OK,' she said reluctantly. 'Go talk to Fadawi. See if he knows anything. But if it's a red herring . . .'

'Then I'm out of here. Spooks' honour.'

He touched a hand to his forehead in mock salute.

She smiled, squeezed his shoulder again and walked across the room. Picking up a cordless phone from its holder on a bookcase beside the door, she disappeared into the kitchen. A moment later her voice could be heard: brisk, businesslike, instructing someone to arrange two emergency passports and check availability on all flights out of Cairo over the next twelve hours.

Flin was right, Freya didn't go quietly.

She reappeared ten minutes later, dressed in the clothes Kiernan had found for her – jeans, shirt, cardigan, plimsolls.

The outfit was a surprisingly good fit, although she'd had to turn up the jean bottoms and the shirt and cardigan were just a little too tight. She hadn't bothered with the bra, which was three sizes too big.

When Kiernan explained what had been decided, that for her own safety she was going to be put on the next available flight out of Egypt, she refused point blank. She owed it to her sister to stay, she said, and wasn't going anywhere till she had seen Girgis in either a police cell or a coffin. They tried to persuade her, tell her that there was nothing she could do that wasn't already being done, but she was having none of it and insisted on going with Flin.

'Here's the score,' she said, standing in the middle of the room with her hands on her hips. 'Either we work together, or I go to the police. Or you keep me here against my will, which I'd like to see you try.'

She planted her feet and clenched her fists as if she was about to launch into a prizefight. Kiernan gave an impatient shake of the head. Flin smiled.

'I think we're fighting a losing battle, Molly. Freya and I will go and see Fadawi together, and if nothing comes of it we'll fly out together.'

Kiernan still wasn't happy – 'For goodness sake, we're not haggling in a bazaar here!' – but Freya was adamant and in the end the older woman was forced to back down.

'Like dealing with a pair of naughty children,' she muttered. 'It's come to a fine pass when I have to negotiate how to run my own intelligence operation.'

She sounded more cross than she looked, and although her voice was sharp, there was an amused glint in her eye.

'Please don't make me regret this,' she said.

Flin got himself showered and changed, his clothes a rather less successful combo than Freya's. 'I look like some sort of gay clubber,' he grumbled, indicating his baggy pink shirt and embroidered jeans. Grabbing her shoulder bag, Kiernan then took them downstairs and out of the building. A couple of blocks along the street a silver Cherokee Sport was parked beside a children's play area.

'You can take my car,' she said, handing Flin the keys, tapping a permit on the inside of the windscreen. 'It's got Embassy ID so it'll get you through any security points without too many questions. You OK for money?'

Flin nodded.

'If what you've told me's true probably best not to call me on my mobile from now on. Or any of my landlines either.'

'So how do I contact you?'

Kiernan took a small notepad and pen out of her bag, tore off a sheet of paper and scribbled a number on it.

'Until I get all this checked out you can leave messages for me here. It's a secure service, no one knows anything about it except me so unless they're monitoring every line in and out of Egypt it should be foolproof.'

She handed the number over and they climbed into the Jeep. Sitting behind the wheel Flin adjusted the driver seat, started the engine and lowered his window.

'Keep in touch,' said Kiernan. 'And watch yourselves.'

'You watch yourself,' said Flin.

There seemed nothing else to say and with a nod, he slid the automatic shift into Drive and they started to move off. Kiernan called after him.

'This has nothing to do with the girl, Flin. You don't owe anyone anything. Remember that. It's history.'

He just tooted and, without looking back, headed down the street and round the corner, pointedly ignoring the quizzical stare he was getting from Freya.

Kiernan waited until the car had disappeared before rummaging in her bag and removing her mobile phone.

'Shit,' she murmured. 'How the hell . . . Shit!'

Cy Angleton had a gun, a Colt Series 70 – a beautiful thing, nickel-plated, and with a rosewood grip inlaid with tiny lozenges of platinum and pearl. It had been given to him years back by a Saudi businessman in return for services rendered, and just as some people like to name their cars or their houses, regarding them not as inanimate objects but as actual people, so Angleton's pistol also had a name. She was called Missy, after the freckle-faced girl who had sat behind him in class when he was a kid and was the one person who'd shown him any sort of kindness, who had not teased him about his size and his voice and all his various medical infirmities.

Although he practised regularly with Missy – blasting cans off fences, punching holes through the target sheets of his local firing range – and always took her with him wherever in the world he travelled, he had never once used her in an operational situation. Never once even come close to using her, preferring to leave her tucked up in the bottom of his suitcase like a baby in its cot, content in the knowledge that she was there if needed.

Tonight was different. Tonight he had brought Missy out, cleaned and oiled her, slotted in a new magazine and tucked her into the buckskin shoulder holster beneath his jacket. Which is where she now rested, cushioned against the rolls of flesh just beneath his heart, keeping him company as he sat in his hire car and watched Brodie and the girl climb into the Cherokee and drive off down the street in front of him.

He'd followed Kiernan out here earlier in the evening. It had been an easy tail despite the heavy Cairo traffic and he'd kept pace with her the whole way, tagging along three or four cars behind and parking in a side street as she disappeared into the apartment block. He hadn't known about that – she was clever, slippery. Twenty minutes later Brodie and the girl had turned up, as he'd had a hunch they might, the three of them remaining in the flat for the best part of an hour before they all reappeared and the younger couple climbed into the Cherokee. Which left him with a quandary. Should he stick around and see what Kiernan did, or follow the car? He started the engine and patted Missy, aware that a swift decision was needed.

They were on to him, of that Angleton was convinced. Why else would Brodie have written his earlier text to Kiernan in some sort of code, the first time he had ever done such a thing? How on to him Angleton couldn't be sure, but his guess was general suspicion rather than specific facts.

It was still a nuisance, an intense nuisance, if not a wholly unexpected one. Things were starting to speed up and narrow down, as they always did on this sort of job. First came the subtle stalking, the game of cat and mouse, then the full-on chase, and, finally, the catch and kill – although who exactly was going to end up dead in this instance remained unclear. Which is why he'd wanted Missy with him. Things, he sensed, were about to turn nasty. Had already turned nasty.

The Cherokee rounded a corner and disappeared from view. Angleton desperately wanted to know what was going on with Kiernan. There were still so many missing pieces. But for the moment instinct told him he needed to stick with Brodie and Hannen. Throwing a final look up the lamp-lit street – was he imagining it or was Kiernan scowling at her mobile? – he pulled out after the Jeep, keeping one hand on the steering wheel while with the other he tapped a number into his mobile and held it to his ear.

In his wood-panelled office Girgis replaced the telephone receiver and sat forward, clasping his hands on top of his desk.

'Make yourselves comfortable, gentlemen. I suspect we're in for a long night.'

In front of him Boutros Salah, Ahmed Usman and Mohammed Kasri were sitting in high-backed leather arm-chairs. Salah cradled a balloon of brandy, Usman and Kasri sipped tea.

'That's it?' wheezed Salah in his throaty, cigarette-scoured voice. 'We sit and wait?'

'That's it,' replied Girgis. 'I'm assuming the helicopters are fuelled? The equipment ready to load?'

Salah nodded.

'Then there's nothing else we can do.'

'And if they're giving us the run-around?'

'Then we allow the twins to do what they do best,' said Girgis, nodding towards one of the closed-circuit televisions banked up along the side wall. The two brothers could be seen playing snooker in a downstairs room.

'I don't like it,' muttered Salah. 'I don't like it, Romani. They could just take off.'

'You have any better suggestions?'

Salah grumbled, taking a swig of his brandy and a draw on the cigarette he held in his other hand.

'Then we wait,' said Girgis, leaning back and folding his arms. 'We sit and wait.'

Ninety minutes earlier, following Brodie and the girl's escape from Manshiet Nasser, he had been apoplectic – screaming and shouting, scratching at himself as though thousands of tiny insects were scurrying across his skin. Now he was calm, collected, focused – unrecognizable. It was the aspect of his character those around him found the most disconcerting: the way volcanic rage would suddenly segue into sober composure before equally suddenly switching back the other way. It made him impossible to predict, to know how to deal with. Left his employees constantly wrong-footed. Which is exactly how Girgis liked it.

A servant brought more tea and the four men once again ran through the logistical details, confirming that all the elements of the operation were ready to slot into place if and when any new information emerged. After which Kasri and Usman drifted away – Kasri into the library to work on his laptop, Usman to amuse himself with one of the girls Girgis always kept on tap to service guests and associates – leaving Girgis and Salah alone in the study.

'I still don't like it,' grumbled Salah, stubbing out one

cigarette and immediately firing up another with the lighter that hung from a chain around his neck. 'It's leaving too much to chance.'

Girgis smiled. They went back a long way, he and Boutros. Kasri had been with him for twenty years, Usman a mere seventeen. Salah, on the other hand, had been there right at the very beginning, the two of them having grown up together in the same Manshiet Nasser tenement. There at the beginning, and still here now, his closest confidant, the one person in the world he would consider calling a friend, although if it came to it he wouldn't think twice about having his throat cut. No room for sentiment in this business.

'It's all under control, Boutros,' he said. 'If Brodie comes up with anything we'll be the first to know.'

'He took out four of our people, for fuck's sake. Nobody does that. Nobody! We should be cutting the bastard's eyes out, not sitting here tapping our feet.'

Girgis gave another smile. Coming out from behind his desk he clapped his colleague on the shoulder.

'Trust me, Boutros, we'll have his eyes, his fingers and his balls as well. And the girl's eyes too, for good measure. But not until we've found the oasis. At the moment that's all that matters. Now how about a game of back-gammon?'

For a moment Salah continued to grumble, before he too broke into a smile.

'Just like old times,' he said.

'Just like old times,' echoed Girgis, sitting down in one of the leather chairs and sliding a marquetry box from beneath the coffee table between them.

'Remember that board we used to play on when we were kids?' said Salah, helping him arrange the pieces. 'The one old Father Francis gave us.'

'Whatever happened to Father Francis?' asked Girgis, laying out his counters.

'For fuck's sake, Romani! We had to waste him, don't you remember? After he found out about the dope, said he was going to report us.'

'Of course, of course. Silly man.'

They finished setting up. Dropping the dice into the leather shaker, Girgis threw. Double-six. He chuckled. Looked like it was going to be his lucky night.

It was 8.30 p.m. when Flin and Freya left the apartment. Paranoid that Girgis might somehow have tracked them, Flin drove around for ten minutes making sudden sharp turns to left and right, glancing constantly in the rearview mirror to make sure they weren't being tailed. Eventually, after a lot of toing and froing, they came back onto the same Autoroute they had travelled along earlier in the taxi – or at least it looked the same to Freya, she couldn't be sure. They continued for another couple of minutes before suddenly, to Freya's horror, the Englishman yanked the steering wheel hard to the left.

'What are you doing!' she screamed, clutching the dashboard as they sliced through a gap in the central reservation and into the opposing lanes of traffic, headlights streaking towards them like tracer fire. There was a cacophony of outraged hooting as cars and pick-up trucks swerved out of their path, Flin grimacing as he threaded the Jeep through the oncoming rush of vehicles and the wrong way down a slip road. They skidded across another busy highway – more rushing headlights and outraged beeping – and over a strip of manicured grass back into a stream of traffic that was moving in the same direction as they were. Flin slowed and took them into the inside lane, looking in the rearview mirror.

'Sorry,' he said, throwing Freya an apologetic glance. 'I just needed to be sure.'

She didn't reply, afraid that if she opened her mouth she would be sick. Hanging off a three-hundred-metre rock face would never seem quite so daring again.

They made their way back into central Cairo and crossed the Nile, picking up a broad, traffic-clogged avenue on the other side. Finally, after numerous jams and hold-ups, they drove out past the Pyramids and the city dropped away behind them, housing projects and apartment blocks giving way to empty sand and scrub, bright lights and neon to a monochrome expanse of moonlit desert. Everything became very quiet and very still, the only sounds the soft purr of the engine and the hiss of the wheels on tarmac. A sign drifted past announcing it was 213 kilometres to Alexandria. They picked up speed.

'You might want to put on some music,' said Flin, tapping a CD rack beneath the Jeep's stereo. 'We've still got a way to go.'

Freya flicked through the rack's contents, passing on the various hymn and sermon compilations – of which there seemed to be quite a number – before settling on Bob

Dylan's *Slow Train Coming*. She slotted the disc into the system, a low, slow pulse of guitar and bass echoing from the speakers, playing in the opening track.

'So who is this Hassan Fadawi?' she asked, settling back and putting her feet up on the dashboard. A staggered string of tail-lights stretched off into the distance ahead of them – small red punctures in the mercury nightscape.

'Like I told you at the museum, he's the guy who found the Imti-Khentika papyrus,' Flin replied, flicking the indicator and pulling out around a battered pick-up truck. 'The greatest archaeologist this country's ever produced. A living legend.'

'A friend of yours?'

Flin's hands seemed to clench a little tighter around the steering wheel.

'Former friend would be more accurate,' he said after a pause, a tension in his voice, as though the subject pained him. 'Now he wants to cut off my balls and kill me. With some justification, to be fair.'

Freya looked across at him, raising her eyebrows, inviting him to tell her more. He didn't, not immediately, just indicated again, this time overtaking a service taxi with a crush of black-robed women in the back. The lugubrious nasal grating of Dylan's voice filled the Cherokee's interior. Giant billboards flashed by, adverts for the Bank of Alexandria, Pharaonic Insurance, Chertex Jeans, Osram Light Bulbs looming momentarily in the car's headlights before disappearing again. She was beginning to think the conversation was closed when, with a sigh, Flin reached out and turned down the music.

'To date I've only made two really catastrophic mistakes

in my life,' he said. 'Three if you count sleeping with my housemaster's wife at school. And of those mistakes the most recent was getting Hassan Fadawi banged up in prison.'

He sat back from the wheel and stretched out his arms, wincing slightly. Whether from distaste at the memory or because his lacerated forearm was hurting, Freya couldn't tell. A lorry hurtled past in the opposite direction, its buffeting slipstream causing the Cherokee to veer and judder. There was another pause.

'We met when I was an undergraduate at Cambridge,' he said eventually, his eyes fixed on the road ahead, his voice low. 'Ironically, at almost exactly the same time Girgis's uranium consignment was plummeting into the Hidden Oasis. Hassan was at the university on a year's visiting fellowship and we got to know each other. He took me under his wing, became a sort of mentor figure – taught me everything I know about field archaeology. Given the age difference it was never really a relationship of equals, and he could be a difficult bastard when he wanted, but you forgave him because he was just such a brilliant scholar. I would never have finished my Ph.D. without his help. And when my MI6 career went tits-up it was Hassan who swung me the lecturing job at the American University, persuaded the Supreme Council of Antiquities to grant me an excavation concession out in the Gilf. He saved my career, basically.'

'So why did you get him sent to prison?'

Flin shot her an annoyed looked.

'Well I certainly didn't do it intentionally. It was more a sort of . . .'

He waved a hand, trying to find the right word. He

couldn't come up with it and instead reached over and lowered the electric side window a few centimetres, his hair flicking and flipping in the breeze.

'It happened three years ago,' he went on. 'I was working with Hassan on one of his projects down at Abydos, re-excavating around the Khasekhemwy funerary enclosure – I won't bore you with details. About halfway through the season he was asked to help with some conservation work in the Temple of Seti I, the main monument at Abydos. The Supreme Council needed a report on the condition of the temple's internal sanctuaries, Hassan was already on site, he was experienced in that sort of thing . . .'

He broke off, slowing and tooting as a pair of shaggy-haired camels appeared in the Cherokee's headlights, wandering directly across the highway. Startled, the animals swung and galloped back into the desert.

'To cut a long and depressing story short,' Flin resumed once they were past, 'Hassan went off to work in the Seti temple and I took over the day-to-day running of the Khasekhemwy dig. Almost immediately I started noticing that objects were going missing from our finds magazine – the secure storage hut where we kept everything we discovered on site. I alerted our site inspector, he put a watch on the magazine, and four nights later they caught someone rummaging around inside, pocketing objects.'

Freya shifted in her seat so she could look directly at him.

'Fadawi?' she asked.

Flin nodded, the glow of dashboard lights illuminating his face with a ghostly sheen.

'Hassan claimed he was just taking the objects away to study,' he said. 'That he was always going to bring them back. But when they searched his lodgings they found a load of other things hidden in his bags and it just escalated from there. Seemed he'd been stealing stuff for decades, from every site he'd ever worked on. Hundreds of the bloody things, thousands of them. Even had some Tutankhamun pieces he'd filched when he was working in the Cairo museum.'

He shook his head, gripping the wheel as another lorry thundered past on its way back to Cairo, its headlights on full beam, briefly dazzling them. Away to their right what looked like an army camp appeared: row upon row of flood-lit huts surrounded by barbed wire and with a line of sand-coloured tanks parked beside the main gate, their cannons levelled menacingly at the road.

'Legend or no legend, the Egyptian authorities take a pretty dim view of antiquities theft,' Flin continued. 'There was a trial, I had to give evidence, they decided to make an example of him. Gave him six years, banned him from ever excavating again. This for a man whose whole life was archaeology.'

He shook his head again, sweeping a hand through his hair and rubbing the back of his neck.

'And as if all that wasn't bad enough Hassan somehow convinced himself I'd engineered the whole thing. Turned him in because I wanted to take over his dig. I tried to go and see him in prison, explain things, tell him how sorry I was, but the moment he spotted me he went berserk, screaming and shouting – the guards had to escort me out. I haven't seen or heard from him since. Only discovered he'd got out a couple of days ago. Broken, by all accounts.'

He slowed as a brightly lit police roadblock loomed into

view ahead of them; just a few oil drums arranged across the highway with a pair of single-storey guardhouses to either side. A car was being waved through by the policeman manning the block. Flin came up behind it and pulled to a halt. Lowering the window all the way down, he spoke to the guard in Arabic and indicated the Embassy ID on the windscreen. There was some chatter and then they too were waved on their way, the policeman scribbling their registration number on the clip-board he was holding.

'And you think he's going to help us?' asked Freya once they were through, picking up the conversation where it had left off. 'After everything that's happened? You really think that?'

'Honestly?'

'Honestly.'

'Not for a moment. I ruined the man's life, for Christ's sake. Why should he want to do me a favour?'

'So why are we going to see him?'

'Because Hassan Fadawi told a colleague of mine he knew something about the oasis, and with fifty kilos of highly enriched uranium up for grabs I reckon even the longest of long shots is worth exploring.'

He looked across at her, then forward again, beeping and overtaking the car that had been in front of them at the checkpoint. Freya dropped her feet from the dashboard and, reaching out, turned up the volume on the CD player. The gravelly whine of Dylan's voice again filled the Jeep's interior, singing something about violence and Egypt, which in the circumstances seemed distinctly appropriate. She glanced at the dashboard clock – 9.35 p.m., they'd been on the road just over an hour – and leant her head against the window. The moonlit desert drifted by, shadowy and nondescript. Far away in the distance a tiny orange flame flickered near the horizon – some sort of oil or gas rig, she guessed.

'What was the first mistake?'

'Hmm?'

'You said you'd made two catastrophic mistakes in your life. What was the first?'

Flin didn't answer, just increased the pressure on the accelerator, the Cherokee's speedometer pushing up past 140 km/hour.

'Only another fifteen minutes,' he said.

CAIRO

The news about Angleton, that after twenty-three years the Sandfire ring-fence appeared to have been breached, had come as a bolt out of the blue to Molly Kiernan, not least because she and her colleagues had taken every precaution to ensure the whole operation remained watertight.

Once the initial shock had passed however, which it did pretty quickly, she had simply knuckled down and got on with things: tough, focused, unflappable. Molly Marble, as Charlie had jokingly used to call her. 'Hard as stone and just as beautiful!'

She had made the necessary calls to the States – her mobile was but one of many communication channels available to her – alerting everyone who needed to be alerted to what was going on, passing Angleton's name across for further investigation. And while her thoughts and prayers were very much with Flin and Freya, it was Angleton who was most on her mind now as she sat in the back of the taxi on her way home to her bungalow in the Maadi district of the city. Who was he? Why was he getting involved? What did he want? She held up the card Flin had given her, mouthing the name to herself. Then, dipping into her bag, she removed the pocket King James Bible she always carried – a 31st birthday gift from her beloved Charlie – and flipped through the pages until she reached Psalm 64.

'Preserve my life from fear of the enemy,' she recited, the passing streetlights streaking the paper with bars of light and shadow. 'Hide me from the secret counsel of the wicked, from the insurrection of the workers of iniquity who whet their tongue like a sword.'

She read it again, then flicked through more pages, to the start of the Book of Nahum:

'God is jealous and the Lord revengeth. The Lord will take vengeance on his adversaries, and he reserveth wrath for his enemies.'

She nodded, closed the bible and clutched it to her chest.

'Too damn right,' she whispered.

THE ROAD TO ALEXANDRIA

The landscape to either side of Highway 11, the main axis road between Cairo and Alexandria, is almost exclusively desert – a low featureless expanse of sand and gravel through which the highway slashes like a line of stitching across a vast sheet of hessian. Occasionally, though, out of nowhere, incongruous swathes of lush green suddenly appear – a golf course, a grove of date palms, a beautifully landscaped garden – muscling aside the emptiness for a brief distance before equally suddenly disappearing as though swept away by the desert's irresistible tide.

As they came level with one such burst of greenery – in this case a large banana plantation – Flin slowed the Cherokee and swung right onto a dusty track that ran perpendicular to the main road. Walls of floppy green leaves pressed in around them like curtains, chandeliers of ripening fruit dangling amidst the foliage.

'Hassan's family used to own Egypt's biggest banana export business,' he explained as they bumped along, the darkness retreating in front of them in the glare of the Jeep's headlamps. 'Sold it decades ago for an absolute fortune which is why he was always able to fund his own digs. Whatever else he's lost at least he's never going to go hungry.'

They jolted onwards, the track disappearing behind them in a fog of dust, moths and other night-time insects slapping against the windscreen, smearing the glass. After about a kilometre the banana plants gave way to mango trees which in turn came to an abrupt halt at a low picket fence. Beyond, bathed in an eerie wash of moonlight, an improbably neat, manicured lawn stretched away towards a large whitewashed house with shuttered windows and a weathervane on the roof. Flin followed the track around the lawn and pulled up on a parking area in front of the building, cutting the engine. A light was on in one of the downstairs rooms; thin strips of illumination seeped out from between the slats of the shutters.

For a while he just sat there, fingers drumming on the steering wheel as if reluctant to leave the security of the Cherokee's interior, the only sounds the chirrup of cicadas and the crack and ting of cooling metal. Then, opening the door, he swung himself out, feet crunching on gravel.

'Probably best you wait here,' he said, looking back in at Freya. 'I'll go and speak to him and if things work out I'll come and get you.'

'If they don't?'

'Then I guess we're on our way to the airport.'

He bounced his fist on the Jeep's roof, steeling himself, then turned and started towards the front door, covering about half the distance before he was suddenly enveloped in a glare of light as a security lamp clicked on. At almost the same instant a deafening crack of gunfire shook the night and the ground at Flin's feet exploded upwards in a shower of dirt and pebbles. He froze, then took a careful step backwards. Another shot tore up the ground directly behind him. He froze again. There was the click of a gun being broken open, and then a voice: rich, cultured, slightly tremulous.

'Oh God, this is sweet justice! Oh God this is just so sweet!'

A figure emerged from the darkness at the side of the building, dressed in nothing but a pair of baggy pyjama bottoms, slotting cartridges into the twin barrels of an ancient-looking shotgun. He came forward to the edge of the circle of light thrown by the security lamp and stopped, snapping the gun shut and raising it to his shoulder. He aimed directly at Flin's head.

'On your knees, Brodie! Like the bastard scheming rat you are!'

'Hassan, please . . .'

'Shut up and get on your knees!'

Flin threw a glance towards the Jeep, raising his palm slightly to indicate that Freya should stay where she was and not make any sudden moves. Then he dropped slowly to the ground, hands hanging at his sides. The man chuckled – a feral, throaty sound, unhinged, like a dog panting – and took another step forward into the floodlight's harsh glare.

'Three years I've waited for this and finally . . . Grovel, you treacherous piece of shit!'

To judge by his high forehead and gleaming blue eyes, and the long narrow ridge of his nose, he must once have cut a distinguished figure. Now he resembled nothing so much as a disintegrating scarecrow, his hair wild, grey and unkempt, his face haggard and lined, half lost beneath a five-day veil of stubble.

'Brodie,' he said, and then again 'Brodie', and then a third time, his voice rising with each repetition until on the last it had worked itself up into a high-pitched yell, like the cry of some tormented animal.

'For God's sake, Hassan,' hissed Flin, sweat rising on his forehead, his eyes glued to the shotgun, the way it was trembling in Fadawi's hands. 'Just put the bloody . . . Shit!'

He ducked, flinging his arms up in front of his face as the gun thundered twice more in quick succession. Sprays of lead shot roared over his head and disappeared into the darkness of the mango orchard. For several seconds he remained motionless as Fadawi broke open the gun and

THE HIDDEN OASIS

replaced the spent cartridges. Then slowly, hesitantly, Flin
lowered his arms and came back up onto his knees.

'Please, Hassan,' he said, struggling to keep his tone calm
and measured, trying to ignore the twin barrels that were
once again pointing directly at him. 'Just put the gun down.
Before you do something you regret. Something we both
regret.'

Fadawi's breath was coming in short ragged gasps, his
eyes manic and dilated.

'Please,' repeated Flin.

No response.

'Hassan?'

Nothing.

'What the fuck do you want me to say?'

Fadawi just glared at him, teeth bared.

'That I'm sorry? That I wish I'd done things differently?
Not a day goes by when I don't wish it. You think what
happened gave me pleasure? Some sort of perverse kick to
screw up the life of someone who'd done so much to help
me?'

Still Fadawi didn't respond. Flin rolled his eyes in
exasperation, looking up at the bright silver disc of the
moon as if it might provide him with some clue as to how to
proceed.

'Look, I can't turn the clock back,' he tried again, 'I can't
change the past, I know what you've been through . . .'

'Know!'

Fadawi came forward another couple of steps so that he
now stood directly over the Englishman, the shotgun
muzzle just inches from his temple. Inside the Jeep Freya
started to reach for the door handle, intending to get out, to

355

try to help. Flin saw what she was doing and gave a barely perceptible shake of the head. Fadawi's finger tightened around the trigger.

'Know what it's like to share a cell with murderers and rapists, do you?' he hissed. 'To go to sleep every night not knowing if you'll still be alive in the morning?'

Now it was Flin who was silent.

'To spend twelve hours a day sewing mail sacks? To have the shits for three years because you can't get any clean water to drink? To be beaten so badly you urinate blood for a week?'

Actually Flin did know what the last of these was like, but kept it to himself. He stared at the ground as Fadawi raged on, the gun muzzle brushing his ear like a pair of nostrils sniffing at him.

'You have no concept of what hell's like, Brodie, because you've never been to hell. I have . . .'

The Egyptian stamped his foot on the ground, grinding his bare sole into the gravel as if trying to crush something.

'. . . and it was you that sent me there! It was your fault, all your fault! You destroyed my career, my reputation, my life. You . . . destroyed . . . my . . . entire . . . fucking . . . liiiiiiiiife!'

He spelt out each word of this last sentence, hurling them at Flin like projectiles, his voice, unlike before, descending the scale, starting as a cry and growing steadily more husky until on the final 'life' it had drawn itself out into an extended, bestial growl. Flin kept his eyes on the ground, allowing Fadawi to talk himself out. Then, slowly, he looked up.

'You destroyed your life, Hassan.'

'What? What was that?'

The Egyptian's left eye had started to twitch.

'You destroyed your life,' repeated Flin, reaching up and gently pushing the gun muzzle away from his head. 'For as long as I live I'll regret not talking to you before going to the authorities, and I'm so desperately sorry for what you've been through, but at the end of the day it wasn't me who stole the stuff.'

Fadawi's face creased into a snarl, the features seeming to crowd themselves down around the mouth as he swung the gun back towards Flin's head, pointing it right between his eyes. There was a silence, even the screech of cicadas seeming to drop away. Then, again, Flin raised a hand and carefully nudged the shotgun barrel aside.

'You're not going to shoot me, Hassan. However much you want to, however much you blame me for what happened. You might want to scare me – and trust me, you're doing exactly that – but you're not going to pull that trigger. So why not put the gun down and let's at least try and talk.'

Fadawi continued to glare at him, his eye twitching, his face contorting as if trying to settle on a suitable expression before finally, unexpectedly, it arranged itself into a smile.

'I know what you want to talk about.'

Suddenly his tone was light, cheery almost, the polar opposite of what it had been just a few seconds before. It was as if a different person was speaking. 'You've seen Peach, haven't you?'

Flin fought to keep his face blank, but it was impossible to hide the fact that Fadawi's words had struck a chord. The Egyptian's smile broadened.

'He told you about the oasis, didn't he? That I've dis-covered something. And you want to know what it is. *Need* to know what it is. That's why you've come up here.'

He was grinning now, sensing the effect his words were having, enjoying it, turning the screw.

'I knew you'd come eventually, of course, but so soon? You must be desperate. Really desperate.'

Flin bit his lip, the gravel digging into his knees.

'It's not what you think, Hassan. It's not just for me.'

'Oh heavens no! It's for the greater good of mankind! It's to save the world! You always were an altruist.'

He chuckled, motioning Flin to stand.

'Something wonderful it was,' he crowed. 'Something extraordinary. Something that will tell us more about the *wehat seshtat* than all the rest of the scattered pieces of evidence put together. The greatest find of my career. And you know what makes it even more satisfying?'

He beamed.

'The fact that you are never going to find out what it is. Not from these lips. The most important discovery since Imti-Khentika and it's all in here.'

He lifted the gun and tapped its butt against his temple.

'Which is exactly where it's staying.'

Flin was standing now, fists clenched impotently at his sides. He didn't know what to say, how to turn the situation round.

'You're bluffing,' he muttered.

'Am I? Either way, you're never going to know. Not tonight, not tomorrow, not ever.'

Again Fadawi tapped the gun butt against his head.

'All up here, safe and sound, under lock and key. Now if

you don't mind I've had a difficult three years, I'm not as young as I used to be and so, delighted as I am to see you, I'm going to have to cut this little reunion short. Goodnight, my old friend. Have a safe drive home.'

He laid the gun in the crook of his arm, patted Flin on the shoulder and, with a final grin, turned and started towards the front door of his house.

'Please help us.'

The voice was Freya's. Up to this point she had remained silent in the Jeep, leaving the two men to play out the scene between them. Now, unable to stop herself, she pushed open the door and stepped out onto the gravel.

'Please,' she repeated, coming forward to Flin's side. 'We need your help.'

Fadawi stopped and turned, cocking his head. Although he had been standing just a few metres from the Cherokee, his attention had been focused so unswervingly on Flin that he hadn't even noticed her. 'Dear me,' he said, tutting and shaking his head as he looked her up and down. 'I knew you were lacking in self-respect, Flinders, but to involve a young lady in this grubby business . . . And such a pretty young lady, too.'

Suddenly his manner was all charm and politeness; a transformation that, since he was standing there in nothing but his pyjama bottoms, came across as not so much endearing as outright creepy.

'Aren't you going to introduce us?' he said to Flin.

'Leave it, Hassan,' snapped the Englishman, clearly not amused by the turn of events.

'Freya. My name's Freya Hannen.'

Fadawi smiled at this, although at the same time a slight frown creased his forehead.

'Not . . .'

'Her sister,' said Flin, fixing Fadawi with a stony look. 'You won't have heard but Alex died.'

The smile remained, but Fadawi's frown deepened, as though different parts of his face were registering different emotions, the one contradicting the other.

'I'm very sorry to hear that,' he said, his gaze flicking from Freya to Flin and back again. 'Very sorry indeed. Your sister was a fascinating woman.'

He raised a hand, swiping at a mosquito that was zinging around his head. Something in his eyes, in the fractional tightening of his smile, suggested a momentary uncertainty on his part, like an actor who has suddenly lost track of where he is in a soliloquy. It was fleeting, and almost immediately his smile broadened and the frown disappeared.

'Yes, yes, an absolutely fascinating woman. And a beautiful one as well. Although I must say, her sister is even more so. Freya, you say?'

'Just leave it,' repeated Flin, his voice now a threatening growl.

Fadawi ignored him, his attention zeroing in on Freya.

'I'm so sorry we have to meet in such unpleasant circumstances,' he said, swiping at the mosquito again before bringing his hand down onto his head and combing the fingers through his hair. 'Had I known you were coming I would have made rather more of an effort with my appearance. As you can see, I'm not quite at my sartorial best. May I?'

He stepped forward and, taking Freya's hand, raised it to his lips, kissing her fingertips.

'Divine,' he murmured. 'Quite divine.'

'That's enough, Hassan!'

Flin pushed Fadawi's hand away and took Freya's arm.

'Come on, we've done everything we can here.'

He tried to steer her back towards the Cherokee, but she shook her arm free, standing her ground.

'Please,' she pleaded. 'We need your help. I can't imagine what you've gone through these last three years, and I know we have no right to ask, but I'm asking anyway. Help us. Tell us about the oasis. Please.'

Fadawi seemed to be only half listening, his gaze locked onto her breasts, the way they pushed against the slightly too tight material of her shirt and cardigan, the outline of the nipples clearly visible.

'Exquisite,' he said, eyes moving down to her crotch and then up to her blond hair. 'I really can't remember when I last found myself in the company of such an attractive young lady. It was the thing I missed most in Tura, you know, the pleasure of female society: their companionship, their laughter, their beauty. I do so love a beautiful lady. The closest I came in prison was a postcard someone sent me of the naked dancer in the tomb of Nakht, which I can assure you was a very poor substitute for the real thing.'

He threw a half-glance at Flin and there was something sly in his look, like a hunter drawing an animal into a trap, excited by his prey's imminent suffering.

'Yes, yes, it's been a very long time since I saw a real woman naked,' he continued, running his tongue across the underside of his top lip, nostrils flaring slightly. 'Hips, breasts, private—'

'Stop this!' shouted Flin. 'You hear me? Stop this now. I

don't know what you think you're playing at, but we're not
standing here listening—'

'You like her, don't you?' the Egyptian purred.

'What?'

'You like her.'

Fadawi was grinning, the sly look now more pronounced.

'You really like her.'

'I don't know what you're talking about.'

'You feel for her, you're attracted to her, you . . .'

'Let's go.'

Flin seized Freya's arm again, more roughly this time,
pushing her back towards the Jeep. Fadawi called after
them.

'I'll tell you what you want to know. About the oasis.
What I found. I'll tell you everything.'

Flin stopped and turned, his hand still gripping Freya's
arm.

'Where it is, what it is, everything you want,' said the
Egyptian. 'Only first . . .'

He paused, smirking maliciously, then closed the trap.

'. . . I want to see her naked.'

Flin's eyes widened in fury and disgust. His mouth
opened, ready to unleash a tirade of abuse. Before he could
say anything Freya wrenched her arm from his grip.

'I'll do it.'

Flin stared at her, aghast.

'The hell you will!'

'Here or in the house?' she asked, ignoring him, addressing herself to Fadawi.

'Freya, there is no way I'm letting you . . .'

'Here or inside?' she repeated.

Flin seized her arm again.

'You are not—'

'Don't you dare tell me what I can or cannot do,' she snapped, pulling herself free and rounding on Flin. 'You understand? It's nothing to do with you.'

'It's everything to do with me! If I hadn't told you about it you'd never have heard of the bloody oasis. I will not have you prostituting yourself to some geriatric pervert because of something Molly and I have—'

'It's nothing to do with you. With Molly. With the oasis. With any of it.' Her face was starting to redden. 'It's for Alex. For my sister. My dead, murdered sister. I'm doing this for her, because *she* wanted to know.'

'If you seriously think . . .'

'What I think is none of your business! It's between me and Alex and that's the end of it!'

'God Almighty, Freya, this is the very last thing Alex would—'

'That's the end of it,' she cried, swinging back to Fadawi. 'So where are we doing this?'

The Egyptian had stood silently through the argument, grinning, relishing Flin's discomfort.

'Oh, in the house, I think,' he chortled. 'Yes, indoors would definitely be best. Away from prying eyes. Shall we?'

He held out a hand towards the front door.

'I will not allow you to do this!' yelled Flin.

Freya ignored him, nodding at Fadawi and starting across the gravel.

'I will not allow you to do this!' Flin repeated, jabbing a finger at her. 'You hear! To hell with the plane, to hell with the oasis. You will not do this!'

She didn't reply, just continued up to the house. Fadawi opened the door for her and ushered her inside.

'We might be a little while,' he said, turning back to Flin. 'So do feel free to wander around the grounds, try one of the bananas. Although I'd ask you to respect our privacy and not peep through the windows.'

He grinned triumphantly, savouring the younger man's outrage, then with a wink and a wave, turned into the house and slammed the door behind him.

Killing people just wasn't as much fun as it used to be. That was the conclusion the twins came to as they hammered balls around Girgis's full-size snooker table, waiting for news of when and where they were next going to be needed. Even torture no longer provided the job satisfaction it once had. Like footballers who have won every trophy there is to win, scaled every height, the hunger just wasn't there any more. It had, they agreed, all become a bit boring.

Once it had been so different. They had used to take a real pride in their work. Craftsmen, that's how they saw themselves, skilled craftsmen. And just as a carpenter will find joy in a perfectly turned chair leg, a glass-blower in a beautifully finished vase, so they too had been passionate about what they did, got a genuine buzz from it. Making that junkie drug dealer eat his own eyeball, feeding the *Al-Ahram* journalist to the polar bears in Giza Zoo, taking out four separate people in the same day up in Alexandria and still getting home in time to make their *omm* dinner – these were things that had given them a real sense of fulfilment.

The magic had been fading for some time, however, and with this current assignment their disillusion had come to a head. Sure the car chase had been fun, and they'd enjoyed cutting up the old pervert down in Dakhla, but flying around the desert looking for a heap of ancient ruins, getting shouted at by that turd Girgis – what the hell was the point of that? They were wasting themselves, no doubt about it. Wasting themselves and wasting their talents.

Which was why, as they potted the final black and started racking up the balls for a new game, they decided that this would be their last job for Girgis. The time had come to make the break and open up their food stall. They'd thought maybe to leave it a little longer, at least until the start of the new football season, but all things considered now seemed as good a moment as any. This one final job and that was the end of it. Aged thirty, they were retiring.

'Should we kill him?' asked the twin with the flattened boxer's nose, rattling the reds in their wooden triangle, carefully positioning it just below the pink spot. 'Girgis. Just to keep things neat.'

'It might be an idea,' said his brother.

'We don't want him giving us trouble.'

'Certainly don't.'

'We'll finish the job . . .'

'. . . it would be unprofessional not to . . .'

'. . . then take him out.'

'Sounds good to me.'

They high-fived, chalked their cue tips and bent low over the table. The brother with the shredded left earlobe slammed the white ball into the reds, sending them careering off in all directions. His twin tapped the cushion with his ring-covered fingers to acknowledge what a good shot he thought it was.

Just think of it like climbing, Freya told herself as Fadawi propped his shotgun beside the door and led her along a corridor. *Executing a particularly difficult move. That's all this is – just one difficult move. Focus, get on with the job, do what you have to, then get the hell out of here. And if he even thinks of touching you . . .*

At the end of the corridor Fadawi opened a door and ushered her into a large, brightly lit living room-cum-study. Sofas and armchairs sat at one end, a desk and bookcases at the other. There was a portable cassette recorder on the desk. Going over to it, Fadawi pressed the Play button before taking Freya across to the far side of the room. A mellifluous female voice wafted around them, rising and falling, curiously hypnotic.

'Fairuz,' the Egyptian explained, adjusting a dimmer switch on the wall to bring the lighting right down. 'One of the greatest of all Arab singers. Wonderful intonation, don't you think?'

Freya shrugged, pushing her hands into the pockets of her jeans, shuffling from foot to foot.

'May I offer you something to drink?'

She declined, then immediately changed her mind and said yes, she would like something. Fadawi opened a drinks cabinet – antique, by the look of it, exquisitely veneered with banded patterns of light and dark wood – and, removing a bottle with a bright green liquid inside, poured two glasses. 'Pisang Ambon,' he said, handing one of the glasses over. 'Made from the Indonesian green banana. Rather delicious, I think you'll find, despite the somewhat un-flattering name.'

'You don't have a beer?'

He shook his head apologetically. Taking the other glass he sat down on one of the sofas, sinking back into the pale pink cushions, his scrawny torso almost exactly the same shade as the material so that it wasn't immediately obvious where the cushions ended and his skin began.

'Well, well, this is cosy,' he said, sipping his drink and leering at her. 'In your own time.'

Freya sipped her own drink, wincing at the sickly-sweet taste. She suddenly felt very exposed and very self-conscious. And she hadn't even started stripping yet. Maybe she should have listened to Flin.

'So how do you want to do this?' she asked, trying to sound more relaxed than she felt.

Fadawi draped an arm along the back of the sofa.

'However you want to do it. So long as it all comes off . . .'

He indicated her clothes.

'. . . I'm happy to leave the technical details to you.'

'I'm not dancing,' she said.

'I didn't imagine for one minute you would.'

'And I'm not . . . doing anything else. I strip, and that's it.'

Fadawi looked offended.

'My dear lady, I may be a voyeur, but I am not a rapist. I wish to admire your body, not paw at it.'

She nodded and took another sip of the liqueur, disliking the taste but needing something to do, some action to calm herself down.

'And you'll tell us what you know about the oasis. After I've finished.'

'I am a man of my word,' said the Egyptian. 'Three years in prison has not changed that. You keep your side of the bargain, I will keep mine. You shall know everything. Provided I see everything.'

He smiled and snuggled even further back into the sofa, his eyes never leaving her. Freya looked up at the ceiling, over towards the door, down at the carpet, anywhere but at him, gathering herself, prolonging things. Then, with a shake of the head and a muttered 'Allez', she downed the remainder of her drink and placed the glass on a sideboard.

'OK, let's get this over with,' she said.

She started with her plimsolls, unlacing them and slipping them off followed by her socks. She tucked them into the shoes and, rather unnecessarily, arranged the shoes neatly side by side, their tips pointing towards Fadawi. Next came the cardigan, which she folded and laid on top of the plimsolls – all the while studiously avoiding the Egyptian's gaze, trying to think of anything other than what she was doing – then her jeans, her long, tanned legs emerging one after the other. Despite the awkwardness of the situation her movements were lithe and graceful; the sound of female singing still echoed from the cassette recorder on the desk.

That was the easy part. Now she was left with her shirt and her knickers, the final two items, the intimate exposure. She took a deep breath, trying to detach herself even further, take herself out of the room and into some wholly different scenario. For some inexplicable reason the first one that came into her head was the afternoon she and a group of friends had been body-boarding off Bodega Bay north of San Francisco and a great white shark had come gliding past, its dorsal fin slicing the water like the tip of a knife. She latched onto this random memory, withdrawing into it as she turned away from Fadawi and started to unbutton the shirt, recalling how she and her friends had gathered into a protective group and paddled the hundred metres back to shore, the shark all the while circling menacingly around them. She became quite absorbed in the scene, almost meditatively so. Slipping the shirt off her shoulders to reveal her smooth, toned back she bent forward slightly and hooked her thumbs through the waistband of her white knickers, ready to pull them down. It was only as she started to do so, drawing the material over the firm curve of her buttocks and down onto her thigh tops, still lost within her thoughts, that she became aware of a voice behind her. For a second she was thrown, not knowing whether it was real or in her mind, then the shark memory dissipated and she was back in the room.

'Enough,' came the voice. 'Stop, please stop.'

Pulling the knickers up again and curving an arm across her naked breasts she half turned towards the sofa, looking over her shoulder, uncertain what was wrong, what he wanted of her. Fadawi was hunched forward, one hand held up, palm out towards her, the other pressed against his forehead, shielding his eyes. His smile had disappeared. In its place was a sort of bewildered grimace, as if he had just woken from a bad dream.

'I don't know what I was thinking,' he mumbled, the teasing jollity of a few moments earlier gone from his voice, which was now frail and quavering. 'Unforgivable of me,

369

unforgivable. To make you ... please, please, put them back on. Cover yourself.'

He came to his feet and, keeping his gaze averted, walked across the room to the desk. Clicking off the cassette recorder, he stood there with his back to her.

'I just don't know what I was thinking,' he kept repeating. 'Unforgivable of me. Unforgivable.'

Freya hesitated, then started dressing again, quickly, slipping the shirt on, stepping into the jeans. Although relieved that she would not have to expose herself, she also felt curiously deflated, as if a part of her had actually wanted to go ahead with the strip. Concerned as well, for if Fadawi had changed his mind about this, maybe he'd done the same about the oasis.

'I don't know what I was thinking,' was all he seemed able to say. 'Unforgivable of me. Unforgivable.'

Freya pulled on her socks and shoes and picked up the cardigan. Throwing it over her shoulders, she started to slide a hand into one of the arms only to take the cardigan off again. Going over to Fadawi, she laid it over his shoulders, feeling suddenly sorry for him, despite what had just happened. He murmured a thank-you, reaching up and drawing the garment around him. The two of them stood there in embarrassed silence, Fadawi staring down at the desk, Freya staring at Fadawi.

'You must care for him very deeply,' he said eventually. His voice was so quiet as to be barely audible. 'Flinders. To be prepared to do something like that for him. He must mean a great deal to you.'

'Like I said outside, this was nothing to do with Flin. It was for my sister. Her I did care for very deeply.'

Fadawi glanced at her – a contrite, shamed look in his eyes – before shuffling round the desk to a bookcase behind it. Running a finger back and forth along one of the shelves, he found the volume he wanted, slipped it out and handed it over to her. Freya recognized the cover instantly: a figure swathed in blue robes walking along a dune top, a vast ruby-red sun seeming to balance directly on its head: *Little Tin Hinan*, her sister's account of the year she had spent living with the Tuareg Berbers of northern Niger. She turned the book over and gazed at Alex's picture on the back. She looked so young, so fresh-faced.

'Flinders introduced us,' explained Fadawi, sitting down in the chair behind the desk and pulling the cardigan even tighter around himself. 'Five, six years ago now. We kept in touch. She sent me a copy of her book. Extraordinary woman, extraordinary. I really am so very sorry to hear about her death.'

He looked up, then down again, opening a drawer and rummaging inside it. A pause, then:

'I'm also sorry about, you know . . . Unforgivable of me to put you through that. Unforgivable.'

Freya waved a hand, indicating that no harm was done and the apology unnecessary.

'I knew it would upset Flinders, you see,' he went on, still rummaging. 'Provoke him. He's a gentleman like that. I wanted to . . . after everything that happened, the trial, prison . . . get back at him in some way. But to use you . . .'

He shook his head, bringing up a hand and wiping it across his eyes.

Freya wanted to prompt him about the oasis, but he looked so old and helpless, so distraught, it just didn't seem appropriate, not for the moment at least. Instead she crossed the room and fetched his glass. Refilling it from the bottle in the cabinet, she brought it over and placed it in front of him. He gave a feeble smile and sipped.

'You are too kind to me,' he said. 'Really, too kind.'

He took another sip. Closing the first drawer he opened the one below, leaning sideways and down so that only the top of his head was visible above the surface of the desk.

'He was right of course,' came his voice, accompanied by the sound of rifling papers. 'Flinders. That it was my fault, I who destroyed my life. I think that's why I was so angry with him – because it was easier than acknowledging where the blame really lay. So much less painful.'

He sat up, pushing the drawer closed. He was holding a plastic cassette case.

'I love objects, you see. Always have. To have them around me, to possess them, fragments of the past, tiny windows on a lost world – an addiction, every bit as corrosive as drink or drugs. I just couldn't help myself. They made me so very happy.'

He sighed – a weary, defeated sound. Opening the case and checking the cassette inside, he leant across and handed it to her.

'You'll need to rewind it, but this is what you want. It's all on there – Abydos, the oasis, what I found. Flinders will understand. You have a tape player in your car?'

'CD,' she said.

'Ah. Then you'd better take this as well.'

He clicked open the portable player on the desk and removed the Fairuz tape, closing it again and pushing it across to her, dismissing her objections.

'Take it, please. No need to return it. The very least I can do after . . .'

He lowered his eyes.

'And your sister's book, you're welcome to that too.'

She thanked him, but said she already had several copies of her own. He nodded and, taking the book back, returned it to the shelf.

'And now I think it's probably time you were on your way. It's been rather a draining night and Flinders will be worried, planning a rescue mission. He never could resist a damsel in distress. The quintessential Englishman.'

Making sure she had the player and the cassette, he led her back along the corridor to the front door. He slipped the cardigan off his shoulders and handed it to her.

'Keep it,' she said, knowing Molly Kiernan would understand. 'Give it back when we next meet.'

'I have a feeling that might not be for a long time, if ever. Better to take it now.'

For a moment they stood there, then, leaning forward, Freya kissed him on the cheek.

'Thank you,' she said.

He smiled and patted her arm.

'On the contrary, thank you. You have made an old jail-bird very happy.'

Their eyes met briefly, then he grasped the door handle. Before he could open the door she reached out and took his hand.

'He thinks the world of you. Flin. Even after everything. He still looks up to you. He'd want you to know that.'

'Actually it's I who look up to him,' said Fadawi. 'The

greatest archaeologist I ever met. A genius, an absolute genius. Best field man in the business.'

He paused, then added:

'Look after him. He needs it. And tell him he mustn't feel bad. The fault is all mine.'

Easing his hand free, he opened the door and steered her through out onto the gravel drive.

'Thank you,' she repeated. 'Thank you so much.'

He smiled again, gave her another pat on the arm and pushed the door closed. Picking up the shotgun he had propped beside it, he curled a finger around the trigger.

'Now let's just think how to do this,' he sighed.

Flin was moving towards Freya the moment she emerged from the house. Breaking into a trot he reached her just as the front door slammed shut.

'Tell me! What did he do to you, the filthy—'

'He didn't do anything,' she said, striding towards the car, Flin back-pedalling beside her, jabbing a finger angrily at the door.

'I'll kill him! I'll kill him!'

'You'll do no such thing. He was an absolute gentleman.'

'Did he make you . . . ?'

'No, he did not make me strip. He changed his mind.'

'So what have you been doing in there all this time?'

'Talking,' she said, opening the passenger door of the Cherokee and climbing in. 'You might be interested to hear he thinks you're the greatest archaeologist he's ever met. A genius, that's what he called you. An absolute genius.'

That shut Flin up, his expression morphing from fury to surprise. For a moment he just stood there staring at the house, apparently contemplating whether to go back and speak to Fadawi himself. Thinking better of it, he opened the driver's door and climbed in beside Freya.

'I suppose it's too much to hope that he told you what he knows?'

She held up the cassette.

'All on here, apparently. He said you'd understand what it meant.'

He took the cassette, turning it over in his hand.

'I assume that's to play it on?' he said, indicating the machine in her lap. Freya nodded.

'He gave it to us. Said we could keep it.'

He pondered, eyes flicking from the tape to the house, then handed the cassette back to her and started the engine.

'We'll listen as we go,' he said. He turned the car round and, with a final glance back, set off down the drive, tyres crunching on gravel, the tape machine rattling and whirring as Freya rewound the cassette. According to the dashboard clock it was now 10.40 p.m.

'Flinders?' she said.

'Hmm?'

'Flinders. Is that what Flin's short for?'

She sounded as if she was about to start giggling. He glanced across, gave an embarrassed shrug.

'After Flinders Petrie. The Egyptologist. For some reason my parents thought it would give me a head start in life.'

She smirked.

'Nice name. Distinguished.'

'Don't knock it. If I'd been a girl they were going to call me Nefertiti.'

They passed through the white picket fence and bumped off down the track towards the highway, a single gunshot echoing from the house behind them, too muted for them to hear above the hiss of the tape machine and purring of the engine.

CAIRO

Cy Angleton sat on the balcony of his listening station in the Semiramis Intercontinental, eating a Mars Bar and gazing distractedly out across the Cairo nightscape, a twinkling mosaic of light stretching off into the far distance. Mrs Malouff was long gone, and although normally the station remained unmanned until she returned in the morning, tonight he wanted to be here, just on the off-chance Brodie called in, tried to make contact with Kiernan.

He had to admire the man, the way he had shaken him off like that, swerving across the Autoroute and into the oncoming traffic, disappearing the wrong way down the slip road. Nice driving, clever. Angleton had long prided himself on his car-tailing abilities – he'd followed Kiernan without her noticing anything, and she was the slyest of the sly – but in this instance he'd had to admit defeat. Trying to match Brodie's manoeuvre would have been tantamount to emblazoning 'You are being followed!' in glorious neon right across the night sky.

And so he'd backed off, returning first to the apartment in Ain Shams in the hope of picking up Kiernan, then, finding she had already left, coming here instead. It was probably a waste of time, but he needed to gather his thoughts and plan his next move.

Every job of this type had a pivotal point, a Rubicon moment where you have the choice of either treading water or ratcheting things up to a whole other level. That moment was now. He knew he still didn't have the full picture – there were still too many variables for his liking – but he needed to track Brodie down and he needed to do it quickly, before events spun completely out of control. So far he had kept things pretty tight, just him, Mrs Malouff and, obviously, his employers. Now, sitting on the balcony gazing at the ghostly floodlit zigzag of the Pyramids – just visible right out on the very edge of the city – he decided it was time to widen the circle, break cover, throw his hat into the ring. Whatever the hell euphemism you wanted to use. He'd already got the go-ahead from Langley, had them make the necessary approaches. With Brodie either not contacting Kiernan, or else doing so via some channel he hadn't yet discovered, he accepted he had no choice but to act. He had to track them down. Brodie and the girl. He had to get to them. Before anyone else did.

He looked out a while longer, finishing his Mars Bar, really cramming it into his mouth, then heaved himself to his feet. Going inside he picked up his mobile from the bed and dialled. Five rings, and then the call was answered.

'Major-General Taneer? Cyrus Angleton, US Embassy. I believe one of my colleagues in the States has already . . . good, good, thank you, that's extremely kind. So, let me explain exactly what I need.'

He went through it all slowly and deliberately, spelling it out so as to ensure the Egyptian not only understood, but also appreciated the urgency of the situation – a sweep of every police checkpoint within a hundred-mile radius of Cairo to see which, if any, had logged a white, Embassy-registered Grand Cherokee Jeep, licence plate 21963. Log times and direction of travel would also be greatly appreciated.

Once he was sure the man at the other end was clear, would come back to him the moment he had any information, Angleton rang off and wandered outside again. Pulling another Mars Bar from his pocket and opening it, he balled the wrapper and dropped it off the balcony. He took a bite and started singing to himself, quietly, to the tune of 'Michael Finnigan'.

> *'Where are you, Professor Flin-i-flin?*
> *Disappeared into air so thin-i-thin,*
> *But it's me who'll win-i-win,*
> *Reel you in again, Professor Flin-i-Flin.'*

BETWEEN CAIRO AND ALEXANDRIA

'Saturday January 21st. Started work in the Horus chapel, the plan being to spend three to four days in each sanctuary, with a week to write my report at the end. Measured up, photographed the walls, made notes on the preservation of the reliefs, ceiling, false-door etc. Some bloody American woman came in and started chanting, sounded like a retching camel. Ridiculous.'

Flin clicked his fingers, motioning to Freya to stop the tape, the Cherokee bouncing and juddering as they followed the track back towards the Cairo–Alexandria highway, dust billowing around them.

'What does it mean?' Freya asked.

He was frowning.

'Well I'd need to listen to a bit more, but from what we've just heard it sounds distinctly like Hassan's work notes, from that last season at Abydos. When he got caught stealing . . .'

He broke off, swerving to avoid a deep pothole. Banana leaves slapped against the Jeep's bodywork like giant hands.

'Hassan always kept two records of what he was doing,' he resumed. 'A detailed dig diary, but also a more informal recorded commentary – thoughts, impressions, general stuff, gossip. In English, for some reason, even though his native language was Arabic.'

He swerved again, this time to avoid a dog that was ambling along the middle of the track.

'What's he talking about here?' asked Freya.

'Halfway through that last season – I mentioned this on the drive up – Hassan was asked to help with some conservation work in the temple of Seti I. The Supreme Council needed a report on the condition of the temple's seven internal sanctuaries, of which the Horus chapel is one. I ended up supervising the Khasekhemwy dig, Hassan took four weeks out to do the necessary survey and write up his findings.'

He scratched his head.

'Although what the hell any of that has to do with the oasis I have no idea. The Seti Temple was built a thousand years after the last recorded mention of the *wehat seshtat* and there's nothing even remotely connected in any of its reliefs or inscriptions.'

'So why's he given us the tape?' she asked as they reached the end of the track and turned left, back towards Cairo.

Flin shrugged.

'I guess we'll just have to listen.'

He leant across and pressed Play. Fadawi's disembodied voice – strong, rich, cultured – once again echoed from the recorder.

'Sunday January 22nd. Couldn't sleep so came to the temple early, just after 5 a.m. No one had bothered to inform the night guards I was working there and one of them damned nearly shot me – thought I was an Islamist planting a bomb or something. Nine years since the Hatshepsut massacre and everyone's still horribly jittery about terrorists. Sketched the King Clothing Horus relief and took more shots of the ceiling vault, which really isn't in very good condition at all. Afternoon tea with Abu Gamaa, who's working on the masonry out in the first court – eighty years old and still the best stone-restorer in Egypt. He told the most outrageous joke about Howard Carter and Tutankhamun's penis which I don't think I can repeat even here!'

And so it continued. Some days received just a few cursory comments, the barest outline of what Fadawi had been doing. Others produced much longer entries, descriptions of his work accompanied by extended monologues on everything from New Kingdom funerary architecture to whether French female archaeologists were better looking than Polish ones (yes, thought Fadawi).

After twenty minutes, by which point they had reached and passed through the checkpoint they had encountered earlier in the evening – the policeman manning the point again noting their registration number – Flin told Freya to start fast-forwarding, leapfrogging segments of the recording in the hope of reaching the part that was actually relevant to them. Still they couldn't find what they wanted as Fadawi's voice chattered on, in brief bursts now, taking them through January and into February, as he worked his way from sanctuary to sanctuary, each apparently dedicated to a different deity: Horus, Isis, Osiris, Amun-Ra, Re-Horakhty. They came to the end of the tape, turned it over, started to play the other side, the two of them looking increasingly despondent as they failed to hit on even the vaguest mention of the Hidden Oasis.

'I'm getting a nasty feeling here,' said Flin as the Egyptian droned on in the background: something about mould damage to the Re-Horakhty ceiling vault. 'That he's wasting our time, taking us on a wild goose chase just for the hell of it.'

'He wouldn't do that,' said Freya, remembering how Fadawi had been back at the house. 'He was genuine. There's something here, I—'

She didn't finish the sentence for Flin suddenly clicked his fingers and jabbed at the recorder, motioning her to rewind. She stopped the tape, spooled it back a bit, pressed Play again.

'. . . with cartouches and offering formulas. As I leant close to it I felt the strangest thing – a slight waft of air on . . .'

Again Flin clicked his fingers, making a whirling motion with his hand to indicate she should roll back even further. The tape rattled and hissed as it spun around its reel. Flin let it go for a good five seconds before waving at her to start it again.

'. . . just found something rather intriguing. I was up on the scaffold at the front end of the Re-Horakhty chapel, taking mould scrapings from the ceiling, the area where the vault joins the chapel's northern wall. There's a stone block up there, forming the very top right-hand corner of the wall, only about fifteen inches by fifteen inches, decorated with cartouches and offering formulas. As I leant close to it I felt the strangest thing – a slight waft of air on my face. Initially I thought it must be coming up from the sanctuary doorway, but when I took a closer look – and you don't really notice this from ground level – I saw that there is a very thin gap, no more than a millimetre wide, running along the top of the block, with similar gaps, even narrower, down each side of it and along the bottom. Everywhere else in the chapel the wall-blocks are so tightly fitted you couldn't get a pin head between them, but in this particular instance there seems to be a bit of give. Not only that, but the fact that you can feel air coming through suggests there is some sort of cavity back there. It's too late to do anything about it today, but I've spoken to Abu Gamaa and we're going to come back in the morning for a proper examination, see if maybe we can move the block. It's probably nothing, but all the same . . .'

Freya pressed the pause button.
'You think this is it?' she asked. 'What he wanted to tell us about?'
Flin just reached across and started the tape again.

'Sunday 12th February. I couldn't help myself, I had to come early to look at the block again, even if it meant getting shot at by trigger-happy guards! The more I think about it – and I've done little else since yesterday evening – the more it seems to me I might have stumbled on something quite significant. The walls between the chapels are at least ten feet thick, and it's always been assumed they're completely solid. If it turns out they're in fact hollow, with cavities between them, that would transform our understanding not only of the temple itself, but also of the way it was constructed. By rights I ought to get permission from the Supreme Council, but that'll delay things for at least a week and I really do want to find out what's back there. Abu'll be here in a few minutes and we can move the block, get an idea what's behind it, then alert the necessary authorities. I really am getting rather excited.'

The Cherokee had come up behind an oil tanker that was rumbling along at less than 60 km/hour. Although the outside lane was clear, Flin just sat there, too absorbed in the recording to overtake.

'. . .4 p.m. and Abu Gamaa's only just arrived – been held up all day on family business, something to do with his brothers, which I must say has been more than frustrating. I know these things can't be avoided, but today of all days! Anyway, he's here now, with his grandson Latif, and we're all up on the scaffold. They've brought a pair of crowbars with them, and a piece of foam matting to lay the block on if and when they get it out and are just starting to work the bars . . . *Khalee barak, Abu!* . . . scaffold's wobbling around rather so I think I'd better put the recorder . . .'

There was a muted clatter, presumably as Fadawi laid his Dictaphone aside. In his excitement he seemed to have forgotten to switch it off because although he was no longer speaking directly into it, the recording continued. The tape echoed with grunts and muttered comments, the creak of scaffolding, the clink and scrape of metal on stone. Every now and then Fadawi's voice could be heard issuing instructions in Arabic – *Khallee barak, Abu! Harees, harees. Batee awee!* – his tone becoming increasingly breathless and urgent, the background grunts increasingly laboured until, after about ten minutes, there was an explosion of jabbering and a sharp rasping sound as of stone scraping across stone, followed by a gentle thud as if something heavy had been lowered onto something soft. A silence. Then Fadawi's voice again, hushed, disbelieving: '*Good God! Good God Almighty, it's full of* . . .'

In front of them the tanker suddenly slowed. Flin only noticed at the last moment and had to veer left into the outside lane to avoid crashing into it. A service taxi that was coming up to overtake them beeped furiously as its driver was forced to slam on his brakes. By the time Flin had rounded the tanker and waved the service taxi past, Fadawi had resumed talking directly into his recorder, his voice now jumpy, excited:

'. . . large cavity filled with stone blocks, all jumbled up together like . . . reliefs, hieroglyphic inscriptions, parts of statues – I'm describing this as I'm seeing it, it's just a mass of . . . Dear God, is that a . . . cartouche, yes, it's a cartouche, hang on, Nefer . . . is that a ka sign? Nefer-Ka-Re Pepi, my God, my God, Neferkare Pepi – Pepi II. I just can't believe what I'm seeing – the remains of an Old Kingdom . . . I have to get in there, I have to . . .'

There was hiss of static and a click as Fadawi stopped the tape. Flin leant forward, eyes bright, willing the recording to resume, which it did after a brief pause. Fadawi's voice sounded calmer, and was accompanied by the background crunch of feet on gravel.

'It's midnight, we have replaced the block and I'm making my way back to the dig house, still barely able to believe what we have found. For so long I've accepted there would never be anything to match Imti-Khentika, that that would be the highlight of my career, and now, suddenly, out of nowhere . . . such a wonderful . . . who would have thought it, who could have guessed . . .'

He tailed off, his voice choking with emotion. For a while the only sound was the crunch of his footsteps before he seemed to gather himself and the commentary resumed.

'As I suspected, there is a large cavity behind the sanctuary wall, about three metres wide and the same length as the chapel itself. What I hadn't foreseen – couldn't possibly have foreseen – is that the cavity has been packed out with the remains of a much earlier structure, in this case what appears to be a temple dating from the reign of Pepi II. It was something the ancient Egyptians did all the time, of course, using the remains of one monument to help build another – the Akhenaten *talatat* at Karnak spring immediately to mind – but I can't think of anything remotely as important as this. I've only had the most cursory look around, but even that . . . the colours are just extraordinary, the inscriptions utterly unique, in some cases recording texts I've never even heard of before, including at least one, and possibly several, relating to the Benben and the Hidden Oasis – just wait till I tell Flinders!'

At the mention of his name Freya glanced across at the Englishman. He was staring straight ahead, a barely perceptible moistness to his eyes. He sensed her looking at him and pointed down at the tape, indicating she should concentrate on that rather than him.

'. . . too early to say, of course, but my guess is that it's not just this one wall that's been filled in this way, but all the sanctuary walls, and possibly others parts of the temple as well. We could be sitting on the greatest collection of Egyptian architectural remains ever . . . I can't contemplate it, I just can't contemplate it. I'll come back first thing tomorrow morning to begin a more detailed study of the inscriptions – I've sworn Abu and Latif to secrecy in the meantime – but for the moment I'm going to take a swift look in the dig magazine, see how they've done today, and then head to bed for a well-earned rest – at my age this sort of excitement really can't be healthy! Unbelievable, just unbelievable.'

The recording clicked off again. Freya waited for Fadawi's voice to return, describe what he'd discovered the following day. There was nothing, just the soft hiss of spooling tape. She started fast-forwarding, trying to pick up the recording again, but the hiss continued until with a clunk the tape came to an end.

'For God's sake,' she said. 'He must have continued on another cassette. We'll have to go—'

'There's no other cassette,' said Flin.

'But he said he was going to—'

'That's it. That's everything.'

She looked at him.

'How do you know?'

His face had gone very pale.

'Because it was on the night of Sunday, 12 February that Hassan was caught stealing from the dig magazine. He never got the chance to go back to the temple. He was locked up in prison.'

The moistness in his eyes, Freya noticed, had become much more pronounced.

'Christ Almighty, no wonder he was bitter. As if it's not bad enough getting banged up for three years, banned from doing the one thing you really love doing, for it to happen just as you make the biggest discovery of your career . . .'

He shook his head and drove on in silence. Houses started to appear to either side of the road. Sporadically at first, lone punctuation marks on the otherwise empty sheet of the desert, then more frequently, single dwellings clustering into estates, and estates swelling into a solid mass of buildings as the city's suburbs swept out to meet them. A brightly lit Mobil petrol station appeared ahead. Slowing, Flin swung the Cherokee onto its forecourt and cut the ignition. An attendant in blue overalls and white rubber boots came over and started filling the tank. Flin got out and trotted across to a payphone beside the kiosk. Freya could see him lifting the receiver and dialling. Thirty seconds later he was back. Three minutes after that they were on the road again.

'I'd offer to drop you at the airport,' he said, 'but I think I'd be wasting my breath.'

She didn't reply.

'Last chance to bail out.'

Freya just sat there. The Pyramids loomed in front of them, a signpost announced that it was straight ahead to Cairo, right towards Fayyum, Al-Minya and Asyut.

'OK,' he said, 'we go together.'

'To Abydos?'

Flin slowed, indicated and turned right.

'To Abydos.'

Molly Kiernan sat on the swing seat in her bungalow garden, swaying gently back and forth. A mug of coffee was cupped in her hands, a blanket wrapped tight around her shoulders for it was late and the night air had turned chill. She'd just picked up the message from Flin. It sounded like a good lead although she'd have to wait a few hours to find out exactly how good. At least it *was* a lead, which was more than they'd had for the last two decades.

She knew she should have felt more upbeat. Would have felt more upbeat were it not for the Angleton situation, which was more serious than she'd feared. Her people had run his name through the system, done a bit of digging and it turned out he had form, a reputation. 'A nightmare,' that's how Bill Schultz had described him. 'Our worst fucking nightmare. The man's a human limpet.'

She gave the swing seat another push. Her laptop was balanced on her knees, its screen filled with the image of Angleton they'd mailed over from the States. Obese, balding, a faint sheen of sweat brightening the curve of his apple-red cheeks. He'd have to be confronted, of course, couldn't just be left to his own devices. The question was when? And how? Twenty-three years she'd been involved in this thing and tonight, for the first time, she felt a genuine shiver of fear. For Sandfire, and also for herself. Angleton, by all accounts, was not someone to be messed with.

She dropped her head back and looked up at the stars. Breathing in the scent of jasmine and bougainvillaea, listening to the creak of the swing and the soft rustle of flame-tree leaves as they swayed in the breeze, she wished more than ever that Charlie was there with her. That she could just curl up and snuggle into the crook of his arm as she used to on their porch back home in the States, all her cares pushed off and held at bay by his warmth and his strength and the certainty of his faith.

But Charlie wasn't there, and there was no point wishing

he was. She'd come this far without him, and she sure as hell wasn't going to crumple now. She looked up a while longer, allowing the swing to slow to a standstill, then, finishing her coffee, she closed the laptop, picked up the Beretta handgun from the seat beside her and went back into the house, locking and bolting the door after her.

'Come on, Flin,' she murmured. 'Bring me something useful. Please, bring me something useful.'

For some reason Freya had got it in her head that Abydos was just south of Cairo. It was south, only rather more than 'just': 500 kilometres, to be precise, a little less than half the length of the entire country, a distance which, even at night with the roads relatively clear of traffic, would in Flin's estimation take them a minimum of five hours to cover, probably longer.

'Doesn't leave us a lot of time,' he said. 'From what I remember the temple opens to the public at 7 a.m., so we'll need to be out of there by, say, 6.45 at the latest or we'll be seen, which believe you me would not be good news. The Egyptians don't take kindly to people breaking into their monuments and pulling them apart.'

He glanced down at the dashboard clock. 11.17 p.m.

'We're going to be cutting it fine.'

'Better get your foot down then,' said Freya.

He did, pushing the speedometer up past 100 km/hour, leapfrogging the sporadic lorries and tankers that were the only other vehicles around at that time. They covered about twenty kilometres, then, abruptly, Flin veered in to the side of the road and skidded to a halt in front of a line of ram-shackle shops. Even at this late hour they were still open. Outside one, illuminated by a bare strip bulb, was a display of building and agricultural tools – brooms, scythes, sledge-hammers, *tourias*. Flin hurried in, emerging a minute later carrying two weighty-looking iron crowbars, two torches and an enormous pair of bolt-cutters.

'We're just going to have to pray there's either a scaffold-ing tower or a ladder on site,' he said, dumping the tools into the back of the Jeep and swinging himself behind the wheel again.

'If there's not?'

'Then we're buggered. Unless your climbing skills allow you to hover in mid-air.'

He started the engine, skidded back onto the road and sped off into the night.

They didn't talk much during the journey. Flin listened to the Fadawi tape a couple more times, cementing the necessary information in his mind, and they exchanged a few half-hearted bursts of chatter. Freya told him a bit about her climbing, Flin described his work in the Gilf Kebir, some of the joint expeditions he and Alex had under-taken. Neither of them went into much detail, they weren't really in the mood for it, and by the time they had reached Beni Suef 120 kilometres south of Cairo they had both fallen silent, the only sounds the purr of the Cherokee's engine and the thud and thwack of tyres speeding over uneven tarmac.

Freya slept fitfully, dozing off only to jerk awake again as they clattered over a deep rut or slowed to pass through a police checkpoint. She got little sense of the landscape through which they were passing beyond the fact that it comprised a lot of scrubby sand punctuated by sugar-cane fields, palm trees and ramshackle mud-brick villages. Around 1.15 a.m. they stopped off in a brightly lit town to fill up with petrol and buy some water – Al-Minya, Flin informed her, just under halfway. Shortly after that they very nearly crashed head-on into an oncoming coach as Flin badly misjudged an overtaking manoeuvre around an oil tanker. Other than that, the drive was uneventful, the speedometer hovering around the 110 km/hour mark, the world rushing dimly past to either side of them, the kilometres ticking away as they sped southwards.

'Freya.'

'Hmm.'

'Freya.'

She blinked her eyes open, disorientated, uncertain where she was or what was going on.

'Come on. We're here.'

Flin was already climbing out of the Jeep. For a moment she remained where she was, yawning, the only sounds the distant barking of dogs and the soft metallic ting of the Jeep's cooling engine. Then, with a look at the dashboard clock – 4.02 a.m., they'd made good time – she threw open her door and climbed out as well.

They were in a large village, at the foot of a hill, a lamplit road running steeply upwards ahead of them towards a mobile phone mast at the top of the slope. A parallel road climbed 300 metres away to her right, fronted, like this one, with a drab wall of shops and concrete tenements. Between the two an enormous rectangle of open space ran backwards into the hillside. At its head – clasped between the arms of the village as though between the prongs of a giant pair of tweezers – was the spectacular floodlit façade of what she assumed must be the temple of Seti I: long, flat-roofed, imposing, lined with a parade of twelve monumental pillars, like the bars of some gargantuan cage.

'The House of Millions of Years of King Men-Maat-Ra, Joyful in the Heart of Abydos,' said Flin, coming up beside her. 'Impressive, eh?'

'Sure is.'

'I'd offer you the full tour, but given the time constraints . . .'

He took her arm and steered her to the back of the Cherokee. Opening the rear door, he gathered the tools from the back seat. He handed Freya the torches and one crowbar, took the other crowbar and bolt-cutters himself and locked the vehicle. She started towards the temple, but he called her back with a click of the fingers and instead led her to the left, down a side street, past a donkey munching on a heap of fodder and deeper into the village.

'The whole area's crawling with guards,' he explained in hushed tones, waving her right up another street. 'We should keep out of sight as much as possible.'

They weaved through the houses, everything deathly quiet save for the dogs still barking in the distance, and, once, the sound of someone snoring. The ground climbed steadily, then started to flatten out. Turning down a narrow alley, they came back out onto the road on which they had parked. They were almost at the top of the hill now, the mobile phone mast rearing to their left, the Cherokee just visible at the bottom of the slope to their right. In front of them a stretch of rubbish-strewn waste ground ran away towards a ragged barbed-wire fence. Beyond lay a confusion of broken columns and mud-brick walls, the tallest of them no more than chest height. And beyond that rose another, much more solid wall made up of a hotchpotch of stone blocks – the side of the temple compound. Flood-lamps bathed everything in a wash of orangey light; black-uniformed guards could be seen patrolling around the perimeter.

'Like Hassan said on the tape, these guys tend to shoot first and ask questions later,' said Flin, drawing her back into the shadows. 'We need to be careful or they'll end up doing Girgis's job for him.'

He peered out, surveying the ground ahead, watching the way the guards moved, calculating the pattern of their patrol.

'There's a blind spot when that guy turns,' he said after a few moments, pointing to one of the uniformed figures. 'We can make it under the fence and in among the ancient store-rooms. When he turns again we go through that small gateway in the corner and down onto the temple portico. OK?'

'What if they see us?'

He didn't reply, just tilted his head and raised his eye-brows as if to say: 'Let's hope they don't.' Thirty seconds passed, then, nudging Freya with his elbow, he started for-ward. She followed, and they hurried across the stretch of waste ground, ducked through a gap in the fence and worked their way into the maze of mud walls. Crouching down behind a row of pillar bases they felt horribly visible, the flood-lamps swamping the area with light, the windows of the overlooking buildings seeming to stare directly at them. They held their breath, half expecting to hear shouts and the crunch of running feet. As it was, their presence went unnoticed, and after another thirty seconds Flin raised his head, took a quick look around and waved Freya on. They kept low to the ground, flitting among the ruins and through a narrow gateway in the wall of the temple enclosure. Four steps took them down to a terrace that ran along the building's floodlit front.

'Stay quiet,' he whispered, drawing her in behind the first of the monumental pillars that lined the façade, holding a finger to his lips.

'What the hell did you think I was going to do?' she murmured. 'Start singing?'

Again they paused, pressing themselves tight against the stone, listening for signs that they had been spotted. Then they began moving along the terrace towards the black rectangle of the temple entrance, scuttling from one pillar to the next, their silhouettes – towering, monstrous, mis-shapen – sliding across the floodlit walls to their left before disappearing again as they slipped out of sight behind each column. There was one agonizing moment when, as they reached the pillar adjacent to the doorway, Freya stumbled and clanged her crowbar against the stone floor. The sound reverberated around the enclosure, seeming to fill the night. They shrank back into the shadows, freezing, listening as footsteps approached across the courtyard in front of the temple, coming right up to the very edge of the terrace.

'*Meen?*' came a voice, no more than a couple of metres away, accompanied by a rustle and a click as of a rifle being unshouldered. 'Who there?'

They stood motionless, neither of them daring to breathe, knowing that if the guard came up onto the platform itself they were sure to be found. To their relief he remained below, pacing up and down before eventually, satisfied there was nothing amiss, moving off, the clump of his boots slowly receding. Flin waited until he had disappeared altogether, then peered cautiously round the side of the pillar. The coast was clear. He handed Freya his crowbar and, clutching the bolt-cutters, stepped up to the iron gate that secured the temple entrance and sliced through its padlock, the cutters severing the metal link as though it were made of cheese. He eased the gate open, stepped through and, taking another glance across the courtyard, waved Freya in, pushing the gate closed after her and pulling her to the left, out of the pool of illumination thrown by the floodlights outside.

For a moment they stood there, catching their breath, eyes adjusting to the gloom, listening. Then, propping the bolt-cutters against the wall, Flin took a crowbar and a torch from Freya and, clicking the torch on, led her forwards.

They were in a cavernous, stone-floored hall. Twin rows of columns marched off to left and right, each column eight metres tall and thick as a tree trunk, every available surface – walls, columns, ceiling – carved with tangled thickets of hieroglyphs. Freya clicked on her own torch and circled it around, gazing in wonder. A couple of years back she had gone night diving on a coral reef off the coast of Thailand, and this had the same mysterious, sub-aquatic feel to it. Her beam cut through the murk, picking out curious shapes and images: figures with human bodies and the heads of animals – hawks and lions and jackals – a man kneeling with hands raised in supplication, three statue heads lined up in a recess in the wall, their empty eyes staring blankly into the shadows. There were colours as well: reds and greens and blues loomed momentarily before fading back into monochrome as she swung her torch elsewhere, as though it were the beam itself that was creating the different hues.

They reached the far side of the hall – the only sound the soft pad of their feet on stone – and passed through a wall into a second huge space, this one also crowded with a forest of decorated columns. Even to Freya's untutored eye it was clear the carving here was of a far higher quality, the hieroglyphs rendered in bas- rather than sunken relief, the images more detailed and subtle. A ladder of moonbeams dropped through a skylight in the ceiling high above. Otherwise everything was utterly black, the darkness so intense Freya could almost taste it.

They made their way across this room too and up a ramp onto a low platform at its far end. Flin played his torch beam across the hall's rear wall, illuminating a row of seven rectangular doorways, deeper voids within the wider one all around. He made for the third door from the left, Freya following, passing beneath a badly damaged lintel and into a long rectangular chamber. Its vaulted ceiling was stained black with mould, its relief-covered walls patched here and there with eczema-like smears of concrete render where the stonework had disintegrated and been repaired.

'The chapel of Re-Horakhty,' Flin announced, still keeping his voice low even though they were now deep within the temple and the chances of anyone outside hearing them were minimal.

He flashed his torch around, then turned to the right and

lifted the beam, directing it into the very top right-hand corner of the chamber, to the point where the wall merged into the curve of the ceiling vault. There, just as Fadawi had described, was a small square block, no more than forty centimetres by forty centimetres, faded remnants of hieroglyphic text just visible beneath the mould which covered its face.

'Now all we've got to do is reach it,' he said.

They went back out into the hypostyle hall and split up. Wandering off in opposite directions, they slashed at the blackness with their torch beams, searching for something – anything – they could use to get up to the stone, neither of them wanting to vocalize the fear that having come all this way they might not actually be able to access the relevant block. Within less than a minute Freya heard a soft whistle. Retracing her steps, she found Flin standing in the doorway of the chapel next to the one they were interested in, a relieved grin on his face. Inside, against the false door in the chapel's back wall and surrounded by sacks of cement, stood a portable aluminium scaffold tower, its legs fitted with castors for ease of movement.

'Appropriate we should find it here,' he said, going over to the scaffold and giving it a rattle. 'This is the sanctuary of Ptah, god of – among other things – masons and stone-cutters. Let's hope it's a good omen.'

The tower was too tall to push through the chapel door as it was, obliging them to remove its upper tier and transport it into the Re-Horakhty chapel in two separate pieces before reassembling it, losing them precious minutes. Once it was erected Flin clicked on the wheel locks and, clutching the crowbars and torches, the two of them climbed up, Freya swiftly, Flin with rather less confidence.

'Jesus, it's wobbly,' he muttered, easing himself onto the platform at the top. 'Feels like it's made of jelly.'

'Stop fussing,' she chided. 'We're only three metres up.'

He threw her a look as if to say, 'That's three metres too many' and, shuffling forward, aimed his torch into the corner of the wall.

From ground level the stone block had appeared as tightly fitted as all the others of which the wall was constructed. Now they were up close, and their torch beams just centimetres away, they were able to see exactly what Fadawi had seen: a narrow gap running along the top of the stone with even narrower ones beneath and to either side of it, each no wider than a pencil stroke. Leaning forward, Flin held his cheek close to the wall.

'Hassan was right,' he said after a pause, eyes gleaming with excitement. 'There's definitely air moving around back there. Come on.'

He glanced at his watch – 4.24 a.m. – and positioned his torch on the platform so that its beam shone directly up at the block, then spat on the palms of his hands and grasped his crowbar.

'OK, let's get to work.'

DAKHLA OASIS

Zahir al-Sabri stood over his son's bed, smiling as he gazed down at the sleeping figure curled beneath him, one arm bent underneath his head, the other thrown out to the side, palm open as though the boy was reaching for something. He remembered the day Mohsen had been born – how could he forget? – the wonder he had felt, the choking surge of euphoria. As a Bedouin it was not considered seemly to show emotion in public and so he had contented himself with giving the wrinkled bundle a kiss and embracing his wife before driving out into the desert where, crazed with joy, he had danced and yelped like a madman, watched over only by the dunes and the sky.

He would have liked more children, a dozen more, for what greater satisfaction can there be than to forge new links in the chain of life, extending it forward into the future? It was not to be, though. The birth had been difficult, there had been complications, bleeding – he hadn't understood the details, only that to go through the same again would have put his wife's life in danger, and that was not something he would allow to happen. Allah gives, and Allah takes. It was how things were. He had Mohsen, and that was enough.

He continued to look down, the moonlight wrapping a silver halo around the boy's head. Leaning forward, he kissed his cheek, murmured '*Ana bahebak, ya noor eanay'a*' – I love you, light of my eyes – and slipped back into bed beside his wife. He stared up at the ceiling. For a while he just lay there, biting his lip, no nearer sleep than he had been four hours ago. Then, rolling to the side, he reached beneath the bed and touched the muzzle of the rifle he kept there, running a finger along the cold steel of its barrel.

He was ready. Whatever happened, whatever was asked of him, he was ready. In that, at least, he would live up to the memory of his ancestors.

'*Ana bahebak, ya Mohsen,*' he whispered. '*Ana bahebak, ya noor eanay'a.*'

ABYDOS

'You really think Fadawi hasn't told anyone else about this?' asked Freya as they worked their crowbars into the gaps around the stone block, Flin at the top, Freya the side. 'Or that other guy, Abu whatever-his-name-was.'

Flin shook his head, pushing with his crowbar, trying to get the block moving.

'I'd have heard about it if they had. Like Fadawi said in the tape, if there's a dismantled Pepi II temple back there it would be one of the biggest finds of the last fifty years. Word would have got out. Come on, you bastard.'

He applied more pressure to the bar. Freya did the same with hers, the two of them falling silent as they focused all their energy on the job in hand, aware that time was ticking away and anxious to get the block moving. Sweat dampened their faces; the room echoed with the laboured grunt of their breathing and the clink of metal on stone. After a couple of minutes Flin changed his angle of attack, yanking the bar from the gap at the top of the block and working it into the one down the side instead, opposite Freya's. They rocked their jemmies back and forth, pushing and pulling. Still the stone resisted and Freya was beginning to wonder if they would ever get it loose when, finally, there was a faint twitch of movement, just the merest shiver, barely noticeable. They adjusted their position, wriggling the bars in another couple of millimetres and heaving. The movement became more pronounced. Flin freed his jemmy and forced it underneath the block, pushing down on it. The block lifted slightly.

'Almost there,' he puffed, eyes wide both with the effort of shifting the stone and excitement at what might lie behind it.

They continued to work their way around the edges, sometimes coming at the block from the sides, sometimes from above and below until eventually it started to creep forward out of the wall – fractionally at first, millimetre by millimetre as though reluctant to show itself; then, as they were able to get a better purchase on it, more swiftly, the clink of their crowbars now accompanied by the grating rasp of stone scraping across stone. When they had prised it some fifteen centimetres out of its socket they laid aside the jemmies and clasped it with their hands, carefully easing it forward, adjusting their holds as more and more of the block emerged. At last, with a final heave, they were able to drag it free of the wall and take its full weight on their arms and shoulders. It was heavy, unbelievably heavy, far more so than either of them had expected, and it was extremely hard to manoeuvre, with the scaffolding wobbling beneath them and the limited space available on the platform. They shuffled a couple of half-steps away from the wall and started to lower it, sweat stinging their eyes, their breathing growing increasingly fast and frantic. They got it about halfway down before both of them simultaneously felt the stone starting to slip through their fingers.

'I can't hold it,' gasped Freya. 'It's . . .'

She stumbled to her right, trying to keep hold before

realizing it was hopeless and letting the block go, leaping out of the way to avoid her feet being crushed. Flin lurched forward and also released his grip, a fraction of a second later than Freya, his momentum propelling the stone to the very edge of the platform and then off into space. The chamber – the entire temple – seemed to reverberate to a dull, hammer-like thud as the stone crashed to the floor below, the force of the impact breaking off a large chunk of its corner.

'Oh God,' Flin groaned, snatching up a torch and shining it down. Heavy wafts of dust undulated through the torch's beam. 'Two and a half thousand years that's been there . . .'

'Screw the block,' said Freya. 'What if someone heard?'

They stood still, listening, the echo of the crashing stone seeming to linger around the chamber's vaulted ceiling, Flin looking as mortified as if he had unwittingly run over a close friend. There were no shouts or footfalls, however, no sign that the accident had attracted the attention of the temple guards, and with a last, pained look down at the shattered block, Flin turned his attention to the newly opened hole in the wall. Stepping up to it, he shone his torch through into the space beyond.

'What can you see?' asked Freya, picking up her own torch and moving in behind him.

He didn't respond, just moved his beam to and fro, surveying the cavity, his back and shoulders blocking Freya's view.

'What can you see?' she repeated, trying to look round him.

Still he didn't say anything and she felt a momentary jolt of fear that maybe there was nothing there, that Fadawi had been fooling with them after all. Then Flin turned to face her, his horrified expression of a moment earlier now replaced with one of startled awe.

'Wonderful things,' he said, giving her a thumbs-up. 'I see wonderful things.'

He shuffled to the left, allowing her to slip in beside him and shine her own torch through the hole. Freya found herself looking into a narrow, shaft-like cavity, no more than two metres across and perhaps twelve metres long, a secret passageway hemmed in between the walls of the chapels. Its ceiling – made up of huge stone slabs – seemed to be on the same level as that of the chapel ceiling, and its floor, she assumed, must likewise be a continuation of the chapel floor. It was impossible to be certain, for along its entire length and up to a point less than a metre below the opening the cavity was packed with a confused jumble of stone blocks, the smallest at least twice the size of the one they had just removed. Some of the blocks were square, others rectangular, some blank, others decorated with images and hieroglyphic inscriptions. The carvings – like those in the hypostyle halls outside – still bore traces of their original coloration: greens and reds and yellows and blues. There were segments of column as well, random pieces of statuary – part of a granite torso; the front end of a sphinx – all of it thrown into the cavity seemingly willy-nilly, everything lying across and on top of everything else. The impression was of peering into a giant box crammed full of children's play bricks.

'Incredible, isn't it?' said Flin, leaning his head in so that his cheek was almost touching Freya's.

He shone his own torch into the shaft, moving the light

around until it had settled on the face of one block in particular, illuminating a pair of what looked like elongated ovals, one beside the other, each encircling a row of hieroglyphic signs.

'Nefer-Ka-Re Pepi,' he read, his torch beam juddering slightly as if he was so overwhelmed by what he was seeing he couldn't hold his hand still. 'The throne name of the pharaoh Pepi II. Like Hassan said, there must have been an Old Kingdom temple on this site that was dismantled and recycled as wall-filling when Seti built his temple a thousand years later.'

He shook his head.

'Christ, Freya, I can't even begin to . . . I mean this is a period of history from which we have almost no material remains. Something like this could completely rewrite . . . Mind-blowing, absolutely mind-blowing!'

They gazed into the cavity for a while longer. Then, aware that time was short, Flin squeezed his head and shoulders into the gap in the wall and started to drag himself through into the space beyond, his legs and feet disappearing as he squirmed down onto the tangle of stone below. Freya followed, rather more dextrously, Flin helping her through from the other side and lowering her gently onto the uneven surface.

'Careful where you put your hands,' he warned. 'The place is probably crawling with scorpions.'

She winced and whipped her palm away from the statue head on which she'd laid it.

Now they were inside, the cavity felt even more cramped and claustrophobic. The ceiling was too low for them to stand fully upright, and masonry pushed at them from all directions, although there was the faintest hint of draught, a barely discernible movement of air – where it was coming from Freya couldn't tell. They gave it a moment, squatting beside the opening in the wall, wheeling their torches about, getting the measure of the space. Then, with another glance at his watch – 4.51 a.m. – Flin started to clamber around, examining the inscriptions, looking for anything that might offer a clue to the oasis's whereabouts. Freya angled her torch beam in his direction to give him extra light, but otherwise let him get on with it. She could no more read hieroglyphs than she could Japanese so there was little other contribution she could make.

Twenty minutes went by, neither of them speaking, the only sounds the scrape of Flin's boots on stone and his occasional murmurs of 'Wonderful. My God, it's just wonderful!' Then, suddenly, he clicked his fingers and waved her over.

'Come and look at this.'

Freya stumbled across to him, head knocking against the ceiling, and crouched down at his side. Flin drew his torch back and played its beam along a length of greenish-black stone. After a moment she realized it was a small obelisk, lying horizontally and partially buried beneath a clutter of other blocks.

'It seems to be some sort of hymn or prayer to the Benben,' he said, indicating the hieroglyphic text with which the stone was inscribed.

'That's the Indiana Jones rock, right?' she asked. 'The one with the supernatural powers?'

He nodded, smiling at her description. Touching a dusty finger to the top right-hand corner of the inscription, he started to recite, his voice – as it had when reading the Imti-Khentika papyrus – seeming to grow deeper and more plangent as though it was echoing from far back in time.

'*Iner-wer iner-en Ra iner-n sedjet iner sweser-en kheru-en sekhmet,*' he intoned. 'Oh great stone, oh stone of fire, oh stone that made us mighty, oh voice of Sekhmet that we carry into battle before us and that brings us victories beyond number . . .'

'Anything about the oasis?'

'No, but this one mentions the Benben too . . .'

Flin moved his torch to the side, aiming the beam at a hieroglyph-covered limestone block, its text picked out in vibrant shades of red, blue, yellow and green.

'. . . and this one . . .'

Now his torch swung over to what looked like a fragment of shattered column.

'. . . which suggests the material towards this end of the cavity all came from the same part of the Pepi temple. Some sort of shrine dedicated to the Benben by the looks of it. And as I said back in the museum, where you find the Benben mentioned you usually find the oasis as well. Around here, that's where we need to look. This is where it'll be.'

He gave a satisfied grunt and resumed his search, examining each piece of masonry in turn, ignoring his own advice about scorpions and burrowing his torch hand deep into the gaps between the blocks in an effort to illuminate those sections of text that were partially buried or else lying at difficult angles.

'What if the inscription we need's right at the bottom?'

Freya asked. 'This stuff must go down another two metres. There's no way we can move it all.'

Flin didn't answer – whether because he was too absorbed in what he was doing or simply didn't want to contemplate that scenario she couldn't tell. Another fifteen minutes drifted by. Freya, sitting on a statue head, felt distinctly useless as the Englishman continued to work his way across the confusion of rubble. Then he let out a sharp yelp and again waved her over.

He was now about two-thirds of the way along the cavity, his torch beam directed at a small block wedged between a clutter of other blocks, its face angled downwards so that he could only access it by lying on his back and looking up. He was grinning from ear to ear.

'What is it?' she asked, craning over him, trying to get a better view.

'It's part of a text discussing how to actually enter the oasis,' he said breathlessly, his fingertips running back and forth across the stone as though he was caressing the skin of a lover. 'Almost certainly from the innermost sanctum of Pepi's temple, where only the pharaoh and the high priest would be able to view it. I just can't begin to describe how important this is.'

He continued to gawp at the inscription, one hand angling his torch beam back and forth while with the other he traced the lines of hieroglyphs. Then, slowly, he began to translate:

'*Sebawy* – two gates – shall bring you to *inet djeseret*, the sacred valley. *Khery en-inet* – at the lower end of the valley – the *re-en wesir*, the Mouth of Osiris. *Hery en inet* – at the upper end of the valley – the *maqet en Nut*, the ladder of

Nut, which is beneath *mu nu pet*, the water in the sky. And these gates alone shall bring you there, only the two, at the bottom and the top, no others shall be found, for it is the will of Ra . . .'

He broke off, the inscription ending at that point.

'The Mouth of Osiris we already knew about,' he said, his voice calmer now, more controlled. 'Although what exactly it refers to . . .'

He shook his head.

'Osiris was the god of the underworld so maybe it's just figurative . . . we simply don't know. This ladder of Nut thing's completely new, however. It's not mentioned in any other extant text, or at least none that I've ever seen, and I'm pretty sure I've seen them all – absolutely fucking extraordinary.'

'What does it mean?' she asked, excited even though the text said nothing to her.

'Well, Nut was the goddess of the sky,' explained Flin, shuffling out from underneath the block, his face and hair powdered with dust. 'And phrases like *mu nu pet*, the water in the sky, generally refer to high cliffs – during flash floods the water would pour down off the top of the cliff as if it was hanging from the heavens. The ladder bit . . . again, it's impossible to know if it's referring to something literal or is just metaphor, but the implication is that the ancient Egyptians used to access the oasis from the top of the Gilf Kebir as well as the side of it.'

He came up into a squatting position alongside Freya, ruffling the dust out of his hair.

'Does any of that help us?' she asked.

'When's there's as little information out there as there is

about the oasis, every tiny clue's important, but no, it doesn't get us any closer to the precise location. What I'm guessing – what I'm hoping – is that if there's a text explaining how to get into the oasis then somewhere around here there's going to be one explaining how to actually find it. We're getting close, I can feel it. We're getting close.'

He reached out and squeezed her arm, then started picking his way over the masonry again, minutely examining every inch of stone. He had been energized before but now it seemed to Freya he became positively manic, hefting aside those blocks and fragments of statuary that were not too heavy to move in order to get at whatever lay beneath them, glancing constantly at his watch, muttering to himself, seemingly oblivious to her presence. His persistence bore swift results. In quick succession he found three more references to the Benben, a text describing the great temple that apparently sat at the heart of the oasis and another inscription repeating the punishments that would be visited on those who entered the oasis with evil intent: *May evildoers be crushed in the jaws of Sobek and swallowed into the belly of the serpent Apep. And inside the serpent's belly may their fears become real, their evil dreams a living torment.*

There was nothing that gave any indication as to where the oasis might be, though, not even the vaguest hint. Another thirty agonizing minutes ticked by, Flin becoming increasingly irate, cursing and thudding his fists against the blocks as if trying to bully them into giving up their secrets. Unable to bear the tension any longer, the oppressive, dust-choked atmosphere, Freya left him to it and clambered out of the cavity and down the scaffolding. She stood a moment stretching her arms and legs – the dull clunk of stones being moved about echoing from the hole above her – then wandered back through the temple towards the front entrance, gulping clean, cool air as she went.

It was past 6 a.m. and the building seemed a completely different place. Shafts of early morning sunlight angled steeply down from the openings set high in the walls, bathing the hypostyle halls in a soft, dreamlike haze, driving the shadows back into the further corners and recesses. Moving cautiously, Freya made her way up to the entrance gate and peered though. Aside from a couple of black-uniformed guards sharing a cigarette, the courtyards outside were empty. Further down she could see coaches drawing up, people milling about, postcard and trinket vendors hawking their wares. She felt a brief shock of alarm that Flin had got his timings wrong and the temple was about to open, but no one seemed to be coming any closer and after a moment she relaxed. She watched a while, then turned and retraced her steps, birds fluttering overhead, weaving their way in and out of the giant columns as though skimming through a forest. Back in the chapel she called up to Flin in a hushed voice, asked how things were going. A despondent grunt was his only response. She climbed the scaffolding and squeezed herself back into the shaft. Flin was sitting right at its far end, bent over his torch, its weakened beam pointing towards the ceiling of the cavity, illuminating his face with a pale, deathly glow. His expression and posture told her everything she needed to know.

'I've gone through it with a fine-tooth comb,' he said, sounding as if he was about to start sobbing. 'There's nothing here, Freya. Or if there is it's buried under a ton of masonry and we can't get to it.'

She crawled over and crouched down beside him. The rubble at this end of the shaft was piled even higher than at the other end, leaving just over a metre of available head-room, hunching them up.

'We can come back tonight,' she said. 'Try again.'

He shook his head.

'The moment they find the hole in the wall, they'll have more guards in this place than Fort Knox. We won't be able to get near it. This was our only chance. There won't be another.'

He glanced at his watch: 6.39 a.m. Only twenty minutes before the temple opened to the public.

'We could try to get the block back up again,' she suggested.

He didn't even bother to respond, both of them knowing it was futile. There was a long pause. Then, with a sigh and another glance at his watch, he said they should think about getting out of there.

'We can hide in one of the hypostyle halls, lose ourselves among the tourists when they start coming in. There's always hundreds of them first thing. Shouldn't be too difficult.'

He showed no sign of acting on his suggestion, just sat with his head thrown back and his elbow resting on what looked like a miniature tombstone – a rectangular, hieroglyph-covered piece of limestone with a rounded top. More for something to say than because she was interested, Freya asked what the stone was.

'Hmm?'

She pointed.

'Oh, a *wd*. A stele. A sort of votive tablet the ancient

Egyptians placed in tombs and temples. They recorded prayers, events, offerings, that sort of thing.'

He twisted and, lifting the stone – it was only about forty centimetres high – hefted it round and rested it on his knees. He pointed his torch at it.

'It got me quite excited, actually. Talks about the *iret net Khepri* – the Eye of Khepri. One of those formulations that always seems to be associated with the oasis, like the Mouth of Osiris.'

He brushed a hand across the stone's face, reading:

'*Wepet iret Khepri wepet wehat khetem iret nen ma-tu wehat en is er-djer bik biki* – when the Eye of Khepri is opened, then shall the oasis be opened. When his eye is closed the oasis shall not be seen, even by the keenest falcon.'

He hugged an arm around the stele, seeming to draw comfort from it, explaining that Khepri was a scarab-headed god, one of the manifestations of the sun god Ra, the name coming from the word *kheper*, 'he who comes into being'. Freya was no longer listening; her attention had been drawn to the upper part of the stele, the area bounded by the arch at its top. There were images in there, separate from the columns of hieroglyphs beneath. On the left-hand side what looked like a red wall or cliff face, on the right the same wall only now there was a narrow green slit running down the middle of it. Between the two images ran an undulating band of yellow from which rose a scythe-shaped black curve, its edges curiously notched and serrated, its uppermost tip opening out into a large, finely detailed eye like a flower at the end of a stem. At first she had thought it was simply an interesting design. The more she looked, however, the more it reminded her . . .

'I've seen that.'

Flin was still discussing the attributes of the god Khepri and didn't appear to hear her.

'I've seen that,' she repeated, louder.

'Seen what?'

'That,' she said, pointing.

He nodded, not particularly surprised.

'Very possibly. The *wadjet* eye's a common—'

'Not the eye. That.'

She touched a finger to the curving black line.

'What do you mean you've seen it?'

'I've seen it. Or something very like it. In a photograph.'

'You've seen a photograph of this image?'

'No, no, it was a rock formation. Out in the desert. It was exactly the same, even the jagged sides.'

His eyes narrowed.

'Where? Where did you see this photograph?'

'In Zahir al-Sabri's house. When I first arrived in Egypt. Alex was in it, that's why I—'

'Did he tell you where it was?' he interrupted.

She shook her head.

'He didn't seem to want me to look at it, hustled me out of the room.'

Flin looked back down at the stele, fingers drumming on its sides, murmuring to himself: 'When the Eye of Khepri is opened, then shall the oasis be opened? When his eye is closed the oasis shall not be seen, even by the keenest falcon.' Minutes passed, Freya acutely conscious that their time window was rapidly closing, but loath to break his train of thought. Flin just sat there, utterly absorbed, until eventually, with the faintest of smiles, he lifted the stele from his knees and laid it back in the corner of the shaft.

'Must run in the family.'

'Sorry?'

'Must run in the Hannen family. A talent for saving the day. Alex was always doing it, and now you seem to be keeping up the tradition.'

He rolled onto his feet and started clambering back along the shaft.

'I don't understand,' she said, following on behind. 'Is it important, this rock?'

'Maybe, maybe not,' he replied, coming up to the hole in the wall and threading himself through, wriggling back into the chapel beyond. 'Between you and me, though, I have a horrible suspicion I've spent the last ten years pissing around with all this stuff and it's going to turn out to be you who's made the crucial breakthrough. For which, frankly, I'll never forgive you.'

He made it out onto the scaffold and turned back. His smile had now stretched into a grin.

'I ought to bloody leave you in there – discovering things without my permission! Purely for the sake of Anglo-American relations, however . . .'

He winked and held out a hand to help her through. She reached for it, only for Flin to suddenly whip it back again and spin. For a moment she was uncertain what was happening. Then she heard what he must have heard – voices. Still muffled and distant, but definitely coming from somewhere within the temple.

'Shit,' he hissed, swinging back again, the smile now gone. 'Come on, we've got to get out of here.'

He reached into the hole and pulled her through, helping

her upright before grabbing one of the crowbars and scrambling down to the floor below, the scaffolding creaking alarmingly. Freya followed and they hurried out into the nearer of the two hypostyle halls. The voices were now unmistakable, coming from the outer hall at the front of the temple; at least two or three people, by the sound of it.

'Tourists?' she whispered.

Flin listened a moment, then shook his head.

'Guards. They must have found the cut padlock. Quick.'

He waved her across the back of the hall, past the last of the chapels and into a narrow corridor. Ten metres along a barred gate opened in the wall to their right. Beyond it a set of steps sloped steeply upward to a second gate and daylight.

'The back of the temple,' he explained, working his crowbar into the lock of the first gate. 'We just need to . . .'

He heaved, the muscles of his neck bulging and twisting, his face purpling with the strain. He removed the crowbar and drove it in at a different angle, putting all his weight behind it, bracing his foot against the wall for extra leverage. Try as he did, he couldn't snap the lock. With a despairing growl, he gave up and led Freya back down the corridor and into the hall of columns again. It was still empty. The guards, it seemed, had not yet come through from the outer hall, although the jabber of voices and thud of boots suggested there were now a lot more of them.

'*Ehna aarfeen ennoko gowwa!*' someone shouted. '*Okhrogo we erfao'o edeko!*'

'Is there another way out?' asked Freya, her voice an anxious whisper.

Flin shook his head.

'Can we hide?'

'Too many of them.'

'What'll they do if they catch us?'

'If we're lucky, stick us in prison for five years and then deport us.'

She didn't bother asking what would happen if they weren't lucky.

'*Ento met-hasreen!*' came the voice again. '*Mafeesh mahrab!*'

Flin looked around, trying to come up with a plan, any plan. With the footsteps and voices now almost at the doorway between the two halls, he grabbed Freya's arm and pulled her along the back of the space again, past the chapel they had been working in and into the next but one along. Unlike the other sanctuaries this one had a doorway in its rear wall that took them through into yet another hall, much smaller than the two main ones. Twin rows of pillars ran down its centre, daylight streamed in through a pair of open skylights in the ceiling.

'Where does this lead?' she asked.

'It doesn't.'

'So why have we—'

'Because there's nowhere else to go! We can't get out through the front, the back door's locked . . .'

He threw up his hands helplessly.

'We're trapped, Freya. I'm just trying to buy us a couple of extra minutes, hoping against hope they might not come in here.'

Outside the chamber the shouts and thud of feet were growing louder as the guards worked their way through the temple towards them, tightening the net.

'*Sallemo nafsoko!*'

'There has to be another way out,' she said. 'There has to be.'

'Sure, there's a magic door and if you wave a wand and say abracadabra . . .'

More shouts, punctuated by a series of shrill whistle blasts. Freya circled her eyes frantically around the hall, looking for something that might help them. Ten squat pillars – two rows of five – smaller rooms opening at either end, relief-covered walls of which the right-hand one was roped off to prevent tourists from touching the inscriptions. Nothing that offered them any hope of escape.

'When they come in just stay still and let me do the talking,' said Flin. 'And keep your hands visible.'

She ignored him, continuing to wheel her gaze around. The shouts and whistle blasts were now accompanied by the barking of dogs.

The two skylights – square blue holes in the concrete slab ceiling – were well out of reach even though the ceiling itself was much lower here than in the two main halls, only about five metres off the ground. Without a ladder or a scaffold they might as well have been fifty metres up. She dismissed them, staring again at the walls, the side rooms, the pillars, the flagstoned floor, back to the pillars. *The pillars.* Squat, trunk-like, made up of drum-shaped sections piled one on top of the other with clear gaps between each drum. She took a step forward and looked up at the skylights again. Each was a good metre and a half away from the top of the nearest column, too far to reach without a handhold. Except that there *was* a handhold – a rusted iron reinforcing bar protruding from the further of the two skylights like some twisted root pushing its way down into the chamber. And the column nearest to it had a metal brace wrapped around its uppermost drum like a garter round the top of a thigh. Up the column using the gaps between cylinders for foot and handholds, finger jam behind the brace, lean out, jump for the reinforcing bar. It was a crazy manoeuvre, impossible, a Deadman into a Dead Hang, something she wouldn't contemplate even in a training climb with safety ropes and a crash pad to break her fall. Crazy. Crazy. But . . .

'I can get us out of here,' she said.

Flin's head snapped towards her.

'What are you talking about?'

She didn't waste time explaining. Waving him over to the rope strung in front of the wall reliefs, she told him to coil it up, then ran across to the column and started climbing. Although narrow, the joins between the stone drums afforded her just about enough space for finger- and toe-holds, and while it would have been easier with chalk and proper climb shoes, she still reached the top of the column without too much trouble. Wedging her fingers in behind the metal brace, she balanced the tips of her toes on the raised reliefs with which the pillar was covered and gazed across at the iron reinforcing rod. From up here it looked an awful lot further away than it had from down below.

Flin was now standing at the bottom of the column, the coiled rope slung over his shoulder. The direction of Freya's eyes told him all he needed to know about what she was planning.

'No way! You'll break your neck!'

She ignored him. Edging her way around the column, she brought herself as close as possible to the skylight, adjusting her toe- and finger-holds to give her sufficient leverage to make the jump.

'For Christ's sake, Freya!'

The shouts and barking were drawing ever closer. With every second now crucial, she threw a final glance across at the skylight, braced her feet and leapt, powering herself away from the column and through the air towards the metal rod.

Her fear had been that either she wouldn't get a proper grip or that the momentum of her leap would break that grip and send her plummeting to the floor beneath. As it was, like a seasoned trapeze artist, she made perfect contact, clasping the bar with both hands, swinging wildly back and forth for a moment before coming still, suspended above the chamber floor. Flin looked up from below, his expression a mixture of horror and admiration. She gave herself a few seconds, head thrown back, staring at the opening above, gathering her strength. Then, taking a breath, she started to heave herself up, hand over hand, towards the skylight. For someone without her climbing experience such an ascent would have been nigh on impossible, requiring as it did uniquely strong musculature in the shoulders and upper arms. Years of pulling overhangs on some of the world's toughest rock faces, not to mention the hundred chin-ups she did every morning to keep herself conditioned, had more than attuned her body to such exertions and she was able to make reasonably light work of it. Biceps and deltoids bulging and knotting, legs flapping as though she were trying to swim upwards, she reached the underside of the skylight. Bringing her left leg up and curling it around the rod, she drove a hand through the opening and clasped its outer rim. She pulled herself up another few inches, got the other hand out as well, heaved and scrambled until her head, then her torso and finally her entire body was out on the roof of the temple.

Down in the chamber Flin watched her disappear through the hole. She dropped her arm back and clicked her fingers and he flung the rope up to her, glancing anxiously over his shoulder. The sound of barking echoed in the sanctuary leading into the chamber.

'*Ehna dakhleen lolo!*' someone shouted. '*Ma tehawloosh teaamelo haga wa ella hanedrabkom bennar!* We're coming in for you. Don't try anything or we'll shoot!'

'Come on!' he hissed.

One end of the rope came snaking back down. Without even bothering to make sure she was properly braced at the other end Flin seized the rope with both hands and flailed his way upwards, the guards now only a matter of seconds away, the bark and snarl of dogs seeming to fill the entire temple. He reached the skylight, heaved and wriggled and kicked himself through and rolled away from the opening, leaving Freya just enough time to yank the rope up and out of sight before a pair of Alsatians came bursting into the chamber below, closely followed by half a dozen guards.

There were shouts, more barking, the thud of running feet, but they didn't stick around to listen. Still gasping for breath, his shirt sleeve stained red with blood from where the wound on his arm had partially opened again, Flin led them across the roof to its rear edge. Because the temple was built back into hillside, this was only a couple of metres

421

off the ground. They jumped down onto the loose sand below and made for the mobile phone mast Freya had seen when they first arrived, picking up the track that descended the hill beside the temple. Five minutes later they were back at the Jeep. Thirty seconds after that they were speeding along the road out of Abydos as lines of police cars passed in the other direction, sirens blaring.

'I never realized Egyptology could be so exciting,' said Freya, the first time either of them had spoken since their escape.

'I never realized rock climbing could be so useful,' retorted Flin.

They glanced across at each other and grinned.

'We've got a long drive ahead,' he said. 'You sure you still want to tag along?'

'Wouldn't miss it for the world.'

He looked across at her again, nodded and floored the accelerator.

'Dakhla here we come.'

CAIRO

Mohammed Shubra had worked on the front desk of the USAID building for the best part of twenty years, and in all that time he couldn't remember ever having seen Mrs Kiernan looking more cheerful. She always had a smile for him, of course, was always polite, but this morning as she strode through the entrance gate and into the building she looked positively euphoric.

422

'Something good has happened,' he said as she came up to him and flashed her security card. 'I see it in your face.'

She smiled and wagged a finger.

'You don't miss a trick, do you, Mohammed?'

'Mrs Kiernan, you would have to be blind to miss this! You have had family news, I think.'

She shook her head.

'Work. It's always work, Mohammed.'

He would have left it at that – it wasn't his place to question her about her business affairs – but to his surprise, and pleasure, she took a quick look around, then leant forward across the desk.

'I've had some news about one of my projects,' she said. 'I didn't think it was going to pan out but now it looks like it just might.'

She had never spoken to him like this before, never confided in this way, and he felt a thrill of excitement, as if he was being let into a great secret.

'You have been working long time on this project?' he asked, trying to sound offhand, as though he talked about these sorts of things all the time.

'Oh yes,' she replied, touching the cross around her neck, beaming. 'A very long time. Since before you even started here. A very long time.'

'It is big project? Important?'

Although she continued to smile, something in her eyes seemed to harden suddenly, as though she had revealed as much as she felt comfortable with and now wanted to close the conversation down.

'All our projects are important, Mohammed. They all

make the world a better place. Now I've got a busy day ahead of me so if you don't mind . . .'

She raised a hand in farewell and headed towards the lifts, only to come back again, fiddling in her handbag.

'One thing. Have you ever seen this man before?'

She laid a photograph on the desk in front of him – a fat, balding man with rosy cheeks and big lips.

'He was here yesterday morning,' replied the Egyptian, feeling that maybe he had overstepped the mark earlier and pleased that he now had an opportunity to redeem himself. 'The director gave him a tour.'

Kiernan nodded and slipped the picture back into her bag.

'Would you do me a favour, Mohammed? If you see him again give me a call, let me know he's in the building?'

'Of course, Mrs Kiernan. The moment I see him. You will be the first to know.'

She thanked him, crossed the foyer, stepped into the lift and disappeared.

'A very nice lady,' Mohammed Shubra told his wife when he called her later that morning. 'Tough as old shoe leather, though. I certainly wouldn't like to get on the wrong side of her.'

DAKHLA

Emerging from the undergrowth, the figure paused a moment as if listening, then hurried up to the side of the outbuilding – a plain, breeze-block structure with a palm thatch roof and a heavy iron door secured with a padlock and chain. It was a man, that much was clear from the way he moved. Beyond that, it was impossible to identify him for his body was swathed in a billowing black robe, his head and face in a *shaal* of the same colour so that only his eyes were visible.

Fumbling in his pocket, he pulled out a small metallic object with what looked like a magnet attached to the bottom. He turned it over in his hands, then returned it to his robe. Clambering onto the old wooden cart parked beside the building, he scrambled through a window set high into the wall – a simple square opening without frame or glass. There was a muffled thud as he dropped to the floor inside, followed by a rustle of movement and a low clunk as of the magnet clamping itself to something. Within a minute he was out again and pushing his way back into the undergrowth behind the barn. Three minutes later there came the sound of a motorbike starting up, its roar slowly receding until there was nothing but the twitter of birds and the low putter of an irrigation pump.

CAIRO

Chaotic organization, that was the best way Angleton could describe it. Or organized chaos. Either way the Egyptian traffic monitoring system was one that, on the face of it, appeared hopelessly shambolic – bored, semi-literate police conscripts standing at roadblocks in the middle of nowhere scribbling down the number plates and driver details of passing vehicles – and yet when all was said and done actually proved remarkably efficient.

Just after midnight Major-General Taneer's people had come back to him with the first batch of results: Brodie and Hannen's car had passed through a checkpoint on Highway 11 at 9.33 p.m., travelling north towards Alexandria, and then back again through the same checkpoint at 10.54 p.m., this time towards Cairo. What exactly they had been doing out there Angleton had no idea, but whatever it was it had merely been a prelude to their main journey. The information had dribbled in steadily through the night and all of it had shown them moving south. First along Highway 22 to the Fayyum, and then along Highway 2 up the Nile Valley. They had passed through Beni Suef at 12.16 a.m., Maghaga at 12.43, Al-Minya at 1.16 – by this point he had asked the Egyptians to concentrate all their efforts on that particular route and its tributaries – Asyut at 2.17, Sohag at 3.21 and finally, at 3.56 a.m., a checkpoint just outside Abydos.

After which there had been nothing for over three hours. Around 5.30 a.m. he'd requested a telephone sweep of every officially registered hotel and guest-house in the vicinity of Abydos to see whether they had stopped off for the night. Zilch. He had started to curse and fret – not at all like him – convinced they had given him the slip. There had been no mobile traffic either, no communications of any sort for his listening equipment to pick up on and he'd all but accepted he'd lost them. Then, suddenly, at 7.07 a.m., he had received word that the Cherokee and its two occupants had once again passed through the Abydos checkpoint. Not only that, but their departure had coincided with some sort of security incident at the temple – a break-in, vandalism of some kind, a chase. He would have liked to know more, but the details were still sketchy and he'd had to content himself with the fact that Brodie and Hannen were at least back on radar. He had punched the air in relief and, sweeping poor old Mrs Malouff up in a bear hug as she came through the door for the start of her shift, planted a kiss on her cheek.

'Game on!' he cried in that girlish, high-pitched voice of his. 'Game on again, you sons-of-bitches!'

Once he had calmed down and Mrs Malouff had smoothed her dress and primped her hair – 'You will please not do that again,' she had told him sternly, 'I am respectable married lady!' – Angleton left her to it and took a taxi to his office at the US Embassy. He had continued his vigil from there (and got a full breakfast sent up from chef Barney down in the kitchen – lack of sleep always made him hungry).

At 7.46 he received word the Cherokee had passed through the Sohag checkpoint again, heading north, and eighty minutes after that the one at Asyut. Clearly Brodie and Hannen were on their way back to Cairo.

Then came a surprise. On the basis of their outward journey, and the fact that there was more traffic on the road by day and so their progress was bound to be slower, Angleton calculated they would hit Al-Minya some time around 10.30 a.m. 10.30 came and went. Then 11, 11.30. He was starting to fret again when, just after 11.45, he got a call to say that, far from heading north, the Cherokee had been clocked at three separate checkpoints on the desert road south-west from Asyut, the last just twenty kilometres out-side Kharga. More info had by this point filtered through on the events back at Abydos. Someone – it was too much of a coincidence for it not to have been Brodie and Hannen – had broken into the temple, smashed a hole in a wall and discovered some sort of secret chamber. As before, the details remained confused, but whatever they'd found or seen, it now seemed to be leading them out into the western desert. Interesting. Very, very interesting.

He went over to the map on the wall, staring at it for some while before going to the window. Part of him was tempted to hold out a bit longer, keep tracking the two of them from a distance, checkpoint to checkpoint. The problem was, that always left him one step behind, and as the crisis of the whole drama approached – as he sensed it was fast doing – one step behind was as good as being out of the game altogether. There was no point asking the Egyptians to put a tail on them: if *he* couldn't keep up with Brodie they sure as hell wouldn't be able to. He toyed with the idea of asking for the two of them to be stopped at the next checkpoint and held until he himself got there, but swiftly dismissed it: a fit, highly motivated former agent against a group of clueless hick conscripts – no contest.

He stared out of the window a while longer, watching as people wandered to and fro in the compound below. Slapping his palm against the glass, he came to a decision and returned to the map. Time to make his move – get in there, find out what Brodie and Hannen knew and then take them out of the picture. The question was, how? And, more pertinently, where? He traced his finger across the desert from Asyut to Kharga to Dakhla and then left and down to the Gilf Kebir. That's where they were ultimately heading. Had to be – in this story all roads seemed to lead that way. Before the Gilf, however . . . He dragged his finger back to the desert highway, moving it between Dakhla and Kharga, to and fro as if playing eeny meeny miney mo before eventually settling on Dakhla. It was a gamble, of course, but then everything was in this game. He hadn't put too many feet wrong so far and he felt deep in his gut that he wasn't going to here. Dakhla was their next port of call, he was certain of it, and Dakhla was where he'd head them off. He rapped a chubby knuckle hard against the map, as if knocking on a door, and crossed to the phone. Snatching up the receiver, he dialled. A brief wait, then a voice echoed at the other end of the line.

'I need a flight to Dakhla,' said Angleton without pre-amble. 'ASAP. And a car at the other end. I'm heading out to the airport now.'

He replaced the receiver and lifted his shoulder holster which he'd slung across the back of his chair. Slipping Missy out, he grasped her handle and sighted down the barrel, aiming across the room at the wall map opposite.

'Cyrus is a-coming!'

DAKHLA

It was just past midday when they finally passed between the giant metal palm trees that mark the eastern limit of Dakhla Oasis. They had been on the road for five hours straight, Flin at the wheel for most of the time although Freya had taken over for the long middle section between Asyut and Kharga so he could catch up on some sleep.

It had been an uneventful, if, thanks to Flin's driving, sporadically heart-stopping journey. First they'd retraced their route back along the Nile Valley with its lush fields and straggling mud-brick villages. Then they'd turned out across the desert – sand, rock, gravel and very little else, the only signs of human influence the regularly spaced kilometre markers and the occasional police checkpoint. And, of course, the road itself: a seam of shimmering black tarmac stretching across the sands like some enormous fissure splitting the landscape.

Fifteen minutes after entering the oasis they reached Mut, where Freya took over the directions, Flin never having been to Zahir's house before. They passed the hospital and police station – it had only been 48 hours since she had been there, but already it felt like part of a different life – and took the road out of the other side of town, speeding through maize fields and rice paddies towards the distant white wall of the desert escarpment. Eventually they reached Zahir's village and pulled up in the street in front of his house. Flin cut the engine and started to open his door. Freya laid a hand on his arm, holding him back.

'You know Zahir, right?'

Flin looked at her over his shoulder.

'Well I've met him a few times. We're not exactly friends, if that's what you mean. I use another guide when I'm out in the desert. Why?'

'I can't really explain it,' she said, staring over at the gateway of the house. 'There was just something . . . He wasn't very friendly when I was with him.'

Flin smiled.

'I wouldn't take it personally. It's just the Bedouin way.

They tend to keep their emotions to themselves. I once knew a guy—'

'It was more than that.'

He released the door handle and swivelled round to face her. Her eyes were red from lack of sleep, her blond hair tousled and unkempt, still flecked with dust from the cavity in the temple.

'How do you mean?' he asked.

'Like I said, I can't really explain. There was just something about him, his manner . . . I don't trust him, Flin.'

'Alex did,' he said. 'With her life.'

She shrugged.

'I just think we should . . . be careful. Not tell him too much.'

'Alex was a good judge—'

'I just think we should be careful,' she repeated. 'I don't like him, he's dodgy.'

He held her eyes, then nodded and climbed out of the Jeep. Freya followed and together they walked through the mud-brick gateway into the yard in front of the house. Skirting Zahir's Land Cruiser with its smashed headlamp, they came to the front door. It was wide open.

Freya had been harbouring a vague hope that Zahir might not be at home. That his wife would let them in to look at the photograph of the rock formation and that they could find out what they needed without having any direct contact with the man. As it was, Flin hadn't even had time to knock before Zahir materialized in the corridor ahead. On seeing them his face broke into a broad smile before rearranging itself into the surly blankness that seemed to be his default expression.

'Miss Freya,' he said, striding towards them. 'I worried. You disappear.'

She mumbled an apology, said she'd had urgent business back in Cairo. It didn't sound very convincing and he clearly didn't believe her, but he let it go. Ushering them into the house, he shouted something down the corridor behind him. Freya caught the words *Amrekanaya* and *shiy*.

'*Ana asif, sais Zahir*,' said Flin, 'I'm sorry, Zahir, but we don't have time for tea. We need to ask you something.'

Zahir's attention switched to the Englishman, the first time he had acknowledged his presence. Although his expression remained unreadable, something in his eyes and the set of his shoulders suggested, if not hostility, at least unease.

'Ask?' He sounded suspicious. 'Ask what?'

'About the photograph,' said Freya. 'The one in the room at the back of your house. The photograph of the rock.'

Zahir shook his head as if he didn't understand what she was talking about.

'Don't you remember? When I came here before, I was looking for the bathroom and went into the wrong room. There was a photograph there, of my sister standing beside a rock.'

She motioned with one hand, outlining the shape, the way the rock curled upwards from the desert like an enormous cutlass spearing through the sand.

'It was on the wall above your desk. You said the room was private.'

'We need to ask you about it,' said Flin. 'Where this rock is. It's out near the Gilf, isn't it?'

Zahir's eyes flicked from Freya to Flin and back again.

He seemed reluctant to answer. There was a silence, then the Egyptian gave a dismissive flick of the hand.

'First we drink tea. Then talk.'

He turned into the sitting room with its television, cushioned bench and knife hanging on the wall. Flin and Freya remained in the doorway.

'Please, we need to see the photograph,' said Flin. 'We don't have much time.'

Zahir turned to them.

'Why you need see this picture?' he asked, a barely discernible hint of aggression in his voice. 'Is just rock.'

Flin and Freya exchanged a glance.

'It's to do with my work,' said Flin. 'I know the Gilf pretty well but I've never seen this formation before and I think it might be important, might . . . have some bearing on our understanding of Palaeolithic settlement patterns in the middle Holocene.'

If he was hoping to bamboozle the Egyptian with technical speak it didn't work. Zahir remained where he was, unmoved. There was another uncomfortable silence, then Freya lost patience.

'Please, Zahir, I want to see the photo,' she said, more sharply than perhaps she intended, but she was exhausted and time was pressing. 'My sister was in it and I want to know about it.'

Zahir frowned.

'*Sais* Brodie say he want know about picture for work. You say you want know because Doctor Alex in picture. I no understand.'

Freya's mouth tightened and for a moment it looked as if she was going to lose her temper. Instead, drawing a breath, she took a step towards Zahir and opened out her hands in a gesture of entreaty.

'Please,' she repeated. 'For Alex's sake, if not for mine, tell us about the photo. She'd want you to help us, I know she would. Please.'

They stood facing each other, the only sound the muffled squawk of geese from outside, Freya staring at Zahir, Zahir refusing to meet her gaze. Everything about him suggested doubt and unease. Seconds passed, then, with a reluctant shrug, he stepped past them back out into the corridor.

'You want see picture, I show picture,' he said, his tone implying that he wasn't at all happy about it. 'Come.'

He led them along the corridor and out into the yard at the back of the house. Freya caught a fleeting glimpse of his wife and son in the kitchen doorway opposite before the woman moved back into the shadows and was lost. Crossing to the nearest of the doors in the right-hand wall, Zahir threw it open and waved them after him into the room beyond.

'Here picture,' he said gruffly, walking over to the desk and jabbing a finger at the photograph, spreading his arms as if to demonstrate he had nothing to hide. They took in the huge, curving spire of black rock with its notched sides and the tiny figure standing in the shade at its foot. Flin in particular seemed captivated by the image, leaning across the desk to scrutinize it more closely, his head nodding slightly as if he had suddenly been presented, if not with the answer to some long-pondered riddle, at least with new hope of discovering the answer.

'You took this?' he asked.

Zahir grunted an affirmative.

'Where?'

'In desert, is obvious.'

Flin ignored the sarcasm.

'Near the Gilf Kebir?'

Another grudging affirmative.

'The Gilf's a big place. Can you be more specific?'

No answer.

'Northern part or southern part?' pushed Flin.

'*Fi'l ganoob*,' conceded the Egyptian, clearly not appreciating being interrogated in this manner. 'In south. I no remember exact place. Is very long time ago.'

Flin studied the photograph for a moment longer, then turned to Zahir.

'*Sahebee*, I am in your house and so I will show you respect. But you must respect me as well. This photograph was taken within the last five months. See here . . .'

He tapped a finger against the image, indicating a thin sliver of silver leaning against the rock beside Freya's sister.

'This is Alex's walking stick. She only started using it when she became ill last November.'

Zahir looked at his feet, shuffling uncomfortably.

'I don't know what you're trying to hide,' continued Flin, trying to keep his voice level, but clearly in no mood for playing games, 'or why you don't want to tell us about this photo. But I am asking you as our host and also as a Bedouin to stop bullshitting and give me a straight answer.'

Zahir's head came up, nostrils flaring.

'You no speak to me like this,' he growled. 'No in my house, no anywhere. You understand? You no insult me or it will no be good for you.'

'Are you threatening me, Zahir?'

'I no threaten you, I tell you. You no speak me like this.'

Their voices were rising and Freya stepped in before the situation spun out of control.

'Zahir, we have not come to insult you,' she said, her tone at once both mollifying and firm. 'We just need to know where the photograph was taken. My sister thought a great deal of you and as I said before, if not for our sake, for hers. Please, tell us where the rock is and we'll leave.'

This time Zahir held her gaze. His anger appeared to have dissipated as quickly as it had come, replaced by . . . Freya couldn't quite pin down what it had been replaced by: a mixture of resignation and apprehension it seemed to her, as though he had accepted he was going to have to tell them what they wanted to know, but was fearful of the consequences.

'Please, Zahir,' she repeated.

He was silent for a moment, then:

'You want go this place?'

Flin and Freya looked at each other, then nodded.

'I take you,' he said. 'We go together.'

'We just need to know where it is,' said Flin.

'Gilf Kebir long way. Dangerous, very dangerous. It no good you go without guide. I come with you.'

'We just need—'

'Long way, long way. You go alone it take three day get there. I come with you, less than one day. I know Gilf, I know desert. I take you.'

The argument continued for some time, ping-ponging back and forth – Zahir insisting on accompanying them, Flin and Freya insisting that all they wanted was the location of the rock – before at last the Egyptian acknowledged defeat. Slumping into the chair beside the desk, he hugged his arms around him, eyes fixed miserably on the floor.

'You know Wadi al-Bakht?' he muttered.

Flin said he did.

'Rock thirty kilometre south of al-Bakht, three-quarter between al-Bakht and Eight Bell. Big cliff there, very high. Rock four, five hundred metre away in desert. You go south from al-Bakht you cannot miss.'

He looked up, shaking his head as if to say 'You don't know what you're getting into.' With no reason to prolong the conversation, they thanked him, made their farewells and moved to the door. As they reached it he called out after them.

'I try help you. Gilf very far, three hundred fifty kilo-metre, only desert, very dangerous. I try help you, but you no understand.'

He was on his feet again, one hand extended towards them, something almost pleading in his eyes. For a moment they all stood there in embarrassed silence. Then, thanking him again, Flin and Freya stepped out into the yard and closed the door after them.

Once they were gone Zahir stood for a long while contemplating the photograph on the wall. Then he made his way back through the house to the bedroom, reached underneath the bed and retrieved the rifle he kept there. He sat and balanced the gun on his knees. Running one hand back and forth along the barrel, he fumbled with the other in the pocket of his *djellaba* and pulled out his mobile phone. He dialled and held the phone to his ear.

'She has been here,' he said when the call was answered. 'With Brodie. They know about the rock. They are going out there.'

A voice echoed at the other end of the line.

'We have no choice,' said Zahir. 'It is our duty. You are with me?'

Another tinny echo.

'*Tamam*. I'll pick you up in thirty minutes.'

He rang off and rose to his feet, the rifle clasped in his hand.

'Yasmin!' he called. 'Mohsen! I must go away! Come and say goodbye!'

The Learjet deposited Angleton at Dakhla airport a little before 1 p.m. and within five minutes he was outside and in the hire car, a lime-green Honda Civic whose best days were clearly long behind it. He'd thought things through on the flight down, consulted the maps, knew exactly where Alex Hannen's house was located – that's where they were going to start from, it had to be – and with the local police under instructions to relay any sightings direct to him, there was no reason to tarry. Mopping the sweat from his neck and forehead – sweet holy Jesus it was hot out here! – he started the Honda's engine, put the car into gear and, tyres squealing on the baking tarmac, roared off across the car park. The guards manning the airport security gate leapt out of the way as he careered past them and out onto the road to Mut.

It was a curious thing, but from the moment she'd first heard about the Hidden Oasis – was it really less than twenty-four hours ago? – Freya had somehow sensed she'd be heading out into the burning wastes of the western desert in search of it. Although that sense had grown stronger as the hours had slipped by and the oasis had come more and more to dominate events, at no point had it ever been anything more than an abstract notion. It was only now, as they tore along the desert track back towards the mini-oasis and Alex's house, that the reality of their impending journey fully came home to her.

'Don't we need supplies?' she asked, clutching the dashboard as they bumped and slewed on the track's uneven surface. 'Fuel and stuff? Three hundred and fifty kilometres is a hell of a long way.'

'It's in hand,' was all Flin would say. 'Trust me.'

They reached the oasis – its dense, tangled undergrowth feeling considerably less malevolent than it had done when she was last here – and followed the track as it looped and twisted through the trees. Finally they arrived at Alex's house, skidding to a halt in a billow of dust. Freya wondered if there would be blood inside. If the old farmer's body would be sprawled on the floor. But the building was empty – cool and neat and ordered, exactly as it had been the first time she had seen it.

'I need you to get some warm clothes together,' said Flin, pointing her towards Alex's bedroom. 'Jumpers, coats, anything like that: the desert gets pretty cold at night. We're going to need water as well – there should be a couple of containers in the kitchen. Just fill them from the tap, it's perfectly drinkable. If you can find any food and coffee, great, but don't go overboard. Hopefully we won't be out there for much more than twenty-four hours.'

'But Zahir said it would take us three days to get there.'

She was talking to herself for Flin had already disappeared into Alex's study.

She hovered a moment, wondering, rather late in the day, if the Englishman was actually qualified for this sort of expedition and whether they should have taken Zahir up on his offer after all. She dismissed the thought – better someone unqualified, she figured, than someone she didn't trust – and went into her sister's bedroom. She found a large nylon holdall underneath the bed. Sifting through the drawers and cupboards, she pulled out a couple of jumpers, a sweatshirt and a heavy woollen shawl; pressing the garments against her cheek, she sensed her sister's presence in each one, then stuffed them into the holdall. She added Alex's old suede travelling jacket from the hook behind the door, swung the bag onto her shoulder and was moving out into the living area when she suddenly turned and went back into the room. Walking over to the picture frame on the bedside table, she removed the passport-booth photograph of her and Alex together as teenagers and slipped it into the pocket of her jeans.

'Didn't think I'd leave you behind, did you?' she said, patting the pocket.

In the kitchen there were a couple of five-litre plastic water containers sitting on the sideboard. As Flin had instructed, she filled these direct from the tap before foraging for various other items: a jar of instant coffee, some chocolate bars, a large tin of baked beans, a tin opener. Adding these to the holdall, she lugged the whole lot outside and hefted it all into the back of the Cherokee.

Throughout all this Flin had remained out of sight in Alex's study, the clunk of opening drawers and the rustle of paper the only indication that he was still in the house. He emerged now, just as she closed the Jeep's rear door, holding a chunky black briefcase in one hand and a book and a couple of maps in the other.

'Know where we're going?' she asked as he climbed into the Jeep, waving her in as well.

'Pretty much,' he replied. 'You get everything?'

She jerked a thumb towards the holdall and water containers in the back. He nodded and started the engine.

'Gilf Kebir here we come,' he said.

He reversed the Cherokee and took them back through the oasis. When they reached the point where the track dog-legged left around a large dirt threshing floor, he swung right onto a smaller track that Freya had not noticed before. It was little more than a glorified footpath and the Jeep was only just able to squeeze between the dense walls of vegetation that hemmed it in, high tufts of grass sweeping the vehicle's underside with a sharp rasping sound. They jolted along for another minute, rarely getting above 20km/hour, passing a sheep pen and a concrete cistern with water pumping into it before abruptly the undergrowth dropped away. They were right at the edge of the oasis, beside the breeze-block barn where Freya had taken refuge two nights ago. Ahead stretched the flat expanse of sand across which she had sprinted to make her escape, the indentations of her footprints still faintly visible on its compacted surface.

She assumed that this was it, that from here Flin would simply drive out onto the desert and off they'd go towards the Gilf Kebir. Instead he pulled over beside the barn, cut the engine and got out. Removing the briefcase, maps, book and holdall and asking her to bring the water containers, he went over to the building's iron door, fished a key from his pocket and undid the padlock. He swung the door open and disappeared inside.

We must be going in another car, she thought as she lifted the water containers from the back seat and followed him in. The building's interior smelt strongly of petrol and was awash with light, partly from the window openings set high in the walls, mainly from the gaping hole in the roof where the downdraught from the twins' helicopter had ripped away a chunk of its palm thatch. A row of 20-litre plastic jerry cans were lined up along the wall to her left, filled with a transparent liquid which, from the pervasive smell, she assumed was petrol. Beside them sat a small orange cool box, a heap of thick woollen blankets and a tray piled with spanners, screwdrivers and other tools. But what really caught her attention – unavoidably – was an enormous object sitting in the middle of the barn and taking up most of the building's length, width and height. What it was exactly she couldn't tell for it was shrouded in a heavy canvas tarpaulin, but it certainly didn't look like any car she'd ever seen before. Any vehicle of any kind.

'What the hell's that?' she asked.

'Miss Piggy,' replied Flin cryptically, squeezing past the mysterious object and moving to the far end of the barn.

Rather than breeze-block, this end of the building was walled in by a heavy steel roller-door. Grasping the chain that dangled down from the roller-wheel above, he started to tug. The door furled itself up and around with a clank and a rattle until it was open, the barn's concrete floor segueing seamlessly into the shimmering yellow carpet of the desert. Again Freya asked what was going on, but Flin simply beckoned her over and, taking one corner of the tarpaulin, indicated that she should take the other. Together they slowly drew it up and over the object, working their way back along the barn until it was completely exposed.

'Say hello to Miss Piggy,' he said. 'AKA the Pegasus Quantum 912 Flex-Wing Microlight. Desert travel, executive style.'

'You've got to be joking,' murmured Freya, standing there with her mouth open. 'No fucking way.'

In front of her sat what looked like a cross between a hang glider, a go-kart and a toboggan. It had a conical, two-seater pod in bright metallic pink – hence the name, she assumed – with three wheels, a propeller on the back and, attached to its tail fin, an enormous triangular sail which seemed to hover over the pod like some giant white bird.

'No way,' she repeated, moving around the machine, taking it all in. 'You can actually fly this thing?'

'Well, Alex was the ace pilot,' Flin replied. 'But yes, I just about know what I'm doing. Enough to get us airborne, certainly. Whether I can get us down, again . . . ?'

He winked and started issuing instructions, showing Freya how to attach two of the 20-litre jerry cans to the saddle-bags slung on either side of the pod while he filled the tank underneath the front seat from the remaining cans.

'Is this going to be enough fuel?' she asked as they worked, still barely able to believe what they were about to do.

'Only just,' he replied. 'It's a 49-litre tank. She uses about eleven litres per hour of flight and it's a good four hours out to the Gilf, so it's going to be tight. Especially since we're at maximum weight capacity. We can take on some extra at Abu Ballas, though, and that should see us through without too many problems.'

'There's a gas station in the desert?' she asked, incredulous.

He smiled, something faintly mischievous in the expression, as though he was enjoying her bewilderment.

'All will be revealed when we get there,' he said with another wink.

Once the microlight was fuelled they stowed the equipment inside the pod – maps, book, water, holdall, blankets, cool box, Flin's black briefcase – only just managing to fit it all in. They then pushed the aircraft outside, its rubber wheels making a soft crunching sound as they rolled onto the compacted desert surface. There were two helmets sitting on the seats, with in-built headsets and intercoms. Throwing one to Freya, Flin helped her into the rear seat and strapped her in, plugging her headset's jack into the socket beside her knee.

'It's all a bit cosy,' he said, squeezing into the front seat and donning his own helmet; Freya's legs extended to either side of him as though she was riding him piggyback. 'And I'm afraid there's no in-flight catering. But if you can put up with that it's actually not such a bad way to travel.'

'As long as you don't kill us I'll be happy,' she said, feeling both nervous and strangely energized.

Flin glanced at his watch – 1.39 p.m. Flicking various switches and turning a key on the dashboard, he jabbed a finger against the starter button. The engine coughed once, twice, then roared into life, the propeller whirring around behind Freya's head. Its rushing draught caused her shirt to ripple and flap although her helmet filtered out the worst of the noise.

'You're sure you know where we're going?' she called.

Flin made a chopping motion with his right hand.

'South-west till we hit the Gilf Kebir,' he said, his voice sounding through the headset. 'Then south along its eastern edge till we find the rock. Shouldn't be too difficult.'

'And you're absolutely sure you know how to fly this thing?'

'I guess we'll just have to find out,' he replied, pushing a lever on the seat beside his hip. The engine's revs shot up and they started to move, gliding smoothly across the sand towards the clump of desert grass behind which Freya had sheltered following her escape from the oasis. After a hundred metres Flin turned them round, steering with his feet, and took them back towards the barn again. 'We need to get the oil temperature up to 50 degrees,' he explained, tapping one of the dials on the dashboard in front of him. 'Otherwise the engine's going to seize.'

They repeated the pattern for several minutes, back and forth across the sands, until eventually the gauge was showing the correct temperature. Swinging round a final time in front of the outbuilding Flin brought them to a halt. He went through some last-minute checks, then craned his head round towards her.

'Ready?'

Freya gave him the thumbs-up. He nodded, turned to the front again and, grasping the control bar hanging from the sail above, eased the throttle forward.

'Piggy Airways welcomes you on board this unscheduled flight to the Gilf Kebir,' he intoned in mock pilot-speak. 'We shall be cruising at an altitude of—'

He got no further. Just as they started to pick up speed there was a blur of movement away to their right. Like a cork from a champagne bottle, a lime-green Honda Civic – mud-spattered and badly dented – burst from the undergrowth, slewing madly on the sands before correcting itself and heading straight towards them, its driver beeping furiously. It was difficult to make out much of him, although even at this distance it was clear he was an extremely large man, his body seeming to fill the entire front of the car. Flin's shoulders tensed and his hands tightened around the control bar, his voice crackling through the headset.

'Angleton!'

Cyrus Angleton didn't speak much Arabic – languages had never been his strong suit – and so it was lucky that the young woman in the Kodak shop in Qalamoun village had a reasonably good grasp of English. Doubly lucky because as well as being able to communicate with him, she also had some useful information. Fifteen minutes earlier, as she was opening up the shop after her lunch, a white Jeep had sped by and turned off onto the track out to the small oasis. There had been two people inside, she explained, a man and a woman. The woman, she was sure, was the young American who had visited the shop a couple of nights ago. Had they come back again? Angleton asked. No, the shop-keeper replied, so far as she was aware they hadn't. Were there any other roads into or out of the oasis? No, she told him, just the one.

'Sweet!' he chuckled.

Wedging himself back into the hire car he sped out across the desert, the Honda bouncing and jolting on the uneven track, clouds of dust billowing behind the vehicle as though it was on fire. He reached the oasis, raced through it, pulled up in front of Alex Hannen's house. No sign of the Cherokee. He got out, went round to the back of the building. Nothing.

'Brodie!' he called, hand slipping inside his jacket, clasping Missy's grip. 'You here?'

No response.

'Bullshit!'

He circled round to the front of the house again, opened the door and went inside. There were open drawers in the bedroom, kitchen and study – someone had been doing some packing. Rapidly, by the looks of it.

'They can't be,' he said out loud. 'Not on their own. They can't be.'

He went back outside and checked his watch. They were fifteen minutes ahead of him and must have spent at least ten of those in the house. If they *were* heading out into the desert he should still be able to spot them. He needed height, though, a vantage point from which he could survey the landscape. He looked around and spotted a rickety-looking wooden ladder propped up against the side of the building. Lumbering over to it, he started to climb. The first rung snapped beneath his weight. The second one held, albeit with a pained creak, and he continued upwards, rivulets of sweat streaming down his face, his breath coming in short, agonized rasps. He took no exercise of any sort, never had done, and what to a normal person would have been a matter-of-fact ascent was to him a major physical endeavour, involving frequent stops to allow his lungs to calm and muscles to recover from the strain of hauling so much weight upwards.

'Christ Jesus!' he kept gasping. 'Christ Jesus God Almighty.'

He made it in the end, clambering his way onto the roof and stumbling across to its far edge. Shielding his eyes against the fierce afternoon sun, he gazed out across the desert, scanning the sands, seeking out the Cherokee. Nothing.

'Son-of-a-bitch,' he murmured. 'Where are you?'

For a minute his eyes slid back and forth across the tangle of dunes and hummocks. Then, suddenly, as if he'd been struck on the back of his head, he wheeled.

'What the fuck . . . ?'

From somewhere behind him the roar of a motor had shattered the torpid afternoon silence. As quickly as his legs would carry him he hurried across to the opposite side of the roof and flung his eyes up and down the oasis, trying to track down the source of the sound. Swiftly his gaze zeroed in first on a barn at the southernmost tip of the cultivated area and then, a fraction of a second later, on a large triangular sail moving out across the sand flat beyond it.

'You bastard!' he roared. 'You idiot limey bastard!'

He yanked Missy from beneath his jacket, flipped off the safety catch and curled a finger around the trigger, aiming in the rough direction of the microlight. Then he thought better of it and returned the gun to his shoulder holster. Not only was it too risky at this distance, but if they clocked someone shooting at them they'd take off immediately and that would be it, chance gone. He had to get down there, he had to get closer.

The microlight had turned and was gliding back towards the outbuilding. Warming the engine, that's what they were doing, which at least gave him a few minutes. He powered back across the roof and clambered down the ladder, puffing and panting. Reaching the ground, he headed for the hire car and jammed himself in. If there was a path or track leading from the house to the barn he hadn't spotted it from above, and he wasn't going to waste precious seconds searching for it now. Instead, he slammed the gearstick into first and, tyres spinning on the loose dusty surface, roared past the house and straight into the fields beyond, churning his way across them and out onto the desert. The moment he hit sand he yanked the steering wheel to the left, slewing in a wide arc before straightening up and speeding on round the perimeter of the oasis. He covered five hundred metres before a sudden, deep trench directly across his line of travel forced him to swerve left back into the cultivation. He bumped across another field, smashed though a brushwood fence and picked up some sort of cattle track that took him round the edge of an olive grove before plunging him headlong into a solid curtain of undergrowth. The momentum of the car somehow carried it through and out the other side back onto the desert. Away to his left stood the barn and in front of it the white sail of the micro-light. He brought the Honda back under control and raced towards them, steering with one hand while with the other he pulled Missy from her holster and hammered the horn.

'Oh no you don't, you son-of-a-bitch!' he yelled. 'Uncle Cyrus wants a word with you!'

Inside the microlight's open cockpit Flin pushed the throttle full forward and grasped the control bar with both hands, his eyes flicking from the car to the dashboard air speed indicator and back again. The Honda was aiming for a point just ahead of them, clearly intending to block their line of take-off, so he angled the nose to the left, trying to buy them some extra distance. The trike rapidly picked up speed, rushing across the sands. But the car was faster. Much faster. It ate up the gap between them, closing in on them.

'We're not going to make it!' cried Freya, her hand involuntarily coming out and grasping Flin's shoulder.

He gritted his teeth and concentrated on the stretch of sand ahead. The car loomed ever larger in his peripheral vision until it seemed inevitable that the two vehicles would collide.

'He's going to hit us!' she screamed.

He held off for a few more heart-stopping seconds, then – at the very last moment – pushed the control bar forward and the microlight rose gracefully into the air and over the top of the Honda as it cut directly in front of them. The trike's wheels cleared its roof by what seemed like a matter of centimetres.

'Kiss my arse, fat man!' whooped Flin, easing the bar further forward and tilting it to the left, the microlight climbing and banking. Below them the car skidded to a halt and its driver clambered out, bellowing up at them, brandishing a pistol. His voice was lost in the roar of the engine and although he let off a couple of shots he appeared to do so more in frustration than with any intention of hitting them. The bullets flew well wide and his rotund form steadily dropped away as they climbed higher and headed out over the desert.

'Who the hell was that?' asked Freya, craning round to look down on their still-gesticulating pursuer.

'A guy called Cyrus Angleton,' replied Flin. 'Works at the American Embassy. Seems he's been tailing us, feeding information back to Girgis.'

'You think he'll come after us?'

'In a Honda Civic? I'd like to see him try.'

Banking to the left he extended an arm and gave Angleton the finger.

'See you at the Gilf!' he called before straightening again and setting a course south-west over the sands. The car, the barn, the oasis, Dakhla, all receded behind them until they had disappeared and there was nothing but the endless rolling wastes of the Sahara.

On the ground Angleton watched until the microlight had dwindled to a minute, indeterminate speck. With a shake of the head, he returned Missy to her holster and climbed back into the car. For a moment he just sat there, staring out across the desert, punching a fist against the padding of the car's dashboard. 'Idiot,' he kept repeating. 'Stupid Limey idiot.' Then, starting the engine, he headed back to Dakhla airport. Time to stop fucking around. Time to deal with Molly Kiernan.

CAIRO

Romani Girgis put down the cordless telephone and folded his arms, gazing out across the gardens at the back of his mansion.

'That's it, they're in the air.'

Beside him Boutros Salah coughed heavily and sucked on his cigarette.

'You sure you want to do this, Romani? Why not let—'

'I haven't waited twenty-three years to take a back seat now. I want to be there, see this thing with my own eyes.'

Salah nodded, took another drag on his cigarette.

'I'll tell Usman and Kasri,' he said.

'The twins?'

Salah grunted.

'Still playing snooker. I'll send them down. Any news on—'

'Being dealt with as we speak,' cut in Girgis. 'It won't be a problem for much longer.'

Salah nodded and disappeared into the house. For a moment Girgis stood where he was, thinking how far he'd journeyed to get to this point, how far he had climbed from those hellish early years in the cesspit of Manshiet Nasser. Then, with the smile of a man whose dream is finally about to be realized, he started down the terrace steps towards the helicopter waiting on the lawn.

OVER THE WESTERN DESERT

Her sister, she knew, had been murdered. She herself had been chased, shot at, very nearly mutilated. And yet for all that the flight out across the Sahara was one of the most wonderful experiences of Freya's life, the all-enveloping emptiness of the desert diluting for a while her other cares and worries, leaving her curiously calm and at peace.

They flew low, no more than a couple of hundred metres above the sands. The air at that height was cooler than at ground level, but still warm, buffeting her face and torso as though she was being fanned by a giant hair-dryer. All around them the desert stretched away as far as the eye could see – a vast, unforgiving wilderness of rock and sand, unearthly in its barrenness. It was as if they had been transported to a different world, or a completely different time within our own world: an unimaginably distant era when all life had withered from the planet and what remained was the earth's bare skeleton. There was something terrible about it, overwhelming, kilometre after kilometre of blank, searing desolation. Beautiful as well, though. Breathtakingly so, the towering sand waves and mysterious twisted rock formations possessed of a grandeur beside which even the greatest works of Man appeared drab and trivial. And while the landscape appeared devoid of life, the further they flew the more it seemed to Freya that this was not, in fact, the whole story. That the desert was, in its own way, very much alive: a gargantuan sentient being whose shifting colours – one minute soft yellow, the next livid red, here blinding white, there sombre black – were curiously suggestive of changing moods and thought patterns. Its varied shapes and textures – dunes slumping into gravel flats, salt pans rearing into rock hills – likewise gave the unnerving impression that the landscape was moving, bunching and stretching itself, flexing its muscles.

Wonder, awe, fear, euphoria – Freya experienced them all. Above all, she felt the most intense sense of connection with, and yearning for, her sister. This was Alex's world, the environment she had made her own, and the further into it they ventured, the closer, it seemed to Freya, she came to her estranged sibling. Reaching into her pocket she pulled out the passport photo she had taken from Alex's bedside table, and the last letter her sister had sent her, which she had transferred from her old jeans when changing her clothes the night before. She clutched them in her lap and smiled, the wild, brooding collage of the Sahara unfurling slowly beneath her.

After about two hours of flying, the sun by now starting its gradual slide towards the western horizon, Flin brought them down on a gravel flat beside a small, cone-shaped hill. The hill's lower slopes, Freya noticed as they taxied up to it, were covered with chunky sherds of broken pottery.

'Abu Ballas,' Flin explained, cutting the engine,

removing his helmet and clambering from the microlight. 'Also known, for obvious reasons, as Pottery Hill.'

Freya removed her own headset and shook out her hair, the temperature seeming to rise dramatically as the propeller slowed to a halt behind her. Flin proffered a hand and helped her out.

'No one really knows where they came from,' he said, nodding towards the mounds of shattered jars. 'The general consensus is that they were part of a water dump for Tebu raiding parties from southern Libya. There are some interesting prehistoric rock inscriptions on the other side, but I think we'll leave those for another time.'

Freya was stretching and looking around, taking in the amphora fragments, the hill, the dunes rolling away behind it – everything bare and still and utterly arid.

'I thought you said we were refuelling here.'

'Indeed we are.'

'So where's the . . . ?'

'Petrol pump?' He smiled, waving her over to a heap of potsherds set slightly apart from the hill. They appeared to have been deliberately piled into a small cairn, with an upturned tin can resting on top.

'The Abu Ballas gas station,' he said. Dropping to his knees he removed a large, shovel-shaped sherd from the pile and started scooping away the sand to one side of the cairn, digging down until he hit something metal.

'It's a trick Alex and I learnt from the early twentieth-century desert explorers,' he explained, brushing the object with his hand, revealing the upper part of a large metal jerry can. 'You leave fuel dumps along your line of travel, insurance in case you start to run low. There are three

20-litre cans down here. We'll fill up with one and leave the others in case we're getting short on the flight back, although with the spare fuel we're already carrying we really shouldn't have any problems.'

He dragged the can free of the ground and lugged it over to Miss Piggy. He emptied the container's contents into the microlight's tank, the air filling with the pungent tang of petrol fumes. Once he was finished he handed the empty container to Freya and asked her to bury it again – 'I'll refill it when I'm next out this way' – while he busied himself opening the maps he had taken from Alex's house. He spread them on the ground and weighed down the corners with stones, poring over them.

'Abu Ballas,' he said once she'd joined him, pointing to the larger of the two charts, to a small black triangle in the middle of an otherwise blank expanse of yellow. 'And here's where we're heading.'

He traced a finger diagonally down the map to an area where the yellow darkened to pale brown beneath the legend 'Gilf Kebir Plateau', giving Freya a moment to get her bearings before sliding the second map over the first. This depicted the Gilf itself on a scale of 1:750,000: what looked like two large islands, one to the north-west of the other, connected by a narrow isthmus and with a scatter of smaller islands floating around them. Their coastlines, if they could be called that, were jagged and broken, pierced by deep, snaking wadis and fringed with minute clusters of words giving the names of exotic-sounding features and for-mations: Two Breasts, Three Castles, Peter and Paul, Clayton's Craters, al-Aqaba Gap, Jebal Uweinat.

'Wadi al-Bakht,' said Flin, pointing to one of a series of

wadis that descended ladder-like along the eastern face of
the more southerly landmass. 'If Zahir's got it right the rock
shouldn't be too hard to find – thirty kilometres south of
al-Bakht, three-quarters of the way between there and
Eight Bells.'

He touched a finger to what looked like a chain of eight
tiny islands stretching off the bottom of the Gilf.

'And if he hasn't got it right?' Freya asked, looking over
at him.

Flin folded the maps and stood.

'We'll cross that bridge when we come to it. For the
moment let's just get ourselves out there.'

He checked his watch: 3.50 p.m.

'And we should do it quickly. I don't want to have to land
in the dark. Do you need the ladies' room?'

She threw him a look and shook her head.

'Then let's get going.'

They flew for another eighty minutes, the sun now dipping
fast into the west, the air growing noticeably cooler. Freya
was glad of the extra layer of clothing they had put on
before leaving Abu Ballas. The desert looked if anything
even more spectacular than it had on the first leg of their
journey, the softening light teasing out its full panoply of
colours – yellows and oranges and a dozen different shades
of red – the lengthening shadows throwing the landscape
into ever sharper and more dramatic relief. They passed
over towering dune seas, vast lakes of pancake-flat white
gravel and strange, primordial forests of shattered rock,
venturing deeper and deeper into the mysterious heart of
the wilderness. Eventually, with the sun balanced right on

the line of the horizon, a hazy band of red loomed into view across their line of flight, hovering in front of them like steam rising off the desert surface. Flin pointed to it.

'The Gilf Kebir,' came his voice over the headset. '*Djer* to the ancient Egyptians – the limit, the end of the world.'

He adjusted their course slightly, taking them higher and bringing them round more to the south. The haze drifted closer, seeming to expand and solidify the nearer they came, its colours to waver and change in the shifting late-afternoon light, red morphing into brown and brown into a soft orangey-ochre. Finally, like a genie rising from a bottle, it gathered into clear focus: an enormous upland plateau rearing 300 metres from the desert floor and stretching away as far as the eye could see to the north, south and west. In places its face was sheer, an impregnable wall of dusty yellow rock, the sands gently swelling against its base like waves against the flank of an ocean liner. Elsewhere it was convulsed, cut by deep valleys and inlets, the cliffs break-ing up into rock shelves and scree slopes which in turn fell away into jumbled archipelagos of buttes and gravel hills, the plateau seeming to stumble down to the desert in a series of huge, uneven steps. Freya could make out distant patches of vegetation – specks and smudges of green against the yellow backdrop – and, as they came closer, the odd bird as well. Hardly teeming with life, but after the desolate tracts over which they had just flown it seemed positively abundant.

Flin had the map of the Gilf in his lap, folded in such a way that only the plateau's south-eastern quadrant was visible. Bringing them closer to the cliffs, he turned due south, setting a course parallel to the massif and slightly above it, working the control bar with his right hand while he held the map flat with his left, his finger tracing their course across its surface. Ten minutes went by, the sun sinking all the time until only its upper rim was visible, the western sky burning with brilliant swirls of green and purple. Then Flin pointed ahead and below, to a place where the face of the Gilf suddenly opened up into a broad, sand-clogged valley.

'Wadi al-Bakht,' his voice crackled. He banked to the right and took them directly over it. The valley snaked eastwards and out of sight, carving into the uplands as though someone had gouged a jagged slit through the bare rock. 'Not far now, just another thirty kilometres. Less than twenty minutes. Keep your eyes open.'

He swung away from the Gilf again and brought them down so that they were now below the tableland's summit. They continued south, the cliffs rearing to their right, dwarfing the microlight as though it was a dragonfly buzzing along the side of a skyscraper. The desert ahead was smooth and blank, a gently undulating swell of sand, devoid of features. They should have sighted the rock formation with ease, even with the sun now gone and twilight thickening around them. Twenty minutes came and went. Twenty-five. And when far ahead to the south a line of conical hills drifted dimly into view, Flin shook his head and started turning back.

'That's Eight Bells. We've come too far. We must have missed it.'

'We can't have,' said Freya, buttoning her sister's suede jacket up to the neck against the increasing cold. 'The desert's completely empty, we would have seen it.'

Flin just shrugged and put them back on a northerly heading, dropping even lower. The two of them scoured the desert beneath, anxiously searching for any hint of the crescent-shaped rock as what little light remained fast ebbed away and the tableland to their left faded into a mist of featureless grey.

Another ten minutes ticked by and it was looking as if they would have to abandon their search for the night and land the microlight before it was completely dark, when suddenly Flin gave an excited shout.

'There!' he cried, waving a hand down to their right.

How they had missed it before Freya had no idea. She recognized the cliffs at that point, which – even though they were now veiled in shadow – still towered noticeably higher and more vertiginously than anywhere else along that stretch of the Gilf. There had been no sign whatsoever of the rock the first time they had passed that way. And yet there it was below them, clearly outlined against the pale desert surface: a vast curving spire of black stone bowing upwards from the otherwise empty sands to a height of some ten metres, dominating the surrounding landscape. What titanic forces of nature had shaped and raised it, had left it standing there alone and surreal like a gargantuan rib thrusting from the wilderness she couldn't even begin to guess. Nor did she care. They'd found it: that was all that mattered. She gave Flin a clap on the shoulder to show that she'd seen it and looked down as he took them in a wide arc around the rock, scanning the desert for somewhere suitable to land. It was impossible to judge the precise state of the surface below, the world having dissolved into a dull monochrome haze. It appeared perfectly flat and compacted, and having circled a couple of times scouting for any obvious obstructions, Flin cut the revs, closed the throttle and descended to within a couple of metres of the ground. Gently easing the control bar forward, he landed the microlight with barely a bump, gliding across the sand and coming to a halt almost directly beneath the spire.

'Welcome to the middle of nowhere,' he said, stopping the engine and switching off the electrics. 'We hope you enjoyed your flight.'

For a while they just sat there, the propeller slowly whirring to a standstill behind them, silence pouring into the void left now that the engine was no longer running; a deeper, heavier, more all-consuming silence Freya had never known. Then, unplugging their intercoms and removing their helmets, they heaved themselves out of the pod and walked over to the rock tower. Its curved, gently tapering length loomed above them, the black stone of which it was formed – obsidian? basalt? – even more eerie and unearthly now that they were close to it.

'I just can't believe I've never seen this before,' murmured Flin, contemplating the summit ten metres above, silhouetted against the night sky like the tip of some gigantic tusk. 'I must have flown over this area a dozen times, and driven through it almost as many. It's impossible I could have missed it. Impossible.'

They wandered around the rock, hands trailing across its surface, which was still warm from the day's sun and curiously smooth, almost glass-like. Coming back to the microlight, they stood staring upwards, the Gilf rearing to their left, an orange moon slowly climbing to their right.

'So what do we do now?' asked Freya.

'We wait.'

'For what?'

'Sunrise. Something happens here at sunrise.'

She looked across at him; his face was only just visible, angular and handsome and shadowed with stubble.

'What happens?' she asked.

Rather than explain he turned to the microlight and rummaged inside its pod, pulling out a Maglite pocket torch and the book he had taken from Alex's house. He'd marked a page about halfway through. Opening it, he handed it to Freya and switched on the torch.

'Khepri,' he said, shining the beam on the page. 'God of the sunrise. Notice anything?'

In front of her was an image of a seated figure, viewed in profile, clutching an ankh sign in one hand and a staff in the other. While the body was human, the shoulders were topped not with a head and face, but with a large black scarab beetle, its oval body culminating in a pair of . . .

'The legs,' she said, touching a finger to the curved limbs rising to either side of the beetle's head. 'They look just like . . .'

'Exactly,' said Flin, lifting the torch and running its beam along the arc of stone curving above them. 'Christ knows how, but this rock's been weathered into almost the exact shape of a dung beetle's foreleg. It's incredible – look, it's even got the barbs the beetle uses to burrow and grip.'

He played the light around the upper part of the spire. Its surface was jagged and notched, giving it a curiously serrated appearance, reminiscent of the barbed protrusions rising from the legs of the scarab in the picture.

'Any ancient Egyptian who saw this rock would

immediately have made the connection,' he continued. 'We already knew Khepri and the oasis were closely linked – remember the stele text at Abydos: *When the Eye of Khepri is opened, then shall the oasis be opened? When his eye is closed the oasis shall not be seen, even by the keenest falcon.* There was always something missing though, some crucial part of the equation. You found it when you recognized the image of the rock on the stele. It would seem that when they talk of the Eye of Khepri the ancient texts aren't just using the phrase in a figurative sense, they're referring to something very specific: this.'

Again he ran the torch up and down the curve of black stone.

'How it all fits together I've no idea – just that there's some interplay between the rock, the sunrise and the oasis. Somehow they all connect, and that connection will reveal the whereabouts of the oasis. Or at least I hope it will. It's a bloody long way to come to find out I've got it wrong.'

He played the torch around for a moment longer, then switched it off.

'Come on,' he said. 'Let's make camp.'

CAIRO

There was a refuelling problem with the Learjet, which meant that it was dark when Angleton finally arrived back in Cairo. He briefly toyed with the idea of dropping into the Embassy for a shower and a bite to eat – his last proper meal had been the previous afternoon – but time wasn't on his side and instead he took a taxi straight down to Molly Kiernan's bungalow in the city's southern suburbs. No sign of her there and so back into the taxi and on to the USAID building where the security guard on the front desk – Mohammed Shubra according to the name tag pinned to his shirt – informed him that yes, Mrs Kiernan was still in the building, working late in her office on the third floor.

'Gotcha,' hissed Angleton, slipping a hand inside his jacket and crossing to the lifts, too distracted to notice the guard behind him lifting his phone, dialling and whispering into the receiver.

The third floor was dark and deserted, the only sign of life a thin strip of light emanating from beneath a door at the far end of the corridor. Kiernan's door. Removing Missy from the shoulder holster, checking the safety catch was off, Angleton made his way towards the light, sweat beading his forehead even though the building's air conditioning was still on. He reached the door, again checked the safety catch and raised a hand to knock, then dropped it. Instead he grasped the door's handle and threw it open, bringing Missy up in front of him as he did so and stepping into the room. Molly Kiernan was sitting at her desk opposite. She started to rise.

'Can I help . . .'

'Shut the fuck up and get your hands where I can see them,' snarled Angleton, levelling his gun at her chest. 'I think it's high time you and me had us a little talk.'

Massawi military airstrip, Kharga Oasis

Romani Girgis stood watching as a steady stream of aluminium packing cases were wheeled out of the hangar and over to the line of Chinook CH-47s. A man in a white boiler suit ticked each one off on a clipboard before pointing out which helicopter it was to be loaded into, everything bathed in a wash of icy light from the dozen arc lamps arranged across the tarmac. As was to be expected, it was all moving like a military operation, a line of figures shunting the crates from hangar to helicopters while others leant over trestle-tables check-listing an impressive array of weaponry – Browning M1911 handguns, XM8 assault rifles, Heckler & Koch MP5 submachine-guns, M249 SAWS, even a couple of M224 mortars. And that was just the stuff he recognized. More than once Girgis had wondered if it was all really necessary, if they weren't going over the top: so much firepower, so much technical gadgetry. After all these years, however, and with so much at stake, he accepted it was better to err on the side of caution. And anyway, it was out of his hands now. They could bring an entire army with them for all he cared, so long as he got paid. As he soon would be. $50 million, direct into his Swiss bank account. About bloody time.

He pulled a wet-wipe from the packet in his pocket and gazed around, looking for his own people. Ahmed Usman was in the hangar, talking with more of the men in white overalls. Mohammed Kasri was pacing up and down beside the Chinooks, talking animatedly into his mobile, relaying details of their flight plan to General

Zawi so they'd be given a clear run by the Egyptian military. And the twins? Apparently they were off using the bathroom. Unbelievable: the two of them even pissed together.

'How long till we're in the air?' he asked, balling the wipe and casting it aside.

Beside him, Boutros Salah sucked out the last of his cigarette, taking it right the way down to the filter.

'Forty minutes,' he wheezed. 'An hour tops. We've already got people on the ground, so we're not going to miss anything. Cairo?'

'Sorted,' replied Girgis, holding up his mobile phone. 'The Lear's on its way now, took off fifteen minutes ago.'

'Looks like we're all set then.'

'Looks like it.'

Salah flicked away his cigarette and lit another.

'And you really believe it's going to be like they say? That it's all true?'

Girgis shrugged, smoothed a hand over his hair.

'Usman certainly thinks so. And Brodie too, by all accounts. We'll just have to wait and see.'

'Incredible. Absolutely fucking incredible.'

'Fifty million dollars, Boutros, that's incredible. The rest of it's just . . .'

Girgis gave another shrug and waved his hand dismissively, the two of them watching as more and more aluminium cases were wheeled from the hangar and out to the waiting choppers.

THE WESTERN DESERT

From a distance it looked like a small white beetle crawling across the landscape, creeping up dunes, scuttling over gravel pans, a single luminous eye peering out into the pewter-coloured wilderness. Only as it came closer did it resolve into its real form – a battered white Toyota Land Cruiser zigzagging through the desert. Its roof-rack was laden with 20-litre jerry cans, a sharp beam of light speared forward from its one working headlamp, slashing transient patterns across the ground as it manoeuvred this way and that. Although the terrain was broken and uneven, folding into towering sand walls and jagged rock formations, the driver seemed to know exactly how to navigate its intricate twists and turns. Even in the most labyrinthine stretches he still kept up a reasonable speed, rarely dropping below fifty kilometres an hour, doubling that across the sand and gravel flats that punctuated the landscape like huge lakes. How many people were inside the vehicle it was impossible to tell for its interior was completely dark, although at one point it stopped and someone emerged from its passenger side, lifted the hem of his *djellaba* and urinated, so there must have been at least two of them in there. Beyond that, and the fact that its driver was clearly in a hurry, everything else about the car was a mystery: a solitary white speck weaving its way through the arid wastes, the growl of its engine echoing across the sands, its nose swaying to and fro as though following a scent that drew it irresistibly towards the south-west.

THE GILF KEBIR

They found a jumble of dried wood neatly heaped under a ledge at the bottom of the rock formation – traditional Bedouin practice, Flin explained, to leave such stashes beside obvious desert landmarks. Borrowing from it, he built a small fire and got it going. They pulled on even more clothes against the night chill and spread blankets on the ground. Opening the cool box, Flin produced various fire-blackened pots and pans and began to brew up some coffee and heat the baked beans Freya had found in her sister's kitchen.

'Reminds me of when me and Alex were kids,' she said, shuffling closer to the flames and hugging her arms around her legs, gazing at the orange wafer moon hovering above the dunes to the east. 'Dad used to take us camping all the time. We'd build fires, eat beans, pretend we were Indians or early pioneers – we slept outside more than we did in.'

Flin sipped his coffee and leant forward to stir the pot in which the beans were heating.

'I envy you. My father's idea of fun was to send me and my brother to the Ashmolean to draw ancient pots.'

'You have a brother?'

For some reason Freya was surprised by the revelation.

'*Had* a brother. Howie died when I was ten.'

'I'm sorry, I didn't . . .'

He shook his head, continued stirring.

'Named after Howard Carter, the guy who discovered Tutankhamun. Shared his name and ironically died of exactly the same form of cancer, although at least Carter made it into his sixties. Howie was only seven. I miss him sometimes. Often, actually.'

He gave the pot a final stir and lifted it from the fire.

'I think these are ready.'

Spooning the beans onto a couple of plastic plates, he handed one to Freya and took the other for himself. They ate in silence, peering into the fire, their eyes occasionally flicking up and meeting. Once they were done Flin cleaned the plates – wiping them with sand and splashing the sand away with a handful of water – and they settled back with mugs of coffee and the chocolate bars Freya had brought. Flin reclined against the rock, Freya stretched on the other side of the fire.

The first stars had already started appearing while they were up in the air, and now the night sky was ablaze with webs of light. Rolling onto her back, Freya looked up, feeling something of what she'd felt during the flight out over the desert: calm, peaceful, contented even, the silence and the stillness wrapping her like a duvet. *I'm glad I'm out here*, she thought. *Despite it all. I'm glad I'm here in this place my sister loved so much, just me and the sand and the stars. And Flin as well. I'm glad I'm here with Flin.*

'Who's the girl?' she asked.

'Sorry?'

She glanced across at him and then up again. A shooting star flared briefly across the hem of the sky, fading almost as soon as it had appeared.

'Back in Cairo, as we left the apartment, Molly mentioned a girl. "This has nothing to do with the girl." I was just wondering who she was.'

He sipped his coffee, poking at the embers of the fire with the toe of his boot.

469

'Something that happened a long time ago,' he said. 'When I was with MI6.'

His tone suggested he didn't wish to pursue the matter and Freya let it go. Sitting up, she wrapped a blanket around her shoulders. The rock spire towering above them felt menacing yet at the same time curiously comforting, as though they were being cradled in the arm of a giant. There was a silence, broken only by the hiss and crackle of burning wood; then Flin lifted the coffee pot and refilled his mug.

'It sounds hopelessly naïve now, but I actually joined the Service because I wanted to do some good. Help make the world . . . well, if not a better place, at least a slightly safer one.'

His voice was low, barely audible, as if he was talking to himself rather than to her, his eyes locked on the fire.

'Although if pushed, I'd probably have to admit that part of it was about pissing off my father as well. He didn't really approve of things like MI6. Didn't really approve of anything outside academia.'

He gave a wry smile, drawing patterns in the sand with his finger. What this had to do with her question Freya didn't know, but she sensed it was important to him and so didn't interrupt.

'I went in just after I finished my doctorate,' he said after a brief silence. '1994. Did a couple of years on a desk in London, then got posted overseas. First to Cairo, which is where I met Molly. And then on to Baghdad. Trying to get the inside track on Saddam and his weapons programmes. Not exactly an easy nut to crack – you wouldn't believe the level of fear and paranoia Saddam generated – but after I'd been there about a year I had a breakthrough with a guy from MIMI: the Ministry for Industry and Military Industrialization. He approached me, said he was willing to pass on info, top-level stuff – just what we needed.'

He looked up at Freya and down again. A jackal howled somewhere in the distance.

'As you can imagine he was pretty jumpy about the whole thing, insisted on using his daughter as a go-between, said it would minimize suspicion. From the outset I was against it – she was only thirteen, for God's sake – but he wouldn't do business any other way and it was just too good an opportunity to miss, so in the end I agreed. He copied papers from the Ministry, she took them with her on her way to school, slipped them to me as she walked though Zawra park in central Baghdad. Simple, only took a couple of seconds.'

Two jackals were howling now, calling to each other out in the dunes to the east. Freya barely noticed them, absorbed in what Flin was saying.

'For a while the whole thing worked fine and we got our hands on some good material. Then, about five months in, I missed a rendezvous. These things happen, of course, but in this instance it was because I'd been on a bender the night before and overslept. I was drinking pretty heavily by that point, had been for some time, Scotch for the most part, although when I got up a head of steam . . . Christ, I'd have drunk paraffin if someone had poured it out and stuck a couple of ice cubes in it.'

He shook his head, rubbing at his temples. The jackals' high, ululating wail, more melancholy than threatening, provided a strangely appropriate soundtrack to the narrative he was spinning.

'We had an absolute rule with the handovers,' he went on. 'If one of us wasn't in the park the other just kept going, didn't hang around. The *Mukharabat* – Saddam's intelligence services – were everywhere, always watching, and it was crucial not to do anything that might look out of the ordinary. I don't know why Amira – that was the girl – broke the rule, decided to wait, but that's what she did. She was spotted, picked up, taken in. So were her dad and the rest of her family.'

He let out a deep sigh, screwing his coffee cup into the sand beside him. The jackals were suddenly silent. Everything was silent.

'Christ alone knows what they put them through, but they never named me. I got out safe and sound, they all disappeared into Abu Ghraib – *that* Abu Ghraib – and were never seen alive again. Apparently Amira's body turned up a month later. On a rubbish dump outside the city, gangraped, teeth pulled out, fingernails ... you just can't imagine.'

He leant his head back and contemplated the rock, his voice a monotone, dull, emotionless, as if he was trying to hold what he was describing at arm's length, avoid engaging with the full horror of it. It clearly wasn't working. His hands, Freya noticed, had started to shake.

'There was an internal inquiry, of course. I resigned, went back into Egyptology, came out here, *really* started drinking. Would have kept right on going if I hadn't met Alex. She pulled me back from the brink, got me dry again. Saved my life, basically. Not that it was worth saving. Thirteen years old, for God's sake. You just can't imagine.'

He brought his knees up and rested his elbows on them,

pressing his forehead into the palms of his hands, the now fully risen moon bathing the desert in a soft mercury glow. Not really sure why she was doing it, hardly even aware that she *was* doing it, Freya stood, moved around the fire and sat down beside him, laying a hand on his shoulder.

'Molly's right, of course,' he said. 'It's what all this is about: Sandfire, Girgis, the oasis – what it's always been about. Trying to make amends in some way, redeem myself for sending a thirteen-year-old kid into Saddam's torture chambers. I can't bring her or her family back, undo the agony she suffered, but at least I can . . . you know . . . try to . . .'

His voice was cracking and he broke off. There was a pause, Flin breathing heavily, then he lifted his head and looked across at her.

'I tell you, Freya,' he said. 'Whatever else I might think about the Iraq invasion – and none of it's particularly good – I can't condemn Bush for toppling Saddam, however badly he botched it. The guy was a monster. A fucking monster.'

He looked away. Stretching out his legs, he pulled his cup from the sand and drained its contents. Freya wanted to say something, to try to comfort him in some way, but everything that came to mind just seemed so pathetically glib and inane, wholly inappropriate to the enormity of the story he'd just recounted. Instead she did the one thing she could think of that would show she understood what he was feeling, that she too knew what it was like to have your every waking moment – and most of your sleeping ones too – corroded by guilt and regret.

'Did my sister ever tell you what happened between us?'

she asked, removing her hand from his shoulder and hugging her arms around her. 'Why we didn't talk for so long?'

He glanced across at her again. 'No. She never spoke about it.'

Freya nodded. Now it was her gaze that was fixed on the fire's embers, the burning wood pulsing and twinkling as though it were alive. There was another silence – she had never discussed this with anyone, ever, it was just too painful – then, taking a breath, she told him.

How after their parents' deaths in the car accident Alex and her fiancé Greg had moved back into the family home so she could take care of her younger sibling. How Greg had always been attentive to Freya, joking and flirting, and how that flirting had increased once he was living under the same roof. How initially it had been Greg who made all the running, but after a while, flattered, Freya had started to make some running of her own. How what had started as kisses and fondles – wrong, of course, but salvageable – had rapidly spiralled into something altogether more sordid, she and Greg hopping into bed together the moment Alex had set off for work each morning and staying there until just before she returned home in the evening. How it had continued even as Alex and Greg were planning their wedding, until her sister had come back early one day and, inevitably – crushingly – caught them together, Greg at that moment going down on Freya, which had somehow made the whole betrayal even more grotesque and humiliating, although she omitted that particular detail in her description to Flin, the memory of it still too eviscerating to share, even after all these years.

'She wasn't angry,' she said, swiping a forearm across her eyes. 'When she came into the bedroom. Shocked, yes, but not angry. It would have been better if she had been, had screamed and shouted, launched herself at me, but she just looked so sad, so lonely . . .'

She choked, wiping at her eyes again. Flin reached out and took her hand, a reflex gesture, comforting, the two of them sitting there in silence, hypnotized by the flickering tongues of flame. The jackals started up again, behind them now, to the north, their wails drifting across the night like some mournful aria.

'Is that what the Hassan thing was about?' he asked after a while. 'Agreeing to strip for him. A way of . . . ?'

'Balancing things out?' Freya shrugged. 'I guess we've both got stuff we're trying to put right.'

His grip tightened.

'Your sister loved you, Freya. She talked about you all the time, your climbing – she was so proud of you. Whatever happened, it was in the past. She'd want you to know that. Want you to know how much you meant to her.'

She bit her lip, touching a hand to her pocket, to the outline of the letter Alex had sent her.

'I do know that,' she whispered. 'What hurts is that I never got the chance to say the same to her.'

She sighed and looked across at him. This time their eyes met and held. For a moment they remained like that, Flin's hand still clasped around hers. Then, slowly, their faces started to come together. Their lips made fleeting contact, then they broke away. Freya reached out and touched his face. Flin brought a hand up and ran it through her hair, before as one they pulled back and stood, knowing this wasn't the time or the place. Not now, not after all that had been spoken.

'We should try and get some sleep,' he said. 'We've got an early start.'

Together they built up the fire, shook out the blankets and settled back down – on opposite sides of the blaze now. Their eyes met again briefly. Then, with a nod, they rolled away and disappeared into their own thoughts, the jackals still calling in the distance.

Four hundred metres away, the figure adjusted his night vision binoculars. He watched for a while longer before sliding down behind the lip of the dune, switching on the transceiver and radioing in. It only took a moment: they've turned in for the night, no movement, nothing else to report. Within a minute he had resumed his vigil – binoculars clamped to his eyes, M25 sniper rifle resting on the sand beside him – oblivious to all save the two motionless forms curled innocently beneath the towering arch of stone. The fire between them slowly burnt itself down until it had reduced to almost nothing, a tiny orange smudge on the vast moonlit desert.

It had been three days since Freya had had any proper rest, and her sleep was deep and dreamless, free from thoughts and worries, an empty black void into which she gratefully sank, as though her mind had been swaddled in dense black velvet. Only as dawn was starting to colour the east, a soft band of pinkish grey drifting up off the horizon, did she slowly return to consciousness. Not because she had slept enough – she could have gone on for a good few hours more – but because she became aware of a curious droning sound that even in the fog of slumber she sensed was at odds with the remote desert setting.

For a while she lay listening, still only half awake, pulling the blankets tighter around herself against the early morning chill, trying to work out what was going on. The sound faded and then strengthened, as if whatever was causing it was moving back and forth, sometimes nearer, sometimes further away. Rolling onto her side, she looked across at Flin to see if he was aware of it too. He wasn't there. She rolled the other way, looking for the microlight, but that too was gone. She jerked fully awake and leapt to her feet, spinning around, scanning the sky.

In the few minutes since she had first woken the world had already grown noticeably clearer and she spotted the microlight immediately, soaring over the Gilf like an enormous white-winged bird. How Flin had taken off without waking her she didn't know – she really must have been out of it – and for the briefest of instants she felt a shock of alarm, convinced he was abandoning her. The thought disappeared before it had even properly lodged itself for he was clearly flying in a circle rather than away. Wheeling and swooping over the flat tableland on the top of the Gilf, he headed south and then north in a broad circuit whose central axis appeared to be on a westward line from the rock formation beneath which she was standing.

She stood watching as the microlight flew right out to the very extremity of her sight, dwindling to a barely visible dot against the greying sky before slowly enlarging and once more coming back into focus. Ten minutes passed, then the aircraft swung away from the plateau and, dropping low above the desert, roared directly overhead. As it did Flin tipped the sail slightly and shouted, gesturing at something on the ground. Freya threw up her arms to show she didn't understand, forcing him to loop round and come back over again. Dropping even lower and gesticulating towards the fire, he mouthed the word 'coffee'. She smiled and gave him a thumbs-up. Flin held out a hand with fingers spread, indicating he'd be another five minutes, then picked up height again and headed back towards the Gilf. The gargling drone of the microlight's engine slowly receded as he resumed his survey of the massif.

She collected wood and tinder, got the fire going and put the water on. Flin circled the plateau a couple more times before peeling off and bringing the microlight down to land, taxiing to a halt beside the rock just as the water came to the boil and Freya poured it into the mugs.

'See anything?' she asked as he clambered from the pod.

He shook his head.

'I've gone twenty kilometres north, south and west and there's nothing, just sand and rock and a few scattered patches of camel thorn. Whatever else happens here at dawn we're sure as hell not going to be finding an oasis.'

Nodding a thank-you, he took a mug from her and slurped.

'I just don't understand it. There's simply no other way of interpreting the text. *When the Eye of Khepri is opened, then shall the oasis be opened*. The oasis is near here, and at sunrise the rock somehow points the way. It has to mean that. You can't read it any other way. Unless . . .'

He took a step backwards, peering up at the curving sweep of rock rearing overhead.

'Is there something on the stone itself?' he murmured, more to himself than to Freya. 'An inscription, a direction marker? Is that what it's trying to tell us?'

He ran his gaze up and down the spire's glassy surface, his eyes narrowed. Walking slowly around it, he searched for marks or incisions or hieroglyphs, any sign of human interference. There was nothing: the rock was smooth and black and bare from its base to its tip, what chips and scratches there were clearly of natural origin rather than man-made. Only one feature seemed to give him pause for thought, something they had missed in their torch-lit examination the previous night: a small fist-size lens of opaque yellow crystal, punching right through the spire from one side to the other, about three-quarters of the way up its length, like a miniature porthole. It was a curious thing, a geological anomaly at odds with the surrounding stone. For almost a minute Flin stared up at it before reluctantly concluding that it, too, was simply a natural part of the formation. With a shake of the head, he turned away and went to refill his mug.

'I'm fucked if I know,' he said. 'The oasis ought to be here, and that –' he jerked a thumb over his shoulder – '. . . ought to point us towards it. I just don't understand.'

'Maybe the rock's a red herring,' suggested Freya, bending over the fire and refilling her own cup. 'Hasn't got anything to do with the oasis after all?'

Flin shrugged and checked his watch.

'Sun-up's only a few minutes away so we'll see what happens then, but on current evidence I have a nasty suspicion you might be right and I've screwed up. Not for the first time, I can assure you.'

He sipped his coffee and looked east. The desert ran flat for a few hundred metres before flurrying into an untidy mess of dunes, the sand slopes growing progressively higher and steeper the further they marched off into the distance. Freya joined him and together they watched as in front of them the dawn strengthened and spread, the sky awash with greens and pinks, the landscape steadily brightening from monochrome grey to pale yellow and orange. A couple of minutes passed, the sky's hem burning a deeper and deeper shade of red. Then, slowly, like a bubble of molten lava, the upper rim of the sun started to show itself above the dune tops, a wafer-thin curve of magenta pushing up through the horizon, the surrounding desert seeming to warp and shimmer as though melting in the face of its intense heat. The air grew rapidly warmer as the curve swelled into a dome and the dome into a circle. Their eyes moved back and forth, flicking from the sun to the rock tower and back again as they waited for something, anything, to happen, some sign to manifest itself. The rock just stood there, black and bent, unchanged, unyielding, revealing nothing as the sun continued its ascent until it was free of the horizon and dawn merged into early morning. Flin and Freya gazed a while longer, the sun's heat pulsing into their faces, fierce even at this early hour, then looked at each other and shook their heads. The hoped-for revelation had not materialized. Their journey had been wasted.

'At least we got to see some nice scenery,' said Freya glumly.

They kicked sand over the fire and started gathering up the camping equipment ready for the flight back to civilization.

'We've still got a fair bit of fuel left,' said Flin as he clipped shut the lid on the cool box and stowed it inside the microlight pod. 'So we might as well have a fly around, see if we've missed anything. I vote we head—'

He got no further, for Freya let out an exclamation and grabbed his wrist.

'Look! There!'

Her free arm was stretched towards the west, at the face of the Gilf. He followed the line of it, squinting, scanning to and fro for a moment before he spotted what she was pointing at. On the towering cliff wall, about ten metres up from the desert floor, a tiny disc of light had appeared, clearly visible against the orangey-yellow stone all around.

'What the . . . ?'

He took a step forward. Freya came with him, her hand still clasped around his arm as the two of them stared at the glinting blob, trying to work out what it was, what was causing it.

'Is it something in the cliff?' she asked. 'Reflecting the light back at us?'

Flin stood with one hand shielding his eyes, brow furrowed in concentration before suddenly pulling his arm free of hers and back-pedalling across the sands, looking away from the cliffs and up at the curving spire of rock. A brief pause, then:

'Oh my God that's wonderful!'

Freya backed off too, coming up beside him, gasping as she saw what he had seen: a tiny pool of molten gold about three-quarters of the way up the rock spire where the sun's rays were pouring through the lens of desert crystal, setting it ablaze and sending a diaphanous beam of light lasering west towards the face of the massif.

'Behold the Eye of Khepri,' whispered Flin, his voice hushed, awed.

They stared up, open-mouthed in wonder as the crystal seemed to burn through the surrounding rock like a flame through black paper, its glow becoming increasingly fierce before slowly, imperceptibly, it started to pale, the beam weakening, the crystal fading back to a dull shade of amber.

'Shit!' cried Flin.

He spun and started to sprint, pounding across the sands towards the rearing flank of the Gilf, eyes fixed on the dwindling patch of light – a ghostly stain on the rock.

'It must only show when the sun's at a certain angle,' he yelled over his shoulder to Freya, who was following on behind. 'Keep looking – we have to see where it's hitting. That's what the inscription means. The rising sun points to something on the cliff face. We mustn't lose it!'

The rock spire was four hundred metres from the Gilf and they had covered less than half of that distance when the beam faded completely, the light spot disappearing, leaving a blank wall of dusty yellow stone.

'There,' he shouted, slowing to a walk and raising an arm, pointing. 'That's where it was. Just above that ledge.'

Freya was looking at the same spot, eyes fixed on the rock face. They continued forward until they were right at the very foot of the Gilf, its cliffs rising vertiginously above them.

'There's something there,' said Flin. 'Some sort of hole. Can you see?'

She could: a small rectangular opening, no more than about fifty centimetres high by half as much across, just

above a protruding rock shelf ten metres up, barely noticeable unless you were staring directly at it, and even then
still hard to spot. It was unquestionably man-made, its sides
neatly carved and dressed, way too symmetrical for a natural feature, and appeared to be stuffed with material of
some sort which helped it to blend into the surrounding
cliff face. She started to ask what he thought it was, but Flin
was already climbing. Wedging his fingers into a narrow
crack, he heaved himself upwards, one toe jammed into a
shallow rock pocket, the other scrabbling for purchase on
the bare stone. He lost his footing and dropped back,
cursing. He tried again with the same result, and again.
Moving to the left he attempted a different route, this time
getting almost twice as high before running out of hand-
and footholds and falling off, tumbling onto the desert with
a jarring thud. He struggled to his feet, spitting sand, and
was about to have yet another go when Freya stepped up
and gently pushed him aside.

'May I?'

Swiftly she surveyed the wall, mapping out a route. Tying
her hair up into a bun, she locked her fingers into the same
crack Flin had tried earlier, toed into the same rock pocket
and was off. A minute later she had reached the
opening and was balancing herself on the ledge a metre
below it.

'I guess I'll just stick with the Egyptology,' Flin
grumbled. 'What can you see?'

'Pretty much what we saw from down there,' she called.
'It's a hole with a load of linen stuffed into it. Definitely
man-made.'

'Any inscriptions?'

She squatted – the ledge was more than wide enough –
and examined the rock around the opening. It was bare,
devoid of anything even remotely resembling lettering,
hieroglyphic or otherwise.

'Nothing,' she called down. 'I'm going to pull the
material out, see what's inside.'

'Be careful of vipers,' he called. 'They're common out
here and we haven't got anti-venom.'

'Great,' she muttered, tweaking nervously at the cloth,
teasing it out of the cavity. It was coarsely woven, dyed a
dull yellowish-ochre – the same colour as the surrounding
stone – and extremely tightly packed, as though to prevent
anything getting into the opening. She'd assumed it must
be ancient, but it seemed remarkably well preserved and
the more of it she removed the more convinced Freya
became that it was in fact modern and nothing to do with
ancient Egypt at all. She communicated her doubts to Flin,
but he waved them away.

'Textiles always survive well in the desert,' he shouted.
'It's the dry air. I've seen five-thousand-year-old mummy
wrappings that look as if they're straight off the loom. Is it
out yet?'

'Almost.'

She continued to pull, more and more of the cloth emerging – there were, it transpired, several separate pieces of it
rather than a single large sheet. Eventually, with a dry sucking sound, a last heavy plug of fabric popped from the
opening and it was clear. She gave the heaped material a
couple of prods with the toe of her plimsoll, still fearful
there might be snakes curled up within its folds, then
squatted down and placed a hand to either side of the

opening. Adjusting her position slightly so as not to block the sunlight, she peered in.

'Anything?' Flin's voice came up from the desert below, expectant.

There was silence as her eyes adjusted to the gloom inside the hole, then:

'Yes.'

Another silence.

'Well what, for God's sake?'

'It's like . . .'

She paused, searching for the right word.

'A handle.'

'What do you mean a handle?'

'A handle, a lever. Like the brake lever on a cable car.'

'I've never been in a sodding cable car!' He whirled his arms in frustration. 'Just describe it.'

A wooden lever, that's what she could see, right at the very rear of the cavity, which had been cut over a metre back into the cliff. It had a leather strip wound around its handle and sat in a deep horizontal slot in the cavity's floor, the latter presumably providing a channel along which the lever could be pulled – to what effect she couldn't even begin to guess. It was a surreal, curiously unnerving sight, like finding a light switch sitting on the surface of Mars, and part of her couldn't help but feel faintly spooked by it.

'Well?' yelled Flin.

She described what she was seeing. He frowned and chewed his lip, pondering. Then he shouted up to her:

'Pull it.'

'You think?' There was unease in her voice. 'I don't know if we should . . .'

'What the hell else have we come out here for? Go on, pull it.'

She didn't move, sensing . . . she couldn't really explain what she was sensing. A vague premonition of danger; an inner warning that by doing as Flin instructed she would be setting in motion a chain of events that they couldn't control, crossing a line that wasn't meant to be crossed. But then as he'd said, it's what they'd come all the way out here for. More important, it's what Alex would have done. No doubt about it. Her sister would have pulled the lever without a moment's hesitation, probably before she was even asked to do so. She paused a moment longer. Then, rapping her knuckles a couple of times against the face of the rock – a pull-yourself-together gesture she used when steeling herself for a particularly tough climbing manoeuvre – she drove her arm deep into the cavity.

It was cool inside, the handle only just within reach, right at the very limit of her stretch. She really had to force her shoulder into the opening in order to get her fingers around it, her palm pressing hard against the leather wrapping, her thumb curling round to secure her grip. She shifted slightly, tested her hold and then started to pull.

The lever was stiff and it took all her strength to get it moving, the muscles of her neck and shoulder bunching and rippling. She moved it a few centimetres, paused to get her breath and adjust her grip and heaved again. The lever started to come more easily, gliding slowly along the slot, its progress accompanied by a curious creaking and grinding as of ropes tautening and wheels turning, the sound issuing from somewhere far below, as if emanating from the rock itself. She dragged the handle towards her as far as it would come, right to the front of the cavity. Giving it a final tug to ensure there was no more slack, she leant out and looked down at Flin, raising her free arm as if to say 'Anything happening?'

He had moved a little way back from the cliff, his eyes running back and forth over the rock face.

'Nothing,' he called. 'You've definitely pulled it all the way?'

She shouted an affirmative.

'I don't know,' he said. 'There's no magic doors opening up, I can tell you that much.'

They continued to watch, Flin below, Freya above, the curious creaking sound still echoing although fainter now, more distant. Otherwise everything remained exactly as it had been before she pulled the lever save that the sun seemed to grow hotter and brighter and the sky an ever paler shade of blue. They gave it a few minutes, the creaking gradually fading away into silence. Seeing no point in remaining up on the ledge, Freya started to down-climb, following the same foot- and handholds she'd used on the way up. As she did she became aware of a new sound, only just audible – a sort of soft, whispering hiss. She stopped where she was, feet toed into a narrow crack, looking around, trying to work out what was causing it. Flin had heard it too and had moved closer to the cliff, head cocked, listening. The hiss seemed neither to fade nor grow stronger, just hovered there in the background.

'What is that?' she asked.

'I don't know,' he said. 'It sounds like . . .'

'Please don't say snakes.'

'No, no, more like . . .'

He broke off, stepping right up to the foot of the cliff.

'Look at this!'

Freya shuffled her feet and leant right out, hand clasped around a knuckle of rock, peering down. At first she couldn't see anything. Then she noticed what he had noticed. At the very base of the rock face, at the point where it formed a rough right angle with the desert, the sand was slipping downwards, trickling away along a twenty-metre stretch of the wall as though through the neck of an hourglass. Flin squatted beside it and pressed his palm on the ground, watching as the sand disappeared around his fingertips.

'What the hell is that?' she asked. 'Quicksand?'

'Not like any I've ever seen before,' he replied. The grains were starting to drain off faster, as though being sucked from below, the trickle turning into a flow, a clear line opening up at the bottom of the cliff.

'Where's it going?' she asked.

'I haven't the faintest idea,' he said, staring hypnotized as the line lengthened and widened.

'Maybe you should move back a bit.'

He nodded and stood, backing off a couple of steps. The sand continued to slump and sink, more and more of the rock wall revealing itself, like the root of some enormous tooth.

'It seems to be undercutting—'

He didn't finish the sentence. With a muted whumph an entire section of desert dropped away beneath the toes of his boots. The hissing grew much louder, the sand avalanching downwards, although where it was going still wasn't clear. Flin stumbled back, lost his footing and fell, leapt up again, frantically retreating as more and more of the desert disappeared in front of him, surging away like water down a plughole, an ever widening and deepening hole rushing out from the cliff towards him.

'Run!' Freya screamed.

He didn't need to be told. Spinning round, he sprinted off across the sands. The hole seemed to snap at his heels, chasing him away from the Gilf. It expanded almost fifty metres from the rock face before it gradually started to slow and, as if satisfied it had pursued him far enough, came to a halt, leaving an enormous crater gaping at the base of the massif.

Gasping for breath, Flin stopped and turned, ready to run again should the crater decide to resume its outward rush. Aside from some gentle slips and trickles of sand as it settled itself, the opening seemed to have stabilized, and after waiting a few moments Freya traversed sideways and dropped down onto the desert at the crater's edge. Moving carefully, she made her way around its lip and joined Flin. The two of them gazed into the depression beneath.

'God Almighty,' Flin murmured.

Below them a steep, semicircular chute of sand swept downwards towards the cliff face. At its lowest point, black and forbidding, like a yawning mouth, a doorway opened into the bare rock, flanked by monumental carved figures – arms crossed at the chest, heads topped with tall conical crowns, beards descending from their chins like tapering stalactites. Below the waist the statues were still buried in sand, as was the lower part of the doorway, the desert funnelling through it and down into the gloom beyond, a pale slide descending into the throat of the underworld.

'The Mouth of Osiris,' Flin murmured, his face strangely blank and expressionless, as if he was so staggered by what he was seeing that he had momentarily lost the ability to work his features. 'A lifetime of Egyptology and I've never . . . I can't believe it. It's just . . . just . . .'

His voice fell away into silence. For a while they just stood there staring down in mute amazement, the sun's heat pressing against their backs, a lone buzzard wheeling high above them, wings silhouetted against the pale morning sky. Then, gathering himself and telling Freya to wait, Flin jogged back to the microlight, returning with the Maglite torch and the black briefcase he had taken from Alex's house. He dropped to one knee, balanced the case on the other and clicked open the lid. Inside was what looked like an orange thermos flask with an antenna protruding from the top of it.

'Locating beacon,' he explained, pulling the object from the protective foam cushioning that surrounded it. 'It'll beam a signal direct to Molly's people in the US and they'll alert their team on the ground here in Egypt. We'll have back-up within three hours.'

He flicked a switch on the side of the beacon, screwed it into the ground and stood.

'Are we going down?' asked Freya.

'No, I thought we'd stay up here and build sandcastles.'

The sarcasm was gentle, and Freya smiled, knowing her question had been a foolish one, that there was no way Flin would just sit up here twiddling his thumbs.

'You think it's safe?'

He shrugged.

'Probably on a par with Manshiet Nasser and Abydos.'

'Well I guess we got out of those OK.'

It was his turn to smile.

'God, you're like your sister.'

She didn't respond to that, just undid the bun on top of her head, shook out her hair and extended an arm towards the opening below.

'Egyptologists first.'

His smile broadened and he started to make his way down towards the doorway, taking the slope sideways on to keep his balance, feet sinking into the sand almost to the level of his thighs. Freya followed. He was about halfway when he stopped and looked up at her. His smile had faded, his expression now serious. Businesslike.

'You'll probably think this sounds silly, but there are things about this place, elements we don't . . .'

He broke off, struggling for the right words.

'Just be careful,' he said. 'When we get inside. Try not to disturb anything. OK?'

He held her gaze to make sure his words had hit home, then, with a nod, continued downwards.

The helicopters flew in formation over the desert, six of them powering above the dune tops: five sand-coloured Chinooks and, lagging slightly behind, a black Augusta. They flew fast, towards the south-west, the rising sun behind them, their line of flight taking them slightly to the north of a lone, rearing crag of rock, which meant they missed the white Land Cruiser lurking in the shade beneath an overhang at the bottom of the crag. Only when they were well past, the insidious whining thud of their rotors fading into the distance, did the vehicle nose its way out into the sunlight. It paused a moment as if sniffing the air, then roared forward across the sands, heading in the same direction as the dwindling choppers, its wheels slewing and skidding as if it was anxious not to be left behind.

'Jesus,' said Flin.

They had reached the doorway. Standing one to either side of it, they peered through into a dim, steeply sloping shaft beyond. Below them the sand chute descended for another ten metres or so before gradually petering out, revealing a succession of rock-cut steps that disappeared into the murk as though into a pool of deep black water.

He switched on the Maglite and flashed it around, examining the neatly cut walls and ceiling, the stone still bearing the tell-tale ripples of ancient chisel marks. Failing to find where the shaft ended he dropped onto his backside and slid downwards, reaching the steps and coming upright.

'See anything?' asked Freya, shuffling down behind him.

'Just steps,' he replied, aiming the torch beam into the blackness below. 'An awful lot of steps. It must go right down under the Gilf. Although exactly *where* it's going . . .'

He shifted, allowing Freya to come alongside him, the shaft just wide enough to accommodate the two of them. There was something oppressive about the space, forbidding – the darkness, the silence, the way the rock pressed in on them from all directions – and for a while they just stood there, even Flin apparently reluctant to go any further.

'Maybe you should wait up top,' he said. 'Let me check where it leads. That way if anything happens . . .'

She shook her head and told him they either went together or not at all. He nodded – 'Just like your sister' – and, with a final sweep of the torch, started to descend, Freya at his side, the two of them stopping every few steps to re-examine the shaft, trying to make out where it was leading. The stairs just continued down, deeper and deeper into the rock, the air growing steadily cooler, the doorway behind them dwindling until it was no larger than a pin-prick, a tiny rent in the enveloping blackness. They counted fifty steps, a hundred, two hundred, and Freya was starting to wonder if they would ever end or just descend *ad infinitum* into the bowels of the earth when, as they passed the three-hundredth stair, Flin's torch beam hit flat rock below. Another fifteen metres and the shaft levelled out.

There was another doorway at the bottom, flanked by the same carved figures as the entrance above. Passing through it, they found themselves in a long tunnel, its curved walls and arched ceiling giving the space a curiously rounded, tube-like feel, as though they were standing inside a gigantic intestine. Unlike the shaft they had just descended, whose walls and ceiling had been bare stone, here the rock had been plastered and whitewashed, painted with a strange looping design which after a moment Freya realized depicted the coils of a multitude of entwined snakes.

'*May evildoers be swallowed into the belly of the serpent Apep,*' murmured Flin, his torch picking out a head with jaws levered open, forked tongue flickering menacingly.

'I'm not getting a good feeling about this,' said Freya.

'That makes two of us,' he said. 'Stay close. And try not to touch anything.'

They started walking, their feet making a dry, slapping sound on the stone floor, the entwined serpents keeping pace with them, coiling across the walls and ceiling. The swaying of the Maglite beam had the unnerving effect of making the coils seem to roll and slither as though the snakes were moving. The darkness amplified the effect, as did the tunnel's shape and somnolent, claustrophobic atmosphere, and more than once they jerked to a halt and wheeled, convinced the images *were* moving, gliding up behind them, jaws stretched. But they were just images, and once they had satisfied themselves it was all in their imagination, a sort of subterranean mirage, they turned and continued on their way. The tunnel ran flat for some five hundred metres, driving in an unswerving line through the bare rock before gradually it started to angle upward, gently at first but then more steeply, pushing towards the surface. They covered another few hundred metres – the tunnel and stairway combined having now taken them well over a kilometre into the underbelly of the Gilf – when Flin suddenly stopped. Clasping Freya's arm, he switched off the torch.

'Notice anything?' His voice echoed along the tunnel.

At first she didn't, the blackness smothering her. Then, as her eyes adjusted to the void, she became aware that above and ahead was a pale thread of light, barely visible, no more than the tiniest vertical crack in the enveloping murk.

'What is it?' she asked. 'A door?'

'Well it's either a bloody narrow one, or a hell of a long way away,' he replied. 'Come on.'

He switched the torch back on and they resumed walking, faster now, both of them anxious to be free of the oppressive darkness. The corridor carried on upwards, the walls and ceiling imperceptibly widening and lifting so that where initially they had only just been able to fit two abreast, they now found they could do so with room to spare. They broke into a stride and then a jog, hurrying forward, yearning for sunshine and clean air, no longer caring where the tunnel led them or what was at the end of it, just wanting to get out. Although the corridor continued to widen, and their pace to quicken, the thread of light seemed neither to strengthen nor to come any nearer. It just hovered on the edge of sight, a tenuous slash of grey that beckoned them while at the same time seeming to hold them at arm's length.

'What the hell . . .' growled Flin, speeding up even more. He started to pull away from Freya, aiming the torch at the floor so as to spot any obstructions before they tripped him up. Still the light remained distant, tantalizing, taunting, and, frustrated, he broke into a sudden sprint, charging at the grey line as if he hoped to take it unawares, get to it before it could recede again. For a moment the tunnel reverberated to the slap of his feet, then there was a sudden jarring crash and a thud as of something soft falling onto something hard. The torch rolled away across the floor with a metallic tinkle, its beam throwing juddering blobs of light over the stone. Freya slowed, peering into the blackness.

'Flin?'

A groan.

'Are you OK?'

Another groan, then, woozily, 'Bollocks.'

Freya reached the Maglite, picked it up and shone it forward. Flin was lying on his back gazing up at the ceiling, blinking groggily, a bemused look on his face, like a boxer who has been flattened by a vicious right hook. Just beyond him, the reason his sprint had come to such an abrupt halt, the tunnel was blocked by a pair of very solid-looking wooden doors. Between them was a hair-thin seam of daylight, the source of the ghostly crack they had seen from back along the tunnel.

'Are you OK?' she asked, hurrying over and helping him to his feet.

'Not entirely,' he mumbled, clasping her shoulder for support, swaying against her. 'Ran straight into the bloody thing. Christ, it feels like I've been hit with a fucking . . .'

He couldn't think what it felt like he'd been hit with. Instead he just stood there, touching a hand gingerly to his forehead and trying to gather his scrambled senses. He remained like that for several moments, then – still looking distinctly befuddled – he took the torch from her and played it back and forth over the doors.

Hung on bronze hinges driven into the tunnel walls, they were twice as tall as he was and so perfectly carved and fitted – their tops arched to match the curve of the tunnel's ceiling – that aside from the minute streak of grey sandwiched between them, nothing whatsoever was visible of what lay beyond.

'Hear that?' he asked.

She did indeed: a faint twitter of birds and, even fainter, the soft plash of running water. Flin pressed his face to the gap, trying to see through, but it was much too narrow. He backed off and aimed the torch at the bolt that ran across the centre of the doors, holding them closed. A length of coarse, thin rope had been wound around the device and secured with a clay seal impressed with an image that three days ago Freya would not have recognized, but which was now only too familiar. The outline of an obelisk, with inside it the looping *sedjet* sign.

'Still intact,' said Flin, tapping the seal. 'Whatever's beyond here, no one's got to it this way for four thousand years.'

'You think it's the oasis?'

'I don't see how it possibly can be, given that I flew over this precise area an hour ago and there was bugger all here. Then again if there's one thing I've learnt about the *wehat seshtat* it's that nothing is ever quite as it seems. I guess there's only one way to find out.'

He reached into his back pocket, produced a small penknife and pressed its blade against the rope. For a moment he hesitated, seeming reluctant to damage the ancient bindings, then started to cut, slicing through the rope and pulling it away.

'Ready?' he asked, easing back the bolt and laying a hand against the right-hand door.

'As I'll ever be,' she said, putting her weight against the left-hand one.

'In that case . . . open sesame!'

They pushed. The doors swung outwards with a soft whispering sound and brilliant daylight rushed forward to greet them. The sounds of birdsong and running water suddenly grew much louder.

The moment the helicopters landed their doors slid open and disgorged figures in full-body radiation suits. Making their way ponderously down to the doorway in the rock, they probed at it with an array of electronic gadgetry, continuing for several minutes before radioing an all-clear up to those still waiting in the Chinooks. Others spewed out onto the desert. Some – heavily armed men in sunglasses and flak jackets – established a security cordon around the mouth of the sand crater. Others began unloading the aluminium equipment cases, carrying them down through the opening and into the shaft beyond. Only when the last of the crates had disappeared did Girgis and his colleagues make their own way down to the door. They paused beside it, Girgis turning and staring up at the figure silhouetted on the crater lip above. Then, with a nod and wave, he turned and the group began their descent into the blackness beneath, the twins bringing up the rear. Hands stuffed into their pockets, they looked supremely uninterested in the whole affair.

When they were children Freya and her sister had imagined that behind the moon there existed a secret world: a pristine, magical place full of flowers and waterfalls and the music of birdsong. Alex had alluded to it in her final letter to Freya, albeit in a different context, and it was the thing that immediately sprang to mind now as she stood gazing at what she could only describe as the paradise in front of her.

They were at one end of a long, deep gorge, hemmed in by towering cliffs down which slim water cascades streaked like dangling threads of silver. At this, its narrower end, the gorge was little more than twenty metres across. As it drove backwards into the Gilf, however – a gargantuan axe-cleft shearing through the bare rock – it rapidly started to broaden, its floor rising at a slight gradient, its sheer walls angling away from each other like a pair of opening scissors. At its far end, Freya guessed, the valley must have measured four or even five hundred metres from side to side, although it was hard to be sure as it was a long way away. Birds swooped and dived overhead; a babbling matrix of streams and water channels cut this way and that across the canyon floor, dampening the sand and giving rise to a rich profusion of plant life: trees and bushes and multi-coloured carpets of flowers. Even the cliffs had been colonized, heavy clumps of foliage sprouting along ledges and from cracks in the stone like explosions of green hair.

'It's not possible,' murmured Flin, head shaking in wonder. 'I flew over here and there was nothing. It was just rock and desert.'

They stepped forward out of the doorway, hands instinctively reaching out and clasping as they peered into the mesh of leaves and branches ahead. It took a while for their eyes to adjust to the tangled interplay of light and shadow, then they started to notice shapes amid the vegetation – curves and angles of dressed stone, sections of wall, columns and sphinxes and giant figures with human bodies and the heads of animals. Here a pair of empty stone eyes glared at them from beneath a face-pack of moss, there a monumental clenched fist punched out from amid a grove of palm trees. To the left the remains of a paved street dis-appeared into the undergrowth, to the right a row of obelisks speared up through the leaf canopy like a line of javelin tips.

'How could they have done all this?' whispered Freya. 'Out here in the middle of nowhere? It must have taken them centuries.'

'And some,' said Flin, moving further forward into the sandy clearing in front of the tunnel entrance. 'It's just beyond anything I could have ... I mean I've read the texts, seen Schmidt's photographs, but to actually . . .'

He didn't seem able to finish a sentence, his voice drifting off into dreamy, awestruck silence. Five minutes passed, the two of them just standing there staring, the sun now riding well up in the sky, which was curious because according to Flin's watch it was still only 8.09 a.m. He looked up, shielding his eyes and shaking his head as if to say 'Nothing about this place surprises me.' Another couple of minutes went by, then, releasing Freya's hand, Flin lifted his arm.

'That must be the temple,' he said, pointing into the far distance, towards the very upper end of the valley where what looked like a vast natural rock platform thrust above the tree-tops. On it stood a dense honeycomb of stonework, including a structure that Freya thought could well be the gateway in Rudi Schmidt's photograph.

'Are we going up there?' she asked.

Although his expression suggested he would dearly have liked to, Flin shook his head.

'We need to find the Antonov first, check what state it's in. Then we can explore.'

Freya looked across at him.

'Shouldn't we have, like, a Geiger counter or something?

In case, you know, any of the uranium containers were damaged in the crash.'

Flin smiled.

'Whatever else we have to worry about, radiation poisoning isn't on the list. Uranium-235's no more toxic than a granite kitchen surface. I could take a bath in the stuff and it wouldn't harm me. Although if you happen to know a Geiger counter store around here I'm happy to get one, just to put your mind at rest. Come on.'

Giving her a playful wink, he led her across the clearing and into a deep glade of trees, acacia and tamarisk for the most part although there were also palms, figs, willows and a lone, towering sycamore. The air was warm but not uncomfortably so, heavy with the scent of thyme and jasmine, alive with birds and butterflies and the biggest, brightest dragonflies Freya had ever seen. Sunbeams poured down through the branches like sheets of gold cloth; glinting rivulets wound to and fro among the tree roots, in some places simply petering out, in others joining up to form pools of clear water fringed with banks of orange narcissi and dotted all over with the cupped pods of blue and white water-lilies.

'It doesn't seem real,' she said, marvelling at the Eden-like beauty of the place. 'It's like something out of a fairy tale.'

Flin was turning round and round, his expression a mix of rapture and disbelief.

'I know what you mean,' he said. 'There's a fragment of inscription in the Louvre which refers to the oasis as *wehat resut*, the oasis of dreams. Now we're here I can understand why.'

They continued onwards, the gorge steadily rising and widening, walls and statues and hieroglyph-covered blocks of stone looming everywhere. Some were perfectly preserved, others cracked and tilted and toppled by the slow bulldozering of tree roots and flash floods. The more they saw the clearer it became to Flin and Freya that what, from the tunnel entrance, had appeared a random confusion of masonry was not so random after all. Far from it – the stonework must once have formed an architecturally ordered environment of streets and avenues and buildings and courtyards, its basic pattern still just about discernible amid the jungle that had overwhelmed it.

'Christ, it must have been amazing,' said Flin, his voice quivering with excitement. 'I always thought it was hyperbole when the texts describe Zerzura as a city, but that's exactly what this was. Blows away everything we know about ancient Egyptian technology.'

They came into a meadow ablaze with poppies and corn-flowers; ibises and white egrets strutted back and forth, cawing and pecking at the ground. The rock platform they had seen from the bottom end of the oasis was much closer now although still some distance away, rearing above the tree-tops like a gigantic stage, the monumental pylon gateway in Rudi Schmidt's photograph clearly visible. They stopped and gazed at it, then walked on, following a stretch of weed-covered marble paving that ran across the centre of the meadow, twin rows of interspersed sphinxes and obelisks running to either side of them – some sort of processional way, thought Flin.

They had covered about half the meadow's length when Freya stopped and grabbed Flin's arm.

'There,' she said, pointing away to the right, to where a dense grove of palm trees crowded up against the side of the gorge. Just visible above their arching fronds, like a tattered white dorsal fin, was the tail of a plane, glimpses of its fuselage peeping through the trunks below.

'Bingo,' said Flin.

Another paved avenue, narrower if equally overgrown, ran off perpendicular to the one they were on. It seemed to lead directly to the grove and they turned onto it, passing a succession of giant granite scarab beetles before reaching the palm trees. They weaved their way through them and into a small, sun-dappled glade. The Antonov slumped in front of them: white and battered and eerily silent, draped with nets of ivy and bougainvillaea.

Although it had crash-landed and then tumbled the best part of a hundred metres into the gorge – the scars of its cartwheeling descent were still plainly visible on the rock face above – the plane was surprisingly well preserved. Its right-hand wing had sheared off completely and was nowhere to be seen, half of its left wing had gone as well and the propellers of its remaining engine were buckled and bent. A ragged hole gaped midway along the underside of the fuselage as if some large predator had taken a bite out of it. It was the right way up, though, lying flat on its belly, and while badly bruised and dented, was still pretty much in one piece, its tail fin rising defiantly through the trees, its nose pressed up against the face of a monumental sphinx.

They took in the scene, then approached the rear of the plane, stopping in front of three rectangular mounds lined up in the shadow of its tail. At the head of each a crude, makeshift cross was hammered into the earth.

'Schmidt must have buried them,' said Flin. 'Hard to feel sorry for him given that he was smuggling 50 kilos of uranium to Saddam Hussein, but even so . . . Christ, it must have been horrible.'

Freya stood beside him, trying to imagine what Schmidt had gone through: alone, frightened, probably injured, scooping out shallow graves, dragging corpses from the plane . . .

'How long do you think he was here for?' she asked.

'A while, by the look of it.' Flin nodded towards the remains of a campfire, the ground around it scattered with empty tins. 'I'm guessing he'd have waited at least a week to be rescued, probably longer. Then, when no one came, he decided to try and walk his way back to civilization. Although how the hell he got out of here I've no idea – certainly not the way we came in.'

They stared at the graves a while longer, then moved along the fuselage to the front exit. Flin put his head through the open door before clambering in and helping Freya up after him. It was gloomy inside and it took a moment for Freya's eyes to adjust. When they did she let out a retching gasp, throwing her hand up to her mouth.

'Oh God. Oh Jesus.'

Ten seats back from where they were standing was a man. Or rather the remains of one. He was sitting bolt upright, perfectly mummified in the dry desert atmosphere, eye sockets empty, skin leathery hard and the colour of liquorice, mouth clogged with cobwebs and stretched wide open as though frantically gasping for breath. Why he had been left there and not buried with the others was not immediately obvious. Only as they came closer did the reason become apparent: the force of the crash had shunted all the seats on the right-hand side of the cabin forwards and into each other, concertinaing them together and trapping the man's legs just above the knees, holding him fast. It looked unbearably agonizing, the kneecaps crushed as though in the jaws of a vice, although it wasn't this that appeared to have killed him. Rather it was the large metal case he was holding flat on his lap and which the movement of the seats had driven backwards into his stomach, mashing his internal organs, compressing his midriff into a space less than ten centimetres wide.

'Do you think it was quick?' asked Freya, looking away.

'You'd hope so,' said Flin. 'For his sake.'

He dropped to his haunches and carefully examined the case. It was still secure and didn't seem to have been damaged or tampered with. A quick search revealed three identical cases on the floor between the seats on the opposite side of the aisle. These too were still locked and in good condition.

'All present and correct,' he said. 'And all in one piece. Come on, let's get out. Molly's people'll be here in a couple of hours and they can deal with all this. We've done our bit.'

He touched a hand to Freya's elbow and she turned, ready to move back to the exit. As she did her gaze again brushed across the corpse's desiccated face. Only for the briefest of instants, but enough for her to notice movement, something shifting inside one of the eye sockets, squirming around. Initially she thought she had imagined it, then, her throat tightening in disgust, that it must be a worm or a maggot. Only when she forced herself to look closer did she see to her horror that it was actually a hornet: fat and yellow and as thick as her finger, creeping out of the corpse's head and onto the bridge of its nose. Another one followed, and another, and then two more, a low buzzing sound suddenly emanating from inside the dead man's skull.

Anything else she could have handled. Wasps and hornets, however, were her primal terror, had been since she was a kid, the one thing she could neither bear nor cope with. Letting out a scream, she started to back away, hands flapping in front of her. The movement startled the insects. The ones that had emerged lifted menacingly into the air, more and more spewed out of the nest behind, buzzing angrily. One got caught up in Freya's hair, another banged against her cheek, increasing her hysteria, which in turn inflamed the swarm further.

'Stay still!' ordered Flin. 'Just stand where you are!'

She ignored him. Wheeling round, she launched herself towards the exit, arms flailing. She only got halfway before her foot snagged on a tendril of creeper and she crashed to the floor, the commotion sending the hornets into a frenzy.

'For Christ's sake stay still,' hissed Flin, easing himself along the aisle and dropping on top of her, shielding her with his arms and body. 'The more you move, the more it agitates them.'

'I have to get out!' she wailed, bucking and writhing underneath him. 'You don't understand, I can't . . . aaargh!'

A searing barb of pain lanced into the back of her neck.

'Get them away! Please, get them away!'

He just grasped her wrists and locked his legs around

hers as if they were wrestling, his cheek pressed against the back of her head, his full weight pushing down on her, pinning her to the floor. She felt one hornet crawling up inside her trouser leg, another creeping over her closed eyelid, two more on her lips, her worst nightmare made real, beyond her worst nightmare. But there were no more stings, and while it was all but unbearable to have them on her skin like that, she managed, with a supreme effort of will and the aid of Flin's bodyweight on hers, to remain motionless. On and on it went, hornets battering them from all sides – how could there possibly have been this many of them crammed inside a single skull? – before, as unexpectedly as the swarm had materialized, it started to dissipate. The buzzing faded: the insects on her face and leg were suddenly no longer there. She remained flat on the floor, frozen, her eyes and mouth clamped shut, fearful that the least movement on her part would bring them rushing back again. Flin must have been thinking the same thing because it was a long time before she felt him raise his head and look around. There was a pause, then his weight lifted.

'It's OK,' he said, reaching down and helping her to her feet. 'They've gone.'

She pressed herself into his chest, trembling, the sting on her neck burning viciously.

'It's OK,' he repeated, arms wrapping around her, his voice calm and reassuring. 'You're safe. There's no danger. Everything's fine.'

For a moment, just a moment, it seemed that he was right. Then, from outside, there came a low, malicious chuckle.

'Unfortunately, Professor Brodie, that's not really the

case. Not really the case at all. From your point of view at least. From mine, on the other hand . . .'

The figures flitted through the undergrowth, two of them, moving swiftly, hugging the side of the gorge. Every fifty metres or so they stopped and squatted down behind whatever tree, bush, wall or statue presented itself, pausing a moment to listen and catch their breath before scurrying on again. Their brown robes merged seamlessly with the surroundings so that even the birds scarcely seemed to notice their passing, the one discordant note being an occasional flash of white Nike trainers as they hoisted their *djellabas* to clamber over rocks and leap streams. They didn't speak, instead communicating with hand gestures and chirruping whistles, and seemed to know exactly where they were going, continuing down through the oasis until they had reached its midway point, whereupon they veered in towards the centre of the valley. They went even more cautiously now, working their way from one piece of cover to the next, looming briefly before melding back into the landscape. They came to a giant dum palm and one of them clambered nimbly up its trunk, hunkering down among the umbrellas of foliage at its crown. The other went a little further before also going to ground behind a colossal granite arm. They popped their heads up and nodded at each other, raising their rifles. Then, as a line of men appeared below, moving through the trees towards them, they ducked and were gone. It was as if they had never existed.

For a moment Flin and Freya remained locked together, too startled to move. Then, as one, they dropped down behind the seats, peering out through the nearest window. It was reasonably free of vegetation and they had a clear view of Romani Girgis standing in the clearing outside, immaculately dressed and grinning. He was flanked by the ginger-haired twins in their Armani suits and red-and-white El-Ahly football shirts, and two other men – one tall and bearded, the other thickset and lumpen, with a cigarette clamped between his teeth and a bushy, nicotine-stained moustache. There seemed to be others moving around in the background, although they couldn't see exactly how many or what they were doing.

'How the hell did they find it?' whispered Freya.

'God knows,' said Flin, trying to get a better view of what was happening outside. 'Maybe they already had people out here watching the rock, maybe they sent people out the moment Angleton saw us taking off ... I've no fucking idea.'

'What do we do?'

'You will please come out,' came Girgis's voice as if answering her question, although he couldn't possibly have heard her. 'And you will please keep your hands where they can be seen.'

'Shit,' groaned Flin.

He looked frantically around, eyes wheeling up and down the cabin before coming to rest on the mummified corpse. It was still fully clothed, the designer shirt and jacket contrasting sharply with the shrunken, blackened body beneath. Peeping out from beneath the jacket was the butt of a pistol. Crawling over, Flin pulled it from the shoulder holster, broke out the clip and checked the mechanisms. Remarkably, it still seemed to be in working order.

'You will please come out,' came Girgis's voice again. 'There's really nothing you can do, so why play games?'

'Can we hold out?' she asked. 'Till Molly's people get here?'

'Two hours with a single Glock and a fifteen-round clip?' Flin gave a derisive snort. 'Not a hope. This isn't a Hollywood movie we're in here.'

'So what? What do we do?'

He shook his head helplessly, eyes again scanning the Antonov's interior. They settled on the three metal cases sitting between the seats behind him. He hesitated, then, laying the handgun on the floor, he leant across, grabbed the handle of the nearest case and hauled it over to him, struggling with the weight.

'What are you doing?'

He ignored her question, fiddling with the case's twin locks, trying, and failing, to get the lid open.

'What are you doing?' she repeated.

Still Flin didn't reply. Instead, retrieving the Glock, he leant back, shielded Freya with one arm and fired off two shots, shattering the locks. He laid the gun aside again and yanked the case open. Inside, held tight in a nest of foam padding, were what looked like two silver cocktail shakers. He eased one out and, holding it in both hands to support the weight, came to his feet.

'Professor Brodie?' Girgis's voice echoed in from outside, sounding more intrigued than alarmed. 'Please tell me you haven't shot yourself. I have men here who will be extremely disappointed if they've been denied the chance—'

Flin stretched across the seats and smacked the container hard against the window, making a loud thudding noise, cutting the Egyptian off mid-sentence.

'Do you see this, Girgis?' he shouted, hammering again, drawing the attention of those outside, making sure they could see what he was holding. 'This is a canister of highly enriched uranium. *Your* highly enriched uranium. You come a step closer I'm going to open it up and empty it all over the inside of this plane. Same with the other canisters. You hear? Come an inch closer, I'll turn this place into a radio-active oven!'

Freya had come up behind him, her fingers digging into his shoulder.

'I thought you said uranium wasn't dangerous!' she hissed.

'It isn't,' he replied, keeping his voice low. 'But I'm counting on Girgis not knowing that – he's a businessman, not a physicist. And even if he *does* know that, his men probably won't. At the very least it'll make them think twice before coming in here and blowing our heads off.'

He gave another hammer on the window, really pounding the Perspex, then clasped the canister's screw-lid and gave it a turn, exaggerating the movement so that it was crystal clear what he was doing.

'You watching, Girgis? Want to see some uranium? Find out what it smells like? Because so help me God you're about to if you don't back off! Roll up, roll up, to the great radioactive poisoning show!'

He gave the lid another turn, and another, and another, waiting for some reaction from outside. None came. Girgis and his men just stood there, their expressions half amused, half bemused. There was a pause, the cheerful twitter of birds providing an incongruously melodic backdrop to the stand-off, then, suddenly, a peal of laughter. Not from Girgis, but from the trees behind him. Soft, vaguely feminine laughter.

'Professor Brodie, you really are a hoot! Now why don't you put that down and come outside and we can talk this through. We're all friends here.'

CAIRO

Ibrahim Kemal was seventy-three years old, and for sixty-five of those seventy-three years he had fished the same short stretch of the Nile just north of Cairo. And in all those sixty-five years he had never, ever encountered a fish as big as the one he now felt tugging on the end of his line.

'What the hell is it?' asked his grandson, arms wrapped around the old man's waist to steady him against the rocking of their boat. 'A catfish? A perch?'

'A whale more like,' sputtered the old man, wincing as the line cut into the palms of his hands (a length of nylon with a hook on the end, that's all he used, nothing fancy like a rod). 'I landed a 150-pound perch when I was your age and it wasn't half as heavy as this. It's a whale, I tell you, a whale!'

He paid out some line, giving the fish a bit of slack, allowing it to run, then started heaving again. Their simple wooden skiff rocked alarmingly, wavelets of river water sloshing across the gunwales.

'Maybe we should let it go,' said the younger man. 'It's going to turn us over.'

'It can take us down to the bottom for all I care!' grunted Ibrahim, drawing the line in, hand over hand, eyes popping with the strain. 'I've never lost a fish yet and I'm not about to start now.'

Again he eased off, lulling his adversary, again started pulling, the rocking of the boat growing ever more pronounced, exacerbated both by the eddying current and the bubbling wake of a Nile cruiser ploughing its way upstream over by the opposite bank.

'Come on, my beauty,' coaxed Ibrahim. 'Come on. That's a good girl.'

The line was coming easier now – whether because his quarry had given up the fight or was playing a game of its own Ibrahim couldn't say. He reeled in some more line, stopped to get his breath and adjust his stance, heaved again, teasing the monster from the depths, drawing it slowly up towards the surface until his grandson let out a yell and pointed.

'There! There it is! Holy God, it's huge.'

Away to the left, between them and a raft of Nile weed drifting downriver, the outline of a fish had emerged just below the surface, although it was unlike any fish they had ever seen before – bulbous and pale and curiously still. Ibrahim continued to pull, slower now, a quizzical look on his face. His grandson released his waist and leant out over the side of the boat, landing net in one hand, billhook in the other, ready to draw the fish in once it was close enough. As he did a wave slapped hard against the creature's flank, pushing it towards them and rolling it, turning it belly-side up so that for the first time they got a clear view of what it was they had caught. It was not a catfish, or a Nile perch, or even a whale, but a man. Enormously fat, he was wearing a bow-tie and a cream-coloured jacket that wafted and swayed in the eddies of the river. A single neat bullet-hole was punched clean through the centre of his forehead.

He drifted right up to the side of the boat and knocked against it, peering up at them through sightless eyes. Ibrahim met the dead man's gaze, shaking his head.

'I think this is one we're not going to be selling at the fish market,' he muttered.

INSIDE THE OASIS

'Molly! I don't bloody believe it!'

For a moment Flin continued peering out of the window, stunned, convinced his ears had deceived him. Then, seeing that it really was Kiernan who had spoken, he returned the uranium canister to its case and, beckoning Freya to follow, hurried back through the plane towards the exit.

'How the bloody hell did you get here so quickly?' he cried, jumping out and turning to help Freya after him. 'I thought you'd be at least another two hours. Talk about the cavalry arriving in the nick of time.'

He was excited, hyped-up. Swinging Freya to the

ground, he turned back to Kiernan, a broad grin on his face.

'Honestly, Molly, I can't believe it. I mean I knew you lot were on top of your game but even so – I only activated the beacon ninety minutes ago. There's just no way you could have got here this quickly, no way. It's . . . it's . . . it's . . .'

His voice stuttered to a standstill, his grin freezing and then fading as for the first time he really took in the scene in front of him: Molly Kiernan, a black walkie-talkie clasped in her hand, standing side by side with Romani Girgis. Both relaxed and smiling, neither seeming remotely uncomfortable in the other's presence. Quite the contrary. They looked, if not exactly like bosom friends, certainly not sworn adversaries either. Business associates, that was the impression Freya got – old business associates who, if their satisfied demeanour was anything to go by, had just clinched a large and extremely lucrative deal.

'Molly?'

Flin's tone was suddenly uncertain, eyes moving back and forth between Kiernan and Girgis and beyond them into the trees behind, where he could see figures moving around in the distance, lugging what looked like large aluminium cases.

'What's going on, Molly?'

Kiernan's smile widened.

'What's going on, Flin, is that thanks to the both of you . . .'

She tipped a nod at Freya.

'. . . we've found the Hidden Oasis. Sandfire's goal has been achieved, the project can be signed off, the world's already a safer place. Smile, you're heroes!'

She held up her walkie-talkie and tapped a finger against

it as though taking a photograph before stepping forward and clapping them both on the shoulders.

'And to answer your earlier question,' she continued, slipping between them, going up to the Antonov and leaning her head through the door, 'we had a satellite tracker on the microlight, were on your tail the moment you took off. A surveillance unit kept an eye on you through the night, we camped forty kilometres away, which is how we were able to get here so quickly. Oh Lord!'

She had spotted the mummified corpse, her face wrinkling in disgust. Behind her Flin was still trying to make sense of the situation.

'Am I missing something here?' he asked.

'Hmm?'

Kiernan withdrew her head and turned towards him.

'Am I missing something, Molly? Who exactly are "we"?'

'I would have thought that was obvious.'

'No, it's not obvious,' Flin snapped, his tone hardening. 'It's not obvious at all. So why don't you enlighten us. Who are "we"?'

'Me and Romani, of course.'

She sounded like a parent explaining something to a particularly obtuse child.

'You're working for Girgis?'

He was wide-eyed, disbelieving.

'Well, on balance I'd say it was more a case of Mr Girgis working for us, although like any relationship over the years—'

'Over the years! What the hell are you telling me, Molly? How long has this been going on?'

'You want, like, precise dates?'

Flin's entire body tensed, his arm coming up, finger jabbing at Kiernan.

'Don't piss me around, Molly. This drug-dealing pimp piece of shit cut a friend of mine's throat, very nearly killed both of us . . .'

He waved a hand towards Freya.

'I'm not in the mood for games. I want to know what's going on and how long it's been going on for, and I want to know now. You hear?'

Kiernan's mouth tightened, as though she was not used to being talked to in this manner and didn't much appreciate it. She stared at Flin, eyes steely, then, with a nod, smoothed down her dress and sat back in the plane's doorway, arms folded.

'Romani Girgis has been working for us since 1986. April 1986, to be precise, which is when we approached him with a view to procuring a quantity of fissile material to aid our Iraqi allies in their struggle against Iran.'

Flin looked across at Freya, then over his shoulder at Girgis – grinning smugly on the other side of the clearing – and then back at Kiernan.

'Your government's behind this?' His voice was incredulous. 'It was your *government* that was going to give Saddam the bomb?'

Kiernan's mouth tightened further, puckering into something just short of a snarl.

'I only wish that had been the case,' she replied. 'Sadly it wasn't. We were happy to finance the Iraqis, give them intelligence, weaponry, even chemical agents, but when it came to providing them with the wherewithal actually to finish the job – to eradicate Khomeini and his Koran-toting madmen – Reagan bottled it. Worse than bottled it – half his goddam administration were supplying *Iran* with arms.'

She shook her head in disgust. A pause, then:

'Which is why a group of us decided we would have to intervene and take control of the situation. For the good of America. For the good of the whole free world.'

'A group of you?' Flin's mind was whirring, trying keep up with it all. 'Group of who? CIA?'

She gave a flick of the hand, dismissing the question.

'I'm not going into that here. Like-minded individuals from across the military, Pentagon, Intelligence – that's all you need to know. Patriots. Realists. People who knew evil when they saw it, and saw it plain and clear in the form of the Islamic Republic of Iran.'

Flin rolled his eyes in disbelief.

'And this group of like-minded realists decided that the best way to ensure stability in the Gulf was to drop an atomic bomb on Tehran?'

'Exactly so,' replied Kiernan, either not noticing, or else choosing to ignore Flin's sarcasm. 'And given what's going on with Ahmadinejad at the moment I think we've been proved about as right as we possibly could have been. Snakes, every single one of them. Snakes and scorpions.'

She gave a nod as if to emphasize this assessment. Unfolding her arms, she smoothed down her dress again, her eyes never leaving Flin. The Englishman had the same dazed, befuddled look on his face as when he had run into the wooden doors back in the tunnel, his mouth opening and shutting as though he had a hundred and one questions to put and wasn't sure where to start. Beside him Freya stood mute and expressionless, no more able to believe what was happening than Flin, the burning of the hornet sting on her neck all but forgotten.

'Why the hell bother with Girgis?' Flin asked eventually, struggling to control his voice. 'If you've got all these people in the military, the government . . . Why not just slip Saddam a couple of your own bloody warheads? It's not like you haven't got enough to go round.'

'Oh please!' Kiernan shook her head, her tone again that of a parent exasperated at her offspring's stupidity. 'We've got leverage, but not that much leverage – it's not like you can just fill out a requisition form or something: "Excuse me, Mr Quartermaster, could you put aside two nuclear bombs, I'll pick them up this afternoon." This whole thing was seriously off-piste, had to be kept way out beyond any normal channels. Sure we set the deal up, provided the intelligence, went fifty-fifty on the finance with Saddam, but we were so far behind the scenes we might as well have been in a different theatre. In terms of day-to-day management, it was very much Romani's show.'

'But with you pulling the strings,' said Flin.

'But with us pulling the strings,' she conceded.

He shook his head and swept a hand through his hair. His face seemed unable to decide whether to settle into an expression of disbelief, outrage, shock or black amusement.

'All that bullshit about tracking Girgis, intercepting the plane . . .'

'Well obviously we *were* tracking him,' said Kiernan. 'Just not for the precise reasons I gave you.'

He gave another shake of the head.

'And when it all went tits up?' he asked, jerking a thumb towards the wreckage of the Antonov.

Kiernan shrugged.

'Again, obviously, we had to do a certain amount of finessing, bury our own involvement – we couldn't exactly go around saying "Sorry, guys, we've lost 50 kilograms of uranium we were in the process of smuggling to Saddam Hussein." To all intents and purposes, though, the narrative was pretty much as I told it the other night. We got on with searching from our end, Romani from his end, the only real difference being that both ends were actually working towards the same end, if you get my meaning. Given the complexity of the situation, I think we did a pretty damned good job.'

'Jesus fucking Christ. And you think Khomeini was the mad one.'

For a moment Kiernan made no response to this, eyes boring into him, jaw set, back ramrod straight. Then, slipping from the doorway and transferring the walkie-talkie to her left hand, she walked over and slapped Flin hard across the face.

'Don't you dare take the name of our Lord in vain,' she spat, her face purpling, her mouth contorting into a rictus of fury. 'And don't you dare presume to judge me. You have no concept, no concept whatsoever of how wicked and dangerous these people are. Oh please sir, please sir . . .'

She raised an arm as if trying to attract the attention of a teacher, her voice slipping into a grotesque parody of that of a little girl, all coy and innocent and squeaky.

'. . . I want the world to be a nice place and everybody to be friends and nobody to do anything nasty. Try living in the real world, asshole!'

She dropped her arm again, flecks of spittle popping from

the corners of her mouth; there was something savage in the way her eyes glared at Flin.

'You think Saddam was bad? Take it from me, he was a goddam saint compared to those rag-head Shia lunatics running Iran. You forgotten the Tehran Embassy siege? The Beirut Embassy bombing? The Beirut barracks bomb? My husband died in that attack, my Charlie, and Iran was behind it, just like they're behind half the terrorist groups across the region: Hezbollah, Hamas, Islamic Jihad . . .'

With each name she snapped her fingers in front of Flin's face.

'They are one of the most poisonous, satanic regimes ever to infect the face of the planet and by the mid-1980s, when you were just a schoolboy pissing around with your pathetic Egyptology, those of us with slightly higher responsibilities were having to face up to the fact that these murdering sons of Cain had a very real chance of defeating Iraq and becoming the dominant power in the entire Gulf. They'd already taken the Majnoon Islands, the Fao Peninsula, they were sinking oil tankers . . .'

Again, she clicked her fingers in Flin's face, hammering home her point.

'It was a catastrophe, unthinkable, the word's key oil-producing region in thrall to a bunch of deranged Stone Age mullahs. Something had to be done. And those of us with enough guts decided to do it. And let me tell you, if we'd succeeded the world would be a damned sight safer place to live in than it is today, you have my word on that, a damned sight safer!'

She broke off, breathing heavily. Bringing up the back of her wrist, she dabbed away the spittle at the corners of her mouth, eyes still locked on Flin, who just stood there, his cheek reddening from where she had slapped him. There was a long silence, broken only by the chirruping of birds and an occasional wheezing rasp as Girgis's thickset colleague puffed on a cigarette. Then, touching the cross at her neck, Kiernan stepped away from Flin and sat back in the doorway of the Antonov.

'I'm sorry for what you've been through these last few days,' she said, smoothing down her skirt again as if to calm herself, her tone softer now, placatory. 'For what both of you have been through.'

This with a glance at Freya, who stared back at her, unblinking and stony-faced.

'And I'm sorry that I've used you, Flin, which I have these last ten years. As I've used a lot of people. I knew your background, what happened with the girl in Baghdad, knew you'd leap at the chance to redeem yourself, would do whatever you were asked to do. I played on that and I'm not proud of it, but the stakes were simply too high to allow personal considerations to get in the way. I did what I had to. For the greater good.'

'It was you that tipped off Girgis, wasn't it?' Flin said, sounding more tired than angry. 'Told him where we were? At the university, at the museum.'

'Like I say, I did what I had to.'

'But you were going to fly us out. Back at the apartment – it was *me* who insisted on staying.'

'Oh come on! Sandfire was everything to you, your big chance to get your life back on track! It doesn't take a psychologist to figure that if there were any stops you hadn't already pulled out, stones you hadn't already turned, you sure as hell would if I threatened to stick you on the first plane back to England. And although I say it myself, it worked pretty well.'

She raised a hand, indicating the oasis around them. Flin sighed and turned, looking first at Girgis and his colleagues, and then at the figures moving in the distance beyond the grove. He caught glimpses of equipment cases, guns, men in what looked like radiation suits, which in the circumstances struck him as excessive. He didn't pursue the thought, his mind too preoccupied with everything he had just heard.

'What about Angleton?' he asked, turning back to Kiernan. 'I'm assuming he was your liaison with Girgis? Did all the running around while you played puppet-master behind the scenes.'

She stared at him, eyes narrowed. For a moment she was silent, then, suddenly, unexpectedly, she burst out laughing.

'God bless you, Flin, but it's comments like that that convince me you might be a fine Egyptologist, but you'd never have got very far in the world of Intelligence.'

Her laughter redoubled. Pulling a tissue from her skirt pocket, she dabbed at her eyes.

'Cyrus Angleton was nothing to do with me, with Romani, with Sandfire, with any of it,' she said, taking a breath, composing herself. 'He was CIA Internal Affairs.'

Flin's mouth opened, then shut again.

'Lord alone knows how,' she went on. 'Because Sandfire was so tightly ring-fenced a goddam flea shouldn't have been able to wriggle its way in, but someone, somewhere in the Agency got wind something wasn't right – unusual payments, strange goings-on in Egypt . . .'

She threw up her hands.

'Who knows what tipped them off? Angleton was sent out to investigate, top-level authorization. Their best man, by all accounts, a legend in the world of internal snooping. Highly decorated. Never failed to crack a case.'

She smiled, balling the tissue and returning it to her pocket.

'Ironic, really, because from your perspective he was the good guy, was trying to help you. He'd worked out Sandfire wasn't exactly what it seemed. That *I* wasn't exactly what *I* seemed. He tried to head you off in Dakhla to warn you, take you both somewhere safe. Yep, he sure got to the bottom of things. Is still there, I expect. Right at the bottom.'

She looked over at Girgis and the Egyptian let out a low chuckle, the two of them sharing some private joke to which neither Flin nor Freya were privy.

'Come on,' Kiernan said. 'You've got to admit it's funny.'

'Hilarious,' muttered Flin bitterly, throwing another glance over his shoulder through the trees. Only a few figures were now visible, the rest having moved on up the gorge, setting up some sort of cordon around the plane he guessed, although as before he was too preoccupied with other thoughts to dwell on it. Everything about him – the slumped shoulders, the hangdog expression, the glazed eyes – bore the look of someone who has just discovered they are the victim of a large and extremely unpleasant practical joke.

'So what are you going to do with it?' he asked eventually, returning his attention to Kiernan.

She didn't seem to get what he was talking about and he had to repeat the question.

'The uranium,' he said wearily, nodding at the plane. 'What are you going to do with the uranium? Given that your friend Saddam didn't turn out to be such a good friend after all.'

She shrugged.

'We're not going to do anything with it.'

'What do mean you're not going to do anything with it?'

'Exactly that. We'll leave it here.'

'Please, Molly, no more games.'

'I'm not playing games, Flin. We're leaving the cases exactly where they are, we're not touching them.'

'You spend twenty-three years and God knows how many millions of dollars scouring the western desert, you kill my friend, very nearly kill me and Freya, and now you've found what you're looking for you're just going to leave it here.'

She nodded.

'What the fuck are you talking about?' His voice exploded, hands clenching into fists, shaking at her, all the frustration and bewilderment of the last ten minutes erupting from him like spume from a geyser. 'Twenty-three years and you're just going to leave it here! Fifty fucking kilograms of highly enriched fucking uranium and after all this you're just going to leave it here!'

She stared at him, unfazed by his outburst. There was a pause, Kiernan and Girgis exchanging another look. Then:

'There is no uranium, Flin.'

Kiernan's voice was calm, curiously matter-of-fact.

'What? What did you say?'

Flin held a hand to his ear, clearly thinking he'd misheard her.

'There is no uranium,' she repeated. 'There never was any uranium.'

He just stood there, gawping.

'Leonid Kanunin, the Russian who was picking up the other end of the deal – he pulled a fast one; took his $50 million and handed over eight canisters full of steel ball-bearings. Someone in his organization tipped us off a couple of days after the plane came down.'

Behind them Girgis let out another throaty chuckle.

'We confronted Mr Kanunin, talked it through over dinner. Sadly he didn't seem to enjoy what was on the menu.'

He murmured something to his companions and they too broke into laughter.

'I appreciate your concern, Flin, really I do,' continued Kiernan, 'but even if al-Qaeda or some such group did happen to stumble on the plane – which given the trouble *we've* had finding it I think is highly unlikely – well . . .'

She smiled.

'I don't imagine the might of the American military machine will be overly troubled by someone launching handfuls of miniature metal balls at them.'

All the colour had drained from Flin's face and his arms hung limply at his sides. He seemed to have aged ten years in the space of as many minutes.

'Don't believe me?' Kiernan came to her feet and held out an arm towards the plane's door. 'Take a look for yourself.'

He did, pushing past her and clambering up into the Antonov. The sound of movement echoed from within the plane before he reappeared with one of the metal canisters clasped in his hand. He unscrewed the lid and upended it. A rush of ball-bearings poured out, pattering onto the sand at his feet with a soft tinkling sound. His face was so pale Freya thought he was going to be sick.

'But why?' he mumbled, his voice dazed, unsteady. 'I don't understand. Why spend twenty-three years looking for a consignment of uranium that didn't even exist?'

'But we haven't been looking for it,' said Kiernan, moving across the glade and taking up position beside Girgis. 'It's not about the uranium. It was never about the uranium.'

'So what the hell is it about?'

'It's about the Benben, Flin.'

His eyes widened.

'That's what we've been looking for all these years, ever since we picked up that last broadcast from Rudi Schmidt, found out the plane had come down in the Hidden Oasis. The uranium was never anything more than a side-show. It was the Benben we were interested in. It's always been the Benben.'

Her voice was soft, almost seductive, her eyes glinting.

'What is it that old cuneiform tablet says? The one in the Hermitage museum. *A weapon in the form of a stone. And with this weapon the enemies of Egypt in the north are destroyed and in the south are destroyed and in the east and the west are beaten into dust so that their king rules all the lands and none shall stand against him nor come against him nor ever defeat him. For in his hand is the mace of the gods.*'

She held the walkie-talkie above her head as though it were a weapon. Beaming, triumphant.

'I tell you, Flin, if this thing is half as powerful as the

sources make out there's not an evildoer in the world that will dare stand against us. Not an Iranian, not a Russian, not a Chink. Not any of those tinpot African or South American oddballs. Nobody. Absolute power, absolute security, a new world order. A *proper* order. God's order. When you look at it like that a twenty-three-year search and $50 million commission seem positively cheap at the price. Don't you think?'

In front of her Flin stepped forward, mouth opening to speak. Before he could, the silence was shattered by a raucous laugh.

'A rock! A goddam rock!'

It was the first time Freya had spoken. Up to this point she had remained silent, standing alongside Flin as the story unfolded, no less shocked than him, no less outraged, occasionally letting out the odd gasp or muttered expletive but otherwise keeping a low profile. Now she could hold back no longer.

'You killed my sister for a piece of fucking rock!' she cried, her voice teetering on the edge of hysteria. 'You were going to cut off my arm because of some half-arsed legend? What sort of madwoman are you? What sort of fucked-up screwball . . .'

She started towards Kiernan, covering about half the distance between them before she felt Flin's hand around her arm, pulling her to a standstill, heaving her firmly back to his side. Thirty seconds ago he had seemed a broken man. Now his entire demeanour was transformed, his body erect and tense, his gaze focused unswervingly on Kiernan.

'Be careful, Molly,' he said, his tone sharp and urgent.

'Whatever you think you're going to do with this thing, please, be very careful.'

Freya yanked her arm from his grip and stared at him aghast.

'You're not telling me you believe this shit?'

He ignored her, eyes still locked on Kiernan.

'Please, Molly. There are things here we don't understand, forces . . . you have to be careful.'

'What is this bullshit!' yelled Freya.

'Molly, I'm begging you, this is not something to fuck around with. You can't just blunder in there . . .'

'We're not blundering anywhere,' said Kiernan. 'We've had twenty-three years to prepare for this. We've got the best weapons experts, the most advanced scanning systems . . .'

'For God's sake, Molly, this isn't something you can just press a button and detonate. There are things going on here, unknown elements . . . It's beyond anything . . .'

He was fighting for the right words.

'We don't understand it,' he ended up saying. 'We just don't understand it. You have to be careful.'

Beside him Freya was uncertain whether to scream in frustration or burst into derisive laughter. She didn't get the chance to do either because at that moment there was a crackle of static and a voice echoed from the walkie-talkie in Kiernan's hand. An American voice.

'That's it, Ms Kiernan. We're all set up.'

She nodded. Lifting the unit to her mouth, she pressed the Talk button.

'Thank you, Dr Meadows. We're on our way.'

Flin started to protest again, but she held up a hand.

'You're a sweetheart, Flin, and believe me I'm touched by your concern, particularly after everything I've just told you. But from this point on the ones who are really going to need to be careful are the enemies of America and our Lord God Jesus Christ. It's His mighty hand behind this, I can feel it. I've always felt it. And let me tell you, Flin, the time is long overdue for that hand to strike down in righteous anger upon the heads of the wicked. Now if you don't mind, I've been waiting many years for this moment and really would like to get up there and see what's going on. You'll join us, of course.'

This last comment was phrased as a command, not a request. She threw a hard, malevolent look at Freya – clearly displeased by her earlier outburst – and turned away, walking off through the grove of palm trees that surrounded the plane.

'Oh, and Romani,' she called over her shoulder, 'you might want to give Professor Brodie a quick pat-down. I do believe he snuck a side-arm under his T-shirt when he went back into the plane.'

'Shit,' murmured Flin.

They returned to the processional way with its weed-choked marble pavement and interspersed sphinxes and obelisks, following it as it climbed gently upwards through the centre of the oasis. Kiernan, Girgis and his two colleagues walked ahead, the twins brought up the rear, guns in hand; Flin and Freya were locked tight in the middle of the group.

'It's a bluff, right?' she asked, keeping her voice low. 'All that stuff about the stone. You're bluffing them, right?'

'I'm deadly serious,' said Flin, his gaze on the rock

platform and monumental gateway looming above the tree-tops in front of them.

'You're telling me you believe all this *X-Files* crap?'

'A lot of different sources from a lot of different places all say exactly the same thing about the Benben, which suggests there must be some truth to it.'

'But it's bullshit! A rock with supernatural powers! Bullshit!'

'Two hours ago I flew over the Gilf and there wasn't an oasis here, and then suddenly . . .' He waved a hand around them. 'Strange things happen. And if the ancient texts are to be believed, bad things to those who misuse the Benben.'

'Bullshit,' she retorted. 'Hocus-pocus bullshit.'

He looked across at her and then away again.

'Well it's all academic because after everything Molly's told us I very much doubt she's going to let us just walk out of here. And even if she does, Girgis certainly won't. First chance we get we run for it. OK? First chance.'

Their eyes met.

'And whether you think it's bullshit or not, when we get into the temple don't touch anything or do anything that might . . .'

'Make the Benben angry? Hurt its feelings?'

Her tone was sarcastic.

'Just be careful,' he said. 'I know it sounds crazy, but please, just be careful.'

He held her gaze to make sure she'd got the message, then looked forward again.

'Bullshit,' she murmured underneath her breath. 'Hocus-pocus bullshit.'

They trudged on, deeper and deeper into the gorge, their

feet sinking into the sponge of moss with which much of the paving was carpeted, the cliffs to either side gradually opening out like the mouth of a funnel. The sun blazed down, its fierce light washing out the rich greens of the vegetation, everything blanching and merging so that the valley looked an altogether less beautiful place than it had when they first entered it. It was hotter too. Not as suffocating as it would have been out in the wider desert, but no longer comfortably balmy either. Flies buzzed and flitted around their heads; they started to sweat.

On several occasions Freya was sure that she glimpsed figures in the undergrowth. They were shadowy and indistinct, and with Kiernan setting a rapid pace in front of them there wasn't time to pause for a closer look. The causeway started to rise at a sharper angle, the trees crowding in closer around them, the temple coming in and out of sight through the foliage ahead. They encountered flights of cracked stone steps. Sporadic at first, they became more frequent as the causeway transformed into a vast, root-covered staircase that carried them upwards at an ever steeper gradient until at last they emerged on the summit of the rock platform. In front of them, swaddled in heavy cloaks of ivy and creeper, rose the monumental pylon gateway they had seen from afar, each of its trapezoid towers carved with the obelisk and *sedjet* sign, its lintel with an image of the sacred Benu bird. Exactly the same as in Rudi Schmidt's photographs but for one difference. In the photographs the gateway's wooden doors had been firmly closed. Now they were thrown wide open.

Flin slowed to a standstill, taking it in. Kiernan and the Egyptians were in no mood to dawdle. Striding up to the gates, they hurried through with barely a glance at the surrounding architecture, the twins herding Flin and Freya through after them. They passed between the towers – soaring cliffs of milky limestone – and into a vast courtyard, its walls cluttered with traffic jams of hieroglyphs, its paving, like that of the causeway they had just ascended, choked with moss and grass and weeds. In places trees – palm and acacia and sycamore – had forced their way up between the stone slabs, heaving them aside, giving the space a curiously broken, crumpled look as if it was slowly folding in on itself.

'Extraordinary,' murmured Flin, gazing around, fascinated despite himself. 'Unbelievable.'

They crossed the court, grass swishing around their ankles, and approached a second pylon on the far side. This one was even larger than the first and also decorated with images. On the left-hand tower a human figure with the head of a hawk held aloft an obelisk in the palm of its hand, while below, much smaller, a line of men seemed to stumble backwards, their hands clasped to their eyes. On the right-hand tower was an almost identical composition save that the human figure was now topped with a lion's head, and the men below were holding their hands to their ears.

'The gods Ra and Sekhmet,' explained Flin as they drew near, pointing left and then right, 'each embodying a different aspect of the Benben's powers: Ra, a blinding light, Sekhmet, a deafening sound.'

'You don't say,' muttered Freya, no more ready to believe any of it than she had been ten minutes previously.

They walked on through this second gateway, across another court – this one crowded with dozens upon dozens of obelisks, some plain, others inscribed, some no taller than a man, others ten times as high – and through a third pylon. As they emerged, Kiernan and Girgis came to an abrupt halt. Even they were now gaping in astonishment.

In front of the group a third courtyard opened out. It was twice as big as the previous two, which had themselves been enormous, its enclosing walls lined with gigantic statues of gods and men. At its opposite end the façade of a colossal temple reared skywards, every inch of its monumental stonework – walls and columns and architraves and cornices – painted in brilliant shades of red and blue and green and yellow, the colours rich and vibrant even in the glaring sunlight, every bit as fresh as when they had first been applied thousands of years previously.

It was not the temple itself that took their collective breath away, however. It was the gargantuan obelisk that erupted, rocket-like, from the centre of the space in front of it. Well over thirty metres tall and covered from base to tip in beaten gold, it gleamed in the rays of the sun, filling the court with a dazzling blaze of light as though the air itself was on fire.

'Holy God Almighty,' growled Girgis.

For a moment they all stood there staring at it, spellbound. Even the normally expressionless twins were wide-eyed with wonder. Then, with a click of her fingers to drag them back to the business in hand, Kiernan led them on. Passing the base of the obelisk – now they were up close they could see that each of its four faces was inscribed with minute columns of alternating *sedjet* signs and Benu birds – they approached the temple entrance.

Three muscular figures in sunglasses, combat trousers and flak jackets stood guard amid the columns lining the front of the building.

'Who's the boy band?' asked Flin. 'Special Forces? Or have you gone private for this particular jaunt?'

Kiernan didn't respond, just threw him a withering look and continued on into the temple. A man in a white lab coat and what looked like a surgeon's scrub cap came forward to meet them, speaking in hushed tones to Kiernan before ushering them forward. They passed through a succession of halls, each, it felt to Freya, as big as the entire interior of the temple at Abydos. Some were filled with towering, papyrus-shaped pillars, others were empty, their walls decorated with spectacular polychrome reliefs. One was overgrown with a tangle of monstrous tree roots, another lined with rows of alabaster tables on which were displayed thousands upon thousands of miniature clay obelisks, just like the ones Freya had seen in Rudi Schmidt's knapsack and the display cabinet in the Cairo museum.

'Christ, it makes Karnak look like a suburban bungalow,' muttered Flin, gazing around.

Further and further they walked, moving ever deeper into the building – the only sounds the pad of their feet and the wheezing of Girgis's cigarette-smoking colleague – until eventually they emerged into a courtyard at what must have been the very heart of the temple complex. It was a secluded space, smaller than the courts at the front of the temple, with a lotus-filled pond at its centre and a giant eucalyptus tree pushing up through the paving against its left-hand wall. Opposite, on the far side of the pond, stood a squat stone building. Plain and unadorned, it was constructed of crudely cut and unevenly laid blocks and seemed wholly out of place amid the imposing architecture that surrounded it. Although she couldn't be sure, Freya sensed that it was far older and more primitive than the rest of the temple complex and had probably already stood on the site for an immeasurable age before the earliest foundations of the adjoining structures had even been dug.

'*Per Benben*,' Flin informed her. 'The House of the Benben.'

Despite his obvious interest, Freya couldn't help but notice a hint of anxiety in his voice.

They circled the pond and came up to the building's single low doorway, which was covered by a reed curtain. A tangled spaghetti of cables snaked out and across to a row of portable generators grumbling in the corner of the yard. The man in the lab coat drew the curtain aside, revealing a short passage with a second drape blocking the other end. Again he spoke to Kiernan in hushed tones before waving them in.

'Whatever happens in there, stay beside me and do what I do,' Flin whispered to Freya as the twins shoved them from behind. 'And don't touch anything.'

He clasped her hand and, ducking, they pushed their way through the two curtains. A sharp icy light enveloped them as the hum of the generators gave way to the blip and squeak of electronic equipment.

Freya had seen many unusual sights in her life – a fair proportion of them over the last few days – but nothing to match the scene that now greeted her.

They were in a large, square room, very basic, with a compacted dirt floor and bare stone-block walls and ceiling, the polar opposite of the ornately decorated halls through which they had just passed, more reminiscent of a cave than something man-made. Four halogen lamps bathed the space in a cold, piercing light; a dozen men and women dressed identically in white lab coats and surgical-style scrub caps pored over an array of monitors and computer screens, the latter bleeping and pulsing, displaying graphs and number sequences and rotating 3-D graphics of strange geometrical shapes.

All of this Freya absorbed in a matter of seconds before her attention zeroed in on the most unlikely element of the whole scenario, and the one that was obviously the focus of everything else that was going on: what looked like a quarantine chamber sitting right in the centre of the space. A heavy, tank-like cube of amber-tinted glass, it had a bulbous ventilation tube feeding into one side of it while on the other a two-door airlock provided access. Enclosed within was a large wooden sled on which rested an indeterminately shaped object wrapped in thick strips of linen. Two men in full-body radiation suits were probing at it with instruments resembling cattle prods – these presumably feeding information back to the monitors outside the chamber – while a third man, also in a radiation suit, was kneeling on the floor with his back to them, examining the sled.

The whole thing was so surreal, so wholly wrong and spooky and out of place, more akin to a film set than real life, that Freya's immediate, disjointed thought was that she must be dreaming it all. Had indeed been dreaming right from the very start and was in fact still asleep back in her apartment in San Francisco, snug and safe and secure and with a sister who was very much alive. For a euphoric instant the thought took hold. Then she felt Flin's hand tightening around hers. It *was* happening, she realized, she *was* in a temple in a lost oasis, and while *she* might have been struggling to buy into the whole Benben script, everyone else in the room was taking it extremely seriously.

'Bullshit,' she repeated underneath her breath. 'Hocus-pocus bullshit.'

For the first time there was doubt in her voice, as though rather than making a confident assertion of fact, she was now trying to reassure herself.

'So what exactly have we got here, Dr Meadows?'

The question came from Molly Kiernan.

The man who had led them through the temple and appeared to be in overall charge – of the scientific operations at least – raised his head from the monitor over which he had bent. Coming across, he motioned them all forward so that they were standing close to the chamber's thick glass wall.

'Preliminary scans are showing a solid core,' he intoned, his voice nasal and monotonous, 'with elevated levels of iridium, osmium and ruthenium, which would tie in with it being of meteoric origin. That's about all we can establish at this stage. For anything more we're going to need full physical contact.'

'Then I suggest we make full physical contact,' said Kiernan. 'Mr Usman, as the Egyptologist here – the *other* Egyptologist –'

She threw a sideways look at Flin.

538

'. . . maybe you'd like to do the honours.'

The figure kneeling beside the sled raised a hand in acknowledgement and stood up, moving around the cloth-swathed object so that he was standing directly opposite them. Now that she could see his face through the radiation hood, Freya recognized him as Girgis's companion from the night back in Manshiet Nasser: plump cheeks, pudding-bowl haircut, thick plastic spectacles.

'Molly, I'm begging you,' Flin pleaded. 'You have no idea what you're playing with here.'

'Oh and you do?' said Kiernan with a dismissive snort. 'Suddenly you're the great physicist?'

'I know what the ancient Egyptians thought of the Benben. And I know they hid it out here for a very good reason.'

'Just as we've found it for a very good reason. Now if you don't mind, Professor Brodie . . .'

There was scorn in her voice as she said the name.

'. . . we've got the future of the world sitting in front of us and I for one would like to take a look at it. Dr Meadows?'

The man in the lab coat gestured to one of his colleagues. The four halogen lamps suddenly dimmed and then went out, leaving just the ghostly glow of the monitors and the beam of a single, small pin-spot angled at the mysterious, cloth-swathed object on the sled. One of the scientists picked up a video camera and started filming.

'If you please, Mr Usman,' said Kiernan, folding her arms.

Usman nodded. Stepping right up to the sled, he reached out, allowing his hands to hover over the object for a moment before his fingers started to tweak at the cloth wrappings. They were tightly bound, and his protective gloves made it difficult for him to get a grip on the material. There was something vaguely comical about the way he fumbled and clawed at it, puffing and muttering to himself, struggling to get it loose. Several minutes passed and both Kiernan and Girgis were starting to look distinctly impatient before he finally managed to prise one end of the cloth free, after which it started to unravel more easily, the material unwinding in a succession of long linen strips like the bandaging around a mummy. He started to work faster, using both hands, circling them round and round, pulling the fabric away, loose folds of material spilling down onto the sled and floor like shedding skin, the man with the camera moving around the chamber, capturing the scene from different angles. Wads of protective linen packing started to emerge, bound in among the wrappings, bulking the object out so that what had initially appeared quite sizeable gradually diminished as more and more of its covering was removed. Smaller and smaller it became, less and less impressive, shrinking before their eyes as layer after layer of its binding was removed until the last of the linen strips fell away and the object within was revealed: an ugly lump of greyish-black stone, squat and dumpy and less than a metre in height, its top blunt and rounded, more like a traffic bollard than a traditional obelisk. After all the build-up it was, to Freya's thinking, a distinct anticlimax. Judging by their nonplussed expressions, it was an opinion shared by both Girgis and Kiernan.

'Looks like a dog turd,' muttered one of Girgis's companions.

There was a pause as they all stared, Kiernan frowning,

her head shaking slightly as if to say 'Is that it?' Then the halogen lamps burst full on again and there was a flurry of activity. More men in radiation suits joined those who were already inside the glass chamber, crowding around the stone, attaching electrodes to it, wires, a barnacle-like excrescence of adhesive pads. The blipping and bleeping sounds suddenly grew faster and louder, the monitors and computer screens more animated as a rush of new information was fed back to them. A printer started chattering madly, spewing out a rush of digit-covered paper; voices babbled, calling back and forth, conversing in a jargon that Freya couldn't begin to decipher or understand. From inside the chamber microphones relayed a high-pitched whizzing sound as what looked like a miniature dentist's drill was applied to the base of the stone, scoring its surface, releasing a gritty residue that was collected in sterile sample bags and passed out through the airlock for further analysis.

'God help us,' groaned Flin, looking on in horror, his hand clasped so tightly around Freya's it was starting to hurt her. 'They don't know what they're bloody doing.'

If he was expecting something to happen – as he clearly was, everything about him bearing the look of a man who has been made to stand beside a ticking time bomb – it singularly failed to do so. The white-coats continued their scraping and chipping and listening and monitoring, Usman all the while gently caressing the top of the stone as though to comfort and reassure it, his voice intermittently audible as he chanted softly: *Iner-wer iner-en Ra iner-n sedjet iner sweser-en kheru-en sekhmet. Iner-wer iner-en Ra iner-n sedjet iner sweser-en kheru-en sekhmet.*

Through all of which the stone just sat there, as in any other circumstances one would unquestioningly expect a stone to do. Mute, motionless, it neither exploded nor screamed nor emitted any toxic rays or whatever it was that Flin feared it would do. A drab, uninspiring spit of murky grey-black rock – no more, no less. After twenty minutes Girgis's thickset companion excused himself and went outside for a cigarette. Ten minutes later Girgis's other colleague and the twins went out to join him, then Girgis himself, with Flin and Freya. And finally Molly Kiernan. She paced up and down beside the pond, talking to herself, her brow furrowed, her hands occasionally clasping and her eyes flicking up to the sky as though she was praying. Twice Flin and Freya tried to edge out of the courtyard, twice – inevitably – they were spotted, the twins trotting over and waving them back.

'Don't even think about it,' said Kiernan, her voice harsh, devoid of its earlier jocularity. 'You hear me? Don't even fucking think about it.'

As she resumed her pacing, the two of them, for want of anything better to do, sat down in the shade of the giant eucalyptus tree. According to Flin's watch it was now 10.57 a.m., although, as they had noticed when they first entered the oasis, the position of the sun in the sky suggested it was much later – mid to late afternoon.

'It's like time moves differently here,' he said.

They were the only words they exchanged. The sun blazed down, the minutes ticked by, the generators rumbled, and nothing happened.

In the end almost an hour passed before they were called back into the room. Kiernan and Girgis looked thunderous.

'So?' snapped Kiernan, not even bothering with a preamble.

'Well there's no question it's a meteorite, or part of a meteorite,' began Meadows in his dreary, nasal voice as he ushered them over to the front of the glass confinement zone. 'As well as iridium, osmium etc. we're picking up significant traces of olivine and pyroxene which are clearly suggestive of primitive chondritic—'

'Just cut the crap and tell me what it can do.'

The scientist shuffled nervously.

'There are more tests we need to carry out,' he mumbled. 'A *lot* more tests, which we'll begin the moment we get it back to a proper laboratory with more powerful spectroscopic . . .'

Kiernan threw him a look and he fell silent.

'It's a primitive chondrite,' he said after an uncomfortable pause. 'A meteorite.'

'Yes, but what can it do? You get what I'm saying? What can it do?'

Kiernan was clearly trying to control herself.

'What can the meteorite do? What's inside it? What's all this stuff telling you?' She waved a hand at the gadgetry ranged around the chamber. Meadows fiddled with the edge of the clipboard he was holding, but didn't reply.

'That's it?' Kiernan's voice was starting to rise. 'Are you telling me that's it? Is that what you're telling me?'

The scientist gave a nervous shrug.

'It's a primitive chondrite,' he repeated helplessly. 'A meteorite. A piece of space rock.'

She opened her mouth, shut it again, stood there, one

hand touching the cross at her throat, the other balled into a fist. Silent. Everyone was silent. Even the electronic blipping seemed to have slowed and quietened as though sharing in the general sense of shocked deflation. There was a long pause, then, inside the glass chamber, the men began pulling off their radiation hoods and tearing away the tangle of electrodes and wires which covered the stone. Flin started to chuckle.

'Oh that's priceless,' he chortled. 'Twenty-three years and God knows how many deaths and all for a worthless chunk of rock. That is just absolutely bloody priceless.'

All his anxiety appeared to have evaporated, the dynamic of the scene the complete reverse of what it had been back at the plane. Now, it seemed to Freya, it was Flin who was savouring the moment and Kiernan and Girgis who were struggling to come to terms with the situation.

'But the texts,' Kiernan mumbled. 'They said . . . The experts, everyone said . . .'

She wheeled round, waving a hand at Flin.

'*You* said! You told me. That it was real, the Egyptians used it . . . you told me! You promised me!'

He held up his hands.

'*Mea culpa*, Molly. I was a crap spy, and it seems I'm a crap Egyptologist as well.'

'But you said, you told me, they all told me . . . it had powers, it destroyed Egypt's enemies . . . The mace of the gods, the most terrible weapon ever known to man!'

She was starting to rage, her eyes dilated, flecks of spittle again gathering in the corners of her mouth.

'Be careful, that's what you said! Don't fuck around with

it, there are things we don't understand, unknown elements! Powers, you told me it had powers!'

'I guess I got it wrong,' Flin said, pausing a beat before adding: 'Come on, Molly, you've got to admit it's funny.'

It was the phrase she herself had used earlier and she clearly wasn't amused at having it thrown back in her face. She glared at him – a more vicious, caustic look Freya had never seen. Then, jabbing a finger as if to say 'I'll deal with you in a moment,' she rounded on Meadows, haranguing him, demanding to see his findings, have them explained to her, telling him he must have made a mistake and would have to run the tests again.

'They told me!' she kept shouting. 'Everyone told me – it's got powers, that's what they said, it's got powers!'

Girgis and his companions joined in, jabbering in a mixture of Arabic and English, yelling at the scientists, and at Usman – now standing alone in the isolation chamber, a forlorn figure in his thick plastic spectacles – and at Kiernan too, insisting that, powers or no powers, they still expected full payment of the money that was owing to them. The heavy-set man with the moustache lit up a cigarette and now Meadows – who had stood meekly taking the abuse – lost his temper as well, demanding the cigarette be extinguished immediately lest it interfere with the electronic equipment. Two of his colleagues came forward to back him up and all at once everybody was shouting and jostling, the twins wading in for no particular reason other than that was the sort of thing they did. The whole building echoed to the dissonant strains of furious argument.

'Time to go,' whispered Flin, taking Freya's arm and pulling her across the room. They reached the doorway, paused to confirm they weren't being observed and started to step through. As they did one of the white-coats – a curly-haired young man who was positioned not far from the door and was, despite the general confusion, still bent over his monitor – suddenly held up a hand and said: 'Hey, look at this!'

It wasn't the actual words that caused Freya and Flin to stop and turn back into the room, but the urgency with which they were uttered.

'Look at this!' the man repeated, flapping his hand to attract attention. On the screen in front of him Freya could see a series of vertical bars rising and falling like the valves of a trumpet. Still the argument raged: the man's voice was lost in the general swell of shout and counter-shout, and he had to call a third time before the hubbub slowly began to subside and he had everyone's undivided attention.

'Something's happening,' he said. 'Look.'

Everyone shuffled forward, crowding around the screen. Even Flin and Freya moved closer, their escape moment-arily put on hold as they waited to see what was going on.

'What is this?' asked Girgis, the signals on the monitor in front of him becoming increasingly animated. 'What does this mean?'

Meadows was craning over his colleague's shoulder, brow furrowed as he watched the bars leap up and down, shoot-ing right to the very top of the screen before dropping back again and flat-lining.

'Electromagnetic activity,' he murmured. 'A lot of electromagnetic activity.'

'From where? From the stone?'

The voice was Kiernan's.

546

'It's not possible,' said Meadows. 'We've been monitoring it for two hours and there's not been any . . . It's just not . . .'

He swung round and crossed the room to the glass chamber, the others following in his wake. Flin and Freya hung back near the door, no one taking any notice of them, all eyes now focused on the Benben. Usman was still standing inside the chamber, one hand laid protectively on top of the stone as though on the head of a child; a collar of wires and electrodes was snagged around its base where they had been stripped away by the men in radiation suits. It looked no different from how it had done when it was first unwrapped: a squat, parabola-shaped lump of grainy, greyish-black rock.

'Harker?' called Meadows.

'It's off the scale, sir,' reported the curly-haired man. 'I've never seen anything . . .'

'I'm getting an increase in alpha, beta *and* gamma radiation,' announced another scientist. 'Quite a significant increase.'

Meadows hurried over and was bending down to examine this new finding when a woman on the opposite side of the room also called out – something about non-sequential ionization – forcing him to break away to go over to look at her screen. Other voices now joined in. Excited, insistent, yelling that they too were getting unexpected readings, bandying words and phrases that meant absolutely nothing to Freya. Meadows scurried from one screen to the next, shaking his head, repeating 'It's not possible, it's just not possible,' over and over. The printer, which had been silent for the last few minutes, started chattering again, even more manically than before, an ever-lengthening tongue of paper jerking out of its mouth. The electronic sounds returned with a vengeance, filling the room with a symphony of blips and bleeps and crackles. The monitor and computer screens swirled with a dazzling kaleidoscope of activity.

'What is happening?' shouted Girgis.

Meadows ignored him. Striding over to the glass chamber, he ordered Usman out. The Egyptian didn't move, just stood there staring down at the stone, transfixed, a confused, vacant sort of look on his face. Meadows repeated his command, twice, each time with increasing urgency. Then, with a helpless flap of the arms he motioned to one of his colleagues, who hit a button. The airlock hissed, closing and sealing, leaving Usman locked inside.

'I'm sorry to have to do that, Ms Kiernan,' Meadows began, 'but I can't risk—'

'Fuck him,' interrupted Girgis. 'What about us? Are we in danger? Is it safe?'

Meadows stared at him, shocked by the Egyptian's lack of concern, then slapped his palm against the front of the protective box.

'This is three-inch-thick, multi-walled carbon-nanotube-reinforced leaded glass. Which is to say there's nothing getting out of here that we don't want to get out. So to answer your question, yes, we're perfectly safe. Unfortunately I can't say the same for your colleague.'

Usman had started to sway back and forth, one hand clasping the rock for support. He was mumbling to himself, eyes glazed as though he had fallen into a stupor, apparently only half aware of what was going on.

'What the fuck's wrong with him?' asked the thickset man. 'Is he drunk?'

No one answered. Usman continued to sway, his free hand coming up and pawing at the zip of his radiation suit, trying to get it undone.

'*Ana harran.*' His voice echoed through the intercom. It sounded woozy and disorientated. '*Ana eyean.*'

'He says he's hot,' Flin murmured, translating for Freya. 'He doesn't feel well.'

'What's happening to him?' she asked, horrified and fascinated at the same time.

Flin shook his head, unable to answer. Usman lurched, regained his balance, got a hold of the zip and started to strip off the suit, fumbling it down over his body and off, revealing blue trousers and a white shirt beneath.

'*Ana harran,*' he slurred. '*Ana eyean.*'

He tugged the shirt off as well, and the trousers, leaving him standing there in just his underpants, socks and shoes. It would have been comical were it not for the fact that he was clearly now in serious distress, his chest heaving as if he was struggling for breath, his hands trembling uncontrollably.

'*Ha-ee-yee betowgar,*' he moaned, pawing at his thighs and belly. '*Ha-ee-yee betowgar.*'

'It's really hurting,' translated Flin.

'Oh God,' whispered Freya. 'I can't watch this.'

But she continued to do so, as did everyone else in the room, morbidly hypnotized by the scene that was playing itself out within the glass quarantine chamber. The printer chattered ever more furiously, the blipping and bleeping grew more clamorous as whatever forces were gathering did so at an accelerating pace. Despite Meadows's assurance that everything was safe, Girgis and the other Egyptians moved back from the chamber. Unlike Kiernan, who had gone right up to it, pressing one hand against the glass while with the other she fondled the cross at her neck, eyes glinting with excitement.

'Come on,' she whispered. 'Come on, baby, show us what you can do. Stone of Fire, Voice of Sekhmet. Come on, come on.'

Usman was now stumbling around, moaning in pain, rubbing his eyes, tugging at his ears.

'*Ana haragar*,' he groaned. '*Ana larzim arooh let-tawarlet.*'

'Christ,' murmured Flin underneath his breath. 'He says he's going to be sick, needs to . . .'

Usman doubled up and dropped to his knees, right in front of Kiernan. A trickle of watery vomit spilled from his mouth, his white underpants turned a pale shade of brown.

'He's shat himself!' laughed the thickset man. 'Look at that! The dirty idiot's shat himself!'

'*Iner-wer iner-en Ra iner-n sedjet iner sweser-en kheru-en sekhmet . . .*' intoned Usman groggily, heaving himself to his feet again and just standing there, his face and belly pressed up against the inside of the glass, his hands hanging limp at his sides. Thirty seconds passed, the electronic feedback dampening slightly as though whatever process was causing it was starting to dwindle and calm. Then, suddenly, shockingly, two things happened in swift succession. A deep, sonorous pulse rang out. Seeming to come from within the stone itself, it reverberated like a magnified heartbeat, causing the entire building to tremble even though the sound itself was not particularly loud. At almost exactly the same instant there was a blinding burst of light – also from within the stone – like a flashbulb going off although far brighter and more intense. It lasted only a fraction of a second and the amber tinting of the glass protected them from the worst of the glare. Even so, they were all momentarily blinded. Arms came up and covered eyes, the printer and monitors fell silent, the computer screens and lamps cut out, plunging the room into darkness. There were shouts, movement, Girgis's voice demanding to know what was going on. Then, as abruptly as they had shut off, the electrics came back on line. The monitors and computers rebooted, the halogen lamps flickered back into life. There was a pause as everyone blinked and adjusted, then screams and the sound of retching.

'Oh my God,' choked Freya, clasping a hand to her mouth. 'Oh God help him.'

In front of them Usman was standing in exactly the same position as he had been before the flash of light, still pressed up against the inside of the glass, still in his underpants, socks and shoes. The one difference was that his skin had gone. His body – limbs and face and torso – was now a glistening, slippery patchwork of tendons, muscles, bones and fatty tissue. Horrifyingly, he still appeared to be alive, for a bubbling growl welled up from his throat, his lidless eyes swivelling back and forth behind his spectacles as he tried to work out what was going on. He mumbled something and tried to take a step back, but the front of his body from the waist up – belly, chest, right cheek – seemed to have fused to the glass. He tried again, his eyeballs rolling furiously, his ribs heaving up and down as he fought to draw breath. Then, lifting his raw arms – how he found the strength Freya couldn't begin to guess – he placed his hands flat against the front of the chamber, gritted his lipless teeth and pushed, forcing himself away from the glass. There was a moist tearing sound and he tottered backwards, thick shreds of flesh remaining glued to the chamber wall. For a brief, sickening moment they glimpsed his jawbone, colon and what might have been part of his liver. Then there was another throbbing pulse, another burst of light and everything went black again.

'We're out of here,' said Flin, grabbing Freya's arm and propelling her through the first of the curtains hanging across the chamber entrance. As he did so Kiernan's voice rang out from the darkness behind.

'Do you see what it can do! Oh my Holy Lord, it's a miracle! A beautiful miracle! Humble yourselves under the mighty hand of God! Thank you, Lord, thank you!'

As soon as they emerged into the courtyard, the shadows now lengthening as the sun dropped west, they started to sprint. Freya was fighting back an irresistible urge to vomit. She no longer cared what happened to Girgis and the others or about avenging her sister's murder. She just wanted to get out.

They didn't take the direct route back through the temple. Instead they left the yard by a side gate and zigzagged their way through a labyrinth of passages and galleries and colonnades in an effort to bypass the flak-jacketed guards at the front of the building. Eventually, more by luck than design, they emerged into the second of the giant courts through which they had passed earlier, the one crowded with an array of different-sized obelisks. They paused to catch their breath, listening, making sure they weren't being followed and then ran on. They had just passed through the pylon at the head of the court into the first and outermost quadrangle when the curious pulsing sound again reverberated behind them, exactly the same volume as it had been back in the chamber. The entire temple complex seemed to shudder.

'We've got to get out of the oasis!' cried Flin, waving her on across the court, stumbling on the uneven, moss-covered paving. 'Whatever they've started, this is just the beginning of it. We have to get out!'

'What's going to happen?' Freya shouted, powering along beside him.

'I don't know, but on the basis of what we've just seen it's not going to be pretty. And that's before you even start factoring in all the curses that are supposed to have been laid on the oasis.'

Thirty minutes ago Freya would have dismissed this last comment with a snort of derision. After the events in the chamber, she took them very much at face value.

'Come on!' he cried. 'We've got to move!'

They reached the first pylon, the one at the very front of the temple complex, and started through, its trapezoid towers rearing above them, a sea of tree-tops spreading away into the distance ahead.

'What if there are more of those men?' she called, remembering the shadowy figures she'd seen lurking in the undergrowth as they made their way up the valley earlier. 'The guys with the sunglasses.'

'We'll deal with that when it happens. Let's just get down—'

There was a blur of movement and a squat, brawny figure stepped out from a niche in the pylon wall and slammed a ring-covered fist hard into the Englishman's face, splitting his lip and knocking him to the floor. An identical figure emerged from a niche in the opposite wall, tripped Freya and sent her sprawling down beside Flin, her forehead cracking on the paving, her palms grazing on the bare stone.

'Hello, Eengleesh,' said a gruff voice. 'You go home?'

'You go grave,' came another, eerily similar voice.

Laughter, and then the feel of rough hands hoisting them to their feet.

The moment the lights had come back on in the chamber and Freya and Flin's absence had been noted, Girgis had sent the twins after them, which was a shame because after two days pissing around doing bugger all things had finally started to get interesting, what with Usman getting barbecued like that. Funniest thing they'd ever seen, fucking hilarious. But Girgis was the boss – for the moment at least – and so off they'd gone, heading straight back through the temple so that they'd reached the front of the complex ahead of the two westerners. Taking up position inside the entrance gateway, they'd pounced the moment their quarry had appeared, giving that poncey Englishman a bloody good thumping, which he'd had coming for a while now.

They hauled the pair of them to their feet, the Englishman wiping blood off his chin and jabbering at them, first in what they assumed was his native language, then in Arabic, some shit about inscriptions and curses. They gave him another couple of punches and dragged him and the girl back into the first of the giant courtyards where they made them kneel side by side while they discussed how best to get rid of them. Bullet through the head? Slit their throats? Stamp them to death? This being their last job before retirement they wanted to make sure they got it right. Went out on a high.

'I vote we put them in with Usman,' said the one with the torn earlobe.

'I don't think they'd let us,' replied his sibling, clearly disappointed by the fact. 'In case, you know, stuff got out. Nice idea though.'

There was a booming thud as another of those weird pulsing sounds echoed around the temple, the ground quivering underneath their feet. Barodi, or whatever the hell his name was, waved his hands frantically, banging on about curses again, forces that couldn't be controlled. They kicked him in the balls – try that for a force! – and he slumped down, gasping. The girl screamed and threw a punch at them, so they gave her a good slap as well. Silly pig. *Ugly* pig. Thin. Way too thin.

They backed off a couple of steps and resumed their discussion while in front of them the Englishman slowly hauled himself back onto his knees.

'You have to believe me,' he pleaded, helping the girl up as well, checking she was OK. 'This is just the start. We have to get out of the oasis. You can do whatever you want once we're out of here, but if we stay we're dead. You understand what I'm saying? We're dead. All of us. You too.'

They tried to ignore him, but he kept on at them and in the end they concluded a bullet through the head would be the best thing after all, if only because it would be the quickest way of shutting the prick up. Decision made, they took another couple of paces back and pulled out their Glocks. The Englishman wrapped an arm around the girl and drew her protectively against him while continuing to rant.

'You want to take him or the girl?' asked the twin with the flattened nose.

'What the fuck's wrong with you!'

'Easy either way,' replied his brother.

'This whole place is going to blow and you're discussing who's going to shoot who!'

'I'll take him, then,' said the first twin.

'Fine by me,' replied his sibling.

'At least let her go!'

'Count of three,' they said in unison, lifting their guns. 'One . . . Two . . .'

'You ignorant fucking shitbags!' he spat. 'So much for Red Devils always looking out for each other!'

'Three.'

No shots. The twins stood there, arms still extended, guns pointing, a faintly quizzical expression on their faces.

'You support El-Ahly?' they both asked simultaneously.

'What?'

Barodi looked ashen-faced, confused, his arm still wrapped around the girl.

'You said Red Devils always look out for each other,' said one.

'Why would you say that unless you supported El-Ahly?' put in the other.

'Are you an *Ahlawy*?' they chorused.

He couldn't seem to work out if they were toying with him or not, playing some sort of sick joke. Beside him the girl was trembling, her eyes darting back and forth in shocked bemusement.

'Are you an *Ahlawy*?' they repeated.

'I'm a season ticket holder,' he mumbled.

The twins frowned. This was unexpected. And troubling. They lowered their weapons slightly.

'Where do you sit?'

'What?'

'In the stadium. Where do you sit?'

'You're about to kill me and you want to know where I sit to watch football!'

The guns came up again.

'West stand, lower tier. Just above the touchline.'

The twins exchanged a look. A season ticket holder. And in the west stand. Just above the touchline. Impressive. Although he could be bluffing.

'How many League titles have we won?'

The Englishman rolled his eyes in disbelief.

'Is this some sort of fucking—'

'How many?'

'Thirty-three.'

'Egyptian Cups?'

'Thirty-five.'

'African Champions Leagues?'

He counted on his fingers, the girl kneeling there beside him, wide-eyed and bewildered.

'Four,' he said. 'No, five!'

The twins exchanged another glance – the guy certainly knew his stuff. There was a pause, then, just to be sure:

'Who scored the winning goal in the 2007 Cup Final?'

'For God's sake! Osama Hosay, from an Ahmad Sedik cross. I was there. Mohamed Abu Treika gave me a complimentary ticket after I took his sons round the Egyptian Museum.'

That sealed it. Orders or no orders, foreigners or not, there was no way they were going to take out a fellow Red Devil. Especially not one who'd done a favour for Mohamed Abu Treika. They lowered their guns and slipped them back inside their jackets, motioning the westerners to their feet, muttering a grudging sorry, didn't know you were Devils, no hard feelings, maybe catch you at a game some time. They all faced each other in embarrassed silence, then, as yet another of the deep pulsing sounds echoed around the temple complex, Barodi started pulling the girl backwards before the pair of them turned and broke into a run. As they reached the gateway at the front of the temple the Englishman slowed and shouted over his shoulder.

'*Entoo aarfeen en Girgis Zamalekawy.* You know Girgis supports Zamalek, don't you?'

And then they were gone, out through the gateway and into the oasis beyond.

'Did he say Girgis supported Zamalek?' asked one of the twins, horrified.

'That's exactly what he said,' replied his brother, equally shocked.

'We've been working for a White Knight?'

'A *Zamalekawy*?'

They looked at each other, uncomprehending. Apart from their turd of a father there was nothing in the world they despised more than a Zamalek supporter – scum, all of them, lowlife scum. And now they'd been told they were working for one. Had been for the last decade.

'Let's get out of here.'

'Girgis?'

'We'll deal with him back in Cairo. Teach him a lesson he'll never forget.'

'Wanker!'

'Wanker!'

They scowled and were about to set off towards the main gateway when the brother with the torn ear suddenly reached out and grabbed his brother's arm.

'We could take a bit of that gold with us,' he said. 'You know, from the big pillar thing.'

He pulled a flick-knife from his pocket, clicked it open, made a sawing motion.

'Strip it off, sell it in Khan el-Khalili.'

'It might be an idea,' agreed the other.

'Buy something nice for Mama.'

'Open another *torly* stand.'

'Make the whole thing worth it.'

They hesitated, the courtyard trembling as yet another booming pulse filled the air. Then, with a nod, they turned and started trotting back through the temple complex, discussing gold, and *torly*, and how they'd like to squeeze every Zamalek supporter in the world into that glass tank, flick a switch and watch them fry.

'What the hell did you say to them?' gasped Freya as she and Flin ran out through the monumental pylon and across the narrow clearing in front of the temple.

'I told them I'm a Red Devil.'

'What?'

'Long story. For the moment I just want to get out of here. Come on!'

They leapt down the steps that led up to the temple platform. Reaching flat ground, they charged on through the trees, slipping and stumbling on the uneven paving, the pulses now coming at regular intervals, each one sending a rippling tremor through the oasis, as though the rock itself was shivering at the sound.

'Wasn't there something about a crocodile? And a snake.'

'The Two Curses,' replied Flin, hurdling a giant root that had driven its way up through the path. '*May evildoers be crushed in the jaws of Sobek and swallowed into the belly of the serpent Apep.*'

'Which means?'

'I haven't the faintest bloody idea. Come on!'

They continued downwards, sphinxes and obelisks lining the causeway to either side of them, the gorge starting to narrow. So insistent was the throbbing of the Benben that it was only now Freya noticed that the screech and chatter of birdsong – previously so pervasive – had disappeared, as had the buzz and hum of insects. She looked around and up, but aside from a couple of what looked like vultures circling high in the sky above, the valley seemed suddenly empty and denuded of wildlife. Flin must have noticed the same thing because he slowed to a walk and then a halt, surveying the trees and cliffs before breaking into a run again, pushing on with even more urgency than before. The absence of fauna seemed to have spooked him as much as, if not more than, the booming of the stone.

'At least all Molly's people seem to have gone as well,' called Freya, pounding along behind him. She'd been scanning the undergrowth as they descended and hadn't spotted any of the shadowy figures she'd glimpsed on their way up through the valley. Her hopes were rising that they might actually make it down to the tunnel and out of the oasis without being challenged. 'They must all have . . .'

Flin came to an abrupt stop. A giant dum palm reared to their left, a colossal granite arm to their right. Ahead, standing in the middle of the causeway, was a man in a flak jacket and sand-coloured army combats, a Heckler & Koch MP5 submachine-gun pushed tight into his shoulder, its muzzle aimed directly at them. A second flak-jacketed figure stepped out from behind the palm tree, also wielding a submachine-gun. Flin reached out and took Freya's hand as another shudder reverberated through the valley. For once he didn't seem to have anything to say.

Molly Kiernan had always loved fireworks, ever since the annual Fourth of July displays in her home city of North Platte, Nebraska, when she and her family would gather to watch in wonder as sparkling explosions of colour lit up the night sky above the Lincoln County Fairgrounds on the edge of town. Since then she had seen bigger, more spectacular displays – the one at the Pyramids to mark Egyptian National Day was always impressive – but nothing came close to the scenes she was now witnessing inside the glass isolation chamber.

Every time one of the deep, sonorous pulses rang out

from the Benben – and they had been coming more and more frequently over the last twenty minutes – it was accompanied by a brilliant burst of illumination. The flashes had grown brighter and fiercer with each repetition and Meadows had insisted they all don radiation goggles as back-up to the protective tinting of the chamber's leaded glass screens. Colours had started to appear inside the stone, faint at first, barely noticeable, minute glittering pinpricks of red and blue and silver and green that flared momentarily within the dark mass of rock before disappearing again. As the pulsing grew more frequent and the light flashes more blinding, the colours grew commensurately stronger and more striking. Pinpricks turned into streaks and streaks into swirls, the entire stone burning with a brilliant kaleidoscope of hues, a dense aura seeming to rise off its surface like steam, enveloping it in a rich golden haze.

'It's beautiful,' cried Kiernan, clapping her hands in delight. 'Oh Lord, it's the most beautiful thing I've ever seen! Don't you think? Aren't I right? The most beautiful thing ever!'

No one responded, everyone in the room gazing speechless as the display intensified in front of them, the monitors and printer now silent, the computer screens blank, the electrics having long since burnt out and died.

'Is it safe?' Girgis kept demanding. With his shiny rubber goggles, slicked-back hair and thin, lipless mouth he appeared even more reptilian than ever. 'Are you sure we're safe? I don't want to end up like that!'

By which he meant Usman, or what had once been Usman. There wasn't much of the Egyptologist left, each successive burst of light having stripped away a little bit more of his body, reducing him layer by layer like an unpeeling onion until all that remained was a bleached crumple of bones lying on the floor at the foot of the Benben. Still – surreally – tangled up with his shoes, socks, underpants and glasses.

'We're perfectly safe, Mr Girgis,' Meadows assured him. 'As I told you before, the glass membrane is unbreachable. Whatever happens inside the observation zone will remain inside the observation zone. Nothing's getting out that we don't want to.'

But as the reaction within the rock continued to gather force, the pulses coming ever faster, the light-bursts growing ever brighter, even Meadows began to look uncertain. He paced up and down, scratching at his balding head and conversing in hushed, anxious tones with his fellow white-coats, all of them clearly wondering where this was leading and whether perhaps they had underestimated what they were dealing with here.

Kiernan alone remained unfazed by the pyrotechnics. Standing well forward of the others, she beamed and clapped her hands like an over-excited schoolgirl, occasionally reaching out a finger and touching it to the glass wall as if trying to connect with what was going on behind it, convince herself it was actually happening.

'Look at it, Charlie!' she whispered. 'Will you just look at it! All these years you've kept me strong, kept me believing! And now . . . Oh my sweet holy Lord in heaven will you just look at it! Beautiful! Beautiful!'

So absorbed was she, so utterly hypnotized by the extraordinary sound and light show playing out in front of her that she didn't notice when someone started calling her name – a crackly-sounding voice with an American accent. Only when Meadows came forward and handed her the walkie-talkie she had left beside one of the monitors did she finally pull her attention away from the stone. Holding the apparatus to her ear, she listened, eyes flicking towards Girgis, her head shaking as if in disapproval. Then, with a curt 'Terminate them', she handed the set back to Meadows and returned her attention to the Benben.

'Oh blow ye the trumpet in Zion,' she whispered as a crackle of static echoed from the walkie-talkie, followed by muffled gunshots. 'Sound an alarm in my holy mountain, for the day of the Lord is coming, it is nigh at hand!'

Shock can play strange tricks on the mind, and for a brief, scrambled moment Freya thought she must be dead and having some sort of out-of-body experience.

It wasn't just that she had heard Kiernan's voice ordering their execution, and then the sound of gunfire and of two bodies thudding to the ground, but that everything had suddenly gone deathly quiet and still, as though the world had come to an abrupt stop and all that was left was a freeze-frame of its final moment.

It only lasted an instant before she realized that, whatever else had happened, she most certainly hadn't been gunned down. She blinked and looked around. Everything was exactly as it had been a few moments ago – the oasis, the avenue of sphinxes and obelisks, the giant dum palm, the monumental granite arm. The only noticeable difference was that the sound of the Benben had ceased, plunging the gorge into a silence all the more profound for the intensity of the noise that had preceded it. That and the fact that the two men in flak jackets – who only a few seconds ago had been about to open fire on them – were now lying sprawled on the ground. One was face down, the top part of his skull blown away, his hair, neck and flak-jacket collar matted with a viscous porridge of blood and bone and brain. The other was on his back, arms splayed, a dark, fleshy hole gaping where his left eye had once been.

'Jesus,' she mumbled, uncertain whether to feel horror at the carnage, relief that their assailants were dead or alarm that this was merely the prelude to some new and un-expected assault.

She glanced across at Flin, who seemed to be struggling with the same slew of emotions. He raised his eyebrows as if to say 'I've no more idea what's just happened than you have', and looked around, trying to see where the gunshots had come from and who had fired them. As he did there was a rustle of branches and something – someone – dropped from the dum palm above their heads, landing with a soft thud to their left. Simultaneously there was a whirl of robes on the far side of the causeway. A figure scrambled over the top of the giant granite arm and hurried towards them, rifle in hand. Flin moved in front of Freya, fists clenched, ready to fight. The figure stopped, held the rifle out to his side and with his free hand tugged away the scarf that was wrapped around his head and face. Flin and Freya gawped.

'Zahir?'

Although the evidence was standing right there in front of her, Freya still couldn't believe it.

'Zahir?' she repeated. 'How the hell did you . . . ?'

She broke off, surprise and relief giving way to suspicion. All her misgivings about the Egyptian came flooding back, memories of that last, tense meeting at his house in Dakhla. He noticed the change in her expression and again held out his rifle to show he meant her no harm. The other man did the same with his gun, reaching up to reveal his face as well – Zahir's younger brother Said. Freya recognized him from her sister's funeral. She relaxed slightly, as did Flin who dropped his fists and stepped back so that he was standing beside her.

'What are you doing here?' she asked, shaking her head in bewilderment. 'How did you find it?'

If she was looking for an explanation, it didn't come. Instead, after standing there a moment, both of them with that stern, slightly dour expression that seemed to run in the family, Zahir came forward a couple of paces and held a hand to his chest.

'I sorry, Miss Freya.'

She frowned, having no idea what he was talking about.

'I sorry,' he repeated, his manner formal, serious, as though he was making some public pronouncement. 'You my guest in Egypt, you sister my good friend Doctor Alex. It is my duty care for you, protect you from all danger. I no protect you; many bad thing happen. I sorry, I very sorry. You forgive me.'

Of all the things that had happened over the last few days – car chases, shoot-outs, lost oases, lumps of rock with supernatural powers – this for some reason struck Freya as the most bizarre: standing there beside two blood-covered corpses and a giant granite arm being apologized to for no good reason by a man who had just rescued her from certain death.

'You forgive me,' he said again, something almost child-like in the earnestness of his tone. Despite herself, despite everything, Freya burst out laughing.

'Zahir, you just saved my goddam life. I should be thanking, not forgiving you! Jeez, you Bedouin . . .'

She whirled a hand beside her head, indicating that she thought he was mad. Zahir frowned, trying to work out whether the gesture was playful or insulting. Apparently settling on the former, he gave a nod and the faintest hint of a smile, no more than a brief upward twitch at the ends of his lips.

'Everything OK now, Miss Freya,' he said, coming forward and nudging one of the bodies with his foot. 'You safe. Both of you safe. No danger. Everything good.'

Curiously they were almost exactly the same words Flin had used after the hornet attack back in the Antonov. Now, as then, she felt a warming surge of relief and well-being, thinking that maybe, just maybe, the odds had turned in their favour, that they were going to make it out of this alive.

Now as then it proved a short-lived respite. Barely had she allowed herself that first glimmer of optimism when, like a volley of slaps across the face, the deep pulsing sound suddenly started up again. Boom . . . Boom . . . Boom . . . echoing around the gorge, causing the rocks and the trees to tremble, repeating at an even faster rate now as though whatever was causing it had recharged itself and now wanted to make up for lost time.

The four of them froze, looking anxiously around. The ground beneath their feet seemed to jump with each pulse, the vibrations now so forceful that for a moment Freya was convinced the sound was not only sending tremors through the walls of the gorge, but actually causing them to move, shunting them inwards towards each other. She shook her head, certain she was imagining things, that it was just some optical illusion. But the more she stared, the more it seemed to her that the walls of the gorge *were* moving, slowly creeping together like a vast closing book, the geology of aeons going into reverse, telescoping into a period of mere seconds. A low, malevolent grinding sound of rock crunching against rock could now be heard, quite distinct from the booming pulse, swiftly building in volume until it had all but drowned the Benben out.

'Do you see that?' she said, her arms coming up, pointing at the cliffs to left and right.

Flin obviously had because he was already sprinting across to the giant granite arm, Zahir and his brother just behind. The three men scrambled up on top of the stone to give themselves a better view.

'What is that?' Freya shouted. 'What's happening?'

Flin was shielding his eyes, his head turning back and forth, his legs braced against the trembling of the arm beneath him.

'The jaws of Sobek,' he murmured. Then again, louder: 'The jaws of Sobek! My God, that's what the curse means! *May evildoers be crushed in the jaws of Sobek!* The oasis closes like a crocodile's mouth. That's what it means. Look! You see how it's coming together!'

Freya did indeed, even from her lower elevation. The

shape of the oasis – narrow at one end, wide at the other, its cliffs forming themselves into a gigantic V – gave the impression, now she looked at it, of some gargantuan crocodile's maw, maxilla and mandible gradually clamping shut, crushing everything in between. Rocks and other debris were starting to cascade down the faces of the cliffs; there was a distant splintering sound as of tree trunks uprooting and snapping.

'But it's not possible!' she screamed. 'How can a gorge just close up? It's not possible.'

'None of it's possible,' shouted Flin, waving his arm around. 'None of it, from start to finish! It doesn't matter, it's happening, we have to get out. We have to get out now!'

He leapt down, closely followed by Zahir and his brother, the Egyptians' brown *djellabas* billowing around them. Although their faces were as blank as ever, the alarm in their eyes was unmistakable.

Flin seized Freya's arm and started moving on down the oasis towards the tunnel, but Zahir came after them and pulled them to a stop.

'No that way. Many men below. We go other way, top of valley.'

He chopped a hand back towards the temple.

'We climb. This how we come into oasis. Always how we come in.'

Flin opened his mouth to ask what Zahir meant by this last comment, but the Egyptian and his brother had already started running, waving the two westerners after them.

'Come!' Zahir shouted. 'No much time!'

'You've been here before!' called Flin, charging along in his wake. 'Did you say you'd been here before?'

His voice was lost within the roar and crack of grinding rock as the cliffs inched steadily towards each other, clouds of dust starting to rise to either side of the gorge as though the oasis was burning.

Vernon Meadows – *Dr* Vernon Meadows BSc, MSc, Ph.D., CPhys, FAAAS, FInstP, SMIEEE – had worked on what he liked to refer to as the 'esoteric front line' of US defence research for the best part of forty years, everything from quantum teleportation to weather disruption programmes, invisibility shields to anti-matter-propelled isomer warheads. And during that time, whatever project he had been engaged on, wherever in the world he had been engaged on it – and there weren't many corners of the globe he hadn't visited on his mission to push the outer boundaries of weapons technology – two basic rules had always stood him in good stead: stay calm and in control, however outlandish the situation; and when you can't stay calm and in control, get the hell out quick.

It was the second of these rules that came into play now as the Benben started pulsing again – no bursts of light this time, which was interesting – and, from outside, there came a heavy rumbling sound which, one of his colleagues informed him, after rushing out to look, was being caused by the walls of the gorge slowly drawing together. Meadows had witnessed a lot of weird shit over the years, but nothing that even came close to this. He went outside himself to assess the situation, then returned to the chamber and called time out, ordering everyone to drop whatever they were doing, abandon the project and run for their lives.

No one argued. Even Girgis allowed himself to be hustled through the doorway by his colleagues, albeit with yells of 'What about the money! I've kept my end of the deal and I want my money! Now, you hear! Now!'

Only Molly Kiernan refused to leave. She remained rooted where she was in front of the glass isolation zone, oblivious to the frantic exodus behind her, gazing at the stone as it pulsed and boomed and once again filled with spiralling curlicues of colour. The hues if anything were even richer and deeper than they had been before – the most vibrant, exotic, mesmerizing colours she had ever seen, as though the rock were merely a window onto some higher and more perfect order of reality.

'Ms Kiernan, we have to go!' cried Meadows, furiously waving at her from the chamber entrance, his legs pulling him backwards through the doorway as if they were working independently of the rest of his body. 'Please! We have to go. It's out of control.'

She gave a scornful flick of the hand, not even bothering to turn round.

'Go on, get out! Run away home to Mommy! Mice! Every one of you! Mice and worms! There's no place for you here!'

'Ms Kiernan . . .'

'This is the time of the strong. Of the faithful. Of the true believers! Our time! God's time! Go on, get out! We'll take it from here! We'll take the world from here!'

Eyes blazing, she gave another contemptuous hand-flick, as though dismissing someone who was trying to sell her an unwanted trinket. Meadows shook his head helplessly, turned on his heel and ran from the chamber. Kiernan's voice echoed behind him, audible even through the booming of the Benben and the grinding of the gorge walls, shrill, euphoric, triumphant:

'Look at it, Charlie! Oh will you just look at it, my darling! See its power! We'll crush them! The evildoers, the wicked ones! We'll grind them into dust! Oh will you just look at it!'

'You knew, didn't you? All the time. You knew where the oasis was. You've been here before.'

Flin was struggling to keep pace with Zahir as the Egyptian led them back up the processional way towards the top end of the gorge. Freya and Said were following close behind, the ground heaving and buckling, the cliffs to either side looming ever larger, creeping inexorably inwards like a closing vice. Dust filled the air; statues and masonry were starting to shudder and topple. The noise was deafening.

'When?' cried Flin, fighting both for breath and to make his voice heard above the chaos around them. 'When did you find it?'

'No me,' shouted Zahir over his shoulder. 'My *in-sis-teer*. Mohammed Wald Yusuf Ibrahim Sabri al-Rashaayda. He know all desert, every dune, every grain sand. He find oasis. Before six hundred year.'

'Your family have known about the *wehat* for six hundred years!'

'We pass one generation al-Rashaayda to next, father son, father son. No tell anyone.'

'But why, for God's sake? Why keep it secret?'

Zahir skidded to a halt and turned to face Flin. Freya and Said were coming up behind.

'We Bedouin.' Zahir slapped a hand to his chest. 'We understand oasis, we respect. We come, we drink water, we spend night, nothing more. We no touch anything, we no take anything, we no hurt anything. Other people . . . they no understand. Oasis powerful.'

The Egyptian waved an arm around.

'Dangerous if you no respect. Like all desert. No safe other people come here. Bad thing happen. Oasis punish. Now come. We no have much time!'

He started running again, Flin, Freya and Said pounding along in his wake. They reached the first of the flights of steps that climbed up towards the temple complex above. Rather than continuing straight on, Zahir swerved right, taking them off the main avenue and onto a path that looped around the base of the rock platform on which the temple sat. It was narrower than the causeway, clogged with roots and fallen masonry, and their progress slowed.

'What about the plane?' Flin shouted, warding off a branch as it switched back into his face. 'You knew about the plane?'

'Of course know about plane,' said Zahir. 'We find four, five week after crash. We know one man live because he dig grave, we search him, but we no find. After this we come many time. We watch. We guard.'

'But you were part of Sandfire! You were helping Alex look for the oasis!'

Zahir threw Flin a glance, his meaning perfectly clear

even without words: I might have helped her *look*, but certainly not to find.

'You were trying to protect us, weren't you?' called Freya, pushing along beside Flin. 'When we came to your house yesterday, asked you about the rock. That's why you didn't want to tell us. You wanted to protect us.'

'I try warn you is dangerous,' said Zahir, slowing to a walk as ahead of them a huge fallen column came into view. Three metres in diameter, as long as a railway carriage and wrapped in dense webs of creeper, it completely blocked the path. 'Oasis dangerous, bad people dangerous, everything dangerous. You my good friend. I no want you be hurt.'

He reached the column, seized one of the creepers and was starting to heave himself up when Flin reached out and grabbed his arm, pulling him back.

'It's us who owe you an apology, Zahir. More than an apology. We mistrusted you, insulted you in your own home. I am sorry, *sahebee*. Truly sorry.'

The Egyptian gave another of those barely discernible half-smiles, and brushed Flin's hand away.

'Is OK, I kill you later,' he said. 'Now we keep moving. Climb out oasis. Please, quick.'

He clapped the Englishman on the shoulder and, swinging around, clambered up onto the pillar, kneeling and holding out his hand for Freya. She scrambled up as well, the movement of the cliffs causing the column to rock and judder as though it were some giant inflatable toy rather than forty tons of solid stone. She took a moment to get her balance, then turned to help the others up. As she did she noticed movement out of the corner of her eye, above and to her right.

'Look!' She pointed.

They were now almost parallel with the front of the temple, although much lower down. A wide gap in the intervening trees offered them an unimpeded view of the first pylon with its creeper-draped towers and open gates. As they followed the line of Freya's arm, they saw figures stampeding out into the open area in front of the temple: men in flak jackets and sunglasses, the lab-coated scientists, Girgis and his colleagues, Meadows and, bringing up the rear, the red-haired twins in their Armani suits. No sign of Molly Kiernan.

'They go wrong way,' said Zahir matter-of-factly. 'They die. We live. Come.'

He reached down to help his brother onto the pillar, Freya doing the same for Flin. Said scrambled up but Flin remained where he was.

'Molly didn't come out,' he shouted. 'She's still in there.'

'Who gives a shit about Molly!' yelled Freya. 'Come on.'

'I can't just leave her there!'

'What do you mean you can't just leave her there? After everything she's done to us? Screw her, let her fry!'

Flin was clenching and unclenching his fists.

'Come on!' screamed Freya again, glancing frantically left and right at the converging cliffs.

'I can't just leave her,' Flin repeated. 'She helped me, despite it all. Introduced me to Alex, gave my life some meaning, however screwed up the motives. I can't just leave her to die.'

'You're mad. You're fucking mad!'

He ignored her, backing away towards a secondary flight

575

of rock steps that snaked up to the temple gateway from the side rather than the front.

'Go,' he shouted. 'I'll catch you up.'

'No!'

Freya swivelled round and clasped a thick tendril of creeper, ready to clamber down off the column and go after him. Zahir grabbed her arm.

'We wait at top,' he said. 'Is better that way.'

She shook the arm off and stood, screaming after Flin.

'What are you doing? She killed Alex! She was part of it. How can you want to save her? She killed my sister.'

But he was already powering up the steps away from her, taking them two at a time, and her voice was swallowed by the booming of the Benben and the thunderous roar of pulverizing rock.

'I pray that one day the ground will open up and swallow you, oh shame of my womb.'

These were the last words Romani Girgis's mother had ever spoken to him and now, as he charged down through the oasis, the cliffs closing in around him like some monstrous pair of pliers, the entire world seeming to fold and collapse in on itself, he had a nasty feeling her dying wish was about to be granted.

He should have known it was a bad deal. Right from the very outset, from the day twenty-three years ago when that mad bitch Kiernan had told him to forget about the plane, that it was the Benben her people were interested in. Whores, drugs, guns, uranium – these were things he could

576

understand, things he could rely on and control. But exploding stones, ancient curses? He should have known, if not twenty-three years ago then certainly earlier that morning, when they had flown over and over the Gilf and found absolutely nothing, and yet the moment they had traipsed through that disgusting tunnel there was the oasis in front of them, as if it had been there all the time. There were forces at work here that he couldn't comprehend, factors he couldn't predict, powers he couldn't bend to his own will. All of which added up to the mother of all bad business decisions.

'I want my money,' he screamed, scratching furiously at his hands and neck as he ran, the obelisks lining the processional way crashing down around him like tumbling skittles. 'You hear? I want my money! Give it to me! Give it to me now!'

He was yelling to himself. Most of the group who had fled the temple with him had by now either stormed away into the distance ahead or else, as in the case of that idiot scientist Meadows, been crushed under falling masonry. Now it was just him and his fellow Egyptians – Kasri, the twins and, lagging behind, gasping for breath, Boutros Salah. His oldest colleague. The one person in the world he'd consider calling a friend. He was waving desperately.

'Don't leave me, Romani! Please wait. I can't keep up!'

'It's your fault!' shrieked Girgis, half turning and jabbing a finger at him. 'You should have warned me it was a bad deal. You should have talked me out of it! And so should you! And you!'

This to Kasri and the twins.

'All of you! You should have warned me! You should have

577

talked me out of it. I want my money! You hear? I want my money now, you dirty thieving *koosat*!'

He continued to rant as they stumbled onwards, flailing his arms, raging at the duplicity of the Americans and the treachery of his own people. They passed the wreck of the Antonov, the rock face behind slowly pushing the plane towards them, bulldozing it along on a churning tide of masonry and boulders and uprooted trees until eventually it was upended and dragged down and underneath the hem of the cliff like a toy boat beneath the prow of an ocean liner.

'How is this happening!' screamed Girgis. 'Make it stop! You hear! That's what I pay you for! Make it stop!'

His voice was lost in the deafening clamour of shearing stone. Even if they could have heard him no one would have taken any notice, all of them focused solely on getting to the bottom of the oasis and back into the tunnel as quickly as possible.

On and on they ploughed, the world growing ever darker as the gorge narrowed, sending billowing clouds of dust and debris surging into their faces. In the end they were to all intents and purposes running blind, the looming blackness of the walls to either side and the slight downward gradient of the ground beneath their feet the only indication that they were still moving in the right direction.

So impenetrable was the murk, so disorientating the thunder of splintering rock that Girgis was already thirty metres along it before he realized he was actually inside the tunnel. The dust cloud slowly dissipated around him, small pools of light gradually came into focus from the portable krypton lamps that had been arranged at intervals along the shaft when they had first come through earlier that morning.

He slowed, stopped, started running again, taking himself well away from the tunnel entrance and the chaos outside, covering another fifty metres before coming to a halt and leaning back against the shaft's curved wall with its interlocked images of writhing snakes. Gasping for breath, he slapped the dust and grit off his hair and suit. The group had become strung out and separated in the final frantic dash for safety and Kasri was now some ten metres behind him. Salah was even further back, just emerging from the dust cloud, choking and wheezing. The twins were not immediately visible and for a moment Girgis thought they must still be back in the oasis, but then he spotted them away to his right, further along the tunnel, two spherical blobs marching off into the distance.

'Where do you think you're going?' he yelled.

They kept walking.

'You stop where you are and wait for me! Do you hear! You wait for me!'

'Zamalek are shit!' came a voice, echoing back up the shaft towards him. 'And *Zamalekaweya* are scum!'

'What? What did you say?'

They didn't reply, just continued on their way, their outlines growing steadily more vague as they slowly merged into the shadows.

'I'll be seeing you on the other side!' Girgis bellowed after them. 'You hear? I'll be seeing you on the other side, you little shits!'

Scratching at his head and neck, muttering expletives, he pushed away from the wall and set off down the tunnel in pursuit, waving at Kasri and Salah to follow. The rumble of the closing cliffs slowly dropped away behind them, growing fainter as they descended ever deeper into the earth until eventually it had faded to nothing more than a distant creaking groan, no louder than the slap of their feet on the tunnel floor and the gravelly wheeze of Salah's breathing.

They reached the bottom of the slope, Girgis still some way ahead of his colleagues. The ground levelled out, the tunnel now running flat, driving horizontally through the underside of the Gilf like an enormous worm burrow, the krypton lamps continuing to light their way – ghostly islands of illumination that if anything only served to intensify the tracts of blackness in between.

'Not far now,' shouted Girgis, whose mood seemed to have mellowed the further away from the oasis they travelled. 'Another ten minutes and we'll be out of this filthy shit-hole and back to Cairo. We'll have a game of backgammon, eh Boutros! Just like old times!'

Salah lit a cigarette and grumbled something about not appreciating being left behind when they were in the gorge. Girgis waved the comment away.

'I'll make it up to you. Buy you a new car or something. Come on, keep up.'

He quickened his step, striding on along the tunnel, trying to ignore the painted snakes that seemed to shift and sliver in the ghostly half-light, coiling malevolently around the walls and ceiling. He walked for about a minute, then stopped, squinting into the shadows.

Although his memory wasn't a hundred per cent clear – hardly surprising given everything he'd gone through – he could have sworn that when they came along the tunnel earlier that morning it had been completely straight. Now there was a bend up ahead, the tunnel wall curving sharply around to the right.

'What is this?' he muttered, starting forward again before coming to another abrupt halt as something very curious happened. There was a dry rustling sound as of hands rubbing across grainy wood and, before his very eyes, the tunnel slowly straightened itself before bending in the opposite direction. He shook his head, certain he must be imagining it. He was tired, after all, emotional, had just been swindled out of $50 million. But then it happened again.

'Boutros!' he shouted. 'Did you see that? Mohammed?'

He swung round, seeking reassurance from his colleagues, but now there was a bend behind him as well, where there certainly hadn't been one before.

'Romani!' came Salah's voice from round the corner, hoarse with terror. 'The tunnel's moving!'

'What do you mean it's moving? How can it be moving?'

Girgis was starting to sound upset again. Very upset.

'The walls are moving,' cried Kasri. 'They're bending.'

'How the fuck can solid rock—'

He was cut short by another dry rustling sound, although now he was hearing it a third time it struck him as more of a dusty slither. As he watched aghast, Kasri and Salah slowly came back into view and then vanished again as the tunnel undulated gracefully from left to right. Walls, floor and ceiling rippled and stretched as though they were made not of stone, but of something softer, more elastic – skin or sinew.

'Stop it!' shouted Girgis. 'Stop it now! I order you to stop it!'

581

For a moment it seemed as if his command had been heeded. Everything stilled, the only sounds the wheeze of Salah's breathing and, from somewhere far off, a muted shout which Girgis assumed must be one of the twins. Five seconds went by. Ten, and he was starting to think that whatever geological forces were at work had calmed and settled when the corridor gave another slow, undulating contortion. This time it kept on moving, swirling sinuously first in one direction and then the other, back and forth, the krypton lamps toppling and rolling, everything blurring in a confusion of light and darkness and coiling serpents. Girgis was thrown to the floor, clambered upright, fell again, started crawling. He didn't even know in which direction he was going, he just wanted to get away. The snaking became more violent, the floor swishing and slithering, the entire tunnel seeming to writhe. A malign hissing sound filled the air, a stench of rotting, half-digested meat clogged his nostrils, causing him to gag and choke.

'Help me!' Girgis screamed as his fellow Egyptians suddenly loomed in front of him, Kasri flat on his face, Salah on all fours, a cigarette still dangling from the corner of his mouth. 'In the name of God help me.'

He fought his way towards them, desperately stretching out a hand. Salah and Kasri also tried to reach out, their fingertips coming to within inches of each other before, to his dismay, Girgis saw the tunnel starting to narrow and contract. Like a puckering mouth its circumference slowly closed around his two colleagues, clamping their legs and torsos in a tightening glove of rock, crushing them. For a moment they struggled, arms flapping, faces reddening as the shaft squeezed ever more ferociously, and then they were sucked backwards and away. Salah's hand protruded for a few seconds longer, nicotine-stained fingers curling into an agonized claw before it too was swallowed and he was gone. The tunnel gave another violent lurch and fell still. The hissing sound faded into silence.

For a moment Girgis knelt there, staring dementedly at the anus-sized aperture through which his companions had just been sucked, shivering and whimpering. Then, with a trembling hand, he took the upturned krypton lamp that was lying on the floor beneath the aperture, rose unsteadily to his feet and turned. *Forget what's just happened*, he told himself. *Forget Salah and Kasri. Keep calm, start walking, get the fuck out of this godforsaken hell-hole.* But the corridor had contracted and closed ahead of him as well – presumably devouring the twins just as it had Kasri and Salah. He was alone and he was trapped, entombed in a minibus-sized section of tunnel.

'Hello!' he cried weakly. 'Is anyone there? Can anyone hear me?'

His voice was barely strong enough to fill the space he was in, let alone penetrate the solid rock all around. He called again, and again, the lamp in his hand – the only lamp – starting to fade as its battery ran down. The shadows grew thicker and more menacing, gathering around the margins of the krypton bulb's weakening glow like a wolf pack around a campfire.

'Please!' he moaned. 'Please help me, somebody. I'll pay. I'm rich. Very rich. Help me!'

He began to weep, and then to scream, a high-pitched, hyena-like wail as he pounded his fists vainly against the unyielding stone, calling on God, any god – Christian,

Muslim, ancient Egyptian – to come to his aid, save him in his hour of need. Everything remained as it was, the silence every bit as intense, the rock cage every bit as solid, and in the end, exhausted, he slumped down on the floor with his back against the wall. Above him, barely visible in the fading light, an enormous painted snake's head hovered, its jaws levered wide open.

'Get away,' he moaned, scratching at his neck and limbs, the feel of cockroaches on his skin more intense and unbearable than ever. 'Get off me! Disgusting! Disgusting!'

His scratching grew more furious, fingers clawing and slapping at himself, the sensation of scurrying insects so loathsomely realistic that, drained and despairing as he was, he couldn't bear to sit motionless and staggered back onto his feet. As he did he caught sight of something dribbling down the wall where he had been sitting. Chips of stone and grit by the look of it, a whole rush of material, although the light was now so weak he couldn't be sure. He leant closer, trying to see what was happening, terrified that the tunnel was starting to cave in. But what he saw was worse than that. Worse than anything he could ever have imagined, his most terrible nightmare made real. Cockroaches, dozens upon dozens of cockroaches, hundreds of them, thousands, were streaming out of the mouth of the serpent on the wall like a surge of dirty brown water. He looked down – they were on his jacket, his arms, his legs, his shoes.

Howling, he reeled backwards, frenziedly trying to slap the insects away, his feet making a moist, crunching sound as he stumbled across the floor. He slammed against the opposite wall and dropped the lamp, its light momentarily shining brighter, clearly illuminating the entire space. There were other serpent mouths – to his right, his left, above, in front – all of them spewing hordes of cockroaches. The entire cavity was alive with movement, a scuttling tide of insects sweeping towards him, surging up, down, across and over his body, enveloping him in a glistening shroud of wings and legs and feelers. The light only lasted a few seconds, just enough to bring home to Girgis the full horror of what was happening to him. Then it dimmed and went out, leaving just darkness, the click and skitter of millions of tiny feet and Romani Girgis's crazed shrieking.

When Flin reached the top of the steps he paused, the extra height affording him a clearer view of what was going on in the oasis as a whole.

The scene was one of spectacular and increasing devastation. The pristine paradise of a few hours earlier was now barely recognizable as the cliffs continued their unstoppable advance, churning everything in their path, palm groves and flower meadows, orchards and pools, avenues and statuary slowly disappearing like debris beneath a pair of industrial vacuum cleaners. At the very bottom end of the gorge the cliffs already seemed to have clamped tight together, although it was hard to be sure because of the swirling dust. Further up there was still clear space between them, a wedge of greenery that grew wider – or rather, less narrow and compressed – the closer it came to the top of the canyon, although even this was fast being devoured as the cliffs swung remorselessly inwards, obliterating everything in their path. Flin guessed he had about fifteen minutes until they reached the sides of the rock platform and started demolishing the temple buildings. And maybe another ten after that before they closed altogether and the oasis was gone. Fifteen at the outside. Not enough time. Not nearly enough time. He turned and started sprinting.

He passed through the first courtyard – the rock walls towering to left and right, the force of their approach causing the paving to warp and heave beneath him – and then the second courtyard, where half the obelisk forest was now lying jumbled on the ground like driftwood. And then the third. The giant obelisk at its centre still stood erect and defiant, unbowed in the face of encroaching chaos, albeit with a ragged patch of gold sheet missing from its bottom left-hand corner, an act of vandalism he barely registered, so intent was he on getting to Kiernan.

He reached the temple building and raced through the succession of monumental halls and chambers. The boom of the Benben, which had been all but smothered by the roar of the disintegrating oasis, gradually became more audible, muscling its way back into his hearing, a repetitive, pulsing counterpoint to the clash and rumble of collapsing rock.

'Come on!' he cried, trying to push himself on even faster, force every last ounce of energy into his legs. Showers of dust and grit rained down from above, chunks of masonry were starting to shift and dislodge – and this before the cliffs had even reached the temple platform and started to exert their full compressive force on it.

He passed through the hall filled with giant tree roots,

the one with the alabaster offering tables, more and more of the building starting to crack and move around him, on and on until eventually he emerged into the small courtyard at the heart of the temple. Its pond was now empty and drained of water, a deep fissure cutting across its bottom, pink and blue lotuses lying slumped and forlorn on the drying stone. With a cry of 'Molly!' Flin ran directly across it and through the doorway of the squat stone building on its far side, barging past the twin reed-curtains and into the room beyond. The external sounds suddenly faded, the pulsing of the Benben Stone growing commensurately louder, filling his ears. 'Molly, you have to get out! We have to go! Come on!'

The room was empty. Flin stood on its threshold, taking in the abandoned banks of monitors, the glass isolation chamber, the Benben itself – its interior ablaze with spiralling rosettes of colour, a soft golden mist seeming to rise off its surface. He was just starting to turn away, thinking she must already have fled, that she'd been with the group they'd seen rushing through the temple gates earlier and they'd simply missed her, when there was movement within the chamber. He wheeled, staring aghast as from behind the stone Molly Kiernan slowly came to her feet.

'Hello, Flin.'

She sounded like she was welcoming him to a tea party.

'God Almighty, Molly, are you crazy! Get out of there!'

She just smiled at him. Perfectly calm, perfectly relaxed.

'You saw what it did to Usman!' he cried, frantically waving at her. 'Get out! Come on! We've got to go!'

Her smile broadened.

'Honestly, Flin, do I look like Usman?'

587

She spread her arms, like a magician inviting an audience to examine him, to reassure themselves that despite having been sawn in half he was still very much in one piece.

'See? It's not hurting me. It's not doing anything to me.'

She swished her hands up and down her body, then leant forward and, to his horror, hugged the Benben, pushing her cheek right up against it. She appeared to suffer no ill-effects and after remaining still for a moment to prove her point, she came upright again.

'It's not going to harm anyone we don't want it to harm, Flin. It's a tool, no more, no less. And like any tool you've just got to know how to use it.'

She reached out and wafted a hand across the top of the stone, the pulsing sound seeming to slow and quieten as if she was indeed able to bend it to her will. Flin looked on in disbelief.

'It's our friend,' she purred. 'Just like it was friend to the ancient Egyptians. What was it they called it? *Iner seweser-en* – am I pronouncing that right? – the stone that made us mighty. And now it's going to make *us* mighty too. That's why it's been revealed to us, why we were led here. It's a gift, Flin. A gift from God himself.'

Around them the walls of the building were starting to shudder, ten-ton blocks of stone trembling and jumping as if they were made of nothing heavier than polystyrene.

'Please, Molly, there's no time! We've got to get out! Now!'

'And this is just the beginning,' she said, ignoring his entreaties, her voice disconcertingly placid and composed, as if she was operating in a completely different reality from the one in which Flin found himself. 'The first tiny glimpse of its power. Think what it's going to do for us when we *really* unleash it, what it's going to help us achieve.'

'Please, Molly!'

'A new world, a new order, an end to wickedness. God's kingdom on earth, with the Benben as security and not an evildoer in sight!'

The ceiling blocks were starting to pull apart, slits of dusty blue sky now visible above.

'You could be part of it, Flin,' Kiernan went on, extending a hand to him, apparently oblivious to the fact that she'd only recently ordered his execution. 'Why not work with us? You know more about the stone than anyone, even me. You could advise us, help us realize its full potential. The others were weak, but not you. Come with us. Help us build a new world. How about it, Flin? Are you with us? Will you help us?'

'You're mad!' he yelled, backing away, eyes flicking from Kiernan to the ceiling and walls of the chamber which were juddering ever more violently, breaking open like a hatching egg. 'It's not something you can control! It's beyond you. It's beyond all of us!'

She laughed, wagging a finger at him, like a Sunday school mistress chiding an unruly pupil.

'Oh ye of little faith. Oh ye of such shamefully little faith! Do you really think He would have gifted us something that we couldn't use? Can't control it? Does this look like I can't control it?'

She spread her arms again and, opening out her palms, slowly brought them down onto the head of the Benben. To Flin's consternation, the pulsing sound slowed and quietened further until it had faded altogether, the colours

within the stone dimming and disappearing. The walls
and ceiling ceased to tremble. Everything fell eerily still and
silent. Flin looked around, unable to believe it.

'My God,' he murmured. 'How do you . . . My God.'

Kiernan beamed.

'Like I told you, He wouldn't give us something we
couldn't use. And believe me, we are going to use it, with or
without your help.'

She drew a breath, exhaled, dropped her head back,
closed her eyes.

'Be silent before the Lord,' she murmured. 'For the day
of the Lord is at hand; the Lord has prepared—'

She was cut short by a deafening rumble. The building
started to shake violently again. At the same moment the
Benben resumed its pulsing, the sound much harsher than
before, angrier, like the growl of a lion. The interior of the
stone once again blazed with colour, just a single shade now:
a livid, furnace-like red, as if everything that had gone
before – the swirling hues, the bright flashes of light, the
golden aura – had simply been a preamble, a warming-up
exercise, and now, finally, the Benben was revealing its true
nature.

Kiernan's eyes snapped open and her head jerked forward, the smile shrinking on her mouth, her arms suddenly
rigid as if she was being electrocuted.

'Out!' cried Flin. 'Get out!'

She didn't seem to be able to lift her hands from the
surface of the stone. She started to shake, her eyes growing
wider and wider, her mouth levering open until it looked as
if the jaw would snap. Flin took a step forward, thinking to
try to help her, to drag her from the glass tank, but even as

he did a patch of her cheek started to turn yellow and then brown, like paper held over a candle, the patch expanding and darkening before suddenly bursting into flame. Other patches appeared – on her hands, her neck, her forehead, her scalp, her arms – these too browning and catching alight, the flames spreading and joining, wrapping around her, swaddling her in a fiery embrace. Her entire body was ablaze, a raging fireball with at its centre something that looked vaguely like the outline of a human form.

For a moment Flin stood rooted to the spot, too shocked to move. 'Charlie!' he thought he heard her scream. 'Oh my Charlie!' Then, as spear-like streaks of light erupted from the top of the Benben, piercing the supposedly im-penetrable glass of the isolation chamber and punching right through the ceiling of the room, vaporizing everything in its path, he spun and ran for his life.

Outside the disintegration of the oasis had progressed faster than he had feared. Much faster. The cliffs were now locked tight around the rock platform, contorting and crush-ing it, towering above him like a pair of converging juggernauts. The temple buildings were starting to fold in on themselves, columns and pylons and walls and roofs swaying, buckling and slowly toppling in an avalanche of dust and debris. Any hope he might have had of getting out the way he had come in, or else through some gateway in the side of the temple, evaporated. With no other option open to him he wheeled and made for the back of the com-plex, praying there would be a rear exit through which he could escape.

Swerving and side-stepping to avoid the masonry crash-ing down all around, a wave of collapsing stone seeming to snap at his heels, he sprinted through a further succession of courtyards and hypostyle halls. The complex went on and on and he was starting to wonder if he would ever find the end of it when he emerged into yet another courtyard. In front of him rose a wall, fifteen metres high and made of solid stone blocks. Without gate or opening, and with similar walls hemming him in to left and right: he realized he'd brought himself into a giant cul-de-sac. He was trapped.

He screamed in frustration, running up to the wall and slapping his hands despairingly against it, knowing that this was it, there was no way he was going to be able to back-track, not through all the chaos behind him.

'You bastard!' he bellowed, slapping again, and again. 'You stupid fuck . . .'

The ground beneath him gave a particularly violent heave and, as if it were made of nothing more solid than children's play bricks, the wall simply disappeared, lurching away from him and out of sight down the incline at the rear of the temple platform. Through a swirling veil of dust, the top end of the oasis came into view directly ahead – a rear-ing cliff of vertical rock along whose face the gorge's side walls were slowly creeping. The sun hovered above it, a ball of fiery red.

Stunned, Flin clambered over the remains of the wall's lower courses and started down through the trees beyond. A pair of kneeling figures were just visible far ahead at the base of the cliff. They seemed to be examining something on the ground.

'What the hell are you doing!' he yelled at them. 'Climb! Start climbing!'

His voice was barely audible to himself, let alone anyone else. He could do nothing but charge on downwards, weaving his way through the collapsed blocks of masonry, the oasis closing around him, another bolt of fiery light erupting from the Benben behind.

The moment Flin had disappeared up the steps towards the front of the temple, Zahir had beckoned Freya and his brother forward, leading them around the foot of the rock platform and on through the trees to the top end of the oasis – a vertical, 200-metre precipice that connected the sides of the gorge like the base of a triangle. When Freya had first entered the wadi earlier in the day – Christ, it seemed like a lifetime ago; a dozen lifetimes – its upper end had appeared to be 400 or even 500 metres across. Now it was only half that, and closing.

'How long do you think we've got?' she cried.

Zahir held up a hand, spreading his fingers, and opened and shut it four times.

'But it's not possible! How are we going to get up there in twenty minutes? I'm a professional climber and I couldn't do it in under two hours!'

Zahir just sprinted on towards the cliff. The trees around them gradually thinned and then dropped away altogether, leaving them running across clear ground. To left and right the sides of the gorge were now clearly visible, surging waves of dust churning along at their base as they steam-rollered mercilessly forward. Ahead, blocking out the sun, carpeting the valley floor in deep shade, rose the cliff face they had to climb. A towering expanse of alarmingly blank, smooth-looking stone, its only noticeable feature – apart from very occasional ledges and cracks and protrusions – was some sort of meandering seam that ran right up the middle of it. Initially Freya assumed this was just a vein of slightly different coloured rock cutting through the limestone. Either that or a thin arête standing proud of the otherwise flat cliff surface. Only as they came closer did she see that it was neither of these – that it was not a natural feature at all, but an enormous ladder. Or rather a whole series of ladders. Wooden, rickety-looking, their rungs held fast by rope lashings, they ascended the rock wall from base to summit like a procession of giant centipedes, picking out a zigzagging route from ledge to ledge, crack to crack, protrusion to protrusion, using whatever natural anchors were available to work their way upwards, connecting earth with sky. Freya stared in wonder.

'The ladder of Nut,' she murmured, recalling the inscription she and Flin had found back in Abydos.

'Very strong,' said Zahir, coming up to the base of the cliff and giving the bottommost of the ladders a hard yank, demonstrating how its frame had been secured to bronze spikes driven deep into the bare rock. 'My family use many hundred year. We fix. We keep good. Long climb, but safe climb. Now go!'

He stood away from the ladder and waved Freya onto it, jabbing a thumb upwards, indicating that she should start ascending.

'What about you?'

'I wait *sais* Brodie. We climb together. Go, go.'

She tried to argue, but he was having none of it – 'I climb

fast,' he insisted, 'like monkey' – and so she did as he said. Stepping onto the ladder, she began her ascent. Zahir's brother followed on behind, his rifle slung over his shoulder, the two of them clambering upwards from rung to rung, steadily pulling themselves away from the valley floor. The cliff face trembled and shivered like the flank of some distressed animal, but the ladders held firm and as she grew more confident in their strength Freya moved faster, the figure of Zahir falling away below, more and more of the gorge coming into view behind. More and more chaos and destruction.

She'd ascended about twenty metres, the length of four ladders, straight up, and was just starting on the fifth set of steps when the cliff gave a violent lurch. On the periphery of her vision, she caught movement above. Years of climbing experience had sharpened her reactions and instinctively she pressed herself flat against the ladder, jamming her head between two of the rungs so as to give it as much protection as possible. A shower of small rocks and pebbles clattered down onto her shoulders followed by three or four much larger chunks of stone which missed her by what felt like centimetres. She remained motionless, clamped to the ladder, waiting to see if the rock fall would continue. Aside from a few more sprays of gravel, that appeared to be it. Cautiously, she eased herself backwards, looking first up and then down.

'You OK?' she shouted to Said, who was a few metres below her.

He raised a hand to show he was unharmed. She started to look away, ready to resume the climb, then jerked round again, leaning further out from the cliff, eyes zeroing in on the ground below.

'Oh no! Oh please God no!'

Said must have seen what she had seen because he had already started back down the ladder, waving at her to continue climbing. She ignored him, following him down, scrambling as fast as she could. The roar of the cliffs, the trembling of the rock face, the collapse of the oasis – everything receded as her entire world narrowed to the small patch of ground beneath, where Zahir lay prone beneath a car-bonnet-sized slab of rock.

She came to within a few metres of the valley floor and jumped. Slamming onto the sand, she scrabbled her way over to Said who was kneeling beside his brother. He was pinioned from the chest down, alive, but only just. His fingers clawed weakly at the top of the rock and a thin trickle of blood crept from the corner of his mouth.

'We've got to get it off him,' Freya cried, forcing her hands underneath the slab, straining to lift it.

Said just knelt there, stroking his brother's forehead, his face set and expressionless. Only his eyes registered any emotion, gave any hint of the torment he must have felt to see his brother crushed and trapped like that.

'Help me, Said,' Freya groaned. 'Please, we've got to get it off him. We have to get him out.'

It was futile and she knew it, had known from the moment she'd first seen what had happened. The slab was far too heavy, and even if by some miracle they *did* manage to move it there was no way they were going to get Zahir up 200 metres of vertical cliff and out of the oasis, not with the sort of injuries he'd be carrying. Despite that she continued to heave at the stone, her eyes blurring with tears, until eventually Zahir's hand crept across the surface of the rock and, clasping hers, moved it away. His head shook slightly as if to say: 'It's no use. Don't waste your energy.'

'Oh God, Zahir,' she choked.

He gave her hand a feeble squeeze and, rolling his eyes, looked up at his brother, spoke to him in Arabic, his voice a barely audible rasp, bubbles of mucousy blood popping from his nostrils. Although she couldn't understand what he was saying, Freya caught the word 'Mohsen' – his son's name – repeated several times and knew instinctively that he was making final arrangements, entrusting his family to Said's care.

'Oh God, Zahir,' she repeated helplessly, holding his hand in hers, stroking it. Tears were now rolling down her face – tears of impotence, of sorrow, of guilt at all the doubts she had had about him, all the bad things she had thought and said, when all along he had been a good man, an honest man. A man who had given his life to save hers. She had wronged him, just as she had wronged her sister. And just as she had failed to help Alex in her hour of need, it seemed to her now that she was failing Zahir too, so that all she could do was to stroke his hand, and sob, and hate herself for the damage she always seemed to cause to those who did the most to help her.

Why do I always get it so wrong? she thought. *And why is it always the good people who end up paying for my mistakes?*

Zahir seemed to understand what was going through her mind because his head came up slightly.

'Is OK, Miss Freya,' he said, his voice now no more than a faltering croak. 'You my good friend.'

'I'm sorry, Zahir,' she cried. 'We'll get you out. I promise we'll get you out.'

She started yanking at the rock again. Not because she thought she had any chance of moving it, but because it was so unbearable to do nothing, simply watch as his life slowly trickled away in front of her. Again Zahir shook his head and pushed her hand aside, mumbling something as he did so. His voice was too weak, the background noise too over-whelming for her to catch what he was saying. She bent right down, bringing her ear within an inch of his bloodied mouth.

'She happy.'

'What?'

His hand tightened around hers.

'She happy,' he repeated, an urgency to his voice, as if he was channelling what small reserves of energy he still possessed into making himself heard and understood. 'She very happy.'

'Who, Zahir? Who's happy?'

'Doctor Alex,' he croaked. 'Doctor Alex very happy.'

He's delirious, she thought, *drifting into some imaginary twilight world between life and death*. Zahir tightened his grip further as if to show her that this was not the case, that he knew exactly what he was saying. Around them the oasis seemed momentarily to fall still and silent, although whether it was really happening or her senses were simply so focused on the figure lying beside her that everything else had been shunted away beyond the margins of consciousness Freya couldn't tell.

'I don't understand,' she pleaded. 'What do you mean Alex is happy?'

'In Dakhla,' he wheezed, seeking out her eyes, holding them, trying to explain. 'You ask if Doctor Alex happy. When you come first day. You ask if she happy?'

Freya's mind spun back, through all the turmoil of recent events, to that first morning in Dakhla, before any of this had started. Zahir had taken her to his house for tea, she had gone into the wrong room, found the picture of Alex on the wall, he had surprised her.

'Was she happy?' she had asked him. 'At the end. Was my sister happy?'

'She very happy,' whispered Zahir, fighting to get the words out. 'We bring her here. To oasis. When she ill. We use rope, carry her down, she see with own eyes.' Despite the agony he must have been in, he smiled. 'She very happy. She happiest person in world.'

And now Freya's mind was spinning again, something pulling at it, some vague memory, some connection demanding to be made. Her thoughts whirred and tumbled before suddenly Alex's voice echoed inside her head, as clear and strong as if her sister had been standing right there beside her. The words she had written to Freya in that last letter, the one she had sent just before her death:

Do you remember that story Dad used to tell? About how the moon was actually a door, and if you climbed up there and opened it you could pass right through the sky into another world? Do you remember how we used to dream of what it was like, that secret world – a beautiful, magic place full of flowers and waterfalls and birds that could talk? I can't explain it, Freya, not clearly, but just recently I've looked through that door and glimpsed the other side, and it's just as magical as we ever imagined it. Somewhere, little

PAUL SUSSMAN

sis, there's always a door, and beyond it a light, however dark things might appear.

And Freya realized that this was what Alex had been talking about all along: not some abstract recollection of a shared childhood fantasy, but something real, something tangible – her visit to the oasis with Zahir. Her last great journey. And while the pain of her sister's murder remained as intense as ever, beside it there was now something else, a glimmer of light. For she knew how much joy it would have brought Alex to see this place, how excited she would have been by it, how very happy and fulfilled it would have made her in her final days. As Alex herself had put it: *When you've seen that secret world you can't help but feel hope.*

'Thank you, Zahir,' she sobbed, clasping his hand, stroking his forehead, barely noticing as the thundering roar of shifting rock started up again around them. 'Thank you for helping her. Thank you for everything.'

A pause, then:

'You are as great a Bedouin as your ancestor Mohammed Wald Yusuf Ibrahim Sabri al-Rashaayda.'

How she remembered the name she had no idea, but his smile widened, the expression barely visible beneath the surgeon's mask of blood that now covered the lower part of his face. He squeezed her hand again, his strength spent, his eyes starting to dim. With a final effort of will, he pulled his hand free and started pawing at his *djellaba*, slowly dragging the material out from beneath the rock until he had found its pocket. He fumbled inside and removed something, pressing it into Freya's palm. It was a green metal compass, chipped and heavily used, with a folding lid and a brass sighting wire on top. She knew immediately that it was her sister's, the one she had taken with her on her rambles around Markham County, that had once belonged to a marine in the battle of Iwo Jima.

'Doctor Alex give me,' Zahir whispered. 'Before she die. Now belong you.'

Freya gazed down at it, oblivious to the raging of the oasis around them. Flipping open the compass's lid, she saw a pair of initials scraped into the metal on its underside: AH. Alexandra Hannen. She smiled and looked back at Zahir, started to thank him again, but in the few seconds her attention had been away his head had dropped to one side and his breathing had stopped.

'He go,' said Said simply. Reaching out, he smoothed his hand across his brother's face, closing his eyes.

'Oh Zahir,' choked Freya.

For a moment they just knelt there, the ground quaking beneath them, the gorge walls lurching ever closer together, what looked like bolts of crimson lightning erupting from the top of the temple platform. Then, standing, Said motioned her back towards the cliff.

'But we can't just leave him,' Freya pleaded. 'Not like this.'

'He safe. He happy. This good place for Bedouin.'

Still she remained where she was, forcing Said to lean down and take her arm and pull her to her feet.

'My brother come here help you. He no want you die. Please, come, climb. For him.'

Freya couldn't argue with that and after gazing at Zahir's broken body for a few seconds longer, she turned and hurried back to the base of the cliff. Said had already leapt onto the bottommost ladder and was swarming up ahead of her.

'I go first,' he shouted. 'Make sure is no broken.'

'What about Flin?' she yelled up at him.

He leant out and pointed back across the stretch of open ground in front of the cliff. The Englishman was running towards them, waving his arms madly, urging them to get climbing.

'You follow me,' Said shouted. 'OK?'

'OK,' she called.

The Egyptian nodded, turned and started up the ladder, moving with feline speed and agility, his feet and hands barely seeming to make contact with each rung as he flew upwards. Freya hovered a few moments longer, not wanting to leave Flin too far behind. Then, with a final glance back at Zahir's body and a murmured 'Allez', she grasped the ladder and started to climb.

All the way down from the temple platform Flin had been bellowing at the figures below, yelling at them to get moving, unable to understand why they were just kneeling there. It was only as he came up to the base of the cliff and saw Zahir's body pinioned beneath the rock that the reason became apparent. He slowed to a halt, looking down and shaking his head, feeling many of the same things Freya had felt – sadness, helplessness, guilt at the way he had spoken to Zahir in his home in Dakhla. There was no time for proper contemplation nor to pay his respects in the way he would have liked. Dropping to one knee, he touched a hand to Zahir's forehead and murmured a traditional Bedouin farewell. Then, jumping up again, he sprang over to the cliff and started to climb. The gorge's walls were now less than 150 metres apart, the air filling with surging wafts of dust and grit, the oasis growing steadily darker.

Already some way behind the other two, he pushed on as fast as he could, trying to make up some of the intervening distance, the ground dropping away below him, the ladders creaking and groaning with his weight. Every now and then Freya would stop and lean out, looking down. He waved her on and continued climbing, trying to ignore the approaching cliffs and the trembling of the rock face and the burning in his lungs and arms and legs, to focus all his energies on just keeping moving.

For the first thirty or so metres the ladders ascended in a perfect vertical line, one directly above the other, and he made rapid progress. Then, at the top of the eighth ladder, the line suddenly stopped dead. A horizontal rope led away to his left, taking him along a narrow ledge – not much more than the width of a cigarette packet – to the base of a second set of ladders. This climbed for a further fifteen metres before also coming to a halt, another rope taking him along another, even narrower ledge – this time towards the right – and onto another brief run of steps. Which is how it went on, the ladder trail now zigzagging its way back and forth across the cliff face. At no point did it ascend more than three or four ladder-lengths at a time before breaking off and recommencing in a different place, the gap between each run of steps traversed by heart-stopping, rope-assisted shuffles along ledges and cracks.

Why the ancient Egyptians had arranged the whole thing in this way, staggering the ladders rather than allowing them to climb in an unbroken vertical, Flin had no idea. Probably because they were having to work around stretches of bad rock, he guessed, where their bronze anchoring spikes couldn't get a proper hold. Whatever the case – and he didn't give it more than the most fleeting of thoughts – his upward progress was dramatically slowed as he was forced into a succession of diversions to left and right, edging his way nervously from one set of ladders to the next.

Behind him the implosion of the oasis appeared to be gathering pace. The temple platform was now nothing more than a crumbling, dust-shrouded wedge of rock, the magnificent buildings a jumbled heap of ruins from the midst of which the Benben continued to emit spectacular, laser-like shafts of crimson lightning. The scene was apocalyptic, like some medieval artist's depiction of Hell. It barely registered with him, so intent was he on working his way back and forth across the cliff, his hands and feet slipping and sliding as he drove himself on ever faster, taking more and more risks in his desperation to keep ahead of the walls closing in to either side.

Once he slipped while manoeuvring along a rope-line between ladders, dangling for a moment with a hundred metres of empty space looming vertiginously beneath him before he managed to regain his footing and scramble along to the next set of steps. On another occasion one of the ancient ladder rungs snapped, the splintered wood slicing a deep gash in his calf, causing him to howl in agony, blood streaming down his leg and into his boot.

He almost gave up hope, convinced there was no way he was going to make it; that the gorge's jaws would snap shut around him before he could reach the top and clamber out to safety. He kept moving nonetheless, refusing to be beaten, zoning out the pain and the exhaustion and the throttling sense of vertigo, summoning every last vestige of strength to push himself on. The valley floor dropped ever further behind him – now completely lost in a fog of debris – the summit of the cliff drew closer above, and eventually despair gave way to hope as he traversed a final short ledge and there above him was a straight run of five ladders taking him directly up to the top.

Freya and Said had been hanging back on the upper part of the climb, not wanting to leave him too far behind. Now they were just below the summit, shouting and gesticulating, encouraging him onwards. He shouted back at them, telling them to get the hell out, and after a brief pause to drag some oxygen into his aching lungs, started on his final ascent. The walls of the gorge were now claustrophobically close. He covered the first of the five ladders, every muscle in his body screaming out in protest. Then the second ladder; the third. He was halfway up the fourth, just five metres from the summit, an excited surge of adrenalin sweeping through him as he realized he was almost home and dry, Freya's screams of encouragement now clearly audible from above, when a jarring tremor ran through the cliff face. Locking his arms around the ladder, Flin waited for it to pass so that he could begin climbing again. As he did he felt the ladder lurch beneath him as first one and then another of the pinions holding its upper end to the rock face started to work free from their housings. He stopped, the steps settled, he moved up another couple of rungs, the ladder lurched again. Now he could see the bronze spikes slipping, inching their way out of the stone, the top of the ladder moving with them, pulling slowly away from the wall. He scrambled, but it was hopeless. As he clawed desperately for the bottom rung of the next ladder up, the pinions came completely free and there was no longer anything to hold the steps in place. For a brief, surreal moment everything seemed to stand still and he had the curious impression he was in one of those old silent movies where Harold Lloyd or Buster Keaton engage in gravity-defying stunts high above the earth. Then, with a sickening sway, the top of the ladder arced backwards and away from the wall and he was falling helplessly through space, hands still gripping the wooden rung, a hysterical scream ringing out above him.

Freya should have known by now that the moment it looked as if things were going to work out OK, something would invariably happen to ensure that they didn't.

As soon as she and Said had topped out – clambering their way onto the flat ground at the head of the cliff – she had swung round and looked down to check on Flin's progress. The gorge had now narrowed to little more than the width of two tennis courts, its floor no longer visible, nothing visible save for the brilliant, burning ember of the Benben as it continued to shoot streaks of fierce red lightning up through the dust clouds into the sky above. In any other circumstances she would have been transfixed by what she saw, by the sheer impossibility of it. But her eyes were locked on Flin, watching intently as he worked his way up the final run of ladders, her confidence rising with each step he took.

'Keep going!' she yelled, hope surging within her as she realized he would be OK. 'You're going to do it! You're almost there! Keep going!'

Even as she shouted the ground beneath her feet had given a sudden, jarring lurch and the ladder Flin was climbing – Christ, he was so near, just a few metres off the summit! – started to pull backwards away from the cliff face. For a few brief, heart-stopping moments it had looked as if he might still be able to scrabble his way to safety. But then the pinions holding the top of the ladder *in situ* popped from the wall and the whole thing had toppled backwards, taking Flin with it.

'No!' she had screamed, burying her face in her hands. 'Oh God no.'

She was distraught, shattered, unable to believe that after everything they had been through these last few days, all the dangers they had faced and overcome, it should end like this, at the very final hurdle. So distraught and shattered that when, a few moments later, she caught a distant cry of 'Hello!' she dismissed it as a shock-induced trick of the imagination. Only when the cry came again, more insistent this time, percolating upwards through the reverberating crash of shunting rock, and at the same moment Said grasped her shoulder, did she realize that it wasn't her mind playing games. She snatched her hands away from her face and looked over the edge of the precipice.

'Flin! Flin!'

He was standing below her, about ten metres down,

clinging to a ladder while another – the one that had fallen away from the cliff – now dangled limply beside it like a shattered arm. She saw immediately what had happened: while the spikes securing the top of the upper ladder had failed, those holding its bottom end – or at least one of them – had somehow held firm in the rock, the steps performing a sort of twisting back flip and slamming into the cliff face below.

By some miracle the impact hadn't knocked Flin loose and he had managed to clamber onto the relative safety of the lower ladder. Freya felt a euphoric rush of joy and relief. It lasted perhaps a couple of seconds, then evaporated as the full picture started to come home to her. He was alive, but certainly wasn't going to be for much longer.

It wasn't simply that the gorge walls were getting nearer by the second, pressing in on him like a gigantic pair of hands about to crush a fly. There should still have been just about enough time for him to climb out of the oasis. The problem was he had nothing to climb up. Between the top of the ladder on which Flin was perched and the bottom of the one that would bring him up to the cliff's summit there were now five metres of empty space. For a brief moment she thought they might be able to get the fallen ladder back in position to bridge the gap, but as she watched the last remaining spike slid out of the cliff face and the ladder plummeted away into the maelstrom beneath.

'Shit,' she hissed.

There was a pause, all of them standing frozen, no one knowing what to do. Flin shook his head as if to say: 'It's no good, there's no way up,' whatever slim chance he might have had growing slimmer with each passing second. Then, knowing it was futile, but also that she at least had to make some attempt to help him, Freya swung herself onto the topmost ladder and started back down into the gorge. Said tried to stop her, insisted he should be the one to go, but she knew that she stood the best chance. Shrugging away his hand, she continued her descent.

Even the most experienced climber feels fear, and Freya was no exception. Sometimes it is low-level, nothing more than a speeding of the heart or a tingling in the gut. Other times it can be more intense, your entire being seeming to recoil and shrivel as you teeter on the brink of your own mortality. Freya had known both extremes and most things in between. But never, ever had she been as frightened as she was now, the ladder jolting beneath her, the approaching cliffs swamping her peripheral vision. Somehow she managed to keep the fear at bay, stowing it in the farthest corner of her consciousness and pushing herself downwards, moving from rung to rung until she had reached the foot of the ladder.

'Don't be fucking ridiculous!' Flin was bellowing, waving her away. 'Go back! Go on, get out!'

She ignored him. Bouncing a couple of times to ensure the ladder was still secure, she hooked a leg through its bottom rung, grasped the next but one rung above and leant out, hanging practically upside down, reaching towards him. Still yelling at her to get away, Flin mirrored the movement, climbing almost to the top of his ladder and extending his hand towards hers. Even at their fullest and most desperate stretch there was still the best part of a metre between their fingertips. They tried again, and again, giving it everything they could, adjusting their positions, elongating their arms until it felt as if the tendons were going to snap, but it was no use and finally they were forced to admit defeat. Flin descended a few rungs, Freya pulled herself upright again.

'There's nothing you can do,' he yelled, glancing to left and right. The advancing rock walls were now at the outer limits of the ladder trail, the wooden steps starting to snap and shatter as a million tons of solid stone slowly ground over them. 'Please, Freya, it's over. Just get out. Save yourself. Go! Please go!'

Again she ignored him, leaning back out and examining the rock face below, trying to see if there was any way of getting closer to him, of bridging that extra metre of space.

There was a clear foothold just beneath her, a jagged hole ripped in the stone when the pinion securing the top of the missing ladder had torn itself free. If she could ease herself down onto that, keep a grip on the bottom rung of her ladder, that would bring her a bit nearer, give her some extra reach.

It still wasn't enough. Frantically she scanned back and forth, searching for something – anything – that might help. A horizontal crack ran across the rock face about two metres above Flin's ladder, just about sufficient to provide a secure finger-hold. Even if he managed to get himself up there, that still left at least twenty centimetres between the crack and the very farthest she could stretch her hand towards him. She howled in frustration. It might as well have been a kilometre. There was no way they were going to make it.

'I'm sorry,' she cried. 'I'm so sorry. I just can't . . .'

She broke off as something caught her eye. Above Flin and a little to his left: a thin flake of what looked like flint protruding a couple of centimetres from the cliff, exactly the same colour as the surrounding stone which is why she hadn't spotted it before. Maybe, just maybe . . .

'Listen,' she cried, struggling to make herself heard above the roar of pulverizing rock. 'You have to do exactly as I tell you. No questions, no arguments, just do it!'

'For Christ's sake, Freya!'

'No arguments!'

'You're wasting—'

'Just do it!'

He gave an exasperated wave of the arm, then nodded.

'You have to get yourself up to that crack,' she called, lowering her foot into the hole the pinion had torn, grasping the bottom rung of her ladder and leaning down. 'You understand? You've got to get your fingers into that crack.'

'There's no way . . .'

'Do it!'

Glaring at her, muttering, Flin started to climb. He got himself onto the fourth rung from the top of his ladder, then the third, then the second, reaching his arms out, pressing his body flat against the stone, hugging it, sliding his way up the cliff face inch by inch.

'I'm going to fall!' he bellowed.

'You're going to fall anyway in a minute. Keep going!'

He remained where he was, cheek pressed hard against the rock face, wincing, eyes closed, seemingly unable to go any further. Then, with a supreme effort of will and a roar of 'Bollocks!' he forced himself up onto the top rung of the ladder and clawed towards the fissure, stretching, straining, wobbling. For a split second it looked like he wasn't going to make it, was going to lose his balance and fall. Then his hand made contact with the crack and he was able to force his fingers inside, clinging to it for dear life while his feet balanced unsteadily on the ladder rung as though on a tightrope. Exhausted, dust-covered, terrified, Freya gave an ecstatic whoop.

'Now for the hard part,' she called.

'You have to be fucking joking!'

She ran through it with him, throwing constant glances to left and right as the gorge walls came to within ten metres of each other. He had to get his foot up onto the protruding rim of flint, she explained, and use that to lever himself up towards her outstretched hand. The manoeuvre she'd used back in the temple at Abydos had been crazy, but this was something else. And he wasn't even a professional climber. There was no other option. It was either this or wait for the walls to knock him off, which they would in the next couple of minutes. Making sure he knew what he had to do, she adjusted her position and reached out an arm ready to catch him, stretching as far as she could.

'Flin, you've only got one shot at this,' she yelled. 'So make sure you do it right.'

'Well I wasn't bloody planning on doing it wrong!'

Despite herself she smiled.

'In your own time,' she called. 'Just make sure it's soon.'

Rolling his eyes up towards her and then back down to fix the position of the flint, he mumbled a prayer even though he hadn't seen the inside of a church for the best part of two decades and hoisted his foot onto the protrusion. A deep breath and he drove himself upwards, unleashing a wild, guttural yell as he released his grip on the crack and flung his hand towards Freya's. She caught it, her palm clamping around his, his other hand coming up and seizing her wrist, his body swinging back and forth like a clock pendulum, feet scrabbling on the cliff face. He was heavy, much heavier than she remembered from Abydos, and she could feel her grip on the ladder rung starting to slip, her shoulder to crack as though her entire arm was going to be ripped away. Somehow she managed to hold on as his feet flailed and after what seemed like hours but must have been only a matter of seconds he managed to jam first one toe and then the other into the rock crevice. Coming up straight, he steadied himself, taking most of the weight off her arm.

'Climb up me!' she cried. 'Use your feet, get yourself up to the ladder. Come on, there's no time!'

He started to do as she said, then stopped, teetering there on the rock face, one hand gripping hers, the other clasped around her forearm, his toes wedged into the crack, the gorge now only six or seven metres wide. Dust spewed up from below, wafting around them.

'There's no time!' she cried, coughing. 'Come on, Flin, climb up me. You've done the hard part.'

All his furious energy of a few moments earlier seemed to have vanished. He just clung there staring up at her, eyes glued to hers, a curious expression on his face – part anxiety, part determination.

'Come on!' she screamed. 'What's wrong with you? We've got to get out! There's no—'

'It was me,' he shouted.

'What?'

'It was me, Freya. I killed Alex.'

She froze, her windpipe tightening as though she was being throttled.

613

'It was me who injected her. Molly and Girgis had nothing to do with it. It was me, Freya. I killed her.'

Her mouth was opening and closing, no words coming out.

'I didn't want to,' he cried. 'Please believe me: it was the last thing on God's earth I wanted to do. But she begged me. Pleaded. She'd lost her legs, her arm, her sight was failing, her hearing – she knew it was only going to get worse, wanted to at least have some control. I couldn't refuse her. Please try to understand. It broke my heart but I couldn't refuse her.'

The gorge walls were now less than four metres apart, towering shadows looming through the dust clouds. Neither of them even noticed. Freya hung from the ladder clasping his hand, Flin balanced on the crevice clutching her arm, both oblivious to everything around them, both locked together in a dimension of their own.

'She said she loved you.' His voice was hoarse, barely audible. 'They were her last words. We sat out on her veranda, we watched the sunset, I injected her with morphine, I held her hand. And just as she went she said your name. Said she loved you. I couldn't *not* tell you, Freya. Do you see that? I couldn't *not* tell you. She loved you so much.'

He held her gaze, his eyes bright. Thoughts tumbled through Freya's head, emotions pulled at her. Everything seemed to spin and convulse as if her inner world had come to reflect the wider chaos all around. At the heart of it, however, holding firm amidst the rush of shock and pain and grief, was a single solid kernel of certainty: she would have done exactly the same if Alex had asked her. And she also knew – from the look in his eyes, the tone of his voice, everything she had seen and learnt of him these last few days – that Flin had done what he had done out of kindness, out of compassion, out of love for her sister, and she could neither blame nor condemn him for it. On the contrary, in a curious way she felt in his debt. He had taken that burden onto himself. He had been there for Alex in her hour of need when she, her own sister, so palpably hadn't.

All of this flashed through Freya's mind in a matter of seconds, time seeming to slow and expand to accommodate her thoughts. Then, with a nod, she squeezed his hand as if to say: 'I understand. Now let's get the hell out of here,' and started to drag him up the cliff towards her. For a moment his face came right up against hers and their eyes met, both of them giving a faint smile of understanding, hardly visible through the choking curtain of grit. And then he was clambering up and over her and onto the bottom of the ladder, the sides of the gorge now practically touching them.

'Go!' she screamed. 'Keep going!'

'You first!'

'Don't be so fucking English! Go! I'm right behind.'

She swung her free arm and gave him a hard slap on the backside to get him moving. Once he was on his way, she pulled herself back onto the ladder and followed him up, climbing as fast as she could, her hands hitting each successive rung just as Flin's feet left it, the steps trembling so fiercely she didn't know how they could possibly stay attached to the rock face. The dust began to clear slightly and she caught a glimpse of Said above, leaning down with his arm outstretched, waving them on. They drove themselves towards him, coughing and choking, the walls clamping ever tighter around them, now barely a metre and a half from each other. Up and up until finally Flin reached the top and Said grabbed his T-shirt and dragged him out. Freya was right behind. As the cliffs touched her shoulders and the sides of the ladder, the steps starting to warp and buckle beneath her feet, the wood to crack and splinter, she found herself seized beneath the armpits and hoisted up into the clean, clear, wonderfully open air on top of the Gilf.

Gasping for breath, they all backed away, watching as the last few centimetres of the gorge closed up. What less than an hour ago had been a broad valley filled with trees and buildings and waterfalls was now reduced to a cleft little more than forty centimetres across, slashes of red light still streaking upwards from deep within it. Now it was just thirty, now twenty, now ten, the crash of grinding rock diminishing all the time, giving way to a low grating rumble.

Even as the gorge sealed itself, there was one final dramatic encore. From deep within the ground there echoed a booming roar – a lion with stone lungs was how Freya would later describe it – and a brilliant blade of crimson light erupted from the last of the crack, the force of it throwing them backwards, slamming them to the ground.

'Don't look at it,' cried Flin, grasping Freya's shoulder and rolling her over, pressing her face into the sand. 'Close your eyes! Both of you!'

Previously the lightning bolts had come and gone, flaring briefly before fading again, like shooting stars. This time the light endured, a gargantuan scalpel of fire that climbed and expanded, slowly forcing the walls of the gorge apart again as it formed into a towering obelisk of flame. It stood there, swaying slightly, the roar growing ever louder, Freya experiencing the curious sensation of being burnt without actually feeling any pain or discomfort. Then, as if it had proved its point, the light receded, withdrawing into the ground like a dying flame. There came one last stony growl and with that the gorge slammed shut and this time it remained closed. Silence.

For a moment Freya lay there, then blinked her eyes open. She saw orange and thought for a confused instant that her retina had been damaged before realizing she was looking into the face of a flower: a delicate orange bloom that had somehow found purchase amid the barrenness all around.

The enclosed flower is a Sahara Orchid. It is, I am told, very rare. Treasure it, and think of me.

She smiled and, reaching out, clasped Flin's hand, knowing it was all going to be OK.

Later, once they had got back to their feet, and brushed themselves down, and gulped in the clean air, and spent a while vainly searching for any trace of the Hidden Oasis, the three of them started walking across the top of the Gilf Kebir, Said leading.

The sun, inexplicably, seemed to have shifted backwards in the sky. When they had fled the gorge it had been well down in the west. Now it was almost directly overhead, bringing it back into synch with Flin's watch, which read 2.16 p.m. They had been inside the oasis for only six hours. It felt like a lifetime.

They trooped towards the north, then turned into a narrow, sand-clogged gully that sloped away eastwards, carrying them gently back down onto the surface of the desert.

'Very safe,' said Said, slapping his hands against the rock walls to either side. 'No close shut.'

'I'm extremely pleased to hear it,' said Flin.

At the bottom end the gully opened out into a small bay in the Gilf's eastern face, where Zahir's Land Cruiser stood parked in the shade beneath a low, umbrella-like overhang. They shared water, and talked about Zahir, and Said produced a first aid box and patched up Flin's various cuts and wounds – 'No be woman,' he muttered disapprovingly as the Englishman groaned and winced. Then they climbed into the 4x4 and set off into the desert, following the cliff-line south, back towards the rock tower and the doorway in the sand.

Except that neither was there any more. They found the microlight easily enough, a garish pink blob that stuck out from the surrounding desert like a paint-spot on a bare sheet of paper. But the curving sickle of black stone had collapsed and broken into pieces, all that was left of it a featureless scatter of glassy rock that gave no hint of its former shape. And where the Mouth of Osiris should have been there was nothing, just flat, empty sand, perfectly level, perfectly blank. Even the rectangular opening in the rock face had gone, that particular portion of cliff seeming to have disintegrated and slid away, reduced to a jumbled heap of boulders piled up at the base of the wall. The only thing they found, the one indication that anything unusual had happened here was a thin triangle of metal that protruded above the sand like a small black fin. It took them a moment to realize that it was the tip of a helicopter rotor blade. Not far away lay a pair of mirrored sunglasses, one of the lenses cracked.

'It's like it was all a dream,' murmured Freya.

'I can assure you it wasn't,' grunted Flin, touching a hand to his cut lip.

'No be woman,' muttered Said.

They drove back out to the microlight, Said waiting in the 4x4 while Flin climbed into the pod and checked the engine. It seemed to be working fine and, leaving it to idle, he climbed out and walked back to the Land Cruiser. Freya stood beside him.

'Are you sure you'll be OK, Said?' Flin asked, leaning down to the open driver window. 'It's a long way back to Dakhla.'

'I Bedouin. This desert. Of course OK. Stupid question.'

It was barely noticeable, no more than the faintest twitch of the lips, but he was definitely smiling. Freya reached in and touched his arm.

'Thank you,' she said. 'It sounds so inadequate after everything you and your brother have done for me. For both of us. But thank you.'

Said just gave a slight nod of the head and, leaning forward, turned the ignition key and engaged the gears, gunning the engine.

'When you come in Dakhla you come my house,' he said, looking up at her. 'You drink tea. Yes?'

'I'd love to come to your house and drink tea,' said Freya. 'It would be an honour.'

He gave another nod, raised a hand in farewell and

moved off across the sands, tooting the horn as he gained speed. They watched him go, staring after him until the vehicle was no more than a distant white smudge bobbing its way across the dunes, then turned and walked back to the microlight. Flin bent down and picked up a small lump of what had once been the curving rock tower.

'Souvenir,' he said, handing it to Freya. 'A little keepsake of your first visit to Egypt.'

She laughed.

'I'll treasure it.'

They refilled Miss Piggy's tank, donned their helmets, climbed into the pod and rode out onto the sand flat on which they'd landed the previous night. Flin ran them back and forth for a while to get the oil temperature up, then increased the revs, eased the control bar forward and lifted them into the air, circling and gaining height. The Gilf's eastern face reared to one side; an endless sea of yellow desert stretched off to the other.

'I'd offer to show you some of the sights,' came his voice through the intercom. 'Jebel Uweinat, the Cave of the Swimmers. But in the circumstances I expect you just want to get back, get cleaned up and get straight into bed.'

There was a pause, then his shoulders tensed.

'I'm sorry, I didn't mean . . .'

He craned round towards her, flustered suddenly, embarrassed. Freya just smiled, winked and dropped her head to the side, gazing down at the desert below.

They flew over the area where the oasis must once have been, nothing there save rock and gravel and the odd stunted bush. And, also, birds. Hundreds upon hundred of birds diving and wheeling and swooping as if searching for something. Flin did a couple of circuits, then banked the microlight and took them towards the north-east, the Sahara rolling away all around – immense and majestic and indescribably beautiful. They flew in silence for a while, then Freya reached out and laid a hand on Flin's shoulder.

'Can we talk about Alex?' she asked.

He took her hand in his.

'I'd love to talk about Alex.'

Which is what they did, the Gilf Kebir slowly dropping away behind them, a new horizon opening up ahead.

The drone of the microlight had faded and disappeared. The birds too had moved off to the north, seeking out new homes in the other wadis further up the Gilf. The desert was wholly still and wholly silent, and wholly empty. Nothing but sun, sky, sand, rock and, down at the base of the cliffs, lounging in the shade thrown by a tumble of newly fallen boulders, a small dappled dune gecko, its eyes rolling lazily, its tongue flicking in and out. Even that scuttled away when a patch of sand in front of it began to tremble. Barely noticeable at first, the tremors swiftly built and became more forceful, the desert heaving and swirling and bulging until eventually its surface tore apart altogether, like a bursting sack. A meaty, ring-covered hand clawed upward into daylight. To the left another hand appeared, thrusting from the sands like some grotesque gleaming toadstool. There was more movement, more swirling, confused glimpses of heads and limbs and torsos and two brawny, ginger-haired figures heaved themselves free of the ground. They staggered to their feet, sand showering everywhere.

'You OK?' asked one.

'Just about,' replied the other. 'You?'

'Just about.'

They brushed themselves off and looked around, taking in their surroundings.

'Helicopters have gone.'

'Looks like it.'

'Guess we'd better get walking.'

'Guess we'd better.'

'Don't want Mama to worry.'

'Certainly don't.'

'Still got the . . . ?'

They delved into their pockets, each producing a gleaming handful of what looked like gold foil. They grinned and high-fived. Then, slipping off their jackets and throwing them over their shoulders, they linked arms and started to trudge towards the east, two tiny red dots creeping across a vast immensity of yellow, the sound of singing drifting behind them:

> *'El-Ahly, El-Ahly,*
> *The greatest team there'll ever be,*
> *We play it short, we play it long,*
> *The Red Devils go marching on!'*

THE REAL ZERZURA – AUTHOR'S NOTE

Of all the many myths and legends associated with the Sahara, few if any have captured the imagination in quite the same way as the mysterious lost oasis of Zerzura.

Supposedly a paradise of lush palms and bubbling springs, Zerzura is said to lie somewhere in the burning wastes of the Libyan desert. Many have argued that it is nothing but a fairy tale, a mirage, an El-Dorado of the sands. That has not stopped people looking for it, and much of the early pioneering exploration of the Sahara was carried out by those hoping to track down this curious forgotten watering hole.

The name Zerzura is almost certainly derived from the Arabic *zarzar*, meaning a starling or a small bird. It first crops up in a thirteenth-century manuscript written by Osman el-Nabulsi, the governor of the Fayyum, who talks of an abandoned oasis somewhere in the desert to the south-west of Fayyum. A more detailed and colourful account appears two centuries later in the *Kitab al-Kanuz* – the Book of Hidden Pearls. A medieval treasure-hunter's guide, the *Kitab* lists some four hundred sites in Egypt where hidden riches can be found, and outlines the various spells and incantations required to ward off the evil spirits who guard those riches. According to the *Kitab*: 'The city of Zerzura is white like a pigeon, and on the door of it is carved a bird. Take with your hand the key in the beak of the bird, then open the door of the city . . . Enter and there you will find great riches, also the king and the queen sleeping in their castle. Do not approach them, but take the treasure.'

The first European to mention the oasis was the English traveller and Egyptologist Sir John Gardner Wilkinson, who in 1835 wrote of hearing about a 'Wadee Zerzoora' – a place of palm trees and ruins located somewhere in the Great Sand Sea. A Bedouin had apparently stumbled on it while out looking for a stray camel, although his subsequent attempts to find the oasis again had proved futile (these two elements – the accidental discovery and the inability to relocate the oasis – are common to almost every tale of Zerzura).

The nineteenth century saw growing academic interest both in the Sahara and in the idea of a lost oasis, especially after the German explorer Gerhard Rohlfs' ground-breaking 1874 journey through the Great Sand Sea. However, it wasn't until the early part of the twentieth century that 'Zerzura fever' really took hold.

This was the great age of Saharan exploration, with figures such as Hassanein Bey, Prince Kemal el Din, Ladislaus Almasy, Patrick Clayton and Ralph Alger Bagnold – to name but a few – travelling though and mapping wide tracts of what had until that point been unknown, unrecorded desert. A fascination with Zerzura formed a key element of these exploratory journeys, and while not every expedition set out specifically to find the oasis, the possibility of doing so was never far from people's minds. The subject was debated in depth in newspapers and learned journals, and there was even an informal Zerzura Club comprising those involved in desert exploration (founded in a bar in Wadi Halfa in 1930, the club came together for an annual meeting at London's Royal Geographical Society followed by dinner at the Café Royal).

The work of Bagnold, Almasy et al. revolutionized desert travel, pushing forward the frontiers of geography, geology, archaeology and science. Indeed Bagnold's *The Physics of Blown Sand* – a study of the process of dune formation and movement – remains a standard text on the subject and was used by NASA when planning its Mars landings.

Their adventures also had a significant bearing on the North African campaigns of the Second World War, with many Zerzura Club regulars putting their expert knowledge to use as members of the British Army's legendary Long Range Desert Group (founded in 1940 by the ubiquitous Bagnold). Almasy alone threw in his lot with the Nazis, something for which his fellow explorers never forgave him.

But through all of this Zerzura itself remained frustratingly elusive. Numerous theories were advanced as to its whereabouts – in 1932 there was huge excitement when an expedition led by Almasy and Clayton made an aerial sighting of two green valleys in the northern part of the Gilf Kebir (later named Wadi Abd el-Malik and Wadi Hamra). While Almasy always maintained that one or both of these wadis were the basis of the whole Zerzura legend, others were not so sure, and the search went on, as it does to this day.

With the Sahara now thoroughly mapped and explored – from the ground, air and space – it is unlikely the search will ever prove successful, but that in no way diminishes Zerzura's mystique. If anything it only adds to it, elevating the oasis from the realms of the earthly into something altogether more potently symbolic.

As the great Ralph Bagnold put it in his book *Libyan Sands*, the power of Zerzura lies less in its actual physical presence than in what it represents – the thrill of exploration, the magic of secret places, the lure of the unknown. In a world in which few corners of the globe remain uncharted, Zerzura gives us hope that there are still adventures to be had and mysteries to be resolved. Seen in that light, Zerzura will always be out there, even when there is nowhere left to explore, for what on one level is simply a lost desert oasis is on another something far more elemental, something that lies deep within all of us: a yearning for the wonder of discovery.

(Note: If you want to learn more about the whole Zerzura story and those involved in it, Saul Kelly's *The Lost Oasis: The Desert War and the Hunt for Zerzura* is by far the best overview.)

GLOSSARY

Abu Treika, Mohamed Egyptian footballer, known as the 'Egyptian Zinedine Zidane'. Plays for El-Ahly. Born 1978.

Abydos Cult centre of the god Osiris and burial ground of some of Egypt's earliest pharaohs. Also home to the spectacular mortuary temple of pharaoh Seti I. Located 90 km north of Luxor.

Ahmadinejad, Mahmoud President of the Islamic Republic of Iran. Born 1956.

Aided A climbing route in which specialist equipment such as pitons, bolts, webbing ladders etc. are used to help the climber ascend. Aid climbing is the opposite of free climbing.

Aish baladi Coarse, pitta-type bread made from wholemeal flour.

Akhenaten Eighteenth Dynasty (New Kingdom) pharaoh. Ruled *c.* 1353–1335 BC. Generally considered to be the father of Tutankhamun.

Al-Ahram Literally, *The Pyramids*. Best-selling Egyptian daily newspaper.

Allez French for 'go'. Used by climbers to encourage each other.

Almasy, Count Ladislaus (László) Hungarian aristocrat, pilot, motor enthusiast and desert traveller, one of the pioneers of Saharan exploration in the early twentieth century. Lived 1895–1951.

Amun-Ra One of the state gods of the New Kingdom whose major cult centre was at Waset, modern Luxor. A conflation of the gods Ra and Amun.

Ankh Cruciform symbol. The ancient Egyptian sign of life.

Apep A spirit of evil and chaos. It lived in eternal darkness and took the form of an enormous snake.

ARCE The American Research Center in Egypt. An organization that funds archaeological training, research and conservation.

Arête A sharp ridge. In climbing terms it generally refers to a vertical feature that can be used to help the climber ascend.

Ash Ancient Egyptian desert god, particularly associated with oases.

Ashmolean A museum in Oxford specializing in art and archaeology. It has an extensive collection of Egyptian artefacts.

Astroman A climbing route up Washington Column in Yosemite National Park.

Atum Literally 'The All'. Primal Egyptian creation deity. Often associated with the sun god Ra, giving the composite name Ra-Atum.

Badarian A Neolithic culture that flourished in the southern part of the Nile Valley around 4500 BC. Named after El-Badari, near Asyut, the site where the culture was first identified.

Bagnold, Brigadier Ralph Alger   One of the great pioneering figures in the exploration of the Sahara in the late 1920s and early 1930s (among other epic journeys he made the first east–west crossing of the Great Sand Sea in 1932). During the Second World War he founded the legendary Long Range Desert Group. He was also a world-renowned scientist whose book on dune movements, *The Physics of Blown Sand*, remains a standard reference work to this day. Lived 1896–1990.

Ball, Dr John   One of the earliest European explorers of the western desert. Discovered Abu Ballas, or Pottery Hill, in 1916. Wrote numerous articles on the desert and the lost oasis of Zerzura. Lived 1872–1941.

Banu Sulaim   A North African Bedouin tribe.

Beato, Antonio   Anglo-Italian photographer who produced numerous images of the monuments and people of Egypt. Lived *c.* 1825–1906.

Bedja   A type of bell-shaped pot used by the ancient Egyptians to mould bread.

Beirut Barracks bombing   A double suicide-bombing in Lebanon on 23 October 1983, targeting the International Peacekeeping Force that had been deployed during the Lebanese civil war (1975–1991). Explosives-laden trucks were driven into the US Marine Headquarters at Beirut international airport and the nearby French Army barracks, killing 241 American servicemen, 58 French paratroopers and five Lebanese nationals. It is generally accepted that the bombings were the work of Iranian-backed Hezbollah militants.

Beirut Embassy bombing   A suicide bombing in Lebanon on 18 April 1983 in which an explosives-laden truck was rammed into the US Embassy building, killing 63 people. A group calling itself Islamic Jihad Organization claimed responsibility, although most analysts believe the Iranian-backed Hezbollah movement was behind the atrocity.

Benben   A conical or obelisk-shaped stone venerated in the ancient sun temple of Iunu.

Benu   A sacred bird closely associated with creator-god Ra-Atum. It was depicted as either a heron or a yellow wagtail. Considered by many scholars to be the prototype of the phoenix.

Bersiim   A type of clover used as cattle feed in Egypt.

Blessed Fields of Iaru   Ancient Egyptian term for the afterlife. Iaru was sometimes spelt 'ialu', which some scholars have suggested is the derivation of the term Elysian Fields.

Blix, Hans   Swedish diplomat who from 2000 to 2003 was the head of Unmovic (United Nations Monitoring, Inspection and Verification Commission), the organization tasked with investigating Iraq's weapons of mass destruction. Born 1928.

Boat Pit   A number of Egyptian royal burials included pits containing full-sized boats. Five such pits surround the Great Pyramid of Khufu at Giza, two of which – discovered in 1954 – yielded intact vessels.

Butneya   An area of Cairo renowned for its thieves and drug dealers.

Cam   Short for 'camming device'. A spring-loaded device wedged into a rock crack to secure a climber's rope.

Carabiner   An oval or D-shaped ring with a spring-loaded gate through which a rope can be threaded. One of the most basic items of climbing equipment.

Carter, Howard   English archaeologist, discoverer in 1922 of the tomb of the boy-pharaoh Tutankhamun, the greatest find in the history of Egyptian archaeology. When he first looked into the tomb and was asked by his companion and sponsor Lord Carnarvon if he could see anything, Carter uttered the immortal words: 'Yes, wonderful things!' Lived 1874–1939.

Cartouche   An elongated oval enclosing the name of a pharaoh.

Clayton, Lieutenant-Colonel Patrick   British surveyor, soldier and desert explorer. Mapped large areas of the western desert in the 1920s and 1930s. Lived 1896–1962. Two other Claytons also played a prominent role in the exploration of the Gilf Kebir during the 1930s: British aviator **Sir Robert Clayton-East-Clayton** (1908–1932), who gave his name to the geographical formation Clayton's Craters, and his wife **Lady Dorothy Clayton-East-Clayton** (1908–1933), who was the model for the Kristen Scott Thomas character in the film *The English Patient*.

Copt   An Egyptian Christian. The Copts are one of the oldest Christian communities in the world, dating back to the first century AD when St Mark brought the Gospel to Egypt. They account for approximately 10 per cent of the population of modern Egypt. The word 'copt' is derived from the ancient Greek *Aigyptos*, which in turn comes from the ancient Egyptian *hut-ka-Ptah* – the House of the Spirit of Ptah.

Cuneiform   Ancient Mesopotamian wedge-shaped script.

David-Neel, Alexandra   French explorer, adventurer, mystic and writer, famous for her travels in Tibet and the Himilayas. In 1924 she was the first European woman to enter the forbidden city of Lhasa. Lived 1868–1969.

Dead Hang Hanging from a hold with your arms completely straight.

Deadman A climbing manoeuvre in which the climber swings his arm upwards towards a difficult hold, making contact with the hold at the very limit of his reach.

De Lancey Forth, Lieutenant-Colonel Nowell Barnard Australian soldier and desert explorer. Served with the Sudan Camel Corps from 1907 to 1916. Lived 1879–1933.

Deshret Literally, 'red land'. The word used by ancient Egyptians to describe the arid desert to either side of the Nile.

Djed An ancient Egyptian symbol of stability depicted as a pillar surmounted by four horizontal branches. Considered to represent the backbone of the god Osiris.

Djedefre Fourth Dynasty (Old Kingdom) pharaoh, son of Khufu. Ruled *c.* 2528–2520 BC. His name is sometimes written Ra-djedef.

Djellaba Traditional robe worn by Egyptian men and women.

Djoser Third Dynasty (Early Dynastic) pharaoh. Ruled *c.* 2630–2611 BC. His Step Pyramid at Saqqara, just south of Cairo, was the world's first monumental stone building.

Duco A cellulose nitrate bonding cement used extensively in the repair and conservation of archaeological artefacts.

Dynasty The ancient historian Manetho divided Egyptian history into thirty ruling Dynasties, and these remain the basic building blocks of Ancient Egyptian chronology. The Dynasties have subsequently been grouped into Kingdoms and Periods.

Early Dynastic   The earliest period of recorded Egyptian history, when the Nile Valley was first unified as a single state. It comprises the first three dynasties of ancient Egypt and lasted *c.* 2920–2575 BC.

Eighteenth Dynasty   The inaugural dynasty of the New Kingdom. It comprised some of Egypt's greatest and best known pharaohs, including Tuthmosis III, Amenhotep III, Akhenaten and Tutankhamun.

El-Ahly   Famous Cairo football club, founded in 1907 (by Englishman Mitchel Ince). Nicknamed the Red Devils, they have an intense and often violent rivalry with the other main Cairo football club, Zamalek. El-Ahly is Arabic for 'national'.

El-Capitan   A sheer, 910-metre granite rock face in Yosemite National Park. One of the world's great 'Big Wall' climbs. It was first conquered in 1958 by Warren Harding, Wayne Merry and George Whitmore, who pioneered a route called The Nose.

Ennead   A group of nine deities ('Ennead' comes from the Greek for 'nine') associated with the great sun temple at Iunu. The group consisted of Atum, Shu, Tefnet, Geb, Nut, Osiris, Isis, Set and Nephthys.

FAAAS   Fellow of the American Academy of Arts and Sciences.

Fairuz   Famous female Lebanese singer. Real name Nouhad Haddad. Born 1935.

Fao Peninsula   Strategically important peninsula at the southernmost tip of Iraq. Scene of bitter conflict during the Iran–Iraq War of 1980–1988.

Fatir   A type of pancake.

Fellaha (pl. *fellaheen*)   Peasant.

FInstP   Fellow of the Institute of Physics.

First Intermediate The first of the three intermediate periods that divided the three great Kingdoms of ancient Egypt. It lasted *c.* 2134–2040 BC and saw the fragmentation of the Egyptian state following the strong central rule of the Old Kingdom.

Free-climb To climb a route without the use of any artificial equipment to aid ascent. Ropes, pitons etc. are only used to provide protection. The opposite of aid climbing.

Freerider A climbing route up El-Capitan in Yosemite National Park.

Gezira Sporting Club A 150-acre sports facility on Gezira Island in central Cairo.

Giza A desert plateau (and town) on the western edge of Cairo, site of the Pyramids, the Sphinx and numerous other archaeological remains.

Great Sand Sea A vast area of dunes covering some 300,000 square kilometres of western Egypt and eastern Libya.

Graeco-Roman The final period of ancient Egyptian history, inaugurated with Alexander the Great's conquest of Egypt in 332 BC and lasting until AD 395. The final native Egyptian ruler of Egypt was Cleopatra, who died in 30 BC, after which the country was ruled directly by Rome.

Hafeez, Sayed Abd-el Egyptian footballer (midfield). Former captain of El-Ahly. Born 1977.

Hall of Two Truths The hall where, according to ancient Egyptian mythology, the deceased's heart was weighed against the feather of Maat, or truth. If the deceased was judged to have done no evil they were allowed to join Osiris in the afterlife.

Hamas Militant Palestinian nationalist Islamic movement, founded in 1987. Hamas is both the Arabic for 'zeal' and a reverse acronym for 'The Islamic Resistance Movement'.

Hamdulillah   Literally, 'Praise be to Allah'.

Hassanein Bey, Ahmed Mohammed   One of the great figures in early twentieth-century Egyptian politics, culture and exploration. In 1922–23 he undertook a ground-breaking, eight-month, 2,200-mile expedition across the Sahara from Sollum on Egypt's Mediterranean coast to el-Obeid in the Sudan, in the process discovering the hitherto unknown Jebel Uweinat and Jebel Arkenu. Lived 1889–1946.

Hatshepsut   Eighteenth Dynasty (New Kingdom) queen, who ruled Egypt *c.* 1473–1458 BC as joint pharaoh with her stepson Tuthmosis III. Her mortuary temple on the west bank of the Nile at Luxor – one of the most spectacular monuments in Egypt – was the scene of a notorious massacre in 1997 when Islamic extremists killed 58 tourists and four Egyptians.

Heliopolis   Literally, 'City of the Sun'. Greek name for the ancient Egyptian temple city of Iunu.

Hezbollah   Literally, 'Party of God'. Militant Shia Islamic group based in Lebanon.

Hierakonpolis   A hugely important archaeological site in Upper Egypt. Known to the ancient Egyptians as Nekhen, it was one of the earliest known urban centres in the Nile Valley, with settlement evidence dating back to 4000 BC.

Hieratic   A cursive form of hieroglyphs. The ancient Egyptian equivalent of joined-up writing.

Holocene   A geological epoch lasting from around 10,000 BC to the present.

Horus   Ancient Egyptian god, son of Isis and Osiris. Portrayed with a human body and the head of a hawk.

Hypostyle hall   A large hall with a roof supported by columns.

Imma (pl. *immam*)   A headscarf or turban. Worn by men throughout Egypt.

Intermediate Period   The three great Kingdoms of ancient Egypt were separated by three 'intermediate periods' during which central authority collapsed and power became localized, with no single king ruling the entire Nile Valley.

Isis   Ancient Egyptian goddess. Wife of Osiris and mother of Horus. Protector of the dead.

Islamic Jihad   Militant Palestinian Islamic group, founded in the late 1970s.

Iteru   An ancient Egyptian unit of measurement, equivalent to approximately 10.5 km. Also the ancient Egyptian name for the Nile.

Iunu   One of the three great cities of ancient Egypt, along with Mennefer (Memphis) and Waset (Thebes/Luxor). Located in what is now northern Cairo, it was a site of huge religious significance, home to a vast temple complex dedicated to the sun god Ra-Atum.

Jihaz amn al-daoula   Egypt's state security service.

Karkaday   A soft drink made from an infusion of hibiscus petals. Popular throughout Egypt.

Karnak   A vast temple complex just to the north of Luxor, with buildings spanning almost 2,000 years of Egyptian history. The complex was sacred to the god Amun, although many other deities were also worshipped there.

Kemal el-Din Hussein, Prince   Egyptian millionaire, royal scion and desert explorer. Discovered and named the Gilf Kebir in 1926. A monument to him still exists at the southern tip of the Gilf, erected by Ladislaus Almasy. Lived 1874–1932.

Kemet Literally, 'black land'. The word ancient Egyptians used to denote their country. 'Egypt,' or Aigyptos, was used initially by the ancient Greeks and is a corruption of the Egyptian *hut-ka-Ptah* – House of the Spirit of Ptah.

Kenem Ancient name for the oasis of Kharga.

Khan al-Khalili A large bazaar in Cairo selling everything from jewellery to shisha pipes, gems to leatherwork.

Khasekhemwy Second Dynasty (Early Dynastic) pharaoh. Built a number of monumental structures including a huge tomb at Abydos. Died *c.* 2649 BC.

Khepri Ancient Egyptian god of creation, renewal, rebirth and the dawn sun. He was portrayed with a human body and the head of a scarab, or dung beetle.

Khet Ancient Egyptian unit of measurement equivalent to 52.5 metres.

Khomeini, Grand Ayatollah Ruhollah Iranian Shia cleric and leader of the 1979 Iranian Revolution. Supreme religious and political leader of Iran from 1979 to 1989. Lived 1900–1989.

Khufu Fourth Dynasty (Old Kingdom) pharaoh, builder of the Great Pyramid at Giza. Also known by the Greek version of his name, Cheops. Ruled *c.* 2551–2528 BC.

Kingdom The history of ancient Egypt covers almost 3,000 years, from the first appearance of a unified nation state around 3000 BC to the death of Cleopatra and the imposition of direct Roman rule in 30 BC. During this vast span of time there were three extended periods of national unity and powerful central government, known as the Old, Middle and New Kingdoms.

Kufra   A large desert oasis in south-east Libya.

Late-Period   As the name suggests, this was the period covering the later years of the Egyptian state, when a degree of central authority was re-established following the confusion of the Third Intermediate Period.

Lead-Line   The main rope used by climbers.

Long Range Desert Goup   A special operations unit of the British Army during the Second World War. Founded in 1940 by Ralph Bagnold, the group operated reconnaissance, intelligence-gathering and sabotage missions across the Sahara.

Lugal-Zagesi   King of Umma, a Sumerian city-state. Ruled *c.* 2375–2350 BC.

Mahfouz, Naguib   Nobel Prize-winning Egyptian author, widely credited with bringing Arab literature to a wider international audience. Lived 1911–2006.

Majnoon Islands   A strategically important area in southern Iraq, site of numerous Iraqi oil and gas fields.

Manetho   A Graeco-Egyptian priest whose *Aegyptiaca*, or History of Egypt, is a crucial source for the study of ancient Egypt. The original work has not survived and it is only known from passages quoted by other ancient writers. Almost nothing is known about Manetho himself save that he lived in the city of Sebennytos in the Nile Delta in the third century BC.

Manshiet Nasser   A district of Cairo, at the eastern extremity of the city. Home to the Zabbaleen, Cairo's rubbish collectors. It is one of the few places in the city where you will see pigs.

Mashhad   Second-largest city in Iran and one of the holiest sites in Shia Islam.

Meh-nsw (pl. *meh-nswt*) An ancient Egyptian measurement, the Royal Cubit, equivalent to 525 mm.

Midan Tahrir Literally, 'Liberation Square'. A vast open space in central Cairo and the hub of the city.

Middle Kingdom One of the three great Kingdoms of ancient Egypt. Comprising Dynasties 11–14, it lasted *c.* 2040–1640 BC.

Mnevis Bull A bull worshipped at the sun temple of Iunu. Seen as the embodiment of the supreme god Ra-Atum.

Molocchia An Egyptian dish made from stewed mallow leaves. Similar to spinach.

Mubarak, Hosni President of Egypt since 1981. Born 1928. His wife, Susan, is a well-known philanthropist.

Muezzin Mosque official who summons the Islamic faithful to prayer five times daily.

Nakht An ancient Egyptian scribe whose tomb on the west bank of the Nile at Luxor is painted with beautiful scenes of Egyptian daily life, including female musicians and dancers.

Naqada A pre-dynastic culture named after the town of Naqada – ancient Nubt – where its remains were first identified (by English archaeologist Flinders Petrie). The Naqada era lasted *c.* 4400–3000 BC and was crucial to the development of a unified Egypt.

Nasser, Gamal Abdel Second President of Egypt, from 1956 to 1970. He was one of the leaders of the Egyptian Revolution of 23 July 1952, and a key figure in twentieth-century Arab politics. Lived 1918–1970.

Necropolis Literally, 'city of the dead'. A burial ground.

Nefertiti Great royal wife of the Eighteenth Dynasty pharaoh Akhenaten. The name means 'The Beautiful One has Come'.

Neith Principal royal wife – and half-sister and cousin – of the Sixth Dynasty pharaoh Pepi II. Neith is also the name of an ancient Egyptian war goddess.

Neolithic Literally, 'new stone'. The final and most recent phase of the Stone Age era. In Egypt it lasted *c.* 6000–3500 BC, although there remains considerable debate about exact dating.

Newbold, Sir Douglas British explorer who travelled extensively through the Libyan desert while serving with the Sudan Political Service in the 1920s and 1930s. Lived 1894–1944.

New Kingdom The last of the three great Kingdoms of ancient Egypt. Comprising Dynasties 18–20, it lasted *c.* 1550–1070 BC. Some of the most famous pharaohs of Egyptian history such as Tutankhamun and Ramesses II ruled during the New Kingdom.

New Valley Governate One of the administrative/governmental regions of Egypt, covering the south-west of the country and including the oases of Kharga, Dakhla and al-Farafra, as well as the Gilf Kebir. Its capital is at Kharga.

Nine Bows The traditional enemies of ancient Egypt.

Nisu The word used by ancient Egyptians to denote a king or ruler. Pharaoh – from *Per-aa*, 'Great House' – only started to be used during the Eighteenth Dynasty (*c.* 1550–1307 BC).

Nomarch Ancient Egypt was divided into forty-two *nomes*, or administrative districts, each presided over by a nomarch. In times of governmental collapse nomarchs often broke from central authority and ruled as lords in their own right.

The Nose A climbing route up El-Capitan in Yosemite National Park. One of, if not the most famous rock climbs in the world.

Nut Ancient Egyptian goddess of the heavens and the sky.

Old Kingdom The first of the three great Kingdoms of ancient Egypt. Comprising Dynasties 4–8, it lasted *c.* 2575–2134 BC. It was during the Old Kingdom that the Pyramids were built.

Omm Arabic for mother.

Osiris Ancient Egyptian god of the underworld.

Ostracon (pl. **ostraca**) Piece of pottery or limestone bearing an image or text. The ancient equivalent of a doodle-pad or Post-It note.

Oxyrhynchus A unique archaeological site near modern el-Bahnasa in Middle Egypt. Ancient rubbish dumps have yielded huge numbers of Greek papyri from the Late Period of Egyptian history, including previously lost or unknown fragments of ancient plays, poems and early Christian writings.

Palaeolithic Literally, 'old stone'. The earliest phase of the Stone Age of human development, when humans were still itinerant hunter-gatherers. In Egypt it lasted *c.* 700,000–10,000 BC, although there remains considerable discussion on precise dating.

Pepi II Sixth Dynasty pharaoh. Last great ruler of the Old Kingdom. His full royal title was Nefer-ka-Re Pepi. Ruled *c.* 2246–2152 BC, the longest recorded rule of any monarch in history.

Peret One of the three seasons into which the ancient Egyptian year was divided (the others were *Akhet* and

Shemu). *Peret* was the season of planting and growth, and lasted roughly from October to February.

Petrie, William Matthew Flinders Archaeologist and Egyptologist. Worked extensively in Egypt and Palestine and established many of the basic ground rules of modern archaeology. Nicknamed 'the father of pots' for his interest in ancient pottery. Lived 1853–1942.

Petroglyph An image or symbol inscribed into rock.

Piastre Basic unit of Egyptian currency. A hundred piastres make one Egyptian pound.

Pitch A section of a climb between two 'belays' or secure anchoring points.

Piton A steel or alloy peg driven into a rock crack to provide support and protection for climbers.

Pre-dynastic The period immediately prior to the emergence of pharaonic Egypt, when the basic elements of Egyptian civilization gradually developed and coalesced.

Ptah Ancient Egyptian god of craftsmen and artisans, sacred to the city of Mennefer (Memphis). In some Egyptian mythologies he is considered the supreme creator god. Represented as mummiform figure with a beard and tight-fitting skullcap.

Pylon Monumental entrance or gateway with trapezium-shaped towers standing in front of a temple.

Ra (or Re) Ancient Egyptian sun god. The supreme deity.

Ra-Atum A conflation of the sun god Ra and the creator god Atum.

Re-Horakhty Ancient Egyptian god combining the attributes of Ra and Horus, one of the state gods of the New Kingdom. Usually depicted as a man with the head of a hawk or falcon.

Relief An image or text carved from a flat stone surface. In bas- or raised-relief the image stands out from the stone. In sunken relief it is cut into the stone.

Rohlfs, Friedrich Gerhard German geographer, adventurer and explorer. Travelled extensively in the Sahara, making a landmark south–north crossing of the Great Sand Sea in 1874. Lived 1831–1896.

Sahebee My friend (from *Saheb*, friend).

Saidi A native of Upper (or southern) Egypt. Saidis tend to be darker skinned than those from Lower (northern) Egypt.

Sais Word often placed before names in Egyptian Arabic as a form of polite address.

Sanusi A Muslim religious order founded in the nineteenth century and centred mainly in Libya.

Sarcophagus Literally, 'flesh eater'. A large stone receptacle in which a corpse or coffin is placed.

Scarab A dung beetle. Considered sacred in ancient Egypt.

Selima Sand Sheet A vast area of mainly flat sand covering some 60,000 sq. km in southern Egypt and northern Sudan.

Senwosret I Twelfth Dynasty (Middle Kingdom) pharaoh. Ruled *c.* 1971–1926 BC.

Seshat Ancient Egyptian goddess of writing, arithmetic, architecture and astronomy.

Set God of storms, chaos, darkness and the desert. Depicted with a human body and the head of some indeterminate animal.

Seti I Nineteenth Dynasty (New Kingdom) pharaoh, father of Ramesses II. Ruled *c.* 1306–1290 BC.

Shaal A large scarf, similar to a shawl.

Shedeh A form of wine made from red grapes. Highly prized in ancient Egypt.

Shepen The opium poppy. Used medicinally by the ancient Egyptians to induce drowsiness.

Shia One of the two main denominations of Islam (the other being Sunni Islam). While Shias and Sunnis share the same basic precepts of faith, there are certain key differences. Primarily the Shia believe that on the death of the Prophet Muhammad leadership of the Muslim community should have passed to his cousin/son-in-law Ali, rather than his friend and adviser Abu Bakr. For the Shia, spiritual authority resides solely with the immediate family of the Prophet Muhammad, and with imams appointed directly by God. The name is a shortening of the Arabic *shia'atu ali* – the followers, or party of Ali. Only about 10–15 per cent of Muslims are Shia, although they are a majority in Iran and Iraq.

Shisha A water pipe. Found in cafés and private homes throughout Egypt and the Middle East.

Shukran awi Thank you very much.

SMIEEE Senior Member of the Institute of Electrical and Electronics Engineers.

Sobek Ancient Egyptian deity depicted with the body of a man and the head of a crocodile. As well as being the god of the Nile, Sobek was regarded as the protector of the pharaoh and the gods Ra and Set.

Solo Climbing alone, without companions.

Stark, Freya Female traveller, explorer and writer, famous for her ground-breaking journeys through the Middle East and Arabia. She was made a Dame of the British Empire in 1972. Lived 1893–1993.

Stele Upright block of stone or wood carrying images and inscriptions.

Sunni The larger of the two main denominations of Islam, accounting for about 85 per cent of Muslims worldwide. Sunnis regard Abu Bakr, the First Caliph, as the legitimate successor of the Prophet Muhammad, and believe that any worthy man can lead the faithful, irrespective of lineage or background.

Supreme Council of Antiquities Part of Egypt's Ministry of Culture. Responsible for all archaeology, monuments and conservation within Egypt.

Taamiya A form of Egyptian falafel.

Talatat Standardized blocks of decorated stone used in the temple-building programme of the pharaoh Akhenaten (*c.* 1353–1335 BC). Later pharaohs tore down Akhenaten's temples and re-used the constituent blocks in their own monuments. Almost 40,000 talatat have been recovered from inside the pylons and beneath the floors of the temple complex at Karnak.

Tamam Good.

Tasian A Neolithic farming culture, named after Deir Tasa, the site in Upper Egypt where it was first identified. Flourished around 4500 BC.

Tebu A tribe of Saharan nomads found in Libya and Chad.

Tehran Embassy siege On 4 November 1979, 300 militant Iranian students stormed the US Embassy in Tehran, rounding up 66 American hostages. A small number were subsequently released, but 52 remained in captivity for 444 days. They were eventually freed on 21 January 1981.

Third Dynasty   The last of the three dynasties of the Early Dynastic period. Lasted *c.* 2649–2575 BC.

Tin Hinan   A mythical queen of the Tuareg tribe.

Tjaty   Vizier. The highest official in ancient Egypt.

Torly   An Egyptian casserole of meat – usually lamb or beef – and vegetables.

Touria   Hoe. Used extensively in Egyptian agriculture and archaeology.

Tuareg   A nomadic tribe descended from the Berbers of North Africa. They inhabit the desert regions of Mali, Niger and southern Algeria and are distinguished by their blue robes.

Tura   A large prison just outside Cairo.

Turin King List   A hieratic papyrus, thought to date from the reign of Ramesses II (1290–1224 BC), containing a list of all the rulers of ancient Egypt up to the New Kingdom. Although badly damaged and incomplete it is a crucial tool for the chronology of Egyptian kings. It was discovered in 1822 by the Italian traveller Bernardino Drovetti and is displayed in the Egyptian Museum in Turin.

Tutankhamun   Eighteenth Dynasty (New Kingdom) boy-king who ruled *c.* 1333–1323 BC. His almost intact tomb, found in 1922 by English archaeologist Howard Carter, is the greatest discovery in the history of Egyptian archaeology.

UAV   Unmanned Aerial Vehicle.

USAID   United States Agency for International Development. US government organization that offers financial and infrastructure assistance to the world's poorer countries.

Wadi   Arabic word for a valley and/or a dried-up river bed.

Wadjet   An Egyptian protective symbol representing the eye of the hawk-god Horus.

Wall Rat   Slang term for a rock climber.

Washington Column   A 350-metre prow-shaped granite rock tower in Yosemite National Park. Extremely popular with climbers.

Wilkinson, Sir John Gardner   English traveller, writer and Egyptologist, often referred to as the 'Father of British Egyptology'. Lived 1797–1875.

Wingate, Major-General Orde   British adventurer and soldier. Launched a foot-expedition in 1933 to search for Zerzura. Lived 1903–1944.

Yosemite National Park   A spectacular, 3,081 sq. km national wilderness park in the foothills of the Sierra Nevada in eastern California. Contains many of the world's great rock climbs.

Zabbaleen   A community of mainly Coptic Christians who collect and recycle Cairo's garbage. Their way of life is currently under threat after city authorities brought in European contractors to take over Cairo's waste disposal.

Zamalek   District of Cairo occupying the northern part of Gezira Island. Also the name of one of the city's two great football clubs. Known as the White Knights, Zamalek enjoy a fierce and sometimes violent rivalry with Cairo's other main team, El-Ahly.

Zawty   Modern Asyut. In ancient times it was the capital of the 13th *nome* (administrative district) of Upper Egypt.

ACKNOWLEDGEMENTS

There are an embarrassingly large number of people without whose advice, help and support this book could never have been written. First and foremost my beloved wife Alicky, who throughout has been there for me with wise counsel and calming words, and who has put up with more than any wife should reasonably have to put up with these last couple of years. I owe her a bigger debt of gratitude than I can ever repay.

The same goes for my wonderful agent Laura Susijn, whose unstinting support has kept me sane and on track, and my editor Simon Taylor, a man of infinite patience and encouragement.

Professor Stephen Quirke of the Petrie Museum provided invaluable advice on ancient Egyptian language, mythology and religion, and I can only apologize for the endless stream of oddball questions with which I have pestered him, and the substantial liberties I have taken with his replies. The British Museum's Department of Ancient Egypt and the Sudan likewise helped plug the numerous gaps in my knowledge of Egyptian history and hieroglyphs. A particular thank you to Drs Julie Anderson,

John Taylor, Renee Friedman, Richard Parkinson, Neal Spencer and Derek Welsby. Also to Drs Nicole Douek, Clair Ossian, Nicholas Reeves and Robert Morkot for advice on, respectively, ancient Egyptian oases, botany, hieroglyphs and obelisks.

Dr Jon Taylor, Curator of Cuneiform Collections at the British Museum, and Dr Frances Reynolds of Oxford University's Faculty of Oriental Studies were kind enough to give me a steer on aspects of ancient Sumerian language; my good friends Dr Rasha Abdullah and Mohsen Kemal did the same for contemporary Egyptian Arabic.

Until recently I knew nothing whatsoever about rock climbing or flying aeroplanes and microlights. Thanks to the following I am now marginally less ignorant: Ken Yager of the Yosemite Climbing Association, Chris McNamara of SuperTopo, Paul Beaver, Captains Iain Gibson and Alex Keith, Lucy Kimbell of the Northamptonshire School of Flying and Roger Patrick of P & M Aviation. I was equally in the dark about the world of nuclear smuggling and uranium enrichment. The following gave generously of their time and expertise to help enlighten me: Professor Matthew Bunn of Harvard University's John F. Kennedy School of Government, Gregory S. Jones of RAND Corporation, Brent M. Eastman of the US State Department's Nuclear Smuggling Outreach Initiative, Ben Timberlake and Charlie Smith.

A huge thank you to John Berry for welcoming me at the US Embassy in Cairo, Neil Gower for his wonderful maps, Lieutenant-Colonel Brian Maka at the Pentagon, Nashwa at London's Egyptian Cultural Bureau, Stephen Bagnold, Suzie Flowers, Dr Saul Kelly, Ken

Walton, Peter Wirth and staff at the British Library.

Perhaps the greatest pleasure of writing this book has been the opportunity it has given me to get to know two very special groups of people.

Thanks to Suzy Greiss, Magda Tharwat Badea and the staff of the Association for the Protection of the Environment (APE), I was able to enter and explore the fascinating world of the Zabbaleen, a unique community who for many years have collected and recycled Cairo's rubbish. You can find out more about them and APE's tireless outreach work at www.ape.org.eg. Sylvia Smith and Richard Duebel supplied me with crucial background information and introductions, and I am greatly indebted to them as well.

Equally unforgettable was the time I spent with the Bedouin of Dakhla Oasis. *Shukran awi* to Youssef, Sayed and El Hag Abdel Hamid Zeydan and Nasser Halel Zayed – for their hospitality, their insights and for many magical days out in the desert. If you ever find yourself in Dakhla, and want to learn more about the Bedouin and their culture, be sure to stop by the Zeydans' Bedouin Camp (http://www.dakhlabedouins.com).

Last, but by no means least, I would like to mention two greatly valued friends – Peter Bowron and Paul Beard. Although not directly involved in the process of writing this book, they have been very much in my thoughts of late. Thanks for all the laughs, guys, and for making my life a richer, brighter, more enjoyable place. You will be sorely missed, and never forgotten.

THE LOST ARMY OF CAMBYSES

PAUL SUSSMAN

In 523 BC, the Persian pharaoh Cambyses dispatched an army across Egypt's western desert to destroy the oracle at Siwa. Legend has it that his army was overwhelmed by a sandstorm and lost for ever...

Two and a half millennia later a mutilated corpse is washed up on the banks of the Nile at Luxor, an antiques dealer is savagely murdered in Cairo, and a British archaeologist is found dead at the ancient necropolis of Saqqara.

The incidents appear unconnected, but Inspector Yusuf Khalifa of the Luxor police is suspicious. As is the archaeologist's daughter, Tara Mullray. Stumbling on an ancient hieroglyphic fragment, their search for the truth suddenly becomes a dangerous race that leads deep into the desert's unforgiving heart...

'Adrenaline-packed...you feel like you've been on a rollercoaster, in a library and down the Nile all at the same time' *Crime Time*

'Tough, sometimes brutal, always engrossing...Sussman knows his Egypt, past and present' Dr Barbara Mertz, archaeologist

'A tremendous adventure...a great novel masterfully written'
Valerio Massimo Manfredi

THE LAST SECRET OF THE TEMPLE

PAUL SUSSMAN

**A two thousand year-old mystery –
a pulse-pounding race against time...**

Jerusalem, 70 AD. As the legions of
Rome besiege the Holy Temple, a boy
is given a secret that he must guard
with his life...

Southern Germany, December 1944.
Six Nazi prisoners drag a mysterious
crate deep into a disused mine. They
too give their lives to keep the secret
safe: murdered by their guards...

**Egypt, Valley of the Kings, the present
day.** A body is found amongst some
ruins. It seems an open-and-shut case
but the more Inspector Yusuf Khalifa of the
Luxor police finds out about the dead man,
the more uneasy he becomes. Khalifa doesn't know it
yet, but he is on the trail of an extraordinary long-lost artifact
that could, in the wrong hands, turn the Middle East into a blood bath...

THE FIRST APOSTLE

JAMES BECKER

An Englishwoman is found dead in a house near Rome, her neck broken.

Her distraught husband enlists the help of his closest friend, policeman Chris Bronson, who discovers an ancient inscription on a slab of stone above their fireplace. It translates as 'Here Lie the Liars'.

But who are the liars? And what is it they are lying about to protect?

Pursued across Europe, Bronson uncovers a trail of clues that leads him back to the shadowy beginnings of Christianity; to a chalice decorated with mysterious symbols; to a secret code hidden with a scroll.

And to a deadly conspiracy which – if revealed – will rock the foundations of our modern world.

A BRUTAL MURDER
A DEADLY CONSPIRACY
A SECRET AS OLD AS TIME ITSELF

THE FIRST APOSTLE

JAMES BECKER

THE MOSES STONE

JAMES BECKER

AN ANCIENT CODE

A clay tablet covered in ancient writing is found by an English couple in Morocco. A day later they are dead, killed in a car crash. But where is the relic they died to protect?

A SINISTER SECRET

Determined to uncover a secret that's endured for two millennia, Chris Bronson follows a trail of clues that lead him from the hustle of a Moroccan souk to the deserted caves of Qumran; from the sinister echoes of a water-filled tunnel under the city of Jerusalem to a windswept fortress whose name spells death.

A DEADLY CHASE FOR THE TRUTH...

Threatened on every side by violent extremists, Bronson is plunged into a mystery rooted in biblical times. For the stone he must find is older and far more dangerous than he could ever have imagined...